BUCKAROO BANZAI
AGAINST THE WORLD
CRIME LEAGUE
ET AL.

A COMPENDIUM OF EVILS

BUCKAROO BANZAI
AGAINST THE WORLD
CRIME LEAGUE
ET AL.

A COMPENDIUM OF EVILS

THE RENO KID

with E. M. RAUCH
PROFESSOR OF ORATORY AND BELLES-LETTRES

THE BANZAI INSTITUTE

BANZAI INSTITUTE PRESS, LTD.
FIRST PUBLISHED IN GREAT BRITAIN IN 2016
SECOND IMPRESSION 2017
THIRD IMPRESSION 2021

DARK HORSE BOOKS
Milwaukie, OR

BUCKAROO BANZAI AGAINST THE WORLD CRIME LEAGUE ET AL.:
A COMPENDIUM OF EVILS

Cover illustration by Julian Totino Tedesco
Cover design by Patrick Satterfield

Published by
Dark Horse Books
A division of Dark Horse Comics LLC
10956 SE Main Street
Milwaukie, OR 97222

DarkHorse.com

First paperback edition: May 2024
Ebook ISBN 978-1-50672-214-6
Trade Paperback ISBN 978-1-50674-064-5

1 3 5 7 9 10 8 6 4 2
Printed in the United States of America

Library of Congress Cataloging-in-Publication Data

Names: Rauch, Earl Mac, 1949- author.
Title: Buckaroo Banzai against the World Crime League, et al : a compendium of evils / by the Reno Kid with E.M. Rauch.
Description: First edition. | Milwaukie, OR : Dark Horse Books, 2021. | Summary: "Still mourning the loss of his beloved Penny Priddy and his surrogate father Professor Hikita, Buckaroo Banzai must also contend with the constant threat of attack from his immortal nemesis Hanoi Xan, ruthless head of the World Crime League. To make matters worse, Planet 10 warrior queen John Emdall has sent her Lectroid legions against Earth with a brutal ultimatum. Or is her true target Buckaroo Banzai? As the apocalyptic threats continue to mount, only Buckaroo and his Hong Kong Cavaliers stand in the way of global destruction"-- Provided by publisher.
Identifiers: LCCN 2020057639 | ISBN 9781506722139 (hardcover) | ISBN 9781506722146 (ebook)
Subjects: GSAFD: Science fiction.
Classification: LCC PS3568.A79 B83 2021 | DDC 813/.54--dc23
LC record available at https://lccn.loc.gov/2020057639

"All the beans and bullets you can eat."

TO MY DEVOTED FELLOW HONG KONG CAVALIERS
LIVING OR DEAD
THIS EDITION IS AFFECTIONATELY INSCRIBED

"What is precious, is never to forget . . ."
—Stephen Spender

AUTHOR'S PREFACE

I am frequently challenged by critics, with tones of ironic superiority: "Why add to the legend of Buckaroo Banzai—scientist, medical doctor, adventurer, trick shot artist, and professional entertainer, *inter alia*—an exceptional man and soft-spoken do-gooder, yes, and not one to toot his own horn, but also no superhero with superpowers?"

My goodness, no, he is no Superman of the comics, but many account him to be the superman of Nietzsche, that perfect balance of East and West, Apollonian rationality and Dionysian appetite: not a superman to rule over others but to govern himself. "But," continue the critics, "is he not also something of a theatrical cowboy given to fist fighting and street grappling and conspiracy theories, no? Not to mention such charming anachronisms as rhymed doggerel! How many men has the trigger-happy fellow killed? Does he not carry six-guns even when performing in public in front of audiences of all ages? And a celebrated medical doctor, no less! True, his face appears on cereal boxes, and his scientific discoveries and musical talents are undisputed; but what of his social influence on children? Certain of his recordings and stage gyrations are indelicate, to say the least . . ." So forth and so on go the familiar objections.

In the face of such self-righteous sanctimony, I offer the simplest of responses: this cowboy saved the world, not once but repeatedly. Regardless of your personal or political feelings about pistol-toting vigilantes and frontier notions of justice and fairness, scarcely a day passes without some media pasha or academic pundit inquiring if I was really there, at that phenomenal battle over the sleepy plains and thickets of New Jersey. Did I truly see with my own eyes the clash, barely above treetop level, that decided the fate of our Earth? Did I rejoice to see our own Buckaroo Banzai land by parachute while the alien John Whorfin's Lectroid ship crashed in a blazing ball? The answer is a self-evident yes, although with the passage of time I occasionally find myself asking the same question. Was I really there? Fortunately, if I forget all that I remember, or when I pass from the scene, my recollections of that fateful day will outlive me—see *The Adventures of Buckaroo Banzai Across the Eighth Dimension*— because I once took the time to put pen to paper. In the intervening years, swelling ranks of partisan readers have lately petitioned me for information about supervening events in the case, particularly in light of that which is whispered as truth but based upon rumor.

While Hanoi Xan's earlier attempt to ally himself with the unfortunate Dr. Lizardo was thankfully only a near thing, the voice of reason itself demands that the uncanny must not remain behind the black veil of legend and mystery. Like any thing in front of us, we wish to get a better sense of it through critical analysis and, if we are speaking of a historical figure, through as much biographical information as possible, so that the outline of the individual may be drawn with both a softer lead and a finer point and by this process come alive in our eyes.

But Xan is different, to put it mildly, and few subjects arouse such heated controversy as the scabrous contagion known for making the life of Buckaroo Banzai a living hell and killing anyone who crosses his shadow—the same man who among the masses is thought to be imaginary, a fictional being, and yet in parallel is known by another name as a trusted intimate of Queen Victoria and a banker to, among others, many of the principal royal houses of Europe, including the Hohenzollern and the last three czars . . . the same man who is mentioned also in French colonial reports from the 1940s as being in possession of no fewer than twenty princely domains in Xinjiang Province alone, as well as having a long string of criminal enterprises and a regular corps of bullies gathered from the pests of society in his employ. How to reconcile such competing claims? I regret this question cannot be answered authoritatively. The simple fact is that no satisfactory explanation exists for the phenomenon that is Hanoi Xan Anthropos.

In part this is due to his network of *dezinformatsiya* and the finest public relations money can buy, but bribery alone cannot account for why the true nature of the creature is shielded from discovery by the public and therefore the calumny he rightly deserves. Indeed, it flashes on the brain that perhaps there are things about the monster that our human minds cannot apprehend, an understanding not entrusted to us, that when we endeavor to speak of him, we lack even a fundamental idea of what we are talking about or even a way to render him visible. What else can be said of a "man" who claims to have been born a snake, hatched from the egg of a black swan, and whom no less a figure than Macaulay has called "a malefactor with no equal in the long record of human iniquity, a creature scarce seen in the light . . . the perpetual enemy of peace and virtue, a bold, bad man who engaged every lust, whose hands are alternately polluted with gold and with blood."

Such words, while not inaccurate, evoke the archetype more than the man: a mysterious figure of epic scale and larger than life. As against such hyperbole, perhaps it is more helpful to characterize Xan rather in terms of what he is not, as the wise Maimonides taught with respect to the Creator: not anthropomorphic, not mortal, not corporeal, not bound by physical laws. Of course I am not saying that Xan is not material, only that even in the flesh he inspires disbelief.

Consider the fantastical travelogue *The Khan of Kathmandu*, a manuscript recently discovered in the British Museum, believed by experts of the Banzai Institute to be in Xan's own hand and dating from the fifteenth century. Ascribed to Sir Edmund Shaa—goldsmith and engraver to the Royal Mint, moneylender to the king, and member of the Privy Council—the fanciful tale recounts the author's travels in the Himalayan kingdoms and his impressions of a mysterious Mongol prince with supernatural powers whom he encounters along the way. At times the author's language reminds us of a conflicted lover—"my legs did still lothe to lodge within his bed"—furthering our suspicion

Xan even may have written the account himself. Indeed the khan offers magical cures for various maladies: "Float bloode on water, mix with pith wick and natural oils which exude, smoothe over maculae and by reason of euphony, repeat, 'You handsome man rascal, you.'" If this concoction somehow fails to produce the desired results, he advises the author to "wash both Old Larry's winged and subordinate phalluses to and fro, in this way to unbosom one's vexations. Forthwith the mutation is wrought and the innermost penetralia of causes may be pressed."

Make sure it's done right, in other words! Erotic, yes, but exactly what happens between the two travelers is left unclear. In the volume's final illustration, they simply go their separate ways, with the moon and the Himalayas rising behind the khan. Other woodcuts depict the same brooding fellow in traditional Nepali dress, holding a musket and standing over a downed mountain cat, while in another he gazes at the night sky through a telescope, surrounded by a harem of beauties. He is never named, identified only as "the Khan" or "the Wretched Khan."

Was Shaa the man we know as Hanoi Xan? Writing in effect about his alter ego and a part of the world he himself had never visited but knew quite well as Xan? Again, our own forensic handwriting experts think so, but Sir Edmund would have been only one of Xan's many identities down through the centuries. Where, then, to begin? Whence comes Hanoi Xan? What does he look like? How old is he?

I can answer only that he is ancient. From oral legends and pseudepigrapha, he is rumored variously to have arisen from Persia, the Euphrates Valley, or the lost Pacific continent of Mu around the time of the great comet swarm of 11,000 BCE—his face the model for the Easter Island statues, et cetera—but the first notice we have of the entity who has come to be known as Hanoi Xan in the historical age comes from a three-thousand-year-old clay tablet fragment, written in Babylonian, upon which is described a demon feathered snake of "circular form," "birthed by a wicked swan" and possessing "a face which is no face" along with a list of other attributes, being both "large-boned and invisible . . . twixt man and monkey . . . of sable beauty . . . [who] affrights and affronts the great people of Nineveh . . ."

In Mesoamerica, too, we find legends of the feathered serpent—called Quetzalcoatl, Kukulkan, and other names—though I cannot attest to a direct connection to our villain.

THE MONGOLIAN CONNECTION

To speak briefly, there always seems to be a new Xan—one may as well use a name generator—which is not to say that he has changed for the better. In Mongol oral tradition, he is described not as Hulagu Khan or a khan of any kind, but variously as a shaman, a spider, a snake, a dream spirit, or the deceitful Talker (the Mongol devil) himself. A later narrative paints him as a "great dark bird of plunder" (black swan?) who leaves behind a bloody trail of outlawry, including grand pyramids of human heads. Captured and brought in chains to the court of the great Kublai Khan, he and his vaunted powers are put to the test. When the secrets of his magical tricks are exposed by the khan's own conjurer—a purported metaphysician and direct antecedent of Buckaroo Banzai who "brought fire against fire," as the story goes—Xan requests a noble death but instead is dipped in blazing naphtha until he reveals, amid the most terrible damnations, the location of his ill-gotten treasures. When his belly is sliced open, legend has it that enough precious jewels come pouring out to fill an entire *tayal*, or grain bag. What is more, in Xan's single teardrop the khan's conjurer lays eyes on the future: accursed Mongol invasion fleets storm tossed like kindling by a divine typhoon and sunk in the Sea of Japan.

What to say of such a lurid tale on the order of a movie plot, and the no-less-sensational accounts of Xan's revenge on the Banzai bloodline down through the generations? The simplest solution, it might seem, would be to put the question directly to Hanoi Xan and Buckaroo. The former is not available to this author, however, and Buckaroo acknowledges his ancient Mongolian roots but laughs at every mention of a thousand-year-old curse from the Old Country. For all of that, however, he has never explicitly denied the feud, perhaps because its existence is obvious. Make of it what you will, dear reader, as we have other fish to fry.

EUROPEAN VIEWS

Turning to the West and closer to home, we have the famed Elizabethan spiritist and psychic investigator Dr. John Dee and his account of the

angelic apparition Uriel, also known as Phanuel or Shanuel, who in the
doctor's scrying glass appears as wrinkled yet "smooth as glass, white as
walrus ivory, sinister and shining . . . the prowdest vaine viper full of
inchaunting tongues and musiques . . . a lewd and vile bastard, a gnawing
vermin, damnable friend of violence and chief procurer for Old Larry
himself . . . yet having a good contour of the nose . . . an atheist, alchymist,
skryer and prackticer of pracktical kaballah . . . [who] doth loathe his
awefull aged side . . . [and] disgorges his stomacke because his closen eies
could not his sight abide . . . [and hence] bathes in the first menstrual
bloode of young maidens and the bloode of women great with chyld."

I will save for later Xan's reported fondness for bathing in the menstrual
blood of virgins and proceed to the famous case of the broad-hatted man
in Vermeer's *View of Delft* whom the painter later erased from the work
for reasons that are unclear. Eyewitness accounts at the time identify the
figure as Xan's alter ego, the Dutch trader van Pfeffersack, the putative
richest man in Europe who made millions in piracy and the slave trade,
along with a financial killing in the famous tulip panic of 1636–37. Most
scholars, Berenson among them, have noted the uncanny resemblance
between van Pfeffersack and Vermeer himself—the reclusive so-called
Sphinx of Delft of whom little is known—and speculate the erased image
may have been in fact a self-portrait. Others, as I have mentioned, go
even further, alleging that Vermeer, Pfeffersack, and Xan are the same
man. At all events, without an actual image of the broad-hatted figure,
the debate is moot; and I can contribute nothing further upon the subject.

The same period gives us Bunyan's thinly disguised account of Xan/
Pfeffersack which, while not naming names, tellingly alludes to the birth
legend of "Mr. Badman": "I will tell you, that from a child he was very
bad; his very beginning was ominous, a malignity conceived by serpent
and enchanted black swan, and presaged that no good end was, in
likelihood, to follow thereupon. There were several sins that he was given
to, when but a little one, that manifested him to be notoriously infected
with original corruption; for I dare say he learned none of them of his
father and mother who found him foreign to them; nor was he admitted
to go much abroad among other children that were vile, to learn to sin of
them: nay, contrariwise, if at any time he did get abroad amongst others,
he would be as the inventor of bad words, and an example in bad actions
. . . the ringleader, and master-sinner from a child."

A century later we have P. Brydone's *A Tour through Sicily and Malta* (1773), in which the author mentions a fellow tourist who introduces himself as Henry Shannon, an Englishman. One need not imagine Brydone's surprise—for he has written of it in a separate letter—upon recognizing Shannon as the Frenchman Charles-Henri Sanson, the latest in a long line of Sansons to hold the office of royal executioner to the court of Versailles. Perhaps because he is describing two men as the same man, Brydone describes him as "prodigious of length" but also "short round," "gaunt" but "bulbous" and "frog-like."

Carlyle, because he was Carlyle, gushes with zeal over the same bloodthirsty individual: "To fix gaze long onto him is to fling away one's soul. He is a lamplighter, an illuminator, the type of the man to come."

"The type of the man to come," just possibly because he never seems to go away. To wit, the son of Charles-Henri, Henri Sanson, would follow in his father's bloody footsteps and chop the head off Marie Antoinette, among others. Like the latter-day Xan, he preferred to call himself a *disciplinaire* rather than an executioner and—if we give credence to the infamous Marquis de Sade—was a "blood drunk" and an avid practitioner of "domestic discipline" as well.

Was either Charles-Henri or Henri Sanson, or even both, the same individual as Henry Shannon, thereby suggesting the possibility of bilocation? It is a neat theory, but keep in mind that we are still dealing with life in the olden days before photography, so there is no "smoking gun" evidence to prove or disprove the case. Brydone seems firm in this belief, however, and in the case of Xan, we have learned the impossible is itself a myth.

Yet for lack of corroborative evidence, I must leave the matter unsettled, likewise the oft-rumored proposition that Xan and the infamous alchemist and thaumaturge Cagliostro walked in one another's shadow and may even have been the same man. While I give the theory some currency, I do not push it since I cannot confirm it—and chasing original sources is a tedious business. The jury therefore remains out while I continue working.

This theme of human quicksilver is echoed by Forbes in his monumental *Oriental Memoirs* (1813), in which the prolific author and draftsman records meeting a mysterious "khan" from parts unknown and in different guises, describing him in one breath as "dark and dense" and yet elsewhere as "a silvered blaze . . . an ominous glitter of something, dimly discerned." An accompanying sketch shows a dark-haired man of about forty, resembling Charlie Chaplin down to his mustache, baggy trousers, and little frock coat.

In the twentieth century, no less an authority than the great heresiarch Jung speaks of Xan as the "Spirit Mercurius," within whom are embodied all opposites, cosmic, physical, and psychic: male and female, light and dark, all mirror images within the nameless Oneness that predates the dawning of light. (It is less well known that during his time in London Jung became acquainted with Shannon, through introductions by Constance Long and both men's mutual quixotic obsession to synthesize all mythologies into a single universal system.)

During approximately the same period, 1913–14, we have Lytton Strachey's biographical treatment of someone who keenly resembles Shannon, an intimate of Queen Victoria and George V and a favorite of London high society for decades; or it is more accurate to say that we do not have such a document, since Shannon acquired the only manuscript for an unknown sum upon learning that Strachey planned to include him in his semisatirical biographical study *Eminent Victorians* alongside such notables as Florence Nightingale and General Gordon of Khartoum fame/infamy.

But the story does not end there, since we now know from evidence available through Strachey's estate that Strachey contemplated returning to the project after Shannon's death in 1922. From his notes in a 1924 letter to a prospective publisher (not Chatto & Windus) we find a proposal to relate the astounding odyssey of a central figure—who can only be the late Sir Henry Shannon—referred to variously as Hulagu Khan, Hanoi Xan, Hong X'an: ". . . a 6,000-year-old demigod . . . who until recently took in breath from the steppes of Mongolia to Belgravia and the steps of Whitehall . . . an English knight who from the comfort of his club chair at the Royal Geographical Society sat at the helm of the modern-day World Crime League." To be included, he promises, are "many of his most fantastic schemes and murders and black rites."

It is not known to me if any publishers ever saw the outline, which is skeletal and in the beginning stages, sparse on detail and likely intended only as promotional material, as I have suggested. In addition, let us be honest: any publisher presented the proposal almost certainly would have thought Strachey mad. The idea of a six-thousand-year-old living creature obviously cannot stand up under rational scrutiny in the twentieth century, so sensibly nowhere in the outline's talking points does Strachey name Sir Henry as the extraordinary individual under discussion or reveal sources to authenticate his wild claims. His caution, moreover, is understandable, given that a certain risk assessment is at play here, and it is likely Strachey was being extraordinarily careful, even after Shannon's "death," not to toss around his name. His very life may have depended upon such discretion, a fact that also may help to explain why he decided to abandon the entire project.

Yet he is not too circumspect in his notes to toss around certain sensational elements of the mystery man Xan's long and colorful history, promising an exotic concatenation of his experiences over several centuries and continents—from the Spanish Inquisition to Elizabethan court intrigues and Xan's connection to Christopher Marlowe's mysterious death; a banquet of sex in the busy boudoirs of Lady Penelope Rich, Catherine de' Medici and Anne d'Aquavita *et alia*; details of his misadventures with the murderous Jacobins, and his early forays into modern organized crime among the likes of Indian stranglers, the Chinese tong, the Camorra, and other assorted rough customers . . .

This is all tantalizing stuff (the more so if true), but the proposal's most astounding allegation is that Hanoi Xan was also none other than the notorious Hong Xiuquan, leader of the Taiping Heavenly Kingdom, the nineteenth-century Chinese religious cult whose call to revolution against the Qing dynasty led to the bloodiest civil war in human history and the deaths of tens of millions. As befitting the younger brother of Jesus Christ—as Xiuquan liked to claim—he met an ignoble end, only to be "resurrected" in a sense when his corpse was exhumed by his enemies, beheaded, burned, and his ashes fired from a cannon!

Was Xiuquan, a.k.a. X'an, the figure we know as Hanoi Xan? More to the point, why did Strachey think so? Was Shannon himself the source for the sensational story? In a letter to his friend Clive Bell, Strachey paints a frightening and lurid picture of his erstwhile biographical subject: "He [Shannon] reeks of iodoform and writes in the hand of an ancient, asking me to believe that he has lived over several millennia and maintained his vital appearance by shedding his entire skin at intervals and submitting himself to profane sacraments . . ."

Even allowing for a degree of senility—or rumored opium habit—in the centenarian Shannon, one finds it difficult to fathom why he would share such a lurid confession, true or not, unless the ambitious younger man somehow had managed to wheedle his way into his good graces in a deeper way than we understand. Or perhaps the old man merely was joking, as he was wont to do. Jung, for example, mentions finding Shannon on more than one occasion dressed as the Easter bunny, which by all accounts was one of his milder masquerades. Even in the presence of royalty or other dignitaries, he was known to clown and wear odd costumes; but his political and religious beliefs were no laughing matter. Ardent British imperialist and friend of Cecil Rhodes though he was, it was nonetheless the German thinkers and romantics who truly tugged at his heart. Wagner and Goethe, Fichte, Hegel, and Herder were his ideological soulmates; and in his dry and rather tedious autobiography, published just before his "death" in 1922 at the age of at least 109, he explains his belief in reincarnation as analogous to Hegel's dialectic, putting forth the theory that all the leading figures in history have been advanced souls who, by virtue of experience gained in prior lives, are a step closer than we ordinary mortals on the road to enlightened "all-knowingness."

He also speaks extensively of his belief in spiritist religion, particularly the teachings of Allan Kardec (more of whom later), and includes a brief mention of an intriguing discussion of the subject with a young Herman Melville on the South Sea island of Nuku Hiva sometime in 1842. Both Shannon and Melville were seagoing young men with vital intellects and we may imagine a vigorous encounter between the two young sailors. Oh, to have been a fly on the wall, or in the native hut!

What I mean to convey is that Xan the impersonator and various of his aliases have been well known for centuries. And yet, the popular masses of the last hundred years remain largely ignorant that the master villain even exists outside the pages of fiction, where he has appeared as the model for more miscreants than I can name. To cite but two, he is said to be Moravagine in the Frenchman's novel by the same name and the Russian nobleman Pechorin in Lermontov's effort a century earlier. I am reminded as well of Conrad—"a shadow darker than the shadow of the night, and draped nobly in the folds of a gorgeous eloquence"—and in the past century, outstanding stories by Philip José Farmer and the putative Harry Ashton-Wolfe. (The question of whether Xan himself wrote as Ashton-Wolfe is a fascinating one that has not been settled to my satisfaction; perhaps a dedicated reader with access to the British Museum might wish to investigate the case further.)

Since my publishing house does not allow for space to reproduce photographic images, I will also leave to one side a visual comparison of Henry Shannon and the Russian impresario known as Viktor Antropos, of whom I will have more to say in the main narrative. I am left, then, to describe the fiend with mere words; and others—as noted in these pages—have said it better. But let us admit I have a bias and invite another opinion, so that my publishers may not accuse me of editorializing and thereby exposing them to Xan's unsurpassed battery of fancy-pants lawyers who buzz like flies over every mention of his name. To be blunt, I am asked by the company to empathize with the torturer, who has demanded publication of the following self-serving statement by the rascal himself. Sickened and surprised that a monster psychopath who has spent millions to deny his own existence writes to set the story straight, I nonetheless am compelled to comply. Will the real Hanoi Xan please step forward!

FOREWORD BY HANOI XAN

TO THE READER WITH GUARDED
HOPE OF FAIRNESS

Yes, it is I, Hong Xiuquan, younger brother of Jesus and Fourth Person of the Holy Trinity, king of kings, the All-Destroyer Man of Sin. With more lofty names and a higher destiny than other men, not to say a meaning liberated from their understanding, I speak now in order "to address honestly my dishonesty," so that the reader may grasp my views on the beauty of that which some men call evil. What I mean by the beautiful is better called artifice, and evil to a man of my condition is simply the reverse of one's aims; that is to say, the shadow of failure. It follows by this calculus that evil is aligned with error and a want of creative and calculating faculties: a poor adaptation to the world in Darwinian terms. *Mundus vult decipi*: is this not the highest teaching of nature? Who is more beautiful than the conniving Hermes or the Cretan art form of deception? How much more artful than the taking of fair Helen was the Greeks' glorious deceit in winning back the pretty prize, or Abraham's cunning ruse to gift his own bride to the smitten Pharaoh!

Indeed, need I mention the Biblical tricksters? Did they not transcend good and evil? Is not "morality" itself a fluid concept derived from one's relative position of power? It is said the true master transcends good and evil to see the perfection of the way things are and thus to adore the god of things as they are, whose only rule is adapt or die. How many arrive at the pinnacle by way of charitable deeds?

The reader may sense from me a certain tone of frustration, which I acknowledge as a man who in the grand scheme of things, in the life of humanity, has committed every crime but the worst, which is failing to live by the cosmic laws of symmetry and the harmony of parts in all of Nature. In the human realm, this symmetry may be translated as the law of "cause and effect" or "live and learn"—in other words, the sum of all laws, after which there is no need of any other, much less what is called "conscience" or guilt or scolding religion. Think on it: what crime did Maldoror (Mister Morningstar, Prince of Light, et al.) and his disciple Pythagoras ever do, compared to the war god's reign of terror? Can you name one, besides the recognition of numinous numbers and their magical ratios which brought order into the world?

Law and order! Heh . . . that I should be accused as a lawbreaker, when none has followed the natural law more diligently than I, nor benefited to such a degree. In this way I remain an amateur criminal in comparison to the self-righteous do-gooders, politicians, and religious cultists of the world who will love you for a nickel and drop you for a dime. Heh! I am thinking of Buckaroo Banzai, who has disordered the natural harmonia of the world and is now paying the price. Having warped time and space, he wonders why his life is "warped" as well! Oh, how he hurts and cries to the tabloid magazines and television cameras, but he chose the dark path when he traveled through solid matter and compromised the precise balance that binds all dimensions!

Now his heart is broken and it breaks my heart! Whaa, whaa, weeping willow! That explains why I am howling with laughter as he attempts to sound as "cornpone" as his "fans," so they will sympathize with this foolish genius—yes, I will give him that. But hopefully you are not a simpleton so simple minded as to fall for his act or be offended by my words. Yet, whereas Banzai's predatory blood spilling is admired, even exalted, I am condemned and called worse than a cancer, a heathen barbarian, an abomination, an execrable villain (e.g., "terrible malefactor of blackest preeminence" and "depravity in its blackest shape") by hack pulp writers who see me behind every curtain.

Was it Macaulay or was it Gibbon who said of me . . . ? Ha, ha! For that matter, why not ask Sima Qian or Herodotus?

But no vulgar novelist has invented more bilge than my various biographers, who design to give goose flesh but, even so, are alleged to be on my payroll. Here I echo my dear Miss Rand, in asking, "Should not the man of industry be called good for what he has, rather than for what he gives away? Should the rich man not be glorified for his art of making profit, as the painter puts his talent to use?" Why this unjust double standard? The reason is obvious and should be kept in view: I live without reverence, make no claim to brotherly love, invoke no higher being in the performance of my works.

Call me Xan, Shan, Shaytan, Waxaklahun Ubah Kan, the Great Khan of the Golden Horde, Prince of the Air who sees all with my soul eyes in light and shadow alike. Yes, it is I, Sir Henry Shannon, "the Face Who Is No Face," the "human chameleon" and greatest stage actor of my generation—or, to my critics and assorted biographers, the Man behind the Curtain, the Puppet Master, Old Granddad, Max Thrax, the Scourge of Burma, Theophilus Krampus, Mr. Badman, the One Well-Pleasing Hadit, Anthropos Pentachrist, *summum malum, l'homme invisible*, the Archaic One and Author of Disorder, the New Weishaupt and Lord of Genius, Earl of

Rochester, Own Brother of Mephistopheles and Rider of the Clouds, Equal of Heaven and Doctor of the Church and Living Martyr, Mother of All Heresies and Fornications, Hinge of Fate and Pivot of Mystery *et tutti quanti*—even the Αντίχριστος—appearing as myself in this realistic rollicking tale of action and intrigue by Buckaroo Banzai's publicist and resident saxophonist "Reno of Memphis": a crab louse hack somehow smushed between the pages of pulp literature, *de sua pecunia!* Unworthy even to lick the master Henty's boots! And how many pages before he refers to me predictably, *pro domo*, as the "exponentially dangerous Hanoi Xan"? Yet if through the present pages the minor reader receives some accidental instruction in the pseudo profundities of life, so be it . . . *mehr Licht!*

So you will pardon me, curious reader, if I, the so-called worst leaf on the family tree of man, must club a spy to death like a seal or slither under a rock with my pitchfork . . . heh, heh . . . although everyone knows the best place to hide these days is in a boys' adventure book or anything penned by the Reno Kid. "If you read only one book in your life, let it be this one" . . . ha, ha, blah, blah . . . I'll be lurking in your prejudiced backwardness, on the dusty road to your death. Of course! Ignore your head and trust your feelings, for in the words of my dear Baudelaire, the lethal fumes of this book shall dissolve your soul as water does sugar! Run, fool! Yet fain you would grow up and become as successful as I, recalling friend Oscar's panegyric: "You will always be fond of me. I represent to you all the sins you never had the courage to commit."

QED. Happy trails!

[Signet ring seal]
Hanoi Xan Anthropos Pentachrist Invictus

IN REPLY TO XAN

Now, if I may respond to the devil, I'll not mince words (have I ever?): Xan Anthropos is not a man who turned to evil, but is the very embodiment of evil, a supernatural being older than any human has ever been and likely not human at all.

That into the bargain, dear reader! In sum, then: a religious oracle and miraculous analog to Christ in the minds of his followers, a sadist and savage to civilized people, he is everywhere and nowhere, his very existence doubted by many—giving credence to the magician's adage that the larger the illusion, the more difficult it is to detect. I mean to say, and this is the paradox, that Xan defies description, even as descriptive accounts of the beast abound. Rather, Xan is a thing, an "it" existing in both the spiritistic sense and the spacetime realm. Like Satan in the mythoi of the Mosaic religions, he is the Destroyer archetype, of whom it is said in the Egyptian Book of the Dead, "Behold I am Set, the creator of confusion and king of lies."

Accordingly, we go around and around. Not for nothing is he called the Face That Is No Face and the Light Beyond Sight, a man who, despite his reputation, can walk unnoticed down any street and seem to blend into the woodwork, yet whose name is a household word. One day the truth will out, however, and even the empty soul Xan will pay for his crimes at the appointed hour. In the meantime his game of deception is regularly investigated and exposed by that unique force of nature and emblem of moral truth that is Dr. Buckaroo Banzai, but not by him alone, for it is a day-in, day-out effort by his namesake institute, along with us Hong Kong Cavaliers and Blue Blaze field volunteers from around the world.

Such is our reality, less glamorous than is generally supposed and far from the sensationalized version in the popular media. When not making beautiful music together, we have scaled peaks from the Himalayas and Alaska in the north to the Andes and Queen Maud Land in the south, hiding in the weeds of Aksai Chin, huddling through freezing nights on the Eigerjoch and the Schreckhorn while discussing every subject under the sun. But I do not write to advertise his wonders, for Buckaroo Banzai needs no panegyrist nor wants publicity from any quarter, least of all in order to put bread on the table. His legions of fans instinctively understand that he is elevated by an uncommonly high intelligence and moral character; yet he lives simply with a sense of uprightness and gratitude and loves nothing better than laughing at himself—values inculcated by his parents, who set him on the straight and narrow, teaching him how to live off the land by the sweat of his brow.

A tabloid profile has described him thus: "Of mixed race, close to the things of the earth, he is equally at home in the solitary desert among the native boys, cacti and coyotes, or with a throng of admirers in magical places only dreamt of in the movies. Known to smile, grunt and roar simultaneously, he is contrarily phlegmatic, tight-lipped and good-natured in the modest manner of the American cowboy or the honorable samurai of old . . . his *kokutai* uncorrupted by greed."

Think also of the precocious John Stuart Mill or the younger Pitt, keeping in mind Hume's adage: "Be a philosopher, but amidst all your philosophy, be still a man." Add to that William James's description of a man "who sees the strange as familiar and the familiar as strange," and you begin to understand Banzai; but perhaps it is the Cincinnatus analogy that fits best: the farmer-philosopher as warrior and peacemaker, Buckaroo as the reluctant citizen-soldier who deputizes himself only as a last resort, saying in effect, "Trouble has come to our neighborhood, knocked on other people's doors, and now is coming up our walk. Where are my six-guns?"

But be careful and wise, dear reader; I am talking neither about Hollywood nor a Whig notion of history that imagines forces of progress at work against backwardness in each generation and age. Show me the science behind such utopian prattle! Think, rather, along the lines of your favorite *shōnen* series, wherein rivals tend to be characters in transition, forced to fight by fate and reasons beyond their control yet still capable of recognizing one another's humanity in the way that iron sharpens iron, in the way that fire makes poor steel brittle and tempers steel of the first rank. Like few others, Buckaroo is fire tested. In other words, if you fix Buckaroo Banzai as a man who cuts the world into two parts—white-hatted hero in opposition to a black-hearted villain—your radius of human experience is too narrow. Do not be dazzled by fantastical supermen, since the distance between good and evil, friend and foe, comedy and tragedy, is only a short arc of the pendulum.

Suffice it to say I will do my best to amuse with the present yarn; but, to fall back upon a weak metaphor, I must also till the field of history, fighting back with the mighty pen against all falsifiers. The kiss of light upon dark corners remains my goal, since it is the youth, our future leaders in chrysalis, who must carry civilization forward. To captivate the young reader and play such an instructive role—yet without undue embellishment—would give me great satisfaction as an author of juvenile books. To that end, I will, as the poet put it, "paint the cot, as Truth will paint it, and as Bards will not." Perhaps I shall fail; on the other hand, who has ever succeeded?

Fortunately, as I am given to telling the truth, so the words tend to write themselves. Nevertheless, credit my account or not, reader, keeping in mind your schoolboy Herodotus: "It is my duty to report all that is said, but I am not obliged to believe it all alike." In that spirit, if I write what may be closer to Homeric legend than history, let us batten down the hatches and hope for a happy outcome to this latest Buckaroo Banzai adventure!

Non sibi sed toti.

Almaty, Kazakhstan, 2021

I. THE IMMORTAL CHEVALIER

> Greatest of men; he held the key to the deepest mysteries . . .
> Behold, what a full tide of misfortune swept over his head.
> —Sophocles, *Oedipus the King*

Hours after presenting a free concert from our hotel rooftop, Sir Buckaroo Banzai, MD, GBE—a voice of moral conscience without parallel in our age and ranked among the top ten minds of all time—attended a dinner in his honor at the Institut de France, where he engaged in a freewheeling colloquy with a roomful of reporters whose long-winded questions inevitably touched upon the human angle: "How did you feel, Buckaroo, already a *chevalier de la Légion d'honneur*, when you heard you were to receive the Grande Médaille from the Académie des sciences, joining the immortal ranks of the great savants like Pasteur, Lavoisier, and Benoit Mandelbrot? . . . What are your feelings at this moment? . . . Where does this rank among your many *palmarès*, such as the Rock and Roll Hall of Fame and the Franklin Medal and the Gruber Prize for genetics? . . . How badly do you wish your wife Penny could be here? . . . Or your unfortunate parents? . . . Or the man who practically raised you, your colleague and mentor, Professor Hikita?"

It is worth noting here that Buckaroo is in many ways the most private of men and well known to regard such questions as tiresome and bordering on intrusive; yet it was hard to fault the reporters, since their audience doubtless would be keen to know the full gamut of the great man's emotions with regard to the sensational events in recent history—although these feelings easily could be guessed. Indeed, the term "peaks and valleys" can hardly do justice to the emotional roller coaster ridden by a man who, in short order, saved the world from John Whorfin and Red Lectroid aliens and experienced the heartbreak of losing the two people dearest to him. I refer of course to the Jet Car crash in Bhutan that killed his new bride, Penny Priddy—a tragedy compounded by the subsequent disappearance of her body from the remote mountain site while Buckaroo himself lay in a coma for days, on the knife's edge between life and death—and the mysterious death of his surrogate father, Professor Hikita.

Finding such personal questions anathema, Buckaroo naturally preferred to change the subject; and perhaps owing to the hallowed surroundings of the French Academy and fortuitous questions put to him concerning the present state of science in the world, he began to ruminate aloud extemporaneously (a long, digressive dialogue that I have edited into a monograph): "First of all, I want to express my very sincere appreciation and gratitude to the Academy, particularly for the wonderful Festschrift given to me in memory of Professor Hikita, my intellectual mentor and sparring partner."

Clearing his throat to remove a lump, he forced a smile and said, "Fellow scientists, distinguished academicians, waiters and food preparers, journalists, and various recognizable members of the World Crime League . . ."

Amid titters of nervous laughter, he pressed on, saying, "All my life, even from an early age, I always had the feeling that I was two people: an exile living in the 'here and now' and a stranger watching myself from another perspective, an inhabitant of another dimension no less real. For some years, thinking this an aberration of my mind alone, I immersed myself in the study of abnormal psychology, yet without finding the answers I sought; and gradually it dawned on me that, rather than attribute the phenomenon to my imagination, I would do well to investigate the actual existence of other dimensions: another way of saying the universal secret of all time, a unified theory encompassing all scientific knowledge. Little did I envision how controversial this field of inquiry would prove to be.

"Around the same time I was reading a lot of science fiction in those halcyon days of youth, and I could not help being struck by the dystopian view of scientific research as inherently dangerous—a byproduct of the post–World War II atomic age. The message in a real sense seemed to be that any semblance of faith in scientific progress as a power for good is overshadowed by the threat it poses to humanity's soul or even our very existence. Since human curiosity inevitably leads to investigation, which may in turn lead to dangerous knowledge and eventually a doomsday scenario—so the argument goes—scientific research must be closely monitored, even curtailed; therefore it follows that human freedom itself must be closely monitored, even curtailed."

With few listening to what had turned into a somewhat esoteric and tendentious discourse, there was a clamor for him to sing something instead. These requests he deflected gracefully, albeit hinting that he might change his mind and joking that once he started singing, people usually had to pull him away from the microphone. Watching him so charm the room, I could not help but be reminded of Freud's phrase—"the light-suffused face of the young Persian god"—when a reporter brusquely buttonholed me to ask the following: "Why do you Hong Kong Cavaliers give yourselves permission to police the world? Explain to me again, Reno—why is it always your job to save the planet?"

As Buckaroo's amanuensis and unofficial spokesman for our group, I had heard the question so many times that it struck a sore spot with me, and I answered as I always do: "It's a valid concern and one I frequently bring up with world leaders, who, after all, grant us diplomatic immunity to do our work, so perhaps you should direct the question to them. And perhaps we should all put our heads together and come up with a better system to stop imminent threats; but if the world is in a very dark place at the moment or your neighbor is spewing trash onto your property, we can't just sit back, particularly if we are the last resort. Rolling over and doing nothing is not in our DNA."

"No worries," he said, his mood changing rather dramatically from coolly professional to warm and intimate. "I loved your surprise show last night at the Olympia, especially the new single, 'Time Bomb Ticking.' Any chance we'll see you in Chittagong this next leg of the tour? Or at least get the T-shirt concession?"

"I'll put you in touch with Mrs. Johnson, head of our international fan club. She's here in town, having a listening party tomorrow night, and knows where all the bodies are buried," I said, and we exchanged contact information.

In return for the small gesture, the Chittagonian could not have been more effusive in his gratitude: "Thank whatever god in heaven for people like you, Reno! You, Tommy . . . Pecos . . . Buckaroo . . . the whole band and all your extended family."

"Family owned and operated. The quality goes in before the name goes on," I said, recalling an obsolete advertising slogan and turning my attention back to Buckaroo, who was still holding forth extemporaneously.

"But the world requires more than better science—it requires better people. Speaking more than seventy-five years ago, Carl Jung said, 'Our technical skill has grown to be so dangerous that the most urgent question today is not what *more* can be done in this line, but how the man who is entrusted with the control of this skill should be constituted.' I needn't remind you how I used to be laughed at when I was the first to warn the world that spying eyes could be watching you through your TV set . . ."

Amid rueful chuckles he said, "Who's laughing now? It was largely in recognition of this problem that I established the Banzai Institute, a place where scientists may develop not as inhuman cogs in the R&D machine, intent on dominating the natural world, but as intrepid adventurers seeking to gain insight into our broader nature as human beings in the grand scheme of the universe . . . or, to paraphrase Vladimir Lenin in a different light, to live with our hearts on fire and our brains on ice . . . but with humility and compassion for all."

Our little band had blown through Paris, at least in part, to investigate a tip that Henry Shannon had set up shop in the city's environs; and as I listened to Buckaroo's keen insights from the back of the room, my eyes were ever watchful for physical threats. At the same time, I could not help noticing a certain ennui among many of the reporters, who seemed to prefer rolling their eyes or staring at their handheld devices to the act of listening to the noblest, most honorable man in the world. Of course their behavior was not surprising to me—it is after all the self-absorbed culture in which we live—and I confess to being distracted myself in the meantime by a certain well-known TV network personality and host of her own fashion and reality show. I am speaking, naturally, of Desdemona "Mona" Peeptoe, who sauntered up to me in her signature fetish stiletto pumps and shoulder pads.

"Way to go, Buckaroo. Get on your soapbox, tell off these elitist media types for their spoon-fed pap," she urged, standing as always in her on-air pose, pushing her pelvis and one provocative foot slightly forward like the perennial talent show contestant she once was.

"How are you, Reno?" she began with an air kiss and a condescending tone and, after a round of awkward pleasantries that skipped over our tumultuous personal history together, started to press me in her best interview style: "And how are things at the Institute? Still sleeping in the bunkhouse, sixteen deep?"

"It's a living," I said, biting my lip so as not to return her incivility. "We believe in equality and family values, humility foremost among them."

"I'm unbelievably impressed. Congratulations on your humility, Reno," she jested . . .

. . . as we were interrupted by Parisian friends of mine: a brilliant thinker and commander of the Legion of Honor, who, along with her celebrated novelist husband, peppered me with French cheek kisses in passing, prompting Mona to roll her eyes in pique.

"One of Buckaroo's old flames," I informed her by way of smoothing her feathers. "Blue Blazes Julia Joy and her husband June Bug. We met at the Institute years ago."

"Never heard of them," she replied while making it clear she was no longer listening to me, but to Buckaroo, who in response to overwhelming popular demand had begun to croon one of our group's best-loved ballads . . . "I Need an Answer" . . . a tune so steeped in heartache, love, and loss that it ironically seemed to attain curative powers, allowing me to drape my arm around her.

"Getting a little misty in here," Mona announced, dabbing at something in her eye. "What a sad thing. And what a terrible sense of survivor's guilt he must feel. Her body could be anywhere by now . . . even in Hanoi Xan's backyard toolshed."

"Don't, Mona, not today on this happy occasion," I pleaded. "Don't even mention that unholy animal . . ."

"And of course you've heard the worst," she continued, "that Penny may have been a shady lady, a spy for Xan all along. Of course I hope the truth is not so ugly."

"I'll pass on your sensitive tip," I told her with only a trace of sarcasm—not that she seemed to give a whit for my opinion.

"I'm just saying Buckaroo looks tired, sounds hoarse, doesn't seem to radiate the old puissance," she said. "His skin looks bad, his bed hair kind of oily . . . or maybe it's just his horrible baby-shit-green suit in homage to *les académiciens* . . . but then the tacky silver boots and awful tangerine bolo tie . . . he almost looks incognito!"

"It's my bolo," I informed her. "I bought it just this morning when I went out pigeon hunting in the Bois."

"Always covering for the boss," she said with another roll of the eyes. "Even so, Buckaroo still needs to talk to a fashion person. He looks ill put together."

"You might look ill put together, too," I said without hesitation, "if you'd just gotten back from the Fifth Dimension and spent three sleepless days performing brain surgeries in a hyperbaric decompression suit."

"The Fifth . . . ? I thought he went to the Eighth."

"He's been to both, plus a couple of others."

"No wonder," she said flippantly. "Probably wore himself out, to say the least . . . I heard him say interdimensional travel is like making love, times a hundred, but then there's the dark side, the dark sectors as well. I just hope he didn't get his cavities probed like some of those UFO people."

"Jealous?" I said.

"Funny," she replied, meaning the opposite. "And funny you should say that. I have to tell you I'm hearing rumors that Buckaroo is not just tired, but a little off these days."

"Off? As in . . . ?"

"As in exponentially out of control with more than a few loose screws, a broken shell of a man on a morphine pump . . ."

"Let's not exaggerate. The screws are in his skull and a fractured pelvis, plus six broken ribs," I told her irritably and apparently without effect.

"I've even heard the neurologists are telling him not to operate a motor vehicle, much less the Jet Car, because of the concussion and possible cosmic-ray damage to his brain," she said . . . another statement I refused to dignify with a response, mainly because I had some idea of what she was talking about.

"Sorry to burst your bubble, Mona," I said, shaking my head. "You make it sound like he sits home all day, trembling in his house slippers . . ."

"What my sources are telling me," she insisted—then, seeing me less than pleased with her line of questioning, moderated her tone: "Perfectly understandable after the Jet Car crash and his brain concussion, not to mention the emotional toll. His heart must be aching, pushed to the brink of madness by such a thing . . . after saving the world from space aliens, only to lose the woman, the young bride, he loved above all else . . . ! Like I said, I can't even get my head around his loss."

"He's lost a lot," I agreed. "But they can't take away his fight against injustice. He consoles himself with work—"

She continued: "And on their honeymoon, with him at the controls. My God, how horrible. He would have given her the world wrapped in a bow, and now . . . look at him, successful in everything and yet all alone and hurting. And then Hikita, his surrogate father, committing ritual suicide. Does anyone really believe that? Who commits hara-kiri in a wheelchair, wearing Birkenstocks?"

I could only reply, "We all wish it could have turned out different."

"So does Hikita," she scoffed. "The whole world knows Xan had the professor done in, and so does Buckaroo. That's why I'm not one to badmouth the poor guy's fashion sense or kick him while he's down . . ."

"Of course not," I said, biting my tongue. "I know you too well."

These words were a nod to our history together, but she proceeded as if she hadn't heard: ". . . the *genius domus* of his eponymous Institute and best-selling author of *Les pensées de Buckaroo Banzai* . . . a man who, as they say, was born in a manger on the Fourth of July, rewrote Newton's second law, and is now about to receive the Grande Médaille from the illustrious French Academy, not to mention guest conducting the Orchestre de Paris tomorrow night. And what about this scuttlebutt I'm hearing that President Monroe intends to appoint him American ambassador to the Court of Saint James's . . . ?"

"Exactly that . . . scuttlebutt you can scuttle," I answered her. "I can promise you that Buckaroo hasn't the time or the inclination to sit and sip tea with diplomats, when he can accomplish so much more on his own . . . and with higher forms of life."

Now she couldn't resist a dig at him: "Oh, pardon us, 'immortal one,' too wise and all important to show us lesser mortals the way . . . !"

I interrupted to say, "Nice try, Mona, but nonsense . . . that's not Buckaroo. He has never claimed to be a guru who can show anyone 'the way,' even if he wanted to. The idea is laughable at best. Even *I* know there is no 'way' to happiness. Happiness *is* the way . . ."

"Happiness," she sighed, giving me a look of longing mixed with outright disgust. "My dear Reno, ever the homespun philosopher . . . and the best worst mistake I ever made. It kills me to my soul the way we left things between us."

On hearing those words, I experienced a future memory of the two of us walking along the river, pausing to kiss in view of Haussmann's façades and a watchful gargoyle or two. But of course this would not happen during this trip, if at all.

"Your high platform-wedge heels grinding me underfoot" was all I said.

"Like my stilettos. And you loving every minute, pouring your heart out!" She laughed and suggested I take her to the Jockey Club later that evening for martinis and some meaningful conversation, provided I could wangle her an interview with Buckaroo.

When I told her I would not be a go-between, she replied, "Very well, since you look sober and bathed, I'll go with you anyway."

A glance at my watch dispelled even that plan, however, obliging me to say, "Next time, Mona. I'm afraid the airport cocktail bar will have to do."

"Oh," she pouted. "Not even a macaron from Carette in the place du Trocadéro?"

"Something's come up," I explained. "I have to leave for Fukushima tonight on a special mission."

"*Zut alors.* How convenient, and mysterious."

"Tsunami science is that, indeed."

"*Last Year at Fukushima* . . . the movie of our lives," she sighed with exaggerated disappointment. "Then at least tell me something I don't know already. For my millions of viewers, care to give us your most amazing Buckaroo factoid?"

"He has a birthmark in the shape of a guitar," I answered without hesitation.

"His true-blue Mongolian spot? That's old news. Everyone knows that," she retorted. "Is this how you treat me, Reno? Your sweet, forgiving Mona . . ."

"Okay. Rumor has it he's got two left feet," I suggested.

"Seriously, Reno? Do I look brain dead to you?"

"If you don't believe me, ask why you've never seen him dance," I said. "Ever see him do a two-step, much less a suicide death drop like me?"

She cocked an eyebrow and cleared her throat, then resumed, "I thought it was because even after two years he must be slowly dying inside, though I guess he'll keep marching on in search of Penny because that's what he does. Where is our friend Xan, by the way?"

"Follow the flies," I said with a shrug.

"In fact, I have it on good authority several of Hanoi Xan's top lieutenants have been spotted in town lately, which would explain why you added a Paris tour stop at the last moment."

I held my tongue, saying only, "The tour's going great guns. Totally sold out the first leg in Scandinavia and the Baltics, cut a rollicking track for the new album with the Swedish Radio Orchestra . . . got detoured to the Gulf states, where we saved a local musician from the gallows."

"Funny business, show. Oh my word . . . !" she cried out, causing me to whirl and look.

AN ATTACK FROM AN UNLIKELY FRENCH QUARTER

Distracted by this exchange, I may have neglected to mention that some unbridled French journalist, doubtless smelling fresh blood, had just interrupted Buckaroo about the monster Hanoi Xan, whereupon Buckaroo, to his credit, tried to reply in a civil way; but, alas, the feeding frenzy had already begun. More impertinent questions followed until, suddenly and in the space of an instant, a member of the Academy—Jean Lafitte, the noted Belgian experimental physicist— shoved his way through the crowd of reporters, waving the ceremonial sword bestowed upon all Immortals and screaming with a maniacal hatred in his eyes, "*Pour Shang-Ti et la martyre! Naître, mourir, renaître encore . . . !*"

At least that was the way my ears heard it . . . as Buckaroo deftly sidestepped the white-haired octogenarian's épée thrust and Perfect Tommy did the rest, materializing seemingly out of thin air to disarm the old fool and drag him across the worn carpeting to a security official.

"Lafayette, we are here!" he shouted.

"Wow . . . Perfect Tommy . . . how'd he pull that off? Reno, why didn't you tell me Tommy was here with you and Buckaroo?" Mona said accusingly.

"*Jamais deux sans trois, tout de* phawking *suite*," I explained . . . as Tommy reappeared a moment later with a partial cigarette, drinking Coke from someone's tossed bottle and moving his body in the slinky way a cat stalks, all without breaking a sweat.

"No matter where you go, there's always a nut on the loose. That shitbird was jabbering about Blue Snow Cone and wanting to die, drunk as a skunk, and carrying a bag of weed," he calmly informed us.

"It can only be for that reason no one was hurt," Mona said.

"Almost a riot situation," Tommy agreed.

"And credit your quick thinking, Tommy," she added. "Nice work . . . although a sword fight would've been a bonus, or a shooting. Too bad . . . the Wild West angle. Or was it all part of the show? What the hell is Blue Snow Cone . . . ?"

Tommy and I traded looks; but where I hesitated, Tommy jumped in, blabbing to Mona like an excitable schoolboy. "Only the biggest blackmail plot in the history of Mother Earth, which Hanoi Xan threatened to turn into a 'blue snow cone' by sabotaging the hadron collider at CERN. It's a long-ass story, but the idea was to cause an experimental mini black hole to release giant clouds of cold atom matter that could freeze Switzerland and the heart of Europe and perhaps even the entire planet. Jean Lafitte probably had a hand in it, but Buckaroo foiled their little game, so now they want his hide more than ever . . ."

"The World Crime League, you mean?" asked Mona.

Tommy nodded. "Along with his brain, his Jet Car, his OSCILLATION OVERTHRUSTER, you name it. Last I heard, the reward on his head was ten million dollars, to be paid in this life or the next."

"Just the icing on the cupcake I needed," Mona said excitedly, already moving away. "Excuse me, Reno and Tommy, nice talking to you . . . but I have a deadline, gotta run. Always a pleasure. Keep your nose clean, Reno dearie. *Je t'embrasse!* Ta-ta . . ."

I watched her sashay away and muttered, "Tommy, you heroic jackass. You just spilled the butter beans."

"Following your lead, old man. *C'est comme ça*," he replied with a shrug.

Meanwhile, throughout the entire episode, Buckaroo scarcely interrupted his remarks to an audience that was by now paying rapt attention.

MORE WORTHY THOUGHTS

"I'm afraid that what has happened is that our well-founded fear of the atom has jaundiced not only our view of science, but our view of humanity as well," he was saying, "and the dystopian, apocalyptic message so common in modern science fiction ignores that powerful capacity for good inside us and teaches instead that humanity is the great antagonist on the planet—Man as machine and insatiable destroyer of Nature—who must be rescued for our own good from science and therefore from ourselves, who can't be trusted."

"Spoken like a true greedy American," griped a Frenchman in the crowd . . .

. . . whom Buckaroo overheard and answered with a grin, "Yes, and you may thank the nonprofit Banzai Institute, not only for its consulting services, but for your mobile Go-Phone and several hundred other technical and pharmaceutical patents that finance our good works in ninety-three countries around the world."

Amid a show of nodding heads and a few knowing smiles, he concluded, "As a scientist who has glimpsed the possibilities of other dimensions all around us, I believe that active curiosity—asking too many questions and eating from the tree of knowledge—is what makes us human. This relentless pursuit of the unknown is both my professional vocation and my passion in life . . . my *Beruf*, as Max Weber would say. We must never stoop to thinking that we are a beastly failed race somehow unworthy of our own habitat, when the simple truth is that we're an immature species who have not been around very long.

"I myself am often painted as a lurid combination of Prometheus and Pandora for having broken the Standard Model of Physics and for the Banzai Institute's nonreliance on government or Wall Street investors, notwithstanding the fact that we perform honest public service and bring music to the world through a variety of aggregations, such as the Bunkhouse Jazz Cats, the Banzai Brass Band, and the Hong Kong Cavaliers."

Now the applause became prolonged, and more than a few beaming faces turned our way, causing Tommy to grin and wave back . . . as Buckaroo began to wrap up his extemporaneous remarks.

"As Beethoven said, ideas of a divine nature come into being through the electric language of music. As we improve our critical-thinking skills based upon facts and data, we must also elevate humanity and its noblest inventions: virtu and the tools of reason in harmonic balance with our animal nature. This was my aim years ago when, in my ongoing quest for the fundamental particles and universal theory of everything, I first established the Banzai Institute, a kind of artists' colony–cum–think tank and summer camp for talented translational scientists and original thinkers, modeled after Yaddo and others, where we ask the big questions in a world grown suspicious of big ideas and self-appointed deep thinkers . . . where our aim nevertheless is to seek truth and do good.

"So call me old fashioned. I still believe in Bacon's *Novum organum* and the modern Enlightenment project, but am also drawn to the Rousseauian argument that human beings have traded their best and true nature for the comforts of civilization. The mystery for me, at bottom, is the meaning of life: to try to figure out the sense of it all by working together with a generosity born of that universal spirit. That is to say, science is always a work in progress, and I am able to view the natural world as full of magical phenomena not yet understood by the Standard Model or Western epistemologies— something like the Buddhist notion of a living, vibrating universe that permits absurdities and even contradictions: the superposition of two states in quantum physics, for example. As we say at the Institute, 'Expect the impossible.'"

A beep from his watch now led him to wind things down: "Sorry, folks, it seems I got a little carried away and rambled on a bit. That's about the size of it. Thanks for hearing me out. *Merci beaucoup . . !*"

Along with applause came a flurry of questions: "When's your next trip in the Jet Car?" "How's your health, Buckaroo?" "Any news on Penny?" "What did you find at the center of the earth on your last trip?"

Of these queries, he ignored all but one: "What did I find at the center of the earth? I found a stone left by the Vikings."

Quite likely, no one knew if he was kidding or not, and he threw everyone further off balance with a snap of his fingers, as if something had just occurred to him.

A STARTLING ANNOUNCEMENT

"I almost forgot . . . a little tidbit you might want to share with your audience. Based on our analysis of multiple transit timing variations in Saturn's orbit—detected by both NASA's *Cassini* probe and our own Large-Array Observatory—the Banzai Institute has discovered what we believe to be a radioactive planetoid of unknown origin parked in one of Saturn's rings, a finding since confirmed by the GRAPES-3 muon telescope in Ooty, India. That's all I can tell you at this time, but the Institute will be issuing a press release tomorrow, and I'll schedule a news conference in the near future."

"A planetoid?" the reporters erupted. "A big one? . . . You mean like a planet? . . . And it's parked in India? . . . You mean like something manmade, Buckaroo?"

"No, I wouldn't say it's manmade," he answered with a cryptic smile, "but possibly nonnatural, made by someone."

"What?! What are you saying, Buckaroo?" arose the clamorous response.

"It's still only preliminary, mind you," Buckaroo replied, choosing his words carefully so as not to provoke pandemonium. "But we believe it may be a probe from beyond our system actively scanning and archiving our transmissions. *Vive la France et vive la vie, mes amis!* And good luck in your future endeavors!"

"*Vive Buckaroo Banzai!*" members of the Academy chanted in response and then looked back at Tommy and me. "*Vive les Hong Kong Cavaliers!*"

"*Garde la foi!*" I returned, raising my glass. "Fraternity! Sorority!"

Armed now with the knowledge of all that was to follow, one cannot fail to look back and imbue the moment with high drama. Yet at the time, I merely recall glancing at my watch, thinking of Mona and the late-night flight I had to catch. Certainly no one in that room, no less Perfect Tommy and I, could guess that our world already stood on the edge of a precipice, the brink of destruction, as Tommy lit a bummed cigarette, gulped the last of his secondhand Coke, and remarked nonchalantly, "*Vive la vie* and *vive la* me."

Again Buckaroo turned to go, but now was hoisted aloft by admirers, leaving only more questions in his wake. A new planetoid? Was this a big deal or a nonstory? Who cared about Saturn and its crazy rings, anyway? But an alien probe and the fact that Buckaroo Banzai himself had chosen to reveal the discovery! That made it newsworthy, and within minutes, even as he crowd-surfed upon the shoulders of his fellow knights and *académiciens*, the headline flashed around the world and beyond.

II. INTO EXILE

> Quell rebellion before it spreads.
> —Emperor Vespasian

Sometime later and millions of miles distant, Buckaroo's announcement of a suspected alien craft in the heliosphere arrived at Her Majesty's siege vessel *Imperatrix* and elicited a tumultuous response from the Empress's Own Household Guards: not the sound of applauding hands but a hissing and flapping of wings from untold thousands of Mottled and Darkling "Adder" Lectroids (both varieties of luteous and ash-gray color, differentiated by wing structure and minor markings), adhering to every interior surface of a man-o'-war planetoid the size of a minor moon. Though hardly a rust bucket, the gargantuan vessel's hull had seen a lifetime of action and better days and bore more than a sprinkling of corrosion and blast damage, withal presenting a tired and smoked look. Constructed principally of ruthenium and two elements unknown on this earth—I may as well call them adamantium and terrylium—the vessel literally had been through the wars.

Whence had the great warship come? Why was it sent to Earth? I will tell you my thoughts, based upon an eyewitness testimony I will introduce shortly—an account I deem reliable (since I have no other) but cannot confirm, since I was not present.

In retrospect, by the time of these events, we already may call the *Imperatrix* a ghost ship, the result of both an unknown contagion and a political decision from on high, born of cynicism and expediency. By this, I mean the warship and its original contingent of half a million fighters had come to be seen as both a physical and a political threat to the established order of their home planet . . . so much so that, far from receiving their due of a triumphant homecoming, they were banished from their own world and sent into oblivion as the ship of the "lost legions"—the guards' own name for themselves—a far cry from the expeditionary force of elite fighters who once sowed terror among their foes with merely the utterance of their name and their unmistakable battle shriek. Unrivaled in battle and in wanton cruelty, they were known also by their darkly humorous epithet, loosely translated as "the Empress's Own Household Stain Removers and Bug Exterminators," famed for "cleansing" planets of native resistance and preserving order on various colonies under the suzerainty, and brutality, of the Planet 10 empire.

But let us not shy away from the truth, even if it is less spectacular for our purposes than a lie. The Lectroids presently inhabited the tenth world—Planet 10—in their long history; and their vaunted "empire" was something of a joke, a collection of planets that were mostly unnamed remote bodies of low desirability, inhabited by primitive species or no life forms at all, and none of them suitable for Lectroid nest building. Seen in this light, their vaunted military prowess owed less to innate superiority than to the desperate realization that their race was in danger of extinction, along with their fading sun. Hence they roamed far and wide in search of new worlds to conquer, looking in reality for a Planet 11, a new promised land to rival their paradisiacal (and perhaps mythical) first world.

What, then, could have brought low such dreaded warriors, from the exalted status of national heroes to *non gratae* untouchables? How could it have come to this mad exodus? I lack the time or inclination here to lay out even a brief outline of the unit's lengthy military campaigns, although we have a history of these, thanks to a lone scribe whom I shall introduce in another moment. Nor is this the time or place to attempt to sort out the tangled history between the Mottled Adders and Darkling Lectroids themselves, and their common oppressor, the poisonous Reds, going back eons. Though the former race suffered mightily under the boot of Red John Whorfin's rule, relations between the two groups are notably complex—and an explanation of these, even in summary form, would doubtless tire the juvenile reader. Let us merely say that the two races, like the owl and the crow and certain others in our planet's taxonomy, instinctively hate and attack one another on sight.

But to return to our tale: during a lengthy expedition to various worlds, the guards' character underwent something of a radical transformation that can only be described as communitarian and religious in nature, an experience from which there was no going back. The turning point arrived not as a single moment but a series of odd events that began when the ship passed through the mystical Photon Belt around the Pleiades.

Relatively minor in and of themselves, these skirmishes set the stage for the brief but savage military campaign on the noxious planet Re55a, whose "singing soldiers" of unsightly physiognomy—one might call them "stick people" on the order of praying mantises—marched in lockstep into the Lectroids' giant grinders with such equanimity that their conquerors could only regard them with a sense of disbelief. Even when the main body of defenders found themselves herded into the boiling volcano known as the "flaming bowl of doom," their comrades came running, armed only with their singing voices and the small black cubes that were sacred to them . . . thereupon to make leaps of faith into the pit to die with their own kind. Death, in other words, held no fear for them, and their childlike devotion to one another caused many of the battle-hardened Lectroid fighters to adopt the cubes as lucky talismans, war trophies to commemorate their latest victory and pay respect to the planet's strange and suicidal defenders. Still, it is unlikely any Lectroid cried over the cultists and equally doubtful any of them danced upon their mass graves. It was simply another battle in a long campaign of imperial expansion.

And the story might have ended there, with the empress's guards on their way home to Planet 10, only too happy to put the voyage and its hardships behind them. But then the epidemic broke out, first presenting itself as an allergic reaction—excretions of smoking slime from all bodily orifices and a stench like rotten vegetables—soon to be accompanied by blindness, terrible open sores, and violent seizures, followed closely by a final paroxysm of exosystem collapse. Moreover, the excruciating pain felt by the gravely ill stole courage from even the bravest of victims, stalwart Lectroids who had endured the worst wars and maladies.

How to describe the sense of panic and desperation that presumably spread among the force! Tired and lonely, yet so close to the sweet fields of home . . . and now a large portion of one's comrades dropping dead to an unseen killer out of anyone's control! So quickly and with such lethality did the affliction spread that it made one fear to leave one's hole in the heap. Was the disease somehow connected to an ongoing radioactivity leak in the ship's climate-control system, the severity of which was a carefully kept secret? Or was there an invisible disease agent which had been acquired from swamp-infested Re55a, their last stop? In that case, did it have to be a germ? Perhaps the ghost of a warrior come for revenge? Or even a demon, as some seemed convinced?

In one variation or another, this Re55a connection to the sickness was quick to be embraced, all the more so since it seemed that those who wore the souvenir cubes on their persons avoided falling ill but were correspondingly more likely to kill themselves—a realization which produced, in equal parts, loathing and attraction toward the simple cubes and the mysterious cult they represented.

I mean to say that while some blamed the little boxes themselves for the deadly outbreak, others attributed to the cube supernatural powers that could provide protection from disease. Hence, no small number of opportunists profiteered by peddling them for substantial sums as amulets. In the same way, the prisoners taken from Re55a as biological specimens were both brutalized and sought out for advice, on which occasions the poor wretches clung to their simple religious faith and shared it with steadfast earnestness—or, lacking the chance to proselytize, tried to kill themselves.

Now, whether their god amounted to something other than superstition, who could say? Who can account for religious beliefs, much less ascertain their worth? I will not comment, other than to say that various miraculous healings were also ascribed to the cultists, who began to attract Darkling Lectroids to their turn of mind, first as sympathizers and then as fellow believers. In this manner a new religion was being propagated among the ship's company, a growing number of whom began to think of themselves as unneedful of the imperial religion and its attendant empress worship. Perhaps it was inevitable, too, that the vessel's high command and official priestly caste should become alarmed and undertake to suppress the growing cult, as in fact happened.

The nexus of the problem lay not only in the new religion's challenge to the imperial priestcraft but in the Cubist doctrine itself, which celebrated a universal god, a universal community of intelligent species, and a single paradise for all believers. Such high-minded precepts were not altogether foreign to the bellicose Darkling Lectroids, who likewise engaged in body mortification and a death cult of their own. We are speaking, after all, of an elite corps of professionals indoctrinated with its own sense of esprit de corps that honored self-sacrifice, albeit in the cause of militarism and racialist doctrines.

So it should come as no surprise that when even a few in the ranks began to mock corrective discipline and question orders, word filtered back to Planet 10 and the queen herself: the Virgin Empress and "Divine Thunderpump" John Emdall, who had sat upon the speckled throne since the overthrow of the brutal "Red Hammer," John Whorfin.

Long wary of foreign influences, not only in the fighting forces, but in the very fabric of Planet 10 society, Emdall rightly believed that in an emperor-worshiping culture, deities posed a danger. Although the lore of the ancient race spoke of an original creator god and traced its path through ten different planets and reckoned with a crowded pantheon of demigods—both benign and malevolent, personifying wild beasts, forces of nature, and various Lectroid attributes—these were mainly on the order of oracles, superstitions, and ancestral totems invoked or thwarted by amulets and charms. In practice, and by law, there was only one legal rallying cry, one official cult, and one manifest godhead: John Emdall herself, the "True Light of Heaven," whose claim to divinity rested largely upon her ability to animate the inanimate, such as stone statues and rocks, and even Mount Wah-Wah, the legendary "talking mountain."

This phenomenon, her theurgical power, was one she did not understand fully; nor did she entirely trust the high priests who kept such secrets. Some she suspected of being sympathetic to John Whorfin or the rogue general John Red and Raw in exile, while others were known to harbor political ambitions of their own: Again, her motives can only be guessed; what is a matter of record is that, by her decree—doubtless influenced by her priests—the *Imperatrix* received a special commendation in absentia but was denied its triumphant homecoming because of an unspecified danger to the "general commonweal." While it is easy to be cynical, it is also difficult to fault her decision, since it was ostensibly reasonable to take precautions against a possible pandemic; and in this she even went so far as to deny the great ship docking privileges and an onloading of fresh stores. But the contagion she feared above all, I believe, was the new religion Cubism—not its doctrine per se, of which she doubtless knew or cared little, but a revolt of her priests against it.

For a military unit as celebrated as the queen's guards, this official snub represented an egregious break with tradition and yet was the second case in recent memory, after a similar de facto exile had been ordered for fighting units loyal to the ambitious John Red and Raw. Like lepers denied even a farewell visit to their family holes or a chance to put their affairs in order, the expeditionary force instead was rewarded with new orders to continue their wars of conquest. While they were expected to be pleased at the prospect of further glory—their warlike culture bred them for no other purpose than to follow orders, to kill or be killed—one easily imagines the demoralizing effect of the knowledge that, for all their heroic exploits in war, they were helpless against a myriad of factors beyond their control: wretched sickness, a diminished store of foodstuffs, rising levels of radioactivity, and now an empress and governing class that had spurned them without ceremony and sent them to what amounted to slow but certain death.

If such ignominy proved a bitter pill to swallow for even the most meager brained of Lectroids, how much more so among those in whom Cubism had awakened something like thinking and self-reflection! In practice, this festering resentment manifested itself in a downward spiral of ever-sinking morale and an alarming increase in converts to the new faith.

A FIRSTHAND REPORT

Note: For this entire account, we have to thank a low-ranking scrivener and "ship-keep," one John Singsong-of-the-Narrows-of-No-Return-Not-Him-But-the-Other-One (full name), a secret Cubist convert given to reflection and deep thought, illustrated by this passage through which we experience something of the exiles' emotions:

We are the Despaired Of, the very hunters for the purpose; therefore do not mourn our loss, though why fate has not condescended to take us unto its breast and fullest confidence, none can say. If our souls be mean and small and obstreperous, our failures in life too many to bear, why has the honor fallen to us? We can only conclude our rashness, the fecklessness of our youth, has somehow won our special destiny . . . we the Despaired Of and unenvied, who once found Greatness against the brown-eared Bul-Bul and the giant pungent ray of Arap. O rascal of fate, grant us pious pilgrims a boon and a lucky direction of the compass . . . !

As the beast herds dwindled and the food shortage—apart from electricity, which the Darklings also imbibed as an energy source—developed into full-blown crisis, the ship's high command imposed the harshest of remedies, albeit the only one available. But the stock of captive slave workers was not inexhaustible, and these, too, eventually grew scarce, necessitating the stopgap measure of harvesting what I will call "barnacles" and "lichens" from the ship's hull. But this process, too, could provide only a temporary respite; and such was the misery aboard the *Imperatrix* that when a speeding mystery object came seemingly out of nowhere on a direct collision path with the ship, a great number of voyagers fairly wept with happiness at the prospect of merciful death . . . then, the danger past, resigned themselves to suicide in the fiery methane lake that supplied the ship's communal soup food.

One wave of martyrs inspired another and so on, greatly reducing the ship's population, while others, principally the Cubists, invoked the name and power of their deity, who was said to have shifted the course of the oncoming asteroid in the final moments. As a consequence, the event was taken as a divine sign—among all, not merely the Cubists—and a great hue and cry arose among the company, demanding that the ship follow the "miraculous rock" wherever it might lead . . . a decision which, as luck would have it, eventually brought them into our own system.

"As the Cube gives us strength, so we feed others the bread of life!" the Cubists preached in the typical way of the Darkling Lectroid, through a combination of song and interpretive dance, pantomime and sign language, speaking incessantly of a second life and a paradise after death.

"At Home in the Mountains of Ouibos" and "Saved by the Cube" were the hymns they sang, asking, "How could we have made it this far without divine help? It is something of a miracle, though nothing so wondrous as the prize that awaits us in Paradise if we love our cohort more than ourselves and surrender ourselves to the Cube, whose four sides—1 + 2 + 3 + 4—miraculously equal 10!"

This assertion naturally was questioned by some who pointed out that a cube has six sides, but in general the Cubist idea of an infinite positive energy and a ghostly world beyond the physical level now met with cautious encouragement from the priesthood and their slavish high command, who valued such teachings as an antidote to the perfect storm of afflictions in which the ship now found itself. Here was the promise of a future, at least—even if the product of shallow thinking—in which to place one's hope! Ah, Paradise, how sweet it is, especially to one with few or no options! Though we presently rot in hell, a garden of delights somewhere awaits!

Indeed the prospect of such a shining new world in all its abundance now found growing support as the ship received official orders and an actual destination: the blue ball we call our Earth and one of the planets constituting the so-called "green belt" of the Milky Way. Although the exact mission was not yet revealed, and there was still no end to the tedious task of sorting out who was to die in order that others might eat, an improvement in daily life was noted nonetheless. Earth! The very planet where John Whorfin previously had emerged from the prison of the Eighth Dimension and perished at the hands of Buckaroo Banzai—yes, the same Buckaroo Banzai about whom they began to gather as much data as possible . . . v.g., the human brain's two hemispheres, the cause of laughter, jokes to be translated and explained, sexual relations to be understood, and of course diverse foods on eating tables—but above all the question of which humans would fight to defend the planet. In that category doubtless our names appeared among the foremost, because we have it on John Singsong's good authority that Buckaroo Banzai, the Hong Kong Cavaliers, and our global auxiliary known as the Blue Blazes were at the top of the list of possible formidable opponents. Never quitters or good losers, we were the ones most likely to slog it out with the invaders, to resist to the bitter end.

As to their means of transportation qua locomotion to our shores, I cannot report authoritatively. The likely candidates appear to be some method of antigravity propulsion or interdimensional travel or a combination of both, as Buckaroo Banzai believes from firsthand observation. Whatever the truth, we were put under the microscope. Although Lectroids could not understand such human fundamentals as humor or the meaning of colors—being colorblind themselves (their quarrel with their Red rivals notwithstanding)—we now know they were fascinated by human behavior, particularly inasmuch as they wished to manipulate it. Without difficulty one imagines the half-starved fighting force poring over our musical performances (rhythmically tapping their claws and carapaces?) and assorted adventures, both real and Hollywood make-believe, although it is doubtful they could tell the difference between the two.

BUCKAROO BANZAI'S EFFECT ON THE ALIENS

But something quite unexpected happened during this process of investigation and discovery. I call the development "unexpected," although I doubt it will surprise my readers. The more the rank-and-file Lectroids became exposed to the totemic figure of Buckaroo Banzai— through whom they looked to understand our broader world—the more they felt their senses positively stimulated by his inspirational speeches and brilliant lectures, scientific papers and charitable works, along with our hit songs and action-packed films and television episodes.

Nor do I believe I go too far in saying that our broadcasts—along with Bulldog Drummond, Joe Friday, and other of their favorites— provided the miserable souls aboard the *Imperatrix* a reason to live. By that, I mean we became the chief pleasure for these unhappy victims of circumstance, during their long journey to our shores. And what a spectacle! If you can, try to picture a great room roughly the size of London or Paris, swarming with buzzing Lectroids, all visibly excited by moving images of Buckaroo and the music of the Hong Kong Cavaliers. It was from viewing such performances, of course, that they learned our cultural practice of whistling as a sign of both approval— which they augmented by slapping their wings, forelegs, or antennae together—and agitation, which they lustily displayed at the merest mention of the villainous Hanoi Xan.

How might our alien admirers react, then, if ordered to destroy their idol, along with the entire planet, if it should be discovered that the execrable Red John Whorfin had not died, as first reported, but was still living among the natives? This possibility indeed became known as a result of an intercepted conversation between John Whorfin and Hanoi Xan which I will relate shortly, resulting in a "visit" to the ship by the Empress John Emdall within a shimmering virtual reality field. Appearing in a provocative battle dance designed to agitate her audience and whip them into a psychosexual frenzy, she declared their unbreakable partnership—"You are my veterans, many of you wartime disabled or on the road to recovery, but all of you my finest!"—and her disgust with "the self-willed, the disobedient, the small-brained shaved primates of Earth . . . whose god is their belly, who hide the venom-dripping Red John Whorfin from the light lest their deeds be reproved and their blackened hearts, filled with uncleanliness, scorpions, and all manner of disease and wickedness, be disinfected by my beloved Stain Removers and Bug Exterminators . . . !"

THE EMPRESS EMDALL'S THREAT

I will pause here, gentle reader, because I anticipate at once your questions and the sense of astonishment that just may have knocked you off your chair. John Whorfin, you say? The same John Whorfin? I surely must be delirious, you say . . . talking through my hat. When last seen, was not Whorfin blown into a thousand pieces by Buckaroo Banzai? Or was the Red Lectroid chief simply too stupid to realize he was dead? What other explanation could there possibly be? In terms of comparison, one finds only the ancient gods, Osiris, Yeshua the resurrected Galilean, and Raktabija's blood seed.

To anticipate Perfect Tommy's reaction: "Jumping shiteballs, I'll be got-damn! You can't make this stuff up."

Alas, no, the point is, I have no need to fabricate. If a university student can gene edit one's own superbug into existence, what might a government do with a pinhead of alien DNA? Or with the capture of a demon from another dimension? Almost any fantasy rattling around in your head will be possible one day, so why not now?

Add to Emdall's continuing rants the afflictions of homesickness, hunger, and disease I have mentioned, as well as the imperial priests' angry fulminations against the Cubists, and you have the makings of deepening discord, even mutiny, aboard the vessel *Imperatrix*.

Now allow me to digress, reader, for there is an added complication, if we are to believe John Singsong when he informs us that Emdall had a prodigious and personal interest in Buckaroo Banzai that perhaps went beyond what one might imagine. As an example, late in the voyage, our reporter remembers watching video footage of Buckaroo Banzai appearing at some publicity event in the company of Miss Universe (actually Tommy's love interest at the time), to be followed by another of Emdall's diatribes.

"Miss Universe?! Miss Universe?! You would expect a better xenotype to rule the universe!" she harangued her troops in a state of vexation, via jittery, dizzying movements. "As you approach the planet of the shaved alpha monkeys and other Earth walkers, remember to apply repellant before you disembark . . . else prepare to itch like hellhounds! My intrepid crusaders, who do me proud, you will once and forever destroy the tumor called Red John Whorfin and capture the alpha monkey Buckaroo Banzai, who has given him a toehold! We must make hot the rock he has crawled under and claim the unholy place for your Empress, bringing her light to a new world of lost souls living in darkness and ripe to pluck! Children of dogs and first nephews of squirrels, the whole baboon convention called humanity shall be wiped off the face of the planet after I give the order . . . ! Pray for good hunting . . . !"

Such was Emdall's astonishing threat and her low estimation of humankind drawn not from the cheerful syncopated rhythms and real-life escapades of Buckaroo Banzai and the Hong Kong Cavaliers, but from our planet's own broadcasts of its many war zones and crime scenes, jarring music, lurid films and television shows, and endless childish advertisements of vapid products. Strangely, however, when her fiery transmission concluded, only a muted huzzah went up, for it was nearing dinnertime and the survivors were signaling that they literally were starving. If there weren't enough volunteers, more bodies would have to be rounded up . . . a lurid scene left to the youthful imagination of the reader.

Now, as promised and without knowing whether to laugh or feel sorry for the string of hapless culprits responsible for the crisis, I will relate the proximate cause of Emdall's fury and the threat to our beautiful world: an intercepted telephone conversation in a suburb of greater Paris.

III. LORD JOHN WHORFIN CALLING

By the bowels of all the devils . . .
what are you saying to me?
—François Rabelais

The embossed invitation held a sweet garden scent and intimated an open bar with all drugs available for the twelve-day Christmas orgy at the Temple de la Gloire—Diana Mitford Mosley's fabled place in Orsay—but it was hardly necessary. It was the Yuletide fortnight and Henry Shannon's birthday rolled into one, after all, with his old friends and fellow magi Allan Kardec (alternately known as Pseudo Zoroaster, Hippolyte the Hierophant, Hippolyte the Hermeneut, and Hippolyte the Chaldean) and the Mancunian Manny Magdalene (OBE, QC, MP, Shadow Home Secretary, and rumored to be Xan's hidden dauphin and next in line to the WCL throne) in attendance as the two special guests of honor. But perhaps a little history is in order.

Not long after Buckaroo Banzai first piloted his famous Jet Car through a mountain in the American Southwest, definitively proving the possibility of extradimensional travel, Hanoi Xan (a variant of *xian*, 仙, meaning "enlightened immortal") cobbled together a series of phone calls to the Home for the Criminally Insane in Trenton, New Jersey, a decrepit nineteenth-century facility that then held the demon-possessed Italian physicist Dr. Emilio Lizardo and a handful of other warehoused wild men. On each call with Xan and his chief scientists, Lizardo was sure to harangue at great length on discrepancies in Buckaroo Banzai's published papers, *prima facie* evidence in itself that he was plainly unstable by any measurement.

Yet we know that despite deeming Lizardo a likely snake oil salesman, Xan facilitated his jailbreak from the psychiatric facility, gambling that the eccentric (to put it charitably) physicist could help build a Jet Car and OSCILLATION OVERTHRUSTER for the World Crime League.

"Your heart is good, Lizzie," Xan would tell him in broken Italian. "You've been hit hard because, like most geniuses, you're an innocent with special needs and the mind of a child. You're probably the most singular person I've ever known."

"*Grazie*, Mama," Lizardo would reply, while his other half, his inner Whorfin—an utter stranger in a strange land—presumably stuck Lizardo's own thumb up his sad-sack fat butt, which had bloomed greatly after decades of confinement.

A key question here arises: did Xan actually believe Lizardo was inhabited by a space alien? Or did he merely think he was humoring a madman who could give him what he wanted? Put another way, did John Whorfin reveal to Xan his natural Lectroid self? I admit I have no knowledge of such an encounter; and going by the rule that extraordinary claims require extraordinary evidence, I will demur and leave it to the reader to decide the point. What we do know is that on the advice of his scientists, Xan invested very little actual money in the joint project.

The rest, of course, is part history and part conspiracy theory: Lizardo's violent escape from the asylum with his alien alter ego Whorfin leading the way to the ramshackle Yoyodyne Corporation, where his fanatical Red Lectroid cohort awaited. What followed was even more dramatic, albeit predictable, by which I mean the mortal threat to Earth from Whorfin's enemies on Planet 10 and, ultimately, the timely intervention by Buckaroo Banzai to save the day in his usual spectacular fashion.

This much, then, is in the public domain. Less well known are certain details of the climactic air battle in which Buckaroo shot down Whorfin's getaway ship. Information about Buckaroo Banzai's Jet Car and the aliens' own technology also was kept under wraps by the

United States government, which obliterated any trace of Yoyodyne and shamelessly advanced the counternarrative that the aerial dogfight had been staged merely as a secret government war game.

All well and good, then . . . the whole business seemed settled, or at least shelved and under wraps for a good number of years until the night under consideration, when one of Shannon's encrypted phones jangled with a call from the western American state of Nevada, masked and rerouted through British GCHQ and the French Directorate-General (DGSE). Despite the caller's state-of-the-art cloaked anonymity, something about his raspy, faltering voice and pidgin English caused Shannon's batman and cupbearer, Satrap, a neutered former captain in the shah's Persian Guard, to interrupt his yoga practice and take the call inside to the second butler, who handed the instrument to the septuagenarian housekeeper, who passed it to Shannon's personal dresser at the doorway to his private quarters. She in turn passed the call to his masseur and physical therapist, who found the old man (at least one of him) in his purification bath, medicated on laudanum . . . his ancient epidermis riven with leprous keloids, yet glistening through a homemade emollient and the haze of a mister spewing pungent, exotic scents.

Even more troubling, a fat worm the size and color of a Mojave green rattler now slithered out of Shannon's bed—where it appeared to have left a fresh mess—and scurried into the bathroom, leaving the shuddering masseur in a momentary panic . . .

. . . as his distraught patron quick-crawled out of the tub and practically jumped into the masseur's arms, exclaiming, "The dragon!"

Only after the worm was seen to slenderize and disappear down the drain of the clawfoot tub did Shannon celebrate his close call, upon which signal his nurses and attendants formed a single line to perfume and lubricate him in preparation for the evening's happy festivities—and it was in the midst of this group activity that the chief eunuch reappeared to remind him of the strange phone call.

"A man, or a Lectroid, calling himself Lord John Whorfin," Satrap explained. "Something about the package from a Mr. French . . ."

Xan searched his memory: "Package . . . French?"

"From Panama, some weeks ago, with the filth and human hair," Satrap reminded him.

With Satrap's prompting, Shannon, revealed to my readers as the selfsame Hanoi Xan, at once recalled the odd compact parcel, labeled LECTROID SHOT AND FECES FOR THE RIGHT PRICE, and its peculiar contents wrapped in Styrofoam pellets and a Las Vegas newspaper: several plastic prescription bottles bound together like mini sticks of dynamite. With the exception of one of the bottles that apparently contained a lock of human hair, Xan's chemists came up empty trying to identify the biological samples in each bottle, whereupon he put his own aquiline nose—pointy as a mosquito's proboscis and resting on a bed of white whiskers—to the task and found odd pleasure in the bottles' musky wild-animal pheromone mixed with something that smelled like automobile transmission fluid.

It may not appear obvious, then, why he chose to accept the call . . . unless one understands that he was floating on opium and on this night of all nights feeling more invincible than paranoid. So perhaps it was no more complicated than that. He also may have calculated that the call, like the nasty package that prompted it, was someone's idea of a gag, a joke at his expense, and he wished to discover those responsible in order to repay them the favor. And, last but not least, he may have had a certain dread of joining the holiday festivities and wished to stall for time before doing so.

Whatever the reason, he allowed several minutes to pass while an acrylic rebase was applied to his fresh manicure, with the masseur left holding the dreaded compact pocket phone. (I have forgotten to mention that Xan also loathed digital devices, much preferring rotary phones and Swiss clocks.) It also may be supposed that he half expected the caller to have hung up after the long interval, in which case the decision would have been taken out of his hands, and he would be free to shrug his shoulders and forget the matter altogether.

In the event, however, the caller did not go away; and as sounds of tinkling glasses and festive gaiety filtered in from other rooms, Xan settled into his favorite armchair in his private study, warming himself from both the fireplace and a bottle of Christmas vanilla flavor that he sipped at intervals. Minutes later, the exit of his masseur left only an overhead fan and a dozen or so caged lovebirds to stir the silence—and only at this point did Xan remember the phone in his hand and surprise himself by saying hello into the mouthpiece.

A TORTURED CONVERSATION

After a few awkward grunts from the other end, Xan's eyes glazed over. He had expected to hear a fast-talking shady operator, perhaps with an extortion demand, but instead now pictured a mental patient calling from a hospital or a sidewalk somewhere.

"You've seen a load of my golden spunk, so I'm thinkin' you know who I am," began the bold-voiced caller, who followed with considerable tongue clicking and foreign chirps of a kind Xan had never heard, all interspersed with references in bombastic Italian-accented English to "my embryo" and "my liquid-gold gel sperm."

"That's cute, but sounds like you might be on the terrorist S-list, so watch what you say, Inspector Clouseau," Xan warned, referring to the alias of a high-ranking French intelligence official with whom he had dined only days before.

"Who?" returned the strange voice at the other end.

"Or is it you, Captain Moonbeam at GCHQ?"

There were many possible candidates, most of them known to Shannon and many on the World Crime League payroll. But the mystery caller had a question of his own: "How I know you the real Hanoi Xan, money man with all them marbles?"

"Interesting question. I don't go by that name, but *you* called *me*, my friend. You must have some idea."

"I havin' some idea we goin' back in business . . ."

". . . that probably involves the idea of money," Xan speculated, his head spinning at the old familiar voice in his ear and the sight of a speck of insubordinate dirt on his Richard Mille wristwatch. Full of doubts, he needed time to sort things out.

"Maybe some freeloader snitch talk," he said. "Or maybe you called to discuss the Hayekian school's founding principles of free markets and sound money. If nothing else, I can give you something to cry about."

"Is your world, Hanoi. But maybe you hearin' of the mixed John Whorfin and Emilio Lizardo, my host on your stinkin' planet, bed-wettin' and fartin' anus caboose express . . ."

"Lizardo," Xan repeated, fending off a rush of old memories. "I knew a Lizardo once . . . a redheaded Italian who won Fool of the Year award, then got himself blown all to hell by Buckaroo Banzai."

Out of nowhere, another voice—American Southwestern, maybe Texan or Oklahoman, Xan guessed—cut in to complain, "Banzai? The USAF shot that bugger down!"

"Or the USAF, if you're stupid," Xan said, left to wonder how many people were on this call.

"To hell and back, Hanoi," replied the original voice. "Now Emilio weak as a baby bird with a broken wing . . ."

"Emilio . . . a redheaded Italian. You a redhead by any chance . . . ?"

"Plenty red John Whorfin. Just sayin'."

"Whorfin . . . Whorfin . . . that's no everyday name, either," Xan said, fishing for more.

"No, is my everyday name. Of Lectroid roots, nothing of human. My roots is Planet 10, Earth being stink crap in my mouth . . ."

"Whoa, watch your language," Xan warned, by now convinced he was speaking to a mere prankster, but possibly to a sophisticated professional disc jockey or someone from an intelligence or law enforcement agency who had the gift of perfect mimicry. But just as he contemplated hanging up, a third voice—weaker and with a thicker Italian accent—came on the line, speaking in tremolo: "*Bon giorno, principessa.* Whom am I-a speakin'?"

For a moment, Xan could hardly believe his ears, for this voice he recognized at once . . . and yet who could believe such a thing?

"Emilio? Emilio, you poor bastard . . . it's impossible. That you?"

There was a sudden outrush of breath from this new persona . . . a gasp of surprise, delight, and heartbreak all rolled into one that Xan found artificial, an outward show of emotion of the kind he detested.

"This-a beloved Hanoi Xan?" the puny voice implored.

"Time will tell, old fella."

"Once upon a time," the voice continued, albeit weakening. "Once upon a time . . . comin' to my rescue . . . you comin' back for me, beloved Hanoi Xan?"

"I'll be there in a trice, Emilio."

"What meanin' . . . ?"

"Meaning, are you still married to John, the power-mad space alien despot?"

"I'm-a still become one with the youngster big John," the quivering voice somehow managed.

"Amazing, after the world gave you up for dead. You've come a long way, old man."

"*Giusto, Mama.* That's-a the blessed truth."

But suddenly, amid hissing noises and terrible moans, the first voice regained control and ranted, "Emperor God Lord John Whorfin bringin' you sunshine, Hanoi! Emperor God Lord John Whorfin, Trumpet of Heaven and Son of Soldier King Lord John Shark Crab . . . huggin' you like a brother, Great Xan the Merciless!"

"Indeed, what a pleasant reunion with the two of you," Xan offered. "Just add one more to your little party and you could be the unholy Trinity."

"Funny you say that," said Whorfin, "because we're tryin' to have a little one."

"A little one what?"

"A little whelp, my own zygote. Been carrying maybe thirty thousand your years."

"Please accept my congrats to both of you. Locked up like two squirrels together, I can't say I'm surprised. You must both be on cloud nine," Xan offered.

"Sky-high rocketin', Hanoi. Now I like to askin' some questions."

Xan spiraled into a daydream but continued to play along. "Fantastic. You both made a pretty big splash once upon a time, but that's been a while. Sometimes in life, one minute you're a spider, next minute you're a fly. Where you been keeping yourself, fellas?"

"Location Earth, Hanoi. Locked in big shindig dump, deep in a hole with shit and corpses," said the one calling himself Whorfin.

"Nevada, you say? Home of the Reno Kid?"

"I don't say Nevada" came the reply. "What Nevada?"

"Screwed over but not beaten, then," said Xan. "Defeated but not without hope. At least you'll have a new companion on your journey. Three mouths? How many heads? How does that work exactly, you and your ball and chain?"

"Emilio my rock, but shittin' lumpy eggnog . . . soon be dyin'," said Whorfin. "The hand of death upon him shoulder soon put me under the posies, too. No gettin' around so good since the accident."

"The accident . . . you mean . . ."

"Banzai shoot immortal Whorfin outta the sky and Whorfin crashin' in the muck. Losin' my will, becomin' shaky-like hollow shell, lost my

energy field, everything exceptin' my pride. Also, Lizardo got chronic
wet butt, blood pressure blastin' to the moon. Is life or death, Hanoi . . .
Emilio little tiny man wastin' away on his dead bed . . . and him ginger
hair fallin' out. If him dyin', maybe Whorfin dyin' . . ."

"Like two mountaineers roped together," Xan conjectured. "The
blind leading the blind with a lack of parenting skills. But if you're
anything like a human being, you're incredibly resilient. I recommend
starting every day with a brisk power walk and eating an ample breakfast
with lots of water and fruit juice, cereal with milk, coffee, and toast with
butter and honey, or a choice of sweet muffin and a cream-filled cheesy
omelet. Then I'd try to get laid. If that doesn't work, go for a restraining
order, unless you'd rather spend the rest of your life constantly looking
over your shoulder."

"Is monkey blabber . . . what?"

"Sucks to be either one of you," explained Xan.

". . . and white-hair ass sittin' in pesthole right now. Naked hungry,
mold and roaches, Hanoi . . . putrid worms . . ."

"Worms?" said Xan with evident distaste. "You mean the CIA?
Uncle Sam?"

"Trash and vermin, thank you, Uncle Sam . . ."

"What, no termites? Sounds like you don't have two wooden nickels to
rub together and you're stressing about it—hence this phone call. Hopefully
your fortunes will improve and it's just a hiccup, a temporary setback. When
the world closes a door, try opening a window. Maybe you could wash dishes
or clean toilets," said Xan, by now rather enjoying playing along out of
curiosity. In the meantime, Satrap was speaking with a contact at the DGSE
in an effort to learn the actual physical location of the caller . . .

. . . as Whorfin continued to wax and wane sentimental: "Hurtin' every
second of every day, tryin' to pick myself up. Whatever the phawk.
Whorfin a fighter, Hanoi. Happiness I'm dreamin' many times, wreakin'
havoc, swallowing galaxies with my little peanut . . ."

"That's the fighting spirit. Take that shot on the chin and pull together
a smile . . . the true meaning of Christmas with new friends and a kid on
the way. Joy to the world," Xan said.

"So Whorfin givin' my hand job to you, great Xan . . . boss of the World
Crime League . . . august being, whom there is none greater. Not without
greatest respect I extend my hand, as how we comin' from common lines."

"We are all a product of our environment, good or bad, John. Sounds like you're from out of town."

"And just as you helpin' me, I hereby announcin' today the pendulum swinging back. You will sitting on my right hand when my havoc army take back my throne on Planet 10! God-Emperor Whorfin and Empress Xan, in the nimbus light of my icy castle on 10."

"Whatever. All you need's the right venture capitalist," Xan said, beginning to feel weary. "You say your planet is a ten, John? If you say so, it must be true."

"I sayin' it, Hanoi. When I givin', I givin' with a passion above and beyond, my big heart fallin' like a rock, like a schoolgirl! Tattoo me you name, Hanoi! Lips and tongues of Red Lectroids everywhere caressin' you when God-Emperor Lord John Whorfin hand you a huge cigar of victory, endlessly warm! Some night, some stolen hour, when we alone on one my worlds watchin' suns set, I carryin' you big golden balls, rubbin' you man tits sexy as we walkin' among the wheats."

"Is that your butthole winking at me, John? All the way from Langley . . . the George Bush Center for Intelligence . . . ?"

"That's-a me, Hanoi, and my baby king crown jewel."

"Whatever that means. That's your brand of booty loving, John—not mine—so keep it in your granny panties. Try gathering your composure."

"Gatherin' my composer [sic], Hanoi, but everything John Whorfin sayin' comin' to pass soon. Never have John Whorfin cry in front of nobody," the caller continued, followed by several seconds of dead air. "You right, Hanoi, but I missin' my handle full of old boys . . . John Bigbooté, John Gomez, John O'Connor, John Cleanup, John Small Berries . . . I walkin' cold evenings alone, unlucky, missin' my own kind specially at Christmas. But is okay . . . I no lookin' for pity party."

"For sure, boyfriend. I like your spunk."

"How you likin' my spunk? Slurp, slurp."

"Passion never goes out of style, Big John. I know the feeling; and I like your fighting spirit—except it doesn't pay the rent, does it? We have a saying on my planet: put up or shut up. And you're babbling like some kind of old fool, a mentally disturbed funny feller," Xan commented with a glance at his foot that was keeping rhythm with the cuckoo clock above his head.

Not surprisingly, the caller took umbrage at these remarks and launched a stream of vile and mostly unintelligible philippics, including the following: " 'Funny feller' . . . don't forget you speakin' John Whorfin! Have a nice buttocks, you earthling son of whores! I punch you skunk face and smelly straw hat!"

"You're a mean bird, fireball. You and whose nutsack?"

With explosive fury, the caller poured out his passion: "Eight million my Red commandos waitin' on Number 6 Moon! Red commandos, winged hussars, and stout mountaineers! Winged Lectroids stuck in Seventh Dimension, singin' songs of steel tentacles and lightning tails! Fire and axe! Scourge of the universe, we marchin' and flyin' high together, one thousand legions screamin' as one harmonious roar of blind killin' spree . . . wreakin' havoc, feastin' on millions dead vermins!"

"Sounds like a fairly genocidal and pathological worldview you need help getting through," Xan interjected, "but why call me? Why are you not gone yet?"

"Yes, my true friend," said the caller, who at last took a breath. "Get my red ass outta Dodge . . . except, like Bonaparte on Elba, I gotta no OVERTHRUSTER and I gotta no voice and no representation on account I'm in a cash shortage and a big fish tank."

"So you got spanked and put in a corner. That's some crybaby laundry, all right. It's always about money, isn't it, my friend?"

"Skunk planet makin' my ganglia twitch!"

"It does seem like your circuitry might be a little twisted. Where were we?"

Perhaps the caller misunderstood, because at any rate he continued blissfully: "Roamin' wild my natural habitat, rollin' down them red salt mountains, trespassin' the big petrification with divine nymphs of Zalvoz, then later ridin' cross the heath, up slopes to the snowy river of Mount Paradise soon flowin' black with blood! Happy their lamentations and ruins of their cities . . . crumblin' under my feet! And then the band playin' my triumphal entry into the sacred capital, stadium full of red-eyed beauts . . . need I say more?"

"Count me brainwashed, John. I wish I was there," snorted Xan.

"Bravo, Hanoi . . . is impossible to be angry with you. I bow you majestic wonder and sanctity suckin' you man toe and fart pipe . . .

walkin' in the rain with you bitch ass . . . just as I lackin' means expression, English. Yearnin' and askin' you hand and nut bag forever."

"Beautiful you, John. Zing go the strings, though your world sounds kind of dark and creepy," Xan teased, only to pause . . . less for dramatic effect than to wonder if he was dreaming this entire absurd conversation. If the boys at GCHQ were listening in, they must be belly laughing and rolling on the floor, he thought. Yet he could not bring himself to hang up, partly because it was Christmas Eve and he was stalked by a thousand years of holiday melancholy.

He therefore signaled Satrap to bring him a plate of caviar and a pickled-headcheese omelet and continued to engage the strange caller: "I'll indulge you because I like a man—I mean red space insect—who lives off the sweat of others and is unafraid to express his feelings with self-confidence. But here's the deal: whatever it is you want, I'm going to need something more than half a pile of crap on some science-fiction planet."

These strong words provoked a second round of outrage from the mystery caller(s): "Pile of crap?! *This* rock pile, moldy dead skunk planet! Roach hotel! Obnoxious sun lighting!"

"Just remember who you're talking to," warned Xan.

"I talking Hanoi Xan on shitebox Earth, prison planet! Buttload of pain! Bloat, slobberglob lazy fat moo moo rear of ends! Enjoy motherphawk you dog, Hanoi, worm slob blobber blood fart poundin' nail you flesh!" the voice spewed anew; and here followed a long, tortured stream of impenetrable gibberish, as the caller flew into a rage and seemed to pour out his very soul—and then say it all backward—before Xan moved the phone away from his ear.

"Good grief, Charlie Brown, stick to the outskirts of Funkytown," he rhymed. "Was that an attempt at the spoken word? I don't speak jive, and I don't like whiners."

Without warning Whorfin's voice faltered and sputtered, amid sounds of a great psychic struggle punctuated by muffled gas emissions and two rivals vying to be heard.

"Shite cabbage, cuss you, cum-sponge monkey boy!" spat Whorfin.

"*Figlio di puttana!*" hissed his Italian twin. "Steal-a my thunder in the Eighth Dimension! You know I cannot-a control my release! Aaaaaaaaaaaaaaaaa!"

Even more terrible noises followed, like the savage howls of a man, or something else, crawling off into the weeds to relieve his bowels.

"*Buon appetito*," said Xan.

"*Per favore*, holy Saint Jude, *apostolo e martire*, grant my *petizione* . . . !"

"What? Speakin' real words, Lizards. What meanin' . . . ?" said the god-emperor parasite.

"Meaning maybe you're not as crazy as you sound. Well done— maybe you're just multifaceted." Xan chortled despite himself, distractedly stroking his crusty wisp of a beard and a phallic-symbol necklace carved from a piece of meteorite, then calmly using the embroidered sash of his royal-blue-and-gold kimono to dab first his mouth and then his age-freckled fingers and catlike fingernail claws, meticulously painted a glitter red and inscribed with tiny black-visaged scorpions.

JOHN WHORFIN REVEALS A SOFTER SIDE

This prolonged activity resulted in silence, during which Xan and Whorfin both seemed to disappear into deep reveries punctuated by a panting dog or a heavy breather, or perhaps both, on the line . . . maybe the American? CIA? Or GCHQ? Russian? French? Chinese? The Banzai Institute? Xan was beginning to feel like he was losing his senses.

"Just long time homesick," Whorfin was wheezing in a dark moment, "missin' my sacred land, the place of my birthplace . . ."

"I understand you're in extremis, John or Emilio—a dark, dark moment. But life evolves, so throw away your crying towel. You're fortunate you're not in a zoo, throwing feces at children. Young people pick up on that . . ."

He was drugged and trying to get a grip, slurring certain words: "You're still the great Whorfin. But on this planet people are judged by their appearance and their smell. Convince Lizardo to get a shave and a haircut, wear polished Florsheim wingtips, and be well attired. Make yourselves look presentable in a short-sleeved collared shirt. Above all, act and dress like a winner but save for the future and live within your means. Take an exercise class, but be sure to shower afterward with a good body wash. Obviously, this is not intended to take the place of professional counseling."

"Suckin' a baboon's long one . . ."

Xan yawned and said, "That's totally up to you, John. Don't pitch a bitch. Instead, live every day like it's your last, because one day it will be. Change your diet by cutting out all refined foods, particularly carbs and sugar. Try more salads, probiotics, and green tea. Go for walks together, help Lizard with the dishes. This is not rocket science, but it has benefited thousands in your situation."

"Rocket science what I'm needin' to get off this rock. Emilio got bats in his head . . ."

"Perhaps that is humor, although laced in truth, John. I would challenge your brilliant mind—the two of you, with your never-ending shenanigans—to put your heads together and come up with a plan. Maybe find a craft hobby you can do together or finish that home-improvement project you've been putting off. If you're excited about putting your best foot forward, Lizardo will start getting excited, too. Remember, you broke into Lizardo, drank his juice, took his virginity, and set his house on fire, and now you've got your hand out looking for a new sugar daddy. And what matters most, after all, is how we treat others."

"What meanin' . . . sugar daddy?"

"Meaning you have to look at yourself. I'm having trouble seeing what you bring to the table, other than choking on drool, or how you return to your former glory with your boot heel on the necks of your fellow insect people. Frankly, you sound very vulnerable, John . . . close to unraveling and going over the edge. If you're in an awful marriage that can't be fixed, there comes a point where you just have to let go before it kills you. Just walk away."

"Walk away how, Hanoi?"

"Get back to your own community of wackos and rebound with a vengeance. Live life to the fullest, instead of being shackled to your ball and chain, so I wish you luck with that one-way ticket to Mars and greener pastures. Soldier on and continue your wild escapades, but leave Earth alone—that's my best advice. If you're worth a shite, you'll run with it. Run as fast as you can."

"Runnin' how, Hanoi . . . ?"

"As far and as fast as you can, John. You're a born leader . . . fly like Superman! Do the old Tennessee long jump! What else do you want from me? A cookie? A lollipop? Here's a postage stamp: 'Return to Sender' . . . !"

"Hanoi disrespectin' Whorfin. Crushin' my pussy cake I givin' you and Whorfin name," the caller complained with unabashed self-pity.

"Truer words were never spoken. You want a warm glass of milk with that? Or perhaps you are lactose intolerant . . . ?"

"Piece of shite dummy face, I no got time you, Hanoi. Get out my lifes!"

"That makes three of us, John. Phawk you and the planet you rode in from."

Whorfin cut him off with an even louder outburst: "Put zipper you mouth! Too bad monkey boy, you! All the sudden bad boy! Whorfin not scary you face! Grindin' you bone dust! Whorfin wakin' up! Red Lectroids readyin'! Brave, my Red sweeties, givin' Whorfin them all! Piece of little shite, monkey boy caveman!"

"Tossing threats, are you, John? Come to my house and see how hard you are—I'll have a little trick waiting for you. Unfortunately, now I'm turned on to your mean ass," said Xan.

"Snot suck slobber, fat toad pigeon, hairy leather dwarf daddy . . . fat munchin' booger picker Hanoi! Fat moo moo rear of ends!"

"Roll it in bullshit and smoke it, John." Much more that was indecipherable followed, until Xan couldn't take any more.

"Aw, I seem to have triggered your raisin brain into a rage, like a wild animal. I thought you were moving your bowels for a minute," Xan snickered, more convinced than ever that he had been duped by a professional actor or someone in law enforcement . . . or perhaps even practical jokers from the Banzai Institute.

"Counting on you, Hanoi."

"The only thing you can count on, John, is your fingers or claws or whatever. Bye now."

But just as he moved to end the call, the American came back over the phone's speaker. "Ha, ha, telling the great John Whorfin to wear Florsheims and work on his love handles! Stay special, Mr. Xan—don't ever change!"

"Who is this? Another spook?" demanded Xan.

"Mr. Hanoi Xan, Your Royal Authority? Blackus Fabulous, the Devil's Own Fire? Hinge of Fate and Pivot of Mystery? Godfather of the World Crime League? Am I speaking with the great Hanoi Xan? If so, I come to give homage and assurance of my highest regard. And to wish you a very Merry Christmas! Don't worry, our conversation is secure and encrypted from my end."

"I'm not worried. I have my own unjackable cloud," Xan replied, although in reality his safety lay in Henry Shannon's extensive political connections with governments and their intelligence agencies.

Certainly he could be forgiven for thinking he had had his fill of starstruck, bullshitting morons . . . but his own curiosity and something about the mystery voice—its monotonal Southwestern drawl, couched at intervals in what seemed to be a poor imitation of a French accent—gave him pause. It did not sound like the voice of a complete mental defective but rather one with only a single train of thought . . . a serious person, perhaps even a hoodlum, but one who at least spoke more or less standard English.

IV. THE MYSTERIOUS "MR. FRENCH"

Think and grow rich.
—Napoleon Hill

"So, in a few words, tell me what you are calling about," said Xan robotically into the phone. "I can understand entire sentences."

"The peripatetic Mr. Xan . . . ! At long last! Did you get my Christmas birthday package, Mr. Xan?" the fresh voice at the other end asked. "The Dr. Grabow pipe covered in Lectroid skin, along with the Lectroid bio samples I sent to you on behalf of Lord John Whorfin . . . ?"

"Who told you I favor a Dr. Grabow pipe?" Xan wanted to know, bringing the phone closer and confirming his suspicion that a small angry dog, most likely muzzled, was snarling ferociously in the background.

"Short list, Mr. Xan. Point being, it's in your CIA file and psychological profile," replied the voice. "I have a buddy with access to that very sensitive information, the kind of secret info that could get me dragged into court and possibly shot."

"Yet you do it without shame," Xan observed with growing skepticism.

"This I do not dispute, because I believe in the miraculous . . . why fate picked me above all men. Something miraculous is happening."

"River deep, mountain high," said Xan. "How wonderful for you."

"Because I've stopped being stupid and doing good deeds for murderers and have asked John Whorfin for forgiveness . . ."

"I believe you," said Xan, rolling his eyes.

"Only the best go on to be test pilots."

"Right."

". . . because I'm a sick man who has begun smoking dope and some other stuff and pissing on fire hydrants, headed for a divorce with a driving need to make some money."

"And break your oath. You must have feelings for me . . ."

"I'm a believer, Mr. Xan, yessir, why I'm reaching out asking you to vouchsafe me your favor. Merry Christmas and a cheery winter solstice and Happy New Year—let me be among the first to wish you the best on this happy occasion with my modest earth-changing gift."

"In exchange for my hard-earned, no doubt," Xan said. "As I said to your so-called John Whorfin fella . . ."

"Ha, ha. Go slow, said the turtle, by way of Mr. Contreras in Panama City . . . maybe you heard of him? I also sent along a secret map of the largest deposits of rare earth elements on the moon, just to let you know I'm no bounder, but a serious person to be taken seriously, having access to US government intelligence of the highest level . . ."

"Of course you do," Xan said. "Looking out your window, what do you see?"

"I don't have a window, guv'nor. I'm in the basement," said the flat American voice.

"Watching the moon." Xan laughed, imagining the caller in a top-secret underground room aglow with computer screens.

"Surveyed by our secret Lawn Boy rover," claimed the caller. "The same used in Afghanistan to map your vast opium-poppy holdings."

Once again it occurred to Xan to hang up; but something, perhaps fate, stopped him. Instead, he salivated over his own reflection in his Jensen silver dinner bowl, where he had been picking at the remnants of the pickled-headcheese omelet. Therein, he glimpsed a gentleman with neither classic good looks nor the face of a leprous crone, in the way many have described him; rather, he was at once something altogether more inviting and imposing. Beneath an absurdly fitting toupee, he bore the tattoo of a single star on his bald pate, indicating that he had assumed divine status, while on one side of his face he found much else to admire—a seductive amber eye more or less the color of his equine false teeth, a floppy goat's ear, and penciled eyebrows to match a snowy brush mustache beneath a nose that did not seem proportional to his face, along with a pockmarked, leathery complexion slathered with beauty ointments and lip gloss. His other side bore the effects of palsy, however, presenting the same facial features but hanging limp and grotesque. Thus sated with equal parts self-love and self-hate, he reached for a dark chocolate with his left hand, whose illustrated palm had begun to itch. As the sensation intensified, the tattoo thereon—a triangle circumscribed inside a circle of esoteric symbols—began to glow and itch even more until he licked it with his slithery, elongated tongue, which he used also to moisten his eyes in the absence of tear ducts.

"Go on, tell me more, if you have my dossier in front of you," he said, gazing into the tattooed eye and beginning to contemplate the possibility of probing this stranger, perhaps cultivating him as a confidential source.

"I don't have it, but I could probably get it," the caller boasted. "Give the devil his due. I admire your *joie de vivre*! I know you own all the opium and emerald mines in Afghanistan and all the Frankenstein corn in Nebraska, Mr. Xan. I am aware also of your eleven-thousand-dollar investment in Yoyodyne to help Whorfin build his homecoming ship back in the day."

"I don't know what you're talking about," Xan replied, forcing a laugh and smelling danger. "Must be something you've picked up on talk radio or read in one of those crusty men's magazines. You obviously have me confused with someone else."

Now it was the caller's turn to laugh hysterically. The antics of a lunatic madman, Xan thought.

"Oh, yes, sorry to cast a blot upon your reputation, Mr. Xan! Haw! You're also into games and naughty fun and seek to establish a totalitarian one-world government with yourself as chief. That's why they call you the evil that pisses gold and throws dust in men's eyes, who steals the sunshine and does not sleep until his enemies are eradicated. I think we both know that man . . . woof! Woof, woof!"

The caller could be heard barking now in tandem with the small dog, whom he eventually interrupted to address in a radically different infantile voice. "I don't give two squirts of piss—what's nagging you? You travel, you eat well, just dawg the phawk up! Take charge of your manhood!"

Xan meanwhile was rolling his eyes and muttering, "Into the valley of death rode the six hundred . . . down the bunny trail."

"What did you say, Mr. Xan? I hope I didn't miss anything."

Hearing the caller's "normal" fake French voice return, Xan said, "You're somewhere out there, aren't you, Mister . . . ?"

"My name is superfluous, but it's Antoine. One Antoine French, the Marquis of Lincoln," replied the caller.

"Of course it is. One Antoine French . . . because you're American. Extra points in the originality department."

"Okay, you got me, sir. I wish I could come back with something sassy. Just call me Amerigo Vespucci, the Duke of Earl."

"I prefer to call you Knucklehead, but I do not give a damn about it, as you sound like an unsavory character with a certain cerebral liability or social disorder who couldn't quite cut the mustard," said the older man.

"Please don't throw cold coffee on me yet, Mr. Xan. Understand I am not some kind of quack, or a half-wit, but am obliged to be a shady phawk for now and walk in the shadows since I am calling from a top-secret American military installation, my pit stop in purgatory."

"Things don't always turn out well, Mr. French. I, too, walk in the shadows and am often mistaken for another," Xan said.

Without warning, French again seemed to bark at someone else. "Cinch up your straps, cowgirl. This is poker but a shite-ton harder."

Xan interrupted to say, "If I told you to phawk yourself, it would probably just confuse you further."

"Ding, ding, good one, Mr. Xan! You can take that one to the bank. I was only a fighter pilot spending my best years cinching my asshole tight, pulling out of tailspins and aerial acrobatics, pissing on terrorist hovels and turning their caves into Funkytown . . ."

"And did our conscience turn black?"

"I killed them like lice, guv'nor, like sugar ants, same as I shot down John Whorfin over Jersey . . ."

"You shot down John Whorfin? You, and not Banzai?" Xan replied, gnawing at his manicure to keep from laughing.

"There has to be a reason, right? Though in reality I'm a man of high morals who tries to live the right way, but unfortunately I'm damaged and have had to shift gears, according to the ineptitude and lame skills of orgasmic pussies who somehow pass for adults and dishonor the uniform—in it for the drama, ha, ha—and the broken world as I understand it. Not saying I'm a hero . . . others have done bigger, badder shite. I only phawked the terrorist monkey while braver men held its tail, so this is not a cue for sympathy. Nor am I asking for your approval, though I do have an appreciation for goodwill. The bottom line is that Lord Whorfin—with whom you were speaking—is alive as surely as I'm talking to you, although in a good deal of pain and on an emotional roller coaster. Naturally, he doesn't trust people. His enemies enslaved his followers and put him out to pasture in the Eighth Dimension, but he intends to come roaring back with a cold, hard bitch slapping."

"Also not to be confused with reality," said Xan derisively. "Sounds like he has more lives than Felix the Cat. Where is he?"

. "In a room secure as a safe . . . but perhaps not for long. He's pregnant, you know—"

Xan fell uncharacteristically mute.

"—and has been imprisoned in a secret government laboratory where his host and compadre Emilio Lizardo lost the sparkle in his eye . . . dying of advanced adenocarcinoma and gestational diabetes, among other things, such as self-inflicted injuries. The docs are trained fools, unfamiliar with alternative life forms, and have taken away his Mexican salsa."

"Big shocker. To summarize your point?"

"God's fruits, the gift of life made of stardust and Mexican jumping beans. But if Lizardo expires, Whorfin gets flushed out his ass gasket. That's why, Mr. Hanoi Xan, I am communicating."

"You want some of my famous 'Hole in Your Stomach' salsa?"

"Haw, no, because I need some big-ass muscle and I'd like very much to get Emilio to a chiropractor in Brazil who thinks he might just be able to kick his smooth bottom into gear."

"A likely story. Are you broke, French?"

"Broke as a joke, guv'nor, but it's not about the greenbacks," the caller claimed, "although if I had your kind of money, I could throw mine in the trash . . ."

"How about a gun to shoot yourself? What caliber hole would you choose?"

The caller dropped his pseudo-French accent for a moment and protested, "Yes, I am trying to advance myself, Mr. Xan. I think most of us are. So if you are not interested in assisting Emperor Whorfin on his homeward flight—as the one person most suitable in the world to help him—please allow me to put another flea in your ear. Might you be interested in acquiring Buckaroo Banzai's Jet Car plans?"

"Jet Car plans?" Xan said, instantly perking up but in no mood for self-torture. "And the OVERTHRUSTER? I don't like games, French, or having my leg pulled."

"Mr. Xan, m'lord, I'm not pulling your leg, believe me. Pulling your leg would be very reckless. I'm talking the entire set of blueprints to Buckaroo Banzai's Jet Car, including the OSCILLATION OVERTHRUSTER, superslick vinyl wrap, and a custom smart-grid timing belt."

"A smart-grid timing belt?" questioned Xan.

"Based on Tesla's 1929 patent but using an improved numerical system for the directed ZQ photon energy beams' x, y, and z pyramidation point—something I strongly recommend if you want to go through solid matter," said the strange caller.

There was a pause as Xan cleared his throat and suddenly had the urge to visit the bathroom. But was it excitement or wariness of overstimulation he was feeling? The caller meanwhile continued: "I don't need to tell you we're talking a Planck temperature somewhere in the neighborhood of 1.41679×10 to the 32nd, Kelvin, in a matter of a picosecond . . ."

"In your neighborhood, Mr. French?" he said. "You must have a straitjacket in every color."

"Well put, guv'nor. Haw, haw, I tip my hat to you, but Mr. Contreras sent me. He thought you might be interested."

"Contreras doesn't have this number."

"No, but don't forget I work for the United States government with a top-level, code-only security clearance. For example, I know something about your ancient feud with Buckaroo Banzai . . . having something to do with the Pythagorean theorem and the value of the hypotenuse. So my point is that I have access to materials thirty-five levels above Top Secret and things could get very messy for me. Just making this call, I'm the accursed fellow incriminating myself . . . damned from the start, sir, so the quicker we wrap this up, the better . . ."

"Now you're making some sense," Xan agreed, glancing at his timepiece. "The quicker, the better."

"The sum total is maybe I've made a blunder, because you do not see my love but think me a schemer rather than a victim of the first order, trying to hand you a key to unlock the power of the universe. But it seems I've dialed a wrong number."

The caller was agitated, breathless, and Xan felt like a cigarette, craving the taste of menthol. Somewhere in the house a door slammed and startled him.

"Don't get jumpy, French," he said. "I'm listening."

From the other end came a sigh, then what sounded like a repressed sob, then a hiccup . . . and finally a snarl and a medley of dog noises.

"What I mean is, I could spend the rest of my life in the Iron Bar Hotel," the American said gravely. "I could go up in flames at any moment. I would need to disappear."

"You would perhaps need to die."

"I've considered that, Mr. Xan, and made arrangements. My bug-out kit is ready, but I'm already in too deep, so I might as well stir some shite. As a guarantee of my good faith, I'm sending another package out to Mr. Contreras. In the meantime let's keep in close touch, though I most look forward to visiting you in one of your imperial courts, where, if you would confer upon me your seal, your World Crime League signet ring, I will happily kiss it."

"Then your knees must become tough as a camel's. But play me and I will vaporize your sad booty."

"Haw. Under your divine left hand, what is not possible on our joyful journey?"

"Most definitely, French. You're a live man."

"Please . . . Antoine."

"Antoine . . . I'm handing you to my assistant, who'll give you instructions so that it arrives in tomorrow's dispatch bag. Thanks for reaching out."

"No. Thank *you*, Mr. Xan. Woof! Woof!"

XAN SETS SAIL

After a brief conversation with Satrap that mainly consisted of coded hand gestures, Xan lit a cigarette and took his customary eyedropper of calomel before resuming his night voyage, floating down a winding river . . . that middle zone between sleep and wakefulness . . . before taking flight and letting his wings take him wherever they wished to go . . .

. . . as through a patch of sky John Whorfin appeared, dressed in white, with a black beard and searing dark eyes, saying, "I am the worst of the worst."

"I respect your game, Whorfin," he murmured. "But there can be only one True Son of Heaven."

Of course he was used to hearing from pranksters and petitioners of almost every nationality, many of whom begged to serve under his flag as errand and whipping boys, even if it meant sticking wires in their heads and being controlled like remotes. Of these, only the lucky champions with "sunlight on their faces" would ever rise to the level of Lasiqs or self-sacrificing companions and assassins. And of these rising luminaries, fewer still would undergo baptism with their own blood and tears to become full-fledged apprentices in the business affairs or propaganda wing of the one-thousand-year-old organization handed down from the khans and the Secret Order of Assassins. Finally, only a minute number of companions would be invited to join the governing bodies, the Diaconate and the Bishopric, and become franchisees in the most elite den of iniquity and society of king criminals ever to exist: the transnational Interlocking Directorate, informally known as the World Crime League . . . the same organization that "Antoine French" now apparently wished to join; and although Xan was preternaturally wary of trading in sensitive government secrets, particularly with someone who seemed slightly off his rocker, in his long and colorful experience spanning generations, it was always the risks not taken that rankled him the most and kept him awake nights.

This man French had not named his price, but if he really could produce Banzai's Jet Car technology, most importantly its OSCILLATION OVERTHRUSTER, the sky was the limit. Moreover, based upon French's delicate mental state, Xan reasoned that the offer was time sensitive. It was also only prudent to assume that French was shopping his materials elsewhere . . . to governments or even to the Banzai Institute itself, the very thought of which caused Xan to ball his fists with hate.

In this context the keen reader may recall the well-known line from Du Fu, favorite poet of both Buckaroo Banzai and Hanoi Xan: "The carp swims early to find the fishermen still unfurling their nets." I have heard Buckaroo Banzai offer something like the very same advice—"Life is short: we arrive late and leave early, when it is better to do the opposite"—and examples of the worth of this truism abound. In arriving sooner than expected, the lone warrior slips past enemies sent to dispatch him; the earlier worm avoids the early bird; the early arriving salesman hears office gossip and gains much valuable intelligence that will serve him well against his competitors. More importantly, it is to be hoped that unaccounted arrivals may constrain the Furies and Fates from acting mischievously in concert.

By the same token, Xan was not one to remain in one locale for long . . . a restlessness owing as much to his mercurial moods as threats to his safety. For decades his favorite watering hole had been the Shepheard Hotel in Cairo, where he kept an apartment. But the Shepheard was no longer the Shepheard of legend, and Egypt was no fun these days. Political events in that part of the world had robbed his tranquility, and it was much the same with his underground mansion at Petra, which had its own set of problems. Old Ma'rib was of course out of the question, and it would be reckless to take his entourage to North America. Of course there was always the annual salt trek across the Himalayas, but good weather was still months away. Nonetheless, the strange call from Nevada had left him second-guessing, obsessing over his own safety. And there were other alarm bells, as it was quickly learned that only a few days earlier Contreras, a worthy assassin and loyal Lasiq, had taken a swan dive into the Panama Canal and failed to come up for a breath.

So now was not the time to dither. Directly French's package arrived in Marseille the following day, it was brought by special courier to Orsay and placed upon Xan's white grand piano.

THE EFFECT OF THE PACKAGE

As Xan examined the crumpled cardboard box bearing the label (in shaky block printing) HANOI XAN, DEVIL'S OWN, WITH AWE AND REVERENCE, he thought, "This has to be a joke. If not, it's even more hilarious."

Untying a red Christmas bow on the box's lid, he delved into a trove of wadded graph paper to find—wrapped in a piece of shimmering, almost liquid-like vinyl material marked SUPERSLICK—a round, fist-sized object spray-painted the color of trophy gold, with various wires and gauges attached. The crinkled pages of the graph papers themselves, smeared with food and coffee stains, displayed numerous crude drawings and fanciful descriptive captions penciled in the same chicken scrawl: SUBMARINE-MOUNTED DARK STAR OSCILLATRON THRUSTER . . . NITRO-FUELED LA-Z-BOY RECLINER . . . HIGH-DENSITY-FOAM NONSAGGING (FIRM) CUSHIONS . . . WITH SADDLEBAGS, NUKE KNOBS, CUP HOLDER, THE LANCE OF DESTINY TACHYON SHOOTER IN TINFOIL (a long Pitot tube protruding from a chaise lounge recliner). Still other pages were covered with detailed designs, elaborate calculations, and additional captions: BLUE AURORA, MEISSNER SUPERSLICK EFFECT, EIGHTH DIMENSION RESONANT FREQUENCIES AND TRAPDOOR ALGORITHMS, DIMENSION-SHIFTING SUPERCONDUCTING OVERSQUARE PUSHROD QUANTUM NANOTHRUSTER, INCREASED ELECTROMAGNETIC TECTONIC TORQUE AND OVERTHRUST ANGLE W/ ZERO RESISTANCE AND DECREASED STROKE-TO-BORE RATIO, TIME THE WARP (FARADAY CAGE WARP BUBBLE VACUUM EFFECT) INTO SWIRLING BLACK HOLE (DARK ENERGY)!!!

Besides these items—and I report it here only for the factual record and the serious student—there appeared at the bottom of the box an added holiday bonus buried in a crumpled *Las Vegas Review-Journal*: two gift baskets—one crammed full of summer sausages and cheese, the other chock-a-block with varieties of fruit—both of these wrapped in red-and-green holiday cellophane. So put yourself in Xan's shoes, dear reader. Taken together with the crude clay model that resembled a human heart or perhaps a child's rattle box, the diagrams and so-called formulae themselves appeared to be a joke, as if sloughed off in a matter of minutes and so shoddily sketched that the accompanying calculations and tech specifications could scarcely be taken seriously, even after Xan slipped on his reading glasses and tried to make some sense of it all. He was after all no physicist, but the sloppiness of the overall presentation suggested either a sick sense of humor or mental laziness on the part of the sender, leading him to deem the documents as likely counterfeits.

"*Tant pis*," was his reaction upon examining the contents of the box and experiencing a sense of disappointment that was almost personal. Whence this feeling?

Handling the absurdly crude clay model of an OSCILLATION OVERTHRUSTER, he could be excused for reminiscing about his earlier association with John Whorfin and the motley band of Lectroid stragglers at the Yoyodyne Corporation. If only . . . if only, he mused . . . if not for Buckaroo Banzai, things might have been different. Despite Whorfin's boundless egomania, a great alliance might have bloomed.

But beyond the dashed hopes represented by French's joke box, there was something else that inflamed Xan's brain, that sent his thoughts in another direction and bears mentioning. By this I mean his loneliness, his alienation . . . indeed his very conviction that he himself was a kind of alien not of this earth. How else to explain his superhuman talents? His inexplicable longevity?

Either he was a god or a being from another world—what else could account for his superiority?

Granted, he did not know the answer. There was no scientific evidence that he possessed actual alien DNA, and his true origins were lost in the mists of antiquity; but in effect he believed himself to be an alien among lesser humans and therefore something of a kindred soul with the Lectroid Whorfin. Paradoxically, however, he also believed aliens of various denominations were fairly commonplace, living unnoticed among us. Proof of their presence could be found in the simple act of watching television and pushing the pause button, thereby capturing people with alien facial expressions.

"Look at that one," he would tease and show others just such a face caught in midspeech. "Zombie or alien?"

But to return to the bundle of papers sent by Mr. French, there was also something else: a loose bundle of government documents stamped TOP SECRET / SENSITIVE COMPARTMENTED INFORMATION. Even skimming the surface of these pages, Xan became convinced they were not to be brushed off quickly and set them aside for future reference; and with a signal he instantly summoned Satrap and his muscular shield maidens, who measured his testosterone against his baseline and gave him multiple injections south of the border, in his nether region: B_{12} with Benzedrine, cocaine and a cocktail of steroids, amniotic fluid, rhinoceros horn, human growth hormone, and perfumed oils he called "arse sweeteners." The same attendants next laced his bespoke oxfords and dressed him in red parachute pants and Charlemagne's supposed seamless robe of Christ, to which overall effect he added a gnarled walking stick said to be carved from the true cross itself—passed down from Constantine and his mother, Saint Helena—and customized with Xan's own adornment, a desiccated stingray tail said to possess magical properties of its own. By means of these holy relics, and like a moth drawn to the light, he flitted several times around the ceiling before directing himself toward a portal flanked by blazing sconces and a quartet of singing castrati carolers known as Death Dwarves. Each pair of these consisted of a dwarfish naked eunuch, tattooed chin to wrist and perched piggyback-style atop a muscular "bottom."

Now, weary of self-propulsion or in keeping with some procedure of long standing, Xan allowed himself to fall into the arms of Satrap, who cradled him like a swaddled infant and led the way, as the King of Crime and his colorful entourage swept forward into the ballroom.

"It's a holly jolly Christmas!" a hundred voices cheerfully intoned, followed suddenly by a manic bout of mariachi music announcing the arrival of Xan and the hundred-dollar gratuities he tossed like confetti.

V. A COURT MASQUE

> Terrible were his crimes—but if you wish to blackguard the
> Great King, think how mean, obscure and dull you are . . .
> —Robert Lowell

You may take it as fact that Buckaroo's new bride, née Penny Priddy, had no memory of the Jet Car crash, nor of her body being stolen and revived from the dead, or near dead, depending upon which version you believe. Indeed, she recalled almost nothing before waking up in a strange room, being stuffed into the trunk of a car, the late-night move to a location called Astor Place, the helicopter and private jet to God knows where . . . but how long had she been here in this dark dungeon? Weeks, months? And what had she been doing before any of that? The story they told her was that she had suffered from a near-fatal case of viral encephalitis, causing severe damage to her hippocampus and near-total memory loss. Try as she might, ponder and ruminate as well as she could, it was all she could do to say even a few words; mostly she spent her days hugging herself and holding her own hand.

Was her brain damaged or chemically altered? She was sure of it, as she often caught her thoughts rambling on senselessly . . . perhaps from the odd powder her strange captor called "unicorn dust" that he liked to blow in her face. How else to explain her inferior state of mind, a mental bloatedness interspersed with migraine jabs, nausea, and wild visions? And this was queer, since she usually thought of herself in such terms as "energetic" and "dynamic," a can-do person (although she lacked any real memory of her past): one of those cheerful, optimistic souls who are fond of saying things like "Turn that frown upside down— we're all in this together," when in fact she was totally alone in her daily life and in any case could barely string a few coherent words together.

Besides the powerful tranquilizers that put her into a kind of catatonic fugue, she was immobilized by physical pain and loneliness, causing her to look forward even to those moments when her mysterious jailer, a coxcomb and apparent man of riches who called himself the Black Rhino, would arrive . . . his approach signaled by the ancient bell he wore around his neck like a dairy cow. Only initially did he appear to her as a rhinoceros; other days he was the Blue Panther Prince or a prancing monkey, but always wearing the rusted bell.

"Do not mistake my kindness for weakness or I shan't come back," he liked to tell her on such unceremonious occasions when it fully dawned on her that this was her new station in life, following whatever had been her former one. But clearly something was afoot this evening; the oxygen in the air seemed more depleted than usual, reminding her of the foul air in the various car trunks that had smuggled her like so much contraband during her kidnapping ordeal . . to this new nightmarish place.

Now the rapid drumbeats—like volleys of shots heard as single cracks and interlaced with a tumult of wild, frenzied voices and the acrid smell of kerosene lamps—sharpened her anxiety to a sense of impending doom. (I can only try to present my conception of her mind, although there are no words to convey accurately the ghastliness of her captivity or the horrors still to come.) A minute later, the door to her dark cell opened and she felt a choke collar looped around her neck by silent hooded figures, followed by a stumbling trek down a *via ferrata* to the cavernous underworld whose blaze of light hit her like successive waves of nausea and a suffocating aspect that caused her to wobble and feel faint . . .

. . . as the mariachi ceased its happy strains and a string quartet began to unpack amid grunts from a pair of midget wrestlers copulating in plain view and an inflatable Père Noël bobbing above the mob of painted revelers—many in Father Christmas attire while others, in animal skins, appeared as wolves or dancing bears—wandering about in a state of drunken euphoria, singing and dancing, beating drums, shaking maracas and bone rattles while riding the backs of others or indulging in public sex acts. The greater part were men, but no small number were women and others of indeterminate biology and even the odd android. Most had the same apparent purpose, however: to fuel themselves into a state of communal ecstasy compounded by pain. With whips and cat-o'-nine-tails, many lashed their neighbors or themselves, while others doubled their pleasure by observing the instruction of their "True Bible," the book of life and black Book of Books, that it is more blessed to give *and* receive than to do either solely. Indeed, this guiding principle suffused the entire mad whirl of motion that greeted her, from which—due to limited time and space and a sense of decorum—I have added nothing and subtracted much.

XAN, THE LAW GIVER

Now she turned to see the slight bird-like figure who on this night wore all blue and seemingly had coalesced soundlessly alongside her, held aloft by a younger, muscular companion, so that the little bird fellow—the aforementioned man of riches in blue plumage and mask and wrapped in a leopard skin—seemed to be as tall as she. Gazing into his peculiar glowing eyes, visible even through the mask, she had to admit he was not a beautiful man, although there was about him both an undeniable sense of solidity and a powerful presence, despite his compact size, not to mention a putrid smell that could not be masked by his perfume that some part of her remembered from a lifetime ago but could not name.

"... the frailty of all that is human," he was saying to her. "Try to stay awake, my sunshine."

"What?"

He merely shook his head, leaving her with the more urgent question of who he was. Who was this crazed man—this thing—responsible for the tragedy that had befallen her . . . the crimes against her humanity? And yet . . .

Why did others cheer him so? A sea of voices hailing him as Shang-Ti, or Huang-di, Pater and Father, or Mr. Shannon? Still others in the mob whispered almost religiously, "Hanoi Xan . . ."

And who was she, for that matter? Was that bridge to her former life—the whole history of who she was, and a sister—burned and lost forever? To hear him tell it, they had both been gods in Greece, the Nile Valley, and then later in Mexico, where the blood of thousands flowed upon his altar . . . until people stopped believing in him, so he became a man and died, only to return because he was a star seed and mother of the night and child of the sun, but she guessed he simply had been out in the sun too long.

A natural fibber, then: "I have told you already that from the first time I laid eyes on you, from the level of intensity, my parietal eye knew instantly we had been lovers across the sands of time, either in this world or some other. I knew you were my immortal half sister, something you will come to recognize as your memory improves and you lose your bourgeois traits and values."

"Then . . . ?" She began a question which he already seemed to anticipate.

"Of course not everything goes our way," he said and proceeded to explain how she had been born without memories of prior lives and misdeeds—of which she had many—which meant that after each rebirth she had to reset and begin anew, whereas he, a dying and rising god among men, retained a memory of who he really was on the other side of the intersection between life and death.

"It's called ancestral knowledge," he explained. "Without the ponderous barriers of time and distance, I carry it all in my head. Nothing of consequence is left behind."

Such talk made her want to beat her head against the wall, and yet she also blamed her poor memory for not giving her a better handle on the meaning of life. He, on the other hand, when he spoke with a certain hypnotic tone, was able to invade her brain against her wishes . . . which she interpreted as his own evil means in the service of his evil purpose.

"I will point you in the right direction, Alisa," he never tired of telling her and now turned her head back toward the theater of cruelty.

Mostly, he called her Alisa, then Pallas or Pulchérie, also Mother Mara the Temptress or Little Pousie or Bon-Bon or some goddess or other whose names she could not remember, much less get straight. But she did not feel like a goddess, not since he had come to her that very first night as a rhinoceros, smelly and unwashed, while sermonizing: "And as a woman, you are fine witted enough to understand that it is in the name of motherhood and sexual morality that the priestly castes in their dark robes have forever held you in subjection. If a woman's chief honor is her worthless virginity, know how little you are valued."

How little she was valued?! Saying this to his pleasure slave! Yet he denied mistreating her and, sensing her desolation, would say, "You are thinking of someone. It seems he played you like a guitar, thinking to keep you on a string, while I have loved you since that first winter in Mongolia when I took you by my right *de jambage*."

His special insight in this regard lay in the fact that, as the son of Zeus and an incarnation of Vishnu, he had sacrificed his own divinity to become flesh, or so he liked to say. His other claims—that he was the First Adam or even preceded Adamic man as a prototype discarded because of his godlike properties—were equally laughable; and yet like the snake in the Garden, he had paranormal talents. Already, she had seen him shoot fireballs out of his hands and kill one of his singing parakeets with but a drop of his spittle, which was nearly black.

Just now, surveying the swirling mass of partygoers below them, he silenced them merely by holding up his left hand, whose shiny signet ring and elaborately tattooed palm had a peculiar calming effect even upon her as well.

"Friends, Romans, countrymen, welcome to my sacred garden! Without further ado I give you Saturnalia and the flower garden of human love!" he proceeded to shout. "Long live Saturnus!"

"Long live Saturnus! Viva! Merry Saturnalia!" they responded in near unison; and upon his signal a middle-aged man, with an enormous distended belly and a single turkey feather protruding from his boxer shorts, entered the subterranean hall like a frightened grouse already sensing his doom. Nor was he mistaken, for in another instant he ran for his life, chased by party guests with cigarette lighters and bags of buttons and button stitchers. As greater numbers joined the frenzied attack and took turns burning his crotch, the unhappy fellow found it impossible to escape or even to scream—his mouth was quickly buttoned shut—and his tormentors trapped him, proceeding to stitch buttons of varied sizes and colors directly onto his skin.

At once she cried and retched, although she still found it impossible to avert her eyes or close them; and in any case, the image of the big-bellied man was already seared into her addled brain . . . along with the same feeling of numbness and immobility that she was unable to overcome on a daily basis. What she did instead was hold her breath in apprehension, feeling she was no longer breathing; yet in another sense she felt she owed it to the pitiful victim to watch . . . almost as if her silent witness could lend humanity or meaning to the scene. So her gaze never left the miserable fellow, even as the mob swirled around him and the string quartet players themselves began to pound their instruments with ferocity and the victim was reduced to gasping for air and clutching his throat.

"Have you ever watched a pack of dogs at play, peacefully running and gamboling about, only to turn viciously on one of their own in an instant?" the man in blue asked her. "It can happen swiftly and not necessarily to the smallest or weakest. A strange dog enters the area, and the entire pack seems to sniff his fear and then turns on him. This stuffed Christmas turkey, by no means spotless, was once the richest man in all of Paraguay, yet look how they prick him. It is simply something that happens, an invisible sign that the odd man out sends . . . a vibe we do not quite understand. Perhaps his energy is not consonant with the other members of the pack."

He was amused by the look of stupefaction on her face as well as her rude awakening—since the very thought of aggressive force was foreign to her notion of the world.

Indeed, her tender nature had been insulted, brought into total disorder by the immediacy of torture and death in front of her. Yet for all her mute protestations, she made no effort to avert her eyes from the brutal sight, nor did the man of riches—or the man of golden nonsense, as she now considered him—seem surprised by her sniveling. If anything, he was entertained by the very thing she feared: her fascination with the grotesque, which by now had raised its ugly head.

"It's all right, my little one. He won't go to waste," he informed her. "At least not his liver and conch meat; it's no harder to peel down a human ear than a banana, and with a jeweler's hammer and chisel, his brain will be a delicacy."

At this he merely laughed and continued: "Don't seek an explanation that is too slippery for you to grasp, because the whole of life is in this little production. It is all about dominance and submission. The mark has rolled over and will be basted in his own bodily fluids, fried like a bug on an electric zapper. His tougher portions will be given to the cannibal monks and the poor, where he will be further appreciated. The very last of him will be made into human hummus, gelato, and vegetable oil, added to dog food, sodas, and pasteurized milk, or even school paste, by one of our subsidiaries."

Poetic words he had in abundant supply, yet she shuddered to think what kind of obscenity this bloodthirsty devil was about to perpetrate, as he prepared for the defloration of her soul by donning a pair of white opera gloves.

Welcome to the natural world, then, a world without mercy; this was his message. She was worried sick about the poor victim, but what else could she do? Scream? Who would hear her? Who would care? And how much worse was still to come, as the plot thickened? Besides, she needed help focusing her thoughts, but focusing on what? Indeed, she seemed to be waiting for instructions, in order to know what should be her own response. So she continued to watch the spectacle without really seeing but feeling dirty all the same, as if lying helpless in a bed of filth and doing nothing more than dreaming of a bath. But it was not her skin that needed cleansing.

"Now death is staring him in the face. It's both poignant and humorous. Once he has been selected by the Selector to propitiate the gods, there is no going back," he said, pointing out a particular face in the crowd that appeared to make him quail: a naked man in horn-rimmed glasses, covered in mud and mucus and other human ooze.

"Selector," she pronounced slowly, as if to commit the word to memory.

"The Selector . . . the Dispatcher, the Rat, the Dragon, the Wyrm," he affirmed, with scarcely disguised loathing. "From Constellation Unknown. He works for Erlik the Mongolian, the Admin. The peacock . . ."

"The peacock?" she also repeated without any idea why. More disturbingly, however, she seemed to recognize the fellow in horn-rimmed glasses, but from where? Where could she have known him? Had she, too, been "selected"? Although she could not recall the exact time and place of her abduction, her mind turned back often to the vague recollection of waking up in a strange place, a cheap room, among masked figures who wielded odd straps and tools and remained unmoved by her cries for help. Perhaps if she had screamed or fought them, she speculated . . . but, no, she disregarded this possibility, feeling hopelessly paralyzed and believing at the time that they were surgeons or even government men, though why she thought this was unclear.

But, in any case, she kept coming back to the riddle: why her? She had told her captors from the beginning that they had kidnapped the wrong woman, obviously mistaking her for someone else; but this was a difficult argument to make, since she had no idea who she was.

"Life is good. The dream is alive," was the answer she usually got— and usually in an accent foreign to her, as almost all were—no matter the question.

This apparently struck them as funny, and she could still hear their laughter ringing in her ears as the Blue Prince now proceeded, "There is an impulse among all mankind to wear a mask of distinction and rectitude, to tell oneself a fable that promotes one's own moral excellence over other men. Hitherto immune to dark deeds, he thinks himself altogether a fair creature and so praises himself profusely. 'Thank God I am not like other men, who revel in burlesque and dishonor,' he says to his own vanity. That this view, at bottom, is false emerges one improbable day when all that he has believed is forgotten and he finds himself an ecstatic spectator at a blood orgy or a public execution. Alas, he has become an enthusiast of the blood sport. To his dismay, his mask has dropped, revealing a wild stranger beneath. Perhaps that is what is happening to you . . . your brain is so stimulated it is shutting down."

"Death!" the fanatical mob was shouting. "Cripple him! Give us his heart! His liver!"

Once more, the Blue Prince elaborated. "Indeed, what happens to the diligent soul who, following the fashion, attends the games and finds beauty in them? I am speaking not only of the athletic grace of perfectly muscled gladiators and fighting beasts, but also of the poetical victim who faces imminent death, erect and alone. The spectator, meanwhile, remote from his own salvation, watches as a man possessed while the stronger takes the weaker and carries his reward. But is there not felicity and divine inspiration in such a violent encounter? Is it not the manner of nature to compete for survival? To kill or be killed? Does not the strong live off the weak? The intelligent off the stupid? Is not nature more beautiful than man's pathetic efforts to distort it through civilization and religion? Is not the life-and-death struggle, the imposition of the stronger will, and the final resignation of the victim exemplary and a thing of art?"

But just at that moment someone below shouted, "Single combat to the last extremity!" And the throng roared as two men in wolf skins began to stab one another in a flurry of jabs until the last one standing gushed blood and received a cheering ovation.

"The point is, there is no such thing as a free lunch," Xan explained, and now, with a wave of the hand, he moved events to a suitable disposition. "*Assez!* To the sacrifice!"

THEATER OF BLOOD AND A MARTYR

At once, the assembly united like so many appendages on a single organism, yielding to his command with servile exuberance, as excitement caught flame and swept through the crowd. Like children panting with exertion from play, the revelers required no acting performance to express their adoration for him, competing with one another for his attention.

"It's the old man! Ho, ho! Hail Xan, our *dragón*! Dionysus, Rider of the Clouds and Spigot of Honey! *Cagliostro!* We will die for you, Huang-di, Great Khan, and Son of Heaven, more beautiful than all the angels!"

And the Son of Heaven in turn addressed them. "I accept your mandate—my power players, lords of industry, my money team! Tonight we light the wick for the new year!"

They bellowed back, "Sickness is good! Darkness is truth! War is peace! Freedom is slavery!"

At his bidding, they again repeated each slogan and raised more vigorous cheers, and he proceeded, "My bravos! My wolves! My birds of prey, scouts and freebooters, my gravediggers, sappers and young blades, men of the best quality! My *guizu*, my *jiangjun*, go flog yourselves!"

The sharp crack of rawhide whips and chorused cries proceeded without abatement for several long minutes, while every eye turned to Xan, who now exhibited his naked left leg and thigh, which thigh gleamed as brightly as burnished gold—as though in a heavenly light. Then, though the reader doubt me, he began to flap his arms like wings and by some infernal device rose off the floor, levitating above the attendees, whose adoration of the gangster surpassed even the power of my purple prose to describe.

"Your love keeps lifting me!" he liked to say, shaking his jimmy in the sign of the cross. "Higher and higher! *Sanctus! Sanctus!*"

"Love?" she questioned.

"Love requires two, my dear: a rump buster and a rump to be busted."

It was, in short, a scene of pandemonium, akin to a kind of chemical process in which the sight of him hovering in the air fused the mob together in a supernatural way. Such was the bond between them—that he would share his treasure with them and they would defend him to the death—and such his thrall over them, that many of their number formed a human pyramid and grappled to attain its summit and reach out to touch him, striving to shorten the distance between mortal and god.

"With our blood and ardent gratitude! Hanoi Xan! Father!" intoned their voices in song.

She had never seen anyone levitate before and now seemed to swoon herself, into Satrap's waiting arms. When Xan's parachute pants flared and brought him back to earth, she stared at him incredulously, as if to ask, "What just happened? You flew? What kind of thing is that?"

He answered indirectly: "I simply reverse the spin of gravity with my mind. It is a custom with us, signifying our holy bond, like a communion wafer. I am the old guy, the OG, their ancient connection going back to the Divine Brotherhood, and they pledge their lives to me. The least I can do is have the decency to say thank you."

And with a mumbled semblance of Sanskrit and a few words in a dead language—possibly Ugaritic or Old Syriac—he held up his left hand for silence, acknowledged them, and gave the order: "Delegato of Paraguay, prepare to pay your debt to doom . . ."

"To doom! *Sacred death!*" the throng cheered.

"To doom and our pact of steel!" Xan returned, scanning the crowd with uncanny intensity, as if registering each individual face in his formidable memory bank . . . meanwhile telling her, "Think of us as family. It is just our way. One trunk from many branches: the One becomes the many, and the many nourish the One. Those nice fraternity boys in ties and blazers are from Skull and Bones, others from the Cognoscenti Society, many present and former heads of state, the Carlton Club, the Carlyle Group, Mensa, FIFA, Rosicrucians, and the Southern Baptist Convention. And of course the ultimate secret cabal: the black nobility, the Jesuits with their crooked crosses. That old man shaking the maracas is a Rockefeller, and the woman next to him in the 'Royal Bitch' T-shirt is the Grande Dame of the Mathematikoi and Illuminati and a member of the British royal family. Half the noble blood of Europe is here . . . dukes, barons, counts, even princes . . . shoulder to shoulder with flesh eaters, Khlysts, and the corpse eaters of Aghori . . . all good people wanting to make a difference."

Here he pointed to a band of naked, emaciated figures covered in ashes and drinking out of cups made from human skulls, adding, "Some of them are a bit crazy, but if they show all signs of being happy and draw no bad repercussions from their filthy habits, form your own conclusions. A little something to think about, though their beliefs are not mine. I am not particularly religious."

What strange things this pungently perfumed man said, she thought! He almost succeeded in making her believe that everything had been set in motion long ago, in which case how could anyone resist even the most terrible acts?

She said nothing, however, because she could not remove her gaze from the terrified human prey, who now wore only a vest of buttons stitched to his own bloody skin; and Xan, who appeared to feel little for the rite and even less for the victim, allowed a mock tiara of Christmas ornaments, paper money, and seashells—with a single twig of laurel—to be placed on the Paraguayan's head in order to appease the crowd. Seeing excitation and joy on the faces around him, hearing their fevered voices urging him to show the world the bloody prize, he decreed, "To doom!"

And once again the assembly reverberated, "To doom! À mort! To doom!"

Of a sudden, the condemned man's eyes flew open, and events now whirled in *dynamis*, as without another word, Xan stepped aside for a brightly painted beadle, who now produced an obsidian dagger (or possibly dark jade) and, gently pushing aside the victim's regimental striped necktie, laid bare his smooth neck; and it was here, at the Paraguayan's visible pulse, that the executioner now directed his aim.

"Why, Father? Xan Khan! *Pourquoi?*" was the question the poor man desperately posed, along with a string of Spanish asking for some explanation of his punishment and filling his lungs to the gasping point, before forcing the air out in a single bellow. "With my last breath, I serve thee upon my knee! What I have, I give to thee! I ask only the safety of my family . . ."

"*Tant pis*," said Xan.

"Behold the sacred martyr!" screamed the crowd and pressed forward, many with cups to gather the victim's blood.

"This is the language of sacrifice!" exclaimed the beadle.

The martyr's lips were still moving, or at least quivering, as his bloody heart passed into Xan's possession with all the respect due to precious things. What an object to behold, what an enchantment, a still-beating human heart! Like a caramelized apple dripping Christmas pudding, the organ demanded to be tasted, but first, the frenzied horde expected Xan to say a few words. (For good reason I have ceased mentioning Penny, who by now was barely conscious and in Satrap's care.)

"Just remember to breathe, my rare flower," she heard Xan telling her, or was he talking to the man about to be eaten? "What a beautiful tingle when two long-lost pieces, missing halves, come together as one, and I see the bereftness in your eyes—because your tears are mine! Even so, don't cry. This won't take long."

With his ancient stick and one finger, Xan first quieted the crowd and said softly, "Quiet, *mes enfants*, you are all my children. At this time of year we take a bite of the heart to remember we are one and there is a bloody world to win. And this is the vessel to take us there! By the martyr's blood, cupbearers, take heart!"

They shouted back, "We take it!"

Then he held the heart aloft and, to the mob's delight, took a bite of it and tossed it to them, proclaiming, "Come and get it! Eat this for the werewolf within you!"

"We eat it! Holy Father! Xan Khan! We will die for you!" the miscreants shouted, fighting over the slippery heart as in a rugby scrum.

"Clap your hands." He commanded them back to order. "*Pai pai shou . . . !*"

This they did as ordered. Many even fell to their knees, groveling to show their devotion but continuing to applaud, for none wished to be seen as the first to cease clapping. Such dedication would be tested, however, as the evening was still young and their dark world was to become even darker over the next several hours.

She, too, clapped lightly but closed her eyes to the coming horrors, none of which were quick and none of which I shall describe, except to note the end result. So aroused was Xan by the orgy of blood that his happy parts throbbed and he began to whirl, ill with pleasure. Thus excited and inclined by nature, he flew with her to his upstairs *secretum* wherein he lit candles of ambergris and allowed the forces of passion to take control.

"I'll enter you first through the ear," he said and laid a tango on the phonograph. Yet on this particular night, he made love only to his feather mask and ordered her to watch, confessing, "I can't deliver the old climax—I am pumped dry—but I'll learn to love again. *Vive l'amour! Sanctus, santus, sanctus . . .*"

VI. AN UNCLEAN SPIRIT

> In my name they shall cast out devils;
> they shall speak with new tongues.
> —Mark 16:17

Some months after the strange phone call between Xan and the one calling himself Antoine French, perhaps an even more bizarre incident took place at the closely guarded American military installation known as Nellis Air Force Base in the state of Nevada. As a pair of USAF force protection officers watched with a mix of apprehension and befuddled amusement, a rosy-hued man dressed as a Franciscan friar, complete with a handlebar mustache, pedaled a vintage Sting-Ray bicycle across the parched salt flat to a rarely transited entry point onto the giant base.

"That's close enough!" called out a young USAF lieutenant, edging one hand to the butt of his holstered pistol. "Where the hell did you come from . . . ?!"

"I am needing an air pump. My house trailer has a flat tire," the Franciscan reported in an Italian accent, pointing back toward a mini motor home far in the distance, barely visible through midday thermal waves rising off the desert floor.

The aforementioned lieutenant, whose name has been lost to posterity, followed protocol and picked up the phone to speak with his superiors. The visitor did not wait for a reply, however, before choosing to continue,

"I'm a Franciscan brother from Italia. I believe I'm expected by the commander. I am Brother Costello, mendicant and Paraclete."

"Did you say parakeet?"

The strange Franciscan either did not hear or did not understand the question, saying simply, "Please . . . hot . . . I have come without shoes."

In fact only one foot was shoeless, though both his feet were nearly black, gnarled, and blistered. The second force protector, a sergeant, nonetheless chose to mock him. "How would you like a shoe up your ass?"

The monk shrugged, saying, "You can see . . . my shoddy feet."

"You mean shitty? Dude, put some lotion on it. Piss on your motherphawk feet," the sergeant simply said and gesticulated, at which point the supposed friar complied with the strange order and urinated on his feet without so much as a complaint or an effort to lift the hem of his tunic.

"Now do it again and get out of here," said the unsympathetic NCO.

"But my pester is empty," said the wayfarer.

"You mean your peter? Then vamoose . . . go away and stop whining. Where the hell did you come from?"

"I come from Route 66."

"The devil's highway? Try again, Padre."

(An odd encounter, to be sure, and one the DOD still refuses to confirm . . . as it does virtually all reports having to do with the secret base. The reader also may deduce why officials might wish to keep the public uninformed in this particular instance, in view of the extraordinary events that were to follow.)

But a moment later the lieutenant got off the phone and waved the friar over.

"Brother Costello . . . ?"

"That's-a me."

Without another word, the lieutenant directed the friar to a general officer's staff car, a Ford Crown Victoria Police Interceptor, where an aide-de-camp held open a rear door. It all made no sense, the guards were thinking; yet Brother Costello climbed into the back seat and found himself next to a major general and a snarling Chihuahua chewing on a mule's jawbone. According to the sworn testimony of the general's driver—the same aide-de-camp, a Captain Bowers—his two-star superior welcomed the humble Franciscan with a fist bump and a small tomato-paste jar containing numerous tiny vesicles swimming in cloudy, reeking liquid.

"This is for the poor who take human form, in the name of our Lord," the general said to the friar, who studied the jar uncomfortably, while a strange vision—lasting no more than a second or two—flashed through his head: a scene of comical martyrdom in which he literally laughed his head off.

"I am a friar-mendicant," the foreigner protested.

"Good for you. That's the best kind, right?" the general said. "I am a wing commander. Wing Commander Wagoneer."

"Life is beautiful," replied the monk, "because we are all in it together."

"Until the crap comes rolling in," the general added and once again pressed the jar upon the visitor, adding, "It's for your boss, Cardinal Wildthing. In lieu of cash or a burnt offering, this is what he wanted. You get my gist . . . ?"

The monk shrugged uncomfortably—not understanding the strange soldier—but nonetheless put the jar in a small leather satchel and said what came to him naturally: "We are all human and make mistakes, but death is not final."

The general said, "I hope not. I even thought about becoming a priest before I met my wife Dorothea . . . Santa Dorothea. Sometimes I still do, just to give you an idea of the mental clutter in my life."

"We all make mistakes," the monk reiterated, sizing up his odd benefactor as an unimpressive physical specimen with a liver-spotted shaved head and the ruddy apple cheeks of an alcoholic. The nameplate above the general's spaghetti-stained breast pocket identified him as WAGONEER.

Intimidated by the unkempt stranger and his angry little dog, Costello hugged his satchel and armrest, wondering why the cardinal had dispatched him to this desert wilderness straight out of the Bible. Outside, the secret American military installation appeared to hover off the ground, amid dust clouds, thermal waves, and a huge plume of acrid smoke billowing out of various holes in the earth, each the size of a truck.

As if reading the Franciscan's mind, the general added with a cough, "Burn pits, like something out of Dante. You know Dante's *Inferno*? Lots of toxic gas, jet fuel used as a fire accelerant . . . then firefighting foam, perfluorinated chemicals, to put it out. I suppose it all jacks with the biology. The whole idea of Dante is that sooner or later we all get what's coming to us."

"Yes," replied the monk. "No matter where you live at."

"Ventilation seems poor today," said the general in a low voice that was almost impossible to hear over the Chihuahua in his lap, whom he now scolded. "Shut up, Mr. Know-It-All. And no fake tears."

"You understand?" the monk asked him, pointing at the snarling animal.

"No, I don't understand him. I don't understand a lot of things," the general admitted and rambled on about other matters—"wounded souls" and "a world without humanity or honor"—that seemed to make sense only to the Chihuahua, who growled thoughtfully in reply.

"You picking up any of this, Friar? He's waiting for your answer."

"No . . . I cannot, I am afraid . . ."

"Don't be afraid of Nostradamus, because he'll smell your fear, and that stresses him. See, he's giving you one of his hard looks, expecting a treat."

"I have no . . . what am I doing wrong? I am a Franciscan. I am loving all beasts."

"They're better than low-functioning people—some, not all. Personally, I put the tally of people I can trust right about zero. But he seems to like you. He's a mental case, but his predictions are usually correct. He told me you would come."

"Some animals is sick," the friar pointed out. "Very sad."

"That's just the reality of the situation. There's some in every crowd, and you have to weed them out—that's why I got in touch with you. I've been walking on eggs, feeling dirty a while myself. You don't look like much either, maybe one step above a drifter, but Cardinal Wildthing told me about your miraculous deeds, healing and casting out demons *in nomine Dei*. The word on the street is you can do no wrong. Thank God for the internet."

"You speak Latin, *non è vero?*"

The general now paused to light up a hand-rolled cigarette and, squinting through *mejideh* tobacco smoke, elaborated. "I was All-American at the University of Oklahoma, where I was discalced for a number of years. I then got a seminary certificate at the dead man Oral Roberts, where I met my cheating wife. Maybe that tells you why I'm no Bible thumper . . ."

"Thumper . . . is hit someone?"

"Hit someone and blame it on somebody else," Wagoneer explained. "It means I know my way around the language of Cicero, apostasy, and Satan's traps. You see, I'm smart in many ways—even called a whiz kid when I was shooting up the ranks—but I'm tired of the bullspit. Do you understand that American word? It means when someone bends you over and gives it to you dirty, yet accuses you of shite. I recently got passed over for another star. You say the sun will still rise in the morning regardless, but that's thin applesauce to a career soldier accused of cooking the books. Like I said before, life's a bitch and then you marry one, *hermano*. It also turns out I have poison in my blood and a 250-pound bug in my head that might be distorting my awareness of my own gender identity."

"Bug . . . ? Some bug, your head?"

"In my head, yeah . . . like flesh-eating bugs or a brain tumor," he said. "It keeps me company, but either way, it needs to come out. I don't fear death or going under the knife, but I believe faith is more powerful . . . although I have drifted spiritually with urges of sexual relief. That's why you're here. I did some networking mojo on you and heard you exorcised the whole Carpathian Forest, including the vampires . . . even did a job on the chief of the Russian military—General Staff—and the prince of Monaco. What was the prince's problem, shite cufflinks? Silver spoon up his ass?"

"You are sick man? *Pazzo?*" inquired the friar . . . more opinion than question.

"Somebody to watch out for, especially to my enemies, let's put it that way. I don't think there's any doubt about that," Wagoneer nattered, exhaling smoke with a hacking cough. "King Kong, smoke a bong, but I haven't touched the turbo dust in years. And after you're finished with me, there's another troubled fool I want you to look at . . . a very unique raving lunatic, not to mention he's on death's doorstep. You're probably hungry—I'll bring you a sandwich when you're done. You probably prefer an Italian submarine."

For whatever reason, Brother Costello now strangely spit into his own hands and tried to apply their clammy wetness to the general's nose and ears—a move stymied only by the Chihuahua Nostradamus, who suddenly stopped gnawing on the jawbone and lunged for the Franciscan's jugular, sending him recoiling in terror before the animal fell onto the floorboard.

"That's always gonna happen. Lucky he didn't go for the cock bite," said the general matter-of-factly. "Maybe better throw some holy water on that bad-boy heathen."

"Bad boy? You are proud your bad boy?"

"You'd better believe it. He's a little high strung, but no purse dog. He polices the grounds and protects his people. I'd like to have him christened and his soup bone blessed also," said the general with parental pride, adding, "but it's important we keep below the radar for the time being. I trust your accommodations at the Ramadan Inn [*sic*] were up to par."

"Very nice," the friar replied and took from his dusty vestment a Jack in the Box antenna ball, which he appeared to cherish like a holy object. "*Molto bene . . . !*"

In any case, we now pass on to further events, since I have nothing to report concerning General Wagoneer's own exorcism or the baptism of Nostradamus . . . other than to say it is doubtful that any good purpose was achieved in the fight against their respective disorders. But thanks to Defense Department whistleblowers, the diligent spade work of my research assistants at the Banzai Institute, and Buckaroo's own account of his later extraordinary meeting with General Wagoneer in the Smithsonian tower, we know the identity of General Wagoneer's "raving lunatic" and have a good picture of the sight that awaited the general and his Franciscan visitor in Area 51's top-secret XO block.

WHORFIN-LIZARDO REDIVIVUS

Let us set the extraordinary scene. Inside a hermetically sealed plexiglass cube, a long-haired bag of bones—one hundred years old at a minimum—with a distended, round belly, lay four pointed, bound to a hospital bed amid various metal trees and monitoring devices. Overhead dangled a massive electromagnet surrounded by a complex system of filters and ventilator tubes resembling ganglia, all connected to a vacuum suction device and steel-reinforced collector bag.

For the time being the gaunt specimen seemed to be sleeping fitfully, doubtless sedated, while a masked lab technician adjusted the old man's spit mask and prepared to jab him with yet another needle.

"You are saying he speaking Italian? Who is he . . . ? How did he . . . ?" the puzzled friar asked the general, but got no satisfactory answers.

"His code name is Desert Lizard, but his name's not as important as his holy soul—that's the only thing you need to know," said the American. "And the only thing I need to know is whether you can smoke the demon out, whether this shite is winnable . . . excuse my French."

"Winnable, General . . . ?"

"I'm oath bound to tell you this is much bigger than you or me. Just focus on that for a minute, for your beloved republic and its beautiful city-states. For Jesus and Garibaldi . . ."

After a lengthy pause during which the friar again spit into his hands and placed them upon the glass enclosure, he appeared to pray in Italian before saying, "I sense a huge and unwanted dark presence veiled in allegory . . . an unknown invader that has bore into his brain."

"A demon, right?" said Wagoneer. "Whatever you just said, you're the demonologist. Poof—be gone, right? You're the wonder worker . . ."

"Sometimes works and sometimes no. I never met this spirit before," fretted the friar. "Such negative, wicked force . . ."

As if in response to these very words, and without warning, the specimen's sad and shallow eyes began to glow from an inexplicable phenomenon that caused the pupils to turn white within irises of black; and the same dark energy radiated through his centenarian translucent skin like high-wattage light through a lampshade, causing the friar to press harder against the viewing glass, in contrast to a nurse inside the cage who backed away from the luminous Desert Lizard in mindless horror until an orderly stepped in and, averting his gaze from the mortifying sight, pulled her to safety.

But the two observers outside the cage kept their eyes riveted on the shining figure.

"You feel it, too, huh? What do you see?" the general asked the friar, who now pressed a gold cross and his face against the glass partition like a child staring into a toy shop window.

When the friar failed to reply and in fact began to rub his own eyes, Wagoneer continued, "I see two entities in one, one human and one alien devil capable of clouding men's minds with an assortment of identities. Is she presenting? Once she starts radiating, glowing, you haven't got a chance. You'll be looking at a candlelight dinner with the works . . . . firm buttocks and breasts, the complete package that'll make you smile twice. What's she got on? Fishnets and a garter belt? A vinyl tennis-skirt vision of loveliness?"

"She is on a golden robust palomino . . . look, it is Palomina, a girl once I know in a village festival as a young man," murmured the friar. "Now . . . hail Mary . . . it is Jesus in a dress . . . !"

"What's he saying?"

"She's crying to me like Jesus."

"She's a psycho. But you see her, right? What color sexy getup is she wearing?"

"No, Palomina, *carina*, you are still my love," the friar said, making the sign of the cross and kissing his fingers. "I will always have your heart, and you will always have mine. But do not let the devil take custody of your soul."

"Be careful," warned the general. "Try to leave and she pulls you back . . . turn away while you still can."

As if to confirm the fact, the friar squeezed his throbbing temples, attempted to avert his eyes, but could not. At last, with great effort, he closed his eyes and stuck his fingers in his ears.

"This wicked devil!" he complained. "Husband-and-wife things! Forbidden foreign lusts!"

"That's it—fight it! Welcome to the club," sympathized Wagoneer. "Make no mistake: the lying demon—this thing, this whatever the phawk it is—is on your doorstep, probing your psychic defenses for points of entry into fantasyland."

"Yes . . . I can't fight it anymore," said the friar with a certain resignation. "It is too strong!"

Suddenly and without warning, the general cried out, "You cold-blooded Cinderella . . . liar with no soul! Self-centered, controlling bloodsucker! Give this Christian boy a chance at happiness!"

By now both men were visibly squirming, but what exactly was the reason? Each seemed to be experiencing a different woman. Was the alien life form John Whorfin reading their minds and desires or simply projecting generic electronic camouflage? Remark either of these possibilities, but also put yourself in the mind of the friar, who knew on this day only what he saw with his own eyes: an emaciated, one-armed old man on a gurney—yellow as saffron, belly round as a melon, sweating and stammering, with odd colorless pupils and papery skin—yet who somehow had the power to impersonate a ravishing beauty.

"How do you call this place? Prison or a hospital?" asked the friar, seemingly in a daze.

"We're more like an asylum of last resort. People come from every damn where," the general explained, pointing at the wizened prisoner. "Once upon a time, he was probably fat, dumb, and happy, originally from Italy. Like most of us, he ended up alone, wondering where his youth went and how he wound up manufacturing firewater for the red man. Well, it's all behind him now . . . just an old desert rat more or less a hundred years old. He lost his map to the Lost Dutchman's mine, and he's been sitting on his pity potty ever since . . . slipping away fast, one foot through death's door. Believe it or not, he tried to chew his own arm off to get out of those cuffs."

"The devil is in him," said the friar ominously.

"God only knows, amigo," replied General Wagoneer. "That's why you're here . . . our last hope."

"Not by myself alone but by the miracle heart of Jesus . . ."

"There you go," said the general. "Mechanically speaking . . . he can't remember simple shite. Aphasia . . . onset of dementia, monomania, leukemia. Can't sleep because he hears voices. His liver's failing. We've been trying to sweat the poisons out of his system, feeding him baby food through that rig in his abdomen, but he's got some kind of kink in his bowel. That's why he looks like a scarecrow, but don't let that fool you. He's full of angry juice, napalm coming out of his nostrils."

"Because that is all that remains. The devil always wants you to feel his pain," explained the humble Franciscan. "That is how he wreaks his revenge on God."

Wagoneer considered these words and resumed. "I hadn't heard that, but a couple of weeks ago I snuck him out and took him fishing at the reservoir, and a little devil crawfish crawled up in his breeches into his downstairs region and never came out, leaving him physically disabled and infantile."

"Crawl fish?" inquired the friar.

"Something like a shrimp, maybe a brain-eating amoeba. I could give a rusty rat's pee-pee what it was—it's been in him festering like a big bowl of ugly ass, giving him a big bellyache and orgasms that make him piss and curse the Lord, begging for raw phawking. I just wish I understood everything going on. Don't tell me you never farted in the bathtub, Father, and bit the bubble . . . ?"

"You are telling the truth? Why do you call me away from Italia, a humble Franciscan at the foot of the cross?"

"As I told your agent, Cardinal Wildthing of Bosnia, I mean to subtract the evil spirit from his body for all eternity—I just want it captured and locked away. The docs say he isn't long for this world. That's why I sent for you, to confess the poor sonofabitch and hopefully exorcise the demon. Tell Satan to shove it up his petticoat. Just tell me what you need."

"I need his true name to ask God."

"His name is Emilio . . . Emilio Lazaro Lizardo."

"Lizardo . . ."

Even after many years, the name sounded vaguely familiar to the friar, who seemed to recall hearing it in grade school as an epithet. To call someone a "Lizardo" meant to say the accused belonged in a nut house.

"That might be his name. On the other hand, he's the world's greatest liar," the general reminded his guest.

"The devil is a liar," replied the friar.

"Tell me about it. What else do you expect or need?"

"I have everything . . . except a strong balloon . . . a *specchietto* . . . a looking glass, a stick of goat butter, and a piece of *carbone*."

"Let me write down this crap. An air force weather balloon okay? And goat butter, you said . . . ?"

"Or Crisco, and a strong balloon. To facilitate the demonic one to exit the body."

"Is that anything like catching a fart and painting it blue?" quipped Wagoneer.

"Yes, color of his energy . . . I never see that color before, or smelled it . . . even through glass. It is not a color I know," the friar said with a grave expression and gestured for someone to admit him to the holding cell. Wagoneer's order was quickly forthcoming, and minutes later the friar—armed with a short list of provisions—entered the cube through double doors and an airlock.

"Bless you, Father. May you unload his burden, although I still feel the evil alien life form inside my head," thought Wagoneer, who settled uneasily into a chair behind a control board and faithfully recorded the extraordinary scene that followed. (While it is not my purpose to report every repugnant detail of the exorcism, understand that I cannot pass over the entire episode in silence.)

We cannot know Whorfin's mind or whether the skeletal middle finger Lizardo raised weakly to Brother Costello signified his realization that the man entering his cage had come to bring things to a resolution at long last. Indeed, it was highly doubtful. Heavily medicated and strapped to the gurney, he had lived through much—a human guinea pig—and his rage was understandable. How could he know if the stranger in the Franciscan cassock was friend or foe? Perhaps he merely saw a priest who he assumed had come to help him die. "Don't touch me!" his wide-eyed expression seemed to be saying, and who could blame him for thinking the game was up? But perhaps he was also greatly relieved.

"I'm here to heal your heart and fix what is broken or clogged. This is my wish for you this Thursday evening," the friar informed him and removed his spit mask. "What is your name? *Come ti chiami?*"

At these sounds in his native tongue, the old man became animated and exclaimed, "*Per Dio, italiano?! Sono Emilio, paesano . . .*"

The friar, who shielded his eyes with an ancient-looking leather-bound Bible, inched slowly forward before spitting into both hands, which he began inserting into the old man's nostrils and ears.

THE ASTONISHING EXORCISM

"You who are cursed—you know your name—go out!" the friar announced. "For by well-watered resting places the Lord conducts his servant Emilio, whom he maketh to lie down in grassy pastures."

Lizardo likewise pleaded in Italian, "*Zitto!* Just do it and get it over with, *delegato!* Don't egg him on!"

The friar continued. "And to you, O Devil, be gone! For the judgment of God is at hand. Depart from Emilio into the eternal fire prepared for the devil and his angels."

"Damn it your name!" Lizardo seemed to protest. "Don't-a piss on my head and tell me it's-a rainin'!"

The dark entity within Lizardo now stirred and greeted the man of God with ambivalence by wailing a kind of Lectroid glossolalia interspersed with serpent-like hisses and bastard utterances that I will not repeat, other than to note that the noises carried an echo effect as if originating from inside a bucket. Among other inexplicable occurrences, Wagoneer and the other witnesses noticed that digital clocks and other instruments began to turn backward and Lizardo's limbs became increasingly restless and twitching, his breathing feverish . . . as if choking on blasphemy.

"Hold my hair while I throw up, signore," the ancient Italian begged.

Brother Costello did his best to oblige, clasping Lizardo's long, lank mane, while the old man threw up a spray of the vilest vomit that caused the friar to doubt his powers and retreat in disgust. In an attempt to refocus, he began milling about the sterile enclosure, sprinkling consecrated rock salt and skunk musk and intoning prayers in Latin and English in an oratorical voice that seemed to come from a foreign source not of this world. "Infernal invader, unclean spirit, by the power of the Holy Spirit I command you to call your name several times . . . !"

When no response was immediately forthcoming, he tried anew: "By the Holy Father and most glorious Prince of the Heavenly Armies, Saint Michael the Archangel, against whom all the world's afflictions and adversaries can in no wise prevail . . ."

A raspy, menacing voice like a smoker's cough now arose out of Lizardo, though not from his lips. "I was a stranger and you did invite me in. I needed clothes and you did clothe me."

Cringing, the friar raised his voice even louder. "Unclean spirit, in the name of Christ our Lord, who shall come to judge the living and the dead and the world by fire, I command you to depart from Emilio, this creature of God whom our Lord hath designed to call unto his holy temple, that he may be made the temple of the living God, and that the Holy Spirit may dwell therein . . ."

From Lizardo's posterior zone came another hoarse reply. "From the tight hole that stays moist, phawk you, ferret face."

Such were John Whorfin's words that caused Brother Costello to cry out, "Father of lies!"

Not only did he feel his blood beginning to boil in anger, he could no longer ignore the wicked thoughts that kept bombarding him, nagging at him, eventually forcing him to pause and light a sweet cigarillo with fumbling hands.

Watching from the outside, General Wagoneer himself returned from a ganja smoke break in the bathroom only to fidget and mutter, "Welcome to the battle zone, Padre . . . Whorfin, you puke pussy, you shite pellet of shite . . ."

As Costello sucked on the cigarillo's plastic tip, he, too, showed signs of angry frustration in his exhortations to the Almighty: "Arm him by the washing of regeneration, and renewing of the Holy Ghost, against the spirits of wickedness . . . unclean spirits, satanic powers, infernal invaders, wicked legions, the dragon, the old walrus and serpent, which is the abomination Satan and his bull demons . . . ! Oh, show Emilio you are here, Father! Gird him in thine holy armor and cast the unholy one into the bottomless flaming pit, teeming with souls of the damned . . . !"

Just then the voice of John Whorfin boomed out, "I'm the one you want! Come and get me!"

"Infernal name! *Diaboli!* Identify yourself!" Costello shouted back.

"Ha, ha, I am John Whorfin . . . commander in chief of the Red Lectroid Army!"

Whorfin's declaration at once caused Lizardo to become undone: "*Vergogna! Porca Madonna!* Trash pig neighbor and trespasser! Subprimate! Save-a me from this hell . . . pushin'-a me over the edge!"

"It's okay, Emilio," the friar assured him in Italian. "God watches over the innocent and will put everyone in their rightful place, like sheep to the slaughterhouse."

But the mutual diatribe and string of threats between the two cohabitants continued: "Lazy blabber Lizardo *stupido!* . . . *Insubordinato carogna . . . alto le mani!* . . . Pimple-ass sissy britches, I'm the best thing that ever happened to you!"

Lizardo gurgled in agony and his flowing, snowy mane began to stand on end as the room eerily turned cold, prompting Costello again to beseech the Lord for strength. Yet he did not panic, for he had developed a considerable reputation as an innovator known for approaching each exorcism fresh and with an open mind, playing it by ear as the need arose. Every case, like every evil spirit or human being, was unique, with each demon showing its true colors in a different way. In his experience some spirits—through the purifying spiritual fire of exorcism—even rose to become angels, while others were consumed by the flames and consigned back to hell. This so-called Whorfin, Brother Costello guessed, could only be one of the hell bound and beyond redemption, demonstrated by its cocky eagerness to announce itself. Indeed, Costello had not felt in the presence of such a powerful demon since casting the infernal spirit of Herod Antipas out of a young Norwegian boy several months prior.

Near a total mental breakdown, Lizardo collapsed and began whimpering in Italian as the friar opened his scuffed traveling case and extracted a pocket trumpet, an antique silver pyx, a camel's shoulder blade covered in ancient Aramaic writing, and a tiny wriggling hamster— along with a pair of spicy chili peppers and sheep's wool soaked in the milk of an ass, which the friar inserted into Lizardo's nostrils so as to prevent any escape by the malignant entity calling itself Whorfin. This was followed by a dose of rock salt in the old man's mouth despite his toothless howls of protest.

"Muthaphawkin' son of Rome!" Lizardo howled through a sinus drip, attempting to throw up a Fascist fist.

"Blessed salt in the devil's eyes," Costello calmly explained and proceeded according to time-honored ritual, while invoking emergency assistance. "Most holy apostle, Saint Jude, faithful patron of difficult cases, of things almost despaired of, intercede with God for me in this great need that I may receive the consolation and help of heaven for the holy authority of this ministry, as I confidently undertake to repulse the attacks and deceits of the devil. Do you renounce Satan, Emilio?"

"*Si, signore*, I do not recognize him," said Lizardo through a mouthful of rock salt.

"And all his works?"

"*Si, signore.*"

"And all his pomps?"

"*Si, signore.*"

Whorfin broke out cackling: "'All his pomps' . . . ha, ha . . . deal with it! Best not layin' hands on me, phooey! Puttin' a cork in your disease cooch! Or how about I throwin' asteroids up your ass like bowling balls!"

"All you have is lies, John Whorfin," countered Costello, who now blew cigarillo smoke through his trumpet in the form of a cross across Lizardo's face and spoke in elegant Italian. "As smoke is driven away, so are demons driven. This is not your home. Time to put your tails between your legs and slink away before you feel the ineffable Almighty's wrath. Come out of my beloved Emilio!"

The stern rebuke elicited no greater reaction than a gust of wind from Lizardo's flaccid hindquarters, along with what appeared to be an oxyacetylene blue flame that burned a neat hole through his diaper.

Aghast, the friar carefully removed the messy garment and felt renewed pity for the old stranger, saying, "You *poverino*, lost and alone, in this strange place with so strange people. Have you any *famiglia*? Loved ones to whom you wish a message?"

Lizardo's reply, if there was one, unfortunately is lost to us, because at that moment Whorfin guffawed, Lizardo screamed, and an avalanche of corn kernels flew from his fundament . . . barely missing the friar, who, incredibly enough, continued his deliberate preparations by holding aloft the blessed pyx and offering a Latin incantation to the triple godhead.

"*In nomine Patris et Filii et Spiritus Sancti . . .*"

"Something make-a my butt pucker? Gotta somebody hand up-a my rear? Disrespectful ass," Lizardo complained, as the friar applied a thick blob of Crisco to his excretory canal and readied the excitable hamster.

"Just a little jelly to make it more smooth, so better," said Costello, who naturally was repaid with insults as Lizardo began straining mightily against his bonds and Whorfin's voice was heard only as a muffled echo, accompanied by another blue flame from the excretory pore.

"I am John Whorfin, Trumpet of Heaven!" he managed to push out.

"Demon, I am God's trumpet! Fly the coop!" Costello shouted back and blew several violent notes on the horn.

"You gotta be a-kiddin'!" interrupted the voice of Lizardo.

"You are loathsome devil! You burrowed, embedded tick . . . out of Emilio's loins!" yelled Costello, who now spread dead chicken parts, chili powder, hazelnut oil, refried beans, and a single piece of charcoal on the camel's scapula and, taking a single fish cracker—not gold but a moldy greenish yellow—from the sacred vessel, rolled it in the concoction and pressed it into Lizardo's slack mouth, then chased it with a brown rubber-wedge doorstop to prevent any escape of the evil within.

"Holy hell! *Carogna! Figlio di puttana . . . !*" muttered the ancient Italian.

Brother Costello tried to give him succor. "Keep your head up, Emilio, and relax your sphincter. I know you will find peace while still on this earth. By the Divine Lamb . . . by whose jurisdiction, and by the power that hath descended forth from thine hand, which thou hast shed on us abundantly, I bind you, John Whorfin, and command you to release Emilio! You, who abide in darkness, come out of him! It's never too late! Go and find your peace, and *Dominus vobiscum!*"

"*Cazzo!* Freeloader, out!" demanded Lizardo, practically in tears, though it was unclear whom he was berating. "Damn you . . . I'll punch the phawking shite!"

"By the weeping angels of the Most Merciful, show yourself, demon!" demanded the friar, and what felt like an earth tremor immediately rumbled from deep inside Lizardo's bowels, churning and expelling.

"Come and get me! Wipe you face off the earth!" shouted Whorfin from within.

"*Basta, diavolo!* Come out, you devil!" commanded the friar, as another flame shot from the old man's sphincter.

"It's coming, all right, clean as a fart whistle!" General Wagoneer gushed in a paroxysm of excitement from the other side of the glass— optimism that was to prove short lived—as Costello worked with deft fingers to coax the hamster's head into the pore, leaving the rest of its writhing body to follow.

"This is very wrong," the friar said dolefully, "but you give me no choice."

"Aaaaagh, what is that?!" came Whorfin's smothered but nonetheless terrified response almost immediately. "Worm! Parasite! Whose eyes them?! Rat! Mamaaaaa!"

Now the blazing pneuma of the Lectroid chief transited the canal of filth, exiting the sphincter with the force of a fire hose and rapidly filling the giant weather balloon, which assumed for an instant in time what Brother Costello later described as the face of Satan.

From a separate vantage point, an astonished Wagoneer watched the great rubber vessel swell and thought he discerned the Hindu god Shiva trapped inside . . . the deity's awful visage, likewise outlined in fiery blue, bringing to mind certain portentous words.

"Looks like Popeye ate his spinach!" the general ejaculated with a sense of awe. "Now I am become death, destroyer of worlds . . ."

As the balloon continued to expand at supervelocity, pressing against the walls of the cube, Brother Costello likewise felt both exhilaration and terror . . . backing away while covering his nose against the gag-inducing stench. In his haste to retreat, he stumbled for no clear reason and fell over, as if tripped by karma. All he knew was that something was happening and it wasn't going to be pretty.

"It's coming, *santo Dio*! It's coming . . . and long overdue! The power of Christ compels the loss of all! The end of the journey is the truth of life!" he cried, peeking between his fingers at the gigantic balloon that now bore the terrifying silhouette of the Lectroid John Whorfin.

"Feel sting my wrath! Bow down to Whorfin!" screeched Whorfin's balloon face that stretched beyond comprehension, settling over the friar and threatening to block out all light as the Franciscan brother visualized the sun setting in a pool of dark sludge and realized he had lost any pretense of protecting himself or anyone else.

"No light without darkness . . . no darkness without light. I think I understand," he stuttered, while a heresy he once read, long suppressed, pushed its way into his thoughts:

"Jesus, have we no Father?"
And Jesus answered him in tears, saying, "We are orphans all. We
have no Father."

General Wagoneer, meanwhile, was now on his feet, seriously wondering if he was living in the real world and whether he should sound the mother of all alarms. Of course the Joint Chiefs would be alerted, and in an instant the base would be crawling with coat-and-tie jackasses, brown-nosing pencil pushers from a dozen secret agencies. In the event, he himself would be deemed the culprit in the great sea of ineptness that was the United States government. The only question would be whether he was competent to stand trial, but of course there would be no trial . . . simply the end of the line, maybe demotion with no general-officer pension and no Winnebago to tour the country.

No, they couldn't be allowed to catch wind of it. Consequently, he pushed emergency drills and the hotline number from his mind and kept repeating, "Let's not throw a fit . . . get all worked up in a fervor. What the hell's going on? Where's Brother Costello?"

This was darkly humorous because Costello was obviously wrestling the giant balloon, somewhere underneath it, perhaps in danger of suffocating . . . if the hermetic cube did not explode first under the tremendous air pressure and take the entire exocomplex with it. Suddenly the general longed for the long-distance hotline but realized that only he had the answer.

"Activate the electromagnet, General?" his men were asking. "And the suck? Do we have suckage or not?"

But before either order could be given, Brother Costello managed a last exhalation on his trumpet beneath the pressing weight of Whorfin's pneuma: "Santa Madonna . . . I have done all that I can. Please accept my own flesh and blood and lay your crimes on me!"

The last thing he remembered in his vanishing oxygen bubble, before the balloon burst and blew its great mass of foul air into his every orifice, was his trumpet, pocket change, and crucifix flying toward heaven and the faint, gurgling voice of Lizardo somewhere off in the distance: "*Pezzo di merda! Arrivederci, Roma!* Until we meet again . . . !"

VII. PHYSICIAN, HEAL THYSELF

> The monk said: "Why don't you cure me?"
> The Master said: "So that you neither live nor die."
> —Pen-chi

Regular readers of the Penguin series will recall Buckaroo Banzai's droll assertions that "the only reason for time is so everything doesn't happen all at once" and "life is a wheel, ended before it's begun." Both remarks were uttered in a somewhat playful vein of Taoist logic yet have been disseminated widely by an undiscerning mass media who either fail to understand irony or are too mesmerized by Buckaroo's celebrity to notice when his tongue is planted firmly in his cheek. Or perhaps it is simply the case that vapid people who live their lives in comfortable, uneventful places really do only care about themselves and the price of things.

On other occasions he has amended the above quotation to read: "The only reason for *the illusory concept of* time is so everything doesn't *seem to* happen all at once." The fact is that the passage of time, as we organize it, is a local arrow, like a river that narrows and swells in places but always flows in a single direction. Normally the flow is smooth and predictable . . . the pulse of the river dull and steady. But at the narrows too much happens quickly, driving us to suffer confusion because we have forgotten the river's true power. Too much time spent swimming in the doldrums has hidden its current from us.

Then, in another instant, we are tumbling over the waterfall, suddenly aware that past, present, and future are happening all at once and in more ways than one.

By *river*, I mean of course the flow of consciousness in which our brain's control center acts as gatekeeper. Only rarely does the dam burst, flooding our neural circuits with too much information: pieces of a multidimensional reality in which everything indeed is happening all at once. In the midst of a nightmare, for example, you are rudely awakened by a sudden jolt and a startled cat leaps from the nightstand, leaving the dreamer to wonder what just occurred. Or, contrarily, you lie paralyzed in that murky world between wakefulness and sleep, sensing night visitors beside you and simultaneously recalling an earlier event . . . when an odd flutter appears in your side vision out of nowhere, only to vanish when your eyes dart back to steering the car or performing other quotidian tasks in a conscious state. Put simply, such interdimensional moments occur daily and far more frequently than we assume, but we are blind to them in the same way our eyes look past the presence of our nose and our senses are unaware of the omnipresent wave fields that surround us.

Remark also, dear reader, the schizophrenic and the clairvoyant who hear interior voices, while I have not even mentioned religious or hallucinogenic visions, spontaneous human disappearances, past-life regressions, or another of Buckaroo's pet subjects, the deep structure of fetal dreaming. What are the little rascals smiling about, after all? What do the unborn—whose microtubules do not yet carry quantum information—fantasize about if not other dimensions? Yes, perhaps they dream only of swimming, but it is also possible they dwell in the bliss of a primordial universal connection to other dimensions without categories or junk language to inhibit them. Do I mean to say, then, that those occasions when we feel we are losing touch with reality— awkward moments when we hallucinate and feel betrayed by our senses—are in a systemic way our sanest? That universal consciousness as particle-wave energy floats freely everywhere and comes unbidden to the open minded? Alas, given the available evidence, such a statement is disproportionate; I simply plant the seed to stir your imagination and urge you to view such unsettling episodes thoughtfully, as learning experiences.

Meanwhile, since our world line flows on through spacetime—
perceived as a chronological sequence of events in Euclidean space—we
return to work and that gentle valley not far from the Banzai Institute
near Fort Defiance, where five Indian trails meet and dark clouds loom
menacingly on the horizon.

INTO ANOTHER DIMENSION AND PAYING THE PRICE

With flashing lights and audio warnings on the dashboard screaming
like banshees, the experimental Jet Car II, a twin-burner 1977 Dodge
Power Wagon with a special reinforced tubular steel frame, gathered
speed as if hurled from a slingshot, rocketing straight toward certain
doom—the sheer rock face of a box canyon—as the digits on the
speedometer climbed steadily to six hundred, then seven hundred miles
per hour, causing the machine to rock violently and even become
momentarily airborne!

"DANGER! DANGER! DANGER! CHECK YOUR SHORTS!" sounded the
GENERATION 3 OSCILLATION OVERTHRUSTER's audio warning through
wafting smoke, which the driver and lone occupant took remarkably in
stride, regaining stability control by flipping off the special ramjets'
afterburners and rear vertical thrusters, much to the delight of a chorus of
voices over his shoulder.

"Thank God! Slow down, cowboy! We'll all be crushed to dust!"

"Either that or alone and abandoned in the freak show Eighth
Dimension! Why press your luck a second time? Are you out of your mind?"

"Delusional at best," weighed in another. "Time to take your
meds, Doc."

"Oh, he'll get his medicine, all right!"

"His last sacraments, if we're not careful."

"We'd better be careful," pointed out his gray eminence Professor
Hikita, who placed a cold hand on Buckaroo's shoulder. "Don't forget
this Jet Car's not insured. What company would insure it? If anything
goes wrong, it means the loss of millions, maybe even the end of the
road for the Institute."

"And it's going to get worse before it gets better, Professor," piped up
Pecos from somewhere in the crowded back seat. "Look at the gauges:

his brain computing power is at its max, but he can't figure out his own jigsaw puzzle . . . what makes him tick."

"Looking for an exit strategy, if you ask me, Pecos," speculated the peerless guitarist Perfect Tommy, "and it looks like he's found it. He's obviously lost the will to live. A suicidal loony, in my opinion. Driving like a maniac, yet claims to be sober as a judge."

"Yep, so cool and clinical, always the scientist," remarked another chorister: none other than the venerable Rawhide, dead these many years but hardly forgotten, while next to him rode two singing cowboys of the purple sage and silver screen, Gene Autry and Pedro Infante.

"Cool and clinical? I doubt it," parried the vivacious cowgirl Pecos. "What a shame . . . to be so gifted and explore the ends of the earth . . . yet he can't even stand to see his own reflection!"

The driver with the power-packed physique wasn't talking, but his silence did not mean that the truth didn't hurt. *Why couldn't he look at himself in the mirror?* Could it be because he was an empty shell who had suppressed his feelings so deeply that he would never be able to retrieve them, much less analyze them? He preferred to blame the glare of a mysterious mini spotlight that seemed to follow his every move or the bank of overhead monitors, rather than a mental disorder; yet speeding toward the canyon's solid wall, he saw no way out, no escaping his fate. In 2.74322 seconds, he would hit the rocks, unless he ejected . . . now!

So imagine his astonishment when a gaggle of voices suddenly rang in his ear: "Pull your head out of those self-righteous clouds, Doc! You'll pay for your arrogance! I hope this little moment of vanity was worth it! What are you hiding, small man? Hypocrite! Scoundrel! All that fancy education gone to waste . . ."

Strangely enough, Dr. Buckaroo Banzai—leading man of his age and yardstick of excellence—found himself nodding in the choking air, unable or unwilling to refute their doubts and insults. He had no idea in fact even where to begin, as it seemed certain that all the good he had done in life, and all the people he had helped get on their feet, was now forgotten, except the potential he had squandered. And now his sanity, too, seemed to be fraying—not that it mattered. In another second he could either be dead or plummeting into the anonymous void of the Eighth Dimension . . . for the fourth time. Or was it the fifth? Yet one more unremarkable milestone in his unremarkable life, he concluded . . . utterly absurd, if he stopped to think about it.

But of course he couldn't stop; there could be no stopping now. He had perhaps still a second or two in which to eject and lose the Jet Car or ride it out, though clearly there was a problem either with the software or the Jet Car's weight-balance dynamic. Like everyone, he had made his fair share of mistakes in life, but this one could be the last. To stay or go? That was the real pressing question. Hit the brakes or roll the dice, as in continue rolling forward with his life in the precarious balance? Which was the easy way out? Which the hard?

For a fleeting instant he was between his parents, a blissful child riding in the front seat down a country lane . . . his father behind the wheel, on the right . . . somewhere in Japan? He felt like speaking, but they both appeared deep in thought, musing to themselves behind stares that stretched on and on.

"Low on fuel . . . and Xan still behind us," the father said, glancing anxiously at the mirror.

"But it will be all right?" said the worried mother, or perhaps someone else, because when Buckaroo turned his head, he saw his true love sitting next to him in a moment of sweet, blessed relief and smiling in the eye of the storm, as if to say, "I'll be fine."

At last he found his voice, long enough to ask, "Penny . . . will we ever be the same?"

"Sometimes you have to say goodbye," she said.

But then her face began to peel, melt, and rot away, and more voices chimed in: "Don't say you haven't been warned! Bent on self-destruction and taking the rest of us with you . . . good job, sport! Now be prepared to take your lumps!"

Glancing back, he recognized an impossible gaggle of friends and old lovers, world figures, shadowy opponents . . . all calling to him and floating in and out of acrid smoke that reeked of burning electrical insulation and sulphurous gas.

"Nothing like a little quality time inside thine head, eh, Hero?" came a voice without a face. "Getting a little cluttered up here in the old attic."

It was a pair of red eyes sitting on his shoulder and doing the talking . . . not in English, but in the old antediluvian tongue of the gods, offering, "I can help with gas, nephew. How far you going?"

Many called him Hero but only one soul presently on this earth called him nephew. That would be . . . a dozen aliases came to mind.

"Why put a name on it?" parried the bird. "Thou knowest who I am."

To this, Banzai could only mutter, "Curse thee, Xan. Why do I allow thee to live in my brain? What giveth thee the right to break into my consciousness and snoop around . . . ?"

"What horrors, give it a rest! I rang the doorbell, Mr. Administrator, because I'm a caring soul, ha, ha! Can I help it if thou art still stewing, searching thine innermost feelings for some measure of justice or, at the very least, an earnest self-evaluation? Perhaps thou art needing therapy in order to become a better person."

"Go kick rocks, Xan—thou art delirious. Is there no end to thy crap?"

"Ha, ha. Good luck . . . the end of the crap! Of course there's an end," squawked the voice of his nemesis. "Tired of the pain, are we? Who's driving the car? Is it not within thy power to ease thy burden and end it?"

"Keep prattling on, Mr. Know-It-All. I'm not feeding the doubt monster," said Buckaroo.

"Not feeding me? Thou hast poked me, I did not poke thee, cowboy, so go beat that dead horse elsewhere. Thou art the worrywart who raketh thyself over the coals—that's where the trouble starts! Thou art the ventriloquist, but I am thy nightmare. No matter where thou goest, there I am . . . two peas in a pod, out for a drive in the family flivver. And yet hatred always wriggles its way in. Why is that? But thou already knowest this, nephew. Thou art the golden child."

"Where's Penny? You festering pus!" Buckaroo erupted and tried to put his hands on the voice, which proved impossible.

"Penny Priddy? A pox on alliterative names," Xan laughed, flapping his eyelids. "I thought thou killed her making kissy face . . . crashed and burned. Were not thou at the controls?"

Against this Buckaroo had no answer.

"I'll never give up," he vowed but now experienced a sudden attack of nerves. Had he forgotten to attach the emergency spool of nylon filament, so he could find his way back home in case he got trapped or lost? And what about the left front mud tire? He couldn't remember if he had replaced it or if he was still driving with the donut spare. And the shock absorbers! How could he have forgotten to replace them? Or check his Jake brake . . .

As if reading his mind, Xan said, "Thou shouldst have gone with the GT package. But don't worry about the flat tire. It's only flat on the bottom. Ha, ha! And the seat covers—is this really the color thou wanted?"

Luckily, a reassuring voice was there, as well. "Don't worry. I've done the due diligence, and everything is within specs. Just drive carefully on your honeymoon, Buckaroo. It seems a target is on your back, as always."

Thank goodness for old Hikita, as usual: an ear to hear and a shoulder to cry upon! Whatever would he do without the old professor? But the nightmare voice only guffawed: "Ha, ha! A spare donut tire on the Jet Car . . . ! Sounds like thou art the one who's scared, running away from voices in thine head and this smoking tailpipe of a jet jalopy? What's that smell, nitromethane?"

The laughing eyes were correct. The odor of the volatile fuel was suddenly overpowering, tempting Buckaroo to decelerate, and yet he did the opposite and pressed the footprint gas pedal to the floor, feeding the surging beast . . .

. . . as Xan continued to blather, "I'm just glad we got to share the last ride because it looks like the Institute will be in a real pinch for cash when thou dost go down in flames! So run away to thy parallel universe where thou mayest forget all thy cares . . . perchance meet thy parents and the alliterative one, ha, ha, ha! But which dimension? The Fifth? The Sixth? The Seventh? Or the Eighth, where thou art at home among pestilence?"

"And thou, Xan? Dost thou not have a crime spree or a cesspool to get back to? Some unfinished road carrion or barbecue in hell to satisfy thy blood lust?"

"Perhaps, or perhaps I am one who mindeth mine own business, and thou art good at making things up."

"So thou wilt not slit my throat?"

"Will I? Thou decidest."

"I'm not giving in to my demon, Xan . . . nothing I can't figure out with a few more computer simulations, playing out all the actuarial probabilities, statistics, and scenarios. More than likely, the supercooled helium has frozen the fuel injectors or the magnetos and O_2 sensors. Either that, or it's a ten-cent wiring issue."

"The wiring issue's inside thine head!"—Xan belly laughed—"ever since thou hast dared trespass into other dimensions, against all laws of

Nature and the moral fabric of all religions, even against the warnings of thine own neurologist! Thou hast rent the moral fabric! Hast thou not heard curiosity killed the cat? And what about Adam and Eve? Thou must needs have standards, cowboy."

"Thanks for that jewel, Xan. Time to break this little wave connection that's not even real."

"No? I feel the love."

"If thou art real, then knock this chip off my shoulder!"

Xan guffawed, saying, "Feelest those butterflies in thy gut, nephew? It's not too late to turn back. Is this the life thou seekest? Performing daredevil stunts on money borrowed from thy poor worshipful fans? Who dost thou think is paying for this little hobby of thine? How much hast thou spent already? What a colossal waste! How many mouths couldst thou have fed? How many charities? Better to go hang thyself in a closet or make mine heart sing by eating one of thy famous six-guns. Or die in thy flaming Jet Car held together with Bondo and primer! Ha, ha, so feel free to add thine own skull to thine office collection!"

"Yeah, enough jabbering to myself," Buckaroo vowed. "Problem solved. Just keep the shiny side up . . ."

"Ha, in thy dreams! In the last firing of thy last neuron, before thou freezest up, I'll be with thee," announced the villain, who against all reason planted an icy kiss on the younger man's cheek, before dashboard alarms flashed and the EPIRB went haywire.

"Steady . . . steady," he cautioned, squeezing the steering wheel and hitting the five-speed shifter lever with its caduceus snake emblem, then manually synchronizing the Jet Car's entry vector and the OVERTHRUSTER's oscillation beam from LO to HI. But was it all a waste of time? Was his escape velocity sufficient? And the choking smoke! Damn these twice-rebuilt pulse-jet engines! How far to the point of no return? Had he bought the road hazard warranty? Inflated the tires? How many pounds of pressure in each Nitto Grappler . . . ? And the catalytic converter? The coolant? The Mopar microchannel plate detector and bell housings . . . ?

His mind drew a blank, something all too common lately and proof of his extremely overwrought mental state, as if the choking odor and smoke were not a sufficient reminder of the moment of decision that awaited him in less than a second now—which is not to say that he felt fear, because he kept telling himself that he was caught only in a nightmare, after all, a trap of his own brain's making. Or was this only wishful thinking?

He could no longer see where he was going. The window tint had begun to bubble and the windshield wipers seemed erratic; and now a passing glimpse of himself in the rearview mirror hit him like a bolt from the blue. Fear was written on his face, but fear of what? Death? The unknown? Or just more of the same?

"Hahahahahahahaha! Have a blast, cowboy—and I do mean a blast! Ha, ha!" The speaker laughed and flew the coop . . .

. . . as two black bands suddenly radiated in both directions from the OVERTHRUSTER's targeting lasers and he hit the sheer rock wall, which dissolved in a terrifying pandemonium of fire, water, wind, and earth. And suddenly the great "hero" was spinning at an impossible rate, along with his gauges. His polar or azimuthal angle? He had no idea, much less his spin amplitude. He tried braking—what a joke! All around, shades of red incident light were passing at high shutter speed, and it occurred to him he no longer had control, no longer had free will or a choice in the matter. Like she said, "Sometimes you have to say goodbye."

Was she wrong? Weren't there two sides to every story?

"You always have a choice," he thought, then corrected himself. "Except in the Eighth Dimension, the dark realm of nigredo, phobias, hopelessness, and horrors beyond words, where there is no before or after."

Sometime later, or perhaps both before and after, he hit the air brake and the Jet Car plunged into the lacuna, tumbling end over end in the blackness of the void—no, not a void, not nothingness, but the in-between, unbounded oneness in every direction. But who was he? He was no one, nothing but the picture of abjection whose name he couldn't remember, accompanied by infinite perceptions and a feeling of both terror and exhilaration from being not in the chaos but *of* the chaos, his original state: a feeling of being at home, sweet home, with a trillion other souls. Was he in the slipstream or not? If not, and without solid ground and a place to land, he could descend forever into the bottomless pit. Damn the blackness and all the epoxy and spot welds holding this buggy together, he thought, instantly remembering he had forgotten to replace the wiper blades! And washer fluid in the reservoir! Of all the things! And where in hell were his lights, his off-road and Q-beams? For some unfathomable reason he couldn't locate any switches—and there was still the little matter of the knife in his heart. How could he be such a dunce, so forgetful?

In irritation, he slapped himself; and now it was the Jet Car's turn to be amused, as the vehicle somehow turned its grinning chrome grille and caduceus hood ornament toward him in full equine profile, plodding its hooves in natural rhythm to the cowboy ditty our little riding party was singing.

> I got spurs that jingle, jangle, jingle
> As I go ridin' merrily along
> And they sing, "Oh ain't ya glad you're single"
> And that song ain't so very far from wrong . . .

WHAT PROCEEDED FROM A DREAM

At that very moment we were approaching the entrance of the Cochise Draw—or Cochise Wash on certain maps—in the basin-shaped desert just shy of the Superstition Mountains, where many a miner has struck near pay dirt and where the old Pony Express trail trends off sharply to the southwest . . . past three dry watering holes bound by narrow bands of saguaro cacti resembling human figures with upraised arms. Nowadays these are simply dead holes, without a trace of water or vegetation; but, lying in a triangular form as they do, they afford a pretty fair rest stop, enclosing a little promontory of perhaps ten acres extant; and it was here—"hotter than the midday Venusian sun," we liked to joke—that Buckaroo seemingly awoke and toppled like a giant oak from his saddle, sputtering, "Don't worry about me! Save the Jet Car!"

Even before he hit the ground, landing amid cacti and jutting stones, I leapt from my own little pinto and hurried to his side, with Pecos on her Spanish barb barely two steps behind.

"Buckaroo! Chief!" I exhorted him, hurrying to his side and taking things into my own hands by blind feel. I was well used to waking him from the throes of nightmares, albeit usually upon a Japanese sleeping mat; whereas to see him now, blanched and contorted, lying in cacti and exposed to the torrid Arizona sun, what tender feelings filled me! As I reached for my canteen, the usually unflappable Pecos went further, squeezing diverse pressure points on his body and peeling back his eyelids, unsure herself how to respond to the magnitude of such an event but seeming intent on bringing Buckaroo around with her sweet-smelling blaze of auburn hair.

"He's really hot, and his heart's pounding like crazy," she announced.

"Probably just sunstroke crazy," I said, shaking my head and lovingly delivering a stream of water to Buckaroo's eyeballs, when we were joined by the Black Russian called Hoppalong and a worried Perfect Tommy.

"Poor Buck," Tommy undertook to say in all earnestness. "You don't think it was that stinky cheese we ate this morning . . . ?"

"It's not his stomach, it's his heart," insisted Pecos. "He blames himself, and it's hard to swallow."

"Or the hot Dijon mustard," Tommy continued.

"He's smoking hot, all right. Maybe it's sunstroke. I have some lip balm," interjected our new resident Fellow from the Max Planck Institute in Düsseldorf, known to us as Li'l Daughter of the Rhine.

"He's just sad, people," interjected Pecos. "Right before he hit the deck, I heard him call out Penny's name and say a curse 'against all the powers of destruction.' I could tell he was dozing off, and I meant to wake him, but I was half drifting off myself. I reached for him to prop him up, but a mite too late. Buckaroo, you with us . . . ?"

She nudged him again, and something came out of his mouth that sounded like "Save the desert salamander," prompting Pecos to draw closer to that incomparable face and listen to the plaintive moan on his lips.

"Pennyyyyyy" came the mournful dirge that seemed to travel on the wind.

"Penny," Tommy repeated, shaking his head. "What a sick, twisted world. He's still looking for her in his dreams."

"Not even death can separate them," I said, suddenly feeling a dust particle in my eye and a chilly breeze. "Looks like it's coming up a thundercloud or two . . ."

"*Mein Gott* . . . look at that sky and the butts [*sic*] in the distance. *Das ist wunderbar*," said Li'l Daughter, admiring the desert vista and adding a few descriptive words in her native tongue. "If I could paint a picture, I would. But I'm sure Reno will paint it with his beautiful words."

Did she mean *buttes*? No matter . . . I mussed her hair playfully, and we both turned our attention back to the plaintive sound of Buckaroo's voice.

"Penny . . . ! Penny . . . !"

"No, it's me, Buckaroo . . . Pecos. Can you hear me?"

"Why wouldn't I hear you, Pecos, old friend?" he said, at last setting his gaze on her worried face. "What dimension?"

"Our dimension. You're home now . . . I mean back in our world, at Cochise Draw," she informed him soothingly. "You got back from the Eighth Dimension three days ago with a dented quarter panel and a blown roof-vent hatch."

"And a pounding headache, vision problems, nocturnal paralysis, and debilitating depression," I thought to myself . . .

. . . as Pecos proceeded, "You told us to watch you and put you under lock and key—which we tried to do—but you crawled out your bedroom window and insisted on jumping on Buttermilk and riding fences with us. Then you picked some of that *ch'oxo* plant you always say we shouldn't mess around with and stashed it in your boot. You haven't been chewing it, have you?"

"Endorsed by medicine men worldwide. Am I not a medicine man?" questioned Buckaroo with a vacant look in his eyes that slowly brightened . . .

. . . as he took in the familiarity of our faces and his faithful piebald mare Buttermilk, who once had been Penny's green-broke filly and now refused to leave his side. Speaking warily, with a sense of childlike wonder, he floated another question. "Or is this the Seventh Dimension? Might I be only a ghost in this world?"

I had to admit that was a possibility we had not considered, but nonetheless I tried to reassure him. "You just had a little accident, that's all . . . a bad dream, or maybe an aneurysm."

"The whole shootin' match. Do you even know which way is up, Buckaroo?" said Tommy with an air of smugness. "Maybe time for a little introspection . . ."

"Introspection . . . ?" Buckaroo repeated wryly and gazed up at the sky. "In the dream, or visualization, if that's what it was, I was approaching an interdimensional nexus in the Jet Car, when a strange spotlight began shining on me, illuminating all my anxieties."

"Naturally," Tommy now told him. "It's through dreams that we work out the conflicts in our subconscious, those internal false images unprocessed by the ego . . . not real," Tommy readily explained, as if to a child. "From the sound of it, you were dreaming of Penny . . ."

"Who else?" Buckaroo said. "I was sleeping and kept reaching out my bare foot to her, trying to find her in the empty bed with this useless second pillow . . ."

Such grief was felt by all of us, but nowhere more than on the face of this man whose life had become a living hell. How could it be otherwise, all that had happened and so much still unresolved? Closure, as they say . . . was it even a remote possibility when his bride of barely an hour, a woman to whom he had dedicated every breath—a woman to whom he would compare all others forever—was killed in the Jet Car piloted by himself over the foothills of the Himalayas?

Sometimes the helper needs help, as the old maxim goes.

"Anybody got any Alka-Seltzer?" he requested, feeling a by now familiar pain in the solar plexus, like a dagger in the heart.

Against my better judgment, Tommy tapped two tablets from a rare vintage Pez dispenser into a glass of now-fizzing water which Buckaroo downed, after which he seemed to regain his bearings and appeared less confused. In the meantime the sky laid out our scenario for what was left of the afternoon, as already the sun had begun fading behind a red border of twilight and heated clusters of thunderclouds.

While the greenhorn or Eastern tenderfoot may readily imagine that the southwestern desert is like a trackless sea, albeit hot and dusty, these vast, moody spaces are anything but empty to the native people and the rest of us fortunate enough to inhabit the territory and ride her trails. To us she is a living thing under whose spectacular skies we wander like hoboes, free as the wind to run the gauntlet of rattlers and coyotes, to make new trails up crag faces formed by the migration of ice when it was still midnight in the world . . . to be young and full of fire, the wild children of the earth.

To learn patience by accident, in other words, whether life throws kisses at you or not—this freedom, I believe, is the chief benefit of being in nature.

And yet destiny rules. How well I recall growing up in my provincial hometown, taking every opportunity to escape into the pages of those roseate adventure books I loved, wherein tales of fleet stallions, outlaws and cowboys, winsome señoritas and flashy gunplay on the wide-open frontier excited me from earliest boyhood! But, speaking of wandering, I digress . . .

Up until now the only highlight of an otherwise hot and uneventful trip around the perimeter of the western Banzai Institute had been our constant battle with the mosquitoes, horseflies, and rattlesnakes that called the Institute's twenty-seven thousand acres home. Little did any of us know the weather was not the only thing about to change, however. There was a much worse storm just over the horizon.

"Maybe we oughtta settle in for the night," suggested Tommy.

Under the circumstances I agreed and signaled as much to Pecos and the others in our work party—the aforementioned Li'l Daughter of the Rhine, Colorado Belle, and Pinky Carruthers, along with Lonely Ranger, Papa Bear, Señor Dentista, Pilgrim Woman, Lucky Masahiro, Honest Dan Cartwright, Cottonmouth, El Cuchillo, Lakota Sue, Leo the LEO, Talla 12 de Pantalón, Red Jordan, Missing Person Slim Greenberg, Buffalo Gal, Jolly Rancher, and Webmaster Jhonny Appleseed—before quickly turning my attention back to Buckaroo.

"Sorry to have taxed everybody's patience. I hope I didn't upset anyone," he said contritely, slapping his hat against his white canvas duster and dungarees. "Maybe you ought to send for the men with butterfly nets to take me away, folks."

"You mean Dr. Doe?" Talla 12 said, referring to our resident psychiatrist, Dr. John Jane Doe.

"Just lay off the *ch'oxo* weed," Tommy cautioned. "It's bad medicine."

"Maybe," acknowledged Buckaroo, "but it helps with my motion sickness. Ever since I got back from . . ."

Here he paused, looking downcast.

". . . from wherever the hell I was. Seems I can't even ride Buttermilk anymore."

"That's what we're here for—team building," observed the hairy Pole known as Papa Bear. "You always give us plenty, so we can give a little back to you."

"Gluttons for punishment, then," Buckaroo said. "Something I need to work on, or else maybe I've got no business saddling up anymore."

Well-meaning Pecos now injected a note of humor: "We'll just get you a seat belt, Buckaroo. All we want is for you to ride safe."

This gave us a hearty, much-needed laugh, whereupon Buckaroo announced, "I'll go chop some mesquite branches for wood chips. Anybody with me? The rest of you can peel spuds or have field rations."

"No, a cookout! I'll make potato dumplings, but no cussing!" chimed in Li'l Daughter.

"But first, an hour of target practice. Carry on," said Buckaroo, as Li'l Daughter, Red Jordan, and Buffalo Gal joined him with their tomahawks and set out toward a clump of mesquites sprouting among red rocks, while beyond, on a distant rise, a lone sentinel appeared to be watching us. A gaunt figure under the shade of an umbrella, he or she could have been anyone—spy, marauder, game warden, Apache scout, even one of the intrepid paparazzi known to dog us without respite—but by the time I reached for my binoculars and turned back, the shadowy figure was gone.

"I think I saw a bighorn up on that knob over there," Pecos said, pointing to the same gray rock.

"Big horn or a dark watcher," I replied.

"Third one today," she said knowingly. "Keeping us in sight."

ON BUCKAROO BANZAI'S INDIVIDUAL CHARACTER

Now, after dining on peanut butter sandwiches, Li'l Daughter's potato dumplings with grated mozzarella and fried cactus, corn tortillas, and walnuts, a shadow seemed to creep over Buckaroo's face and he feverishly excused himself from the campfire. Thinking perhaps he had caught a bug and taken sick or gone for another dose of *ch'oxo*, I quickly learned I was mistaken, for he headed straight to the remuda, where he exchanged a few words with Red, our wrangler du jour, and commenced to give Penny's Buttermilk a strong but tender massage—to which I would add that his slightest whisper in the mare's ear caused her to neigh, toss her golden mane, and prance in place. What magic or black art was this? Yet with each loving stroke of the horse's sweaty flesh, it was not hard to guess where our chief's mind was that evening, or understand the hellish demons he still had to endure the best he could. Interrupting him at one point with an offer of roasted marshmallows and hot chocolate, Pecos and I were taken aback by his steely-eyed look of annoyance that unnerved us two old-timers but also gave us cause to smile in the knowledge that our chief was feeling more like himself.

But more like himself in what way? For better or for worse? How many times have I heard this line of questioning, even more so since Penny's mysterious fate and his broken heart! To these inquisitors who have never left the beaten path, I reply, "None of your business. Do you expect me to squeeze his soul? A million light years from home and in another dimension, a few changes can come over a man. You probably wouldn't believe his thrilling experiences, anyway."

If any still persist, I pose to them this conundrum: "Have you ever been the same man you are at this moment?"

As Buckaroo's unofficial biographer, however, I recognize this is legitimate ground on which to dwell for a moment, but let me be brief. Like many, if not most, towering intellects—Einstein comes to mind— the most remarkable quality he possesses, in my humble view, is his simplicity and trustfulness. When he is happy, the sun rises in his tanned and weathered face, and he bowls merrily along from one herculean task to the next, with nary a cross word to anyone. When he angers, however, and however unexpectedly (typically brought on by what he calls "the demons of stupidity"), it is almost to the point of distraction. The term *havoc* suggests itself but is far too mild. Suffice it to say that his indomitable will, brought to a rampageous head of steam, is terrible enough to prevent all intelligent description of it, and of such unpleasant moments—few enough that I can count them on both hands—there is little uplifting to be had. The genial and familiar Buckaroo is unrecognizable; and there is nothing for it but to retreat, for few things in life are to be feared more than the prospect of one of his famous fits at close quarters.

Believe me, I have seen grown men brace themselves for his temper like naughty schoolboys, cross themselves, and mutter prayers before throwing themselves into a mad dash or headlong dive for cover: a bathtub, beneath a bed, even into a food freezer. Indeed, how well I know!

On this particular occasion, when we approached him with marshmallows, I admit to feeling a similar fright, inasmuch as we had no way of taking into account the unknown effects of interdimensional travel, particularly the massive gamma bursts, on his physical and mental well-being.

"Buckaroo, you sure you're all right?" I asked him. "You don't look right . . ."

"I don't see right, either. My vision's muddied and my head's full of rocks," he muttered. "Get my saddlebags, Reno. I need a shot of dopamine and a big sleeping pill."

"Is that the only way, Buckaroo? I mean, if you're trying to block the pain, isn't it . . . ?" I tried to argue, somewhat pointlessly.

"I'm a doctor, Reno—don't waste my time!" he snapped. "Or do I have to get it myself?"

I exchanged troubled looks with Pecos; but ultimately I went and retrieved the chief's black bag. When, moments later, he returned to the campfire a happier man, I believe it was Tommy who spoke for us all, saying, "I think we're all a mite sleep deprived. Maybe we should just get some z's."

"The sky's starting to hemorrhage. I think I'll stay up for the late show," Buckaroo said, feeling a raindrop or two and stiffly craning his neck to study the canopy of clouds overhead.

But it was not the veil of clouds that fixated him; rather it was a single bright star poking through them, or at least a star in outward form, that we all noticed.

"Peeping through a keyhole," Pecos remarked. "The well-conditioned gears of a clock . . ."

"Funny, I don't know that star," Buckaroo replied. "Anyone . . . ?"

None of us knew.

"A star we don't know, one out of ten jillion," Tommy observed, only to have a passing notion pop into his head. "Buckaroo, is it true clouds come from people steaming their vegetables?"

Was he serious? With Tommy, who could tell?

"Amazing powers of observation, Tommy," said Li'l Daughter, who had a more sensible question: "When was your last good night's sleep, Buckaroo?"

"I don't think I've had a good night's sleep since I left the ICU," he replied.

"In Bhutan?" She reacted with surprise. "But that's been months!"

"I don't recommend it," he said. "There's only so much a man can tolerate."

"I'm sure I'd be close to suicide, too," Tommy helpfully pitched in.

The campfire was spitting now; and with rain squalls now upon us, cracking thunder and lightning made sleep difficult even after an arduous dawn-to-dusk spate of riding fences. Instead, we burned the midnight oil, huddled in our plastic macs, listening to coyotes and discussing the day's events, urging Buckaroo to recount more fully what he now believed to be a repressed memory of his recent trip into the Seventh Dimension and perhaps not a dream at all.

VIII. WHEN DUTY SUMMONS

Truths are illusions which we have forgotten are illusions.
—Nietzsche

A palliative for karma is atonement; and Buckaroo was now convinced that his earlier "daydream" had been something more: a repressed memory of an accidental foray into the Seventh Dimension—that hotbed of the imagination and artificial realities—when his actual target had been the storehouse of sense information in the Fifth.

". . . flipping end over end, half-unconscious," he was saying by lantern light, peering out from beneath a rain-slick poncho, "when I managed to shake out the cobwebs sufficiently to right the ship and suddenly found myself at the emergency entrance to Columbia-Presbyterian Hospital, where a porter waved me inside. In another second I was speeding down what seemed like an endless corridor . . . doctors and nurses scrambling to get out of my way. I hit the brakes and hopped out of the Jet Car, only to realize I was still in my stage costume and drenched in sweat, my every step traced by a spotlight.

"Still in the light and now pursued by saber-toothed tigers and a woolly mammoth, I raced into the brilliantly lit operating room, only to find Rawhide, one of my surgical team, pointing to the operating table that was inexplicably also a cafeteria buffet, complete with a plexiglass sneeze guard. Even more macabre, a leg—which I recognized at once as belonging to a Raggedy Ann doll—protruded from a large bowl of chopped lettuce.

"'Table for one, Dr. Pariah?' Rawhide greeted me and handed me a pair of salad tongs; and when I flinched, he said, 'What's the matter? Can't take the truth?'

"Meanwhile the other members of the team, including Hikita and my parents, had begun singing the melody to 'I've Got Spurs That Jingle, Jangle, Jingle' in the key of G-sharp. Then someone handed me a Garden Weasel, one of those tools advertised on television.

"'But I'm not a doctor,' I said.

"Of course they wouldn't listen and kept on singing, calling me Dr. Pariah . . . telling me I was late. 'What kept you? You should be ashamed! A sawbones of your stature and star power!' I said I was sorry and couldn't apologize enough . . ."

At this point Tommy interrupted the tale long enough to say, "If there's one thing I hate, it's an incessant whiner."

"Yes," Buckaroo said. "Couldn't apologize enough for all my big talk and little action . . . all the bad I've done and all the good I've failed to do. But, through it all, this strange spotlight never left me . . ."

"It's the spotlight effect, our critical self-conscious eye watching ourselves, assuming the rest of the world is doing the same," explained Pecos confidently.

"A possibility," Buckaroo acknowledged. "I'm sorry, guys, if this is tiresome . . ."

"No, go on, Buckaroo. This is cathartic stuff," Pecos stressed, urging him on.

"In any case the next thing I knew, I pulled the doll's leg, only to discover she had the head of a dolphin and a fish hook with a wriggling worm embedded in her pincushion face . . . which pierced my lip as well when I bent to kiss her. Thus joined together, I saw Hikita-sama—who now wore the cassock of a priest. 'What God has joined together, let no man put asunder,' he said, and at the same moment the dolphin doll screamed, 'What once was love has turned to hate!' That's when I must have cried out from the pain."

"You called out the name Penny," Tommy said, "and you fell off Buttermilk."

"Yes, I was in a great rush to lift her from the table and lost my balance. Our lips were hooked together and she spat water in my face."

"That was me," I interjected. "I tossed water in your face. No hocus-pocus about that."

"And we were all singing 'Jingle, Jangle' before," Lonely Ranger pointed out.

"Also in the key of G-sharp," Jhonny remembered. "I know because I have the gift of perfect pitch."

"And that spotlight could have been the hot sun blazing down," said Pecos, "while Penny and the rest of it had to be just your grief and sense of loss. But you can't keep blaming yourself to the point it affects your well-being."

"I blame long days," I volunteered. "Too many long days, too many irons in the fire . . ."

"Nobody does as much as Buckaroo Banzai and still finds time to travel to other dimensions, weather permitting," Li'l Daughter ventured . . .

. . . as Jhonny spoke up. "I, too, often feel a disconnection with everyone and everything, particularly around normal people, as if I am in a dream or in another dimension. Who has not had this feeling of pieces that do not quite fit?"

"Or just discouragement with a life that feels manipulated, feeling like a stand-in for someone else," pointed out Lonely Ranger, who had made a fortune on Wall Street before deciding to follow his various flights of fantasy. "Or sticking out so obvious everywhere you go, just wishing your time in the sun could be over."

"Yes," agreed Buckaroo. "Sometimes we are all tempted not to go on, to just disappear. That can be a rush, as well, to leave this world and all its connections, and yet something causes us to cling . . ."

"Like an autumn leaf," said Li'l Daughter. "Not ready to drop until the last minute."

A PHILOSOPHICAL DISCUSSION

"Like a la-la land far, far away," trilled Tommy, contemplating the animal spirits and their constellations in the sky. "Far away in the sense of a quantum dimension, a bizarro world of spook particles which even I don't quite understand."

"Not to worry, Tommy," Buckaroo reassured him and seemed to perk up, as always, whenever the conversation turned to speculative matters. "To paraphrase Feynman, if you think you understand the quantum, you don't understand it, in the same way that 'the Tao that can be spoken is not the real Tao' . . ."

"Or," suggested Li'l Daughter, "in the same way that nothing outside the mind can be said to exist, since if it can be said to exist, it is already inside your mind."

"Good point, Daughter," said Buckaroo, "illustrating the need to expand our minds."

"What I know about the quantum, I could probably stick in a wisdom tooth and not even feel it," interjected Señor Dentista. "I am given to believe it is something like the microstructure of corpuscles, which are everywhere but very elusive."

"Don't worry, Señor," Tommy reassured him, but in a condescending tone. "Only three or four guys, tops, really get it. A lot of very bright people get stumped by the quantum."

Rather bemused, Buckaroo continued, "It costs nothing to pay attention, Tommy. Another way of saying it: you either get fooled or you fool yourself. At the same time quantum theory threatens to undermine the entire foundation of logical thinking . . . the basic laws of thought, much less physics."

With my own fair share of vanity, I now quickly spoke up: "The law of noncontradiction, the law of the excluded middle, and the law of identity. Nothing less than a Copernican change, I'd say."

"Hell, yeah, the raw truth, negative-number worlds," agreed Tommy enthusiastically. "Because the All Hidden is hidden from us for a reason. Not to put too fine a point on it, but it's too phawkin' freaky—right, Buckaroo?"

"There's no right answer to the wrong question, Tom," Buckaroo said. "We just need to recognize that our senses can be impediments, as well as helpers, in the process of discovery . . . like a dirty window that impedes the passage of light."

"Famous dying words, something about the wallpaper," I recalled. "Aren't our limited, and limiting, senses something like the wallpaper?"

"And our limited vocabulary," added Li'l Daughter. "All our words come from our own minds and our own mouths—it's all so circular. We're like babies with our primitive faith in our own rational thinking."

"Yes! Like babies, asking the eternal inexplicable: why is there something and not nothing," said Pecos.

"Not nothing is something," Tommy pointed out.

"So hard to dig deeper," Li'l Daughter posited and questioned Buckaroo further. "But you've done it, Buckaroo—pierced the veil, gone through the wallpaper into the alt-universe! How many dimensions? There are eight, no . . . ? We live in the Fourth, in spacetime, the *Welterfahrendesleben* . . ."

"Let's keep it clean," cautioned Tommy.

"The Fifth is our internal tape recorder, an archive of all our sense memories," I volunteered. "A faithful reproduction of every detail in our sensorium, everything we've done in three dimensions and the Fourth, as well as the substrate of repressed memories, including the womb and perhaps our prior lives . . ."

I made a point of again looking at Buckaroo, thinking he might wish to speak, but he merely stared at the ceiling and muttered, "Hard to describe, really, with no sense of context . . . and I'd rather not."

"But that's only eight," noted Li'l Daughter. "Could there be more?"

"Eleven, as far as I know, Daughter, but there may be no upper bound," Buckaroo replied.

"An infinity of dimensions—that's my theory," our dear Rhinelander postulated.

"Some infinities are bigger than others," Tommy helpfully reminded us.

"Mathematically speaking, Tommy's right," Buckaroo said. "But I haven't solved the problem of what lies behind even one universe and probably never can. Although all my life I've been obsessed with the idea of breaking barriers, particularly the parameters of our world, consciousness is the one barrier that can't be broken, even in other dimensions. To ask questions we lack the means to answer seems to be the curse of our race."

"No matter where you go . . ."

"You are, in the end, what you are in the dark," I said helpfully. "What we *were* in the dark before we were. Does that sound crazy?"

"True enough. But at the very end . . . there is the supernal flame, no? The sublime truth in the castle keep . . . ?" Webmaster Jhonny asked earnestly, leaning forward in rapt concentration.

"The famous interior dome light . . . I'll let you know when I see it, Jhonny," Buckaroo told him, "if you're talking about the Eighth Dimension and the ecstatic oneness with everything and nothingness. As we've been saying, other dimensions—other patterns, other reasons why things happen—are creeping in all around us, and dreams and waking phenomena may be simply memories from one of these or from what we call the future."

"Memories from the future . . . so we can tell what is going to happen," continued Jhonny. "Not to be Chicken Little, but I have been lately having terrifying dreams of fighting in battle, then feeling a bullet and falling . . . at a loss of understanding . . . into a sports car seat of soft velvet. Then quickly seeing it is very narrow, then realizing I am riding in a coffin."

"Feeling powerless over your expiration date like every other human being, Jhonny. But sometimes a dream is only a dream," Buckaroo assured him.

"Yes," Jhonny replied. "The soothsayers I have consulted back home cannot agree among themselves, so thank you."

"Cool story, bro," Tommy said, interrupting Jhonny. "Let me just close with this, skipping the psycho-wanko. Buckaroo, I'm willing to bet the ranch your so-called dream is memories from the Eighth Dimension, although I can't prove it. The point is, you were head over heels over Penny and blame yourself for the crash, even though we strongly suspect it was sabotage. But that's the bottom line: guilt. At the same time, you want to believe she's still alive, represented by her body on the operating table."

"But why a dolphin?" Buckaroo wondered aloud. "And the next part? Someone handed me a guitar and told me they were waiting for me onstage. Even from the operating room, I could hear an audience that sounded like a stadium crowd of thousands. And I was suddenly caught in the roar of the crowd, walking out onstage, and not just any stage, but the middle of the Roman Coliseum . . ."

"The Roman Coliseum . . . ?" I queried, keen to know. "How about us Cavaliers? Were we there, too?"

"An all-star lineup. Even Muscatine was there," Buckaroo said.

"Muscatine Wu? The girl wonder?" We reacted as one.

A NAME FROM THE PAST

Like few others, the name Muscatine Wu burned a hole through our memories: Muscatine "Magnum" Wu, perhaps the greatest bluegrass lutist and banjo player who ever lived and arguably the first to play the augmented banjo with a bow . . . who in her quieter moments was also a world-class roboticist and a wonderful down-to-earth, hard-working, fun-loving tornado chaser and motorcycle rider, among her other pursuits. How well I recall making music and robots with her and enjoying the pleasure of her mischievous smile both onstage and off, particularly during those periods when she was clean and sober! The penitentiary is full of such women, brought low by childhood trauma and addictions, but only a tiny few resolve to get at the root of their problems by entering the Banzai Institute's harsh counseling and detoxification program, led by Dr. John Jane Doe and Mrs. Johnson.

Quietly, Buckaroo now made a comment to no one in particular. "It's true Muscatine struggled with a tall order of personal problems, but we all have to walk our own paths."

"Yep, we're all fighting our own battles, just a hop, skip, and a jump from ending badly," Pecos reflected. "Life is messy—we all know things have a way of turning south in a hurry."

Meanwhile, Tommy, not content to let sleeping dogs lie, remarked, "She was a thief, plain and simple. She violated the morality clause, so she had to go."

"Just because she used to help herself to your favorite guitar plectra," returned Pecos.

Tommy was prepared to argue the point, when at that very moment Colorado Belle inclined her head sleepily against my shoulder and stared at her handheld device, which she switched in a flash from a video game display to a screen of scrolling text.

"Talk to me," the tatted beauty muttered to herself.

"What is it, Belle?" I asked. "From Mrs. Johnson?"

"Oh, nothing, Reno," she said, skimming her messages. "Just the usual personal threats and terrorist alerts from Jill of All Trades back at World Watch. Someone's threatening to 'put a bullet behind Buckaroo's ear' . . . someone else trying to feed us a virus . . . others wanting their sexual jollies . . . another call from that scientist group in Fukushima . . . a medical question from Columbia-Presbyterian Hospital, also asking about Buckaroo's promise to deliver a lecture series at the med school . . . still those pesky bedbugs in the bunkhouse making people highly irritable . . . also a reminder that the county fire department's showing up in the morning to make sure the new particle collider lab is up to code . . . and Jack Tarantulus called again about the upcoming European tour, something about another royal command performance at Buckingham Palace . . . also an Apache kid who was brought in with a bad dose of Rocky Mountain spotted fever that Big Norse and Ladybug took care of . . ."

"Spotted or rat-bite fever . . . ?" Buckaroo wanted to know, reaching for her phone.

"And look, this just in," she said, indicating the message on her screen. "Lucky says Postmaster General Mantooth called, looking for you . . . !"

"The postmaster general?" Buckaroo responded, nonplussed. "A.k.a. Rainbow Trout?"

"Says she's calling on behalf of President Monroe," Belle said.

"Interesting," he remarked. "A call he feels he can't make himself."

"Maybe because you and the president had that public falling-out after you gave him an earful in that spat over the World Health Organization," I reminded him.

"You mean over his undescended testicles," he jested, exhibiting a flash of his famous temper, which heartened me. At the same moment, however, Buttermilk whinnied loudly from the remuda and Buckaroo himself scrambled to his feet, listening intently to the usual sounds in the night . . . and I heard it, too, like a fart on the wind. Something had intruded.

RAIDERS FROM THE SKY

"We've got company," Buckaroo announced suddenly, and seconds later the others began to hear it, too: a low-toned thumping noise in the distance, but not too faint to be identified.

"Thunder? A stealth chopper!" Tommy shouted, prompting Red Jordan to stir awake and come running with his massive Smith & Wesson 500, as the approaching sound—a muted *thwack-thwack*—drew nearer.

"What's the plan . . . our tactic?" a nervous Pilgrim Woman wondered aloud.

"Maybe go back to your day job," someone else said.

"I saw somebody stalking us on that ridge before we pitched camp," Red recalled, pointing.

"No sense obsessing. We'll find out soon enough," said Pecos, anxiously stroking her H&K machine pistol and squinting with the rest of us at a lightning flash that revealed with extraordinary vividness the heavens opening and a glint of metal between thunderclouds.

"Running lights dimmed, must've gotten sidetracked," Tommy conjectured. "A flawed flight plan. Maybe Drug Enforcement or Immigration."

"Could be either one, because it's really stupid flying a whirlybird into an electric storm," said Pecos.

"No foolin'—that thing's a flying coffin," said Tommy, just as a streaking bolt appeared to strike the mystery ship and send it slow-spiraling to earth, its motor clunking, not two seconds later and not too distant.

"Who's got my kit?" Buckaroo called urgently over his shoulder, already mounting Buttermilk. Then, with the goad of a well-placed spur and a giddyup he was off to the proverbial races, leaving the rest of us to eat his dust . . . all of this as the wayward mystery ship seemed to hit a false bottom on its way down, furiously revving its rotors and rising for a second or two, only to resume its free fall. But the drama was only beginning, and seconds later our entire group rode up in time to see the smoking aftermath: a large matte black helicopter having landed with force and now resting precariously halfway on its side and a quartet of spectral-looking American commandos in three-dimensional camouflage standing over one of their own, whose minor wounds Buckaroo wasted no time in treating.

The first thing one notices about most soldiers—I am talking about the highly trained combat variety—is actually two things that at first seem contradictory: a watchful gaze coupled with a don't-give-a-damn attitude, as if to say, "I'm looking right at you but don't really care about any of it, unless you make a move, in which case I'll be obligated to use this tool they gave me and shoot you." One such man, a young captain named Jackson with greasepaint on his face and a 160th Special Operations Aviation Regiment patch on his desert camo ghillie suit, looked us over for several seconds, making certain his ducks were in a row before heeding our questions.

"Night Stalkers . . . ?" I asked him once more. "A long way from Kentucky . . ."

He failed to answer but a minute later seemed to scrutinize our group for the first time with his bedazzling flashlight. "Nice out here . . . pretty remote. Y'all weird? Got nothing better to do than camp in the rain? Seriously?"

"And looks like somebody couldn't wait to share in the fun," I ventured. "What brings you out tonight, Captain? War games?"

"You got a problem with war games, Mister?" he demanded.

"No way in hell. Absolutely no problem," I clarified. "I'd say your chopper and a couple of your injured men have a problem, though."

"The trailing bird should be here in two minutes. The C-in-C's in a pickle and needs Buckaroo Banzai," he said, with a nod in Buckaroo's direction.

"The C-in-C . . . ? The prez must need Buckaroo pretty bad, not to call ahead."

"Supposed to be in and outta this mudhole in ten minutes. My duty is to bring in Buckaroo Banzai, by any means necessary."

"By any means . . . ?"

"Any means, Reno. Any reason why not?"

So he had recognized me; I touched the big revolver on my belt and said, "As long as you know who I am, three fifty-seven reasons why."

"Huge turn-on to meet you, sir. But an iceberg's chance in hell."

He used even more flowery language than that, but this was the gist of it; and he had a point, for a second helicopter now traversed the disk of the moon and landed nearby, whereupon Buckaroo turned his patient over to two military stretcher bearers and took a phone call.

Not privy to his conversation (with President Monroe, to no one's surprise), I engaged in one of my own with Pecos, who informed me that she had notified Mrs. Johnson to issue a call to general quarters until our situation came into clearer focus. Our dialogue was cut short, however, by the persistent presence of Captain Jackson, who seemed to enjoy hovering within earshot and talking mainly to himself.

"Pretty intense . . . crashing a bird in a damn desert monsoon," he complained to anyone within earshot. "This weekend was supposed to be mine to enjoy with my vehicles and my dog—that's what I want to be doing right now."

"Crazy," Pecos remarked.

"Go on with your crazy," he spat, along with some blood. "The world has lost its mind."

"I know the feeling," I said. "You all right, Captain?"

"Fine as frog's hair," he informed me and spat out blood again. "Just a regular Joe."

It was an idle comment but one conveying a kernel of truth. I doubted that he had been raised by wild hyenas on a diet of raw meat and roots, as Pecos had been, or been subjected to the psychological terrors of captivity: having his teeth busted out or his head placed in a noose or sleeping next to a prisoner's corpse whose eyes were rotting out of its head. Yet although we carried different weapons—his Mark 18 carbine and my Winchester rapid-action pump—we were both soldiers of a kind who understood the rigors of discipline and deprivation and long days that were the norm. Perhaps our unselfish devotion to a higher cause was a character flaw to be blamed on idealism or simple-mindedness, albeit one that benefited society; and I have not even mentioned the allure of danger—adventure, if you prefer—an addiction to the adrenaline rush of the unexpected lurking around every corner . . . along with the necessity of sleeping with one eye open or not sleeping at all.

But this was not to be our parting conversation. Minutes later, when Buckaroo signaled Pecos, Tommy, Li'l Daughter, and me to join him in the second chopper, Captain Jackson bade us goodbye, but not before snapping pictures of us just as the doors closed.

"Good luck and salty nuts, Cavaliers! Good travels and good fortune!" he yelled over the muffled rotors and tossed me a ration of peanuts and a can of energy drink called Go Fast, bearing a likeness of Pope Innocent the Mercātor under the legend BOTTLED AT THE RIVER JORDAN, CARBONATED . . .

. . . which, as I opened it, gave me the distinct sensation of opening a can of worms.

EASTWARD, HO!

It was understood now that Washington was to be our eventual destination, but, for the rest, only Providence could say whether a walk

in the park or a meat grinder awaited us. With the possible exception of
Buckaroo Banzai, none of us as yet knew our mission or its likely
duration, but this was a life we had chosen and these were concerns we
were used to shutting off. Our most pressing priority for now was to
resist our nagging unease concerning air travel, after what had happened
in Bhutan barely eighteen months earlier.

One glance at Buckaroo's taut face told this story better than any
writer's words yet could only hint at his painful thoughts: his bride's face,
her screams, the spinning earth coming up to meet them, the horrible
crash and worse aftermath . . . most of all the overwhelming survivor's
guilt, the same unbearable sense of responsibility that had led Hikita to
blame himself as the one who had approved the Jet Car's flightworthiness
on that happiest and most tragic of days.

It would take a long time, then, to cauterize, much less callus over,
such a raw wound; and yet when the great man caught a glimpse of
me at that moment and our eyes happened to meet across the helicopter
aisle, he managed to give me a glimmer of encouragement that perhaps
because we were the last slender hope of someone somewhere, all would
be well.

He smiled through bloodshot eyes, and I turned away before I
teared up.

We were of course thankful that no soldier had died or lost body
parts in the rough helicopter landing and that we were leaving the
Institute in the capable hands of our brothers and sisters. But speaking
for myself, at that moment I cared more about the taste of peanuts and
the highly caffeinated drink in my other hand; it mattered little to me
if all the day's drama—the hours in the sun spent stringing wire and
patching fences, Buckaroo's fall from his horse and his odd revelations,
the helicopters bearing special operators to fetch us—sank into the
earth forever without leaving so much as a footprint. But of course this
was so much wishful thinking. Someone somewhere had misstepped,
and under the rules of linear time, nothing could be over before it
began; therefore erasures of events were not permitted, at least not in
our dimension.

"To sleep, perchance to dream—ay, there's the rub . . ." Weary to the
bone, my brain closing down, all I wanted was to shut up and stare at
the hundred billion galaxies out my window. Yet one last glance at

Buckaroo, still at work on twin handheld devices, reminded me of a pressing worry and the question we were all asking: when would the man sleep?

IX. A THREAT FROM THE DEEP SKY

> We have nowhere else to go . . . this is all we have.
> —Margaret Mead

At the risk of stating the obvious, the fishbowl effect of life in the Imperial City dictated that Buckaroo and the president meet out of view of the public eye. To do otherwise—given the glare of publicity—would be uncomfortable and counterproductive for everyone, except perhaps the president's normal cheerleading squad, who enjoy such media stunts; but to Buckaroo Banzai, who gets hit with twenty questions everywhere he goes, such attention is unwelcome, even less so when the world teeters on the edge of oblivion.

Of course this was entirely my own thought process regarding the seriousness of the present threat, based upon what little information I was able to glean as our government car—with what looked like a shotgun hole in the windshield—wound its way through the white-sepulchered city, past soaring monuments to the greatest Americans, and Tommy grumbled, "Which building is the Ministry of Truth and Love? And where are all the public serpents, the resident gutter rats with Samsonite briefcases full of brother-in-law deals?"

"We can disagree without disagreeableness, Tom," cautioned Pecos.

"Is there anything we can do about it, Tommy? Do we hold the whip of power in this country?" I reminded him and watched him struggle mentally.

"Maybe not," he said, "but I'm gonna look deeper into this shit."

Buckaroo meanwhile traded calls with Postmaster General Mantooth and Jill of All Trades at World Watch One, the nerve center of our worldwide intelligence net back at the Institute. From these snippets I was able to form a pair of tentative conclusions: our immediate task had to do with stolen Jet Car technology, and Buckaroo was growing angrier by the minute, directing his ire at more government agencies than I even knew existed.

Thankfully, I was not the target of his wrath (which I have discussed already), but as his trusted secretary and sometime amanuensis, I sat directly opposite him on the ride in from Andrews Base and felt the weight of his worries as he juggled text messages on both of his handhelds.

"Want to talk about it . . . ?" I ventured, point blank. "How much trouble are we in?"

"A world of it, looks like," he said, going on to relate how a disgraced high-ranking American military officer was accused of transmitting to the World Crime League classified data having to do with our research into dark-energy velocity fields and interdimensional nexuses, ambiguity bits, and the OSCILLATION OVERTHRUSTER tachyon generator, along with blueprints of the Jet Car and its superslick, antielectromagnetic molecular coating.

"The whole kitchen sink, bugged by technology, in other words," Pecos groaned. "Do we have a name?"

"Just his initials, which I make out as General William Wagoneer, commander of Nellis Air Force Base, home of Area 51. Our number one fan . . ."

"You know him?" asked Pecos.

"He's written me a ton of fan letters over the years," Buckaroo said. "I'll go so far as to say he thinks he's me. He thinks he shot down John Whorfin."

"What? And he's in charge of top-secret Area 51?" Pecos erupted in disbelief. "That's outrageous! He needs to be put down like a rabid dog. How is such a thing even possible?"

"Bunch of government buzzards blowing smoke up our ass, in other words," interjected Tommy. "Any of this ring a bell? It's only about the hundredth time we've had this conversation. You don't think a traitorous sleeper mole, maybe one of our own . . ."

Irritated by the suggestion, Buckaroo said, "Anybody in mind, Tom?"

"Start with that keyboard player who turned out to be ATF or that crazy runaway who jumped into the hog pit . . ."

"Or the same people who put spyware in our Wi-Fi and have been cutting our fences and our cables," piped up Pecos.

"Yeah, creepy Webmaster Jhonny needs to go. Not a good fit," said Tommy.

"You're wrong, Tommy—Jhonny's a good man. Let's not have any witch hunts," Buckaroo cautioned . . .

. . . as Tommy demurred and peered out the window at the Capitol dome, grumbling, "The corridors of power . . . ha, ha . . . nothing but snakes, lizard lobbyists, and fat cats, thieves with briefcases, armchair quarterbacks, and pencil pushers. I don't even know why we come here . . ."

"Because the pot goes to the kettle, not vice versa," Buckaroo explained. "When we heard reports that the Pentagon was trying to hack into our networks and was sneaking spies into the Institute to steal the blueprints for the Jet Car and the OSCILLATION OVERTHRUSTER, I didn't want to believe it, despite the fact that I felt in my bones something was amiss and the signs were there . . . such as that small detail of a pretty good knockoff OVERTHRUSTER for sale in that Spanish bazaar a while back. But when we asked for help from the intelligence community, I was given the runaround . . . their usual strategy of lullabying you to sleep, then back-shooting you because that's the way it's done in this town—making a mess and then denying authorship."

"A mess of historical proportions . . . thousand-dollar hammers and toilet seats," Tommy reminded us. "I think we all know where that money went. Hanoi Xan must be laughing his ass off."

"Yeah, of all the deceitful . . . power-tripping leeches," muttered Pecos. "But we were ninety-nine percent sure no one got through our cybersecurity safeguards."

"True," said Buckaroo, "but there's always the one percent, and the one hundred percent chance we don't know what we don't know. And then the Jet Car crash . . . the disappearance of the wrecked OSCILLATION OVERTHRUSTER, not necessarily due to souvenir hunters."

"Reverse engineering?" I suggested. "From Uncle Sam? Perish the thought . . ."

Buckaroo ruminated long and hard before answering, "So many rumors . . . and overall ignorance . . ."

Tommy continued to seethe, declaring, "Lying polecats don't sit well with me. Spying is stealing, and body snatchers are the lowest . . ."

When Buckaroo flashed a twinge of pain, Tommy corrected himself just in time: "There's nothing lower than scurrilous officials abusing their power."

"Pathetic drivel from the mouths and egos of the high and the mighty predatory cronies," added Li'l Daughter in her Bavarian accent. "By now it's practically in their DNA."

"Whose DNA?" Pecos wanted to know. "That's the question. How high does it go? Even President Monroe?"

"And how much info could they have gotten?" I wondered aloud.

"The Jet Car's supervinyl wrap and smart-grid timing belt?"

"A lot but not everything," Buckaroo speculated, pointing at his head as the ultimate storehouse. "My hunch is even President Monroe is not altogether aware . . ."

"Not hard to believe. He was probably medicated from the get-go," suggested Pecos.

"Not the brightest bulb," I agreed.

"Probably couldn't pour piss out of a boot," said Tommy. "Or feed himself if you dropped him in the middle of a farmers' market."

"Enough, Tommy," Buckaroo objected. "He's a decent man, but without getting into palace intrigues, it's possible the wolves are running the show without him."

His furrowed brow and cowboy hat were reflected in the limousine's supposedly bulletproof glass, a self-image he studied briefly in restless contemplation; or perhaps he was looking beyond the smoked glass at hot dog carts, bottled-water vendors, and sidewalks full of bundled-up homeless and tourists in Bermuda shorts. Whatever he saw when he turned back and scrolled simultaneously through hypertext on both handhelds, it became apparent that the bad news was getting worse.

At one point I thought I heard him mutter, "Lizardo . . . ?" But this was only a momentary lapse in his intense concentration, as I noticed that in addition to our conversation, he was intently watching a baseball game on his mobile. Broadcast in Japanese, the translation now came to us, courtesy of Buckaroo: "Bottom of the ninth . . . two out, Naruta batting . . . Otagiri on the mound . . . hurls a splitter. Damn the day! Damn you roundly, Naruta, and the day you were born! Damn his eyes . . . long live the Hiroshima Carp . . ."

"I wouldn't know a Hiroshima carp from a Louisiana catfish," said Tommy.

Buckaroo merely let his head droop and lamented, "A ninth-inning home run. The Giants win. Down goes Hiroshima, plummeting out of first place."

"I'm sorry, Buckaroo," I said. "But it's just one game in a long season. Find strength."

"Right, no sense wallowing," he admitted, at the precise moment his second phone, his most private number, suddenly jangled loudly with an avalanche of dissonant ringtones I had never heard before; nor, may I say, had Buckaroo, who stared at the message screen in amazement.

"Something rotten in Denmark . . . ?" I heard him mutter.

AN INCREDIBLE MESSAGE

"What is it, Buckaroo?" I asked; and precisely at that instant what appeared to be a blinding apparition burst forth from his device, causing Buckaroo to drop the glowing phone like a hot rock and shield his eyes from its intense light that did not seem to be a hologram, but rather a more tangible presence, like a flesh-and-blood visitation. Squinting through my fingers, I beheld a shimmering form—vaguely female and humanoid, save for her splay-toed, furry feet—who wore the angular headgear and costume of the Nova Police.

"Greetings from the Secretariat of Nova Police to Buckaroo Banzai, remarkable luminary of blue horizons and fullness of vigor whose deeds are surely immortal," the apparition began and now flashed an electronic badge. "May you enjoy ease of heart and days of joy in these end times."

"What?! End times?" Tommy interjected, momentarily drowning out the mysterious visitor's voice. "Shut up!"

"No, you, Tommy! Be quiet!" ordered Buckaroo.

The emissary continued: "This is a high-level information bulletin that is not open to replies. Please save time by not replying . . ."

Strangely, the otherworldly messenger now turned by coincidence in Tommy's direction and demanded to know, "Who is the hothead? I request respect."

In point of fact, however, the hologram was not interactive and to the keen eye displayed a fair amount of buffering, lacking the capability to respond to our comments. Instead it merely continued with the prepared script.

"You do not know how much trouble you are in. Why this warning knock on Buckaroo Banzai's door, of all doors? Why Buckaroo Banzai, amid a dwindling pool of honorable humans, who combines cunning with a first-class scientific knowledge and has more than a nodding acquaintance with the criminal fugitive John Whorfin? Tough and tenacious Buckaroo Banzai, whose brain is his weapon, who lives virtue in his daily life, values hard work, and encourages good citizenship . . ."

"Yes, yes . . . the fairy tales, everything good and perfect in the world . . . but let's not beat a dead horse," Buckaroo said impatiently, objecting to such profuse flattery.

". . . yet who failed to put an end to John Whorfin . . ." the message continued, prompting Buckaroo to jump nearly out of his seat.

"Failed to put an end to Whorfin . . . ? Confound you! What are you talking about?" Buckaroo pressed adamantly . . .

. . . as Tommy again interrupted, shouting, "Shite on a sheet, Buck! Careful! For all we know, Hanoi Xan sent this joker!"

"Information lately come to us. I have the extreme displeasure to inform Buckaroo Banzai that real terror comes by attack from Planet 10, a single man-o'-war siege vessel and planet destroyer, largest of the Planet 10 attack planetoids with pos-ion torpedoes, has entered your near beyond, on the rumor that the shadow of John Whorfin yet lives and is waiting in the wings, a free subject in your world—"

"!"

"What?" we ejaculated nearly in unison.

"Then the rumor is wrong," an astonished Buckaroo exclaimed. "In what hell or alternative universe is John Whorfin alive?"

"I speak of a war party of several million strike-master Lectroids of the mottled ringneck variety . . ."

"Several million . . . what? 'Strike masters' . . . ?" Buckaroo demanded to know.

"Traveling under charter from the Virgin Empress John Emdall, who has detected a sighting of the animal Whorfin and will herself do the monumental work of destroying his genetic information and every Earth mammalian . . . without a doubt. This is the full truth I am given to report, without adding particulars. Godspeed—whatever that means. You do not know the first thing about terror."

With that parting shot, the visitor froze in front of our eyes, leaving us miserable witnesses to rave and carry on under the weight of her words.

"Hell, she's flaky as pie crust. You've got a smart mouth, lady!" Tommy scoffed and aimed his middle finger at her and the universe in general. "No way this thing's on the up and up! It's pure devilment, phony to the phoniest!"

"A phony-baloney," concurred Li'l Daughter of the Rhine. "Isn't that what you mean, Tommy? A scam of some sort? Some phony-baloney going on?"

And I had my own doubts, thinking out loud, "Virgin Empress John Emdall . . . ? The same John Emdall who . . . ?"

"John Whorfin's archnemesis on Planet 10," Buckaroo recalled, still uncertain whether his comments were reaching the now mute and motionless oracle.

"That's idiotic," I objected. "A damnable lie!"

"I say we don't pay any attention—now I'm plain-ass mad!" swore Tommy, who, ever loyal to Buckaroo, suddenly launched himself blindly at the emissary with the intention of throttling her . . . but managed to grasp only a handful of air.

"Tommy, Son of Thunder! Sit down!" demanded Buckaroo.

"Yeah, Tommy!" yelled Pecos. "It ever occur to you this might be important . . . as in a scary situation?!"

"I could give a red rat's ass!" Tommy retorted. "Makes me want to break something!"

"Can you hear me? Are you still there? How can I reach you?" Buckaroo was still asking the lifeless figure hovering in midair. "What if we capture John Whorfin? Is there a way to reach John Emdall?"

Suddenly, without so much as a sound, the image of the messenger vanished, leaving us to look at one another with the stark realization that we were alone . . . and on our own.

CONSTERNATION FOLLOWS

"Talk about the long arm of the law," Tommy piped up, voicing our collective sentiment. "I'll be got-damn. Like a bad replay come to life."

"And a lack of imagination," noted Buckaroo, who gingerly picked up the overheated phone and still looked deeply worried. "If true, John Emdall has fallen once again into a Thucydides trap and gone into mad attack mode, envisioning John Whorfin as Hitler, Jesus Christ, and Harry Houdini all rolled into one."

"Our old friend John Emdall," Pecos mused. "Surprise, surprise . . ."

"How did the Nova Police get Buckaroo's private number?" I wondered aloud.

"Maybe they know everything," Pecos surmised. "If they can send a message across billions of miles . . ."

"Easy," said Tommy. "Hot energy always goes to a cold spot, and Buckaroo's the coolest dude on the planet."

"I think I got it all, at least most of it," I said, passing Buckaroo my Go-Phone, which I had found the presence to switch on during all the excitement.

"I'm guessing astral projection of an extremely high mental order or, as the message said, a Nova Police quantum network bouncing a signal off the magnetosphere, either through a Chinese server farm or induction loop antennas buried in the pavement beneath us," Buckaroo replied, simultaneously attempting to reach the return phone number of the caller on his own device.

"Is the number not archived, Buckaroo?" questioned Li'l Daughter.

"Oh, it's archived," Buckaroo confirmed with obvious irritation, holding the phone carefully up to his ear.

"A sex talk hotline wanting credit card info . . ."

"Phawking sweet," Tommy said. "That explains it . . . we've been spoofed, scammed, trolled, whatever. Either that, or it's maybe time to buy gold . . . put our assets in precious metals, like lead bullets."

It was a simplistic explanation we were eager to grasp. "Tommy's right," I asserted, though it pained me to agree. "How do we know someone's not putting one over on us? Some kind of mind games. How could John Whorfin be alive? In which case, are we talking about Emilio Lizardo being alive, too? At the ripe old age of what? A hundred and some odd . . . ?"

"Extremely odd," said Pecos.

Tommy proceeded, "I'm just spitballin', but this whole Lectroid posse . . . how much damage can one ship do to a whole planet?"

"Do we want to find out?" asked a pensive Buckaroo. "And perhaps not just one ship—a large man-o'-war, probably a mother ship—but most likely carrying a fleet of smaller attack pods."

Still fiddling with his other handheld device, Buckaroo added, "Of course, you could all be right. It's too early to dismiss any possibility, and the possibility of a hack or a prank—someone stirring the pot and trying to rattle us—was certainly going through my mind as well; but I can think of no explanation for what just happened, other than an astral-traveling Nova cop sent to warn us about that mystery planetoid, whose existence we first posited mathematically after months of tedious work . . ."

"My God, I hadn't thought of that," said Pecos, "but the mystery object does seem to have jumped like a flea and left Saturn's orbit. Could it be the Lectroid man-o'-war?"

"Or could it be the source of the astral messenger," I conjectured aloud, "begging the question: if the Nova Police are aware of the threat to us, why did they wait so long? Why don't they do more to help?"

"Anything's possible, Reno, although you're assuming they possess the means to do so. You're also assuming we matter or that we even merit an explanation in a galaxy with billions of planets. It's hard to imagine an interstellar sheriff. There's a big difference between sending a warship vast distances and a simple warning by quantum packet or psychic wave, perhaps amplified and bounced off cellphone towers, mimicking a phone call to my private number," Buckaroo went on, studying his revolutionary full-spectrum Go-Phone and its impressive array of electronic tools. "On a frequency of fifty-one point five hertz . . ."

"Fifty-one point five . . . ?" Pecos said. "No wonder I didn't see it. My extrasensory spectrum sucks."

"Mine's pretty damn good," Tommy insisted with typical bluster. "Nothing much gets by me."

"Except fifty-one hertz," I pointed out. "You're not synchronized, obviously."

"Why do you think they call it Area 51?" said Tommy.

"And the same incline angle as the Great Pyramid at Giza," Li'l Daughter recalled.

". . . above the range of ordinary neuronal firing but within the realm of expanded consciousness," Buckaroo explained. "Think of a dog whistle. But how did they get my private number? Only a handful of people have it. If bad actors are behind this, they're plenty good."

Pecos added, "We could run to the government, but why do I feel they might be involved in this for their own purposes?"

"Not cool," Tommy said. "Definitely not cool."

"All vital points, from all of you," said Buckaroo, "but, given the stakes, we have to assume the worst-case scenario and get a handle on it. Where do we begin to look for an Italian centenarian with an alien alter ego?"

THE CENTRAL MYSTERY

Indeed, our heated discussion kept coming back to the crucial New Jersey resurrection story . . . and Buckaroo was talking mainly to himself: "Unfortunately, we didn't have control of the crash site; but based on what I saw, the intense fire that enveloped Whorfin's ship would have incinerated every trace of life, although perhaps not every scrap of burnt carcass, due to the Lectroids' hard protein coating which might carry their genome and twisted DNA, in addition to their microRNA . . . I suppose theoretically it could have transferred horizontally when Whorfin and Lizardo melded in the Eighth Dimension . . ."

"And all this time we've just been sitting around, doing nothing in good conscience," Pecos groaned . . .

. . . as Buckaroo continued his musings. "Let's not forget that according to our old pal New Jersey, his uncle Ira actually managed to retrieve a piece of alien tissue before the feds moved in and swept the area clean . . ."

"Alien tissue . . . ?" said Li'l Daughter. "You mean a piece of a Lectroid? How in the Sam Hill . . . ?"

"New Jersey's uncle lived near ground zero, and smoking Lectroid meat landed on his patio," Pecos explained to the young German. "But he was a well-known UFO geek and a heavy drinker, so no one took him seriously, even when he tried to sell the stuff in town. Then when

Uncle Ira died, Sidney stumbled upon the sample in his garage and did the responsible thing as a medical professional by calling the Health Department. But after that, his life changed. His home and office were broken into, and he started getting wiretapped and shadowed everywhere he went, forcing him eventually, for his own peace of mind, to accept an invitation from the Vienna Boys' Choir to become its musical director . . ."

"That's all true," Buckaroo verified.

"And he claimed the US government continued to stalk him and the whole choir," I said.

"Rumor had it," Buckaroo reiterated, "although I may have simply come to believe the story, having heard it so many times . . . perhaps like the aerial dogfight itself . . ."

"What? But, Buckaroo, you saved the Earth!" we exclaimed unanimously. "We all saw you blast Whorfin's ship out of the sky over Yoyodyne . . . blew it from here to Hades."

"Did I?" he commented evasively. "Maybe in some dimension. Who can say for sure?"

"Then some special effect . . . ?" Tommy suggested. "Maybe we only imagined the whole thing. Damned ironic . . . shades of the Orson Welles radio broadcast, in which imaginary Martians landed in New Jersey . . ."

"But they weren't imaginary," Pecos said, reminding Li'l Daughter of the epic radio hoax orchestrated by "the traitor Welles."

"Traitor?" questioned Li'l Daughter. "The great Orson Welles was a traitor . . . ?"

"A traitor to our planet," Pecos patiently explained. "He took money from Hanoi Xan to make his first movie, *Citizen Kane*. But in return he created this big radio show to smuggle red aliens in from the Eighth Dimension, where they had been exiled for thousands of Earth years."

"Martians?" Li'l Daughter guessed.

"That's what he said over the radio, but they weren't red Martians. They were Red Lectroids from Planet 10 by way of the Eighth Dimension and with powers of telepathic camouflage . . ."

"Oh my," the young German marveled and turned up her nose in disgust.

PUTTING TWO AND TWO TOGETHER

"Exactly right, Pecos," said Buckaroo. "Now let's assume that if Sid's uncle Ira found one piece of Lectroid remains on his barbecue grill, there may well have been others that the federals missed. It's just possible that someone found Lizardo's ass with that knucklehead Whorfin still in it."

A palpable silence now overcame us all. We were—take your pick—flabbergasted, exhausted, mystified; and only Buckaroo seemed determined to continue our gab session, albeit with himself. As we stared into space or at our handheld devices, only his voice could be heard, debating himself. "And no shortage of secret government agencies out there . . . all depending on whether Whorfin's genetic value has been degraded, and by how much . . . so yes and no. He could be said to exist and also not exist at the same time. More than two possibilities, certainly . . . I just wish the Nova Police deputy had given us a hint or two where to find him . . . assuming he's in one single place."

"As in the foggy world of the quantum, perhaps? Two places at the same time . . . ?" Tommy broke in with his most erudite voice.

"Maybe we're splitting hairs or atoms here," said Buckaroo.

To this Tommy remarked, "I just mean no whole truth at any given point. All is induction and supposition, not certainty."

"Kind of like, the more you know, the less you know, Tom?" I ventured.

As we laughed wholeheartedly, Buckaroo continued. "In fact there are probably a lot of clues we've missed. Maybe the lesson is we've all been on the go a lot recently . . . working on solo research and recording projects, getting various treatments, visiting loved ones, going on adventures and outings . . . and I've withdrawn myself since Penny's disappearance. Looking for answers by traveling to other dimensions, investigating my own psyche and the superstructure undergirding our universe. Yet it seems our own infrastructure, our world, may now be in mortal danger . . ."

Changing the subject slightly, I posed the question, "Why do I smell the hand of that cancer of humanity, the World Crime League and its puppet master Xan, in all of this?"

Buckaroo had the perfect reply. "You could be right, Reno, but also wrong. The World Crime League may be the nastiest cancer on our planet and yet still only be an elementary school bully compared to an existential threat from outer space. What's our defense against something like that?"

Indeed, it was time to get serious. "Progress Over Protocol"—direct action—was of course our mantra, our allotted mission in life, and yet what were we adventurous souls to do? From an inexplicable message out of the blue—or black of space—we had been given to understand that the portal to hell, the fiery abyss, was about to open because John Whorfin might be alive and well . . . though how such a thing was possible, like the exact nature of the threat against us, was not clear. What was the horrible fate soon to be visited upon us? I don't think we wanted to find out, though our ignorance was in no sense bliss.

Whereas only minutes earlier our most pressing concern had been a case of presumed-stolen Jet Car technology and a possible connection to Hanoi Xan and the World Crime League, all of that suddenly seemed a distant concern in light of the mysterious messenger's dire warning. It was necessary to regroup; and what was needed at this moment was a plan to find the master brain John Whorfin, whose present appearance and location were unknown. At a minimum, a necessary first step involved attempting to communicate with the alien man-o'-war and even reestablishing contact with the Lectroid empress John Emdall. If this proved impossible, the collective psychic energy of Blue Blazes everywhere, some sixty thousand strong, would be employed in a mighty community effort to open a telepathic channel to either of these targets.

In more practical and earthly terms, we tasked ourselves to come up with a disposition matrix of behaviors—a kind of psychoanalytical algorithm—matching John Whorfin and Emilio Lizardo's known personality profile. From there, a few keystrokes on our pocket Go-Phones might in mere seconds find close matches in the Banzai Institute Security Index and its archive of villains and case histories, which we could also share with our handful of trusted contacts in the intelligence community.

"Make a note, Reno," Buckaroo told me. "Let's find out for sure if there's the slightest trace left of Yoyodyne . . . any leads to follow. Also send a 'be on the lookout' email blast to all Blue Blazes worldwide, along with Lizardo's file photo . . ."

"Or just a picture of a warthog," Tommy cut in. "They'll probably think it's a joke anyway."

"With fire shooting out of his ass," Pecos added. "Wouldn't hurt to scour every police blotter from here to Timbuktu."

"Just remind our volunteers what they're getting into right up front," urged Buckaroo. Perhaps I'll know more after I talk to the president and find out what he knows, but in the meantime, let's familiarize ourselves with every detail of Whorfin's dossier and Lizardo's bio, everything in our files. Just a hunch, but international travel would be difficult without a passport. Of course someone could have supplied one, but my hunch is they're still here in the USA. Check food stamp rolls and men's stores—we know Lizardo likes expensive clothes from the 1930s."

Compiling such a laundry list was admittedly a long shot, but doubtless a better use of our time than filling in the spaces with our fertile imaginations. But there was also the business still before us: Buckaroo's scheduled rendezvous with a certain rheumy-eyed general whose United States Air Force wings had been clipped, pending a top-secret investigation.

X. A SECRET PRISONER

> Show me the man and I'll find you the crime.
> —Lavrentiy Beri

In the north tower of the venerable Smithsonian Castle, there is a sepulchral room unknown to all but a few . . . a place of prayer and monastic contemplation not much larger than a jail cell and as tightly sealed. Its existence is mentioned only rarely in popular literature or on secret tours of the capital, and actual entry to the windowless chamber is barred to all but members of the secret society of Saint Anthony Hall and its college affiliates—and even these find entry barred if the room is locked from the inside or guarded by government and Pinkerton men, which happened to be the case the afternoon of our arrival . . .

. . . as two public figures, both instantly recognizable anywhere in the world, ascended the tower's narrow stairway with their escorts: three Secret Service bodyguards, a nondescript man carrying the United States missile and bomber launch codes, and myself. Buckaroo Banzai carried a medical valise and a battered cowboy hat that he had doffed on entering the great museum, while President James Monroe II—hefty but reasonably fit, short, and bespectacled with lank, sandy hair—wore a red jogging suit and clutched a bag of fried chicken tenders or nuggets, from which he plucked at will. Although I could hear only snippets of their conversation, plainly it was between old friends.

"Thank you for your time, Buckaroo. You look like you could use a little meat on your bones, but I know how busy you are, like me. But it's important we stitch up our differences and get back to serving the common good . . ."

"I want nothing more, Mr. President. I always enjoy being taken for a ride, especially by the Night Stalkers."

". . . because we share a special bond others can never know . . . two peas in a pod with a purity of commitment, of staying true to the cause, fighting evil without fear . . ."

Already impatient, Buckaroo interrupted, "How's it going, Mr. President?"

"It's going super," the president said reflexively before changing his tune just as quickly. "No, I'm sorry; I don't need to cover up the truth from Buckaroo Banzai. Not to give you the whole story, but I'm in a very bad place emotionally . . . not even eating decently."

He sipped contritely from a pocket thermos and, between bites from his greasy bag, said, "Believe me, Buckaroo, I'm embarrassed and ashamed. I had no freaking clue about the Jet Car espionage program—most likely rogue troublemakers out in Langley, but I can't know everything our vast intelligence apparatus is doing, much less things that happened before I took the helm or when my own people feed me horse manure. As for the how and why, I've pretty much washed my hands of it all."

"With all due respect, Mr. President, you can't run and hide; and I've warned you that bipolar drugs affect people in different ways."

"Please, Buckaroo, call me James or Jimbo."

Buckaroo ignored the offer and continued to make his displeasure known.

"Mr. President, the truth is foreign to false people. Many of those around you are poseurs, professional butt kissers only interested in feathering their own nests."

"An old boys' club, yes, Buckaroo. Even as president, I have to go with the flow, always the same stupid. Why do you think I turned to Postmaster General Mantooth as my most trusted adviser . . . ?"

"Hopefully not a case of too little, too late," mused Buckaroo. "Spying on the Institute is one thing, but putting the whole planet at risk is another. It's about the survival of the planet right now."

"A bit of overstatement, surely, Buckaroo?"

After a flurry of indistinct whispers between them, it became apparent that the president had not been briefed by the Nova Police, or likely even heard of them. Only when Buckaroo played my blurry, low-quality recording of the emissary's message did Monroe turn ashen faced, virtually the color of this page you are reading . . . although that is not to say he fully comprehended the gravity of the situation.

When a second playing of the space messenger's dire warning concluded, he visibly trembled and said, "My God, what a predicament! And you think it's legit? I've never heard of anything like this—a hologram from outer space?! And why didn't they come to me, as well? I'm the phawking main man around here. Now all of a sudden my gut hurts. And you think not mumble jumble, a yarn about a yarn, then? This is the real deal?"

"I ask myself the same question," Buckaroo replied. "After all, how could that low-down bacillus John Whorfin still be alive? Since the Defense Department and the FBI secured the crash site, elements in the government would almost certainly have to know . . ."

"May I rot in hell if this is the end of Earth," the president vowed.

"In my humble opinion, Mr. President, the prudent course is to proceed on that assumption, that it's an existential fight for our planet," Buckaroo said gravely, "although of course it's always possible they're only interested in tribute and taking custodial ownership, if in fact they're privateers more inclined to self-interest than taking orders from a distant sovereign. It's worth remembering that they can always go elsewhere, but we can't."

"Damn sure worth a try," the president conceded. "Our policy is never to pay ransom, but I won't obstruct you as a private citizen. And mark my words: if we're on the verge of saying bye-bye to life on this planet as we know it, in my short time left here on this earth I will devote every waking hour to getting to the bottom of this and finding this freak John Whorfin."

"That would be helpful, but we may be set up for failure," said Buckaroo. "You can start by getting me access to all the records of the cleanup, disposal, and so forth . . . and the Yoyodyne file."

The president looked like he had been hit with a bucket of ice water and processed this request by taking a deep breath. Behind the voids of his eyes and their tiny pupils, something was wreaking havoc with the activity centers of his brain. Dark thoughts were seeping through.

"So, yeah, wow," he sighed at length. "I'll do what I can, using every instrument of governance at my disposal, even if it endangers my sorry butt."

"I applaud your backbone and wish you a long life," Buckaroo said with a wry glance in my direction. "My priority right now is John Whorfin, but since you brought me here, suppose we get to the point."

"It's General Bill Wagoneer, whom I've relieved as commander of Nellis Air Force Base," the president continued, sadly shaking his head. "We also suspect him of selling your Jet Car technology to the World Crime League in order to overthrow America."

"'Wild Bill' Wagoneer?" questioned Buckaroo. "I heard he was something of a hotshot, but a turncoat? My first question would be how he came by the secret Jet Car data in the first place. I'd have to be stupid to believe the government wasn't involved."

"The circumstantial evidence does seem strong," the president agreed. "We're still trying to wallow through it all, but keep in mind there are certain things I can't tell you. What I can tell you is that the man is a traitor, a scammer, a consummate actor, and a festering psycho who blew up a multimillion-dollar Defense Department lab, causing injury to numerous military personnel under his command."

More than a little curious, Buckaroo inquired at once, "What kind of lab, Mr. President?"

"There are conflicting stories. Like I said, it appears the whole chain of command's been hoodwinked. Just so you can understand my concern, it was a tank built inside a special enclosure inside Area 51, wrapped in mystery and a black budget, leaving a big hole in the taxpayers' pocket. This cannot be pointed out enough. We had to break into his secret bunker with a battering ram, and even now I feel like he's phawking with us, with his childish baby words and absurd stories of space aliens fed hallucinogenics or even made into tasty meals served at the Officers' Club. Tastes like chicken!"

He forced a laugh and swallowed the nugget he had been chewing, giving Buckaroo an opportunity to say, "Nice to know we're still the apex predators . . . at least so far. But how is such a thing possible?"

The president meanwhile was saying, "I sent for you because it's been a nightmare trying to get a statement out of him, trying to get his rambling stories straight—yet your name always seems to brighten his stupid grin and he's been asking for you. Just pathetic, a real circus."

"But not unusual for a sociopath. In some weird way, he identifies with me and has been writing me for years with certain odd theories about things," Buckaroo related, thinking back on Wagoneer's long letters full of gibberish. "While it occurred to me Wild Bill might not be firing on all cylinders, he's far from alone, and I never got the feeling he was a threat or a disloyal American. And he's in this joint because of the big blowout at 51?"

The president looked uncomfortable and chewed before answering, "Not technically. We can't afford to put that out there for national security reasons, and that's why I sent for you secretly. So far, he's here on a violation of the uniform dress code for slovenliness and theft of a two-peso Mexican gold coin from a Panamanian stripper."

"Panama . . . ?"

Monroe nodded. "He's already tried to kill himself a couple of times, which is also why I thought of you, the man of the hour and always our last and best hope. On the other hand, he may just be faking it . . . as I say, more hoodwinking. You see my point?"

"I see we're up a creek and need some answers," said Buckaroo. "Is that it?"

THE MAN IN THE BOX

It is this historian's good fortune that Buckaroo has seen fit to share details, many never before revealed, of this first pivotal encounter with William Wagoneer and the perplexing circumstances that likely delivered the traitor into the arms of Hanoi Xan. Most authors have presented the case that Xan somehow got his hooks into the general and corrupted him, whereas the truth in front of me—Buckaroo's own faithful notes—tells a different story.

While it is not in my purview to comment upon the legal debate concerning the general's arrest for a minor infraction and his subsequent incarceration at a nonmilitary secret location, the fact of the matter, as I view it in retrospect, is that extraordinary (and extralegal) measures were regrettably justified under the circumstances. Although the public was not yet paying attention—and we ourselves were not yet aware of the extent of Wagoneer's perfidy or Hanoi Xan's involvement—the warning from the Nova Police, strange as it was, had cast into sharp relief the true scope of the crisis. Given what we now knew, we had no choice but to proceed under the assumption that the world truly had been painted into a corner and would survive or perish according to our actions.

"Could I borrow a couple of your chicken tenders?" Buckaroo asked the president.

"Only if you agree to be my ambassador to the Court of Saint James's," President Monroe replied, only half in jest. "I'm even prepared to throw my support behind your worldwide campaign to save the bumblebees."

"Good news, Mr. President, but no time for that now, though I'm sure certain people wouldn't mind seeing me leave the country," said Buckaroo, who palmed the still-warm nuggets and headed past a pair of plainclothes guards into the tower's hidden room.

Without difficulty, young reader, you can imagine the tingling sensation that the occupant of the spartan chamber must have felt when his cell door opened to reveal a pair of plainclothes federals with their illustrious visitor in tow. As I say, one may imagine it, but the fact is that the unclothed prisoner lay in a fetal ball atop an air mattress with his eyes tightly pressed shut and consequently did not see Dr. Buckaroo Banzai duck beneath the archway and step into the small, unventilated enclosure that smelled of human gas.

From Buckaroo's perspective, he saw a marshmallow of a middle-aged man—nude except for shite-stained riding boots and a spiked dog collar—rolled into a Mylar thermal blanket and audibly sobbing. On a nearby table rested a dozen prescription drug vials, a leather-bound Bible, a plastic food tray, and a cafeteria-style dinner plate holding a wilted piece of lettuce in a soupy brew of gravy and crimson Jell-O.

There were also twin folding chairs, presumably for officials and interrogators, since Wagoneer was not permitted visitors. Other furnishings included a trashcan, a chamber pot, and the aforementioned air mattress that now made a rank farting noise as the general sat up with convulsive suddenness and a gaping canine-like maw.

"Chicken? Is that the Colonel I smell?" he said, adding a holler and a whoop at the sight of his famous visitor. "Buckaroo Banzai . . . by Jesus!

Knock, knock, who's there? Buckaroo Banzai, cool as the breeze! To your credit, sir! To your credit . . . and our relationship!"

"General Wagoneer—?" said Buckaroo.

"Please, the name's Wild Bill. The general stepped out, but I rise to show respect! I'm his mouthpiece," the general sputtered, his Adam's apple bobbing like crazy. "Still trying to get my head around this—I guess somebody upstairs listened to my pitiful-ass plea! Buckaroo Banzai—I feel fine now, Mama! Just a touch of distemper. I've been expecting you . . . welcome to Uncle Sam's distemper doghouse, the kill room."

He extended his right hand; but as Buckaroo started to grasp it, the general simply took the chicken nugget out of Buckaroo's other palm and greedily devoured it.

"I've been tightlipped until now," he said. "I think we both know why you're here, and it's not to change my dressings."

"I'm here as a physician, General, nothing more, at the request of psych services and your primary care provider, Dr. J——."

"The old crisis response team, eh, Doc? Then I'm just gonna go out on a limb here and say welcome to the nut hut. Feel free to monitor my performance while I nut . . ."

Failing to finish his thought, he pointed secretively at the overhead fluorescent light and the covered chamber pot in the corner—actually a piece of antique cookware likely borrowed from the museum—and raised a finger to his lips for silence.

"Quiet," he whispered. "You can hear the warblers and thrushes, the sweet ravens who mate for life . . ."

Through the thick walls there was of course nothing of the sort to be heard, leading Buckaroo to inquire, "Are you in pain, General? Do you hurt anywhere?"

"Hurts all over," the prisoner said. "It's unacceptable that this should happen in America, much less inside the Smithsonian."

When a full minute passed without another word, Buckaroo decided to indulge the odd character's tenuous grip on reality by announcing, "What if I told you I'm really here to do a prison album like Johnny Cash?"

The general's face suddenly lit up and he said, "There's Johnny Cash and Buckaroo Banzai, and the rest is just pretend, Doc. But how about a TV movie? Maybe the Reno Kid could play me, but nobody would ever believe my story."

"What *is* your story, General?" Buckaroo asked.

"Borderline criminality," Wagoneer replied, looking the great physician squarely in the eye. "But only borderline because my mother needed a kidney and I tried to do the right thing. I didn't sell you out, Dr. Banzai, nor my country. That is a scientific fact and I can back it up."

"That's good to hear," said Buckaroo matter-of-factly. "I'm happy you did the right thing."

"So be it and so help me God," declared the general, happily believing he had cultivated a favorable impression of himself in Buckaroo's mind with such little effort. But he had more to say. "Why would I go to a lot of trouble, even deadly trouble, for very little money? Besides, some sixth sense warned me."

"Nice to know you had misgivings, General."

"Even so, it seems I have duly kept my appointment in Samarra."

"Fate can be mighty cruel," Buckaroo observed. "Just look at the mess that lies all around us."

"You're right, Doc. We're all just toys of chance, and I feel its sharp eyes—the eyes of the phawking infinite—upon me. The drama hastens on, even for the snow-white sacrificial lamb," the general said, losing his train of thought while trying to capture a housefly. "Sorry the place isn't spick and span. I guess I won't be getting any Mr. Clean awards—I just took a chili-fueled prison crap on the bastards' miniature bugging device—because my intestines are twisted up in knots. Can you imagine—a proactive guy like me, with my level of intelligence? I hope you brought some cigarettes and a little something for the pain, Doc. Drugs are expensive in jail."

"Quite true. If we could only be as smart as we think we are," said Buckaroo. "Any addictions besides nicotine? Prescription medications . . . ?"

"My heart pills, Doc, so I've been doing what I can with the cards I was dealt. I don't suppose you brought Nostradamus . . . ?"

"Nostradamus?"

"My main man, brother Chihuahua, and spiritual soul twin. He told me this would happen. In fact, he saw the whole thing coming down, also foretold in the Book of Famous Amos," the general said.

"Would you mind undressing? I understand you tried to mutilate yourself," Buckaroo informed him.

"Hey, they don't call it the Smithsonian Institution for nothing, Doc. Looks like I've been institutionalized, but I get it—it's a blackmail move to make me crack. Half my ancestors made it to the Tower of London. In fact I was trying to geld myself, but thankfully I'm hung like a bull terrier and lacked the necessary implements. So I stabbed my demon ball with a plastic spork, trying to give myself a reprieve from this spider hole, like my great mentor in life, Professor Hikita."

"So you know the good professor?" Buckaroo said, giving the general the long nose. "When did you meet?"

"We saw him here just yesterday . . ."

"We . . . ?"

"Me and Nostradamus . . . and the person at the door. Somebody's coming up the walk now."

Noticing Wagoneer turn and stare intently in the direction of the bolted door, Buckaroo saw no one and may have turned away briefly to keep a straight face.

"I had no idea this place was humming with such activity. Expecting trouble?" he asked the agitated inmate, as straight as he could manage.

"I hear trouble rattling my front door," the general went on and now shouted at the invisible companion. "Did you hear me? We're closed! I have very little money on the premises!"

Buckaroo jotted himself a note and said, "More like a desperate cry for help, then, rather than *seppuku*."

"Looks like it worked. You're here, aren't you, Doc? So far, so good."

Wagoneer stood there in the nude, smiling blissfully as if proud of himself. Crazy as a loon or crazy like a fox? Buckaroo had difficulty deciding, but said, "I'm a health care provider . . . it's what I do. As you've told me, all of this must be very painful for a man of your position, with your brilliant career."

Wagoneer forced a bitter laugh, muttering through his teeth, "What position? You mean the doggy position? Yep, it's pretty raw, Doc, a raw deal. One minute I'm a hero riding a float in my hometown parade, lots of good folks and good barbecue . . . and the next thing I know, I get hit by a Roman candle, presto PTSD, causing me to soil my dress whites. People say it's a wonder I didn't get blown clean off the float, but I guess I should've expected it. Nostradamus warned me, being the black sheep of the British royal family. Next thing I know, I'm busted. Either show me the evidence against me or grant me the liberty of being in America! The freedom of this land! What is my recourse?! Where are the charges and strict-ass laws I broke?! My life's on the line here, Doc! Repeating myself like a flippin' parrot when I say my fate's already sealed. The Bill of Rights is as useless as tits on a bull, assholes on an elbow. I could go on and on . . ."

"Please do. The British royal family?" Buckaroo probed, trying to calm the excitable fellow.

"Straight outta Buckingham Palace," the prisoner affirmed. "With nothing better to do than rake my rocks over the coals, the twenty-third illegitimate grandson to the king of England. On a mission to take me down because I was his little experiment . . . stick me over here in no-man's land . . . no visits, no phone calls, no Wi-Fi, no clean bedding, no means to shower the fecal or get away from the radiation."

As it so happened, Buckaroo was carrying a Geiger counter and much more in the palm of his hand: his Go-Phone with its Doc-in-a-Box application, containing x-ray, sonography, spectrometry, interferometry, CT scan, and a slew of other functions with instant links to the Banzai Institute and Columbia-Presbyterian Hospital in New York City. With a mere pass of the device over a patient, he could have a second, third, and fourth opinion from other world-renowned specialists within minutes.

A WALKING TEXTBOOK OF MALADIES

"No matter where you go, there you are—am I right, Doc? Takes all kinds to make the world go around. Trouble is, no matter where you go, they're there, too . . . fleas, lice, scabies, shite-grinning backstabbers, four stone walls, all the stewed tomatoes, bologna sandwiches, and Jell-O I can eat . . . all aimed at my chemical and intellectual sterilization, where depression and regurgitation is my only activity. What does it mean when your dark piss smells like vinegar? DNA mutation?"

It was at this precise moment (Buckaroo confided to me later), when he passed his interferometer over the general's filthy face, that he realized he was staring into the mad eyes of either a consummate actor or a pathological narcissist. Yet he hid his personal opinion and merely said, "And now you've ended up here. Seems kind of like overkill, just for soiling your pants. Might it have something to do with espionage or dereliction of duty? Something about being in league with Hanoi Xan . . . ?"

"You said a mouthful, Doc," the general said, appearing to pay attention before just as quickly drifting away. "Can you at least tell the DOs to let me have a hammock? Just charge it to my credit card on file. Somebody throw me a damn soup bone . . . but, hell, why do I even bother? They'll never let me out, because I know too much!"

He was wheezing at a fever pitch by now, his chest rising and falling like a petulant child's, when he suddenly pumped his fist and delivered an infantile kicking tantrum, taking out his wrath on the flimsy table and sending it flying, along with Buckaroo's instruments, an Episcopal prayer book, and a food tray, bellowing, "It's like I've fallen off the damn planet! I was good to you, USA, so throw me away! Worm food! I sipped the Kool-Aid, played by the house rules for thirty-odd years and fought for it, paid in blood, guns a-blazin', old school! Put on the helmet and flew the bird in a leadership position, unlike the rear-echelon motherphawkers! Faced down Russian Bear bombers over Alaska and made thunder rumble in the 'Stan. Ha, ha, I stepped into the breach and now am cast out! Phawk off, we murder!"

Calmly retrieving the strewn items, Buckaroo warned, "Sad, sad situation, but let's acknowledge one another civilly, General, before things go really wrong. Otherwise you're destined to end your life here, perhaps an untimely death, sick and alone. Or maybe you'd be more comfortable with a military physician."

"No, no, please—peace, love, and happiness, Doc—don't be upset . . . no reason to get annoyed . . . I'm in crisis here!" swore the general. "I'm sorry, but crazy is living in my head, and before I go down for the count, I'd like to dance with my wife one last time . . . dance like it's my last day to live before I go to heaven."

"Your wife? So . . . a lump in your throat . . . swollen lymph nodes. It appears science backs you up," Buckaroo said, simultaneously examining the general's cranium with his tomographic scanning application.

"She played, got laid; now she sleeps in the bed she made. Unfortunately, she took Nostradamus with her, and I haven't heard from either one. Whatever happened to true love, Doc?"

In his case notes jotted down later, Buckaroo would describe the once powerfully built male Caucasian in his Jockey briefs as "midfifties . . . approximately 6'2" and ramrod stiff in the military way but with clumsy gestures, moving as if in a torpor, robotic, b/c fusion of L5 and L6 vertebrae (horse-riding accident) . . . his face oily, blotchy, alcoholic or fetal alcohol syndrome? . . . gray, limpid, wide-set eyes, double chin . . . thyroid goiter . . . noticeable neck swelling . . . his pate liver spotted and bald . . . steatopygia . . . overly long, tapered fingernails giving his odd scaly hands, also liver spotted, a feminine aspect . . . presenting signs of palsy and hemolytic jaundice, drawn looking and fatigued, ample belly (swollen), malnourished? . . . alternately ecstatic and insouciant, annoyed, borderline manic . . . other signs of mental anxiety . . . speaks of grief, thoughts of suicide . . . his breasts abnormally swollen, bilateral gynecomastia . . . his genital area hairless (razor stubble) . . . herpes pustules . . . an undescended (left) testicle . . . continually playing with his penis hidden behind a cotton ball and a Band-Aid . . . frequent episodic retching . . ."

"Please don't pleasure yourself when I'm talking to you, General . . ."

"What, this?" Wagoneer said. Stretching his foreskin and trying to turn it inside out would be a more accurate description of what he was doing; in any case he did not cease doing it.

"Those dry scales on your hands . . . ?" Buckaroo asked him. "Have you been working around cleaning solvents? Methyl ethyl ketone . . . ?"

"Meth . . . ?"

"Not methamphetamine. Methyl ethyl ketone, a highly toxic chemical that produces dioxin when burned."

"Well . . . I worked downwind from the burn pits for years, drank perchlorate, radioactive contaminants, melted plastic, and medical waste every day in the drinking water, along with the rest of my fighting men," the general said and audibly retched. "Like I told Abbot Costello . . ."

"Abbott and Costello . . . ?"

"The abbot Costello, Doc," Wagoneer informed him. "Chief exorcist of Perugia."

THE GENERAL'S ASTONISHING CLAIMS

Searching his memory, Buckaroo realized he had heard of such a man, a humble Franciscan whose growing body of work, healings, and other miracles had made news in Italy and elsewhere, particularly in the tabloid newspapers. By coincidence, High Sierra in World Watch One had informed Buckaroo recently of a rumored miracle, of which it was said that the holy infant Jesus had appeared in the company of Abbot Costello, who recently had performed a feat no one had managed in one thousand years: manually removing San Galgano's sword from its resting place in the famous stone at Montesiepi Chapel in Tuscany.

Of course such stories—particularly this version of events, filtered thirdhand through the tabloid media and local villagers—were often exaggerated, even though the hole in the rock where the famed sword was once lodged had become a new object of veneration overnight. But whatever the truth, Abbot Costello was not a name to be taken lightly.

"He finally got rid of my tumor," claimed Wagoneer. "Logically impossible, I know, but nothing compared to what happened next with Lizardo . . ."

"Lizardo? Emilio Lizardo??" Buckaroo uttered with surprise, wondering if the general could have heard his conversation with the president moments earlier. The prospect seemed far fetched, but no more so than Wagoneer's unbidden remark out of the blue.

"I thought that'd grab your attention," the general chuckled perversely. "What would you say if I told you that Dr. Emilio Lizardo—the famous scientist Lizardo—and the alien Whorfin inside him somehow survived the shootout over the Garden State?"

"I would say it's now the second time I've heard it this morning, but 'somehow' does not explain how, since I blew him to kingdom come. You'll have to work harder than that, General. I also think I see your plan."

"I swear, Doc. I buried him myself not six months ago. He's in the ground at S4, behind the TR-3B and antigravity flying disk hangar, lying right next to Elvis."

Buckaroo gave him the long nose but humored him, asking, "Elvis Presley? Now you're piling it on many layers deep. Seriously?"

"As serious as it is Thursday, Doc . . . it is Thursday, right? I kicked dirt over him myself. You wanna know something else? Just to prove I'm on the level, the autopsy determined that they both died of a broken heart and a megabowel. Only fitting they're buried next to each other."

"You must think I'm very gullible, General," said Buckaroo. "I have a pretty keen sense of what's wrong in the world, but I hadn't heard that bit of news. Why were you keeping Elvis?"

Wagoneer merely shrugged, as confounded on that score as anyone else.

"The secret-agent boys at Langley had him frozen for years, was all I knew," he said. "Then I heard they moved him to the secret Coca-Cola vault in Atlanta before shipping him out to us in a special refrigerator car."

"The same vault where they keep the Coca-Cola recipe?"

"I wouldn't be surprised. You'll have to ask the alphabet boys—CIA, NSA, DIA—how come. Maybe they just needed the room."

"Room for the Diet Coke formula?" ventured Buckaroo skeptically. Indeed, by now he was more skeptical than ever of the general's whole preposterous tale.

"Could be. I won't call you a liar," replied Wagoneer. "I understand they also have the bones of the biblical Goliath. This is just between us, though, right, Doc? I've seen what they do to squealers."

"The alphabet boys . . ."

"You may or may not be one yourself, Doc. I don't wanna know."

"Relax, General—there's such a thing as doctor-patient confidentiality. Tell me about the explosion . . ."

"Explosion? What explosion?"

"Turn your head and cough for me, please."

"The old short-arm inspection, huh, Doc. Shinbone connected to the knee bone," sang Wagoneer, coughing up a glob of sputum and feeling Buckaroo squeeze his oversensitive privates.

"I'm not easily shocked, General, and it also happens that I'm nobody's fool," Buckaroo assured him. "I think you'll find that's how I'm known through the streets of the world . . . a straight shooter, not a mind player. I think most people are also aware of the fact I don't work for any government."

"Then you're lucky you've never been on the federal titty. I gotta admit you make shite happen, Doc, and stand up for what's right and just," Wagoneer conceded. "Loyal, caring, and a great man. If I can't trust Buckaroo Banzai, one of the white hats and friend of the common man . . . oww!"

By now Buckaroo had moved one hand over Wagoneer's sunken chest, from which he jerked out a hair and examined it with the spectrographic feature on his handheld Go-Phone, saying, "Right now I'm more interested in this Whorfin business. How did you bring Lizardo back to life? Was that the explosion?"

"I don't remember the explosion they keep talking about," Wagoneer continued. "A little out of my field and pay grade. It was the R&D guys in skunk works who got a pretty payday for growing the bastards back from the dead by Frankensteinian methods, after you fried the hair off their nuts, Doc. I'll never forget that day as long as I live. They all looked like they'd been through the scrapper, but Whorfin was a tough bird who refused to let the Lizard die. As for the others, cloning techniques and a baby-chick incubator did the rest."

"The others?"

"I used to see little pieces of Lectroid carcasses outside the containment unit, little baby dills hanging with clothespins or growing like floating spud turds, marinated in packets of shite cake and who knows what white sauce. My God, the things I've seen, Doc . . ."

"Chop the weed and ten more grow back?" Buckaroo grimly remarked.

"Ten, twenty, a hundred—beyond the pale, Doc. A reality many find hard to believe."

"So they undergo a curing process, is that it . . . ?"

"Among other things . . . pretty much just throw 'em against the wall and see what sticks. Ignorant carapaces with very little brain to work with, at least in the beginning, but with a pace of evolution that blew our minds."

"How many are we talking about? Do they reproduce?"

Wagoneer nodded and proceeded to say, "Little fetuses, or larvae, in the throat. They carry them around in their mouths . . . not sure for how long. I heard they're like frogs or clownfish, able to be whatever sex they want to be, but since the lab boys didn't always clue me in, I can't swear to it . . . hard-shelled carapaces around big blobby silicon-based genomes. I personally know guys walking around in the skins of the poor butchered bastards . . . fancy vests stitched from corded lines of their tough, silver-threaded DNA . . ."

"Capsids, then? Conductive body armor?" Buckaroo guessed. "That might explain their phototrophic conduits that enable them to harvest electrons from any electrode source."

"They don't follow our laws, that's crystal clear. But then again, neither do we," said the general, eyeing another nugget and licking his chops. "I doubt even President Monroe knows about all our bloodthirsty jackassery. I'm just telling you what I've seen: sick, twisted, pants-crapping shite that would break your heart . . . space aliens in cages like a cheap carnival freak show . . . surgery on baby aliens crying for their mamas who we assume have zero human emotion. We outstanding moral humans built the little blighters a set of electrified monkey bars, then encouraged them to play king of the mountain for chocolate-covered peanuts that they sometimes chew, sometimes stick up their excretory pores. Then they roll over and die. No biggie. Same with Coca-Cola. After that, we grind the dead up into flakes, like cereal, and spread 'em on Lectroid turds and watch 'em sprout into new ones."

"Peanuts, you said?" Buckaroo continued to question, pondering the possible implications. "Could peanut protein allergy be the kryptonite that breaks down their capsid? Or the mycotoxin aflatoxin in peanut butter spread?"

"You heard right. It's disgusting, Doc, unphawking real, all courtesy of the giant alien brain in the special cooler . . ."

"Alien brain . . . ?"

"I'm talking hush-hush dealings . . . the big gray blob who gives the orders to his Neo followers . . ."

"Neo? Nazis?"

"The Church."

"The Catholic Church?" Buckaroo queried. "Or do you mean the alphabet boys?"

"Maybe I've said too much. They'll tear me apart. They've already removed me," the general said, suddenly cautious. "I just meant to plant the seed . . . revealing certain ethical boundaries that have been crossed."

"You wouldn't have any hard evidence, by any chance? Pictures . . . ?"

"No pictures. But for another piece of chicken, I'll trade nuggets of info," the general offered . . .

. . . as Buckaroo placed his hand over his patient's heart, from which he was able to determine that the general suffered from an arrhythmia but might be telling the truth, or at least the truth insofar as he believed it.

"For a bite of chicken . . . where does Hanoi Xan come into all this?" said Buckaroo, fishing the last of the president's fried pieces out of his pocket and dangling it in front of the salivating prisoner.

"Xan . . . ?" the general said in a whisper. "The walls have ears, Doc. I talk about Xan, I'm a tombstone."

"Since when does Buckaroo Banzai fear Hanoi Xan . . . ?"

"Right. I don't fear anybody . . . not even the cawing of the crow. The only thing I fear is being in a big bed by myself."

These words had their due effect on Buckaroo, who was beginning to think the general was stupid, but not laughably so; and after a moment of deadly silence, asked, "Were you scared when you shot down John Whorfin?"

"I almost wet myself," Wagoneer answered, adding, "But did I fear death? Flying from this world to Hogfat City to collect Buckaroo Banzai's reward? Hell no! But even the palace of heaven is lonely without your missus and little pooch. But maybe you don't know the meaning of loneliness . . . ?"

"I know lonely," replied Buckaroo. "Do you know who I am, General?"

The general paused, thoughtful. "You're the guy in the movies. You play me in the movies."

"That is gold!" Buckaroo said, stifling first an oath and then a laugh. "Pure gold."

"Why am I here? I've been here too long," General Wagoneer replied, his bloodshot eyes full of bewilderment. "I'm not a Chihuahua . . . I'm a guinea pig. With drugs and booze I could handle it for a while, but then a holiday rolled around and I went down to Central America, where I got the idea of running a sting operation to infiltrate Hanoi Xan's operation and reveal his links to the British throne. Have you ever heard of the Fabian Society?"

"The political movement or the famous singer? What is your interest—"

Cutting Buckaroo off in midsentence, Wagoneer jabbered on. "Instead, Contreras and his boys somehow slipped me some devil's candy at a titty bar—four bars of Xanax and some noxious weed—and put me in bed with a hooker, then stuck my head in a toilet when I protested. Seems I got caught in their snare with a foreign gold piece somebody put in my pocket. Fast-forward, maybe I was a little too glib with the police. Am I making any sense at all . . . ?"

Buckaroo leveled his steely gaze at the general, doing his best to read his tumultuous mind, before saying, "So . . . blackmail . . . pulling the wool . . . destroying people . . . what the World Crime League does best. Smoke and mirrors. If Contreras was who I think he was, he happened to be the nephew of Carlos the Jackal. If I'm not mistaken, MI6 drowned him in the Panama Canal not long ago."

"Thanks, Doc, I didn't know that, but he was a poor excuse for a human being, with the morals of a horse trader," Wagoneer said. "Obviously, no good deed goes unpunished. I got in over my head, and slander from cowards did the rest. Now I ended up here in the tower, needing help in the worst way. What it boils down to, Doc . . . Buckaroo Banzai needs your help."

For an instant Buckaroo thought his own mind was sliding down a black sinkhole, but he said merely, "You have my help, Buckaroo. Tell me more."

"I'm talking a giant, resounding CIA skullphawk against the United States Constitution," replied the general with obvious passion. "The powers of the president of the United States have been usurped by CIA's MK-ULTRA and a giant red brain called the Nexus that looks like a candy-coated Sacred Heart of Jesus with one big eye, floating in an aquarium of liquid nitrogen. I only got a glimpse of the thing once, behind a human wall of prancing yea-sayers, but I swear on all the buried dead at Arlington it's the holy damn truth. I'm just telling you to keep a cool head and know what you're getting in for. I also have traveled to the stars, but maybe that's a whole other story."

"Undoubtedly. I hadn't heard about the big-brain puppet master, but I've had some experience with Lectroids and their puppet master Whorfin," Buckaroo said. "They love their sweets, as I recall."

"Yes and no. Sweets, electricity, and yellow cake uranium," the general went on. "Not only are peanuts their crystal meth, it turns out they're hydro corn syrup intolerant . . . violently so. This is classified thirty-five levels above Top Secret, but their kryptonite—a single drop or two of the pure hydro corn syrup—seems to provoke some kind of chemical warfare inside their measly brains. And their mouths are fake-outs. I'd see them in the rec room slurping up cola beverages with their other orifices, watching that powerful movie *Scarface* over and over again, then literally keeling over, one by one."

"How Lamarckian. Sounds like we humans share the same phenotype," remarked Buckaroo.

"I don't know about that, Doc, but when I tried to complain through channels that it might have something to do with their diet and that we were putting them in a very bad situation by teaching them our human behaviors, I was ignored by certain dubious people . . . causing me to question everything I ever learned about the Geneva Convention. Totally unnecessary."

"But they didn't necessarily die . . . the Lectroids?"

"Die, hell. They're like things from the sewer, grown even stronger and more violent. Kill 'em, sprinkle 'em with catnip, and they somehow pop right back up and multiply by releasing methane gas and inseminating their own feces."

"Catnip?" Buckaroo muttered to himself. "Nepetalactone?"

"I'm no scientist," confessed the other. "All I know is it's a mess to clean up."

Buckaroo marveled, thinking aloud, "But is it the fructose or the insecticide in the corn syrup that triggers the macrophage activity and immune response?"

The general failed to bat an eye and merely resumed, "You got me, Doc, but they seem to be evolving pretty damn fast, almost generationally. They used to stink a mile, for starters. But the latest generation smell like pumpkin lavender."

"So, epigenetic inheritance . . . ?" pondered Buckaroo.

The general concurred. "Plus, what they have is the power of suggestion, being able to tunnel into your head until you feel eaten up with weirdness. That swindler Whorfin trick-bagged me, posing as a sexy temptress, playing on my guilt for playing God and shooting him and his boys outta the sky . . . commanding me to oil up Lizardo and give him irrigation and other little happenings, until one day I saw him as he really was: a horde of tiny demons only interested in his own particular world. We were involved for nearly a year."

"Go figure," said Buckaroo, no longer surprised by anything that came out of Wagoneer's mouth—or went into it, for that matter.

"That's how I came to understand the devil was in him, commanding me to clean his moldy body parts and help him . . . so I pulled some strings and called the Vatican, who directed me to Cardinal Baltazar, who recommended Brother Costello, whose juju is as badass as they come. That's the last thing I remember."

"Before the explosion?" Buckaroo guessed. "There was an exorcism?"

"Very limited and with all the sanitary protections. I must have blacked out," said the general, tapping his skull. "Maybe it's all up here in my jelly sack. I just don't remember a lot after the big bang . . . just the voice of the Lord speaking to me, saying, 'Stop being a mama's boy. You shall slay them with the jawbone of an ass, like the biblical Samsonite.'"

Was this dialogue real? Or the entire scenario, for that matter? Buckaroo could not be sure, feeling a sense of claustrophobia, of being trapped in the windowless room inside a dream or even another dimension. Strange days were coming, he thought, looking at this plainly delusional individual who was circling the drain in his own outer orbit.

XI. DOCTOR'S ORDERS

A physician is not angry at the intemperance of a mad patient,
nor does he take it ill to be railed at by a man in fever.
—Seneca the Younger

After a few minutes, it became apparent that Wagoneer's relationship with his overbearing father—the "phawking king of England" who frequently belt-whipped him—had caused him to see himself through the authority figure's eyes and view himself in fact as both Buckaroo Banzai and a Chihuahua dog. But how far to plumb the general's troubled psyche, as against the existential problems of the entire planet? This was not only a metaphysical question but also a professional one.

Now Dr. Banzai aimed his otoscope at the general's right ear before donning sanitary gloves and, with the effortless technique of someone who had performed literally thousands of posterior rhinoscopies, applied a tongue depressor.

"Say ahhhh . . ."

"Ahhhh . . ."

"Good job. I see you've had a sinuplasty . . . and a lot of leukoplakia. You still smoking?"

"Like a napalmed carcass, Doc. Ever see one of those smokin' beauties? I've seen plenty."

No sooner had Buckaroo inserted his steel tool into Wagoneer's mouth, however, than the general caught a glimpse of himself in the scope's tiny mirror and began to snarl, showing his teeth.

"There's my little ball of fury! That's my boy!" he gushed, gripping Buckaroo's hand and making clownish faces into the miniature looking glass. "How's Daddy's little bug eyes? Woof! Woof, you lewd little mutt! Look at that little clown! All you can do is laugh, Doc."

Feigned nonsense? Buckaroo was watching for the signs, but so far the general passed inspection, seeming legitimately crazy.

"What do you see in the mirror, General?"

I would have loved to see the look on Buckaroo's face as Wagoneer began to bark, but I cannot imagine it was greatly dissimilar to the expression of President Monroe, who reacted to the disturbance by coming to a full stop in the middle of a stretching exercise out in the narrow corridor. Resting one foot on the stairway balustrade, he bent and nearly touched his toes.

"Listen to that noise. Sounds like we've got an attention hound on our hands," he remarked over Wagoneer's dissonant barking and howling.

"That's pretty funny, sir," I ventured.

"And getting old in a hurry—give it up, Wagoneer. God, he's breaking my heart," President Monroe lamented sarcastically. "If the people out in the country could only see us now . . . boggles the mind, doesn't it?"

"Probably more than they could cope with," I replied. "Even I'm having trouble . . ."

"*You're* having trouble?" said Monroe, pausing to pinch himself. "Every day I ask myself what I'm doing here . . ."

Looking at him, I could read his mind. Here he was, a man who had shot to the pinnacle of power based on his famous lineage and little else, the secret love child of Jack Kennedy and Marilyn Monroe . . . when it seemed all he ever really wanted was to be loved.

"I suppose that's everybody's innermost ambition, Mr. President, to be loved and appreciated."

"People call me a dumb phawk, don't they?" he said, without the slightest prompting from me. "President Dumb Phawk or President Hose Bag . . . a loose cannon and a national embarrassment. They say I'm hyperactive and can't sit still."

Keep in mind, reader, this was astonishing language to my ears as well. To my recollection I had only spoken to him twice before in my life, and never in such close quarters and under such fraught circumstances; yet I felt a responsibility to ease his mind.

"I haven't heard those names," I lied to him. "People say you have a great presentation . . . great smile, great teeth."

"My father's teeth. I'm damn lucky but also damaged," he said. "But I've come to peace with it. Reno, will you join me for a moment of praise and worship for our planet?"

He held out his hand, and I consented to hum along while he sang a hymn softly. Then we briefly prayed together before I assured him, "You'll gut it out, Mr. President, because I know what you're made of."

He hesitated but said, "I hope you're right, Reno. It's true I've been busy with work and school, getting an online master's degree from the Banzai Institute, but it's not true I can't find my own ass with both hands and a mirror on a sunshiny day, like my detractors allege. A few summers ago, if you'll remember, Buckaroo invited me out west, where I got a little sun on the bum, listened to the sounds of silence, and had to hunt to survive out in the rough. Do you remember my nickname, Reno? Tell the truth."

"Puss in Boots? I mean, Pants in Boots?" I said.

He laughed like a good sport and continued, "Pants in Boots! Talk about a greenhorn! I still have my marksmanship and cross-country navigation certificates hanging in the Oval Office. I learned to find bugs under rocks and cook bushmeat on a cow-turd fire and how to heat a cold can of pork and beans with a hot gun barrel. Helocasting, fast rappelling Aussie-style, beach assault, demolitions . . . I did it all, learned leadership, and omitted the word *try* from my vocabulary. I envy you Cavaliers. You've found your tribe, but I'm still looking. But maybe, just maybe, this is my moment, when worlds collide . . ."

The more I listened, the more it occurred to me that I had heard him speak in a similar vein around the campfire at the Banzai Institute. If he needed a sounding board and I could provide that patriotic service, I was willing to oblige. Perhaps there was no one else in his life with whom the president could share such things . . .

. . . as he continued, "If the Nova genie's on the level, we could be talking the end times, Reno, and massive amounts of blood on my hands . . . the end of our planet and our name on the lease, plus north of seven billion lives. Do I wish I'd done things differently? Sure . . . I'm not proud of myself. I heard rumors we had aliens out there at Area 51, and had allowed them to germinate, like something out of horror movies, things in retrospect I should have gotten worked up over or demanded to know more about. Now I curse their names, but in the past the bow tie boys posed as my protectors, and I just looked the other way, more concerned with screwing Hollywood celebrities and raising money at the cost of everything else. No doubt history will have its own judgment of me, if we survive, but there's also partisan bickering and lots of finger pointing to consider, possibly even treason. Did you know our own intelligence assets even snaked a microphone into my Oval Office through the wall sockets? Not only that, we found a little Nazi toy soldier behind an electrical light switch cover. What does that tell you? Do you have any idea what I'm talking about? You ever heard of the Church?"

"The Catholic Church?" I asked, feigning ignorance.

"The Company . . . CIA," he said with a nervous laugh. "Or a secret part of it. They're like the weird kids at school . . ."

"I think I know the ones you mean," I told him. "The short beards with quiet dispositions who do no honor to their country. Like bad doctors, they bury their mistakes."

"Speaking of which," he said, turning the conversation personal, "I've made arrangements for my funeral. My casket will ride on the same gun carriage as my father. I'll also have a riderless horse, followed by Buckaroo and the rest of you fellows down Pennsylvania Avenue."

In response I hardly knew what to say. I think I must have stammered and blurted something inane, such as "I look forward to it."

"Just keep fighting the good fight," he said. "We could be in for fifteen rounds of very dirty pool with these aliens, and then some. We're going to need all-night cowboys, one hundred and ten percent guys going the distance. I wish I had your BMI reading and your code of honor, the way you carry yourself, Reno . . . with no need to impress others despite your many accomplishments."

"You're no slouch yourself, Mr. President," I said, no doubt reddening. "I like your shoes."

"I have an obsession with footwear. I try to get my jog in, eat lots of fruit, get to bed by nine o'clock, no matter what, but it's not easy," he said before dipping and leaping like a ballet dancer. "Obviously this conversation never happened . . . our conversation, this secret tower room at the Smithsonian . . . none of it ever happened."

"You have my word as a Hong Kong Cavalier. I know nothing about any of this," I assured him.

What was going through the mind of the elected leader of our country, I recall wondering, as he performed more deep knee bends and General Wagoneer continued to howl at the top of his lungs. No doubt both of us were thinking the same: an estimable American general with crucial national secrets had lost his way, perhaps even his sanity, and the only man capable of rectifying the situation now stuck his head out of the secret chamber to ask, "Mr. President, do you have any more tenders?"

PRESIDENT MONROE HAS QUESTIONS

While I readily confess my disappointment that I was not invited to join them in the general's cell, it is simple enough—based on Buckaroo's ample notes of the meeting—to pretend that I crossed through the portal alongside the president, who quickly encountered some difficulty lifting his shoe soles from a certain sticky mess on the floor.

"Jesus, what is this shite?" the president grunted . . .

. . . as he handed the greasy paper bag to Buckaroo and turned his eyes to the hairy male nude who once again had curled himself into a fetal position on the air mattress. Between little yips and barks, Wagoneer wept openly and wiped his snot on his chest hair. "Maybe I gave of myself too freely . . . comforted too many bitches when I should have spent more time exploring and loving what's wonderful about me: my companionship, loyalty, and playfulness. Maybe it's time to finally love myself and be me."

"You feel like you've lived up to your end of the bargain, in other words," remarked Buckaroo.

"I just need to get back on top, top dog," the general kept chattering. "Get my shite straight and feel like the old me again . . . use my mind for better things. Doc, did you ever wonder if you're already dead or just stumbled into the comedic side of hell? What a phawked-up species we are . . . and I still smell chicken. Who's got chicken? Some kind of fresh torture . . . ?"

Taken aback by the general's wild soliloquy, the president exchanged looks with Buckaroo, who reluctantly confirmed, "I think it's important we don't leave him alone."

"You poor, suffering man," the president began. "Obviously a sensitive soul and a boatload of bananas."

"And a cautionary tale," Buckaroo chimed in, "reflecting what we have become as a society, the pernicious influence of bullying and greed. I wonder what your father would say, General. I've heard of him: Bulldog Wagoneer, a big guy who held the American record in the Romanian deadlift. Wasn't he heavyweight boxing champ of the armed forces, as well?"

The general noticeably trembled, but replied at once. "Weightlifter and a boxer, right . . . short-haired boxer, two hundred fifty pounds of corn-fed muscle, and full-bird army colonel. Green Beret, paratrooper, grunt, 11B, a soldier's soldier who hated me on account of I only had one ball. I used to hide in his closet behind his uniforms. You're opening some old wounds here, Doc."

"Sometimes wounds need fresh air to heal, General," Buckaroo said, focusing his penlight and ophthalmoscope at Wagoneer's pinpoint pupils. "So a bully, then . . . not exactly a nurturer to light your path. Did he hit you often on the frontal lobe?"

"You mean here, in front? Since I was a kid. That's when the strobe flashes started, and the voices. When I told the coach I had a brain tumor, he just called it tinnitus, and when I told the Colonel, he'd smack me upside the head with his belt and say, 'Brain tumor? Then put on a hat. Is your name Wagoneer or Fagoneer? Man up and get over it, you whiny sniveler! Why'd you leave the kitchen lights on? If you were a car, you'd be a sour lemon. You want to talk about pain? I'll trade you my pain! I didn't come here to play!' Then he'd smack me on the head, so the bruises wouldn't show through my hair. Multiply that by football hits—I was All-American at the University of Oklahoma—and that puppy starts to get real."

"He 'didn't come here to play.' So you were always in your old man's doghouse," said Buckaroo.

"Always in the doghouse, just like now," replied the general, who opened his eyes wide and stared at Buckaroo in recognition of a startling insight. "I was always the black sheepdog, the skinny runt of the litter. Then at the age of fourteen, I dropped to my knees and accepted the gift of salvation and turned my life around. But it wasn't until he passed away that I felt truly free and realized I'd been slowly bleeding to death my whole life."

"Did he ever say he was sorry?" Buckaroo asked.

The general shook his head, recalling, "He died without a word. The only real advice he ever gave me was his prized Ranger handbook.

Ironically, he got brain cancer and died a couple of months before I made general officer, so I never got to outrank him. In the end an aneurysm took him, so maybe he got lucky. They say you don't really become a man until your father dies."

"I can attest to that," said Buckaroo, "although we all process pain in our own way and at different stages of our psychological development. I lost my father when I was just a boy. They tell me I even tried to climb into his casket."

"I can relate to that," said the president. "And now you've lost Hikita. I can understand. When I first found out JFK was my dad, I slept with his picture for months, maybe years."

NEW INFORMATION ABOUT JFK'S DEATH

"My condolences, Mr. President, from a justice-starved man," piped up General Wagoneer. "It might interest you to know I saw the secret file on Oswald at Area 51—the real stuff, not the pap they fed the American people. Turns out the big boy behind the operation was Aristotle Onassis. The head fake was Sam Flood, but the secret wiretaps from the Armory Lounge in 1959 reveal Xan brokered the whole deal with the Chicago Outfit for ten million."

"My God, please keep your insaneness to yourself, General," sputtered President Monroe, stunned by the sensational news, despite long having believed it.

Nor was Wagoneer by any means finished.

"Listen up, don't make me repeat myself—I've seen the transcripts. Ari always wanted to get his paws on Jackie. Like the Trojan War."

"So, cherchez la femme?" Buckaroo said, arching a somewhat skeptical eyebrow.

"What is that, French? What the phawk?" the general questioned. "The fat Greek was lonely. He just wrote the checks while Hanoi Xan and his boys did all the rest. It was Jack Ruby and Jimmy the Greek on the grassy knoll watching it all go down."

"That sonofabitch. That's utter bilge," blurted the president, but a glance at Buckaroo told him otherwise.

"A little before my time, but I won't pretend it's something I haven't heard before," said Buckaroo glumly. "Though I've never seen the hard evidence. There's a photograph of Oswald with a man we think is the British magnate Sir Henry Shannon, one of Xan's guises, that we've never been able to authenticate. But certainly Xan's organization could have pulled it off, as well as the cover-up, with its PR and mind-control media tools."

"Then I won't rest until I get my hands on him and make him spill his secrets," the president vowed, still dazed . . . looking to Buckaroo for a translation as the general suddenly went off on a babbling tangent about Lucifer in the British House of Lords.

"There are a couple of things going on," Buckaroo told the president in a clinical tone of voice, as he studied the hair-follicle test results on his Go-Phone. "First off, he's a walking septic tank of antibodies, full of picograms of crippling environmental toxins, and then there's what I would characterize as BPD: deep-seated sexual and social adaptation disorders arising from a sense of helplessness and repressed rage. By his own admission he has identity and abandonment issues and seems to have been dominated by his father and his wife, both of whom left him, along with his pet Chihuahua and confidant, with whom he identifies to a psychotic degree."

All the president had to do to recognize this truth was to glance at Wagoneer, whose yipping—choked with ragged sobs—was almost too poignant to bear.

"It's time to talk about your future, General," Buckaroo announced, as he knelt and delicately fed Wagoneer a chicken nugget, which the general merely sucked on ravenously like it was a piece of fruit. "I'm giving you this spicy chicken chunk of rational thought to help you get over your inner turmoil. It's going to clear your mind of unwelcome thoughts, okay? Now I think the president has something to say . . ."

"The commander in chief? Woof, okay by me," the general said, before the wet morsel of chicken accidentally rolled out of his flaccid mouth. "Dang, I lost it. Somebody help me chew this bad boy."

Buckaroo pressed the nugget back into the general's mouth and even allowed him to gnaw on his Latex glove, saying, "Mr. President . . . ?"

President Monroe cleared his throat awkwardly and began, "It's about your level of immaturity, General. Obviously this is a messy situation, which is why we had to lock you in the bear cage up here in the turret. The alternative would have been to string you up with a barbwire rope,

since this is some damn scary national security business people don't
need to hear about from the media . . ."

"I know it's all my fault. I'm a user and a loser," offered Wagoneer
meekly with his tongue sticking out of his mouth, as if to show Buckaroo
that his palate was clean. "I just want to do the right thing. It's not an
act, either. I just wish a train would hit me and smush me like a rodent,
but then someone would have to wipe up the crap, which is what I'm
made of. Sometimes I feel like my whole life has been an acting gig,
hustling myself as Buckaroo Banzai. What an asshole."

"I hear you," said the president. "You have a very fertile imagination,
but I don't have time to accommodate your dysfunction, so don't get me
started. We've already got enough on you to put you away for life, but
what happens to you doesn't really concern me. Please ponder that and
stop acting like a bell-ringing idiot."

The general merely continued to grovel. "I know I've been hurtful and
I'll always carry the stench of my stupidity. I'd be the first to admit my life
went sideways, but now my own government's turned it upside down,
phawked me to hell like a stray thrown out in the street! Like I'm being
strangled with the torn and tattered ROE . . . only one major incident on
base during my watch and very few perversions, because I gave my troops
Bible-study tools for self-help and practically rewrote the whole AFSC
playbook. Made all civilian workers wear jeans and a collared polo to look
sharp, even the gardeners. Ran a tight ship, kept lollygagging to a minimum,
never jobbed the system for selfish reasons. So for all that, getting it done
against all odds, they stick it to me on a technicality . . . uniform-code
violation . . . stick me in here and sheep dip my whole record! That way
they don't even have to give me an Article 15 and strip me of my pension.
Now I'll just end up a vagrant, eating out of a tin can with my SRK, trying
to rebuild my credit. God bless and thanks for listening."

"I'm listening, General," Buckaroo confirmed. "I'm not a big fan of this
whole spectacle, but I am beginning to question the integrity of the process
that put you here. Whether or not you stole my OVERTHRUSTER specs . . ."

"Then I shouldn't be left alive," the general whined. "Law and
order, baby . . ."

". . . and then sold the one you stole," Buckaroo continued, "you do
seem to have been targeted for special treatment, and shockingly so. I'm
no expert in the workings of the military judicial system, but they seem

to be doing all in their power to dishonor you and cause you psychological harm. But by whose authority . . . yours, Mr. President?"

"Hardly," the president dissented unconvincingly, "but secrecy dictates . . ."

"Then why did you call me," Buckaroo retorted, "if you're confident about your national security team and the advice you're getting? But we'll deal with that later. Right now the threat to Earth eclipses everything else."

"Devious bastards! They'll phawk us rubberless if we let 'em!" General Wagoneer spat out.

"Good God, he's touching himself," the president informed Buckaroo Banzai, watching the general with obvious distaste. "Does he not realize what the hell he's doing? Get a hold of yourself, General."

"I got a hold, all right," replied Wagoneer, who continued stroking himself. "Look, I'm at full salute!"

"Something has to be done, I agree, but . . ." the president stammered. "Again, I take your point, Buckaroo. What do you suggest?"

"In view of our pressing global emergency, I'm recommending you release the general to my personal care."

The president reacted predictably. "And let this depraved worm off the hook for jeopardizing American lives . . . ? Make a mockery of the judicial system . . . ?"

Buckaroo doubtless stifled an urge to laugh at the irony of General Wagoneer's extralegal situation, saying merely, "Hardly off the hook, I would say. You can always bring charges against him at a later date— assuming the planet's still in one piece—but based on my preliminary examination and certain statements he has made to me, which I can't share with you due to protected health information under HIPAA . . ."

"If it's a deal breaker, I waive it," said Wagoneer. "I'll even pull back my billion-dollar lawsuit. All I ask is to be reunited with my brain."

BUCKAROO'S SURPRISING OFFER

Buckaroo stepped closer to President Monroe and lowered his voice, although his whisper still resounded within the tiny enclosed cubicle . . . as was his intent.

"Of course he gets under my skin as well, Mr. President, and all the pharmaceuticals are only adding to the turmoil. I haven't looked at my *DSM*, the *Diagnostic and Statistical Manual of Mental Disorders*, in some time, but I remember enough to know our friend appears in every one of the chapters . . . multiple personalities with borderline narcissistic personality disorder, for starters. But he has been fairly open with me, not to mention the fact that he is a gravely ill man, most likely as a result of routine exposure to toxic agents at Nellis Base that probably turned his liver to shoe leather, as well as causing his child to be stillborn, contributing to his marital problems, which eventually mushroomed into a midlife crisis . . . followed by the Fourth of July firecrackers that sent his PTSD over the edge and caused him to soil himself on a patriotic float. Then the unexplained lab explosion at Area 51 nearly took his life, leading to an abuse of painkillers and loss of his command, his military career, his marriage, and his freedom. While these factors alone might not have led him to betray his country *sua sponte*, they undoubtedly made him more vulnerable to foreign brainwashing techniques, especially when you consider that he may have been developmentally disabled since boyhood and with severe self-esteem and masculinity issues . . . obsessed with lengthening his penis by stretching it."

"Ha, ha, malpractice at its finest," grumbled the general.

"Too bad," said the president to Buckaroo. "He brings this pity on himself."

"And his paranoia, which may be justifiable. I'm also ordering an EPI test, and his pH level needs adjusting," Buckaroo elaborated. "He has a fairly large hernia on the left side, residual fibrosis in one lung, and bilateral hearing loss, also irritable bowel syndrome that causes him chronic back pain. I need to get him off the Mogadon, not to mention naproxen and ten other drugs, and, judging from his rhinoplasty, it's also safe to assume he's done a fair amount of self-medicating in the past. Right now his body is highly stressed, iodine depleted, acidic, and dehydrated, as well as suffering from scabies, pubic lice, a flare-up of fibromyalgia and what I suspect are high blood-lead levels, low thyroid, abnormalities in the basal ganglia and hippocampus, and some autoimmune issues that might explain his claudication and skin blotches. I'm also detecting elongated areolae with increased nipple sensitization to go along with his gynecomastia and an abnormally high level of estrogen . . ."

"Estrogen?" questioned the general. "You mean hermaphroditism?"

". . . perhaps caused by exogenous lifestyle factors like fatty diet and high alcohol consumption, which can cause gene mutation and tumors in certain tissues. Then there is the acute chronic insomnia, idiopathic intracranial hypertension, COPD, and several more serious ailments: a high-enzyme-count liver, congestive heart failure, and possibly a transverse sinus thrombosis resulting from a horseback-riding accident . . ."

"Add a general burr up my ass and under my saddle. I'm talking idiot mode," proclaimed the general. "Maybe some Percs to keep my head from exploding. Or lemme just go to my mother's house . . ."

"What a douche," interjected the president, whom Buckaroo continued to bring up to speed:

"The fluorescent lighting in this room also aggravates his generalized hyperreflexia and schizoaffective disorder, making it difficult for him to focus on my questions. More than palliative care, he needs a good power washing, a PosTEP regime to back up his T helper cells, followed by a slew of tests and an MRI. My hunch is clinical depression brought on by the scabies and an HSV-2 genital outbreak, bone-on-bone arthritis, stage-three liver fibrosis, hepatic encephalopathy with some brain deterioration, and possibly the onset of vascular dementia . . ."

"Whoa. I'm beginning to understand him a little better," said the president. "What else?"

"This will take a little while. In addition we're talking mild strabismus and fibromyalgia brought on by long-term exposure to environmental toxins, exacerbated by chronic abuse of antidepressants, muscle relaxants, and anti-inflammatories such as cyclobenzaprine and ibuprofen eight hundreds, among others, that have wreaked havoc on his GI tract, not to mention angioedema of the small bowel, enteric parasites, and possible gastric ulcers caused by *H. pylori*, spread by the fecal-oral route. In other words, pardon my French . . ."

The general interrupted in a huff: "French? The hell with the French! Sounds like I'm being publicly shamed for my patriotism. Hell, just patch me up with a little monkey blood, mercurochrome, and I'll be shipshape."

"Geez Louise," groaned the president as the general garbled what might have been a song lyric, possibly a barroom ballad: "Ting-a-ling, goddamn, find a woman if you can. If you can't find a woman, find a clean old man . . ."

"A cautionary tale, to be sure," Buckaroo continued in a throaty whisper to the president, though obviously still intending to be overheard by Wagoneer, "and if he dies in secret custody, you may be forced to do a lot of talking, because you'll have a mess on your hands, Mr. President. But at the Institute he'll get integrative medicine—the best of Western and holistic treatment, from acupuncture and the sacred healing herbs of Old Saxony mixed in a Champion juicer to our cutting-edge pharmaceutical research department, along with full psychogenic and pathophysiological evaluations and an IQ developmental index, including the Minnesota Multiphasic and the Iowa Test of Basic Skills—all while working part time to pay for his keep and repair his Vitamin D deficiency: planting tomato seeds and winter rye grass, castrating sheep, polishing horse tack, scrubbing toilets at the friendless shelter . . ."

"Ha, scrubbing toilets! A straight flush beats a full house!" declared Wagoneer, as he devoured the last fried nugget and rolled over on his back into a playful puppy pose, purring like a furry cub. "Beats going down the booby hatch! I'll work a shite ton! I'll work for cookies!"

". . . indeed earning what amounts to bread crumbs, company scrip redeemable at the Institute trading post," Buckaroo proceeded to inform the president, "but also learning to use a bamboo bow and earning callused working hands. At the Institute we believe hard labor is ennobling and empowering. True, he lacks both character and credibility, but let's not forget that he did take an oath to protect the Constitution as a member of the military and stepped up to the job for many years."

"I stood in the damn gap doing my bounden duty! With the walls closing in!" the general cried, trying to wrap himself around Buckaroo's leg . . .

. . . as Buckaroo continued, "I've given him a mild sedative, which seems to have calmed him. But he's obviously bitter and bearing numerous grudges—indicating an imbalance of his humors, an excess of yellow bile—and having problems separating real from unreal, possibly due to progressive dementia that may have gone into overdrive; but I believe he still has at least a semblance of a social conscience, which we'll discover through psychoactive drugs and advanced mind-reading analytics . . . despite what I have noted as strong indications of *pseudologia fantastica*, or pathological lying. It's just possible he doesn't know the truth or honestly believes his own lies. But if he proves to be uncooperative, I'll tar and feather him myself and send him right back here to the tower, or maybe Guantánamo."

"Guantánamo . . . ?" said the general with a sneer. "Guantánamo would be a piece of cake compared to the Smithsonian!"

The president merely massaged his temples and croaked hoarsely, "I just . . . I need time to think . . . I can't be expected to . . . in this manner of a short time frame. You make a fine speech, Buckaroo, but you're way ahead of me. I can't go there yet."

"I understand," replied Buckaroo. "Don't think I take treachery lightly. The lowest level of hell is reserved for the turncoat, but this man's technically not charged with treason or espionage. He's charged with wetting and soiling his uniform on the Fourth of July. Try to picture that juicy courtroom drama going viral in the media."

"Technically true," replied the president thoughtfully. "And you tell me these alien bugmen have got us by the short and curlies . . . and all set to tighten the screws. God only knows what they'll do to us if we fall into their hands. And yet to them, in their upside-down world, we're probably the savages."

"They might sucker-punch us, no matter what, but we have to do all we can to control what we can, starting with finding John Whorfin. And I believe the general knows more about that than he's letting on, which leads me to worry about his safety from certain greedy elements in our own government," Buckaroo said, turning his attention back to the prisoner. "How about it, Wild Bill? Ready to sweat out all that toxicity? Stand up and be counted . . . ?"

The general literally jumped at the chance, springing to his feet and exclaiming, "Not to blow my own horn, but you just called Strategic Air Command 911! I realize I have a lot of self-work to do, but I beat a mean bongo and a Chinese gong! Knock me down and I rise like yeast!"

President Monroe could only frown and twist his lips into an awkward pucker, saying, "God, what a clusterphawk. I'm doing everything in my power to say no. I don't know shite apparently, but I'll go with your gut, Buckaroo, to give me right guidance . . . at least for the time being. I hereby lay my seal on your neck and guarantee you sweeping immunity, from the east to the west—but I can't have my fingerprints on this. I even suspect my own phone and wall outlets are compromised, so you'll have to liaise with Postmaster General Mantooth."

"You mean Rainbow Trout?" replied Buckaroo. "Holly Mantooth's been a Blue Blaze for fifteen years, so I know she grieves for the state of the world and, unlike most, is willing to do something about it. I look forward to working with her, Mr. President. And of course you have my oath of personal allegiance as well as that of all my Cavaliers and other notables pledged to me."

"That may be," said the president, "but in the immortal words of JFK, it's not because it's easy, but because it's hard. Damn hard. I'm also going to have to insist on an ankle monitor for this sonofabitch, because I don't want him loose in the world."

"Not without restraints," agreed the general. "I don't trust myself."

"That won't be necessary, Mr. President," replied Buckaroo. "I'll radio chip him, but I wouldn't worry. He won't get far in the great Sonoran Desert. In the meantime, the first rule of the game is to protect the king; and as long as this cult of aliens headed our way is flying under the radar, I'd feel better if you kept a low profile and entrusted yourself to Postmaster General Mantooth's personal security detail."

The president agreed. "Whatever you say, Buckaroo, as long as you keep me up on developments. I won't blow the whistle until you give the word. Until then, the kitty's got my tongue."

Even so, he had one last request, and gazed at Buckaroo with arms outstretched.

"I'm lonely and having a meltdown," he said. "I need a hug."

XII. IN THE GARDEN OF EVIL

> There shall you heare the Nightingale . . .
> How prettily she tells a tale
> Of rape and blood.
> —Sir Richard Fanshawe

On our flight back to the Institute, Buckaroo described our present murky situation as "speeding full bore down a cul-de-sac." We were of course careful not to publicize the mysterious Nova Police message of impending doom. President Monroe insisted, and we agreed, that there was no reason to incite panic around the globe or raise an international battle cry over something as flimsy as a single thirty-second transmission of unknown provenance; and as weeks went by without a follow-up to the original message, the president's reluctance to speak publicly of the threat appeared to be the sensible course.

At the same time, we had to assume the doomsday clock was ticking, so we could not afford to be idle. Among our first steps was to prevail upon the president and friendly Pentagon contacts for admittance to Nellis Air Force Base, while simultaneously casting a worldwide net in search of clues, namely those thousands of Hong Kong Cavalier fans who also count themselves part of our citizen army, the Blue Blaze volunteers. As against these good intentions was the troubling reality that it was practically impossible to give chase to a phantom. If John Whorfin had escaped his host

Lizardo and somehow entered a new host, it was next to impossible even to imagine where to begin searching for him.

Yet Buckaroo's nagging conviction that the hologram communicated an authentic threat meant that it would have been imprudent also not to utilize all resources at hand, including the legions of the World Crime League—those nameless galley slaves who lived tethered to their lives of crime, strung along and milked, slaving day and night to enrich Xan and the rest of the Interlocking Directorate bosses. It bears repeating that Buckaroo felt the presence of Xan as background noise on a continual basis and was also mindful of certain inherent risks to his own safety, and ours; but at this moment of utmost importance in world history, he also believed it in our planet's best interests to rise above old disputes. As he phrased it, "If Whorfin's enemies succeed in driving Earth into a ditch, we'll all be in the car together." Accordingly, he had the hope, naive or otherwise, of enlisting Xan's extensive intelligence network in the search for Whorfin.

Since Xan's present location was not known to us, we sent a number of cordial entreaties. These letters in invisible soybean ink— handwritten by Buckaroo in Old Enochian and Linear B—went out to Golden Boy Pizza and the Bohemian Club in San Francisco; the Burj Khalifa in Dubai; the World Crime League's Wild Casino Land in Laughlin, Nevada; the Bush family holdings in rustic Paraguay; Wilkes Land in Antarctica; and a handful of other known Henry Shannon boltholes: Davos, Monte Carlo, Penang, Darjeeling, Hong Kong's Deep Water Bay, Hamburg's Reeperbahn, and Cairo's Shepheard Hotel.

But this is not to say we had the goods on Xan, since, in addition to the above, he likely was hunkered down in one of his numerable fortresses of solitude—his secret cave on Mount Rushmore, his mountain redoubt in Bhutan, or his private coral atoll in the South Pacific—so that we had no choice but to put our message in the bottle and more or less toss it into the sea, stressing the threat Whorfin posed to our common planet without being more specific and certainly without mentioning General Wagoneer, whose communication channels to the League's new Panamanian representative, a man named Valdez, we sought to maintain at all costs through repeated offers of more classified Jet Car data for sale.

A POSSIBLE SIGHTING

By some coincidence during this period, a low-level mobster in Rome, nicknamed Il Pugilato, reported to his superiors that he had met a queer fellow pretending to be a Catholic monk who spoke as two separate personalities, like a man either possessed by a demon or blessed with the gift of speaking in tongues. One of his personas was Italian and called himself Brother Costello, while the other—claiming to be someone named Lord John Whorfin—had stolen from a gelato vendor and terrified witnesses to the theft by baring his breasts, spewing hatred at random, and asking for a "Lectroid kitchen."

"I am sick but not a liar," the monk told the Mafioso. "I am heavy with child and under the sway of the devil. Kill me with a bullet, but do no harm to the unborn."

Although neither of the names—Costello or Whorfin—meant anything to the young street tough, the personality calling himself Whorfin had insisted he was known to Hanoi Xan, so Il Pugilato thought the encounter worth mentioning to his capo. Perforce, then, let us return to the Temple de la Gloire and the eternal brigand. Independent of anything I have related, but for reasons of timeliness, I include the following.

To the extent that it was brought to his attention, Xan was understandably unmoved by news of the minor incident, finding the so-called Il Pugilato's account simply annoying, and dismissed it, as he did a second report concerning the same monk's attempts to surrender himself at a fire station and a pregnancy support center. When the desperate abbot broke a window and staffers swatted him away, he fled . . . only to take refuge in a fruit stand and then a porta-potty, where it was said he guarded his meager belongings.

Whatever the truth of the story, Xan could make no sense of it— although he did manage to smile at the part where a pickpocket pointed at the odd monk and shouted, "That's Abbot Costello! A true man of God! He lives in the *gabinetto!*"

The name made Xan giddy to such an extent—although unable to smile or laugh in the way of ordinary mortals—that he felt like biting his tongue and pissing himself, claiming to have known the popular comedy duo back in their Hollywood heyday, marveling moreover at how time flew.

What we now know and did not know then was that Xan suffers from a cancer of the blood and was on the verge of moving to his impenetrable fortress in the Rift Valley of Ethiopia when he was laid low by a particularly vicious round of flu and consumptive fever that left him intermittently delirious and with numerous complications, including colitis, a hoof-and-mouth infection, and anorectal sepsis. When, after more than a week, these conditions gave no signs of improvement, he came to the conclusion that he had been invaded by the Death Wyrm and ordered his trio of doctors from the Institut Pasteur to insert pigweed and other miracle cures into his bowel. This radical course of action they at first rejected by arguing that his pneuma was simply old and irradiated, not to mention full of hormones and antibiotics; but as his insistence left them no room for maneuver, they soon complied, inserting skunk cannabis and a large section of wapiti horn, as well as aerating him with small puncture wounds to the liver and other organs in order to let his excess black bile escape.

Then, fearing to confess that one of them had nicked the intestine—leading to bleeding and rectal prolapse as Xan labored mightily to expel the foreign object—the doctors finally threw up their hands in despair and made haste to depart. In this they were frustrated, however, as Xan forbade them from either leaving or transporting him to a hospital, even as his feverish rants grew more bizarre and his caregivers continued to treat him with daily purges, healing stones, and poultices, including a fresh cow's bladder placed over his face and lithium batteries on his tongue.

XAN'S TALE OF LIFE AFTER DEATH

"Feeling so low and down, oozing from the behind," he began one such ramble in Penny's presence, sucking on a Dr. Grabow, his nose in a favorite Henty novel. "A pinched sciatic nerve, they're calling it, but I can see through them. Their faces are like open books, the whole panel of jokers . . ."

His voice tailed off, and he mumbled almost inaudibly, ". . . crucify them upside down and make them disappear into the wall, so that it will appear not a stone has been dislodged . . ."

"Who?" was a word she managed to form, but he appeared not to hear in any case.

"My enemies are all around me, not making words but laughing something awful behind my back," he said, seemingly time traveling through various gradations of consciousness . . . his gloomy voice from far away. "You try to protest, but the sound catches in your throat. Then dragged behind your own horse, stabbed and thrown into a shallow grave . . . the suffocating dirt, and all goes black and silent, except your panicked breathing and pounding heart, your hands clawing, your mouth screaming, but only the vermin hear you . . ."

"Where?" she asked, not overly interested.

"It was more like a cave. A long time, maybe a hundred years," he tried to explain. "Not a big death, as deaths go . . . more like a dead end, or what is called a 'pale death,' in which I felt no pain and my head continued to think, unaware of time passing or the new form my body was taking. Needless to say, common sense could not apply in such a situation. Different rules come into play, and I could no more put the pieces together than the man in the moon. It never occurred to me that I had all but vanished from the world, no more missed than an unripe grape."

"How?" she asked with a certain breathlessness herself.

"I needed to work on myself," he said, gazing at the ceiling before resuming his account. "Then one day I awoke with a craving for a cigarette, only to discover that I had turned into a beetle and was pushing before me a fruit seed from the Tree of Life, deep underground. But that was not the issue."

"How not the issue? That doesn't sound right," she said.

"With the realization that the seed was wrapped in a ball of others' filth, yet what I was pushing was actually my own negativity and bitterness that my world had come crashing down," he replied. "At a given moment I decided to stop blaming others and to be the master of my fate, to return to the world not as a miserable bug or even a prince but as a man with the power to move mountains, richer than Croesus, perhaps a great khan or even a god. I'm talking about the importance of keeping a little money and a retinue for the afterlife. Never again will I die broke and alone. That's why I sleep with these little bags of gold dust and gold coins around my waist . . . because you can always buy a higher court. Meat rots at the drop of a hat, but what happens after that depends on how the cards fall and who you know and whether you can get an appointment . . . which is why I deliver many bodies of my enemies who will serve me in the afterlife, not to mention a good woman to keep me company during cold nights in the dirt, and a fast horse. That's what I'm talking about, hiding a little stash for the winter."

She gave him a blank look, then feigned interest in the book he had been reading, a story about pirates . . . as he continued, "Of course this would not happen overnight. I was even told it had never been done that a dumb excrement dweller, lowest of the low, a dung bug, could rise from the darkest spot of my life into the light of day . . . but only after learning an important lesson. The more I pushed my little ball of dung—the ball of my questioning and therefore of dissatisfaction—the more it inhibited my rise to the light. You see, the harder I worked at pushing the ball, the fatter it grew, and the more hopeless the situation became; and this was the truth of it, that until I had the revelation that I was burdened by a dung ball of anger and self-pity and, above all, haunted by regrets and a search for explanations—I could never push my way to the surface. Instead of greedily layering and layering my dung ball until it became too large to push another centimeter, I had to arrive at the understanding that I could only move forward by forgetting the past and not questioning things . . . to be of no mind, as the monks say . . . above all to have no self-pity, indeed no pity of any kind! No meaning, no theorizing! All is nature, and in nature there is no mind, only self-preservation, and the commerce of nature is adaptability and patience. I was unlearned in these ways but am now giving this esoteric knowledge, things I have learned over the course of my life, to you. Perhaps you have even found it out for yourself."

"Possibly, but it is a sad use of knowledge to bully others," she said, drawing a connection from his tale to certain things she had seen with her own eyes.

"No, it is the sad story of one little bug, pure and simple, and out of cigarettes. Not everyone can mentally handle it. I had to learn to stop in my tracks and take stock of myself, to dump all that is rotten and bitter and plant the seed of a new life. Understanding this—the invisible design of nature or whoever is running the game—by which I mean letting the supernatural do its work—I ate the dung of my cares and planted the seed of a new life, then hibernated in darkness and gathered my strength, waiting for the seed to sink roots and sprout and, finally, to bloom many years later. Then making my way to the surface as I knew not what, I emerged not as a dung beetle but as a frog . . .”

She had no idea what he was talking about but believed it all came back to the idea of sanity, saying, “It sounds like you need to talk about this with someone.”

It occurred to her that perhaps this was her function, the answer to the question of why her life had brought her here: to help this miserable man heal by offering him a place of understanding and compassion. But he was too hard for her to understand, except when he said the world was full of pathetic liars.

Now he squeezed her hand, making her skin crawl, and from somewhere these exact words made themselves heard: “. . . a noble line of horses who, if they get overheated and are hunted down, bite open a vein to help themselves breathe more freely . . .”

He stared at her carefully for a moment before asking, “What did you say? Did you just say Hallelujah . . .”

“Hallelujah,” she repeated, feeling embarrassed yet also increased in strength. “Just something that came back to me . . .”

“It’s Goethe, Mother. Yet also very much in the Mongol groove. You often said those words inspired your entire philosophy, your fierce commitment to freedom at all costs. It is truly amazing . . . you are her, my Alisa in the flesh. Yes, long live the wild thoughts of freedom!”

“Long live,” she concurred with these words that seemed to carry her upward. “The wild thoughts of freedom . . .”

“Worth their weight in gold,” he added and returned to his narrative. “Even a scurrilous bug, I did not cry and blubber, but ate the dung and lifted my head for freedom, overcoming everything that stood in my way.

“Another thing,” he said curtly, touching the bell around his neck. “Do you see this little bell? It is a leper’s bell. I wear it to remind me of the leper colony in Uttar Pradesh, where I spent many years. To remind me of the men who lit my hair on fire. Still, I never pitied myself. If I looked for explanations, it would bother me no end, but it is just nature’s way, the supernatural way. Does the wolf cry over her pups or apologize to the sheep? The crow over her eggs? Of course not, because even they know what we have forgotten: there are no rules, only rulers."

Quite by accident, she happened to turn and notice a fat centipede crawling on the wall, but did not trust herself to kill it . . . until she saw her captor paralyzed with fear.

"Don't squash it!" he implored her.

"But . . ."

"He will only gain in numbers! Let him come and go," he pressed, his mouth forming even more sounds that did not come out.

But she killed it. Without any sensible explanation, she smashed the hideous creature to pieces with a decorative stone she picked up from a night table.

"You Judas," he reproached her sternly; but in fact he seemed relieved and refused to let her wipe the spot.

"No?"

"Confined to a space, he will be easy to keep an eye on . . . Anyway, you get my drift. Let's see what's in the larder for a snack. How about a movie and some hot chocolate? Or a peanut butter sandwich? A comedy, perhaps?"

THE MONSTER'S CONDITION

These days he was treated daily for depression by his astrologer and soul-integration guide, Hippolyte the Chaldean, who at last located a piece of broken wapiti horn and an entire carbolic atomizer in his patron's rump amid a maggot infestation, culminating predictably in Satrap's fierce retribution against the doctors, whose gruesome tortures I am reluctant to share in a book for youngsters (preferring instead a moment of respectful silence).

As soon as Xan began to grow stronger, he summoned her more often—usually requesting her bathed in Eau de Lily or lavender toilet water and in one kind of brunette wig or another, styled either short or gathered in a simple chignon—to fluff his pillow, read him to sleep with a nostalgic tale from his boyhood (G. A. Henty, Horatio Alger, something of the sort), or feed him his favorites: the headcheese omelet I may have mentioned, along with limpet broth, raw oysters and shrimp chow mein,

stuffed partridge, kippers and Russian jam, Nutella chocolate pudding
and digestive biscuits, with a vintage bottle of Sancerre or Jerez and a
samovar of tea to wash it down. (He did not eat flesh meat, other than
pork rinds and human placentas for their antiaging properties.) After
dinner and before his bedtime, he was just as apt to smoke his pipe and
engage her in a game of marbles as to pull a blade or a pistol on her
playfully—to laugh at her exhalations of fright—or have her put on a
silly hat and join him in a game of *World Domination* on the computer.
Indeed, one is led to wonder how many unsuspecting game players
glimpsed Penny Priddy in a mask or encountered Xan in a fez or WCL
baseball cap without guessing that one was presumed dead and the other
was the planet's most deadly criminal!

"My *Luftwaffe Sturmgruppen* crushes all comers!" he would revel with
delight. "The world is ours, *meine Kameraden* . . . ! All others, banned
from the board!"

Lest I give the wrong impression, however, his lighthearted moods
were often followed by long hours of darkness and opium, as a terrible
pressure surged within him—arising from an enslavement of the spirit—
that he wished to share equally with others in the form of physical pain.
This, I believe, explained his predilection for torture.

A kitten or a cobra, then, depending on his mood. His screen name,
for the sake of the record, was Vastatio, a Latin word meaning
"scorched earth" that also described his style of play all across the table.
If his situation became hopeless, he would decline to resurrect his
Kamaraden by hitting the revive button, preferring to go into Hitler
mode or bunker mode—wheeling around against his own forces and
destroying them utterly, rather than fighting to the last man and giving
an opponent the satisfaction of victory. Or, knowing all was lost, he
would turn the game over to her, after which she would go to extreme
lengths to save his reckless strategy before tending to his physical needs,
such as cleaning his joke shop set of dentures, massaging his prostate
gland, or preparing his pink bubble bath—pinkish from a witch's brew
of goat's blood and virgins' menses—while he worked in his sketchbook.
Claiming to be ambidextrous and dyslexic like the great Leonardo, he
drew with both hands simultaneously, preferring mostly pornographic
and architectural subjects recalled from his own past, such as memories
of having worked on the Egyptian pyramids or Hadrian's wall.

In any case I again direct the reader to Bunyan's estimable biography: "When he was but a child, he was so addicted to lying that his parents scarce knew when to believe he spake true; yea, he would invent, tell, and stand to the lies that he invented and told, and that with such an audacious face, that one might even read in his very countenance the symptoms of a hard and desperate heart this way."

It goes without saying that he was always right and never wrong, at least in his own mind. Worse, when he came down from his opium cloud, his inability to face the music for his actions led him to find equanimity in the pain of others—this despite his frequent claim that anger was beneath him and a tool of the unenlightened. (Never mind his infamous birthday party which I have mentioned!) Though she escaped the worst of these bloodthirsty snippets, for every occasion when he tried to lift her spirits with rope or amateur magic—the trick of making his dentures chatter and talk in their soaking bowl, for example—there were his sadistic sexual tastes, which he inflicted on her by pinching and pulling, or by depilating her with tweezers, asparagus tongs, or an oyster shell. During these painful sessions in which he plucked her nose hairs and scraped her eyebrows and the stubbly hair on her legs and pubis, it was nigh impossible for her to keep from crying; yet how she fought the tears, knowing that any expression of suffering only encouraged him to ratchet up the level of pain, particularly around her scarred-over injuries!

"We are always discovering new wounds," he would remark. "I myself am losing my old skin, which is nothing but a wrapper, nothing more than a shadow. When I handle your legs or rub them with different fabrics, I feel the most surreal release, like my emotions become uncorked and I have the whole earth to myself. Because love is the greatest gift two people can share and our mirror neurons have lives of their own, like a lantern through the ages enabling our separated souls to find one another."

This was excuse enough for him to beguile the tedium of a lazy afternoon by dabbling in his hobby of phrenology, as he drew his fingers over the contours of her face and its particular points, measuring their correspondence and the overall dimensions of her skull.

"Some say the reading of faces is a foolery, but its truth resides in the learned skill of the user," he once said, while tapping her forehead with his knuckles. "You are definitely her, the very same . . . and equally fatal to me."

In this manner it was his general habit to pinch faces and thump people's heads, sometimes quite painfully, in order to discern personality traits and relative intelligence—a curious process that almost always led to sex talk or discursive monologues on the subjects of religion and eschatology.

"Your deepest intimacies are open to me, but it isn't your little firebox that ignites my passion—it's your spirit and our destiny to bring forth life together that consummates our union," he once said.

This suggestion of having a child disturbed her, for she had come long ago to the conclusion that he was human in outward form only; and even this dim view of him she believed overly optimistic, given his vestigial scorpion tail, bristly neck mane like a horse, and scaly skin that he seemed to be shedding like a snake; and it was true his shadow no longer seemed to follow him but did as it pleased, following his movements only occasionally.

As he liked to say of this phenomenon, "The thing is free to come and go. With any luck it can latch on to another poor devil . . . just one of the effects of advanced age. In the same way our muscles lose tone and we lose hair, a man doesn't even control his toenails."

SUNLIGHT AND SHADOW

The reader may picture the two of them on a crisp winter's day, after she had turned sexual foreplay to her benefit and persuaded him to step outside for sunshine and a breath of air, such as the afternoon Satrap made a barbecue on the sacrificial grill of Pallas—modeled after the great altar of Pergamon—which stood in the garden between a decrepit child's swing set overgrown with roses and myrtles and three upside-down crosses that doubled as trellises.

Caught in real sunlight without his shadow and his usual cosmetic powder to fill his pockmarked face, Xan wore only his rubbers, stained baggy boxers, and a threadbare greatcoat, while Penny in leopard-print pants toted a small Louis Philippe vase that served as his male urinal. Nearby, one of Xan's singing girls in a dirty taffeta gown pounded millet with a stone pestle and a pair of bodyguards rolled up the last of the crucified physicians in a bloody duvet, prior to depositing him, still alive, into a hole in the wall.

As always, the wind chimes ceased to ring as Xan drew near, leaning on his gnarled cane and pausing to withdraw dainty chocolates from Penny's chinchilla muff. These he employed to make a trail which the local rats followed in a kind of charmed state, before he caused them to hover in the air by means of his magical stick and then go flying into the electrified razor wire he had installed around the property. How terrible to see their fur fly, the cruel way he treated other living things! Yet what envy she felt, wishing she had the courage herself to run into the wire and so cease to exist in a great shower of sparks!

Until now she had not noticed a fat black crow perched upon the gate—a sight that produced in Xan a powerful effect, as if the visitor's vested meaning was intended for his eyes alone.

"There, do you see it? Sitting upon the gate?" he asked her. "From my friend and intelligencer, the crow, I am given to understand that a plot by lesser hands is brewing this very night."

"The bird . . . ? Some trick . . . ?"

"He bears news," Xan said and crept closer in order to stare into the crow's beady yellow eyes . . . behavior she did not find odd in light of his frequent comments that, of all the creatures in nature, he was most like a bird for the simple reason that "birds eat and splatter where they please and wander farthest, respecting no one's superior claim or reputation."

That same evening, it was she who finished the session with Bengay, patchouli, and other essential oils and used the electric trimmer to groom his goat-like chin tuft, then combed his bed hair and forelock, cleaned his ears with a World Capital Lending ballpoint pen (she could have killed him easily then, with a single thrust), and rubbed laudanum on his eyelids, causing him to lapse into a kind of vigilant coma, his eyes wide open but in a dream-like trance.

These were the times when she performed as expected but nonetheless scolded him for his opium use, which he did not defend except to say that he was a slave to the pipe and had tried many detoxification programs, all to no avail.

"I have had so many 'clean dates' but the dragon will stay until I die. It's coming for me and will kill me, sure," he said. "The Wyrm, the dragon. There . . . !"

He pointed to the Ba Gua mirror hanging next to the piano, then with his finger traced a path past a marble bust of Pallas to the four-poster

bed—which itself was surrounded by strategically placed bowls of water—
and a nearby horsehair sectional sofa, the spot where his gaze now became
fixed. It was there, in such a state between sleep and wakefulness, that he
often saw the dragon: a Death Wyrm which he believed, despite its
formidable size, capable of wriggling its way somehow into his ear or
some other orifice and swallowing him from the inside out. Other times
he saw himself riding the same fat and disgusting creature toward his old
tomb on Arslycus.

"No. Look, he's here. That's all she wrote," she said and pointed to
the stain on the wall where pieces of the squashed centipede still
dangled—indeed, if anything, these appeared fresh and perhaps even
larger, as if growing.

Xan shook his head. "All she wrote? I've killed him many times before.
Open him up and there are at least two of them."

She then surprised even herself by asking, "Maybe the worm is all in
your head. Are you a magical thinker? Believing in magical forces?"

Her words took him aback, but he patiently explained, "Scientific
laws do not require thinking or belief, my little gamine. The present
vessel dies, but the vital spark travels on across magnetic fields, perhaps
to other universes, yet with all its baggage and negative and positive
energy. I have told you already that there is the taste of dung in my
mouth, but to this one becomes accustomed. Ha, ha! But so long as
you have not experienced this, to die and gather your resources, you
must realize 'du bist nur ein trüber Gast auf der dunklen Erde.' Bodies are
not meant to last forever, but they can be enhanced to have extended
life. All the same, you must get out of the habit of thinking in terms
of beginnings and endings. Only states of being have beginnings and
endings, not the being itself, since we are both star seeds and certain
to live again."

The mere thought plunged her deeper into mad despair, and she wished
for nothing more than to be conscious of nothing. Better the wormy earth
than this wretched life. Yet at that very moment, he tried to suck in a
labored breath and reached out to her for physical support . . . forcing her
to make certain necessary calculations about this wrinkled, subhuman
monster who stunk of rancid fish, who had kidnapped her, drugged and
blindfolded her, used her body for every vulgar indulgence; yet here she
was—his Sweet Pousie, his little kitty, the one he called Mama and

Mother—in some kind of twilight zone that lacked any sense at all, where he sought her help and she did not reject him.

"Would you take away your hand from an old man with the French disease and gout?" he chided and placed her hand upon his leathery scrotum.

Understanding that he was a man—or a man-devil—with many harems around the world, she always worried that he had put some little bug or gremlin inside her. Lately, in fact, she had dealt with daily dyspepsia and a certain effluvium in her throat that carried an offensive odor.

Yet she rationalized that illness might be her best defense against his indecent demands, so she said nothing except, "Who are you, really?"

He laughed and joked, "Who am I? I am the unique alpha they have not yet run to ground with their Christ mind, the hunter archetype whose testosterone level disconnects my temporoparietal junction. By following the law of nature, I break the little laws. Does that make any sense? What do you see when you look at me?"

"An eyesore about to topple over, but then you slither away," she replied and cringed, awaiting his angry reaction that never came; nor did she particularly care. Unlike his worshipful followers who lived in fear under his controlling behavior, she did not bother to think twice before speaking as she pleased. In this respect, at least, she had a little freedom.

"I am who I am. *Je suis* . . . the butcher," he told her. "They call me the butcher, the 'face without a face.' Do you like the sound of that better? Have I not made you very comfortable? You lack for nothing."

"Lack for nothing . . . ? I have a different view," she started to say, along with other things she had no time to express before he kept on talking, repeating the whole litany of his gifts to her: a Russian dacha on five country acres, with fifty serfs (or so he said); a ten-thousand-acre wildlife preserve in Africa, complete with a symphonic sound system, where he claimed to have killed "almost every animal on Noah's ark except a unicorn"; and a castle in Uruk (wherever that was) with nine hundred towers. More intimate presents included exotic Parisian lingerie and an old-fashioned chastity belt he described as "a device for lady liars," whose key he entrusted only to the eunuch Satrap.

Often he would twirl a globe and say they should get ready to move to this or that city, meanwhile telling stories about properties he owned around the world, lessons he had learned over many centuries, large business deals he had made. All of this she found endlessly fascinating, especially since she was never permitted to leave the grounds of the Temple.

"What is the Jesus story but metaphor, after all? The story of a struggling man in a dangerous situation," he told her, inveighing as always against the hypocrisy of sham religion and its tortured categories of good and evil that "do not tally with the composite picture. Take, for example, two identical paintings of naked lovers caught in varied acts of coitus—how many bodies, male or female, you may decide for yourself—the point is that both portrayals are exactly the same in all respects. Yet let us allow the first of our twin images to be commissioned as *Heaven*, in which case it will be condemned as dark and pornographic by the cultural noblesse, while its identical twin, called *Hell*, is deemed by the same gatekeepers to be a work with a proper moral theme. Since the two works are precisely one and the same, their difference can only lie in the viewer's eyes and emotions. By pairing sexual functions with guilt, the pharisees create the law and enable the rulers to control the populace. If a man must ask permission of the religious authorities to express even the passions of his heart and body, does it not follow that he must submit for their approval the rightness of all his actions? For good or bad, external order depends upon the interior control of a man. Otherwise, how could the privileged few lead the horde? Always remember, if there were no rich, the poor would be content, and it is for this purpose—the opium of the masses—that the lie of religion was contrived."

But these long soliloquies—above all, his insufferable attitude that had her pinned for such a fool—only made her think, "All I want is to get out of this hell, to build a bridge back . . . to where exactly?" Here she became stuck. "All I want is to be free! To be free again, but I can't remember when that was . . ."

She went on to say that in a just world he would be cooked and eaten like the hapless Paraguayan, but of course these words were useless and he was used to hearing them from her. To make matters worse, just as she was in the process of saying he was a monster who did not belong in the world, he experienced a choking spasm and she patted him on the back, albeit with perhaps more than adequate force.

"It's nothing—it's trivial," he said, wheezing and squeezing her hand. "We are a couple of scamps, aren't we? How alike and alone we are . . . a couple of conjoined twins, misfits with a capacity to transform from one incarnation to another, who have partaken of hell before finding heaven . . . who were lost but now are found."

"Like a recording, playing the same tune," she said, recalling the tango singer stuck in a record groove. Devoid of any feeling except despair, she begged, appealing to his "goodness," to be released from this existence she compared to being an animal in a circus.

"Goodness . . . ?" he laughed. "My goodness, what is goodness worth? Not even the envy of others!"

XIII. NOSING AROUND AREA 51

> Be thou comforted, little dog, Thou too in Resurrection
> shall have a little golden tail.
> —Martin Luther

Another of Buckaroo's fears, not unrelated to Whorfin, was that Lectroids could be walking disease factories—or as he put it to me, "outbreak monkeys with who knows what communicable pathogens, against which we humans have no resistance."

"It would seem to be a simpler matter to be on the lookout for them," Pecos joked. "Even with their electronic camouflage powers, they're easily spotted with their dirty looks and bad vibes."

"Crazy about pizza, sweets, and suicidal carbonated beverages," recalled Li'l Daughter. "And Wild Bill says their favorite movie is *Scarface*."

"Which rules out exactly no one in America," Pecos pointed out.

Yet no matter the existential threat from whatever direction, people did not stop falling ill with the usual maladies, and the good doctor continued to tend to the welfare and happiness of individual human beings . . . always a physician's chief concern. Nor did he fail to share with those around him his usual ration of camaraderie and good humor.

Naturally, the normal operations of the Institute had to be maintained, along with our individual research projects and experiments, weekly radio program, and band rehearsals. Sometime during this same period—if my memory holds—we recorded several tracks with the

Budapest String Quartet, who arrived at the Institute as artists in residence. Likewise, the Falstaff Players and Acrobats, our amateur theatrical and improvisational troupe, mounted its full slate of stage productions, while the Anime Collectors, Anxiety and Meditation Workshop, Birdwatchers Anonymous, Rock Stars (rock and fossil collectors), and the Philosophical Society continued to hold regular meetings. Our nightly clothing-optional Tang Soo sparring sessions, open-mike comedy shows, Lonely Hearts Club meetings, Taco Tuesdays, and Wednesday movie nights all went on as usual; and the Institute's Banzai FC and sponsored teams in table soccer, pickleball, jet dragster racing, skeet shooting, bass fishing, orienteering, and *yumi* archery likewise experienced no interruption in their travel schedules. We made our annual Colorado River float through the Grand Canyon, and Buckaroo continued his regular trips to the CERN accelerator in Switzerland and to numerous far-flung speaking engagements and academic colloquia the world over—all of this in addition to keeping his normal volunteer hours at the Apache reservation health clinic, coaching an Apache youth soccer team, and working on several scientific papers, at least two of which deserve mention here.

"Come, let's have a *chavrusa*. I've been reading Velikovsky's lost manuscript," he remarked one day out of the blue, tapping a stack of yellowed typed pages at his fingertips.

"Seriously? I've always had my concerns about Velikovsky," I said. "Bunch of smoke and mirrors, if you ask me."

"Only natural, I suppose," Buckaroo agreed. "But scamming us? Hustling? I don't think the man had it in him. I've been studying the original manuscript for a couple of days now. His estate, under pressure from the government, never allowed it to be published, and I can see why. He offers a pretty compelling argument that life on Earth was almost entirely wiped out at least three times by alien invaders, and there is some radiopotassium and mitochondrial DNA evidence, as well as cave drawings by early man, to support these quasi extinctions."

"I'll be a sonofagun," I replied, whistling through my teeth. "Exactly in accordance with Hopi legend and others."

"Quite a few others, including the Voynich manuscript, which I've been working on like a crossword puzzle with missing pieces, but it seems to be an arcane gynecological treatise. Perhaps Velikovsky didn't have the right angle on everything, but it is interesting that the Nova Police message indicated that this wouldn't be the first time the planet's been degraded, with dominant life forms destroyed and others elevated to take their place. I've been talking with the Bogdanoff brothers and Val Valerian, who has an interesting theory about swamp gas—"

"Isn't everything?" I said.

"Everything what?"

"Isn't everything swamp gas? Velikovsky, Voynich, and Val Valerian . . . I can't help seeing a pattern," I noted.

"All the *bien-pensants*," he quipped. "Don't forget Vorilhon and Vishnu, possibly our last line of defense if we're really living in the late stages of the Kali Yuga, the last Hindu eon."

I reminded him, "And yet here we are. Big wheel keep on turnin' . . .'"

"Big wheel keep on turnin' . . . so far," he echoed. "And we have no choice but to trust nature, by which I mean the direction of our growth, the ladder of souls as governed by *jo-ju-e-ku*."

"You mean the cycle of life," I said. "Rise and fall, death and rebirth. Recurrence. So does what we do even matter?"

"Correct, we've had this discussion before," he recalled. "Whether or not we're in charge of anything, even our own actions . . . or whether we're just house-trained pets or mere avatars of aliens or humans from the future . . ."

"Even our own words in this conversation might be from the mouth of someone else telling our story," I conjectured. "I mean, do you ever wonder who's talking inside the quotation marks?"

"Let me ponder that," said Buckaroo. "It gets back to the free-will question. Think of all the forces in the universe that have brought this moment into play, but we can't function on that basis. Otherwise, we're no better than ants, genetically programmed to sacrifice themselves for the greater good—a worthwhile result in the insect kingdom but not for the human condition."

For some time now, Buckaroo had also been dissatisfied with the conventional scientific literature concerning the navigational prowess of certain ants, including some of the familiar types we saw at the ranch every day. I personally had seen him spend hours in apparent deep concentration, his eyes trained upon a single ant carrying its cargo unfailingly to its destination, typically its nest. Putting aside the astounding strength of the ant and its homing skills, Buckaroo was struck by the ease with which the little pack animal found its way even when its line of sight was blocked. While the ant's reliance on polarized sunlight, and even celestial navigation, has been widely documented, Buckaroo was baffled by his own experimental results showing something else—the spooky ability of the lowly creature to reach its destination successfully in darkness, under various types of artificial light, in a spinning ball, indeed even in a weightless environment— leading him to conclude that the ant's internal guidance system functions by receiving homing signals through an encoding process, not yet fully understood, of quantum entanglement. In these pages Buckaroo proposes that Einstein's "spooky action at a distance" operates at a subatomic biological level, allowing for something he calls "telepathic navigation" between two points even miles apart. It is nothing less than an astounding theory, and one I am ill equipped to explain in this space.

Why do I tell you this? Perhaps the resourceful reader will recognize the obvious implications of his research for interdimensional travel; and more importantly, for the young scientist, let it serve as yet another example of a scientific discovery hiding in plain sight.

And there is also Buckaroo's comparison of the social network of ants to our own Blue Blazes, which I will paraphrase as follows:

"As a lifelong student of systems of all kinds, what intrigues me about the ant on a social level is how individual ants, operating within simple rules and assigned roles, nevertheless give rise to highly organized complex societies. Of course human beings are not ants, but taking the ant model and adding a little fun and games, we have the Blue Blazes, a worldwide crime-fighting collaborative of people doing basic tasks, not out of a biological imperative but of their own free will."

"Bravo," I said, and we continued to discuss strategy and analyze input from the public: rumors and reported Lizardo sightings that poured into World Watch One from every continent. But mostly we sweated and simmered, restlessly awaiting a new development in the case. When permission to visit Nellis AFB still had not come through after two weeks, we decided to show up at the secret base unannounced, regardless of personal risk.

A BEASTLY REUNION

Only days earlier, Buckaroo had brought General Wagoneer together with his wife Dottie—or Doggie or Doxie, as the general called her—in hopes of improving his mental state, but the effort was doomed from the start . . . a farewell visit, as it turned out. She was tall and rangy, a freckled redhead milkmaid type, snake hipped and double jointed with a barbed smile on a face that seemed too small for her magnificent slinky skeleton. She explained that their marriage had hit the rocks after her miscarriage, for which the general blamed himself.

Although the plan was to leave the two of them alone to clear the air and perhaps repair their relationship, Wagoneer requested that Buckaroo remain, for he had a certain fear of her temper (besides "Big Red" and "Doxie," his less flattering sobriquets for her were "Kill-a-man-jaro" and "Kraka-my-toa"); and after a few anxious moments and an awkward exchange of greetings, his addled mind seemed to give way under the strain, and he thumb wrestled himself, flashing emotion only when Nostradamus appeared.

"You're the furry sonofabitch who stole my Doxie!" he declared, taking the little dog in his arms and kissing him. "How you must have suffered!"

"Oh, piss up a rope, Billy. Who's the bad dog? Who's the bad dog, huh?" Dottie yelled at him shortly afterward and stormed out, only to return some weeks later for an appointment at the clinic. Under obviously sadder circumstances, Buckaroo explained to her his theory of things.

"After everything he went through with his domineering father, as an object of ridicule and the butt of his jokes, Bill spent his life trying to prove Bulldog Wagoneer wrong . . . chiefly by surpassing his military career. Like a psychic cage fighter, he at last believed he had conquered his demons—at least this was the picture in his mind—only to learn that his own unborn son Chico, his pride and joy, was malformed with serious disabilities . . ."

"He got all tripped out," Dottie tearfully recollected, "like it was his fault."

"Because in his mind it was reaffirmation of his father's disapproval and his own inadequacy, causing him to revert to childhood, to the point of soiling himself in public like an infant—like the infant you lost. After that, all bets were off," Buckaroo explained. "I've heard him refer to himself as a lemon, or a defective automobile . . ."

"Yes," she recalled, "with 'pretty windows and a dirty interior.' Those were his father's derogatory words, I believe."

"What ugly nonsense," said Buckaroo. "No matter what we think, every one of us combines good qualities and bad."

She nodded and said, "He used to point to his head and say, 'There's stuff in here. I'm gonna call him on it one day.'"

"Stuff put there by his old man. What kind of disgraceful father ridicules his own son and laughs at his failures . . . ?" wondered Buckaroo.

"And leaves the rest of us to cover the costs," she said, stroking a contented Nostradamus. "I finally left him when he stuck my finger in his guillotine cigar cutter. I'll miss you, Chico, but it's over . . . time to move on down the road."

AREA 51

With reason, our marital counseling had failed, though perhaps we had attempted the impossible. The man-and-canine reunion was more successful, however, and days later I observed Wagoneer and his implacable beast peering out the helicopter window as we nervously approached Nellis AFB, ignoring reputable threats over the radio to shoot us down.

"Don't you recognize my voice, you moron?" the general snapped repeatedly into the microphone. "What's your name, airman? . . . So call your poodle general! And I'd like a steak and champagne when I get there!"

In this manner the threat from the ground subsided, and the general—resplendent in holiday cowboy duds and a gold-braided US Cavalry hat—stroked the snarling little fellow in his lap and nattered to himself and anyone who cared to listen.

"Poor snuggum wuggums . . . he just suffers from social anxiety. Fact is, he's a little bit of a recluse, unless bitches come around," he droned on. "Of course this old war dog used to be the same way. Back when I was a big bull-cocked terrier, a sucker for pretty smiles, too . . . and I've met plenty. I'd make 'em melt, give 'em the 'meat and greet.' Then I met the love of my life. Unfortunately, she married the uniform and not the man . . . suffered from a bad case of frigid fanny and gave me bruises—I've got pictures—but of course I never reported it. What kind of American general or classic man gets whipped by his own lip-injected mutt mix, who then runs off with a worthless Chihuahua who thinks he's God's gift to bitches? God, I miss Mama's wolf scent, even if she was cold to my love and used to pummel me to a pulp, not to mention the issue with my vas deferens and red string around my shaft."

"No wonder shit is like it is," said Tommy, appearing at most mildly interested.

"One fine motherphawker . . . a freak in the sheets," Wild Bill continued, paying no attention to Tommy's tactless remark. "Bitches think he farts gold, and that's no empty brag. He tries to mind his own business, but there's a lot of expectations. He's rutted dozens on the sly . . . big ones, little ones, short haired, long haired, Yorkie poos, even foo-foo show dogs . . . hits 'em on the head with his Easter ham, makes them literally mouthwater. It's like his Chihuahua dink is his money roll, whereas I whip out my wrinkly dinky and even my Doxie ran away. Remember Mother Hen, Chico? Now I couldn't get laid if I was a Fabergé egg."

"Always the last girl left at the table, huh, General?" Tommy remarked. "And here I thought you were a heartbreaker . . . love 'em and leave 'em."

Wild Bill shook his head, confessing, "Been with two, married one. Happily ever after . . . right, Chico? Old jaws and claws . . ."

Saying that, he kissed Nostradamus on the mouth until Pecos became uncomfortable and commented, "So you feel your wife took your manhood . . . ?"

"The miscarriage. After that it was all over, Rover, bend over in the clover. The sex was always lame to nothing, but after I was diagnosed with reclusive penis syndrome, up went the ice wall. Then she locked me out, cleaned me out, took my pillow and blankets, too. Why is it the nice guy always winds up with the passive-aggressive Chihuahua?"

When Nostradamus understandably objected to this characterization, Wild Bill hastened to stroke him, repeating over and over, "It's not your fault, baby. No one can hurt you now."

As I say again, we were for the most part tuning out the odd couple, but that was before the general unexpectedly said, "Maybe that's why I sympathized with Whorfin carrying John Emdall Thunderpump's love child. I'm a sucker for a good romance. What I wouldn't give for one more romp with a female human—"

"What did you say? A child?" interrupted Buckaroo, who had in fact been listening attentively. "Whose child?"

"Who the so-called father, John Emdall Thunderpump, is, I have no idea," said the general, "but I believe John Whorfin dearly loved that titty rat he was carrying inside for thirty thousand years. One day he told me the whole story, the two of them phawking like rabbits at their secret rendezvous in the dark vortex of Neptune, having to sneak around like Romeo and Juliet, being of different warring species . . . and how the baby king would have amazing powers, like a god. And his name should be Crown Jewel Ban-Lon."

I have seldom seen Buckaroo Banzai at such a loss for words as he appeared at this moment frozen in my memory. Or was he simply lost in thought?

All I could say was "Wowza . . ."

Tommy, too, felt the need to voice his opinion. "This is some Santa Claus–ass shite. Aren't Whorfin and Emdall Thunderpump deadly rivals? Red infantry against the black and blue flying species . . ."

"Doesn't mean they couldn't have been lovers thirty thousand years ago," Pecos pointed out. "Love has a way."

"My advice to you," Wagoneer cut in, "is don't take your health lightly."

By now we were swooping low over the top-secret base, and Wagoneer told the excitable Chihuahua, "Look . . . our old stomping grounds. You need to piss on this place and every single thing in sight. Over there's where that German short-haired pointer and that mixed pooch tried to chew your ears."

Taking our cue from the unaccountably ebullient general, we landed in the midst of heavy security and bluffed our way forward with a jaunty air. Of course it did not hurt that we were Buckaroo Banzai and the Hong Kong Cavaliers and affably complied with every photo and autograph request. As a result the only portions of the base to which we were denied access (despite our protestations and direct calls to President Monroe) were a pair of R&D bunkers and several heavily guarded hangars, all of which, even from a distance of a kilometer or more, registered elevated levels of radioactivity on

Buckaroo's interferometer. Our exclusion from these skunk works sites was of course disappointing, since it was Wagoneer's contention that we would find within their walls an array of experimental and extraterrestrial spacecraft, a Jet Car prototype based on Buckaroo's stolen plans, and a specimen lab–cum–hatchery ward housing various species of aliens, alive and dead, including Lectroids and the gargantuan alien brain the general also professed to have witnessed. But in our efforts to see such *miracula* for ourselves, we found ourselves stymied by shadowy higher-ups, the nomenklatura of the Pentagon or various three-letter agencies.

As for our impromptu interview with the new base commander and our visit with the white lab coats, there is little to say, except that the laboratory had been practically emptied and scrubbed to gleaming perfection with gallons of whitewash, almost as if someone knew we were coming! Working on tips from General Wagoneer, the four of us—Buckaroo, Tommy, Pecos, and I—passed out our business cards and muddled through the standard questions about buried bodies and skeletons in closets with a handful of remaining technicians and a ranking officer. Although without exception these turned out to be proper garden-variety paper pushers (courteous but robotic and seemingly unenlightened sticklers for rules) who claimed to know nothing of Lectroids or Lectroid eggs—not to mention Elvis Presley or the large alien brain described by Wagoneer—their attitude was not unexpected, and perhaps a certain terror in their eyes told us more than they intended.

One project manager, when I asked what kind of work he was involved with, nervously told me, "The stuff of dreams . . . I can't talk about." Another answered the question by saying that he was in charge of the deep space team's Gamma Quadrant, but when I jokingly made a comment about Salusa Secundus, he did not miss a beat in speaking about the planet as though it were not imaginary! Yet a third engineer turned the tables by asking me questions about the Banzai Institute's own deep space antennas, after requesting a photograph of us together!

The experiences of Buckaroo and the others were by all accounts similar, although of course I was not present during all these encounters. As Tommy summarized our reception so quaintly, "There's more bullspit here than in a cow pasture."

"Psychoville" was the word Pecos used.

But there were in fact consolation prizes to be discovered: the advanced "flying saucer" spy plane; caged laboratory animals with various designer sexual diseases, such as memory-erasing (pseudodementia) viruses; bionic spy geese and salamanders; and the Jet Car's crown jewel, a crude OSCILLATION OVERTHRUSTER tachyon-generator prototype, which Pecos found in a coffee cupboard and surreptitiously pocketed.

As Buckaroo would say later in the middle of a scathing indictment against whoever built the clumsy device, "What little rabbit brain designed this? Never mind the duplicitousness—it's the sloppiness that will be our undoing. Even my baseline of trust in my own government, low already, is now gone."

"Trust is a special gift," I said. "Hard to gain and easy to lose . . ."

"Damn it, if we didn't care so much, we wouldn't care!" declared Pecos emphatically.

The same passion dominated our thoughts—we were all maniacs champing at the bit for a little action by now—but we would have to be patient. The learned lesson of our little escorted tour of the nation's most closely guarded military facility was simple: if we intended to unravel the mystery of John Whorfin, we could not expect help from official quarters. Word had apparently come down from on high warning us that even the president's order was not sufficient to peel back the layers of secrecy surrounding the government's most sensitive projects.

As mentioned, during our time on the base, General Wagoneer was something of a changed man. His pulse seemed to quicken, a glow returned to his face, and he actually seemed to grow physically. As darkness gathered and we followed the path from the Area 51 compound back toward the helipad, he took a sudden detour and gazed out over the still-smoldering burn pits, where Buckaroo could be seen gathering any half-scorched pages of documents he could find . . . despite warnings and the threat of arrest.

"It's slipping away, but I get it . . . all the bad shite that happened. A captain goes down with the ship," the man we called Wild Bill reflected. "I fear I'll never have this again, this sweet aroma."

Buckaroo reminded him, "That sweet aroma from the pits is toxic, General. Remember, it's not about having, but about giving all we have."

"Together as one," the older warrior said. "I get it."

He then turned to salute Old Glory waving in the distance and set down the Chihuahua, who at once scampered off toward a field of prairie grass and began to sniff and scratch at a noticeable barren patch.

THE REMAINS OF DR. LIZARDO

"I stood right here watching my karma burn, then buried him over there in a Hobbit hole, a curse on his lips," Wild Bill said, pointing at the same location. "I knew then I'd be shat upon bigtime."

"Lizardo . . . ?" Buckaroo assumed, as we wound our way toward the spot, past a number of air vents carved out of the earth that suggested hidden underground facilities.

"Septic tanks doubling as bomb shelters," our helpful guide explained . . .

. . . as we arrived finally at what was now a mountain of loose dirt presided over by the frantic Chihuahua, who now aimed a stream of piss into a freshly uncovered hole.

"Look at him raise one leg, like a god!" the general exclaimed admiringly.

"Looks like Nostradamus and the coyotes beat us to it," Pecos observed, pointing at what appeared to be a gnawed human foot protruding from a shallow grave; and although we would have freely declined to commit such a blasphemy under ordinary circumstances, we were at peace with what was a necessary procedure . . . so we dug, albeit not for long. When at last the old man's putrefied ruins lay exposed, Buckaroo knelt with his collection kit while the rest of us hung back, covering our noses with our neckerchiefs at the sight of Dr. Lizardo's remains—mere pieces of him, smoke dried like beef jerky, organs turned to jelly and wrapped in tattered yellow vinyl and stray Styrofoam beans. According to General Wagoneer, he had been buried for approximately four months; yet beneath his orangish stringy hair and desiccated residue, the old man's prune face and blank gaze maintained their fearsome power. Even dead, the eyes seemed to bore right through us.

"Sweet blue-eyed Jesus," Pecos said, crossing herself. "Maybe we should pass the hat or use the money in the swear box to buy him a cheap coffin."

Our accusatory looks naturally turned toward Wild Bill, who said merely, "Blame me for the right things, lady pants. In the heat of the moment, I was the angel of mercy . . . buried him inside a beanbag chair with full military honors."

"I'm confident you did the best you could," Buckaroo said.

"I think I see the missing synapses in old Lizardo's brain," joked Perfect Tommy.

"Be careful with your moral superiority, Tommy," Buckaroo warned. "Even with his predilection for Mussolini, you have to respect his intellect. He might have been a great scientist if he hadn't become reckless—a case of hubris and haste made waste—and then had the bad luck to collide with John Whorfin at the border of the Eighth Dimension. After that, everything went south."

"Yeah, years of sociopathic hell, spent two-timing Earth," Tommy said.

"It wasn't all his fault. A good scientist with a bad record," Buckaroo summed up. "The poor devil simply had no tools to resist the strange attractor."

"Strange is an understatement if you're talking about Whorfin," stated Pecos confidently.

I shook my head, begging to differ. "I don't think that's what Buckaroo meant. The attractor is the force between them, right, Buckaroo? Whatever held Lizardo and Whorfin together . . ."

"Exactly right—the secret sauce," he said. "I doubt it was love."

"Any hope of finding the damn thing?" asked Tommy.

"Only enough to stir my imagination," answered Buckaroo, who now stuffed most of Lizardo into a plastic trash bag, clasped his kit, and slowly stood, while doffing his Stetson. Although we had little in the way of high sentiments to offer, what followed was a brief spiritual moment.

"Any words?" he asked us.

"The great one Deity, the light from above the entirety," volunteered Pecos.

"The all-seeing eye," I said. "Do unto others."

"And leave no trace," Tommy elaborated. "As we continue to probe the eternal mysteries, following the example of Jesus and Erasmus . . . open sesame to the voodoo sky . . ."

"Should we dig up Elvis?" Pecos pondered aloud, half imagining herself enticing the great entertainer out of the land of shadows with the bottle of Coke in her knapsack . . . when all he probably wanted was to be left alone.

Oddly enough, from somewhere afar came a gust of cold air at that very moment and the sound of a lonesome sheep bell, seeming to toll mournfully . . . joined by Wild Bill humming taps while simultaneously thumping his cheeks percussion-style. Yet how tired and joyless he seemed, although I suppose you could say that about any of us under the unusual circumstances!

It had been another long, mostly fruitless day full of feverish excitement and little progress, other than what I have related. With the planet perhaps hanging by a thread, and with the understanding that life deals random blows to everyone—Lizardo, Elvis, even Buckaroo—we nonchalantly kicked more dirt on Lizardo's grave and turned to leave . . . when suddenly off in the distant sheep pasture a violent fracas broke out between two creatures. (I can only call them *creatures* since I'm confident neither of their kind has existed anywhere else on the surface of the earth.)

THE ROSWELL BOYS

Amid angry, hellish cries, they flew at each other headfirst . . . one with ram-like horns while the other slashed with fangs and tusks. Any more than that I could not make out in the dim crepuscular light, and yet General Wagoneer seemed anything but fazed by the remarkable spectacle . . . merely commenting, "There's an added bonus round . . .

"Oñate! Javelina! I'm sick and tired of this!" he calmly shouted at the two and once again ordered into action his furious Chihuahua phenom, who in a matter of seconds not only broke up the fight but shepherded the two antagonists toward us. What a moment of high strangeness, as the pair of freakish fellows—prodded by the angry Chihuahua—came loping toward us on all fours, but clad in ratty human clothing! When one of them found a tin can and began to chew it, I was not alone in reflexively moving my hand to my gun belt . . . which naturally I had been ordered to leave in the helicopter.

At this delicate moment, Buckaroo later told me, what crossed his mind was a recurring nightmare, first encountered in the Eighth Dimension,

in which all the men he had killed could see him from hell. Yet he also
had the presence of mind during this stunning turn of events to recall
words of wisdom from Hikita: "The way of living things is a wide gate
. . . so deign to be kind, Buckaroo. Everyone is fighting a battle."

General Wagoneer simultaneously assured us, "It's okay. Say hello to
the Roswell Boys, Oñate and Javelina. Looks like they're just blowing off
a little steam, having fun . . . or maybe out foraging because they're hungry."

"Any chance they're meat eaters?" asked Pecos anxiously.

"They'll eat anything, depending on their hunger pangs," explained
Wagoneer.

Not entirely reassured, Pecos replied, "Oh, in that case—for a minute
I was worried. Now I'm flipping off my safety, except I had to leave
my gun."

Now for the proper vocabulary . . . at least the best my human mind
can do. The horned creature that Wagoneer called Oñate, roughly the
size of a man, resembled in remarkable ways a satyr, its rear legs cloven
hooved but its two forward appendages inordinately long and sporting
alien hands, each with only two lobster-like digits. Its head seemed too
large and ill sized for a body covered by a dozen gradations of wooliness,
white mixed with darker shades, while its face was ovine with curled
horns, as I have noted, and a pair of utterly black and opaque eyes that
seemed to emanate flesh-piercing rays. Do you not see my difficulty now,
patient reader?

As for the other, the so-called Javelina, I could not help but be
reminded of Odysseus's crew, whom the goddess Circe turned into swine.
Despite a bristly, pig-like snout with wild tusks and the diminutive body
of a large-headed extraterrestrial, there was something almost human
about the fellow (in fact I had no clue if it was male or female or both)—
perhaps its dark eyes, not fathomless and impenetrable like its sidekick's,
but two warm, reflective pools radiating, dare I say, enlightenment . . .
something resembling a higher evolved state.

But in the result, the telepathic message emitted by both beasts was
one and the same: "I won't let anyone tread on my toes, but I trust we
shall be friends."

"Don't show fear, Reno. Don't shrink back," Wagoneer instructed.

Perhaps my nervousness was simply in anticipation of what was about
to happen, as we suddenly became aware of a flying squad of military

police and their baying guard dogs headed our way . . . a moment of truth surely at hand. On occasion one can reason with humans but not with guard dogs, and one glance at Buckaroo dissolved our doubts.

"A picture speaks a thousand words," he said. "Let's hightail it."

"My life has flown. I accept my death. It will be here now before I know it," declared Wagoneer stoically, until Buckaroo scooped up his beloved Chihuahua, and the general naturally followed on the run.

Tommy likewise wasn't sticking around.

"Kiss my butt, suckers, and sayonara," he ejaculated and took off.

Now we made a beeline for the chopper, half expecting to hear gunshots whizzing over our heads at any moment, or worse, depending on the temperament of our pursuers. After piling into our seats and waiting an extra second for the slow-footed General Wagoneer, we had liftoff in the nick of time, and of course all eyes turned back to the scene we had left behind . . . only to discover, to our amazement, the two freakish beasts had performed an impossible leap at the last moment, grabbing hold of the chopper's undercarriage, and now seeming to be shrieking with delight, and in tandem, as we gained altitude, leaving the guards and their baying dogs helpless below.

"If they escape the perimeter, they'll have to be destroyed like the others and ground into tacos," the general remarked with palpable concern.

I think we all must have squirmed uneasily, feeling sudden pity for these frightfully queer hybrids whose squeaky, cartoonish voices contrasted with their beastly appearance and mismatched eyes. Part of me wanted to say the general was incorrect, that no harm would come to them if they were recaptured, but I also had no difficulty believing that our shadowy government might choose to exterminate the creatures to prevent their exposure to the public.

So what to do with their lives in our hands? Bring the wild specimens into the passenger compartment? Take them back to the base that was no place to call home? Back to their cages like zoo animals in all their vulnerability? Just as I glanced at Buckaroo and tried to read his mind, however, we hit a patch of turbulence, and he dove out the door, much to our collective panic. Only seconds later did we collect our wits sufficiently to poke our heads out and observe Buckaroo hanging on to the landing skid and a wailing Javelina, whose companion had fallen to an uncertain fate.

"Get my kit, and a rope!" Buckaroo shouted.

"Keep him busy, Buckaroo!" Tommy called back and wasted no time grabbing Buckaroo's medical bag and a rappelling rope and climbing out to lend a hand . . .

. . . as we spent the next quarter hour retracing our flight path and circling close to the ground in search of the wayward Oñate. But in the gathering darkness we found no trace, and by now fuel and muscles were both running low.

"Let's head for the hills. Home!" Buckaroo announced, and he and Tommy at last secured the tranquilized Javelina with rope and lifted him into the cabin . . .

. . . as General Wagoneer spoke baby talk to the semiconscious beast, recounting to us the story of how the parents of the duo survived the famous crash of their spaceship back in 1947 and escaped for a time into the rugged rural countryside around Roswell, New Mexico, where they had sexual congress with a variety of local wildlife before being tracked and shot by hunters. Autopsies revealed they had several shiny brains, each no larger than a marble or an acorn, some even the size of a BB. Although another known hybrid had been captured and dissected, Oñate and Javelina were—as far as was known—the only living offspring of these unorthodox couplings and, according to this chronology, had been at Area 51 for roughly six decades . . . which explained their reasonable English fluency.

"Monkey men," I heard the creature moan, spitting the words like a curse.

"The honeymoon's over, old man," Tommy told the beast. "I guess you have no love for the opportunities this country has provided, such as the astronomical amount of dollars for quality long-term care in a nice facility."

When we seemed amused by Tommy's crude attempt at humor, Buckaroo rebuked us by saying, "Put yourself in his shoes, all. He may be part wild animal, but a trace of him may carry atavistic memories of a lost world before he was imprisoned in this one without justification or perhaps without even the power to deduce why this was happening to him."

"Maybe Texas hunters killed his parents. I'd be bitter, too," Pecos speculated and suddenly drew her hands up to her throat as if something was strangling her.

"Everybody loves their mama," Tommy observed.

Thus suitably sanctioned, we sank back in our seats and tried not to look at the haggard beasts or at Pecos, who was still clutching her throat and making gargling noises.

"A downer, all right," I duly noted . . .

. . . as Pecos all at once freed herself from her own death grip and gasped, "My God, do you feel it? It's like I'm going under in the deep end and can't come up for air, because he won't let me!"

"They're masters at it," related the general from personal experience, "but nothing compared to the big alien brain or John Whorfin, who pushed even me beyond my limits . . . drove a good man into the exponential fire of hell."

"Not this kid," Tommy joked, grinning and removing his Stetson to reveal a crude skullcap of aluminum foil. "I fear nothing from a squealing pig! Heavy-duty ply . . . ha, ha!"

Good old Tommy, always good for a laugh! While the rest of us chortled, Pecos teased him, "Tommy . . . my knight in shining aluminum armor."

I defended him by saying, "Our brains are bioelectrical power stations, so there's nothing wrong with protecting them. Way to use your head, Tommy."

I could swear I heard Buckaroo laugh in his sleeve as well. So in that manner we flew back to the Institute while the rest of us could only exchange looks . . . in equal parts relieved, worried, and airsick. Other than these remarks, I will spare you the details of the flight that lasted the greater part of two hours.

XIV. PIPE DREAMS

We must not only punish traitors,
but all people who are not enthusiastic.
—Louis de Saint-Just

"Every week Satrap counts the hairs on my head. It can happen anytime. It has happened before, as I have described," Xan told Penny, adding a favorite passage from the *Ramayana*: " 'She had lost her heart the minute she recognized him, the prince she had always dreamt about. She had known him since the world began, through many lifetimes.' "

When he drifted on smoke, he claimed to stare into the past with vivid clarity and reminisce over lost loves and the good old days in Mongolia or the Roman Empire or Chicago or Hollywood. "Strange to say how our senses are never emancipated from memory . . . the savor of a particular food or fragrance cannot be erased from our recollections. I said as much to Proust and Garibaldi: we do not outgrow these things, unlike passing thoughts and utterances which we freely transcend. A taste of sweetness, a tender touch . . . though such sensations may be centuries old, I recall them as yesterday and am instantly prodded back. No mind can avoid these apperceptions, for they are inseparable from who we are and therefore transcend time and space."

On another occasion, they were standing in the cluttered basement, not far from a Jet Car prototype mounted on a rail and powered by a fanjet engine, when he told her, "This was where I resurrected you with a little piece of sand art and sea foam."

By "sea foam" she was made to understand he meant his semen, and she was still trying to fathom this miracle when the sicko helpfully drew some sort of family tree with his left foot in a bejeweled house slipper.

They were standing on an artificial putting green that he blamed on a chronic condition that often kept him awake until dawn.

"Too many lonely nights," he said. "Night after night, week after week . . . you start to fester and think of conspiracies. Finally, it was either put a bullet through my head or take up golf."

"Too much thinking. That will get you going," she replied, speaking from her own experience.

She also knew he liked to howl at the moon and in a strange way enjoyed listening to him; it was his endless talk that made her want to brain him with a rock or stuff his face with anything handy.

"But my point is that for many centuries we were not together but were nonetheless connected. Don't you see, I could not have resurrected you, any more than the Selector could have, if we were not both historical people with the souls of gypsies . . ."

It would be up to the magus Hippolyte another day to show her a heavy scrapbook containing yellowed newspaper clippings and several photographs of a writer called Ayn Rand and a young dandy in a zoot suit.

"Look at her," Hippolyte said. "Her masculine, squarish jaw, her mischievous mouth and generous lips, her eyes the same dark pools as yours and Marie Antoinette's . . . it is you, Alisa . . . goddess Pallas. Until now, I could not be sure, but . . ."

"Goddess . . . ?"

"Can you deny it? Try to have an open mind. And that is Viktor with you. He is a *strannik*, like you: a holy traveler across the generations. Look at you, two Russian émigrés, how much you are in love. It was bound to happen again . . . two gypsy souls with one heart between you."

Holy travelers, gypsy souls. This idea gave her pause, especially when the seer followed with an explanation of the life and fate lines in the palm of her hand, explaining, "It's not possible, but this is real and has happened to many . . . like moths to a flame, or should I say a pair of flames drawn together in every age by a kind of strange gravitational or magnetic attraction. In fact one might say you were divided for the sake of love, so that you might find one another."

This seemed nonsensical to her, but time was slipping by, so she said nothing.

Hippolyte resumed, "The world is full of these strange attractions and sometimes the world spirit snakes back to form a loophole in the law of the universe. We may call it genetic memory, but in truth it is something without explanation that cannot be controlled. Your imprint goes back thousands of years to the very beginning, even to the roots of magic, even to the primal flux and primordial atom. You are his mother and lover, the goddess Pallas."

"Mother and lover . . . ?" she replied, feeling a sudden wave of sickness.

"That is my understanding," chortled Hippolyte. "Why else do you think that, of all the women in his seraglio, he does not send you out to gather firewood or fetch water from the well?"

She had seen other women in the house—some fine boned and delicate as porcelain dolls and others more stalwart and intimidating who roamed the halls with full independence, enforcing the rules—but her thoughts now were only of the woman in the photographs who presented not the sunlit sheen of herself, but rather an Old World version, the dark hues of the palette infused with a large stock of even darker wit bubbling in her sly, almost whimsical smile. How like a slinky cat! But those eyes! It was there she recognized herself more than in the physical similarities; in those deep, liquid pools that spoke of a world of troubles, she could see herself . . . an exalted woman after her own heart, even a goddess.

"There is another theory, however," cautioned Hippolyte, dropping his voice to a whisper. "Long ago during his winter campaign against the Ming, the khan stole you from your father and his own brother because he could not resist your beauty. Fearing his brother's anger and yet not willing to commit the second dishonor of killing him, he fled the camp for the cold, desolate steppe. He gave up his world for you. It is said that very shortly afterward he sickened and died and became a ghost horseman . . ."

"And me?" she said, curious to know the rest.

"Legend has it that, carrying a fortune in jewels and three captured keys to the kingdom of heaven, he made his way out of Uzbekistan to

Hollywood, California, traveling not as Timur the Great but as the
Russian émigré Viktor Antropos. But even among all the beauties in
that magical realm of Hollywood, it was you—your invisible fire, your
force of personality—that made him pick you over the many shallow
actress types with all the trappings."

She had become convinced that all people were either wicked or
stupid; and she was never more certain of this than the afternoon she
walked with him hand in hand in the *hortus conclusus* and he pointed to
a low branch of a tamarisk, where a pair of jays vied with one another
for a still-wriggling insect.

"Look, I know the feeling, on both sides, ha, ha!" he said. "I have
been the bug and the bird wetting her chops."

It was his extraordinary claim to be able to remember virtually
everything from all his incarnations on this earth, for well or ill; and he
was thus able to recall with perfect clarity, or so he said, their first
encounter in the MGM cafeteria when he looked up from cumbersome
table talk with Louis Mayer and Walter Pidgeon . . .

"Walter the Pigeon?"

. . . and chanced to enjoy the show: a room so fragrant, full of perfumed,
golden youths free-ranging among themselves, ravishing actors and
actresses, demigods, heroes of the popular imagination. Yet it was the dark
Russian writer who with one curl of her full, spicy lips mesmerized him.

"The way you got up from the table and walked with your head held
high," Xan went on, "no doubt someone already had whispered to you,
'Do you know who that young man is? That is the Russian millionaire
Viktor Antropos. You should go speak Russian to him—he could help your
career—but be careful. It is said he works for Stalin's NKVD and may have
been playing chess with Trotsky only hours before his skull was split.'"

"What did I say to that?"

"You would know better than I. Perhaps you said we had already met
in earlier years. I explained to you that I lived in Paris but owned a
company involved in motion picture sound technology, which I had
brought to the attention of Mayer and other studio chiefs. Now I found
myself alone in Los Angeles with all its peculiarities, not knowing what
to do with myself. We both agreed that the City of Angels was noted
for a certain degree of loneliness and narrowness of culture, but you said
we each have to take the blame for our own unhappiness."

"I said what?"

"More than once . . . on bicycles at the beach and one evening in my rooms at the Chateau Marmont, where we discussed other realms and the music of Stravinsky."

"Who?" she said.

"Another human being. It doesn't matter," he replied. "You don't remember making a swan dive into my bed and afterward we sent for Chinese food and I showed you some of my sleight of hand tricks?"

"I can't remember if I remember," she said.

"Of course my claim of loneliness was a lie, since I was actually engaged in negotiations to buy a large share of Metro studio and was hardly starved for social engagements. In truth, my biggest fear was that I might die from a farrago of too much carousing with teenage ingénues and have to be buried in a sunny grave overlooking the beach."

He seemed deep in thought as they walked on, passing the pigeon coop and on to the goat shed, where he paused to stroke one of the nannies. Then out of nowhere he said, "You may think I care only for business but I have commissioned many of the world's great works from artists and composers . . . movie makers. Do you remember Orson Welles?"

"Who?"

"I tapped him to make a movie called *Citizen Kane*. We were living in New Jersey then . . ."

"We . . . ?"

"Antropos, Shannon, and I by the old ruined mill . . . Grovers Mill . . . where we were the best neighbors in the world. Welles gave me a script he wanted to film and said he had been turned down by every vulture in Hollywood. Looking back, I am surprised by what good spirits we were both in despite death all around us. I told him I would finance the picture, but he would have to make a special radio broadcast for me and a friend of mine. And do you know what he did?"

She shrugged. "He made the movie?"

"He ran and jumped in the pond like a little boy," Xan recalled and tried to laugh. "That was how he was. With artists, the line between childhood and adulthood is always wavering and uncertain. But I said to him, you'll have to make the picture darker. That didn't exactly cheer his heart but I think he did his honest share."

"I like cowboy movies," she said, her voice trailing off. "I don't know why."

Perhaps an alarm bell sounded in Xan's head. In any case he added, "In a movie everything seems to come to an end. In real life you have to make other plans. Hollywood, where all things gravitate toward money, was the great disillusion of my life . . . where I lost hope in a better world to come, yet I learned a valuable lesson. As a result of my philanthropic activity in America, I learned that gift giving pays even better than crime and that for each rung you climb in society, you meet a lower class of people."

A BUSINESS MEETING

At just this lighthearted moment, however, Hippolyte the Chaldean and four of Xan's senior councilors emerged from the house and shunted her to one side. The councilors, known as the Tetrarchy, the Quorum of the Four, or the Committee of Four, included Xan's home secretary and chargé d'affaires Manny Magdalene and the trio of quaestors known as the Musketeers: Xan's chief scientist, artillery engineer, and overall grease monkey Dr. Paraquat; his manager of human capital and special projects for the WCL's Securitat, Fariq Bulbus; and Wadsworth Longfellow, director plenipotentiary of the Axis Fund and head of corporate giving. Their purpose that afternoon beside the lily pond was an impromptu briefing session touching upon budget matters and the day's good news: record profits for Transglobal Insurance, IG Farben, Sequoia Petroleum, World Capital Lending (its global narcotics trade and chain of "laundries"), and the amusement park and entertainment sectors—indeed all the League's zaibatsu—including its hugely successful personal-development speakers' bureau and online university of real estate and business administration.

Almost overlooked in the stellar numbers was Quaestor Paraquat's analytical report—on the whole positive—concerning the assorted confidential Jet Car documents sent by the American mystery man, Mr. French. Xan's response to this news was to allocate a considerable sum to purchase a commercial jet engine and undertake further large-scale experiments at the main research laboratory in Borneo. Tackled last, and intentionally so, was the not-so-pleasant bookkeeping matter having to do with pension benefits owed to an Afghan tribal chieftain for a lifetime of service and an update on a contentious dispute with a fellow World Crime League princelet and sitting member of the European Directorate: Cardinal Baltazar of Bosnia, otherwise known as Pope Innocent's personal manager.

At the very mention of Baltazar and that distant Balkan republic, Manny detected a flash of rage in Xan's feverish recessed eyes.

"Yes, Baltazar, who has been strangely uncommunicative, other than to give himself a huge performance bonus," Manny continued with a slight roll of his eyes. "He writes merely to let us know, in response to our 'bookkeeping query' concerning the pope's endorsements and hair salon franchises, that he has built fifty bell towers to commemorate the faith. Soon every church in Bosnia, and even a mosque or two, will have its own bell tower, but he has yet to build stairs and add the actual bells. Instead, we have learned he has converted the bell towers into lighthouses and also built air-conditioned treehouses, quite a number of them . . ."

Xan angrily clenched a fist, which he used to grip Manny's shirt and draw him closer, spitting his words: "Treehouses? Built with our percentage? My percentage!"

". . . as well as stealing several pope souvenir trademarks," Manny said, meanwhile urgently looking to Paraquat for assistance.

"Not exactly treehouses, but of a special kind," explained the brilliant Paraquat, "especially three giant ones atop the secret pyramids of Bosnia . . ."

"Pyramids of Bosnia . . . ?" questioned Longfellow.

"Outside Sarajevo," elaborated Manny. "They are said to be the biggest pyramids in the world . . . the Pyramid of the Sun, the Pyramid of the Moon, and the Pyramid of the Dragon . . ."

"Big gorilla searchlights shining into space, looking for visitors," Paraquat said.

"And to think I gave that fat rat the power of the keys in exchange for a miracle healing spark," ranted a still-seething Xan. "What does he have to say for himself?"

"He says nothing at all," Manny informed him. "For two weeks we can't find hide nor hair."

"And I noticed he wasn't at my birthday ball," said Xan, obviously deep in thought. "That was very noticeable."

By now he had heard enough to make up his mind but first wished to hear from Hippolyte, who had been listening intently and now spoke in his usual calm and judicious manner. "Two years ago Cardinal Zoran Caiaphas Baltazar asked me to do a special reading, and the card that kept coming up was the hierophant reversed, indicating a narcissist with a messiah complex. Likewise his name's numerical value, using Chaldean numerology, is 66. Interesting, no?"

"Practically the devil's number," commented Manny.

"And his Pythagorean number?" Xan inquired, then quickly added, "Never mind—I'll work it in my head . . . 87 . . . so 15 . . . therefore 6. There is the third 6 . . . 666, the number of the Beast."

This remarkable revelation produced a moment of taut silence. Then Hippolyte said, "That is the reality. Clearly, this man Zoran Caiaphas Baltazar is a megalomaniac, even the Antichrist, and therefore never mistaken. No one else's opinion matters to him."

"We'll see about that," vowed Xan, "after I lift his lid with a can opener! I have to go in tomorrow for a transrectal ultrasound, but I want this taken care of. Baltazar has been in my thoughts lately and my dreams. He has gone down the wrong road, and his churlish ass must be dismantled, his power of the keys revoked."

But the goateed Fariq ("Rick") had lingering doubts. "Still, here is a man who—his basic needs being met and having met him at our franchisees and budding entrepreneurs conference last year in Milan—I would have thought is the last of my worry. He is not a man to make a strong impression, much less steal a trademark . . . more like a workhorse with a hard-on to be somebody."

Wadsworth Longfellow had to shake his head in response, respectfully disagreeing. "Looks can be deceiving, Rick. I remember him carrying an old-fashioned brown briefcase like a door-to-door salesman might lug around with all his samples . . . a meticulous organizer type who moves at a slower pace. And yet this is the man who has revolutionized the pope's business affairs and is making millions from his product endorsement deals and hair salon franchises. I remember speaking to him about insurance, of all things, and coming away impressed. He is in fact a certified life insurance underwriter, although he may be struggling with his sexuality."

Xan seemed to digest all of this but merely said, "He is shit for a human being, crazy right out of a movie."

"He needs to step into the big-boy room for some daddy time," agreed Manny. "He needs a therapeutic moment in his life for dipping into your wallet . . . to open his eyes to the truth."

Xan pondered the matter for a second or two before replying, "Go to Bosnia or Schleswig-Holstein and bring him here. If he refuses, kill his family, his mistresses, even his secret children and his pets . . . so that I may put to him the question directly."

"Of course, Huang-di," said Manny. "I won't blow him kisses."

"Or dangle him from the helicopter," Xan commanded. "Do it . . . or your name will be added and a grave prepared."

"Consider it done," Manny wheezed, visibly fading into the background.

Except we now know, of course, that no such success occurred; and in the interest of painting the big picture, I will note that it was probably around the time Manny was traveling to Sarajevo with his favorite assassin's tool, a billhook, that I received a cryptic message from Mona Peeptoe, asking if I had heard anything about the "Aqua Velva business." As I had no clue what she was talking about and told her so, and she did not reply to my follow-up questions—"What about Aqua Velva? What's going on with Aqua Velva?"—I thought nothing more of the episode . . . though in short order, of course, I was able to connect the dots.

XV. MORE QUESTIONS THAN ANSWERS

Equations know more than we do.
—Werner Heisenberg

Some weeks later, we received two-part replies to our peaceful entreaties to Hanoi Xan. By this I mean to say that each of our emissaries was returned to his tactical commander in two parts, in sloshing five-gallon buckets. All had gold Krugerrands in their mouths and had been cut up pretty badly—though I suppose that is stating the obvious when a man has been cleaved in two. Hell naturally followed; how we howled and wanted to spill Xan's blood! For days, we were so many beasts in a state of wild desperation.

But the world did not end, at least not yet. One of the torsos was also accompanied by a bloody Chinese New Year card that I chanced to handle at the breakfast table before passing it around. Other than the embossed holiday greeting, I could make no sense of either the card's private message in an unknown language or the provocative drawing of a cowboy riding a penis-nosed dolphin toward a pot of gold coins, while three observers on dromedaries watched from a nearby promontory.

"I recognize the Three Wise Men, the Manchu and the Mongolian, but this language here, these scrawls . . . what is it?" I said, handing the card to our house mother and chief nutritionist Mrs. Johnson, who gazed at it quite intently for several seconds.

"Wow," she said, "my Linear B's a tad rusty, but I studied a little Old Enochian at the state normal school—or maybe it was Old Etruscan—as transmitted by the angels to the Archons' Assembly of Divines and Eternal Elders. The way I read it is 'When you have drunk all the water in the Yangtze River, I will tell you where she is.' Then he offers Penny in exchange for the location of the Great Khan's treasure, passed down from your ancestors . . .'"

"Penny? Meaning her body?" Tommy blurted out.

Mrs. Johnson seemed to nod and shake her head simultaneously while saying, "According to Xan, she crossed the Rainbow Bridge, but somehow in some sick and twisted way she's back . . . resurrected from the dead. This goes beyond disrespect. Not acceptable."

"Not acceptable, but not out of the ordinary," Buckaroo commented with a pained expression, taking the card from Mrs. Johnson and turning it over in his hands with utmost care. "The Face That Is No Face, who 'needs no introduction,' says, 'This message confirms all tidings' . . . that one of his sorcerers has changed Penny into a river dolphin . . . and that's where she is now, somewhere in the Yangtze. If I don't believe that nonsense, she's working as a courtesan in the Yoshiwara or starring in the Takarazuka. Either way, he's offering to return her if I pay tribute: the Jet Car, the OVERTHRUSTER, and the location of the Great Khan's tomb, plus additional charges."

"Additional charges? Dear God, that sadistic, belly-crawling, egg-sucking crème de la slime is lower than snake scum, lower than a one-celled amoeba," grumbled Mrs. Johnson. "Makes me want to take two showers even touching this filthy greeting card. This low blow will not go unrepaid. We need to nail his ass, good and hard, once and for all."

"Tall tree, a rope, and a horse," suggested Pecos.

"You got that right. I spit Beech-Nut in his snake eyes," Tommy added and spat into a tin can . . .

. . . as Mrs. Johnson continued, "The Yoshiwara is in Tokyo, is it not? What a beastly ass, and that poor, sweet girl tossed into a brothel . . . it pulls the heartstrings. Also, even with my limited Mongolian, I notice in the message that Xan mentions his own name before yours, Buckaroo. Isn't that considered a gross insult?"

At this, I suddenly experienced something like a light bulb moment.

"Your nightmare, Buckaroo, or whatever it was!" I reminded him. "Wasn't Penny a dolphin in your vivid dream . . . ?"

"You're right, Reno, and with an exaggerated nose," he replied. "Good catch. Maybe I was on to something."

"Maybe you were *on* something," Pecos corrected.

"Like death by a thousand cuts," Buckaroo muttered to himself, seeming lost in a reverie. " 'Round and round flew the raven, and cawed to the blast. He heard the last shriek of the perishing souls' . . ."

"What, Buckaroo?" I asked him.

" 'Right glad was the Raven,' " he said softly. " 'They had taken his all, and Revenge it was sweet!' "

"Hell, yeah, looks like shit stain Xan's circling the wagons, spoiling for a fight," said Tommy.

"And hate-filled to the top," replied Buckaroo.

To whom was he referring? Xan or himself? At that moment I tried to read his demeanor as he stared long and hard at Xan's missive before slipping it into a drawer; but whatever hurt or cold fury he was feeling, he masked it well by turning his attention to his prized crickets and back to the job at hand.

By now we had self-organized into small interdisciplinary ad hoc groups, having delegated tasks, and set about to analyze our situation as scientifically as possible and plot a way forward. In this strategy the thoughtful reader will recognize the theory of precession at work, by which I mean subplots at right angles to the main action, such that the reader who might expect a pulse-pounding chapter—or, at a minimum, the development of a clear plan of action—encounters instead a certain sense of drift and a bare patchwork of narrative threads, but only so many as are at your modest author's disposal.

There was of course the suspected traitor General Wagoneer and the supposed sale of Jet Car plans, which he continued to claim were slipshod imitations, flawed in such a way as to be worthless to any buyer. But we were still waiting for the president's promised trove of secret government data or any other elaboration of a possible Xan-Whorfin connection (the worst of all possible worlds) and were therefore off to a fitful start; indeed, how could it be otherwise when high-ranking military brass and government intelligence officials feared being held accountable for their shortcomings more than any other outcome? To put it bluntly, the

imminent threat to our world mattered less to certain palace mandarins
than getting blamed for it; and without assistance from the Department
of Defense and the various alphabet intelligence agencies, unwilling allies
all, we could not know if the general was telling the truth.

Applying his own lie detector test—his hand over Wild Bill's heart—
Buckaroo believed the general to be clinically insane, incapable of
distinguishing fantasy from reality; and in any case, while the matter of
the Jet Car weighed on our minds in a personal way, the bigger question
of John Whorfin and his political opponents' threat to destroy our world
had to take precedence in our efforts. But on this score, too, the truth
would prove elusive, since our own observatory, and others with whom
we were in constant contact, had lost track of the mystery planetoid,
indicating that it had either left our system or was somehow flying under
the radar, likely cloaked in stealth-mode technology.

But which of these hypotheses was correct? Had the sword of
Damocles hanging over us been lifted? Sad to say, there was really no
earthly way of knowing. While it is tempting to blame ourselves for
our lack of progress during this period, I will go to my grave secure
in the knowledge that we left no stone unturned in our search for
answers. To that end, we prized our late-night roundtable discussions
in the Huddle Room, putting our heads together and analyzing
intelligence, advancing theories, grilling Wild Bill Wagoneer in his
more lucid moments, and following up rumored sightings of countless
old men resembling Lizardo—"bobbing for horse apples in a punch
bowl," as Tommy so colorfully put it.

And even an enhanced clinical understanding of Lectroids did
little to help us answer the crucial question of whether the pneuma of
John Whorfin still existed in a vital state, either as a free entity or
in the body of another human host; and along these lines there was
another possibility that we were as yet unwilling to entertain.

General Wagoneer had frequently mentioned the Abbot Costello.
When queried, however, he professed to have little memory of their
actual encounter beyond the prelate's powerful trumpet that he
theorized had brought the laboratory crashing down like the walls of
ancient Jericho.

As scientists and presumably empiricists—and we were all cothinkers
in this—none of us put stock in the notion of exorcism, whose results

could not be empirically verified. I will go further: the atavistic ritual of driving out demons, present in virtually every primitive society, was offensive to our coldly logical thinking, particularly since Whorfin was not of the religious spirit world—at least not in the traditional sense that we think of it—but rather had entered our dimension and the physicist Lizardo's body through some actual physical process that we ironically had taken to calling transubstantiation. How this all had come about, scientifically speaking, was, to put it mildly, an enigma; and the brain-addled Wild Bill was of precious little help even under hypnosis. As for the perennial mind-body conundrum—unsettled even for our own species and a problem Buckaroo has wrestled with for the greater part of his life—I will avoid dipping even my toe in it.

MYSTERIOUS TRANSMISSIONS

It was in such a woeful state of general ignorance that we thus played a waiting game and felt increasingly useless in our efforts to trace both John Whorfin and the mystery planetoid that was nonetheless beginning to make its presence known in a somewhat perverse way . . . by which I refer to the uncanny disruptions to worldwide radio and television broadcasts by a generic middle-aged individual going by the quaint title of Archangel Brother Deacon Jarvis, who appeared onscreen as a digitized simulacrum swathed in sublime light and molded in the image of the white-haired Quaker on a certain oatmeal container.

While engineered to sound human, his pasty white face never changed expressions in an otherwise flawless impersonation of a radio evangelist whose inflamed religious zeal and mangled speech he seemed to have copied from life.

Herewith, a sampling: "Beware of the evil Red one! Promising you a new vehicle with all the bells and whistles! A promotion at work! Money in the bank! A hot new cutie pie! Just kiss the devil's hairy lip and you've got it made in the shade, right? Lemme tell you, folks, Red John Whorfin is the rat of the world—can I get an amen, a hallelujah, and a cheeseburger? I'm willing to pay."

At this point an image of the appalling-looking John Whorfin in his natural state as a Red Lectroid—dead black orbs in a craggy face that hinted at the void within—normally filled the screen, along with a rolling chyron announcing a "FAT REWARD" and the phone numbers of the Banzai Institute, Interpol, and a special United Nations hotline.

"Tie that snake up and toss him into the fiery pit of the Book of Revelation—better yet, back into the Eighth Dimension! Rebuke him! Tell him your traveling preacher, the old country boy Archangel Brother Deacon Jarvis, said, 'So long, loser, fallen overlord, scumbag of the universe, bald-faced liar, treacherous subjugator and seducer, unutterable beast kicked out of heaven by Her Highness, Empress John Emdall Thunderpump! Hallelujah be her name! Mother of Wonder, Star of Hope and True Light of Heaven, Light Who Begat Light, warning you to clean up after yourselves or heads will roll and she will mess with your axial tilt! Amen and hallelujah! So forget the scratch tickets and try the full, warm feeling, folks! But time is limited and this offer may expire without notice! I'm talking happy and fat, all sorts of wonderful stuff—remember you won't get a lemon from Toyota of Orange. Tell 'em the old traveling preacher Brother Jarvis from the Love Connection sent you!"

"Are you kidding me? What is this thing? Words fail" fairly summarized our collective reaction on seeing this synthetic throwback to an old-time country evangelist who always appeared on the verge of having a heart attack at any moment.

But here was a clue—"Toyota of Orange"—that gave him away, when a viewer from Orange, California, recognized him as an ex-car salesman turned tent evangelist who had miraculously disappeared in a car crash some months earlier. As no foul play was expected, the strange case was never investigated, and now the mystery only deepened. What was his face doing in the sky? Was he still in one piece? Possibly abducted and digitized by an alien exploratory craft? Were the strangers, then, already among us?

These questions were unnerving, to say the least. As noted, these electromagnetic storms flared sporadically and without warning, other than a short, melodic prelude of tubular bells, in virtually all nations and in many tongues, often accompanied by changes in the actual weather, including incandescent lightning and hellacious cracks of thunder. And yet, lacking an explanation for the incidents, most world leaders followed the lead of the United States and variously attributed the Jarvis phenomenon to Russian dirty tricks, a pirate radio ship operating off the coast of Africa, or a Mexican border transmitter perhaps financed by Toyota of Orange.

Even given the advanced state of spy satellite technology, it was impossible to trace the original source of the transmissions, much less a location in space. The question for us—assuming the outbursts were from the planetoid, as we suspected—was whether they were intended as disinformation or merely a means of demonstrating their alien power over our world and thereby laying the psychological foundation for our future subjugation.

We nevertheless continued to aim our call signal and weekly radio show in the general direction of the invisible Planet 10's last known quadrant, though well aware of the obvious folly of such an endeavor. Even putting aside the immense distance such a signal would have to travel, what did we expect to happen if by some chance the alien ship intercepted our radio signal? A return call? A slightly less far-fetched plan—a last desperate hope, more accurately—involved the previously mentioned possibility of instantaneous brain wave transmission, or telepathy, a subject in which Buckaroo had long been interested.

"If we could tweak the electrical frequency of our theta brain waves, a technical application utilizing human telepathy might be doable," Buckaroo speculated one day. "Remember how the World Crime League, working with the KGB, almost succeeded in electronically programming an entire generation of American kids through antennas disguised as mouse ears and raccoon-tail caps. Luckily, somebody at Disney blabbermouthed to J. Edgar Hoover during sex or we'd all be Russian-speaking phone zombies."

"Yep . . . something to think about," I said, already suspecting that he was miles ahead of me. "Luckily, the epidemic of premature facial hair on prepubescent kids gave the plot away, only to have the brainwashing technology find its way into our own government's nefarious thought-control projects, like kids' braces and emulsified lipids in tattoo ink, all capable of subliminal radio reception."

With a friendly grin he reminded me, "Not to mention the increasing number of crypto-blipverts we're seeing lately on virtually every television channel and new streaming service. I think we both know how things work and who's behind the curtain . . ."

"I think we both know how things work," I replied.

He nodded thoughtfully, saying, "We have to tread carefully here . . . a whole field of soft science we need to analyze in depth. You know I've long been fascinated by this but keeping my work under wraps for security reasons. But let us suppose there is a universal psychic frequency and let us further suppose, for the sake of experiment, that the frequency to connect all isolated clusters of ganglia to the greater universal community is fifty-one point five or four hundred thirty-two hertz, further supposing . . ."

He fell silent, momentarily lost in thought, before adding, "Anyway, Mrs. Johnson is working on it and, because of the emergency, I'm also putting together an ad hoc group over in Special Weapons to complete development of my shock wave Bubble Gun, ASAP."

"I'll get right on it," I said immediately.

But he demurred, informing me, "I'm putting Pecos and Li'l Daughter in charge. What's the status of the directed energy beam project?"

"The Jelly Beam? We've been working like dogs to miniaturize it, still diagnosing a couple of—"

Buckaroo cut in impatiently: "Ready for field tests or not?"

"I'm not sure," I replied, at once seeing a certain misery invade his face and wishing I could take back my words.

" 'Not sure,' Reno . . . ? That's a fake answer, Reno . . . the answer of a politician and a weasel. What are the only answers we accept?"

"Only two," I recalled at once. " 'I don't know' or 'I know for a fact' . . ."

"So which is it?"

" 'I don't know' is my answer."

"Then find out. We're clear?"

"Clear as a bell," I said, perspiration trickling down my back.

"Sorry to be testy, but we're under the gun," he explained. "I also need you to focus on a weaponized aerosol for now, perhaps our Graco paint sprayer or a kid's hydrosoaker. I'm thinking you, Jhonny, the Marchioness, and Hoppalong . . . I want a potent insect killer with additives of dextrose monohydrate, chlorpyrifos, aluminum salts, and peanut butter."

"Nasty. Weaponized corn syrup and insecticide . . . ?" I said.

"A little extra green energy and killing power," he replied. "Empty the soft drink fountain dispenser in the bunkhouse cantina. Mrs. Johnson will know what to do and how to mix the whole concoction with emulsifiers and saturated vegetable oils . . . and also maybe add a malodor function, something stinky that a Lectroid might like."

With difficulty I swallowed my pride, as well as my inherent objection to putting my imprimatur, as it were, upon what promised to be a dreadful killing tool, and I merely replied, "I'll get right on it. With any luck we can design a cheap, functional apparatus that anyone can use. I'll even throw in a mess of heavy metals and free radicals to maximize oxidative DNA damage."

"You're right, Reno," he said with the merest trace of a smile. "I don't like killing any better than you, but neither are we a rug to walk over. What have we come to if we don't defend our home for future generations? If need be, we'll give these wind-up monkeys a hot welcome they won't forget."

BRAINSTORMING WITH BUCKAROO

Indeed, the future of our beloved Mother Earth was at stake, so now was not the time to sit around and feel sorry for ourselves or our enemies, much less debate ethical niceties. Although we knew next to nothing about the inhabitants of the planetoid, the example of John Whorfin—a Red Lectroid known for his vile atrocities against all comers—predisposed us to expect the same belligerence from these new arrivals. "Hope for the best, prepare for the worst," as always, was a sapient motto, along with Tommy's corollary: "Hope means Jack and shite, and Jack left town."

Our confirmation bias in this regard doubtless reflected our growing frustration from circular discussions that went nowhere. It also did not help—and here I can only speak for my own working group (Hoppalong, Pilgrim Woman, the Marchioness, and Pinky Carruthers)—that Buckaroo's own thoughts were mostly kept from us, revealed only in our daily general sessions, when he listened to the ideas all the *chavrusas* had managed to generate . . .

. . . such as the possibility of Buckaroo traveling via another dimension to Planet 10 for a face-to-face meeting with John Emdall Thunderpump, who was thought to favor him. But as Buckaroo explained to Li'l Daughter—whose suggestion it was—the odds of the operation actually succeeding loomed impossibly long, especially on a first attempt, given that one had to consider not only distance and our dearth of information about Planet 10's erratic behavior but also the Earth's rotational and orbital speeds, not to mention the rotational speed of the Milky Way and our galaxy's own velocity through space.

"Keep in mind, even if I were certain of Planet 10's location and somehow devised a flight plan through the proper bog hole"—he did his best to explain to us bemused, puzzled listeners—"remote-control guidance doesn't work from one dimension to another. Navigation is strictly by the seat of my pants and three orthogonal accelerometers, as well as certain vibration techniques I've learned through trial and error . . ."

"Not much room for error if you miss the exit ramp," Tommy blurted after a good laugh, thereby exacting a stern look from Buckaroo . . . who continued:

"Thanks, Tom. What I'm getting at is that I may well miss the proper portal, which can be no larger than a crack in a sidewalk, or else I get through and find it a one-way pivot, expecting to arrive at Planet 10, only to learn I overshot and there's no way back."

"You mean even the tiniest variance in trajectory could throw you off by a million miles and a dimension or two," gushed Mrs. Johnson, who arrived just at that moment with a tray of caramel flan and crumb cake.

"Not only that," said Buckaroo, "but emotional information also affects the electromagnetic field. I can't explain yet why this is so, but I've learned that a shift in my emotions produces a marked effect on vibrating corpuscles and wave-particle duality, as measured by my new, improved SQUID . . ."

"So feelings, not facts?" asked Pilgrim Woman, our new genomics researcher and reigning *Guitar Hero* champion.

"Feelings are facts," answered Buckaroo, "in the same way that words left unspoken are still words. They may only exist in the rearview mirror, however."

"Your squid, Buckaroo . . . ? Is that what I think it is?" said Mrs. Johnson, still butting in.

"My superconducting quantum interference device," Buckaroo tried to explain . . .

. . . as Tommy interrupted to clarify, "Consisting of a tunnel-barrier sandwich . . ."

. . . whereupon Mrs. Johnson appeared to experience a frisson of delight and declared, "I love it when you talk about tunnels and your squid thruster, and especially the power of our feelings, Buckaroo—"

"It's a mite more complicated than that," Buckaroo said with a slight grimace.

"Complicated, my rear end," she replied, "even if it is only a starting point for further investigation—which we may learn somehow ties in with the hermetic principle of vibration."

"As well as the Buddhist—a logistical nightmare, but essentially you're correct, Eunice. What my gizmo, the OSCILLATION OVERTHRUSTER, does is twofold," he said with a childlike gleam in his eyes. "It simultaneously synchronizes and amplifies submicroscopic wave energy below the electron level while also shooting subatomic tachyons, exciting the oscillating frequency of dark energy, and loosening attractors at different energy levels, creating a waterfall effect and allowing the superslick Jet Car to acquire negative mass and pass through resistance—vibrating solid matter—on a single Bose-Einstein macrowave that interestingly enough produces the high beat frequency and complex waveforms characteristic of motile eukaryotic organelles. Of course it's not quite that simple . . ."

"This is so much fun," Mrs. Johnson interrupted in her husky smoker's voice, albeit in the same lighthearted vein.

"You mean to say that you pass through solid matter vibrating at the frequency of subunits of living cells? Cilia, flagella, and all that?" Lady Asquith-Gillette inquired in her upper-crust Oxbridge accent.

Buckaroo nodded, saying, "A very Buddhist notion, no, Marchioness? Everything vibrating as one, perhaps allowing us passage through . . ."

"Peace and love, indeed," I said.

Of course there was also the variable of interdimensional slippage or leakage to consider, a phenomenon Buckaroo described in this way: "Think of the multiverse as a giant onion or a series of concave circles . . ."

"You get onion rings with that?" wisecracked Li'l Daughter.

"All you can eat and the best you ever had," replied Buckaroo in the same bright spirit. "That's why I prefer to visit the Fifth Dimension, a field of retained experience I call the *Book of Life*, where every traveler is on familiar ground."

"The Fifth is like a scrapbook," Mrs. Johnson explained proudly, "containing everything you ever did, right, Buckaroo? The Sixth is like your rusty altered memory, the Seventh your ideal fantasy, and the Eighth . . ."

"The Eighth . . . the highest rung of heaven or bottom rung of hell," Buckaroo mused. "The only thing we have to fear is fear itself."

Li'l Daughter couldn't resist mouthing the credo herself. "The only thing . . ."

"The depth of your soul crushed under the weight of your doubts," he continued. "A sacred domain beyond the comprehension of any who've never seen it. Black and trackless, and cold, without pattern or form . . . no up, no down, just expansive nothingness that lends itself to greater velocity if you can stick to your course. A fellow can get lost pretty easy, especially if he has car trouble . . ."

Here he opened a drawer and produced what looked to be a miniature OVERTHRUSTER duct taped to an automatic .22 caliber pistol, a bottle of bubble liquid, and a modified Ryobi power pack, saying, "I've been working on a little something . . . haven't quite worked the bugs out . . . oops!"

In a veritable split second, we all reacted to a gunshot and a superheated strobe beam that suddenly crackled from the device and blasted a hole in the ceiling, raining down plaster.

"Sweet hellacious Jesus!" Mrs. Johnson yelped, still with fingers in her ears despite the fact that the mini sonic booms and the blinding ray of light had ceased almost as soon as they had begun. "What the—?"

"A sonoluminescent beam, Mrs. Johnson," Buckaroo elucidated. "Basically light resulting from microbubbles of sound and excited to a temperature hotter than the sun, produced by a mega-kilovolt battery and a miniature OVERTHRUSTER. I call it a Bubble Gun."

"I'll be got-damn—that's one serious ass-kicking .22," Tommy marveled, as Buckaroo carefully reaimed the device at a life-size human torso of ballistic gel and pressed the trigger, igniting another blinding blast that caused the torso to smoke and vibrate and then dissolve into what appeared to be a swirl of invisible syrup. In fact, except for a flurry of dancing dots before our eyes, it seemed the whole world had vanished in a heartbeat, except for the smell.

"Where's everything gone?! I can't see! Anybody else?" Tommy shouted.

"Did we croak?" said Pecos. "Smells like something dead, rancid!"

"What are those little specks banging together? Surely not big mosquitoes?" the Marchioness wanted to know.

"Not mosquitoes, Lady G," Buckaroo replied. "You're looking at fading electron bursts, my tracer bullets in the Eighth Dimension . . . sorry for the skunky smell."

"Sorry . . . ? My stars, the alt-universe! Seeing it with my own eyes!" exclaimed the noblewoman with awestruck reverence . . .

. . . as our vision and the room now returned to their prior normal state, except for several jagged bullet holes in the ballistic-gel torso and the wall behind it, leaving Buckaroo to attempt to explain. "Still doesn't feel right. It's a bad job—still learning some hard lessons—but it could make a great little tool in a pinch. If nothing else, you've all seen that when we think of solid objects, we're actually just imagining things."

"And the wallpaper! Look!" Li'l Daughter exclaimed with glee, pointing at the bullet holes in the wall. "You peeled it away, Buckaroo, just like we were talking about! Are you telling us you could walk through that wall?"

"Walk? Not recommended. Only if I had a jet thruster, perhaps," cautioned Buckaroo.

But, unable to resist, Tommy now rushed toward the wall in question, saying, "Hello. I'm tired of reality lying to me."

Then, without another word, he ran smack into solid matter, giving us all a needed laugh and a welcome dose of common sense.

STRAIGHT-SHOOTING THE BREEZE

Small wonder that, even today, these discussion sessions are crystal clear in my mind's eye. Some dozen of us are seated cross-legged on tatami mats (though Tommy often occupied the lone winged club chair, complaining of soreness) . . . while our chief kneels, *seiza*-style, at a low shittah wood table in front of several plastic milk bins full of fan mail, a rack of antique katana swords, an upright piano, and his enormous cabinet housing anthropological specimens from around the world: particularly shrunken heads, pickled brains, and a collection of abnormal human skulls. Too, out of the corner of my eye, I see the cats—Penny's fluffy calico Gertrude Stein and Buckaroo's black-and-white Tux—curled up together on a windowsill between a colorful mix of Indian corn and cut flowers in *kutani* porcelain. Next to them, a floor-to-ceiling bookcase is chock-a-block with vintage pistols, his mother's Arriflex 35 mm camera, and an eclectic selection of volumes: *The Prince*, the *Encyclopédie*, *The Art of War*, essayists on the order of Bacon, Mandeville, Marcus Aurelius, Li Zongwu, and a range of Chinese and Japanese poetry from Du Fu and Li Bai to Basho, along with others with whom I am regrettably less familiar. Leather-bound first editions include Dumas (*père*) and Walter Scott, Lavoisier's *Elementary Treatise*, Newton's *Principia Mathematica* . . . while in a special illuminated shelf of honor reside works by various of Buckaroo's friends and lovers (Kristeva and Nussbaum, among others) and Galileo's famous "Letter to the Grand Duchess Christina."

The walls themselves are mostly bare, both by his choice and because his medals, photographs, gold and platinum records, honorary degrees, and other memorabilia are displayed in the visitors' center. Here in his intimate study, we see only an honorary Hiroshima Carp baseball jersey, a few Currier & Ives prints of frontier scenes alongside a Virgin of Guadalupe, a Grandma Moses, an old lithograph of the outlaw John Wesley Hardin, and a triad of *nobori* streamers with kanji letters. The first of these, a stark black-and-white flag, carries a single message in three parts:

AT PEACE UNTIL DISTURBED

WE WILL FIGHT

BY THE RULES OF ANCIENT LIBERTY

On the second appears the legend PROGRESS OVER PROTOCOL. And on the third, the four sides of a black diamond in a white field are formed by the words FARMER, ARTISAN, SCHOLAR, WARRIOR.

Taken together, the three banners capture the essence of who we are—although to the military brass and government nomenklatura in the Pentagon and elsewhere, we represent the late entry in the race; yet it would be up to us, coming from behind, to bring benefit to the world community and, with luck, even save the planet from the enigmatic alien race known as Lectroids, of one sort or another.

To achieve that end, however, we needed solid leads to pursue; and the first of these came to us in the form of a plain envelope bearing a

Vatican postage stamp, a woman's fine handwriting, and no return address. Inside were pictures of a blank-looking Lectroid and photocopies of a pair of highly unusual invoices revealing that a total of "35 Lectroids . . . assorted partial Lectroids and Lectroid products" had been sold for "1,000 liquid greens" (most likely $100,000 cash) to something called the "Equestrian Order of the Holy Sepulchre of Jerusalem."

"That's precious," I said, examining the photocopies. "Can this be real?"

"Why not the Knights of Columbus, while they're at it . . . ?" remarked Tommy. "Could always be a fake, but I guess it's worth checking."

"Could be legit, Reno," added Buckaroo thoughtfully. "I recall a report going around a couple of months back that one of the Bulgarian Army's old Shilkas was stolen by a similar chivalric order . . . and never recovered. A similar story with that surface-to-air missile system stolen off a freight train in Belgium not too long ago . . ."

"Probably happens more than we know," remarked Pecos.

"A Shilka," I said, recalling from memory a page from *Jane's Defence Review*. "Russian: a ZSU 23-4, *zenitnaya samokhodnaya ustanovka* . . . mobile antiaircraft gun . . . actually four autocannons on a modified light amphibious tank. A moldy oldie, but probably still lethal enough, even without being converted to a TEL for a SAM pod."

Buckaroo nodded and pointed to some scribbling at the bottom of the second receipt.

"Notice the sloppy shorthand . . . 'services of Abbot Costello for issues large and small,' in addition to the hundred grand, signed by the Marquis of Lincoln," Buckaroo said, trying to keep a straight face. "Not the first time we've heard that name or seen this handwriting."

"General Wagoneer . . ." Pecos correctly guessed. "Bizarro. I wonder if Pope Innocent knows anything about this Abbot Costello."

There was an easy enough way to find out. With one hand Buckaroo now reached for his phone and placed a call to the pope's private mobile number, and with the other he released several of his prized Japanese hunting crickets from their bamboo cage. These appeared to amuse him no end as they went hopping merrily across his desk, traversing numerous maps and drawings of fanciful mechanical devices in the style of Leonardo. Elsewhere amid the clutter sat bottles of various colors and a miniature distilling outfit with a rack of test tubes, Buckaroo's morning coffee and brandy, a few broken lumps of Mrs. Johnson's black bread, a mathematical proof that he appeared to be midway through, the disassembled pieces of a Walther pistol, and a short stack of books, among them a musty old volume of Virgil in the Latin and a fine leather edition of Thackeray's *Vanity Fair* that transported me back to the day he purchased it from a bookseller along the Seine in Paris.

"Strange," Buckaroo interrupted as if he hadn't heard us, abruptly hanging up the phone after several minutes of silence. "Getting hung up on by a rude somebody after ten minutes of the Vatican's medieval on-hold music. I never had trouble getting through to Pope Innocent before."

"Maybe he's out watching over his flock," suggested Pecos.

"Or kicking back and sipping a cold one," joked Tommy.

"Let's hope one of you is right," Buckaroo said. "Truth be told, perhaps the pope merely misplaced his phone or left it in his other robe. The incendiary individual who answered his phone wasn't exactly helpful. Yet another anonymous psychopath."

Absorbed in deeper matters, he now peered off into the ether and said, "The situation in which we find ourselves is strange. Waiting for some startling bit of information, feeling in subjection to an unseen menace, an invisible authority that is threatening to destroy us. But let's say Lizardo is indeed dead and we capture John Whorfin, assuming he still exists but in some other corporeal form . . . then what?"

"We kill him," said Tommy. "Phawk being a gentleman."

"And the gentleman, or woman or child or animal, whose body he might presently inhabit?" Buckaroo asked. "How do you split them?"

"I don't know and I'm not real belly-ached about it," Tommy retorted with a shrug. "Maybe just unstaple them . . . or with a machete or a chainsaw, after he's dead."

"After who's dead?" Buckaroo pressed.

"After they're both dead. Get a grip, Buckaroo," said Tommy. "We're talking about saving the planet, so what's one life—?"

"One planet versus one life," Buckaroo pondered, turning the question over in his mind while pretending to accept Tommy's argument. "Even in survival mode, it's important not to lose sight of our principles. And what makes us think we can trust the word of someone who threatens to destroy our world, killing billions? What's to say they won't blow us up anyway? If they would kill a planet, what's a lie to them?"

AGAINST THE WORLD CRIME LEAGUE ET AL.   253

"Good point, Buckaroo," I cut in. "But isn't doing nothing the far greater risk? I don't see that we have that luxury, especially if we're just a fun-size snack for these guys in their mighty warship. What are our options, really?"

Buckaroo nodded and framed the question as a thought experiment: "What if we captured Whorfin—let us say alone and in his pure form—and I gave him the key to the Jet Car, so that he could leave Earth? What incentive would his enemies have to destroy us, then?"

"Maybe because it'd be one sick twist that would royally piss off the space monkeys," surmised Tommy. "Why not just tell everybody in the world to put all their belongings on the front porch so the thieves can have easy pickings and maybe leave us alone . . . ?"

"Bringing me back to my original point of why we should trust them," Buckaroo said. "Or jump to their every string pull . . ."

"Or, by the same logic, why take the Nova Police seriously," I pointed out.

"Does their mere word cut it, in other words?" echoed Mrs. Johnson, who had remained in the room to listen. "I hate liars. That stuff really heats me up."

"Thank you, Mrs. Johnson," Buckaroo said. "But Reno is probably right. Given the existential nature of the threat against us and the technological disparity between our two species, I suppose we have to trust the Nova Police report on the ship's stated intentions . . ."

"I could bring up more points but I don't have one," Tommy said.

Buckaroo nodded without comment and continued, "At the moment, as I see it, we have three big problems: the rumored spaceship, the illegal transfer of Jet Car technology and possible Lectroid biomatter to parties unknown . . . and the whereabouts of . . . Whorfin."

He had very nearly said "Penny" before correcting himself, and serious strain was evident on his face. "Of these, the priority is naturally Whorfin, but, as we all know, to unravel one secret usually helps unravel another."

"There's also the shitbird law," remarked Tommy. "Every shitbird has a left and a right wing, thereby giving each wing plausible deniability. But they're both stirring the punch bowl of shite—mark my words. Something phawked up is going down."

"Very astute, Tommy," Buckaroo said. "Something like the magpie theory, then . . . digging up whatever goodies we can use from different places to build tiers of information. It is certainly possible that either of the other trails—the stolen Jet Car docs or the Lectroid body bits—might lead us to Whorfin, if he is in fact still with us, as well as his human counterpart, Hanoi Xan. But at this point it appears the only common link between the two is the man who may have opened this can of worms in the first place, General Wagoneer . . ."

"Stewing in his own dark juices, with zero self-esteem," Mrs. Johnson observed astutely. "Bound on a hellish crusade to wreak vengeance . . . on himself."

"That's the way I read it, too," said Buckaroo. "I'm afraid what he really wants is a ticket home, a painless death."

Their assessment was certainly valid. Wild Bill Wagoneer's past was littered with failed relationships, if we were to believe his story; but that was precisely the question: how far to trust him? We could be forgiven for being naturally wary, but what choice did we have but to care for him and nurse his festering psyche along?

Certain of our doubts were answered a few days later when Wagoneer was "heart-checked" by Mrs. Johnson—by which I mean she took a ruler to his knuckles, took away his lunch and finally his dinner, before he decided to stick up for himself and "pitched a bitch," as she put it. With a small group of us hooting and hollering, the two of them wrestled out by the old chuck wagon and at one point appeared to simulate animal sex—with Mrs. Johnson on top—before ultimately calling it a draw.

"Get your fat-ass carcass off me," protested the general.

"He's a scrapper, he's got heart," Mrs. Johnson announced, giving a thumbs-up verdict. "He'll do."

XVI. A GAME TWO CAN PLAY

> One day the great European war will come out of some damn
> foolish thing in the Balkans.
> —Otto von Bismarck

Meanwhile, Manny Magdalene's unannounced trip to Bosnia began with visits to various of Baltazar's odd treehouses, all unmanned and spread across Bosnia and Herzegovina, their huge spotlights controlled entirely from a remote location. Their message, aimed at the heavens and flashed hourly in Morse code, was "You are not alone. I am the head man to talk to."

On his arrival in Sarajevo, he likewise found no sign of the cardinal, who in recent months had taken to calling himself Cardinal Shine Shine and sacrificing domestic animals in church. Manny also learned from local criminal contacts that the cardinal had departed for Rome some days earlier with a large retinue of local and out-of-town paintball enthusiasts. While such trips to Rome were not uncommon for him, he had left hints on this occasion that he might not return, going so far as to leave the keys to his house and luxury automobiles with his bishops.

Navigating the city on his folding bicycle, Manny found both defenders and detractors of the cardinal among ordinary Sarajevans. Although his critics seemed somewhat fearful to speak, virtually all agreed that Baltazar was on his way to high places, perhaps even the throne of Saint Peter. This prospect was spoken of with much local pride and appeared to be a goal that Baltazar enthusiastically shared. A photograph discovered by Manny on a visit to a local newspaper showed the cardinal dressed like a medieval knight for a paintball competition, while two others showed him on a visit to the Church of the Dormition of the Theotokos on holy Mount Athos in Greece. In one of the latter, he is seen holding hands with an Orthodox primate, while in the other he sits insouciantly on the throne once occupied by Byzantine emperors, with other primates looking on uncomfortably.

Later, winding his way inconspicuously in a borrowed Trabant 601, Manny arrived at Baltazar's rustic mountain retreat, whose twin gold-plated, Russian-style onion domes he recognized at once as machine gun turrets with sweeping views of the so-called Pyramid of the Sun and the road by which he had come. No one answered his knock, but a window offered admittance to the chalet's single great room, where tantalizing clues about its part-time resident abounded: signs of a hasty departure, timber-and-chink walls decorated with taxidermied animal heads and posters of professional wrestlers, and atop a large crate marked CLAYMORE MINES, toy army men girded for war on a biblical map of the Plain of Megiddo. In a far corner, a full suit of antique armor lay like a corpse upon a bed, next to a wardrobe full of vintage military uniforms of obscure provenance—some of which even Manny, a Sandhurst graduate, could not identify. Out back stood a portable privy, a military-style obstacle course, a hot tub apparently used both as a baptismal font and a cockfighting ring, and dilapidated spartan barracks littered with food wrappers and swaths of graffiti scrawled in Old Church Slavonic.

Most damning of all, the detached garage housed a pair of Lamborghinis, a mini laboratory, and a pair of refrigerators full of pickle jars of bizarre biological specimens in murky liquid, the putrid smell of which instantly reminded Manny of a papaya health drink or those septic Lectroid shot samples sent to his employer Hanoi Xan earlier by the pseudonymous Mr. French.

In a number of jars there were, in fact, papaya seeds and their hybrid Lectroid sproutings, hideous beyond description, that appeared to be influenced by demonic forces. Taken as a tantalizing whole, the clues suggested to Manny a far bigger conspiracy than he had envisioned, apparently linking Baltazar to the mystery man Mr. French; but what did it all mean? Was Cardinal Baltazar's consuming interest in paintball merely a hobby or a harbinger of something more dangerous? And what of the stream of apparent visitors to the site? The cardinal's neighbors— at least the two who would speak to Manny—told of hearing gunshots and foreign languages in the woods at all hours.

Although none of this made sense to Manny, he nonetheless took diligent notes, photographs, and even chemical samples; and his one-man fishing expedition might have ended without event if he had not suffered a running attack of local dysentery and felt the urge to relieve himself in the outdoor latrine, where he was surprised by containers of catnip and tiny screech-like noises from down in the shite hole. Something—or someone—was down there; and Manny, bending over, could make out movement in the darkness . . . a vague scurrying of small rat-like creatures, but hard as nutshells . . . prompting him to flick on his cigarette lighter for a better view. In that instant before all went black and he and the johnny were blown skyward, he glimpsed a cesspool of half-developed Lectroid nymphs spitting and writhing, sending a weak salvo of baby darts in his direction.

BLUE BLAZES TO THE RESCUE

The next thing he saw, besides bright flashlights, were the faces of a pair of youthful Blue Blazes in Hong Kong Cavalier T-shirts. For a dazed moment he thought they were angels, then nurses; but neither young woman was smiling and things clearly had gotten physical. One of them was pulling his hair, while the other spanked him repeatedly with a black leather shoe.

"You're hitting me hard!" he yelped. "I'm a nice guy!"

"Enough! Hey, Mister, can you hear me . . . ?" said his paddler in a thick Slavic accent. "It's okay—we have ambulance on the way. Your wife just called your phone. You are really him, Brit home secretary, half-assed member of the British Parliament, yes . . . ?"

"I don't know what you're talking about," he said reflexively before they slapped him again.

"You fear us, no?"

"*Da*," Manny replied groggily, but frankly he couldn't be sure. Too many questions. And he seemed to be bleeding.

"Then why are you wearing a gaudy World Crime League Rolex . . . ?"
one of his interrogators wanted to know.

"With Hanoi Xan's initials . . ." added the other.

"Take it," said Manny, aching all over and on the point of a nervous
breakdown. "I give it to you. Just stop hitting me."

But the sharp blows continued, along with the questions. "You are
terrible person. What kind of example are you putting out there for our
youth? Tell the truth or we will drink your little tears."

Manny closed his eyes and wondered what sky he was staring into,
how much trouble he was in, and whether he had left his spirit animal,
the hyena, back in the shitehouse. What had just happened seemed
surreal; and never mind the baby darts the monstrous little creatures
had fired at him, what would he say to his humorless chief, Hanoi Xan
("heed my word or face my sword")?

For that matter, what would he say to these two impertinent women,
one of whom kept paddling him, harder and harder, saying, "What is
Baltazar's business? Where is Hanoi Xan? Where is Penny Priddy?"

To these questions and others, the two might have extracted answers
by employing the interrogation techniques found in the Blue Blaze
handbook, had not an ambulance and a small force of police arrived to
whisk Manny away. But all was not lost, as our dedicated Blue Blaze
sisters—Darinka Water Moccasin and Zoyenka Racehorse—
kept Manny's phone, which they promptly sent to the Institute for
forensic analysis.

Information concerning Cardinal Baltazar's intentions would remain
in short supply, however. It was as yet unimagined that the respected
cardinal was cheating the World Crime League out of its share of local
rackets and the international drug trade, as well as papal royalties, nor,
in a more fundamental sense, could we begin to guess what kind of
psychological wound or errant teaching made a man of the cloth cynical
enough to betray his oath before God. Who, in other words, was
Cardinal Baltazar, and what was his long game?

It is also likely that we shall never discover precisely how or what
Manny communicated to Hanoi Xan from his convalescent bed in
Sarajevo, although the subject of Baltazar's treehouses was doubtless part
of the conversation . . . as it was part of ours. Although our own Blue
Blazes had uncovered the existence of the structures some weeks

previous, the report had stalled somewhere in the pipeline; and in any case, what would we have made of the news without more pieces to the puzzle? As I have said on many occasions, we did our best, but even the most fastidious investigator inevitably misses certain clues that in retrospect should have been obvious. Were our best efforts for naught, then? A waste of time? Do not think I have not asked myself that very question and yet found solace in Gandhi's words often quoted by Buckaroo Banzai: "Whatever you do will be insignificant, but it is very important that you do it."

BACK AT THE RANCH

Around the same time, however, Contreras, Xan's operative in Panama (or someone acting in his name), wired a message to General Wagoneer's "Antoine French" account, using a previously agreed upon code word. The sender posed several technical questions concerning material Buckaroo had sent as "Mr. French" in a previous email; of particular interest was the Meissner effect as it related to Heisenberg's early oscillator and the so-called Lance of Destiny.

"Was not von Braun's friend Meissner working during Operation Paperclip along similar lines on a giant superconducting, dimensional-shifting balloon that expands and expands until it warps time . . . ?" inquired the author of the email (who we now know was Dr. Paraquat). "I am talking about a squirting warp bubble . . . which some have called Meissner's Folly . . . and yet . . ."

This particular section gave us reason to smile, since the "warp bubble" effect had laid the foundation for Buckaroo's vaunted Bubble Gun, a hypersonic acoustic-blast weapon theoretically capable of superheating sonoluminescent microbubbles to a temperature exponentially hotter than the sun. More technical jargon and a specific list of questions followed, along with a promise of twenty thousand dollars and an invitation for Mr. French to travel personally to Panama with more documents—to which Buckaroo promptly replied in French's name, answering Paraquat's questions convincingly while demanding one hundred thousand dollars and a personal meeting with Hanoi Xan in exchange for any further information.

"We've chummed the water. Now to drag the shark into the light," he told me.

"Wouldn't mind lighting up Xan's world," I said, "especially after the way his boys lit up our emissaries of peace."

"So we pay them the same?"

"I feel like we need to," I replied.

"You think I mean to let it go, Reno?"

"Of course not," I said defensively. "Just imagine the heartache of our Blue Star families, that's all."

"I don't have to imagine. I've spoken with them," he informed me somewhat sharply. "We'll have something to say about it in good time, so direct your concern elsewhere, Reno . . . on finding John Whorfin, for example. Is that acceptable?"

End of discussion.

Thus awaiting an answer to our proposal for a meeting with Xan, we wrestled with bigger questions, such as the end of the world and the irony that everything—and yet nothing at all—seemed to be happening all at once. There was still no actionable intelligence concerning Penny's whereabouts, no news from space, and no proof that John Whorfin had escaped the rotting residue that used to be his earthly host, Dr. Emilio Lizardo . . . although Buckaroo's autopsy revealed evidence of copious amounts of immunosuppressants and organ and skeletal dysplasia of a kind never seen.

Yet he also knew from his experience as a physician and a scientist that while a knotty problem might be cracked occasionally with a lucky hypothesis, it was far more likely that a thousand and one attempts, and much digging, would be required to find a solution. For this reason he has made it a point always to stress the importance of not rushing to judgment until all the data has been collected, sifted, and weighed. Even a so-called fact can have two faces like a coin, as it relates to the position of the observer; and Buckaroo freely admits there are more esoteric secrets in the world than even he can explain.

This is not to say that Buckaroo Banzai is a religious man. His remarks likening religion to a pathogen have been widely disseminated, and widely misunderstood. By comparing a little religion to an inoculation against the full-blown disease, he was recognizing the beneficial aspects of religion—ethical credos and humane praxis—while warning against any claims of absolute truth.

Yet, even as someone to whom organized religion was largely irrelevant, Buckaroo had certain qualms about a Catholic pope endorsing a brand of vitamins or shoelaces or men's grooming products; and the possibility that Pope Innocent's decisions were no longer his to make was even more disquieting, particularly if his agent Cardinal Baltazar had ties to the World Crime League. It only made sense that Baltazar was behind the purchase of the ZSU 23-4, approximately three dozen grown Lectroids on the international black market (a rounded number, and highly suspect, to be sure), and assorted Lectroid bits and pieces by certain chivalric orders used as his straw men. But to what end? What was his next trick? To put his collection on display or sell them, either to governments or wealthy collectors? Or invite the apocalypse, the time-honored agenda of death cults?

And again I must mention unnamed pinstriped generals in the intelligence sector of the United States government, whose wrath over the loss of two of their prized mutants we had yet to feel but expected at any moment. On this score, Postmaster General Mantooth and even President Monroe could not help us or even tell us where the battle lines were drawn in all of this. In the end, it was just another case of us against the many.

Doubtless the possible confluence of these vectors—rogue church elements, government agents, the World Crime League, and alien Lectroids—kept Buckaroo awake at night; and he looked forward to having a chat with the man whose real name was Zoran Caiaphas Baltazar, equal parts hustler and impresario, who reportedly left his seminarian training in Djakovo for several years in order to become a third-rate professional wrestler and a joke of a matador in rural Andalusia. In both professions, he was known for his flamboyant capes and a murderous rage that drove him to attempt to impale his opponents—man or beast—with deadly weapons. Later, as a bishop in Schleswig-Holstein, he assumed a prominent executive role with the local orchestra and was known to enjoy conducting by popular request, likewise sporting a sword and cape on such occasions. Was he the reason Buckaroo had been unable to speak to Pope Innocent in these many months? It seemed so, but of course other conclusions were possible.

In view of such questions, Buckaroo convened an unusual meeting in which it was agreed to bring Baltazar under closer focus, using all means at our disposal.

"Perhaps Baltazar is only a red herring and a greedy opportunist, but we're talking about the lives of billions of people and the survival of the planet. This is one of those times when we can't afford to wait to find out that he's a worse person than we think," said Buckaroo, looking at High Sierra and the rest of the World Watch One cohort.

"Frontal attack or a backdoor hack?" High Sierra asked.

"All we want now is the truth. Not interested in giving him even a black eye at this point," Buckaroo replied. "Just mine everything in his background and monitor his communications . . ."

"With the help of the Blue Blaze community, we could get passwords a lot quicker . . . throw a net over the entire Vatican," High Sierra pointed out.

Buckaroo frowned but said, "Blanket surveillance, hiding behind our keyboards—a kick in the teeth of everything we stand for. But we're in dire need of information."

As for Manny, we had neither the time nor the resources to spearhead the case against him but could take credit for putting MI6 onto him some time earlier. It was equally obvious, however, that Manny was a clever fellow who likely could smuggle a donkey past the queen's Household Guards; and just as Buckaroo made hasty preparations to travel to Bosnia to interview him, the British Embassy quietly whisked the problematic MP out of the country.

Still, Manny's phone and some Lectroid samples had fallen into our laps—a boon, to be sure, but also a source of some added frustration, as his phone log read like a celebrity roll call, including most of the royal houses of Europe and a good number of its ranking political leaders. Frequent calls to a Malay number were of particular interest to us, as Henry Shannon was known to maintain a large base of operations in Penang. And what of the captured Lectroid samples, the reader may well ask . . . ?

EXOTIC DISHES

"Hold on to these and tell me if I'm crazy. I don't quite trust my senses," Buckaroo said to Pecos, Tommy, and me, taking two sealed biological-sample dishes from his cabinet of curiosities one afternoon before Thursday Table—a detail I recall because on this occasion we had decided to combine the weekly roundtable with our winter potluck regimental dinner. (Every summer we had an annual fish and mountain oyster fry.)

Need I mention, with some irony, that our chief's demeanor was no longer that of someone staggering at death's door? With the fate of the Earth at stake, he was once again the cool professional, reverting back to the Buckaroo of old whom we knew and loved . . . a vigorous competitor who loved nothing so much as a good contest. On this particular evening, we had concluded a spirited game of double-deck contract pinochle which included a free-ranging discussion of our progress (and frustration) on the current case, all of which might have explained his stirred-up look; but taking into account the telltale vein in his forehead that seemed to be atwitter, I knew different . . .

. . . as he deposited the twin sample dishes atop an old dog-eared issue of *The Psychoanalytic Quarterly* and began to strum a suspended A-chord on his favorite Stella guitar while ruminating aloud.

"Based on a quick analysis of these Lectroid pupae and cells lifted from Dr. Lizardo's remains, these are pretty remarkable creatures, lacking brains and other organs as we know them . . . which helps explain their ability to survive a destructive event and even regenerate, with the help of Miracle-Gro and an electrical current."

"Didn't we already know they were brainless?" said Pecos.

"I don't necessarily mean stupid," Buckaroo replied. "They're maybe on the low end of an IQ scale but possess extremely sensitive body awareness. They're noncarbon-based rhizomes wound helically around a vertical axis, essentially screws . . . giving them extraordinary structural strength. Their brains, indeed all their organs, are basically tangles of silicon-phosphate nerve circuits in a red feldspar exoskeleton, which helps explain their powers of luminescence and electronic cloaking—not dissimilar to the direct neuron-pixel circuits that give certain mollusks, like the squid or the octopus, a camouflage adaptation—as well as their unusual ability to slow their metabolism to just about zero, making them damn near immortal. As communal replicating machines, they're able to regenerate as well as reproduce clones of themselves both sexually and asexually, indeed possibly even through cannibalism and autophagy . . . like cancer itself, after a fashion."

"Whoa," said Tommy, laughing despite not understanding the meaning of some words. "You mean they're hermaphrodites? So just tell 'em to go phawk themselves . . ."

"I realize this might not compute, Tommy," Buckaroo explained, "but when I say they're likely capable of self-reproduction, I mean they're even able to impregnate their fecal material in a pinch . . . though exactly how, I can't say without more time to study them myself."

"Yuck," Pecos said, squirming.

"My reaction exactly, Pecos," Buckaroo informed her, "although it doubtless depends on a host of environmental factors."

"All the more reason to slap 'em down as quickly as the bastards sprout," I volunteered.

"Palm or backhand?" Tommy said half in jest . . .

. . . as Buckaroo piled on playfully, saying, "Reno, since you have a green belt in a dozen styles of martial arts, including underwater kajukenbo, that's up to you. Of course your signature move is the heartbreaker."

"Indeed," teased Pecos, her eyes gleaming. "No woman is immune to Reno's touch, not even Mona Peeptoe living the millionaire's life."

"I won't fib, no matter what the tabloids believe," I said. "She is rich, but we're just friends."

"That's what you always say, isn't it?" remarked Buckaroo. "Hear anything lately . . . since the famous Aqua Velva business?"

"Nothing," I said. "Zilch. Zippo. But we're not close—we're cordial. She's Canadian."

"Sounds like a new drink or a new song possibility," he wisecracked, prompting us all to laugh heartily, as he now turned back to the subject of the nature of Lectroids and pushed the petri dishes nearer to Tommy and me.

"Wow, what a fragrance," I said, sniffing with gusto.

"What do you smell, Reno?" Buckaroo asked.

"I smell flowers, jasmine," I replied.

"I smell the whole universe and see it through an entirely new prism," said Tommy.

"Interesting," remarked Buckaroo.

Yet the same scent instantly plunged me into an emotional funk, causing me to wish to gripe about this or that; I mean the messiness of his desk, the knickknacks, the photograph of Buckaroo's parents, the smell of a wet mop by the door, and the pungent odor of the small bowl of soup which he drank without a spoon, even the intent expression in his eyes as he watched me reach reluctantly for one of the sample dishes in which could be seen a dark porridge of wriggling matter.

"As you know, Señor Dentista's been running some experiments on the Lectroid samples from Bosnia, giving us some interesting insight into their hive mind . . ."

"Hive mind?" questioned Tommy.

"Or a collective soul, since it seems to lack a physiological basis, if you want to get downright spooky about it," Buckaroo replied. "He took two groups of samples, passing an electrical current through the first group at the signal of a beeping noise. As these experiments typically go, the excitement generated by the electrical shock soon came to be associated with the mere audio signal itself without need of the shock . . ."

"Smart little swamp creatures, right down to their bits and pieces," observed Pecos.

Buckaroo nodded, affirming, "Not only that, but when he placed only one of the conditioned samples into the second group, which had not been a part of the experiment, members of the second group mimicked the learned behavior of the first group, becoming excited at the mere sound of the beep."

"Freaky," Pecos said.

"This seems like woo," I opined.

"Things we don't understand we call woo or pseudoscience," observed Buckaroo. "But there may be a little more to it in this case. What's interesting is that further experimentation revealed that physical proximity of the messenger was not necessary for the exchange of information to occur. Up to a distance of fifty feet and through office walls, we see the same phenomenon."

"The hive mind? Or the power of the quantum?" I postulated.

"Interesting comparison, Reno. But protecting the hive, above all, for the greater good of the species," he continued between sips of soup. "Self-sacrifice for the greater good appears to be their only directive, even at the cellular level . . . along with an electromagnetic camouflage capability to fool their enemies."

"So in one way they're mentally weak," I said, "in the sense that they're servile and simple minded, and yet their mental powers in themselves are formidable."

He continued: "Recalling my friend Masaru Emoto's hypothesis, I placed several Lectroid samples in water and froze it. The frozen cubes contained amazing crystal patterns, which I first attributed to the Lectroids' chemical properties, but then I froze a second batch and placed the Lectroid samples close by but not actually in the water . . . and the result was the same. The mere proximity of the samples had the same effect, somehow causing the formation of the same unique crystal structures."

"Fascinating," I said. "If not woo, damn spooky."

By now, I was holding the dish not quite at arm's length but close enough to study its murky, disgusting contents—small critters swimming in a gravy-like glob. In merely staring at the tiny organisms, almost at once I began to feel woozy, experiencing the distinct sensation that my organs were melting and everything in my brain, every chain of thought that was not nailed down, was being sucked into an alien consciousness with which I nonetheless seemed acquainted, even comfortable. The sensation was like an ecstatic sexual release; the heavens opened and the angels sang . . . all while their alien fingers, like tiny daggers, probed me mentally for more private information.

Somewhere off in the distance Buckaroo was still talking: ". . . an ability to bypass the human eye's rods and cones and communicate directly with our synapses, perhaps by adding resistance to our neural circuits or even blocking synaptic processes altogether, somehow detemporalizing our mental states. A kind of brain fog can be the result. Merely to stand in the presence of Lectroid genetic material is to experience a certain mental unbalance, nausea, and chaotic negative feelings . . . by a process I still can't fully grasp."

"Like the legendary basilisk," I thought I heard Pecos say, and was aware, but only vaguely, of Tommy saying something else; but for the longest moment words were stuck in my throat, before I blurted out, "Good God, what's happening to me? I'm going into a time warp!"

XVII. BRAIN WAVES

> If you want to find the secrets of the universe, think in terms of
> energy, frequency and vibration.
> —Nikola Tesla

For a period of time—I have no idea how long—I was back in my
childhood, which appeared not in three dimensions but as a flat
representation . . . as a stranger watching myself on a screen, without
experiencing my own feelings of being left in the dust when my parents
divorced and then suddenly having the sensation of gripping a flaming
horseshoe, of all things.

"How did they know Daughter and I were just out in the yard pitching
horseshoes and I had the hot hand?" I asked, still flabbergasted.

"And no doubt anxious to get back to your competitive game,"
surmised Buckaroo correctly, handing Tommy the other sample dish.
"Try this one, Tom."

"No fair using my electron microscope?" asked Tommy.

Buckaroo shook his head, saying, "Just tell me what you see, Tom.
And don't feel bad, Reno—the same thing has happened to me. By
some unknown mechanism, they're able to conceal themselves behind
affective projections, projecting false scenes, desire images. That's
how they're able to operate outside our awareness . . . some sort of
electromagnetic camouflage emitting a strange psychosexual energy
that, for lack of a better word, I'm calling *orgonic* because of its

apparent ability to stimulate and produce tiny explosions at the neuronal level."

"And arouse a fella's loins . . . ?" Tommy asked.

"You're kidding," Buckaroo said.

"Just a little. Old Oscar Wiggly," Tommy replied, conspicuously feeling his crotch.

"So, orgonic energy is real?" posed Pecos skeptically. "Loony Wilhelm Reich was on to something?"

"Perhaps only in part, a universal frequency at which neurons vibrate," acknowledged Buckaroo, "but still I'm puzzled by how well they seem to know our brains . . . the exceedingly strong psychic, or mirror neuronal connection, accounting for their skills at affective mimicry."

"Is it my imagination," Tommy now commented, staring into the petri dish, "or is this dish crackling with phosphorescent baby batter and mirror neurons—bluish and aqua greens, for the most part—in which I see the laughing face of John Whorfin disguised as Lizardo? And now on closer inspection, that crazy asshole Cardinal Baltazar, smirking and ridiculing us . . . ?"

As an experiment, Buckaroo screeched *hoo-hoo* softly: a wise owl indeed and near enough for me to hear him shake his wings. A moment later his mournful hoot became the animated howl of a cold north wind that shot through Tommy's veins, chilling him to the bone and taking control of every part of his body.

"Damn," exhaled Tommy, apparently having entered an alternate reality. "Flying, then, observing my shadow on the earth far below, as I rose like Augustine the Hippo, through all bodily things to heaven and even higher, deeper into my own mind and beyond, to the region of never-failing plenty."

"Then why are you making a face?" asked Pecos.

She had a point. As if in a daze, Tommy leaned his head back and stared at Buckaroo's ceiling light, whose facets of etched glass shone like sapphires and diamonds.

"My solitude, as I see it in the shifting kaleidoscope of dreams . . . it does make me feel kind of hopped up on something," he said with a dramatic air, when suddenly a diatribe of unrepeatable profanity escaped his lips, causing him to set the petri dish down and scoot his chair back with alacrity.

"Yes, by all means, save your hot breath, Tommy," Buckaroo commented with a knowing smile, indicating the two dishes we had just held. "Reno's sample was Lectroid pupae. The second one, yours, the placebo, contained only flesh-eating screwworms in a mixture of celery and cream cheese."

It goes without saying that Tommy was open-mouthed. What could he say except what in fact he did say: "That hurts. So it was all in my head? Not the Lectroids?"

"Yes and no," said Buckaroo. "The power of suggestion, the power of the active subconscious, is a formidable thing. Let us say the Lectroid connects with us in some sense we don't understand. It wouldn't need control, just the power of suggestion, and our own mind does the rest. The aliens sense our fear and reflect it back to us in spades . . ."

"As plain as the eyes on your face," said Tommy. "I guess I dropped the ball, and I say that without pomposity."

"I compare it to the euphoria of a scuba diver's bends," Buckaroo was saying. "Apart from the Lectroids' electromagnetic, possibly telekinetic capability—I remember falling backward from what seemed like an inexplicable jolt at Yoyodyne—we know they favor the shock chop in close quarters, along with nerve poison darts fired from the mouth and their cloaca."

"Rawhide," murmured Pecos ominously. "Poor Rawhide."

After a second or two of silence, each of us spoke of our great friend, with Tommy putting it succinctly. "He never once let us down"—a sentiment shared by one and all.

"Damn butt darts," I recalled vividly. "I was nearly on the wrong end of one of those suckers."

Nodding, Buckaroo replied, "Of course that doesn't take into account Emdall's so-called 'Darkling' or ring-necked Lectroids, their different anatomical features and whatever weapons they're bringing. Also, now that we know—if the general is to be believed—that Whorfin is pregnant with John Emdall Thunderpump's embryo, the picture becomes even more cloudy . . ."

"If the general is to be believed . . ." Pecos said. "A big *if* . . ."

"On the one hand, Emdall Thunderpump might not know of Whorfin's condition," Buckaroo theorized. "On the other, she might not want it known back home because it might not sit well with her own kind . . ."

". . . that Whorfin is carrying her offspring," I said. "The Virgin Empress's offspring and scion of her tribe's archenemy."

"Exactly, Reno," he replied. "Put yourself in her shoes or Whorfin's. Without knowing the particular moieties or Malthusian math of Planet 10 Lectroids or their evolutionary chain, my educated guess is that the two Lectroid races once constituted a highly advanced civilization. But that was likely before overpopulation led to genocidal civil wars, which in turn decimated the gene pool, with the result that both groups now fight fanatically over the planet's scant resources and the crumbs of its former glory . . . leading to imperial expansion abroad and civil war at home, with both Whorfin and Emdall Thunderpump feeding off this mutual hatred to consolidate their own positions of power."

"That makes sense," Tommy agreed.

"But now imagine a threat to them both, a spawn born of their sexual congress, possibly with the unique royal lineage and moral authority to unite both groups, to bring them together and end the war . . . indeed usurp their power and consolidate it."

"Then he, she, it must die," I said, "or else the civil war might end, and the status of the militant elites of each faction would be jeopardized."

"Sound familiar?" asked Pecos rhetorically.

"That's what I'm thinking," Buckaroo replied, "although of course it's also possible that the raiding party has no knowledge of Whorfin's pregnancy. On the other hand, don't forget also that Whorfin is a con artist whose word is worthless. Who knows what the truth is . . . but it's always the demagogues on every planet, the same pathetic pack of clowns and their stupid followers easily led astray. Most civilizations, at least in our world, do tend to point in an authoritarian direction over time. We see the same thing happening here. Even so, people still have dreams on a Saturday night, and these alien interlopers have no right to be threatening or making demands of us."

"Damn right. Fighting words," I said, pointing at the straw mat lying atop the fine Persian rug next to me. "Though for all we know, there could be a Lectroid sitting on this very tatami mat."

"What tatami mat?" Buckaroo replied with a perfectly stolid face, prompting us both to break into laughter, however short lived.

"It occurs to me," I said, "that if these creatures are able to mess with our minds, then possibly all our perceptions of them are false . . ."

". . . the perceptions on which to base our conclusions," Pecos agreed, appearing tired and deep in thought as she leafed through the latest issue of *Philological Quarterly*. "Or how do we know for sure they didn't just plant that very thought in our heads?"

Lacking a suitable response to this conundrum, Buckaroo changed the subject, saying, "There's a kind of weasel, I forget its name, who kills much bigger prey by dancing for them. It dances so well they become too mesmerized to notice it's moving closer. Then it strikes the throat with razor claws for the kill."

"Lectroids are weasels, all right. But can they dance?" Pecos asked in good fun.

MOOD SWINGS

Buckaroo by now was staring into faraway space with a distracted air, as if wishing to unburden himself, and I made bold to ask, "How are you feeling these days, Buckaroo?"

The great man rose to his feet and responded, "I'm a scientist, meaning someone who draws on his sensory apparatus and similar experiences of others—knowledge gleaned via observation and experimentation—in order not to arrive at the great imponderables but to formulate probabilities. An empiricist, a materialist, in other words, to my very core. Yet there is this entire other mentality that afflicts me, the unevolved human mind in all its subjectivity, that makes me go round and round . . . even around the bend, by all accounts. What is this thing?"

"This thing called love? Oxytocin?" I wondered.

"The soul . . . that supernatural thing that gets flamed when we die," Tommy suggested.

"Or when we don't die," Buckaroo replied cryptically, taking a tentative step toward the door. "In the Fifth Dimension, I saw the two of us walking in the Serengeti in the moonlight and tried to jump out of the Jet Car, but trying to open the driver's door that was stuck, I veered off course and landed in the Seventh, where I saw her and spoke to her as clearly as I'm talking to you."

"I hate to burst your bubble when you're reevaluating your life," Tommy cut in, "but maybe we oughtta be thinking about saving the world and maybe you oughtta get a live woman. Maybe that would be a tad more productive . . ."

"This *is* productive, Tommy. He's getting things off his chest," Pecos scolded him and turned worriedly to Buckaroo. "What . . . what would have happened to you if you had managed to jump out?"

"If I had jumped out of the Jet Car . . . ? I probably wouldn't be standing here in a state of solidification," Buckaroo said. "Of course there are too many possible vectors to know the details, but my next experiment will involve just such an unusuality."

"Wow, can I share that close call with my readers?" I asked.

"But only with your readers and no one else," he said with a smile and then made a remarkable admission. "Tommy's right, of course. Here I am wallowing in the past when we need to put our hats on tight and cinch our saddles. No sense crying the blues when there's work to be done."

"We've been in tough scraps before," Tommy announced in a more encouraging vein. "If there's one hope for the world, it's us and our great intelligence."

"The only easy day was yesterday, old pard. Yes or no?" Buckaroo said and slapped Tommy on the shoulder as we all got up to leave.

"And yesterday was once tomorrow," I told myself, trying to decide which was the correct answer, when Buckaroo seemed to remember something and produced from his pocket a piece of ruled paper.

"Nearly forgot . . . here's our set list for the next leg of the tour," he said. "Of course feel free to tinker, as long as they're in the key of G-sharp. I was half-asleep when I scribbled it. Thoughts?"

A TOUR IN THE WORKS

"Going back on tour?" I asked, surprised. "Given the circumstances, I—"

"In exactly two weeks. Mrs. Johnson is already blasting the news worldwide," he replied calmly, disconcerting us even further. "Since we have to go to Europe anyway . . ."

"A couple of weeks? But rehearsals . . ." I reacted in shock, meanwhile looking over the song list and passing it to Pecos and Tommy for their perusal.

"I can't help wondering," Pecos said, checking the program. "Why all in G-sharp? That sucks ass. Any particular reason?"

"Fifty-one point five hertz," Tommy at once theorized in his best squinty-eyed, wishing-to-appear-thoughtful pose, adding, "G-sharp vibrates at approximately a frequency of fifty-one point five hertz. Everybody knows that, and that's the same frequency as the pyramids—"

I interrupted him to ask Buckaroo, "What's our lineup?"

"You're the tour wizard and musical director, Reno," he said. "It's in your hands, and I know you'll make wise choices."

"I'll try," I vowed, all too aware of the weighty responsibility. "But what about a bass player?"

"Keeper of the bass flame is always difficult," he conceded. "Between Papa Bear and Hoppalong, I'll leave it up to you."

"Well . . . Hoppalong just bought a new Fender Jazz Bass," Pecos said. "I have it on good authority."

"Mrs. Johnson . . . ?" asked Buckaroo.

Pecos nodded and replied, "He took out a loan for six weeks' wages from the commissary."

"That shows commitment," Buckaroo admitted.

"I wouldn't want him to think he threw his money away. Oh, and there's Webmaster Jhonny," I said, with a sidewise look at Pecos. "Jhonny is mighty set on coming. He's bent my ear, intent on sampling what he thinks is the extravagant lifestyle of the concert tour. He may also feel he has something to prove to someone."

I glanced again at Pecos, who averted her eyes.

"No reason why anyone should be exempt," said Buckaroo. "He can do his job from the bus, but it's up to you, Reno. And one more thing: I've made a slight change to our itinerary. I've moved up our Rome engagement. The tour opens in the Coliseum."

"The Roman Coliseum . . . ?" we all uttered in amazement. "Just like in your dream . . ."

"I thought it would be a good idea," Buckaroo said, "especially since Mayor Agostinelli is a big fan and we'll be appearing the same day as an international DeMolay pep rally at which, according to a Vatican press release, the pope plans to reveal the fourth and final secret of Our Lady of Fátima . . ."

"The fourth secret . . . ?" I said. "I thought there were only three."

"Apparently, someone dug a little deeper and found another . . ."

"Someone?" I questioned him.

"Someone in a position of power," he confirmed. "Neither Pope Innocent nor his agent Cardinal Baltazar is taking my calls. They seem to be indisposed or away from their phones almost like clockwork, so something had to be done. I'm especially anxious to meet this fellow, Abbot Costello, who has apparently gone underground . . ."

"I love the old-time comedies, too," I said. "Well, we've pestered you long enough, Buckaroo. With the exception of Tommy, we've got to get back to our slow cookers for tonight's potluck dinner. Right, Tommy? Frozen turkey loaf again this year, in the original wrapper?"

"My rotisserie chicken, with fried taters and coleslaw," countered Tommy defiantly. "What real men eat, along with quality beef."

"No cookie or a biscuit?" I respectfully inquired.

"Not this year. Putting you all on a diet," he replied, before quickly reconsidering. "Depends what's in it for me."

"Surprise vegetarian goulash and green bean casserole from me," revealed Pecos.

"No surprise there," said Buckaroo. "And, Reno, *andouillette* again this year, in your special *solera* with all the fixings?"

"It seems to be what I'm known for," I chuckled good-naturedly. "That, and my juicy buttered yams."

"Yes, I seem to recall they set off quite the mad scramble last year. Reminds me I need to check my own pot of *brodo di polpo*," he said, adding, "Don't worry, guys, it's just the first leg of a long race to wellness. Let's have a great evening. Nothing shows love like a home-cooked meal."

"I agree a hundred and ten percent," I declared, not knowing exactly what sort of dish he was preparing, but certain it would be wonderful. In this way relieved of the burden of unhealthy competition, we walked out together in a spirit of great conviviality.

THE DOCTOR MAKES HIS ROUNDS

From the same window, I watched Buckaroo cross the community garden and continue past the honeybee colony, the craft brewery and visitor center, the greenhouse-herbarium, and the stockade to the site of the old chicken coop that by now lay mostly demolished, courtesy of Red Jordan and Honest Dan Cartwright, who were presently busy scavenging copper wire from old air conditioners. At that moment, however, what arrested my attention was the sight of Red Jordan on his hands and knees, attempting to retrieve a child's ball from what I assumed was a drainpipe. Nearby, a young Apache girl, whom I recognized as the daughter of one of our nurses, spoke anxiously to Buckaroo. What words were exchanged between them, or between Red and Buckaroo, I can't say, but I continued to watch with fascination as Buckaroo took something from his doctor's case.

From remarks he made to me during my preparation for this project, we have his account: "Tall Crow's daughter Yolanda had dropped her little ball into a pipe too narrow to admit my fingers or any other object without likely puncturing the ball. Yet when I sprinkled in a packet of Alka-Seltzer, its foaming action on the liquid beneath the ball caused the ball to rise sufficiently to become easily grasped. The delighted look on Yolanda's face, and a single tear of joy that ran down Red's cheek, more than justified my modest effort."

Again, a thoughtful reader may reasonably wonder why I include such a seemingly trivial occurrence in the present narrative—to which I would reply that, in addition to providing a window into Buckaroo's unparalleled ability to improvise, the incident presaged bigger things to come . . . even a pivotal event, perhaps.

Now Buckaroo paused to pet one of the many wild flamingos roaming about the place and continued a short distance to the urgent care clinic, before making the rounds of the ten-bed hospital and descending the stairs to its world-renowned laboratory—the cytology section, to be precise—where he donned a sanitary gown and Dansko surgical clogs with blue paper shoe covers, then found Señor Dentista and Colorado Belle hard at work on the Lectroid-papaya hybrid specimens sent to us from Sarajevo.

"Anything interesting?" said Buckaroo, peering over Belle's shoulder.

"I'm not sure these two have any future together," she answered through her plexiglass face shield. "Miss Papaya must have had a lot of makeup on when Mr. Lectroid came calling. Or maybe the light was bad. But if you add a little catnip—"

"Then—?"

"Some very disturbing chromosomes that look like Frankenstein ate Frankenstein," she said. "Makes you wonder why anyone had the idea of marrying these two."

"I think I know, Belle," replied Buckaroo. "From the few writings that Cardinal Baltazar has published, he seems to belong to a small clique of church thinkers who believe that the original forbidden fruit in the Garden of Eden wasn't the apple but the papaya, whose seeds are thought to contain individual demons released as phlogiston."

"Seriously?" she questioned. "So—"

"If every seed is a demon, he might be trying to bring into fruition an army of Lectroids with demonic powers. Let me know at the first sign of deviltry or black magic."

"That's so childlike, it's almost cute," she said. "Almost."

THE GENERAL'S QUARTERS

Upstairs in a freestanding Faraday cage that doubled as an orgone energy accumulator, Buckaroo found Wild Bill Wagoneer still with an orangish tinge despite daily sessions in the Institute's pressurized oxygen chamber and regular enemas of buffelgrass, stinging nettle, and juniper ash. In addition, Mrs. Johnson had been giving him injections of rooster comb, along with foot rubs with Watkins liniment, and regularly accompanied him outside, where they threw knives and tomahawks in friendly competition . . . until one day she caught him mixing contraband Ativan with his daily prescribed glass of Ovaltine. Needless to say, the incident led to an inconclusive investigation, a certain unraveling of their friendship, and a week in time-out for the general.

"Where are all the goodhearted people? Another attempt to keep them from reaching me!" he wailed sporadically during this period.

Later, when his skunk-oil treatments also forced him to live apart from others, even from the livestock, loneliness again became his major complaint. Afternoons and evenings typically found him hunched over his Bible in the old hay barn converted into a lazaretto, where Mrs. Johnson nevertheless remained his constant visitor . . . applying permethrin to his genitals and tossing him high into the air, Mongolian-style, with the aim of flipping his liver.

Through it all, the general continued to engage in strenuous exercise under the same Arizona sun that had toned his muscles and given him an even more jaundiced hue and a vigorous mustache. His behavior raised eyebrows, to say the least, and there could be little doubt that he had acquired a nervous disease; but meaningful therapy proved next to impossible, since Wild Bill's knee-jerk reaction to Dr. John Jane Doe's attempts at psychoanalysis was to play with the buttons on his shirt or "stretch" his penis . . . before apologizing for having forgotten virtually everything in the immediate aftermath of the lab explosion.

"Anybody find my brain or did I leave it in the quack shack?" he might say. "Or did Lord John Whorfin steal that, too, the thieving sonofabitch? No wonder I suck and keep drifting. There's gotta be an evil element involved or maybe I'm just simple. Of course there's a fifty-fifty chance I'm wrong."

Or else he would become insufferably arrogant and patronizing to one and all: "Lemme get on my know-it-all horse and let's review. Or did your mother not tell you what the Intelligence Integration Center is and how it interfaces with the Global Information Infrastructure to coordinate UCAV strikes and directed-energy weapons?"

On this day, Buckaroo slipped into the chamber and began by engaging him in a short conversation concerning a new battery of tests that had confirmed signs of liver cirrhosis and other toxicological organ damage, as well as spirochetes in the general's blood and lymph.

"Good news and bad. We can rule out syphilitic dementia, but spirochetes are frustrating little critters," Buckaroo informed him. "They might be Lyme disease or something else causing your clumsiness and neurological problems. We'll stay with the celery juice, topical skunk oil, and Watkins liniment. I see Dr. Doe also has you on ibogaine, loco weed, and oleander . . ."

"Doc told me it was ragweed for my sinuses," Wild Bill interjected.

"Don't buy a used car from them," Buckaroo said, only partly in jest. "Since there's no standard of care for your condition, they're trying a number of things across the spectrum. You should be all right as long as you don't operate a forklift."

"Or go skateboarding with that crazy Mrs. Johnson. Anybody home? She's wacko . . ."

"Good point, General. I know the two of you have tangled on more than one occasion," Buckaroo remarked, looking over Wild Bill's medical file. "Depending on your hormesis response, we may have to look at an intensive antibiotic regime. I'm also still worried about your elevated viral load, so I'm upping the accumulator's bion output."

Wild Bill merely stared at his Bible for a moment before replying, "Whatever you say, Doc, but I wish you'd save your time and money to help the less fortunate. The little germ bastards can look me in the eye and know I'm not someone to phawk with. Or they can eat me up until all my body parts fall off. I'm still not going on meds or messing with my bodily fluids. I'll try the natural cure in Mrs. Johnson's castor bean gumbo. I know caloric intake is critically important."

"As well as good sleep . . . still showing a sleep deficiency. Just an educated guess, but I see your spirometric numbers are looking better on the gradient treadmill tests. How was your therapy session with Dr. Doe? I understand you got angry and tried to snatch their keys."

"Who?"

"Dr. Doe. They say they suffered bruises when you grabbed for their keys."

"Good and bad, like you said," replied Wild Bill. "Snoozing and passing gas, cursing myself, wondering how I could have missed so many things before they put my crazy ass in this insane asylum. Hopefully, the little shrink with the big whiskers can get me recalibrated in no time."

Buckaroo nodded and scribbled something, humoring him. "I'll make a note in your file for Dr. Nostradamus. In the positive column, the good news is that your gut flora are blossoming and the ammonia levels in your brain are coming down, but I'm worried your erythrocytes may be red shifting on me, possibly to the tipping point. Perhaps a little vibrotherapy will open your bile ducts, as well as pick up your spirits and jar your memory by regenerating axons. But if the chelation and vibrotherapy don't help, your only shot may be a liver transplant, platelet-rich plasma therapy, or even my new experimental serum that I'm ready to test."

Wild Bill declined the offer, explaining, "First and foremost, Doc, give it to someone more worthy. I'm just a war criminal basking in my own piss, a leech lacking the manual dexterity even for physical labor."

"You're too modest, General," Buckaroo informed him. "I suspect you're underestimating yourself. That's why I'm giving you a choice of desert-survival trekking with Papa Bear—"

"Oh, God, no. He's a lost puppy with a shady past," said the general, cringing.

"—or spending a few days at the old Ghost Mine's magnetic vortex about ten miles from here. There's a powerful hidden ley line through there that could boost your solar plexus chakra in a relatively short time."

"Win, win, win," said Wild Bill. "I cannot thank you often enough."

The usual questions only elicited more of the usual answers on this particular afternoon, as Buckaroo reviewed certain previous conversations between them and Wild Bill's childlike sketches having to do with the shadowy Brother Costello and the violent exorcism of Emilio Lizardo, which the general likened to "sucking a donkey's ass through a straw" . . .

STILL AT A LOSS FOR ANSWERS

"Okay, let's try again," Buckaroo said and proceeded to ask the usual questions concerning the mysterious explosion at Area 51 . . . to which he received the usual hazy and mostly nonsensical answers, from which he nonetheless always managed to ferret out bits and pieces of information.

"See something, say something," recalled the general. "I was witness to the whole twisted agenda."

"That's right, and it's not too late to make a clean breast of it," Buckaroo said.

"Ha, 'a clean breast' . . . what I wouldn't do for a good rubdown and pipe cleaning."

"How about cleaning your conscience?"

"If I still had one, Doc," the general commented with resignation. "I'd even do Christian outreach, ride a bicycle with the Mormons, but, alas, my name is tarnished like the forlorn Judas . . ."

After several more minutes of this exhausting exchange, Buckaroo asked questions like the following: Did Lizardo say anything before he died? Were statements taken from any witnesses? Were there photographs, security video, or any kind of audiovisual records of the incident that might exist anywhere? What was Costello's condition? Did he make a statement to anyone present? How long did the friar remain at the scene after the incident? Did he get off base under his own power? How had he come to the general's attention in the first place? Who paid for his ticket from Italy? How much money changed hands? Who was the middle man, this so-called Holy Office?

"Is this your signature, General?" Buckaroo asked, showing him the receipts for the Lectroid body parts. "This bill of sale to the Holy Office, any memory of that?"

"Sharing is caring. Forgive me for sounding like a child, but it does look familiar."

"Maybe because I showed it to you yesterday."

Wild Bill scratched his chin, clenched his teeth, and thought some more, slapping his head violently as if to remove the cobwebs before admitting total defeat. "One too many concussions, capped off by the big one, the big-ass firecracker that stole my dreams. That's what the flight docs said, dating from my childhood of abuse. I'm ashamed, but I don't know what for: I want to say a wild thing . . . an emotional pussycat of a mother I couldn't protect . . ."

"Just keep working through it," Buckaroo urged. "If anything occurs to you . . ."

Wagoneer glanced around as if appraising his surroundings for the first time, then dug deeply and pulled a slimy finger from his nose.

"I feel the pull of psychosis, Doc. Lots of repressed memories there . . . hit me right between the eyes," Wild Bill began, staring at his nose-picking finger, which he now waved in front of a grateful Nostradamus. "For the love of humanity, Buckaroo, I don't know what went wrong, unless maybe static electricity and my adjutant's hair spray . . ."

"You're talking about the explosion that night at the base . . . ?"

Wagoneer both nodded and shook his head, saying, "Most God-awful beating I've ever suffered, Doc. Had to be some astronomical high levels of propellants to throw Costello and Lizardo clean across the loading dock and out the service entrance. God bless America, flew like damn dolls . . ."

"Well, matter is energy, so it stands to reason mysterious matter can produce mysterious energy," Buckaroo theorized.

"I mourn their loss. I mourn the loss of every soul," the general said solemnly.

"Who was lost, General?"

"The little Italian the size of a child and the other Italian . . . I showed you where I buried him and the wiseacre John. They were a hoot."

"John Whorfin."

"The light sleeper I shot outta the sky."

"But now you know that's not true. Why do you think he lied to you?"

"No one was more surprised than I was," the general said. "No question he tapped into my pity bank, but I don't think he'd fib about something like that unless maybe he lied to keep from going insane. I could do a whole riff on this, whatever the deal is."

"What is the deal, General? Do you know what the deal is?"

"He came from a pretty tough neighborhood," the general continued, clutching one hand in the other and rocking back and forth in a troubled manner. "Maybe he gave to everyone and no one gave to him and he couldn't stand to be alone."

"Maybe he's not alone. Any chance he and the little Italian stepped out of the world for a minute and returned together?"

The general seemed to be thinking hard about this and even closed his eyes before answering softly, "Then why did they leave me? I buried them, I hefted them down the trail like a pallbearer."

Buckaroo paused, reluctant to bring up an ongoing issue, but felt again the need to ask, "Do you know who I am, General?"

"You're a helluva entertainer . . . and maybe the better man."

"What makes you say that?"

"Because you're Buckaroo Banzai. And where does that leave me by comparison?"

Just at that moment the general removed his finger from the Chihuahua's slavering maw, causing Nostradamus to howl like a wolverine.

"Before I go," Buckaroo said. "I'd like to see what he remembers about that day at Area 51 . . ."

"Fire away," the general said, "but he's a bullshit artist—hard to tell when he's kidding, so take it with a grain of salt."

XVIII. OUR REGIMENTAL DINNER

> What is each man but a spirit that has taken corporal form briefly
> and then disappears? What are men if not ghosts?
> —Thomas Carlyle

Leaving the clinic, Buckaroo continued along a path that would have taken him past the bunkhouse and general store, horse stables and veterinary hospital, minigolf obstacle course, sweat lodge, food pantry, and petting zoo, and within sight of the cemetery and main gate, where Lonely Ranger and Buffalo Gal were on duty . . . reinforced by a network of CCTV cameras and aerial surveillance linked to the Institute's sophisticated communications center. Without revealing the system's technological prowess or its vulnerabilities, I simply will say that protecting the Institute and its working ranch and thousands of acres of desert wilderness was in many ways an impossible job even for a small army, which we plainly were not. On an average day—not counting tourists and hostel guests but including visiting scholars and preceptors of both the higher and lower faculties—our population hovered around four dozen; and perhaps half that number could be found weekly at Thursday Table, seated beneath Mrs. Johnson's handcrafted whiskey-bottle chandelier in the great Gathering Hall, known also as the Hall of Heroes or the Hall of Ambassadors, where we typically ate, drank, reviewed the week's events, and discussed needed modifications to our modus operandi. Depending on our mood and how much we imbibed,

we might also perform little skits and extemporaneous impressions of
one another or recite ribald limericks, while never failing to acknowledge
random acts of kindness as well.

As I have mentioned, owing to the unique threat to the planet and
our impending European tour, we had elected to combine Thursday
Table with our annual regimental dinner and its long-standing custom
of honoring our comrades, dead or living. Unspoken, of course, was the
thought that this little reunion might be our last.

After the rising of the house and the awarding of medals—mostly
barbed wire clusters for bravery—we were treated to a briefing from the
editorial staff of the Institute's newsletter concerning the government's
proposed nuclear waste dump on disputed Apache land and a projector
display of our annual IRS form 990 and our capital campaign under
Rule 506(c), after which the lord president pro tem (Papa Bear, in this
particular instance) gaveled the meeting to order with a ramekin of hot
sauce and at once threw the floor open to In Tray and Out Tray, a
segment of time devoted to housekeeping and official business, yet
proceeding always in accordance with Robert's Rules. Among the first
matters broached was the necessity of identifying who in our midst had
brought in the onslaught of German cockroaches and who was the source
of confidential information recently leaked to celebrity gossip magazines.
(Might it even be the same person?) In addition there was news of recent
skirmishes with cattle rustlers and the next day's scheduled delivery of
liquid helium to cool the Institute's superconducting magnets, leading
in turn to a frank discussion concerning our weekly natural disaster
simulations, our educational film division and Junior Science Learning
Kit giveaways around the globe, and our mobile library, help desk, 4-H
Club, and job-training program right here at home (in accord with
Buckaroo's belief that teaching is the most effective form of charity).
Next, we were all reminded of the importance of projecting a positive
image of the Institute both on and off the clock and given an instructive
talk on permaculture by Li'l Daughter—complete with a display of
heirloom seeds—followed by a Q&A on hydroponics and the ideal
growing medium for chili peppers and certain medicinal herbs.

Next came a status update on the endangered rusty-patched bumblebee
and our lobbying efforts against neonicotinoid pesticides and a week's
worth of reports from our optical tracking facility, our E-2 Hawkeye,

and our very large array astronomical radio observatory. These readings, taken from different angles, were strongly suggestive of a large stealth object approaching Earth; but, given the inconclusive data and lacking a suitable plan of action in any case, we moved on to an update of our various revenue-generation streams—e.g., flow charts of livestock and crop sales, royalties from our entertainment division, and scientific patents—which continued for no small period of time until Buckaroo announced, to much cheering and backslapping, "And a ten percent across-the-board pay increase, effective immediately!"

"Hear! Hear! For he's a jolly good fellow . . . !"

Indeed, for what were we saving our endowment in these parlous times? If ever there was a rainy day, it was now. When our celebration became a little too rowdy, however, good Mrs. Johnson materialized to remind us, "But still no parking in the red zone! Or skateboarding! And the next one who throws crap down my disposal, I'll hang from the highest tree!"

"Jail food!" someone muttered, but the source of the remark was never clear . . .

. . . as Mrs. Johnson rolled in a giant wheel of goat cheese and the discussion moved on to other matters: our creek drainage problems and trash and waste recycling; brief highlights of our individual and joint research projects; a feasibility study of a plan to convert the old wastewater holding tank into a swimming pool or a skate park for all ages—followed by a moment of respectful silence in memory of Pinky's beloved redbone hound dog Lulu, killed by a big tom puma. Pinky in turn choked back tears and thanked everyone.

"He got mind control over her and dragged her down a thirty-foot rocky embankment," he said. "Every dog needs a person in their life, and I'm so happy I could be that person in Lulu's."

"We're happy, too," said Li'l Daughter. "She was super friendly."

Pecos then went over a list of odd jobs around the Institute that needed doing "in case anybody needs some extra spending money. I'm talking important work at the rate of twenty dollars in cash."

Next up was Buckaroo with the eagerly awaited news of operationally ready dates for our long-awaited compact fusion reactor, our biosafety level 4 (BSL-4) laboratory / proton therapy center with a new underground hot room, and three more big-blade windmills. His patient efforts to give us a comprehensive understanding of the exciting new additions were undermined, however, by mundane complaints about long lines at our snack bar's single microwave oven and unauthorized midnight refrigerator raids, the anonymous ownership of the abandoned sofa outside the gaming lounge, and the recent spate of fence cuttings and probes on our perimeter by suspected city slickers claiming to be itinerant sheep shearers. Directly this conversation concluded, Webmaster Jhonny reported on recent attempts to compromise our web server, and Leo the LEO discussed the troubling increase in unidentified drone activity in our airspace, leading to a suspicion among many of us that odd underground noises, heard in various locations but most conspicuously in the wine cellar, were interfering with the sleep patterns of humans and animals alike and perhaps portending an even more serious danger.

"Sappers? Tunnel rats?" suggested the Marchioness.

"I'm guessing moles or gophers overpowering our defenses," Tommy argued. "Just yesterday I wrote a work order to check all battery-operated radon detectors and gopher spikes."

The Marchioness shook her head, dissenting. "I mean the human kind of varmint, like those supposed Army Corps of Engineers and Bureau of Land Management impostors we keep spotting in the northwest arroyo behind the speedway . . ."

"Or that creepy panel truck with the revolving antenna on top and without plates," said Mrs. Johnson. "Or those weirdos asking to lease our property for a Christmas tree farm."

Since she chose to point fingers of blame, raucous debate of this matter went on for several minutes until a proposal was made to undertake a thorough review of our electromagnetic defense force and form a special volunteer committee of the most capable experts to address all physical threats—especially at this fraught moment in our history—and propose solutions, including improved air and water filtration systems, radon mitigation, and an integrated network of acoustic listening stations and seismic-sensitive weathercocks.

"The bunkhouse is sick with germs and chiggers and leaves a bad taste in my mouth—this is a proven fact," Li'l Daughter said, citing comments by the Marchioness.

"But entirely fixable. Let's see what the committee comes back with. Sorry about your pooch, Pinky," Buckaroo said with honest concern before calling upon Quartermaster Honest Dan Cartwright to give a summary report (more flow charts) on the Institute's assorted livestock populations, including our new ostriches, and our general store's inventories of beans and salt pork, hot sauce, Folgers coffee, MREs, animal feed, propane, gasoline and diesel fuel, potable water, cotton bed sheets, groceries and kitchen supplies, adobe bricks and concrete masonry units (cement blocks), toilet paper, soap, baby formula, silver bullion, and ammunition.

Buckaroo then issued a call for a new volunteer calisthenics leader and a wheelwright / assistant blacksmith, before becoming embroiled in a discussion about a missing extension cord and the pros and cons of purchasing new dinette booths for the bunkhouse snack bar and a dozen office chairs of "rich Corinthian leather" for the library.

"Lots of goodies," Tommy said, raising a valid complaint. "I know 'rich' Corinthian leather's really just a stupid advert and nothing special, so why not get real Naugahyde? It's longer lasting and strong as steel. And never mind the damn extension cord, what about the missing millions?"

"There are no missing millions," Pecos assured him. "Honest Dan is sick and tired of the question, and he already explained to you . . ."

"Nothing but wild rumors. This is the fourth time you've asked me, Tommy," a displeased Cartwright complained. "I didn't earn my nickname for nothing. I'm as honest as the day is long, so why are you beating me up?"

"If you've nothing to worry about, why so tetchy?" Tommy muttered.

But now it was for the person at the head of the table—Buckaroo Banzai—to weigh in: "I appreciate your concern, Tommy. Nothing against Dan, who also does beautiful lapidary work, but it's best not to wear blinders in these situations. Mrs. Johnson and Missing Person Greenberg will be going over the books with a fine-toothed comb in the coming days."

His concerns thus eased, Tommy saw fit to flash his famous maniacal grin, while Pecos could not be silent in the face of such hypocrisy, saying, "Nothing wrong with pampering ourselves a little. Besides, you already have silk sheets, Tommy, and probably leather ones, too—paid for with the money you took from the community swear box!"

"Oh, hell no," argued Tommy. "You mean the jam jar? That was for a new foosball table that was desperately needed! Buckaroo's a witness of that . . ."

But Buckaroo merely scratched his head, leaving it to Mrs. Johnson to scowl and utter in protest, "And meanwhile I'm short staffed, busting my culinary butt, clipping coupons and saving pennies for a new spot welder and a new sewing machine motor . . . ?"

"I'll work on your motor, Mrs. Johnson, once I fix your marred friction shifters," offered Webmaster Jhonny. "I'll even share my sewing kit until your machine is on the mend."

"Thank you, Jhonny. Great way to be," she gushed. "Computers, bicycles, appliances—you're my handyman buddy, a real crowd pleaser."

"No, Mrs. Johnson, the crowd pleaser is your sweet cupcakes that rule the rooster," Jhonny said.

"You mean 'the roost.' But much obliged, Jhonny," she replied.

By now we were hungry and thirsty and ready to cut loose. Buckaroo, as was customary, provided the *itadakimasu* prayer, and Red Jordan said Christian grace, after which we broke into toasts and a medley of silly songs, followed by a series of spontaneous musical jams, a mock awards ceremony (truncated when we ran out of medals and participation trophies), and irreverent speeches. As usual, we shared many a hearty belly laugh with our agent Jack Tarantulus, a large and expansive man and a storyteller of the first rank, who had flown in for the occasion and did his best to dampen our levity with a recurring gripe about Pope Innocent the Mercātor.

"I'm about to nail down Old Spice for one of my athlete clients when all this satanic shite mysteriously goes viral, orchestrated by the World Crime League and the Vatican, claiming Old Spice is 'of the devil'—the old lava boss himself. Then I had a cinch deal with Aqua Velva," Jack was saying in his freewheeling manner, gesticulating wildly with a glass of Jacques Selosse in his hand and spilling nary a bubble. "Or at least I thought I had a deal . . . Perfect Tommy as the worldwide face of Aqua Velva! Then, the next thing I know I'm watching one of those louche tabloid news shows, and some blowhard is talking about Pope Innocent's new endorsement deal as the new spokesman for Aqua Velva and his own signature cologne, Heaven Scent!"

"That was on Mona Peeptoe's show," I mentioned.

"Yeah, Mona Peeptoe's *Come Clean* show. You would know, Reno," Jack said bitterly. "I mean, this is the shite I have to put up with, people laughing behind my back when we gotta compete with the pope. What's next, pope-endorsed jockstraps? Bread and circuses, children. Bread and circuses."

"Blame Cardinal Baltazar," said Buckaroo. "I'm sure these product endorsement deals weren't the pope's idea. Fact is, I don't care for some of my own endorsements, although we put the money to a good cause."

"Yeah . . . I blame Baltazar. I wouldn't mind hurting his health. Thanks for letting me get it off my chest," said Jack.

"Thank you, Jack," replied Pecos, patting him on the knee.

But Jack wasn't finished venting. "Him and his fat Vatican bank account . . . never mind the Cayman Islands and several tons of authentic Parmesan cheese he's got stashed in a private safety-deposit vault. That stuff's gold . . ."

WEBMASTER JHONNY IS TESTED

It also happened that our attention was at that moment diverted by an audible spat between Pecos and Webmaster Jhonny, perhaps due to the language barrier and Jhonny's weakness for charcoal-filtered bourbon.

"You have some gall, Jhonny, you stinker," Pecos chided without interrupting her rhythmic drumming on a practice pad. "Out of neighborliness, I welcomed you as a friend, and you are dear to my heart, but I've had enough of your privacy violations and extreme eye contact and little pranks like unfastening my Velcro sneakers and messing with my candy stash in my locker. Oh, and your bug-eye sunglasses and Groucho eyebrows and blue hair aren't as slick a disguise as you think. I've recognized your scented pomade peeking through my bed curtains—truly an identifying mark of a jackanapes, not to mention criminal etiquette."

Jhonny accepted the criticism with humility and the added benefit that he seemed to enjoy it, saying, "Thank you, Pecos. Yes, neighborliness. I am complex of a man but with a good heart. I dance original and love a good party . . . even if drunken foolishness rankles me to no extent."

"That's for sure, Jhonny," she agreed.

"God-fearing and a sense of humor, but deep as a redwood tree whose beauty you do not see," he went on slurring, plainly under the influence. "Yet I submit my will to you and will always stand in your line of defense, even if I am hurting. I will take the hit and love you only in silence, even you are the light of my life, my beloved woman and my conscious [sic], without whom there is no existence worth living. I am sadly gone and have not been received your love [sic], for the pure fact maybe it is the wrong dream to be one with one another."

"Aw, that's so sweet, Jhonny, but also nothing short of ridiculous," she said, alternately moved and puzzled by his heartfelt confession of love. "I can't turn a blind eye to your games, and a few kind words don't mean I'm interested in you romantically. You wear your heart on your sleeve, but you have odd ways of thinking and maybe aren't the hotshot you think you are."

Sensing all was not lost, he proceeded by reminding her, "We have traded wallet pics, on which you even wrote something on the back. Do you remember what?"

"No, I'm sorry, Jhonny. I don't . . ."

"You wrote, 'To a real gentleman.' Later, you sent me many emojis when we farmed runes and settled Catan together on my custom gaming machine. We played canasta and poker for matchsticks and you let me pedi-paint your toes and troubleshoot your Go-Phone, while I let you into my fort built of pillows at scary movie night and darned your socks and broken belt loops . . . my golden dream lady, sugar and spice and everything nice. Let me put it this way: in the past when I have hugged you on Valentine Day, I have felt no bones, only a curvy curve figure and torrid muscle like a side of beef with very little adipose . . . so much awesomeness packed into your flannel Pendleton work shirt. So when sleeping in the bunk next to yours, at the peak of my alpha sexual meditation and dreaming you hoovering [sic] over me, I am not too pridefully [sic] to admit I have felt arousing and often counted your vertebraes and inhaled your hair and body spray fresh as green-cut grass, pining for you, dreaming of snapping your bra strap preliminary to a nursing relationship between your chests, because I sleep with nightmares . . ."

"That's gross. You and your mommy issues, Jhonny," Pecos replied with a frown. "The point is that you took advantage of me. And to think

I held you in such high regard. Is everything you have ever said to me a lie? I feel used, Jhonny."

"Yes, because you have been my guiding light and I have no couth and only I am to blame. Treated worthless in my native land where nothing ever happened, I summoned energy to write Mrs. Johnson and the admissions committee, who saw something in me. I arrived here for a year of internship and learning new surroundings and the following year won the international programming Olympiad. Then came the chance to reinvent myself and ply my skills in the Institute's famous experimental lavatory [sic], even with nothing on my bank account, seeking only a positive prospective [sic] on life and adventures to be manifested with the great Buckaroo Banzai . . . able to learn jujitsu and healthy behaviors and meet a woman to suit my standard. Yet now I find myself lower than the station of dogs. Why did I ever dream how your velvet skin would be like to surrender and rise together [sic], pillow partners in purity, eternally forever in our happy home?"

"If wishes were fishes and pigs had wings," Tommy hooted derisively.

"Sounds like your ego is doing all the talking, Jhonny. Cry me a river or a landfill," said Pecos, unimpressed by his flowery speech.

In response, Jhonny swallowed a huge lump and poured out his heart: "Yes, my love be damned and buried. The compost pit is what I deserve, because you are the crème de la crème, so hot, and I am so not."

"Enough self-loathing, Jhonny," she pleaded. "I don't like to see a man grovel."

"Yes, your infinite wisdom . . . you have brought happiness to my life, even though I am nothing, only a sweater guy who loves you to the fullest. I try to use the right words but I am terrible at best, so I knit sweaters and enjoy to get dressed up . . ."

"You're the king of sweaters, Jhonny . . . and I see no problem being keen on them," she assured him. "I even gave you a sweater for Christmas, if you'll remember. Maybe you are overthinking things a little."

"Because I have search [sic] for you all my life," he sobbed, "even if, as of recently, my soul is already crush [sic] and I am fallen from grace, so what is left to lose? So now I am out in the cold, destroy [sic] for no reason, shit out of luck, SOL, and will continue to be the odd loner. May God have pity on my soul if I am lie to you [sic] and have ever foul desires or think about undoing your Annie Oakley braids."

"Nothing wrong with your soul, son," Tommy butted in testily. "Pecos is a total phawking prize . . . Just knock the fire out of him, Pecos. Dump his weak BS."

"Ha, ha, bipolar Tommy who cannot even spell BS," cackled Jhonny.

"BS," Tommy refuted him with a vengeance.

But full of liquid courage, Jhonny was now feeling his oats. "You should use a straw, Tommy, because you suck. Ha, ha, you gotta love it! I would call you butter but you are not on a roll!"

"Ha, ha, how about I give you some strawberries and bruises?" Tommy returned against what he saw as Jhonny's growing impertinence. "You need to mute your spiel, buster, before I up the ante."

"What does that supposed to mean? I will be beatened [sic], like back in my home country?"

"I see your point: right there at the top of your little pinhead," jested Tommy. "Don't worry, I won't blame your mama for one bad seed . . ."

"Okay, Tammy! Tommy is Tammy, ha, ha! Don't talk about my mama, Tammy!"

"Looks like I've turned Jhonny's flank!" Tommy crowed in kind.

Things were indeed getting nasty . . . something that would have been perhaps laughable on a less solemn occasion but was plainly out of place under the circumstances. Still, neither man seemed ready to end the exchange of tawdry insults.

"Ha, ha. You are the cowardice psychotic [sic]. Please remove my skid marks from your dirty face, Tammy, or can I call you Patsy?"

"Try it, I'll knock you on your funny bone! By which I mean the one in your pants!" threatened Tommy, who now feinted an aggressive move with his Martin guitar at Jhonny . . .

. . . who retaliated by hurling a feta-stuffed olive and announcing, "They call me the Webmaster: the coolest, realest [sic], baddest hombre this side west of the Pecos!"

As if moved to action by the mention of her eponymous river, Pecos ominously raised a plastic drumstick and prepared to hurl it like a spear at either of them, and in response Tommy jumped up onto the table and demonstrated a series of supposed fighting positions, shouting all the while, "Cat stance! Horse stance! Samurai stance!"

"How do we win?" I called out.

"We cheat!" yelled Tommy.

"Why do we use kicks?" I shouted back.

"The leg is longer and stronger, Reno! Train hard, fight easy!" he returned.

"What's the strongest punch in jujitsu?"

"Reverse!" he cried loudly. "Recognize! React! Reverse!"

By now sharing in the fun, Pecos lowered her drumstick and shouted, "Where does danger come from?"

"From the left! From the right! Backlash!" Tommy yelled and, with another kick, fell off the table, thereby earning Buckaroo's remonstrance.

"Tommy, good to know you're awake, but please stop playing the fool. Why are you tilting at Jhonny?"

"I don't know. Just kind of bored, I guess . . . sitting around, itching for some real action."

"Be careful what you wish for, Tom," Buckaroo warned. "Sounds like we've all got a touch of cabin fever. Including you, Jhonny, a deserving young man who I thought mature for your age, you've been on a downward path that seems to have spiraled. You need to stay focused on the job and forget your fascination with Pecos, which may be giving rise to a dishonest narrative. Remember, a little courtesy goes a long way in the workplace," Buckaroo continued. "You seem to disrespect her boundaries, which amounts to a personal betrayal that can get you banned from the family or even put in check."

"Put in check," Jhonny repeated. "What means . . . ?"

"It's bad," I told him.

"It means you're more than just an ugly eyesore," contributed Tommy.

"Some people never come back," added Pecos.

"You can't expect any help," Tommy said. "Leave us out of it."

Amid our solemn looks and his own nervous breathing, Jhonny swallowed his pride and said contritely, "Yes, I want to just cry. It seems I have become a dreg [sic] on the Institute. I do not have all the brains, and by operating in love I seem to have awakened the sleeping giant of jealousy, in the meaning of human beings everywhere [sic]. Perhaps I saw her big earrings and took that as an invitation to a pity lay."

"A pity lay?" Buckaroo said and continued to educate him. "Jhonny, this is the United States of America, where hoop earrings do not imply a willingness to give sexual favors. You didn't ask Pecos how she felt and didn't believe what she said beforehand, so it was an invasion of her privacy. You simply made assumptions because you believed she suited your purposes. Never mind that this isn't the appropriate time for that—it's unacceptable, like your habit of grabbing your crotch in public. The worst part is that you're apt to ruin a good friendship, if not team chemistry and the orderly flow of things, which could result in our people getting hurt and your exile from our circle forever. And Tommy, once you take the bait and respond in kind to Jhonny's teasing and name-calling, you give him control over you. Need I say more? Let's give Pecos the closure she needs and move on. Let this be a turning point."

"Yeah, let's pump the brakes, boys," Pecos suggested.

"Tommy is a donkey hole," seethed Jhonny.

"Somebody give them a crying towel," I said.

"Because Tommy is compulsed [sic] to push the hater button," continued Jhonny, who likewise lowered his head in apparent repentance and murmured indistinctly something like the following. "So, alas . . . close but no cigars. I am sorry, Pecos. Even if I am false accused or loss good friends [sic], whatever you say, I am okay of it. I never was chase any woman [sic] and am still on a journey of opening up my heart to another, and I had a dream of giving you my promise ring and having childrens . . ."

"I'm anti-procreation, Jhonny, but let me see the ring," said Pecos. "A diamond? Where's that rock?"

"I must have left it in my other dungarees," Jhonny replied, feeling his pockets.

"That there is funny. Whale of a tale, Jhonny Appleseed," laughed Tommy . . .

. . . as Pecos clenched her jaw and said, "I accept your apology, Jhonny, but Buckaroo is right: you need to learn that there are boundaries, especially in our circle of trust. Otherwise, you can ride your high horse outta town."

"Yes, I am a very talented and clever person with a higher mental capacity than ninety-nine percent and good hygiene," Jhonny boasted, "but I have my limits in personal settings and sometimes I can become rageful. I joined the group to smash down the doors of stupidity, but I seem not to know when I am out of my depth. Forgive me for thinking you were in rut and desiring to be my Honey Bunches of Oats when I am about to bust a spring. Bad dog, Jhonny . . . no biscuit."

"What? In a rut? I didn't catch all of that," she said, leaning in closer.

Nevertheless she seemed genuinely touched by his ungenuine show of remorse and returned to drumming on her practice pad, thereby earning Buckaroo's praise.

"Thank you, Pecos," he said. "You, too, Jhonny. You both raise good questions. Now that we're all loosened up sufficiently, why not have our usual freewheeling get-acquainted round robin. Why did we all join up? What has brought us all here together . . . ? Let's hear your stories. Jack, care to lead off? What brings you here today? Looking for excitement?"

CONFESSIONS OF BEFORE AND AFTER

Note: The immature or uninitiated reader may wish to skip ahead to chapter XIX, as the following section includes mostly unredacted material from my notes.

—Reno

"Excitement? Out here in cactus land? A heart attack would be more exciting. I'll tell you what brought me: my Cessna jet parked out on the strip," announced the ever-cynical Jumbo Jack Tarantulus, albeit with an affable smirk. "That, and these contracts in my pocket."

"Same here. The hope of something more," several of us agreed.

"Because I like to eat every day," quipped Jumbo Jack.

"Right. The hope of something more," we teased.

"Tired of feeling like a robot. I needed to cleanse, deprogram myself," someone said.

"For the sunsets," someone else contributed, garnering oohs and aahs of agreement.

"Sitting on the porch in our rocking chairs!"

"Thinker and problem solver," said the next. "Just wanted a bigger skill set in my toolkit."

"My blood pressure, morbid obesity," piped up another. "Disappointment after disappointment in my life. Buckaroo told me to get in the saddle and throw away the Lipozene."

"To take a stand for wildlife, all the critters whose backs are against the wall."

"Positivity" . . . "soul renewal" . . . "unrequited love," several answered.

"Level five executive consultant, then PTSD . . ."

"Mental illness is real."

"Gotta agree."

"One emotional meltdown after another. Then my food truck burned down and I would've been cooked without a small business loan from the Blue Blaze Opportunity Fund. Three years later I returned the loan with interest and decided to pay it forward and help others out, so here I am to right the scales of justice."

"Me, too. Bad credit, along with a pet. Landlords treat you like you're a parasite of society or a career criminal."

"Pet interviews, ha, ha!"

"Or try having a therapy animal. People freak," said another, showing off a tiny green reptile. "Like my little feller, Louie the Lizard. Is this the face of a societal drain or career criminal?"

"The exercise and advanced training techniques . . . the wide selection of sports, not to mention survival skills."

"Collegiality and the free flow of information among other thought leaders," someone pointed out.

"Thought leaders? Seriously? The desert echoes with laughter."

"We're not Olympians, just people leaving the light on for humanity."

"All that stuff. It's an awesome place with tons of incredible talent. Expect the impossible at the Banzai Institute!"

"Yes," replied Li'l Daughter of the Rhine. "Like many of you, I was a troubled person, so when Buckaroo offered me an official chair at das Banzai Institut, of course I pulled up stakes . . ."

"Nothing more American than pulling up stakes," someone pointed out.

"Yes, and forging a new path," Li'l Daughter said. "An *ausserordentlicher Professor* at Heidelberg and later at die Max-Planck-Gesellschaft in Berlin, where Buckaroo saw me in a small role at die Staatsoper Unter den Linden, the State Opera, and encouraged me to come to America to hopefully set up an opera company here at the Banzai Institute and even to bring my cats."

"I've heard you and your cats practicing," various people said. "You hit some real high ones."

"Yes, I was excited by this, since I was working long hours, probing deep into little microscopic things but eating a lot of white sugar and other trigger foods while losing sight of the larger picture and my health, part of a series of bad choices . . ."

"Amen . . . a 'series of bad choices' leading to a dead-end life," said Pilgrim Woman, an Australian astronomer by training, or so she said.

"Life is a lesson. Poor decisions caught up with me, too," admitted Honest Dan Cartwright. "Caltech, PhD, student loans, straight to rehab, so much anger inside. This place has been a lifeboat for me . . . painting, plumbing, laying floors and roofing, operating heavy equipment, working my way up to quartermaster because I'm good with numbers."

"Numbers don't lie. How about you, Hoppy?" Buckaroo asked our resident wrangler and chief ion collider engineer, Hoppalong Krilovsky. "Judging by your furry *ushanka*, I'd say you're Russian or a trapper, right?"

"Black Russian," said Hoppalong in his noticeably Slavic-accented English. "After American Civil War, bunch of former slaves volunteer to go to free republic of Liberia. But through crazy clerical error, we end up Siberia, instead."

"Seriously, Hoppalong?" we queried him incredulously. "Siberia instead of Liberia? Sounds like a bad sitcom."

With an ominous nod, he confirmed, "Free republic of Siberia, so help me, Black Jesus! Funny how switching little letter of alphabet changes not only one life, but lives of generations to come. So I grow up Russian and learn to ride and rope with Cossacks much like yourself, Buckaroo, but my love was always particle physics phenomenology. When my *podruga* bit me square in my ass and left me feeling blue and broke in university in Vladivostok, I sent in my application to Banzai Institute, just for hell of it . . . what to lose? *Nichevo*."

"'Blue and Broke in Vladivostok.' Sounds like number one on the hit parade, a real toe tapper," Pilgrim Woman chimed in.

"More like tearjerker," Hoppalong replied. "Most exciting thing in Vladivostok is smoking cigarette," he said. "Is kind of town full of money grubbers and bad food, but at least portions are small."

"Unlike here, where portions are large," someone pointed out, and we all agreed . . .

"Sounds familiar," Red Jordan interjected. "I earned my Special Forces badge—SF A-team, combat engineer my MOS, mainly EOD— and went to war, was taken prisoner, freed myself, won a couple of medals, only to come home to court judgments in the thousands and the wolf at the door . . . thanks to my two-timing ex, whose drug-infested mouth I found on the repo man."

"What's the old saying? A ring can't fill a hole," Mrs. Johnson said.

Red did his best to laugh, and our new shooting instructor, Talla 12 de Pantalón, related her own war story: "Just out of high school, I was just another *de las chicas en apuros*, knocked up, no money. I was just lost. My boyfriend had joined the Marines, so I followed him, ended up loving it, and learned a lot that helped me deal with my anger. Everyone's got a story to tell, and talking with them was better than any counselor. Semper Fi all the way, I made gunny sarge and wore the blood stripe proud as hell. Served in A-stan, PMI with BUD/S training in Coronado, attached to MARSOC, special operations. My new boyfriend couldn't understand my postcombat stress migraines, why I couldn't get back into cooking and cleaning or getting pregnant again . . . after helping bury little babies."

Who could feel the impact of such hair-curling words without desiring to change the subject?

"That might affect you, all right," Li'l Daughter said, clearing her throat. "Everybody seems a little uptight, so I'll go next. Some of you have asked if I have an allergic reaction. The truth is, I have a rare condition of a brain too large for my noggin, causing headaches all my life and my odd bulging eyes. I went to the best specialists of Europe, all of whom ignored my complaint or said I was just wrapped too tight. But then I heard about Buckaroo, who opened a tiny invisible port in my skull and introduced peas and applesauce . . . which, when the peas absorbed the applesauce, expanded and stretched my cranial sutures and also made me realize that my real problem was not my big brain but a metaphorical hole in my heart, a lack of optimism and faith in humanity, something I was wanting and missing. So it was that I packed a small suitcase, left Max Planck, and came to stay at the Institute to begin riding bulls and studying bovine cloning."

"Does anyone call you 'pea brain'?" someone lamely quipped.

Another asked, "Is that why you always wear that rubber helmet?"

"One of the reasons," Li'l Daughter replied with growing embarrassment.

"I had a similar problem, with a big ego and a swollen head," someone else jumped in to say, "so Buckaroo put me in a helmet, too—a pressure hat."

By now everyone seemed to want to talk at once.

"I think we're all big brains here," gushed someone intemperately.

"I think what we're talking about is hiding in the shadows, scared of what might be waiting around the corner . . . namely, to be out in the sunshine and living life," I volunteered.

"And maybe coming up with the next great idea to change the world," Pecos added.

"Yes, you are right, Pecos," said Li'l Daughter. "Isn't that why we are all here? To set the world on fire? To elevate humanity?"

Others were more modest, repeating a by now familiar refrain of personal struggle.

"Maybe in the same place I was, bored, filthy, and broke, bad smoking habit and a rejected dissertation on quantum chromodynamics due to a certain retaliation," said one of our young teaching interns. "Now I'm clean and stable and change clothes every day. More important, I got over my butt-hurt by catching the pedagogic bug. I really enjoy teaching the young ones."

These sentiments were echoed also by others.

MORE TEARFUL CONFESSIONS

Then the Marchioness spoke up to say, "Whatever happened to morals and decency, simple things like courage, honor, and sportsmanship? A place where people's best instincts are valued. I was Catherine of Aragon by way of Luxembourg, married to the great industrialist Wadsworth Longfellow and doyenne of snooty London high society. Even with the world on a silver platter, one day I realized I was tired of living happily ever after in a thousand-year-old fairy castle, on the dodge for billions in taxes. What I really wanted wasn't gallant Prince Charming on a white charger but training quarter horses for barrel racing and perhaps even traveling to other dimensions someday. I guess I was tired of being spoiled and pampered and still wanting more . . . wanting to change the world rather than merely change the color of my hair."

"Bully for you, Miss Silverspoon. Let them eat cakes. What's really tiring is being dirt poor, ramen-noodle poor, and therefore treated like dirt," confessed an irascible neighbor, who wishes to remain anonymous like most of the others. And so it continued, on around the table.

"Ramen-noodle poor, yes, yes!"

"Here's my arc, from pole dancer to exploring the Poles, North and South, finding out there's a whole lot of world out there that doesn't involve showing cleavage, spending time in the pokey, or money-riding some spoon-fed rich guy . . . or gal."

"Congratulations . . . I kind of went in reverse," confessed the mysterious Missing Person Slim Greenberg. "If you saw me then, at first glance you'd see all the superficial markers of a great success, but inside I didn't give a damn. I was lonely, cold, and burnt out. The funny thing is that the more I wanted to get shitcanned at the internet startup where I worked, the more I kept getting promoted . . . until one day I lost control. Everything went red and the rage took over."

"Is that why they call you Missing Person? You had to go to ground? Duck out?"

"That pretty much sums it up," he murmured contritely, so softly almost no one heard. "I did my time, paid my debt . . ."

"We believe you," the Marchioness replied, turning to Papa Bear. "You wanted to say something, Papa, out of brotherly solidarity? How long were you in the nick?"

"Do I need to say?" said Papa Bear.

"Oh, do," she pleaded.

"Two psych hospitalizations," Papa Bear began. "Then I did fourteen tight, in San Quentin—long enough to teach myself the trivium and quadrivium and discover my love of Euclid—then a five-piece, with administrative segregation tacked on, for shivving my first prison wife when he wouldn't wash my underwear and his mom stopped putting money on my books."

"Wowser, prison norms are weird," someone said amid a slew of similar comments.

"The blade cuts both ways," Papa Bear declared cryptically. "We settled it later like adults. My incarceration did not define me, because I'm not the same person I was then."

"None of us is," someone else pointed out. "What the Institute is all about: transformation and second chances, expunctions of our mistakes. We've all got stuff on our backgrounds . . . done time or been tampered with, one way or another."

"Sounds like me. I was on the design team of the F-35," revealed Honest Dan. "I'd rather teach, but it's all about the metrics."

"You mean the metric system?" Tommy inquired mischievously.

"So tired of it being all about the metrics," added another partner, "fighting for space and resources at State U even with eight thousand individual citations and an *h*-index of thirty-six . . . published in polymer-application trade magazines the same time I was rejected for tenure and told, 'We were good before you got here' . . . ha, ha. Then looking for work, pee-tested by drug court for three years, then told I'm a poor candidate for a slam-dunk job, then getting rejected even at the blood plasma center and absentee sperm bank . . ."

"The World Crime League is always hiring," joked a relative newcomer known as the Last Mapuche, a Canadian snowbird who had arrived recently on a ten-thousand-dollar bicycle.

And on and on it went, tales of lopsided geniuses becoming poorer in cookie-cutter jobs before finding their true calling and personal fulfillment at the Banzai Institute.

"Hello, I'm an addict with six years' clean time. Coming from academia with my credentials, I was given four choices at the employment office: call center or call girl, tortilla roller or door greeter. How pathetic is that?"

"Door-to-door junk mailer here, a thousand fliers a day for maybe five bucks an hour before I crashed and burned, ate a jar of mayo . . ."

"I made good money tutoring billionaires' kids and even started a couple of enrichment camps. But I was rotting inside, shouting obscenities and within a couple of seconds of jumping off the Verrazano Bridge when Blue Blaze Brooklyn 2000 passed by and lured me down with a Buckaroo Banzai lanyard and key fob . . . not to mention the possibility of a new identity out west."

"Same here," confessed Colorado Belle. "I'm new. I come to you from Denver, Colorado, the Mile-High City, where I worked for animal causes, a Brechtian interactive theater troupe, and against the agents of evil. Thanks for being so awesome, all of you."

When others returned the praise unduly, she changed gears, saying, "Unfortunately my own life was a lost cause: the original x-woman, because everyone tried to x me out, including myself. I drank cleaning supplies, tried to drown myself to get insurance money for my kid . . . survived a suicidal car wreck and an exploding meth house, lost my soul working for a multinational company that by proxy made me complicit in the deaths of millions. I'm a survivor but just barely: I cut vertical instead of horizontal, else I would have bled out. I was roommated with a psycho liar and stuck in a lease, so I moved out and lived in an outside porch and then a rabbit hutch, dreaming of the person I could be if I wasn't the person I actually was. Wishing on a star and a ten-dollar rock, in other words . . . just another street rat sleeping under a bridge."

"Greetings from the tent camp, fellow dweller," someone offered . . .

. . . as Belle continued, "Small wonder I ended up a gutter tramp in tweaker town—a truck stop hooker and head junkie with only three teeth, then in the Castro sleeping in squats that didn't pass the smell test before I found a home with a dom daddy in a swinging kink community. Lots of good and bad adventures. It was beautiful and it was filth. If I hadn't gotten busted for banging an Elk in front of a Lions Club in Boise, I'd probably still be taking my love to town or else be a statistic by now. Still, I wouldn't trade the experience for the world because it made me a better country singer and got me a record deal on Buckaroo's label."

Amid expressions of congratulations, she paused to add, "I see myself every day here at the rehab clinic, people of every description going hard on dope: cowboys, Apaches, truckers, businessmen, hipsters. We all know stories that would curl your hair, but with my new smile I can give them hope."

"Ain't no life like the low life," Tommy remarked, ever the skeptic. "You say you lost your teeth. Then how did you open a gunpowder pouch in hardening camp? You need four front teeth, minimum."

"The Institute provided me free dental implants and also free veneers. Thank you, Señor Dentista . . ."

"De nada, Belle," replied Señor Dentista, whose own teeth were somewhat crenellated. "I got free male enhancements and no longer have to hide behind a wall of shame. And I give the same to the impotent. Love is still possible."

ON THE THEME OF LOVE

"Love . . . good luck. Love is not the strongest drug. Ask anyone who ever loved a needle, or loved a needle freak. Love can't fix it—that's on the real," said Papa Bear, speaking from sad experience.

"Peruvian snuff powder," added another. "The white devil will clean break you."

"In more ways than one. Your mouth makes a promise your body can't keep," agreed a neighbor.

"Don't tell me about junk," said High Sierra, our current shogi champion. "I worked on Wall Street in crypto, sitting in front of a light box and algorithms sixteen hours a day, doing nothing but making mega cash, plucking hairs out of my head. One night I just sat down on a sidewalk and ate tainted Halloween candy, thinking how many people I had scammed . . . lives destroyed . . . tired of the crap being shoved down all our throats . . . and I reached for the kill switch, flipped the safety off my repeating pistol."

"Yet here you are. Aren't you glad you didn't . . . ?"

She nodded, elaborating, "Here I am, a certified master naturalist and Reiki teacher, because at the last moment I realized it wasn't my life I wanted to end—it was just my lifestyle. Now I'm high on life."

"We love you, High Sierra," said Leo the LEO. "With me, I wanted to be a cop, even a top cop, until I opened my eyes and realized the whole justice system—er, the travesty-of-justice system—is a waste of time, a sick joke. Your day in court? Tough luck, the joke's on you! Guilty or innocent doesn't matter. Since I refused to squash the innocent and take kickbacks from the guilty, here I am, due to an array of factors including self-preservation."

"You might say you saw the cop lights," someone said.

Leo nodded and said, "I saw the bubble lights and put down the jelly doughnuts, that's right. And thanks to the Institute's vocational training program, I moved up from security to millwright and recently earned my diploma in Jet Car technology."

"Hear, hear! Raise a ruckus for Leo! Congratulations!"

The Last Mapuche also nodded, saying: "No matter where we go, there we are with our truth. I came out here a Rousseauian, anarcho-primitivist Neopagan, wanting to get off the grid and visualizing a vast wilderness. I guess I was only half right."

"For me, it was either here or back to the AA clubhouse," revealed Colorado Belle. "Yet here I am, in charge of the Banzai basic clothing line and our celebrity-endorsed items with worldwide sales in eight figures last year. I nearly died in hardening camp and the purification rites but never looked back."

"I nearly died for real, too," Papa Bear revealed. "I keep giving my all, shaving my wool, only to get my heart ripped out and then blaming myself. Losing hope in love. Is 'happily ever after' even a thing anymore, or are there only workout buddies?"

"There's nothing wrong with being a woolly bear," more than one person said. "Looks and credentials don't matter. It's what's inside that counts . . . being a good person of the earth."

Someone else conspicuously cleared her throat and confessed, "Like Buckaroo says, everyone is fighting a battle and everyone is filling a void. Maybe my struggle is not on a par, being personally a vegan and also a waiter running hot wings to tables . . ."

Of all the comments, this one created possibly the biggest uproar.

"Umm, no . . . eww, the worst . . . no amount of greasy money is worth that! Is this something you even want to talk about?" many exclaimed with earnest disgust, causing the poor ex–table server to get up and leave the table.

Meanwhile, Sir Roger P——, a top international scientist and Distinguished Visiting Fellow (who wishes to remain anonymous), took a bite of blackened fish and spat it out, muttering, "My God, what child died and went into this deep-fried pig snout? Anyone know the secret code for a stomach pump? A culinary cry for help?"

Unaware that he was being watched by Mrs. Johnson—whose cooking had gained long ago the reputation of being beyond criticism—he continued, "As part of Mrs. Johnson's ongoing war on constipation, there seems to be something hissing in my slop, none of which I ordered—"

"What's that you say, motor mouth?" she fired back at the distinguished Englishman with a threatening wave of her cheese grater. "Words of wit, you wimpy little tenderfoot? You had the seafood captain's platter, right? My catfish is good food."

"Catfish *is* good food, Mrs. Johnson, but perhaps that is not a valid refutation, as catfish technically don't live in the sea—they live on a farm," the knight braved, pointing at his plate. "Also, I requested the butterfly shrimp and received these popcorn shrimp by mistake. Could I not have a bean burrito instead?"

"Maybe the butterflies weren't biting, you frigging anarcho-Bolshevik," fired back Mrs. Johnson, whereupon a timely under-the-table kick from

Tommy saved the Englishman from further harm at her hands and prompted him to amend his remarks:

"Yes, maybe just a bit more tartar sauce and it will be fine," he said hastily. "And everyone tells me I definitely need to try your famous expired-milk-and-graham-cracker pudding for dessert, Mrs. Johnson. I can't wait to taste your special creamy creation."

"There might not be enough for everyone, sugar face," she replied archly, still eyeing him suspiciously but now smiling. "The slide rule may be mightier than the sword, but not Boss Mama Johnson's butcher knife and melon baller. Ask me about my world-famous fried mountain oysters."

"Please, not the melon baller—I beseech you, Mrs. Johnson!" the jittery Sir Roger begged. "Because you are merciful, thank you."

"You're hilarious," Mrs. Johnson said.

"Could I have another glass of moo juice, ma'am?" Tommy tactfully interjected in a bid to distract Mrs. Johnson; but in this he failed, for she was not yet done with the knight.

"Because this is why your crazy ass is alone, Sir Roger. If you want your pudding, you've gotta eat your meat!"

"I'm trying to loosen up. Thank you, Mrs. Johnson," Sir Roger persisted.

"I'll see you in purification rites, if you last that long, but maybe you'd do better in a nursing home," she warned, then turned to the rest of us. "And who left a hand grenade in my freezer? Rules are rules in this house. Want me to close the doors? I will, despite my record-setting success . . . !"

"How about shorter chow lines!" some brave soul piped up, a complaint instantly echoed by others.

"Lead or get out of the way! . . . Hear, hear! . . . Change starts with us! . . . Zero tolerance for frozen grenades, ha, ha! Down with hand grenade popsicles!" we bellowed over Mrs. Johnson's threats, leaving her fuming and cursing like a truck driver.

"I hear you, Mrs. Johnson," said Sir Roger, shoveling down his seafood hash. "And I believe I will have a glass of moo juice also, just like my colleague Perfect Tommy, along with another splash of the Pichon-Longueville Baron."

"Work hard, party harder!" someone yelled.

"Viva the Institute!"

"*Que viva!* Progress over protocol!"

"Never bettered, never bested!" a fresh chant began. "A shovel and a shoulder to cry on, all the beans and bullets you can eat!"

"Banzai!"

"Banzai!"

MORE NAMES WITHHELD BY REQUEST

"I came for the space travel because I believe space is our destiny . . ."

"Beats selling gym memberships to mouthy wimps with mental issues. So tired of the double talk, the work-life balance, temp-to-perm, manager-potential crap . . . like all these twenty-first-century jobs with no future . . . nothing but street smear under the boss man's shoe. And bullshit negativity. Just turning into another rat-racer debt slave. They invite you in with a smile. Entry-level professional, they say—oh, sure— counting on you just being willfully stupid and in denial, cynical about your broken dreams and excuse making . . ."

"For sure. Try being a young rising star in complex systems by day, and by night a divorced adjunct prof working for formula and diaper money, just another broke-dick zombie with a pay-the-bills job . . . every day a self-hate crime. Not realizing one iota of a damn's worth of my full potential in a beatnik coffeehouse . . . tired of deadbeat panhandlers wearing better shoes than my black supergrips . . ."

"Can't fire me 'cause I'm not playing!"

"Winning!"

"And if you have a sense of humor, it's even worse! Nobody gets sarcasm!"

"But why? Why is sarcasm so phawking hard?" someone else questioned.

And so on, each with a not dissimilar story: "I arrived here broke and with migraines so debilitating, I threw a childlike tantrum expecting pity. But I was in for a rude awakening, especially when Buckaroo found that I was being radio tracked and slowly poisoned by World Crime League electronic tattoos, which he removed. Now when I run a marathon or lay my head on my pillow at night without my brain in scanning mode, I thank heaven for the Banzai Institute and its support network, the best of the best, where the impossible becomes routine . . ."

Still another declared, "Sounds like. I came for a boob job and butt boosters, but then Buckaroo made me realize the foolishness of wanting manmade bolt-ons to attract a real man, so instead he wangled me a grant from the National Science Foundation for my revolutionary technique in gene transference . . ."

"I won the National Spelling Bee and a free ride for the Banzai Institute Semester at Sea program. That scholarship got my foot in the door and changed my life many years ago," an older gentleman said, looking around at the many faces in the room . . . some familiar, some new. "Pretty select company."

"I'll say. I came for the Institute's summer festival and music academy and never left except for three years with the Philadelphia Orchestra . . ."

"Same here. Eagle Scout competitive shooter, I won junior top prize for shooting clays and went on to the Olympics and a gold medal. But the steel guitar was always my first love. Unfortunately, I was super freckled . . . always insecure. Then the call from Buckaroo that changed my life . . ."

"My skin was messed up, too . . . acne, psoriasis . . . always working on either weight loss or fat acceptance, so I went crazy for tattoos and pretty much inked myself all over. But what was I trying to hide?"

"Was I bitter?" Honest Dan suddenly interjected with obvious intensity. "Damn right I was bitter, living in immiseration with nothing going for me except scratch-off tickets, but better a restless Socrates than a happy pig in slop . . . plus the pure baloney they feed you like unhealthy food, when you're just another well-oiled lab drone chasing the rat wheel and trying to kiss up to penny-pinching bosses. Just so tired of living on the edge with no tomorrow, in a perpetual state of mediocrity, going nowhere and just waiting to die of ass cancer and not being able to afford a casket . . . chasing the proverbial mechanical rabbit around the proverbial track, just a number on a spreadsheet until I had a meltdown one day and happened to see Buckaroo on TV talking about Buckminster Fuller's theory of precession, how positive motivation leads to positive effects and vice versa. Seeing that, I quit my dead-end job and immersed myself in my research that I had given up on as too mind blowing. Six months later Peking U called about my breakthroughs in superfluid vacuum theory and oscillatory dynamics, which eventually led me to observe a physical effect of deep meditation on quantum tunneling and randomly generated numbers, leading in turn to a couple of nice lottery prizes and gigs in Las Vegas and the Princeton Engineering Anomalies Research lab. But by then Buckaroo had already lured me here to the Institute. Like I told my old lady, I'm out the door to better things . . . a bigger stage, a bigger narrative."

"Your old lady . . . ?"

"My mother."

"I can relate," said Li'l Daughter. "I thought I'd be married or at least chasing sunsets with the 'one,' instead of fishing for a guy with a job and decent credit and catching nothing but fake personas and taken men or guys with a lot of guns and heathen children, or STDs . . . *scheiss* terrible days, ha, ha . . ."

"Shitty, terrible days, ha, ha . . . luckily I can't have sex, because it hurts. Small wonder I have trust and intimacy issues! Still, I count my blessings, lucky to be alive and living at the Banzai Institute . . ."

"I had big plans, too, but could never quite get rolling," confessed the anonymous triple amputee in black who had arrived only recently in a hippie van with a hydraulic hoist. "But I vowed to die on my feet, joined the army, and passed the SFQC, then traveled the world for many years, played in a thrash metal band, did some octagon fighting and even a stint in the French Foreign Legion over in the Sudan, where I slept inside the gutted carcass of a camel and survived two bullet wounds, a blowgun dart, and numerous knifings from a hundred-some-odd modern-day slavers . . ."

"Not exactly a picnic," I remarked.

"Not a picnic at all," said the ex-Legionnaire, "but nothing compared to hitting the beaches of Italian Somaliland as a counterterrorism specialist or auditioning for the Hong Kong Cavaliers . . ."

"Italian Somaliland? The inside of a camel?" someone questioned. "That's quite a struggle story."

"Yep. I guess I've used eight of my nine lives and three of my four limbs," said the new arrival.

"Scary."

"Super scary," said someone else, before posing a question to all: "What's the scariest thing about coming to the Institute, everybody?"

"For me, learning to shoot a gun," said a grubby stable hand whose nickname I no longer can recall.

"And running up mountains . . . the hardest of ways, loving and learning . . . from caterpillars to butterflies."

"Oh my God, the screening process," someone fondly reminisced. "Those grueling interviews and personality assessments! All those wacky questionnaires!"

Practically in unison, we screamed with laughter and shouted back, "Do you strongly agree? Somewhat agree? Not sure? Somewhat disagree or strongly disagree? A, B, C, or D?"

"How the phawk did we survive without losing our marbles? Or did we?"

"Team building! Character building! To go where none have gone! When the going gets tough—"

"On guard for Canada!" interjected the Last Mapuche, raising his goblet.

At this Buckaroo also had to chuckle, saying, "Pat yourselves on the back, people. Well done, well played!"

XIX. THE CAVALIERS LET THEIR HAIR DOWN

> With your equipment they all began.
> Get hold of yourself and say: "I can."
> —Edgar A. Guest

"Can I ask you something, Reno?" Li'l Daughter now interrupted and, heartened by my head nod, proceeded to ask, "Why do you call yourself the Reno Kid? Are you from Reno, the Biggest Little City in the World?"

By no means new to this question, I replied, "When I was younger and in and out of trouble, I spent a little time in the ring, and my trainer gave me that name. 'Kid Reno' he called me, but then we got in a bind because there was already another Kid Reno, a lightweight, so I became the Reno Kid, even though somebody had that name, too. But by then I was getting out of the boxing game, so I kept it. It just kind of stuck with me through all my wanderings and dark days at NASA."

"Never a straight answer at NASA," joked Pecos to rollicking laughter.

I chortled as well and said, "Pretty much. Luckily, there was the Indian Institute of Science and then my own startup and think tank in Bangalore and then the Banzai Institute . . . or else I don't know where I'd be. In a world of hurt and a bullying culture, you just have to try a little harder . . ."

"Don't be afraid to say those three little words: I need help . . ."

"And ask the question: am I a sociopath or a truly superior being?" said a jokester.

"I'd probably still be in lockup," admitted Papa Bear. "Nothing leaves this room, right? I came into contact with Mrs. Johnson—the 'lunch lady,' she called herself—who wrote me in care of the USFPS. Through her, I learned that the Institute was background friendly, so my second prison wife sent her a letter of recommendation. Then, lo and behold, I heard back, from the Cavendish Lab at Cambridge, letting me know they'd have a spot for me if I got early release, so I took them up on it and renewed my love of musical theater by joining the Cambridge Footlights. From there, it was just a hop, skip, and a jump to the Institute. Thanks, Mrs. Johnson."

"Glad to help, just happy to give something back through our Write-A-Prisoner program," replied Mrs. Johnson. "The Banzai Institute has been good to me, too. Buckaroo encouraged me to market my cake molds, flatware, and homemade rejuvenizing creams, and I just signed seven-figure deals with CorningWare and Banquet TV dinners."

"Mrs. Johnson! Mrs. Johnson! Action taker! Raising the positive!" we all shouted. "The power is within you . . . you have the power!"

By now emotionally worn out, we all soon fell silent, until Buckaroo spoke up to remind everyone of an important truth. "Don't give up. We can complain all we want, but that's life: learning how to compromise, never knowing what the universe has planned, making something positive and drawing life lessons from our battle scars . . ."

Here he paused, obviously considering his choice of words and his own emotional wounds, before Tommy came to his rescue, in a manner of speaking: "That's right. Too many dang crybabies in their inner hell but still stealing my peanut butter."

"That'd be me, Tommy," confessed Honest Dan Cartwright. "I'm an insulin-dependent diabetic, sane and sober, and greatly honored to be your quartermaster and parts manager."

"Indeed, a strategic partnership," Buckaroo pointed out somewhat cryptically. "I predict big things for you, Honest Dan, with your eye for quality merchandise."

Note: Sadly, Tommy's suspicions proved to be prescient when Quartermaster Cartwright and the triple amputee in black disappeared scant days later. Last seen woolgathering and picking up bottles and cans along the main highway, they

have not been heard from since, and our efforts to locate either of them—as well as a considerable sum of money from our household account—have proved fruitless, forcing me to admit the nice things I have said about "Honest Dan" were not only phony but insincere.

—Reno

"Bottom line, we're all fortunate to be alive," Buckaroo continued, once again making the long nose at Tommy. "When you think things are bad, remember there's a thin line between being a victim and a willing participant. We have to always ask ourselves whether we are a victim or a volunteer . . . and whether what we're experiencing is real suffering or self-centeredness."

"But isn't that an impossible test, Buckaroo, since we experience what we experience, whether it is based on concrete reality or not?" inquired Li'l Daughter. "I know you know the meaning of depression, and I've been depressed myself and once spent a month alone, trying to lose myself deep in the Black Forest and rebirth myself."

"Yes, I often see you walking alone in the orchard," said Buckaroo. "Remember, depression is not something you need bear alone. We have wonderful mental health resources here at the Institute."

"Something to keep in mind yourself, Buckaroo," ventured Pecos. "I hate to think how many days you've spent cooped up in your study all alone, doing nothing but reciting Kūkai's Ākāśagarbha sutra so loud you even vibrate the walls, and blowing your *shakuhachi* along with Beethoven's Third Symphony or the Mormon Tabernacle Choir . . ."

"Kūkai, yes," replied Buckaroo thoughtfully. "In the caves of Muroto, just as I . . . since Penny . . ."

"Just as you, in your own cave, like Kūkai, stare into the gloom," she continued. "Your punishment is your own mind, and it almost breaks my heart to think you might be slipping into *hikikomori* mode. You need to love yourself and get out more, live a little."

"Raise Cain, stay up late with the late-night crowd," Tommy echoed.

"Maybe what we need is a new rip-roaring adventure," I suggested hopefully.

Tommy seconded the idea at once: "Back in the saddle! Boots on the ground! Sooner the better!"

"Maybe when the time comes. But careful what you wish for, fellas," Buckaroo cautioned. "Like everyone else, I have despondent moments, but I've learned that even in suffering, it's possible to find meaning and something like enlightenment. Sitting in the dark, I wish for nothing, not glory, not power, not even revenge, only calm and Ryōkan's lines: 'ten days of rice in my bag and, by the hearth, a bundle of firewood.'"

Li'l Daughter cleared her throat and mused dreamily, "A sense of peace away from this crazy world . . . flow like water . . . I'm there with you, Buckaroo."

"I'm with him, too," Pecos icily warned the young German. "Remember Krishnamurti's words: 'I don't mind what happens.'"

"His secret of happiness. Good advice, and I try," said Buckaroo. "Yet there are many moments when I bemoan my own stupidities and hear a crazy voice . . ."

"Whose voice, Buckaroo? Hanoi Xan's poisonous venom?" Tommy queried him, drawing our ire, although Buckaroo responded with good humor.

"Excellent question, Tom. Let's just say a crazy voice in my head that makes me sick to my stomach and keeps insisting, 'You're out of your league, Buckaroo. No one who kills himself has ever regretted it.'"

"Never? Not even one of 'em ever lived to regret it?" said Tommy in all earnestness.

"You make my brain bleed, Tom. Try to keep your signature dumbassery on the low," I told him with annoyance, while the thought of a suicidal Buckaroo elicited a collective reaction of horror from us all, doubtless causing the great man to regret giving us reason to worry.

"But the reason I listen to the *Eroica*," he explained, "is to remind myself that the composer had lost something precious, even his hearing, and was left with feelings similar to my own when he wrote it. And yet he produced this amazing work, even when we would say he was not at his best, emotionally or physically speaking."

As we listened with rapt attention, he searched our faces and continued, "I find it helpful to remember that example, and I thank you all for standing by my side, especially since each of you has the opportunity to go somewhere else . . ."

"We wouldn't dream of it, Buckaroo," said Pecos.

"Proud to stick around," added Tommy with uncustomary modesty. "We're still the best team going, even if none of us is perfect. Not even me."

"Exactly the point, Tommy. We're only as free and as useful as we allow ourselves to be. We have to learn to liberate ourselves from false realities that we spin or that the world spins for us—even idealized images of ourselves—lest these become sources of frustration and unhappiness. I don't mean to be preachy, but . . ."

"Preach, Buckaroo. Thanks for owning up to it," Pecos urged . . .

. . . as Buckaroo continued: "Perhaps if we are falling short of our goals, the blame lies not with our own efforts but with our inflated expectations, or those expectations imposed on us by others. We needn't punish ourselves so long as we're doing meaningful work that needs doing. I've often told the story of how some of the best people I ever met, and among those with the greatest natural dignity, were my coworkers when I was working as a garbage helper and recyclables gleaner at Columbia College of Physicians & Surgeons. What struck me was how they were less despondent on average than many of my fellow med students—because they were not bedeviled by an expectation of being smart enough to outfox disease and death—and yet the work they were doing was just as vital. On the downside, because society undervalued them and they were often flat broke, I had to remind them that their junk food diets were the equivalent of the garbage we collected, or worse."

His analysis was not whimsical, and perhaps for that reason (his appeal to our best natures), it failed to receive the acknowledgment it deserved, as we continued to focus on our own insecurities and tales of the woe that had befallen us.

"I just have to laugh," said Li'l Daughter. "This is so true."

"By the tag on their pants, you shall know them," said a listener. "I was always the land whale, the fat kid on the seesaw with a thyroid problem, and I'd still be sucking in my belly, wearing size fifty-six jeans with 'Ride or Die' across my butt if I hadn't run into some Blue Blazes putting up a display table at my local flea market, so I rode my Harley with Screamin' Eagle pipes out here to the desert, to the Last Chance Saloon for a gastric bypass, but instead Buckaroo put me on some Get-Right and scared the holy beejeebus out of me, and so far I've lost one hundred eighty-five pounds of blubber ass and have a thirty-one-inch waist . . ."

But Tommy was not impressed, grunting under his breath, "That's a crock of bullcrap. You and your electric-start Tonka-toy Harley—hell, why not just ride a Sportster with racing stripes? American iron, my ass. No disrespect intended, but at least ride a Shovelhead . . ."

"Then phrase it another way, Tommy," Buckaroo suggested to our perpetual *enfant terrible*. "What are you trying to say?"

"What I'm trying to say is, make it work, people!" Tommy said with uncommon passion. "Just chalk it up to a lesson learned! Whatever happened to just putting one foot in front of the other, hitting a road bump, and sucking it up and moving on, until, by the grace of God, we drop dead in our tracks just like our ancestors? This way we all sound like a bunch of whiners looking for pity. Who in this world hasn't wanted to be heard by eating a shotgun or crashing into a bridge abutment? Let's just admit we're all the same monkey trying to screw the same football and nothing special."

When his colorful outburst naturally raised eyebrows, I remarked, "I don't know, Tom, sounds kind of special . . . and a great mental picture. Care to translate for the rest of us?"

This task was left to Buckaroo, who speculated, "Maybe Tommy's talking about an identity crisis . . . a monkey mistaking a football for a sex partner or a life goal. A primary cause might be carrying a false image of ourselves because we lack meaningful connections with other people. I know because there's nothing scarier than struggling with your own mind on a daily basis."

Tommy nodded and replied with a sanctimonious tone, "Pretty much the reason we're sitting here bringing all this stuff up again . . . just a bunch of bridge burners who came to the Institute and found our best selves by putting ourselves to the test and learning to dig from deep within, such as how to be a man on a real Shovelhead with open pipes instead of a fatty cakes on a Harley cruiser."

Pecos now waded in, saying, "I'm not trying to be a man at all, so I'm not fully persuaded. But tell us, why did you sign on, Tommy?"

"Just catching a lot of junk in my life, but you go first, old girl," he said. "What made you put your John Henry on the dotted line?"

"Let's see how fast I can make this," replied Pecos, not given to telling stories about herself. "I grew up the daughter of missionaries, lived in lots of beautiful places, grew our own food, and never lived high on the hog . . . a couple of brothers and a sister . . . we also shared miseries together, struggled to get by. When the you-know-what hit the fan, we had to make do or sometimes make a run for it. My father and two brothers were kidnapped by corsairs off the coast of Zanzibar, and my mother drowned in the Zambezi River, where I was miraculously saved by a crocodile and then adopted by a mama hyena. After Mama Hyena was killed, I entered into marriage with a nomadic cattle drover . . . where my duties significantly expanded."

Plainly having us now in the palm of her hand, she paused to take a sip of *reishi* tea and continued her tale. "After our church paid my ransom of two milk cows, I left the marriage and went to live with my aunt, also a missionary, and continued to travel. I eventually learned a dozen languages and at the age of fourteen became a translator for the Wycliffe Bible Society. Two years later, at the age of sixteen, I entered Caltech and earned a doctorate in nuclear spin tomography. When Buckaroo came to campus for a talk about interdimensional travel, he looked me up and offered me a pair of silver spurs on the spot. It so happens I was the first woman ever to wear them."

Of a sudden, and already bored of the topic, she announced, "Hugs, everybody. How about you, Tommy? Any confessions to share?"

Tommy appeared thoughtful for a moment and replied, "Not to steal your thunder, Pecos, but I do have one confession. In high school I was hot mustard. They called me Mr. Touchdown."

Amid groans and much tooth grinding, Buckaroo interrupted, "Thanks for being so transparent, Tommy, but since we are something of a brotherhood and sisterhood of lost causes, tell us why you decided to become a Hong Kong Cavalier. Was it just for the three hots and a cot? The stipend and the benefits?"

Tommy now appeared to undergo a rare bout of introspection, revealing, "It wasn't for the money. I don't know what any of this has to do with the price of groceries in China, but when I was a kid back in Mizzou, I got diagnosed as an Indigo Child with superpowers, meaning a power child and an empath, among other things. I also got placed into guardianship like a hound dog."

Indeed his face and ears appeared to droop and he chewed his lip with some bitterness, despite Mrs. Johnson's well-meaning attempt to lighten his mood: "I think the last time I saw Tommy this upset was when I wouldn't let him lick my chocolate beaters, or the time I told him we were out of legs and thighs."

"That had to be a desperate feeling," Dr. Doe said softly. "A feeling of inadequacy."

Tommy shot back a wounded look and continued, "Yeah, sucks and blows. I ran away three times, just hopped the choo-choo train to the next town over, and then the next . . . how I come to find out there's always a 'next town over' and a mighty big world out there. Next thing I know, my school principal went apeshit on my teenage buttocks, because of which the judge put me on psych meds and puberty blockers and sent me to Father Flanagan's Boys Town, where I went on to develop into a superhuman athlete and also launched the worldwide Ritalin abuse campaign that won me the MacArthur Wile E. Coyote genius grant, making me the youngest winner ever. I finished my pseudo education at the Wanton School of Business . . ."

"Tommy, when's the last time you were drug tested?" Li'l Daughter asked with concern.

"And never went through puberty? That would explain a lot, especially about your prefrontal cortex," remarked Pecos.

"Tommy, do you mean the Wharton School of Finance?" inquired Jack.

"Yeah, the Wanton School, after which I went up to Balliol College, Oxford, to study history and mathematics, and soon to become its master," Tommy continued, unfazed by snickers of ridicule and a few catcalls.

"Master of Balliol! Oh, bullshit," interjected Jack. "Tallyho, old chap! I'm looking that up."

"Sure, enjoy yourself, Jack," Tommy replied nonchalantly. "Anyway, I always wanted to be ringside, where the action was . . . the tip of the spear . . . so when the docs sent me to another seventy-two hold for running the biggest stud service this side of the Mississippi, I bailed on the day of—gave away all my junk except a big wardrobe box with my guitars, barbell, fishing tackle and big-bore Henry, my stack of *otaku* fanzines and Game Box—and said adios to the old hacienda. Just started driving down back roads in my low-ridin' Midnight Special, baby moon hubcaps, listening to the silence, except for my loud Boss 429 Mustang exhaust and trunk-thumping subwoofers, from the Ozarks to the wild frontier. My dream was to sow some oats and maybe become a head

turner, a Starfleet officer, or a young *shinobi* in the harsh desert—either
that or kill a man for every year of my life, like Billy the Kid. I guess I
wanted people to know my name."

"That's Tommy, all right: guitars and cars," observed Li'l Daughter
affectionately.

"You just showed up without an invite, in your classic muscle car?
With furry dice no doubt," Pecos said, making a face. "I can only imagine
the unsanitation."

Tommy shrugged and said, "Hell, not even so much as an appointment.
I got lost. I wasn't even sure where the Institute was. I just walked in
with one of my premier smokes, took the entrance test, and knocked it
outta the park, scoring three deviations above the mean."

"Mr. Touchdown," teased Pecos.

"Because we all know you're never wrong, Tom," I complimented
him, doing little to hide my sarcasm.

"Not always," said Tommy. "I thought I was wrong once, but, mirabile
dictu, turns out I was mistaken."

Jack now turned off his phone with a somewhat stunned expression and
muttered, "Damn, Tommy's right. He was master of Balliol College . . .
Balliol College, University of Oxford, England . . . for three years."

Buoyed by Jack's research, Tommy responded by dropping some of
his cocksureness: "Of course I make mistakes—I'm only human. I wasn't
groomed for greatness, not one of those pinheaded guys educated beyond
their intelligence. What I mean is, maybe my tallywhacker's bigger than
my heart, and my heart's bigger than my brain."

"At least you have no illusions about yourself," Pecos said in an ironic
jest that passed over Tommy's head . . .

. . . as he resumed his account. "Like I said, I was always a professed
loner and wild child, a born iconoclast and nomad raised in a whirlwind,
who roamed wherever. Never had but about two friends my whole life,
even though people loved to be around me. It was around this time that
I began putting smiles on young ladies. Then I came to the Institute,
where I realized I could do bad all by my damn self but needed to work
with other people in order to do good in the world. Like Buckaroo always
says, to achieve success at anything, you need two things: desire and a
partner. And maybe a plan. All that I am today, I owe it all to Buckaroo
and the Banzai Institute."

Buckaroo chortled in turn and said, "Tommy showed up and literally got his foot in the door, then refused to remove it unless we let him in. As I recall, Mrs. Johnson vouched for him because he gave her a hand in her canning and pickling efforts."

"I only taught him how to pickle. He already knew how to butter a girl up," recalled Mrs. Johnson fondly.

While we cautiously applauded such sentiments, Tommy pulled her leg, saying, "And my other motivation was to eat Mrs. Johnson's buffet long enough to get sugar diabetes. I think I will have another helping of Pecos's vegetarian goulash and a *dhaba* bowl of your famous gunpowder chili with jalapeño cornbread, Mrs. Johnson. Doesn't get any better than that, or worse."

Seeing Mrs. Johnson smile, we had all the laughs.

"Stay special, Tommy," I said and gave him a good nudge in the ribs.

FOOD FOR THOUGHT

I turned my head as Mrs. Johnson nudged me again. "How about you, Reno? Another trip to the trough? Another splash of variety chili?"

"No thanks, but I think Rawhide's due for another," I told her, indicating the empty seat to my right that was occupied only by our dear, departed friend's ragged Stetson hat . . . while across the table otherwise empty chairs were claimed by Penny's sombrero and Professor Hikita's blood-smeared spectacles.

"Definitely, Rawhide will go for another bowl," Buckaroo said. "And Hikita-sama as well. Nobody does primeval chili like you, Mrs. Johnson . . ."

"Lots of protein. And cheaper than a deworming," joked Tommy.

"Oh, you're just saying that . . . so full of baloney," Mrs. Johnson said, turning to Rawhide's empty chair in a moment of poignancy that escaped no one. "That goes for you, too, Rawhide. But save room for banana pudding and your favorite . . . my peach cobbler. And be sure you chew your meat at least ten times and roll your tongue five. Damn those Lectroid buzzards."

Her voice faltered and she lowered her head for a moment to hide evidence of her tears, and I must confess many of us did likewise before

Pecos and High Sierra chorused poignantly and raised their glasses in a toast. "Hear, hear, raise a cup! 'Up, up, tonight we sup—though tomorrow we die of the revel!' A cup of remembrance to our fallen brothers and sisters in arms!"

"Hear, hear! Long live the Institute!" shouted Hoppalong, Red, and Pinky. "To hell with the World Crime League!"

"Nuke 'em! Piss anywhere we want!" hooted a thoroughly soused Tommy between bites of one of Mrs. Johnson's famous Dijon mayonnaise and fried catfish sandwiches, while Buckaroo prepared to read the annual list of our fallen martyrs. But first Li'l Daughter had something she wished to say and so recited Antony's soliloquy over Caesar's body, albeit in German.

When she finished, we naturally whistled and applauded and began clamoring for vengeance against Hanoi Xan. "How many more sick crimes? How many more murders? Haven't we allowed the monster to fester long enough?! Avenge Hikita! Avenge Penny! C'mon, is this the best we can do . . . ?!"

"Silver hollow point!" the Marchioness declared and slammed a rifle bullet down on the table. "One hundred sixty-eight grain . . . double tap to the T . . ."

"And a thirty-two-round mag," Mrs. Johnson added, invoking a curse. "Hex, hex, two by two, Xan, you rodent, I put a hex on you . . . and your long hair and all your names! Drop you like a bad penny!"

Her unfortunate choice of the last word caused a momentary pause to descend upon us all, which Buckaroo interrupted to say, "Big talk and big guns, sisters. How about just burying the rascal under the jail and tying the key to a jackrabbit . . . ?"

"Hear, hear, a jackrabbit! Push the envelope! Find the rock he's hiding under and kick it over! Hold the bozo accountable!" came the rowdy responses from the body of the room.

"Blood in the mud! And double rations of rum!" called out Tommy . . .

"But leave nature undisturbed! Leave it better than we found it!" Mrs. Johnson cautioned . . .

. . . as Buckaroo resumed, "Thank you, Mrs. Johnson, for reminding us of the importance of being good stewards of the environment, and thank you, Daughter, for the moving tribute to our fallen martyrs. And thank all of you, first-class people one and all, for sharing your stories.

Each of you is a rare find who by your very actions rejects the crime of narrow thinking and possesses the ability to see around corners like Tommy—"

Here he was interrupted again by Tommy, who, by now quite tipsy, expertly rolled a cigarette with one hand and proclaimed a toast with the other.

"I believe it was Plutarch or Pluto who once raised a Roman glass," he announced. "To Kentucky horses and Tennessee women! And our small band of badass! And the nectar of the bacchanal!"

Seeing his words elicit little response, however, he indignantly got up, fell down, and performed his trademark backward crawl dance out the door . . . in order, he said, to "catch a drag or two and process my food . . ."

"Godspeed, Tommy," announced Buckaroo, continuing his little talk. "We *are* the lucky few, looking at the world through clear eyes and from a place of gratitude, free to chart our own course in the knowledge that the secret is not to seek acceptance, but rather not to give a damn for it . . . not to wait for opportunity to come knocking, but to knock on opportunity's door, although running toward gunshots is always voluntary."

Allowing for a ripple of laughter, he pushed on with a brief commentary on the Buddha's Turning of the Wheel of the Law sermon before concluding, "As you know, we're living in significant times; and at a moment when we face dangers perhaps unprecedented in the annals of our planet, I'll just close with what you've heard me say many times: it matters not how a man cuts his peas, but the quality of his mind and character, so on this eve of potential calamity let us drink to our friends around the biosphere and the biosphere around our friends . . . and never forget we're alive!"

"We're alive!" we all confirmed.

"And getting better!" announced Lucky Masahiro. "Kaizen!"

"Kaizen! Institutional memory!" we all chimed in. "Banzai!"

UNWELCOME VISITORS

One last toast of *baijiu*, and it was time for Buckaroo to read the honor roll of our fallen martyrs from the beginning forward. When this was done, we sat in respectful silence, save for the sound of a robotic floor buffer in the foyer, which Buckaroo stepped out to investigate en route to tending the fire in the *chashitsu* tea room, inasmuch as it was customary for him to boil the water, prepare the tea, and serve it to all of us in the spirit of *wabi* . . .

. . . when of a sudden we heard him utter an involuntary gasp of surprise, and Nostradamus, almost simultaneously, threw back his head with a mighty howl of his own. Need I say his angry disposition fit our own as we rushed into the tea room to find the phantasm Professor Hikita sitting in golden light on a traditional *zabuton* floor cushion!

I will not describe the great scientist and Buckaroo's mentor other than to say he was plainly a shade and a younger version of himself and not, as some (who were not present) have suggested, a talking corpse. After the brief ensuing hush—verified by comparing our notes afterward—the following exchange occurred.

Buckaroo, taking a tentative step forward, asked incredulously, "Hikita-sama . . . ? Can you hear me . . . ?"

Since there was no sign that this was the case, Buckaroo produced his Go-Phone with its pocket interferometer and fired a visible bolt of static electricity directly at our special visitor, who plainly felt the brunt of the charge and immediately toppled off the cushion . . . albeit with no expression of disagreeableness. In fact his face, transparent as it was, bore no trace of emotion whatsoever.

"Buckaroo!" he exclaimed, suddenly turning our way with a blank look. "Am I late for dinner?"

"But just in time for tea," Buckaroo told him. "Where are you, Chichi? Who's with you? What dimension are you in?"

"I am in 1958. I saw your father only yesterday."

"My father . . . ? Tell him—"

But just then Hikita and the golden light began to flicker and fade, along with his voice.

"I have no power here," he complained, seemingly talking to himself in limbo land. "Life . . . so strange . . . a balancing act where you die at the end . . ."

"Who killed you, Chichi?" Buckaroo called out desperately.

Hikita's voice still lingered but seemed to be moving out of range, or to a different frequency. "Magdalene" was the word that floated back to us, followed by, "Manny did it . . ."

And then our ethereal visitor was gone, leaving Buckaroo with clenched fists and a solemn vow. "I knew your wounds bore the cut of a billhook. I'll crush him, Chichi. I have marked him as my own."

Buckaroo's words were cut short, however, by his own irritation with the noise of the automatic floor buffer, which by now had been joined by a robotic high-pressure washer just outside our window. But even above this combined infernal racket, Buckaroo's acute hearing seemed to detect something else in the air, a troubling sound unnoticed by the rest of us and yet now confirmed by a message over Buckaroo's earpiece and echoed with urgency by Wild Bill. "Not to interrupt you, *comandante*, but Nostradamus informs me he hears a muffled attack chopper, approximately six klicks due north and headed for us."

Neither warning came a second too soon, as Buckaroo tapped his ear and verified the worst: "Buffalo Gal and Ranger Nick reporting . . . a convoy of Pinkertons, or someone who looks an awful lot like 'em, coming up Paint Creek Road . . ."

"Maybe not *federales*, then?" I said.

"Is it a fire drill?" others called out.

"Lockdown, folks! You know your stations!" I shouted and hustled alongside Buckaroo on his way out.

"Could be the new Joint Special Operations Task Force from DARPA we've been hearing about. Nothing we haven't been expecting, since they probably think we stole their favorite mutants . . ."

"Including Wild Bill?" I inadvertently quipped.

"On top of everything else," he said, turning and heading out the double doors into the lobby, where a dozen others were already waiting in improvised field gear and body armor, awaiting developments.

"I'm not looking for trouble, folks, unless somebody doesn't have a search warrant," Buckaroo cautioned before giving Tommy and me our marching orders. "Reno, I think it's time to remove Wild Bill's ankle monitor. You and Tommy take him and the quad racers, split up, and meet up at the haunted mine . . . north adit."

"What about you, Buck?" Tommy asked with urgency. "What are you gonna do?"

"I need to make my rounds with the patients at the clinic—they'll be upset by all the commotion—then try to reach the president before somebody gets more than their feelings hurt!" our chief replied with a sense of urgency and more than a little moral outrage. If there was one human trait he could not abide, it was the abuse of power, particularly by jealous government officials who guarded their turf better than they guarded the planet. Knowing him as I do, however, I also recognized that he loathed this quality even more in himself, even in the tiniest portion.

XX. INTO THE LAP OF THE APACHES

> The soldiers never explained to the government
> when an Indian was wronged.
> —Geronimo

Scarcely five minutes later, after clipping Wild Bill's ankle bracelet,I made a beeline with him and Nostradamus across open country. Racing toward the foothills of the San Francisco Mountains on a highly modified Honda Rubicon 550, I could not see directly the look on their faces; but I believe I can picture it perfectly: both the general and his scraggly Chihuahua with eyes closed, mouths open, and tongues lolling in the wind.

"Hang on tight!" I threw my head back and shouted at him above the din of the high-performance engine, simultaneously steering with one hand while pulling my Vepr 12 from its scabbard.

"Beautiful country! Look at that full moon!" he yelled, eyes half-open. "Looks like some great solitude! Never mind the vultures!"

I did not disagree. In fact, I could be forgiven for not replying at all, as at that point my attention was riveted not on a buzzard but on a small flying object, perhaps seventy-five yards off to our left, that had been dogging us practically since we left the Institute. As I steered with my left hand and leveled the scattergun in the crook of the same arm, he continued to chatter.

"Devoid of the human condition! Of course the Sonoran Desert's nothing. Ever been to Ma'rib? The vast Saudi Arabian Empty Quarter?"

At least that was as much as I heard, as at that instant I pulled the trigger and momentarily used both hands to choke the weapon and fire again, resulting in a semicollision with a cactus patch and a quick overcorrection on my part that nearly tipped us into a nasty spill.

"Aaaaagh, what's all the excitement? I just tossed my salad! And that stank you smell is Nostradamus!" exclaimed the general . . .

. . . as suddenly a roaring cloud of dust came careening alongside and we swiveled our heads to see Tommy on a Yamaha quad, riding hands free and clutching his beloved big-bore Henry rifle.

"You see Henry shoot down that drone?" he asked cockily.

"*You* shot it down? Hell, I shot it down!" I fired back.

"Dang right you shot it down! Destruction of government property— that's thirty years in the hoosegow!" he shouted and proceeded to make a hairpin turn right in front of us, forcing me to execute a perfect doughnut to avoid him.

"Eat my dust, brother!" he hooted.

"Tommy, you tool! We're supposed to split up!" I yelled back and quickly flew into a furious chase without ever letting off the throttle.

"He's got an ornery streak a mile wide!" I yelled at the general, whose anguished reply about being an old fighter pilot I could not quite decipher, as he held on to his US Cavalry hat for dear life and our path became more tortuous . . . winding upward through a staircase of boulders and creosote bushes . . .

. . . until in the distance I spotted Tommy, standing on the saddle of his Yamaha, his rifle barrel glinting in the silvery moonlight while, nearby, several Apaches scrambled over sun-bleached rocks to surround him . . .

"A snowball's chance in hell!" I heard him blurt out—an utterance accompanied by a thundering gunshot into the air and the sudden flight of bats and wild pigeons, as I goosed the quad forward . . . drawing Tommy's attention just long enough to fishtail up the narrow trail and brake to a stop right behind him.

"Tommy! Don't be a complete jackass!"

"I can handle this business, Reno," he said, seeming short fused and still waving his pistol. "I know who they are. Don't they know who I am?"

"Since when does the great Perfect Tommy need an introduction . . . ?" came the voice of an elder Apache, who now emerged from a hidden hole in the mountain and came toward us, signaling his warriors to lower their automatic repeating rifles.

Seeing me, he raised a hand of greeting, saying, "And since when does the great Reno Kid, who runs with our people, need an introduction . . . ?"

"Greetings, great Black Cloud," I said. "I know you're probably not expecting us . . ."

"But *this* man needs an introduction," the Apache continued, pointing at the general.

"This is General Wild Bill Wagoneer, now one of us," I said. "He has come to spend some time in the mine's magnetic vortex with our friend Javelina. How is the wild child?"

"Still yapping and jabbering about nothing, probably his missing compadre," replied Black Cloud. "He ate beans and shat for about a week."

"I look forward to seeing my old friend and perhaps powwow, smoke the sacred pipe and a bowl of weed," said Wild Bill with a forced smile. But plainly Black Cloud regarded him and his growling animal with some suspicion.

"One of the Long Knives," the Apache elder said, eyeing Wild Bill's blue hat with the crossed sabers.

Unfazed, Wagoneer bowed slightly and replied, "By your magnificence. Yes, by the red man I am called Pontiac, son of Oklahoma, sent by the Great White Father. That is how I am often portrayed, but in truth my own government has left me a broken arrow. I come as a man of peace and one-quarter Ojibwe, as is my adjutant and mystical sage, Mustang Sally Nostradamus."

"Then you are both welcome if you come in peace, Mustang Sal," said the elderly Apache. "But this is Apache land and I have received no notice from Buckaroo of your arrival. Therefore you cannot enter the ghost mine . . ."

"How come?" Tommy wanted to know.

"Because phawk you, Tommy," answered Black Cloud. "That is how the real world works."

"Fact is, Buckaroo might be a little tied up right now," I explained.

"Then I shall call him on the red hotline," replied our Apache host.

But Buckaroo—we were to learn—was incommunicado, being held under guard by unidentified masked raiders who ransacked much of

the Institute, looking for the Roswell Boys . . . and General Wagoneer
. . . and the Jet Car. Or simply to teach us a lesson—as one of the
shadowy operators said to Buckaroo—"not to stick your schnoz where
it doesn't belong."

So for the next couple of hours, we sat on the mountainside around
a crackling fire of sage and mesquite wood, talking about the value of
friendship but also the importance of respecting the other cultures that
inhabit the sacred hoop of all humanity. As might be expected, Black
Cloud had many stories about white men who had tried to run his people
off their land, especially certain ones lately who claimed to be from the
Bureau of Indian Affairs and wished to connect all the local mines in a
giant underground city capable of housing thousands of tons of "precious
gringo treasure."

"Salt in the wound" were the words the noble native used, lamenting
all his dealings with white people. "It is a poor place to outsiders but not
a hellhole. It is a holy place where our brother, the wind, looks for a door
to open and come in and live among us, and the water talks to you . . .
where you can feel the energy that flows between the mountains, the
earth, and the endless sky. We have survived their split-tongue deceiving.
We have survived the unsurvivable, a wound so deep it cannot be sewn."

"Makes you wonder, Billy Jack," Wild Bill Wagoneer said, scratching
his head, "if humanity's not at an all-time low. I have watched on TV
how, against impossible odds, your ancestors fought the white-daddy
government whose handshake never meant dick, just meaningless words
spoken with a cloven tongue the color of green wampum and bullshit
status symbols made of plastic."

"Money is king," Tommy concurred. "It all goes back to the iron
horse and firewater . . . lyin' promises made by Dale Carnegie [sic] and
the robber barons to the red man. They had a handshake deal, too, if I
recall."

"Don't forget Hill's rail and Jackson's Indian Removal Act and the
long hunger marches," said Black Cloud. "Don't forget our D-day was
in 1492. Five hundred nations, that's how many we were . . ."

"I've not walked in your moccasins but have ridden Hill's rail and
seen the picture of the white buffalo hunter standing atop a mountain
of buffalo skulls," replied Tommy, "and the rancheros who have diseased
the red man, sickened many, and taken his lands."

"Perfect Tommy is correct," Black Cloud agreed. "What they could not take or plow, they poisoned."

"And plundered all the red man's Krazy Korn. Working for the Jesuits and the English Crown," interrupted Wild Bill.

"Yes, starting with the Five Nations, the paleskins hunted the red man like the deer and the buffalo. May the hill winds know their names," declared Black Cloud in a soft voice whose cadence could mesmerize a listener. "And now all hell is going to break loose in our Garden of Eden, and our brothers, the Aboriginal Australians, tell me the same, that we have shat upon our Mother. Let us not forget that the eternal living waters come from our Earth Mother, not the clouds. But what if these waters—our water table and watering holes—are now evaporating? It's like I told the Dalai Lama at Buckaroo's environmental symposium, we are sun people with a big problem in the earth's heating alarms that are going off: earthquakes, strange sinkholes and pestilence, tumors on our cattle caused by fertilizers, a two-headed rattlesnake, a war eagle that fell out of the sky, glittery skin walkers, and other tricksters I do not recognize. A tribal elder, a shaman who sees such things, has been cursed with weeping boils on his face. And now this talk from the government of a nuclear dump site on tribal land and the strange man on every channel of the television—this devil Jarvis—speaking of annihilation. Can the black snake foretold in our legends and the ancient petroglyphs be far behind? Some say it has already crossed the Animas River."

"The river of souls . . . we're talking ancestral spirit ground," said Tommy, "where I've eaten peyote and seen the winged serpent and a white jaguar."

"The white Jaguar is the casino manager's car," the Apache resumed. "But Perfect Tommy is always correct. He has perhaps seen a *nagual*, because the younger generation is waking up. The balance has changed, and our maps are no longer accurate . . . the whole southwest lands. We have also seen a flaming quetzal in the sky multiple times."

"From the Apache gods . . . ?" I queried.

"And the gods from the Iipay to the Iroquois and the good white god who will pull Earth's abominators out by the roots. Strange-shape cloud formations and a strange blue star," he replied, pointing at a patch of sky that revealed nothing out of the ordinary, at least to these eyes.

"A blue star . . . that will stick it to the corrupt white eyes and their tricky-ass salesman tricks."

"Yeah, try that on for size, Whitey," said Tommy.

"And now in a new situation we can't escape from," Black Cloud warned. "The spirit life—to follow the good red road—needs space to roam, and many nights we can no longer see the Milky Way, much less the sky dancers, like our grandparents. My great-grandfather knew the great Paiute Wovoka, who told him we'll be held accountable in a timely manner, when all earth's bounty will dissolve before our generation's eyes . . . unless there is an all-out effort, because we are meant to be stewards. So what are we going to do about it?"

"Yes, that's just how it needs to be said.. Sometimes we forget that lesson, that we are all immigrant inhabitants of the earth," I commented.

"Made of stardust," said Tommy.

"Yes, even the desperado has a soul for a reason," he replied. "Because ultimately there is nowhere to run. The earth will find him, like it has found all who have come before."

"That could be an understatement. Time to walk the talk up the old Chisholm Trail and find a sheep to shag," interrupted Wild Bill, who now got up and began to "walk the talk" by tugging his penis and dancing to a secret rhythm in his head . . . juggling disco moves, a Mexican hat dance, and an odd galloping gait suggestive of riding a broom or his boyhood stick horse.

Such eccentric behavior was not lost on Black Cloud, who observed, "He looks like that crazy trader on TV in Tucson who sells refurbished clunkers that are 'clean as a whistle.' The 'buy here, pay here' dude. This white cheeks, too, has the utmost audacity . . ."

"White cheeks," chuckled Tommy. "Take that, Wild Bill, paleface."

I readily agreed, saying, "And he has broken a federal law, which is why we are under attack and wish to entrust him to your care for the time being . . ."

"To break rocks in the magnetic vortex?"

"Yes . . . with the tribe's consent," I replied.

Black Cloud studied Wagoneer carefully before asking testily, "Torn from his family and his home by the devious government which has committed worse robberies?"

"Left with only his little dog," I answered in the affirmative.

"That the government wants to chip and deport," Wagoneer added. "With the help of your big magnet, we wish to prove our mettle to your people and the whole Apache nation."

"Because White Cheeks is like the fool on the hill no one seems to like because they can tell he is just a fool," Black Cloud said and found his thoughts drifting. "But we will make a man out of you, one way or the other . . ."

"Thank you, brother. More power to you," offered Wagoneer.

Black Cloud appeared not to hear and continued, "I saw this in a dream . . . the mangled ruins of cities, families splitting up, the rise of fire and the end of water, the wobble of the earth and even its chemical footprint. We must listen to our Mother, though her cry is less than a whisper, and all of this has been foretold, because we are the seventh generation . . . also the four colors of the medicine wheel."

He paused here to answer his vibrating phone and spoke into it animatedly. "Buckaroo, my friend. I am here with these dangerous men I have prevented until now from entering the ghost mine. My only question is whether to hang their scalps from my lodge pole—what is your advice? Yes, I understand. Here is that silver-tongued devil Reno . . ."

He passed me the phone as I heard a coyote nearby and listened to Buckaroo's weary voice deliver bad news, leavened with instructions and travel arrangements. Following a few questions I posed to him—in the vain hope of hearing more about the fires and the evening's excitement—he asked to speak again to Black Cloud, who retrieved his phone and carried on the conversation . . . while I signaled to Tommy and glanced at Wild Bill and Nostradamus, both of whom appeared to be scratching flea bites.

"Would you like to see the latest Jet Car, General?" I asked.

"Hell, yeah, I'm wired!" Wagoneer said with such astonishment and wonderment that he did not have to say a word before scrambling to his feet and cracking his knuckles—yet he could not contain himself and barked, "Let's see that speed demon!"

HARD FEELINGS

Last notes: it was time to head in. After Wild Bill and Nostradamus both paused to urinate in unison on an ant mound, our little band continued

up the mountain toward the concealed mine entrance and its myriad
tunnels and cathedral-like caverns that hid our mini particle beam
accelerator, vacuum and simulated-weightlessness chamber, workshops,
and laboratories . . . all haunted and guarded, so the story goes, by the
inner circle of Apache ghost warriors.

At last, near the summit, I paused to look back again in the direction
of the flames whence we had come. The Institute, or at least a healthy
part of it, was ablaze. As a warning? A failed attempt to capture the
Roswell Boys or the Jet Car? Doubtless all of the above, but do not expect
me to dwell here on the Pinkertons' raid—or I should say their rampage—
visited upon the Banzai Institute by two dozen federals who refused to
identify their agency or branch of service. Thanks to the worldwide
network of Blue Blazes and our friends in the media, among them Mona
Peeptoe, news of the agents' lawless behavior has been widely disseminated
and rightly lambasted . . . although of course the actual targets of the
raid have never been disclosed. How could they be, given that all were
closely guarded national secrets, or so they say?

It is true we had freed two alien hybrids by accident but had done so
not out of any desire to line our pockets; and none of us had stolen
intellectual property, such as the Jet Car technology. Nor were we
ordinary sheep who might have taken such a blunt warning to heart; we
were big boys and girls—Hong Kong Cavaliers—and we weren't going
anywhere except about our business.

For tonight, at least, our travels ended here beneath the starry blackness,
on this winding trail that led into our beloved Mother Earth. And as I
checked my Go-Phone feed and gazed at the fire on the horizon, then
upward at stars that had never looked brighter or closer—twinkling like
thousands of eyes, their movements giving me a sense of vertigo—a
half-forgotten haiku crossed my mind:

> There was beauty there,
> A universe peeking out,
> A thing in itself!

My reverie, such as it was, steeped in profound grief, was rudely
interrupted, however, by the sickening sound of oxygen tanks exploding
in the distant blaze.

"Goat-phawking damn, some crazy fireworks," Tommy lamented, watching the distant glow of flames and intermittent showers of sparks on the horizon. "We oughtta be in the middle of all that . . ."

"Buckaroo said to stay here and await orders," I reminded him.

"What if Buckaroo's been hit? What if he's . . . ?" he said, raising a morbid possibility I conceded, albeit only intellectually. The thought of Buckaroo's actual demise was more or less inconceivable, which is why I told Tommy how little I thought of him for mentioning it.

"Enough naysaying. Don't get sappy, Tommy. Buckaroo can't abide defeatist talk, so do us both a favor and shut up."

"Yeah, not to worry, I'll bet you a chocolate malted and a store-bought cookie the boss is still upright," he asserted. "Even if he's buried in rubble, he's probably breathing through a straw, like that time at the watering hole in the Sahel. Hopefully we didn't lose anybody . . . but looks like the relativistic heavy ion collider and the new proton lab for sick people, all that workmanship and millions of dollars, up in smoke."

Just at that moment, however—either from sheer luck or the providential hand of the Great Spirit—the winds shifted, bringing us the faint but thrilling sound of Mrs. Johnson's clanging dinner bell.

"The 'all clear,' thank heaven." I sighed with relief, listening closely to the pattern of the ringing notes. "And no losses . . . all survived."

"Good news," Tommy remarked, though his sullen expression remained. "Still burns my pucker—nothing but an act of pure–ass cowardice by those soldier boys, probably Pinkertons from DARPA, if it's who I think it was . . ."

With a burning intensity to match, I said, "Could've been a lot of people. A sick joke on sick people and the sick planet."

"Hardly a joke. It's an act of war on all the old–school values and slow-moving people of the earth, the hewers of wood and drawers of water," claimed Tommy, dabbing at something in his eye. "We fools, we proud, we band of gypsies, butt-phawked in our own sandbox by our own bum-ass government that has sold this country down the river. And don't even get me started on acronyms."

"Gotta start somewhere," I said.

"Exactly, Reno. Now the mantle falls on us. Not just to keep talking truth to bullspit, but to make a response with extreme prejudice, loud and hard, while we still have some of the rights that generations have fought and died for from the beginning of this great nation based on freedom. I'm talking about the right to walk the walk of a free man, to call no man master, but that only makes sense to those with a knowledge of history and the philosophy of democracy."

"Don't give up, Tommy. Things'll get better—it'll take more than a bunch of goons and a coordinated campaign of *Zersetzung* dirty tricks to break our spirit."

"I'm not broken," he said. "Instead I'm reminded of Beowulf's victory over Grendel, or that lone sentry dude at Pompeii—the one who never left his post despite the wave of red-hot lava rolling his way, until his head exploded."

If the analogy was murky, I at least shared the sentiment: "War's their moneymaker. Wild Bill says certain shadowy Neo elements of the government may be taking orders from that supposed giant alien brain in Area 51—Project Nexus, he called it—along with stoking hatred and worldwide obesity. There's zero good reason to believe that, although he did pass the polygraph with flying colors; but we do know lots of government secret operators are in cahoots with the World Crime League, some even acting under color of authority, so they poison our wells and salt the earth because they fear the idea of us freethinkers infecting the sheep farm. I guess the question now is whether they've gone the extra yard and issued direct kill orders to a bunch of trigger-happy nutjobs."

"Hard to tell the actors anymore. I can't believe this happened on American soil," Tommy lamented, whistling on the intake through his teeth.

"A crime against America, tampering with our shite," I concurred.

Note: Facts relating to this ill-conceived attack on the Institute by rogue government elements on the payroll of the World Crime League have been placed under seal by order of the Foreign Intelligence Surveillance Court (FISC), although a version may be found in foreign sources, particularly *Théories du complot, réalités du complot* (Conspiracy theories, conspiracy realities) by Philippe Sollers.

—Reno

"That they fear us and our personal code is an added bonus," Tommy added. "Remember Chairman Mao's quote from our military history seminar: 'It is good if we are attacked by the enemy . . . still better if the enemy attacks us wildly and paints us as utterly evil and without a single virtue; it demonstrates that we have not only drawn a clear line of demarcation between the enemy and ourselves but achieved a great deal in our work.' "

"Background music by Wagner," I quipped bitterly as he knitted his brow and sighed a note of resignation.

"When I can't stand on my own two feet, bury me Apache-style, in a hollow tree trunk with my left-hand Stratocaster . . . at one with creation."

(Tommy is ambidextrous, equally proficient on a left- or right-hand-strung guitar.)

"In the meantime, know these truths to be self-evident," he resumed. "They'll eat karma someday because a storm is coming. They've disturbed a hornet's nest, and I, for one, refuse to lower my standard, even if chivalry's dead. Wherever the bird of liberty chirps, wherever the distant crow of freedom's cock is heard, I'll be there to fight liars and their tricky words. May they live forever in perpetual shame."

To this extraordinary pledge I could add little except "Life, fortune, and sacred honor . . . and, through it all, the thread of common decency . . ."

"All we can hope for is a good death and peace in the boneyard . . . because to the masters of propaganda and their running dogs, we're a virus, and stepping on us is the antidote. Just a matter of time until they corral us, and our peashooters and pop guns won't be enough."

"No rest for the weary," I affirmed, "until we pay them back."

"Until destiny finds us and we climb the natural ladder of liberty all the way to the stars. That goes double for me . . . triple," he replied.

In my gut I felt the same defiance and determination; yet I also knew that we could not allow anger or bitterness to seep into our hearts or outweigh what Buckaroo called our *telos*, our purpose, which was to create a new future for the planet. Collecting our revenge, and thereby improving the human gene pool, would have to wait.

XXI. XAN'S FUNK

> Man when living is soft and tender;
> when dead he is hard and tough.
> —Lao Tzu

But let us return for a moment to Hanoi Xan and the Temple de la Gloire in recognition of the fact that wherever the reclusive Xan hangs his hat becomes a major migratory center, drawing future and former jailbirds of all feathers. Although he was accustomed to juggle many balls at once and maintain an unfaltering façade of confidence, his sureness of foot was no longer what it had been once upon a time. Whereas on a typical day his staff still managed to machine-gun out hundreds of memos and responses to his manifold enterprises and World Crime League operatives around the globe, the principal matters occupying his personal attention these days were the anonymous Mr. French and his pilfered Jet Car plans; the overly ambitious Cardinal Baltazar; and, to a lesser degree, the mysterious Abbot Costello: the delusional schizophrenic who apparently was still running the streets of Rome and carrying on his odd activities, which included simultaneously trying to get arrested and fleeing back underground.

By now, Dr. Paraquat and a small group of trusted assistants had succeeded in building a lounge chair prototype in the chateau basement, but significant question marks remained with regard to the specifications for the OSCILLATION OVERTHRUSTER and its mounting on the tip of the

Lance of Destiny—information which Mr. French had lately promised to
provide in exchange for one hundred thousand dollars. This sum, based
upon the always cautious recommendation of Paraquat and his best scientists,
Xan subsequently approved in a directive to Contreras's Panamanian
replacement, who communicated the news to French (effectively our own
World Watch). Details concerning the exchange of the cash payment and
OVERTHRUSTER data were left to be figured out, however.

As for Baltazar, Xan had sent repeated "words to the wise"—counterfeit
wishes for a reconciliation—to the wayward cardinal through
intermediaries . . . all to no avail. As a consequence, he was left to rant
(a daily occurrence), promising to squeeze the cardinal's brain out
through his ears and nostrils, but the time and place of such a reckoning
were held in suspense.

"He will never know what day," Xan would scream and shudder at
his own threats, "I will jump from the bushes, give him the goodbye
look, and castrate him with his own zipper! His pendulous balls will fall
into my lap! He is a gone man."

These were harsh words and doubtless no empty threat. As is well
known, Xan loves nothing more than following a blood trail and slowly
eviscerating his prey, forcing a man to tap-dance while extracting his
own intestines. This tends to be the particular fate of those to whom
Xan feels a personal connection, in the way of a jilted lover—the type
of fatherly affection he once felt for Cardinal Baltazar, believing him to
be a fellow occultist and demigod, an Rh-negative man of renown, et
cetera, dating back to the earliest days in Gondwana among the Nephilim.
Perhaps he was right, perhaps he was wrong; but the more Xan reflected
upon the image of the scoundrel in an old Christmas card, the more he
became convinced that he had seen that face on a younger man over a
century before.

PITCHING WOO

There is not enough space here to list all such clues leading to his
conclusion, but one morning not long after Manny Magdalene's
unsuccessful mission to Sarajevo and his interrogation by MI6 at
Blenheim Palace, Xan awoke suddenly from a restless sleep. Having gone

to bed debating whether to have Manny killed, he woke up instead with Baltazar on his mind, albeit Baltazar by another name.

"What made me dream of that bastard corsair Barbarossa?" he asked himself.

He endeavored to answer his own question during an unpleasant conference call with Magdalene and the Chaldean, during which he waxed nostalgic: "I was soundly sleeping when I sensed a prowler in my mind. Then I perceived a distinct tug from him, imbued with light. I recognized the image at once as opening night at Bayreuth, 1876."

"1876," Manny said, keeping the game alive. "Was I there?"

"With your bootblack box. Who could forget?" recalled Xan with a mocking tone, still not having forgiven Magdalene for his spectacular failure at Sarajevo.

"It was like a fairy tale," Xan jokingly continued. "Your presence with your little shoeshine box outshining even Nietzsche and Wagner, the guest of honor. I remember like it was yesterday . . ."

"I wish I could remember," muttered Manny unhappily.

Xan went on, "Of course I recognized him as a brother occultist, a fellow elder, in the process of sloughing his skin, when he came up to me and, in a self-centered attempt to squeeze himself smugly between me and Nietzsche, pulled aside his shirt to reveal that he was cold to the touch and also missing his areolae. When Nietzsche wandered away a moment later, the brother whispered in my ear, 'I have a secret. I recognized you at once as a fellow son of Enoch and a follower of the esoteric truth, the true philosophy—whom the gods have granted me the opportunity to know, which means our paths may be intertwined deep in the past. Did I not know you in the Old Guard?'

"To which I answered, 'I rode with von Blücher and died upon the field at Waterloo. Perhaps it was there that we met.'"

Awaiting a reaction to his account and hearing only silence, Xan now angrily barked into the phone, "Hippolyte, are you there?"

"I'm writing it all down" came the reply of the Chaldean. "And what did the fellow say then?"

Xan continued, "He laughed and said, '*Jedem das Seine, Herr*' . . .

"'Shannon, Henry Shannon,' I introduced myself, and when that failed to make an impression, I dropped my veil and informed him, 'Timur the Terrible; Ivan the Terrible; Edwardus Primus, Hammer of the Scots; Hassan bin Sabbah,' and finally, 'Xan von Französisch-Indochina.' Naturally, I could not help but notice the dramatic effect the latter name had upon him. Why, he practically fell on his face—or on his walking stick, as the case may be—but in any case a glass or two of schnapps put him at his ease; and for a few minutes before the storm of *Das Rheingold* began, we were able to reminisce in a civil fashion about the Enochian elders of old. He admitted he had served only in the Seven Years' War and never met the Little Corporal, but was now in the service of Otto von Bismarck. Though I gave him merely a small dose of my lineage, he had trouble looking me in the eye. Overall, the miserable chap seemed at loose ends, like a sad and withered flower, dressed poorly with bad creases in his stained pants, and bitter . . . full of gas and ugly and unacceptable insults toward the great men in our midst. A malignant, power-hungry narcissist with a total lack of integrity, rot and filth in my humble opinion . . . and though I had forgotten the incident until now, I am convinced Baltazar is that fellow. I believe he called himself Lycurgus the Spartan, alias Schwantz . . . *ja, ja* . . . Arsch Lecken Schwantz from Schleswig-Holstein."

"Meanwhile, what was I doing?" Manny had the temerity to inquire, even speaking from the relative safety of England. "I thought I was a historical individual—I have the tattoo to prove it."

Xan laughed, saying, "The SS bolts on your ass? Ha, ha . . . Sexus Servus! I am Tiberius Gracchus. You are the simpleton leather boy, the one they called the baker's niece, understanding how insignificant you were—like the rest of Carthage, something sticking to my sandal boot, begging to be buggered. While you jostled in the arena grandstands with the motley crowd, I sat with the beautiful people and threw down spit upon you from above . . . better than you deserve after your pathetic withdrawal from Sarajevo. Don't try to play me, because I am unplayable! You're lucky to be alive."

Manny no doubt lowered his head and babbled contritely, "Thank you for your vote of confidence, Huang-di, but don't forget I saved you at Agincourt with my longbow and also cared for you when you were Alexander of Macedonia. I brought you milk and let you eat from my plate and crawl all over me. And when Diogenes the Cynic cynically insulted you . . ."

"Enough! Because our safety and well-being demanded it," Xan reminded him.

"I only wish I could remember," Manny said. "And I wish I could remember my name."

"I told you: Sexus Servus. Polonius. Or Culus Paterculus, if you prefer," suggested Xan. "Or perhaps you were thinking Ajax . . . ?"

"Yes . . . Ajax the Extra-Large Trojan, and your dauphin," said Manny hopefully.

"My dauphin," Xan replied with a smile and a hint of affection. "I know that is your prayer."

With his pride apparently restored, Manny now cleared his throat and began to talk about Abbot Costello. "I've been made aware of certain events . . ."

NEWS FROM ROME

He went on to describe what we at the Institute were also busy learning: a high-ranking Roman Mafioso had reported that Cardinal Baltazar had offered an exorbitant reward for the return of his client, the abbot Costello, who supposedly had become weak minded, possibly schizophrenic, and prone to getting in and out of street fights, throwing fits in public, or even punching himself and banging his head intentionally against the pavement in some reported cases. This little nugget of information reminded Xan that he had heard a similar rumor weeks earlier about the same mad friar running amok, entering a women's health center to seek an abortion, and later visiting the famous Bocca della Verità, where he proved his truthfulness by sticking his hand into the mouth of the mask and withdrawing it safely.

"This is the same mad monk?" Xan asked. "The rambling Rasputin I was once promised by Baltazar to look into my backside? Who sent me the piss water for drinking?"

"I assume so, Huang-di, but I am guessing."

Yet just another religious kook gone awry, Xan believed—a self-deluded holy man like the cardinal, who had made the mistake of believing what he preached and forgetting his place in the actual scheme of things—and even now Xan had his doubts about the fellow's importance. In his scientific view, so-called healers and exorcists were schizophrenic almost by definition, no different from the average tribal shaman; and yet he tried them all.

"Something is fishy," he said.

"Obviously, Baltazar is afraid of losing his meal ticket" was Manny's response. "His fat commission has come to an abrupt end because the mad exorcist named Abbot Costello thinks he's pregnant and ran away . . . maybe with gender issues and possibly armed with the holy sword of San Galgano."

Xan at once sat up straighter, remaining so for the duration of the conversation, as Manny outlined the fantastic circumstances involving the abbot named Costello, the saint named Galgano Guidotti, and the legendary sword in the stone. For his part, Xan of course was intrigued— the prospect of gaining such a priceless relic could not fail to excite the collector in him—but his poor opinion of Italians in general, made him skeptical.

But Manny was not finished, saying, "You will recall the phone call from Mr. French, which we traced as far as the state of Nevada. You looked upon him as something unpleasant, an arse sniffer or possibly a full-tilt psycho. Yet we are now prepared to make a purchase of the extraordinary scientific material he has offered."

"Stay on the topic," cautioned Xan. "We were speaking of the mental disorder of the nutjob abbot."

"Thank you for the admonition, Huang-di," Manny went on. "I wish only to relate that a few days after French's call to us, a public records search reveals that Abbot Costello was arrested on Fremont Street in Henderson, Nevada . . . after fleeing a Red Lobster on his little bicycle . . . heh, the long arm of the claw . . ."

"A lobster in Nevada?" questioned Xan.

"A restaurant named the Red Lobster," Manny clarified. "He was arrested for trying to leave the premises without paying for shrimp Alfredo and numerous bloody marys and had the appearance of being deranged, speaking in odd voices out of both sides of his mouth . . ."

"The schizoid," noted Xan.

". . . wearing only an Indian blanket and a beaver pelt, naked and bruised as if he had been in one hell of a scrap. When the trooper asked him to explain himself, he simply crumpled into the officer's arms, and they sold him to the jail system."

"Nevada sucks," Xan declared. "Las Vegas blows like the desert wind. I wouldn't be caught dead anywhere in Nevada."

Manny continued, "This was some days before he appeared before a county judge, *pro se, in forma pauperis,* since he had neither money nor identification. The transcript therefore reads like the ravings of a madman interrogating himself. Of greater interest, however, is the fact that he gave the court his correct name and listed two addresses: a doss house in Rome and our affiliate in Bullhead City, where he was presumably headed . . . and where he had spent the night two days earlier, prior to renting a small caravan and heading out to Nellis Air Base . . ."

At the mention of Nellis, Xan's floppy ear appeared to twitch.

"Nellis . . . Area 51," he mused. "What does his agent, the weasel priest Baltazar, have to say?"

"Again, nothing. Not even a how-do-you-do so far to my inquiries."

His blood slowly boiling, Xan kept repeating under his breath, "No one runs a game on Hanoi Xan. I'll hang him by his ham hocks, have his head on a plate like the Baptist . . . !"

"Who, sir?" asked Hippolyte over the phone. "The monk or the cardinal?"

"Baltazar, damn it! All of them! *Trahison des clercs!*"

Manny promptly echoed the sentiment. "One of us or no, the man's a mediocrity . . . a lawless deviant who has thrown off allegiance to you. He has raised up on us, so we must slap him down before he inspires others by his bad example, causing irreparable harm to our intelligence-gathering system of priestly confessionals. I fear it's much too late to handle this in a diplomatic manner if we wish to keep our community shite free, and indeed I question whether he still deserves to walk the land for his grave blunder."

"I'll stick a lance up his ass and gnaw on his liver!" again vowed Xan, who by now was doing his customary ants-in-the-pants dance. "He'll be picking up tin cans and cigarette butts by the time I'm through with him, and feeling lucky to do so before I stick splinters up his fingers! Find his bank accounts, reduce him to penury! He must be curbed, which is more than he deserves."

"I suggest limiting the sonofabitch out of existence, after we have taken back all his bonuses under the malus clause," Manny offered helpfully.

"Yes, I'll take everything, including his dreams. He will give me his robe, his garments, his sword, even his girdle. Then he must be eliminated from the equation of life," Xan ultimately agreed, his anger to be assuaged only by a timely plan to take care of business. "Time to bite back hard and clear my mind of this Balkan bastard. I'll have my balls on his forehead and cook him au jus! But I want more than his head. For my trouble I want a trophy. I'll sack the Vatican as I sacked Baghdad in 1258."

He remained convinced that Baltazar was no mastermind and had to be working for someone else. But who . . . ? With Satrap as his witness, he fashioned a matchstick figure representing the rogue Baltazar and tore it to pieces, prior to signing the official assize with his Montblanc Meisterstück and announcing his intention to head a mission to Rome himself. For the first time in years, then, he would personally lead an armed cohort of World Crime League partisans into battle. Even if Baltazar was not open for business and holed up in the Vatican, Xan the Pitiless would not fool around; he would raze the holy city and give the cardinal a hard dose of reality or, as he put it, "lube him with his tears, horse-phawk him until he squats to pee and quacks like a duck."

Moments later, after the Chaldean had consulted his charts and the entrails of a pigeon, Xan gave orders to Manny over the phone. "We break camp at dawn. Twenty bravos. Pack my hedge trimmer and high-pressure nozzle, my passivator, and two five-man coffins. I'll wear my iron teeth. And I'll need my mobility scooter . . . a rolling toilet chock full of chemical weapons . . . my field kitchen . . . the 75 mm field gun . . . and my flying carpet, the tartan one . . ."

"I am in shock. That could be reckless," Manny said. "Anyway, I'm in London."

"You're overcomplicating things," replied Xan in a flat tone that made Manny shiver. "If anything happens to me, everybody is to be slaughtered, to the last bravo . . ."

"I'll see to it, Huang-di, my lord."

". . . before you kill yourself, of course . . ."

"Of course . . . in that order," agreed Manny, having just come from a long day at the House of Commons and looking forward to a chilled bottle of champagne and his naked visitor who was holding it.

"I'll be on the first flight," he promised and made two obeisances, all but choked with emotion.

Almost even as they were speaking, Xan's informers and agents continued to scour Rome for Abbot Costello. His arrest in Nevada and his subsequent court testimony had also come to our attention, along with the address he provided to the court—a false lead, it turned out, as our Roman Blue Blazes learned quickly that his landlord had evicted him for nonpayment and other various violations of his lease, such as attempted arson. Rumor had it he had fled down into the city's ancient catacombs.

His admission of guilt nonetheless gave us a view into his tortured soul, as it did the Nevada judge before he fined the abbot five hundred dollars, a sum paid by the local diocese. The court's own translation of Costello's statement is instructive: "Before Mighty God and judge of Nevada, I who am the biggest liar on earth . . . a pretender . . . cannot tell right from left, me from the Dark One. No longer know where I stop, and he, the demon spirit of sickness, begins any longer. I am like the lobster in the boiling pot, eaten by the king crab of lust, devoured by the octopus in a hurricane; I am the small and sad firefly who cannot outlast the darkness, my shameful appointment with fate. All exits are blocked to me. There is only the devil with open arms whom I rebuke to no avail in my lamentations. I have lost my way with lustful urges and perhaps am no longer even capable of shame. I have not slept in days, I am urinating fire and accepting humiliating defeat . . ."

At this point the judge rebukes him for long-windedness, followed by an apparent fainting fit by the abbot and the release of his dark inner soul / alter ego in a stream of turgid curses: "wormsack . . . purple wood pole . . . phawk you with God's finger." Although it is difficult to tell from the transcript, an interior wrestling match then apparently ensues between the two personalities, requiring the intervention of several deputy sheriffs.

Looked at from all angles, the court transcript and the feverish fit that afflicted the abbot made little sense, at least to me. Both seemed like a bad joke, the eruption of a man simply lashing out in anger or experiencing a mental breakdown or, worse, the effects of an unknown pathology.

Perusing the same report, Xan threatened, "Find the little puffer! Turn his neighborhood inside out! I'll show him which way the wind blows!"

In the abbot's case, and our own, all winds now blew toward Italy.

XXII. THE ITALIAN CAMPAIGN

> I will not hurt a cleric or a monk if unarmed . . . I will not burn
> houses or destroy them unless there is a knight inside.
> —oath of Robert the Pious

Before the epic battle of Rome, we bivouacked at the University of Pisa, alma mater of Galileo and Fermi, then traveled by helicopter to visit sick children in the hospital of Careggi, built on the grounds of Cosimo de' Medici's ancient villa near Florence. As Buckaroo busied himself advising resident physicians and even performing a number of surgical procedures himself, the children's cheerfulness in the face of their torments and personal tragedies both instructed and inspired us, elevating us from our travel fatigue to a higher plane of gratitude. Such are the inspirational effects bestowed by a courageous child upon the selfish skeptic accustomed only to his luxuries and caprices or the physically healthy man who bears a grudge against the world. We in turn did our best to animate patients and staff, contributing photographs, stories, and, hopefully, uplifting happy thoughts, before departing for our papal audience at the Vatican.

But, first, there was to be an unannounced detour to San Galgano Abbey, rumored scene of Abbot Costello's greatest miracle, where the smell was of scrambled lavender and rosemary and the crisp air of the mountains, and the only sound a shrill fife from somewhere down the road. Here, far from the noisy city and the chaos to come, we found a moment of solace and inspiration . . . a little scented corner, seemingly a thousand miles from paparazzi and assorted panjandrums, klaxons, and choking smoke! And how many flowery festoons, ducks, shimmering pigeons, geese, turkeys, and guinea fowl around us! On our foot tour, I even saw a forlorn wild peacock, latest in a long procession of his species, many of whom (according to our guide) have been memorialized as far back as the Roman emperors; and in yet another moment of quiet epiphany, I witnessed the return of a small flock of sheep and their driver to a farmhouse some might call dreary—its dilapidated straw and earthen walls whitewashed but otherwise barely touched in centuries—yet it was cozy and peaceful, a place for shepherd and his flock to sleep from sunset until dawn behind closed shutters.

Then voices: a Hungarian television crew, a timely reminder that it was time to collect ourselves and return to our purpose, as our own friendly local shepherd pointed out certain details, such as the deserted ruins of the great cathedral and the small chapel where, to our consternation, the knight Galgano Guidotti's broadsword lamentably was missing from the massive rock. But how had it happened? And who could have passed such a test?

I am not here to judge, although our guide informed us there had been witnesses to the miracle, villagers drawn by the terrifying sounds of wild animals wailing loudly in the night and other evil omens, such as a plague of mosquitoes, snakes, and rats; rabbits laying chicken eggs; birds flying backward, and thunder in a clear sky . . .

". . . so that no one could get a wink of sleep. The entire village was in a snit until God heard our agony," the gravelly-voiced local said, opening his mouth to reveal a small cross placed under his tongue, then going on to relate that after many prayers from the community, a Holy Bible signed by San Galgano appeared in a local barbershop without explanation.

"How cool. But the *bestie*?" Pecos questioned him. "Wild beasts fighting *nei boschi*?"

"Or one at war with itself . . . turning their internal conflict outward," speculated Buckaroo, who we could only assume was speaking in jest.

"Over what . . . ?" I wondered.

"Fear . . . uncertainty. The ever-present human urge for corrective discipline, sometimes called a conscience or a control," he said.

Our guide, who had lived all his life in Montesiepi, affirmed that numerous neighbors had heard the odd screeches and cries of both a man and a creature definitely not human—something indeed hair raising and terrible—and had come running, armed with pitchforks and shotguns, only to witness the most incredible sight of their lives: what some saw as the luminescent Christ and others recognized at once as the cowled Brother Costello floating in midair, his eyes like fire, illumined by the locals' camera flashes.

There was also this: next to the levitating monk stood an oddly shaped alien shadow that never left his side. It, too, appeared on multiple videos that capture the entire uncanny sight of the monk, airborne and seemingly panicked, as the holy sword of San Galgano rises magically into his startled grasp, whereupon the monk turns the supernaturally glowing weapon against himself! Before he can fall on the blade, however, he shimmers like the sun and both he and his dark shadow dissolve into a holy flame. Needless to say, any screams from his lips are drowned out by the hysterical reactions of eyewitnesses to the miracle.

"Yes, many people saw him take the sword," said our guide emphatically. "You can see how part of the stone has crumbled. Then the cathedral bells began to ring, by themselves, for no reason."

"Bells?" questioned Tommy. "There's not even a roof on the joint, much less a bell."

The guide, who was wearing a Saint Anthony pendant, crossed himself and agreed, "Yes, there are no bells, Tommy, and yet they began to ring like crazy, confounding our ears."

"Did Brother Costello say anything before or after he burst into flames?" Buckaroo wanted to know.

"Only to himself," reported the guide, "in a voice none could understand."

"Speaking in tongues . . . or just loco?" pitched in Pecos.

"A kind of baby talk, double talk, like a man arguing with his relatives," recalled the guide.

As all of this seemed true and yet hopelessly improbable, I traded looks with Buckaroo and the others—Tommy, Pecos, Red Jordan, and Li'l Daughter—all thoroughly flummoxed by the guide's tale and the inconclusive photographic evidence to support it. Buckaroo meanwhile knelt beside the rock and scraped at a dark bloodstain with his all-purpose

Swiss tool, preparing a sample which he put into his miniature gel electrophoresis machine.

"And then the strange cries stopped?" Buckaroo wanted to know.

"No, for some hours after, we heard them like donkey cries or a mad raccoon, until the *cardinale* arrived. Some of us wished to retrieve the relic; but by then we knew it was a miracle from God, so we were no longer angry, only frightened."

"Praise God and hallelujah," commented Pecos.

"The *cardinale* . . . ? The cardinal?" Buckaroo asked.

"In the village they said he was a cardinal," said the guide, a chatty pensioner with a sense of humor. "I didn't see him myself—but I saw his Lamborghini, into which he tried to pull the abbot, who at first consented but then swung the holy sword, with which he chopped the Lamborghini into pieces, while the cardinal yelled like an insane *pazzo*."

Our group exchanged looks of amazement over such a tale, which the good fellow now concluded. "Then the abbot fell on his knees and seemed ashamed for what he had done. But then he ran away again, still clutching the sword—some say he rode the sword into the great beyond, others say south toward Rome—and nothing more was said of it except the television people, who think we are all crazy peasants who stole the relic ourselves."

"Rest assured none of us thinks that," Buckaroo informed him.

In any case the shepherd merely shrugged, seeming unconcerned about what we thought.

"Life is too short to be sad for long," he said. "In fact without the sword hanging over us, and all the religious pilgrims who came to see it, the village seems a happier place."

We again looked at one another but said little—what little there was to say—as we retraced our steps through the once majestic cathedral, now a mere shell, and listened to the wind whistle through the lancet windows above the choir. Could the howling wind have been mistaken for a wild animal's cry or the devil himself? It seemed doubtful . . . but, then, the whole affair seemed to make little sense. Could some sort of mass hysteria have been at work among these superstitious country folks, as Pecos theorized? Then there were the media, who deemed the whole affair a local hoax designed to garner news coverage and attract more tourists.

Or, in Tommy's words, "Country people get their kicks in funny ways."

"Such as a funny prank? A staged event? Fabricated eyewitnesses? Doctored photographs?" I questioned, although we had watched the video evidence ourselves.

"Maybe to cover their tracks with more bullshite," suggested Pecos. "A relic like that could raise a lot of money for a tiny village on the black market."

But as Buckaroo said, "I think we're compelled to take the video and eyewitness testimony at face value, not to mention Baltazar's wrecked Lamborghini that apparently is still sitting in a farmer's garage. As for the crazy abbot, it could be that he was going through a particularly nasty schizophrenic episode and needed an out-of-the-way sanctuary for a couple of days, a place for him to battle whatever demons or psychosis—perhaps even another personality—might be afflicting him. Remember the story not long ago about his attempted self-lobotomy in Rome? Clearly, he is a deeply disturbed fellow trying to blot it all out . . . a soul in turmoil, carrying a powerful psychic energy that must terrify him."

"Like a fart in a ziplock bag, needing a release," said Tommy.

"Good analogy, Tommy. Your stock is sky high right now," Buckaroo replied in a matter-of-fact tone, nonetheless prompting Tommy to raise his head and puff out his chest like the cock of the walk . . .

. . . as Buckaroo continued, "A manifestation of an alien consciousness needing release or leading sooner or later to a blowout, as the manifestation flows into another host like a parasite . . ."

"Like an evil spirit," I said. "Like an exorcism . . . ?"

There . . . I had said it. I will never forget how Buckaroo looked me straight in the eye and spoke with the wisdom of a thousand years. "That's exactly what I'm talking about, Reno, though it's obviously something that doesn't seem to work within our laws of biology. Under the right conditions, however, an explosion of a certain magnitude might generate sufficient force to convert the manifestation—demon, evil spirit, or any uninvited guest from another dimension—into a high-powered projectile, or plasma . . ."

"That would be some ejaculation," said Pecos. "So the Abbot might be possessed . . . an exorcism gone horribly wrong that could have opened the door to Whorfin?"

"The explosion at Area 51," Buckaroo explained, as he studied the preliminary results of his gel electrophoresis test. "I'm almost certain of it. General Wagoneer brought him in to heal the dying Lizardo by divine means, but a violent exorcism resulted, and Whorfin somehow infiltrated Costello . . . which would explain Baltazar's desperation to get him back in the fold."

I didn't quite follow his line of reasoning but asked instead, "What do the DNA markers say?"

He looked at his versatile Go-Phone and replied, "The panel resembles the Lectroid samples sent to us by Blue Blazes Darinka Water Moccasin and Zoyenka Racehorse from Sarajevo, with an important distinction. Human DNA and human digestive tract bacteria are also present, but without access to a centrifuge, I can only confirm the mix is a bloody mess: lots of molybdenum and some kind of weird Planet 10 elements. But let's not get ahead of the science."

As Buckaroo noted, the science would have to wait. We all agreed there was nothing for it but to hike back to the chopper, but not before we posed for pictures with the Hungarian film crew and Li'l Daughter rescued a broken locust, which she insisted on taking with us.

"I'll be your friend," she said, sheltering the little biblical pest in her hands; and as fecund fields and vineyards and the timeless Apennines unfolded below us, I could not help thinking she had brought aboard a bad omen.

THE HOLY SEE

What obtrudes in my memory of Rome that fateful day? Apart from our famously truncated concert in the great Coliseum and certain other staggering events that I shall recount in the pages that follow, there are the smiles and Roman sunshine that accompanied us wherever we went in the city. Though regrettably confined within a circle of publicists, carabinieri, and the local media—"*Buckaroo Banzai e suoi favolosi Hong Kong Cavaliers in concerto, nel Colosseo!!*"—we were welcomed, as elsewhere, like uncrowned royalty, and not only of our own time. False modesty aside, we represented something more substantial than born aristocrats: the epic world of heroes and the ideality of man.

If I were less than honest, I would cast us in a simple light and say we were surprised by our spectacular reception in the Italian capital, but the truth is that we were long ago benumbed to such wild elation on the faces of complete strangers. Far from giving us goose flesh, such giddy scenes have exhausted their significance for us. We find our public veneration at best something of an irritant and a perverse paradox, given our espousal of ascetic living, self-sacrifice, and humility. Yet we continue to grope our way, sleepwalking mechanically through press conferences, multilayered paparazzi, and television crews, then on to never-ending soirees and (rarely) juvenile all-night romps worthy of Nero . . . affecting our public roles to the point of parody, albeit purportedly for a good cause: our justice and charity work.

Followers of this series know that we Cavaliers have never been comfortable being called superstars, much less "supernovae"—Mona Peeptoe's description of us, doubtless referring to the vast amount of explosive energy in our stage shows—yet in truth, like all human beings, we sometimes fall back upon our laurels and play too easily the role of jaded hedonists in a parade of debauchery, rock stars who have come to expect life on the road aboard a two-million-dollar bus and royal treatment from our adoring partisans and the world at large.

Have I exposed myself in public, dear reader? Then let the record reflect that I am no saint, also that I never claimed to be. Ordinarily—given all of the above and the dire situation of our planet at the time under consideration—I would bridle at wasting space on an account of our arrival at the Apostolic Palace and our perfunctory meeting with Pope Innocent, whom Buckaroo had known for more than a decade. Such occasions are for the most part little more than photo opportunities offering trite banter and the usual encomia, but this particular meeting with Pope Innocent in his sitting room merits ample discussion for reasons the reader will readily discern.

"Thank you for the stuffed animal and the cowboy boots and bottle of Banzai Institute handmade mezcal. Oh, and the lovely Japanese porcelain," the pope told Buckaroo, indicating the tea set laid out before us on an antique coffee table . . . alongside a cheese tray, a tin of English biscuits, and dainty chocolates on filmy lace. "Like you, it has traveled a great distance across the great flat water that sits on the four pillars."

How oddly wonderful, his quaint beliefs and baroque language, I thought to myself. Was the pope serious, or was this mere playful banter between His Holiness and Buckaroo? I could not be certain, even in light of Buckaroo's reply.

"We came by silver bird instead of wooden ship, Your Eminence, as God pleased to guide our path by astrolabe . . ."

"Because the world is round. What goes around, comes around," giggled Pope Innocent.

"Yes, each of us gets what we deserve, our just fruits," Buckaroo stated. "This is affirmed in Brahmanism and most religions."

"And what of your religious beliefs, Dr. Banzai?" inquired a horse-faced cardinal nearby who looked up from his phone long enough to absorb our conversation.

"What of them? I consider myself a skeptical Taoist," Buckaroo informed him.

"But that is an intellectual project, not the one true faith," the cardinal responded airily.

"Pick your poison," said Buckaroo . . .

. . . whereupon the pope, sensing a fracas, cut in to remark, "In my homily just the other day, Buckaroo, I borrowed something you told me during my visit last year to the Vatican Observatory in Arizona . . . how our decision to kick Pluto out of the solar system demonstrated the arrogance of the strong against the weak and the importance of fostering humility, rather than vanity, ignorance, and irrationality. At all costs we must not lose faith in the fact that God wills change, but his will is changeless."

"And faith matched by deeds is a good sight stronger," said Buckaroo. "Congratulations on your latest product endorsement deals, Your Holiness. No doubt you're keeping your accountants up late burning the midnight incense."

"Yes, let us join hands and give thanks," replied the pontiff. "You'll notice that all my television advertisements have hidden meanings."

"Most certainly. And I'm sure the royalties you earn will be put to good use," professed Buckaroo, casting a wary eye at the same cardinal I have duly noted.

On this score the pope seemed uncertain and looked to the others in that ornate vaulted room: the Vatican photographer; purple-hooded members of the household staff; a shirtless peg-legged penitent wearing a diamond crucifix pinned to his hairy chest; and of course the aforementioned cardinal, who now spoke.

"The money goes into a special fund, Your Sublimity, to fix up old lighthouses, remember? To serve as navigational beacons for our sovereign's return," the latter explained to the quizzical pope before raptly turning his attention to his handheld phone, on whose screen—unless I was mistaken—I glimpsed the face of Brother Jarvis.

"Or come what may. All avenues are open to our Lord," said Pope Innocent, relaxing and returning to the meandering discussion that continued for several minutes more. While now is not the time to relate the entire train of small talk—as if I could recall it somehow—what follows may convey a sample.

"Even the bathtub will kill you," Pope Innocent was saying, in response to Buckaroo's contention that life is precious, chiefly because death does not always signal its approach and hence looms as a possibility anywhere and at any moment.

"Food additives that are nothing but food poisoning, never mind household products," added Pecos, "many of which interfere with our natural immune systems."

"Nine out of ten accidents happen at home, which is a good argument for travel," I said lightheartedly in an attempt to steer the conversation back to the eternal delights of Rome. Just then, however, the cardinal's phone beeped; and, glancing at it, he made a curious remark that seems all the more significant in retrospect.

"Rome, without an army, is not Rome," were his words, which led to an awkward silence and an opening for Tommy to say something that literally had been on the tip of his tongue for several seconds.

"This chocolate is incredible," he remarked, indicating the small wet cube of chocolate on which he had been sucking.

"It's five hundred years old and quite precious," the cardinal informed him and, seeing our consternation, went on to tell an astonishing tale. "The conquistador Pizarro sent it as a gift to the Spanish regent King Charles I, who saw fit to share a portion with Pope Clemens Septimus. It is said to come from a long-extinct Indian tribe who engraved their entire history upon it . . . an entire history of a people written on chocolate tablets. You can see something of it by the strange carved symbols in what you are eating . . ."

Tommy at once ceased to savor the chocolate on his brown tongue and laid it carefully on his napkin with these words: "As a famous man once said, 'Good luck with that, amigo.' Bad, bad stuff."

Staring at my own little chunk of chocolate, with my teeth marks still upon it, I myself suddenly felt ill, and gauged a similar effect among the others—a reaction the cardinal appeared to find rather to his liking. With swollen eye bags and a scraggly red beard, he had the look of Torquemada himself. Although he had greeted us with handshakes and the word *peace*, his immediate use of hand sanitizer and his sullen glare—as well as his biretta in camouflage colors, Roman sandal boots, and giant gold crucifix—helped us understand that here was a man who liked to get to the crux of a problem without getting caught up in niceties; indeed, he made it clear in not so many words that we were trampling his toes, very much intruding upon his private fiefdom.

I say this while having had no special motive at the time to form a strong impression of him or guess his outlook on life, save that he had the puckered face of a red snapper and the unorthodox ability to turn his head all the way around, like an owl. Of course it is possible I only imagined these things, or daydreamt them, just as I saw his mouth pop open to exhale cigarette smoke or catch a housefly. "Cardinal Fat Cat" we named him afterward, for his Rolex, jiggly girth, and short stature. Or as Tommy put it more colorfully, "Ten pounds of shite in a five-pound bag."

In the meantime, Buckaroo changed the subject. "As if we both don't know the powerful forces opposed to our work: the World Crime League and their worldwide disinformation machine."

"Yes, people with an overabundance of self-worth standing in the way of unconditional love," His Holiness replied, as the cardinal now gestured to the peg-legged fellow—a Pomeranian flagellant, we learned—who, turning to leave, revealed a colorfully tattooed backside highlighted by a zebra's pattern of fresh, oozing stripes.

"It's a mean world out there, full of human lice," the cardinal readily agreed . . .

. . . as the Pomeranian returned seconds later with small plastic bags full of trinkets—bejeweled shoehorns, key chains, and Ace pocket combs, all with the pope's personal emblem, along with various discount coupons, prayer cards of diverse saints, and souvenir comic books of Pope

Innocent's travels and homilies—which he proceeded to distribute to Buckaroo, Tommy, Pecos, and me.

"In honor of our special relationship," declared the pope.

"I share the sentiment. Words cannot express my gratitude," said Buckaroo, leafing through one of the comics. "The *Baltimore Catechism*, a gift I'll long remember. How thoughtful, Your Holiness."

"Yes, the thought that counts," the pope said and then spouted the television jingle with which we are all familiar: " 'A Deluxe shoehorn and an Ace comb, your ace in the hole, like our Lord who took up our infirmity.' "

To my eyes, at least, His Holiness appeared overly medicated and burdened by the sins of the world we could only imagine. These days his traditional white cassock sported a garish hodgepodge of corporate logo patches—Aqua Velva, Ace combs, Buster Brown shoes and laces, Champion lip balm, Knights of Malta lube job, and Go Fast sports drink, among others—but the familiar sparkle in his eyes was missing, along with his former youthful vitality and purity of heart. It was as if someone had squeezed him half to sleep and wrung half the life out of him as well, so that throughout our meeting it seemed our conversation was taking place through an unwelcome filter or a buffer, an invisible wall of lies. Or, more likely, he was merely inebriated, as rumors of his drinking habits had reached our ears for some time.

"Tell me all the latest about the world tour, Buckaroo," he said, summoning a rare bit of real enthusiasm and flashing humorously what I recognized as a plastic Buckaroo Banzai flashlight ring on his right pinkie finger.

After a scant few minutes, the one-legged Pomeranian received a message on his phone, whispered something to the cardinal, and limped out of the room without a single word to us. His hurried withdrawal, I believe—and the cardinal's open hostility and constant obsession with his enormous Rolex wristwatch—had the effect of accelerating our own departure. Whether this was his modus operandi, and somehow orchestrated with the Pomeranian, was not immediately obvious to me; but a profound undercurrent of tension, palpable danger, and treachery nonetheless emanated from his presence.

THE SINISTER CARDINAL

I have noted already, with regard to General Wagoneer, in what low regard Buckaroo Banzai holds traitors. What can be worse than betrayal from one we trust? Is not even a sickness unto death more bearable than the pain of seeing a trusted intimate turn Judas? What perfidy in nature so pierces the human heart and corrupts its faith like the secret Satan who assumes the role of selfless comrade or faithful servant, yet is alienated from all goodness of heart and human decency? Such a creature is not born of a loving mother; he is made from anomie, like a poisoned apple or a heap of rubbish, whatever word you wish to use: the jealous man who never achieves what he wants in life personally or professionally because he is a defective soul mistakenly allowed into public circulation. Yet rather than fault his own nature or will himself to change, he places the blame elsewhere. Because he has never been wanted as an artist or a lover, he is a man alienated from all but his imaginary victimhood; and this, too, he deems the fault of others. In his distorted world, there is no lack of candidates who sabotage his purpose or whatever glorious enterprise he claims as his own, and he hates them for it. It follows, then, that to invert positions, to embrace a friend or mentor with glib flattery while secretly undermining him, confers the status and meaning the turncoat desperately covets.

Perhaps I stared at the caped cardinal longer than I realized, for Tommy nudged me and whispered, "I don't blame you. Don't turn your back on that weasel face."

When I cautioned for quiet, he muttered under his breath, "Not only that, these guys look like coloring books."

Here he rolled his eyes toward the pair of uniformed Pontifical Swiss Guards flanking the doorway of the Holy Father's private apartment, both of them in their traditional gaily striped doublets and loose slops . . . an ensemble topped off by their rakish raspberry berets and enormous *Zweihänder* swords.

Shifting my attention back to Buckaroo, I heard him say, "Long time in the making, Your Eminence, but the tour is finally happening, thanks to the persistence of our millions of European fans. We hope to see you this afternoon at the Coliseum."

"Without fail, Buckaroo," vowed the pontiff. "Excellent medicine, since I've been feeling down in the dump."

"Not ill, I trust . . . ?" queried Buckaroo.

"Not to the point of serious, but perhaps I should talk to someone," the pope slurred nervously.

"Perhaps the world-renowned healer, the abbot Costello?" Buckaroo inquired slyly. "I've heard so much about him. Am I to understand he works miracles and even made off with the sword of San Galgano?"

The pope, utterly puzzled, could not find his voice, but the cardinal allowed this much: "Even I do not fully comprehend the mysterious ways of God, and I am his agent. I mean to say that I am God's agent on this earth and also blessed to represent the abbot for his many personal appearances without understanding his great gift, a rarity over which he has no control."

"A mystery man, then," acknowledged Buckaroo. "Perhaps I shall meet him on another occasion."

"Almost certainly," the cardinal declared and abruptly pointed with apparent annoyance at his watch. "His Eminence wishes you could remain, but the truths of this world intrude. He has many appointments and much work to do concerning this evening's major announcement to the DeMolay cadre . . . and the entire Christian-speaking world."

"Major announcement . . . ?" inquired Buckaroo.

Baltazar smiled like a crocodile, saying, "He has decided to make public the last portion of the third secret of Fátima. In fact it is a fourth secret and an earth-shattering event, I promise you . . . to be broadcast to a global audience at the conclusion of your concert. Hopefully you will all stay to listen and perhaps learn something."

"Most definitely," Buckaroo said. "I'm always keen to be let in on a secret."

I may have snickered involuntarily at this remark; and for a brief instant the cardinal's sidewise glance met my own, chilling my blood and reminding me that the cardinal was the type of false character who, at the touch of a switch, could spew hot or cold bullspit from the same tap . . . neither the smartest man in the room nor the strongest, but the most ruthless sort of megalomaniac capable of sticking cutlery into the back of anyone in his path.

With any luck we would bring him to a screeching halt. But just who was this cocksure little cardinal in his fiftieth year, who reminded me of a slick-haired thug and yet seemed so proud of himself that he strutted around the pope's private apartments with a sense of superior status and utter insolence? I have said that he was a showman and a former circus barker, a man whose chief connection with the world was always money. Why he had become a priest was anyone's guess, but my own theory was that it enabled him to have sway over others and thus obtain more easily the spoils of life via the power of moral persuasion.

That Pope Innocent was cowed by him was evident to anyone, as was the fact that he had invited us eagerly into his company before something appeared to strain our relationship. This was noticed in the Holy Father's outward manner when he appeared to slip into a nervous pause (almost a cowed silence) at the first word from the cardinal. It was as if he desperately wished to purge his soul but feared his judge, who was apparently Baltazar and not God. But for what reason? And what to make of this fourth secret of Fátima business?

It seemed we had gained important clues but could only speculate on their significance, by which I mean the cardinal's intentions. While I am tempted to say I could see through the façade of the cardinal—that is, give him some character development—the best I can offer in this regard is to pass along the rumor that he habitually laughed himself to sleep.

Whatever the unique bond between them, there was something blatantly sinister in the cardinal's overbearing tone of voice and all-too-obvious manipulation of the Holy Father, a simple *carbonaio* from the Bergamo Alps who rose from humble beginnings and was said to have wrestled the devil on multiple occasions with his bare hands. What gave the cardinal the right to speak to such a beloved man in such a rude manner? So it was with a sense of weary resignation that Pope Innocent raised his portly frame from his antique chair and insisted, "Let me walk you out, Buckaroo."

XXIII. ALSO SPRACH BALTAZAR

> The worst of madmen is a saint run mad.
> —Alexander Pope

The cardinal predictably accompanied us and hung on our every word much too closely for my liking . . . though I had the feeling the pope managed to whisper something to Buckaroo just as our party paused to view a giant oil painting of a red-bearded, bare-chested crusader riding a burro across a bed of palm fronds. Wearing only a flowing Superman cape and a cardinal's square hat with a knight's visor, the powerfully built knight held a sword in one hand and a blazing cross in the other . . . evidently meant to portray a heroic Jesus or even Napoleon, to judge by the grand eagle of the Légion d'honneur tattooed over his left breast. And yet I had my doubts all was as it seemed.

"I don't remember this work—it's new, isn't it?" Buckaroo asked the pope with a skeptical eye. "Signed by Arnold Böcklin . . . executed in his dream-like style, and yet . . ."

The pope merely shrugged, admitting, "I rarely know a thing worth knowing about art, having no good discernment. I like small, happy paintings that give apostolic wisdom and encouragement. Cardinal Baltazar is the art expert."

"His Holiness is too generous, but I know what I like," the cardinal interjected with false modesty and seemed to be experiencing a moment of ecstasy in front of the painting.

"And that sword," said Buckaroo.

"The sword of San Galgano!" Tommy whistled.

"Yes, I believe you could be right," said the cardinal with feigned surprise . . .

. . . as we all stepped closer to examine the rider and burro. Elsewhere in the spacious canvas, a pair of winged cherubs fluttered overhead with streamers and cheerleader pompoms, and a gap in the roiling clouds revealed the light of heaven and a classical Greek Adonis reclining on a cloud à la Titian's Venus, naked except for wrestling tights and a golden sash bearing the painting's title: *Fire and Steel, pro Roma et Schleswig-Holstein.*

"For Rome and Schleswig-Holstein?" questioned Buckaroo.

"*Gott mit uns,*" the cardinal commented with one hand buried inside his cassock. "I acquired it only recently for the Vatican collection, to celebrate my own bloodline through history's great captains and God's blessing on my appointment as cardinal secretary of state, *pontifex maximus* of the Priory of Sion, commandant of the Praetorian Papal Knights and Penitent Boys of Rome, as well as personal secretary and spiritual vicar to Popius here, by whose order I have been tasked—not wishing to sound proud—with rewriting the Catholic Bible."

Making it clear this list was far from complete, he stopped here, gazing at Buckaroo, who had cocked a skeptical eyebrow.

"Popius . . . ?" Buckaroo said.

"Or Pope-sicle or Sweet Pickles, if you prefer," replied the cardinal airily, glancing at the blushing pope. "We're not formal or picky around here when there is so much work to be done."

"Right, thank you so much for being so amazing," mumbled Tommy under his breath.

"Certainly. Congratulations, Cardinal," said Buckaroo. "I'm sure the world cannot say thank you often enough."

"He is an angel," offered the pope.

"I'm no angel," scoffed Baltazar, blushing. "Only a humble cardinal."

AN UNFORTUNATE INCIDENT

Pecos and I meanwhile alternated our gazes between the cardinal and the painting, as if recognizing a certain facial resemblance between

Baltazar and the reclining Adonis, at least insofar as the amateurish artist
had rendered him. It is also possible Tommy experienced the same flicker
of recognition, for he now commented acerbically, "Doesn't look like
any Napoleon Louie I ever saw or Bochephus either, except for his two-
foot-long crank . . ."

Indeed, incredibly enough, it had escaped our notice until now that
the little donkey appeared to need help carrying its elongated penis that
was out of all proportion to the rest of its body.

"Yes, poor Bocephus," I said.

"Who wouldn't take a ride on that?" Pecos wisecracked.

"Doubtless you mean Bucephalus, Tommy," chided the cardinal
condescendingly. "Or did you mean Marengo or the white Coco?"

Beginning to anger, Tommy closed his eyes and appeared to be
counting to ten.

"The nightmare never ends. If I open my eyes and you're still
here . . ."

These words were scarcely out of his mouth before the cardinal
chortled condescendingly under his breath and ribbed Tommy: "This
is not the gunslinging Old West. What does a barbarian cowboy know
about great European art?"

By this insult, however, he invited the wrath of Tommy, who now
stared the cardinal down with his steely gray eyes, saying, "You're the
wizard of smarts. You tell me."

I confess I could not contain a smile, as Tommy proceeded, "I know
two shits about art, but enough to recognize the wrestler in the clouds
as Satan by Guido. I'm sure you know the painting—they say Satan is
Cardinal Pamphili's twin, and therefore yours."

Taken aback by Tommy's unexpected familiarity with the Baroque
period, Baltazar replied arrogantly, "I know the painting you mean . . .
Cardinal Pamphili, who became Pope Innocent X."

At this mention, the present Pope Innocent leaned further forward
and pricked his ears, as Cardinal Baltazar concluded, "But forgive me
if I see nothing of myself in it. Indeed the painting you mention—not
by some Guido but by Guido Reni, his full name—which used to hang
not far from here in Our Lady of the Conception of the Capuchins, no
longer exists. A satanic fungus befell it, and unfortunately it had to be
destroyed for obvious reasons."

Tommy reacted as if the cardinal had punched him in the groin. "A Guido destroyed? That's some fake cheese and you're a gum-flapping liar. I reckon I'll see you in liars' hell!" . . .

. . . as the cardinal responded dismissively, "Yes, I'm sure there is a special place in hell for decadent pop stars who corrupt the youth with their satanic example and godless filth."

"Like I'm sure there's no shit under your hood," countered Tommy.

The cardinal flinched at the profanity but boasted, "Because I have overcome the urge to possess a woman physically, the communion of saints is my true bride."

"I knew your bitch ass was kinky," spouted Tommy.

At this opportune juncture Buckaroo interjected a word on Tommy's behalf. "Cardinal, perhaps you don't know that Tommy contributes much of his time to motivational speaking at schools and orphanages, donating his time to more than a hundred events a year . . ."

"To all who seek out help," Pecos helpfully pointed out. "Rodeos, state fairs, high schools, trade conventions, support groups . . ."

The cardinal seemed amused and peered up his long nose at the taller and younger Tommy, saying dismissively, "Perhaps this explains his overinflated ideas of himself. You may be famous but hardly perfect, Mr. Perfect. 'In all thy works be mindful of thy last end' when you shake your bottom for money and sexual jollies . . ."

"And you keep this in mind," Tommy riposted. "No one phawks with Perfect Tommy unless Tommy wants to be phawked with . . ."

The cardinal arched his brows and responded, "Then I am no longer laughing in my sleeve. I demand satisfaction."

"A duel?" Tommy snorted derisively.

"Or an auto-da-fé . . . the choice is yours, Mr. Tommy."

"Any way you want it, considering the magnitude of your douchebaggery," said Tommy, as several of the Swiss Guards now began to stir, taking notice of the escalating contretemps that by now featured Tommy rolling up his sleeves and assuming a fighting pose.

"Then by the power of heaven, I declare you infamous and anathema. I cast you out," replied Baltazar, pretending to wash his hands like Pontius Pilate . . .

. . . as Tommy shot back menacingly, "Wanna repeat that, red bird? You can't cast me out, because I'm leaving. Else I'm gonna go cold in a minute and release the eye of the tiger—"

"Oh dear," pantomimed the cardinal.

"—and cock you one, if this weren't a respectable joint," Tommy threatened more ominously, taking a step toward the cardinal but finding his progress blunted by Buckaroo, who urged him quietly but firmly to calm down.

"Easy, Tom, don't be a hothead. Your anger only feeds his ego. Slow it down some; let your brain breathe for once . . ."

"After I remove that stick from his tight ass," Tommy muttered, still seething and taking his eyes only reluctantly from his nemesis, and only at Buckaroo's insistence.

"And feel gratified to have done your part with schoolyard taunts, but that's enough. Whatever you do, don't release the eye of the tiger," Buckaroo told him in a hushed tone nonetheless loud enough for the others to overhear. "There is something in what you say, Tommy, but I suspect the cardinal is only playing devil's advocate, perhaps trying to get a rise out of you."

"Perhaps so," the cardinal volunteered with a crooked smile. "Perhaps the devil's advocate is my game. I certainly bear him no ill will and lament the tragic loss of his soul to black mascara and plucked eyebrows."

"Well, that ain't gonna happen, 'cause you're nuttier than a squirrel turd," said Tommy, as Pecos led him by the hand out of the papal apartment, leaving Buckaroo and your reporter to take a fuller measure of the insufferable cardinal who plainly fancied himself the intellectual equal of Buckaroo Banzai.

THE PUGNACIOUS CARDINAL

Buckaroo meanwhile had begun to comment on the wretched painting I have described, saying, "All knowledge is a gift, and to paraphrase Saint Thomas, no knowledge is wholly false and without some mixture of truth . . . as with the portraitist, who is often engaged by the client to flatter the subject by omitting the odd blemish."

Pope Innocent seemed to mull this over and affirmed, "That is true. I myself have suffered at the hands of an accurate portraitist who has left me feeling not so proud . . . ha, ha, merciful Jesus! But if we can no longer distinguish between true and false, Buckaroo, it is a dangerous development . . . if we fail to hold steady to the glue of church teaching and God's revelation. Truth exists whether we like it or not. That which is gained by way of dishonesty, no matter how appealing, is illegitimate, because it is based upon a lie."

"Agreed, Your Holiness," said Buckaroo, who was looking at an unhappy Cardinal Baltazar, even as he directed his words at the pope. "But without questioning convention, one may become bogged down by dogma, which may become a comfort blanket. Let us also agree that certain subjects are natural actors who do their utmost to conceal their true selves."

"One may view every man as a work of art, with his true heart known only to God," the cardinal argued through firmly clenched teeth, not taking his worshipful eyes from the painting. "I especially like Böcklin's use of space and bleak dreariness, as if staring into the smoking abyss of Gehenna. Look at the old order of Europe, symbolized by the valley of Megiddo in the distance and the heathen swine, portrayed as actual pigs, cowering from the Scarlet Knight and the Second Coming!"

Buckaroo and I now exchanged questioning looks because, incredibly enough, not a word of his description came close to being true. At least nothing of what he described could be seen in the painting, where no such multitude of figures appeared.

Still, the cardinal pressed on, sputtering with excitement verging on a nervous disorder. "Just imagine the might of the Corsican's armies with the holy cross and the holy sword of San Galgano going on before! Give me a hundred warriors like Jesus and I'll conquer the known world!"

"*Und mit der Sieg Heil*," I muttered.

"For the Second Consulate and the Holy Roman Empire!" the cardinal concluded breathlessly, trying to retain his wits about him.

"As if we didn't have enough embarrassments who call themselves princes of the church," I said quietly to Buckaroo . . .

. . . who gave me a knowing nudge and spoke up. "I think the fraud analogy is apt. I didn't want to create a stir, Cardinal, but in my view the painting itself is a lie, a forgery. The canvas even retains a faint odor of lacquer . . . and someone has an eye for a good joke. Why, if you look closely you can even see faint human lip imprints amid the brush strokes, as if someone has covered the painting with kisses . . ."

"An observer perhaps inflamed by the Messiah's throbbing sinews of steel," speculated Baltazar.

"The Messiah . . . ?" I pondered audibly.

"The horseman upon whom God's blessings . . ."

"Or a similar amount of cocaine," I ventured . . .

. . . as Buckaroo pointed to the figure in wrestling tights peering through the clouds. "And this, Cardinal . . . ? Looking down from the uppermost vault of unutterable experiences, who is this?"

"He is the Holy Justicer, antidote to the netherworld . . ."

"Based upon the marble bust of Caligula in the Louvre?" suggested Buckaroo.

"I am incredulous, but, yes," the cardinal replied with a dour face, awaiting Buckaroo's final judgment.

"Böcklin didn't paint this. The truth is, this artist is subpar, an average amateur at best," pronounced Buckaroo.

"Still, almost a work of genius," opined Pope Innocent as a conciliatory offering.

Baltazar continued to brood but nonetheless replied cautiously, "I take your point, Dr. Banzai. Interesting how you saw through the poor forgery. I intend to look into the matter, so please carry on planting your baby seedlings in Amazonia—you and your small vision of the world—while we build the New Consulate of Europe. You are looking at the Black Crown Prince of the New Rome! You will toast me when I rise!"

"Go forth and be great, then," said Buckaroo with a cocked eyebrow. "Certainly I will toast you in one form or another, if and when the need arises."

"What is your point?" Baltazar asked breezily before continuing with his delusional rhetoric.

Perhaps never in my life have I had to endure such a mindless, blathering diatribe; yet out of respect to the place, Buckaroo and I said nothing to contradict him, so he continued to propound his nonsense while the pope, mostly looking down and playing with a little bell on his tassel, at least pretended to agree with him, conceding, "Of course you are right, Cardinal Baltazar. Perhaps we are tilting at windmills.

The moral lesson is the important thing, to be liberated from perversion and remind people of the miracle of salvation. Even a photograph is not unequivocally correct . . . only a pale image of God's creation, which is love."

Here he paused, and I took it upon myself to pose a profound question: "But what is love, Your Holiness? Candy kisses and unicorns?"

"Hardly," the cardinal disagreed before the pope could answer. "Augustine said that love may require a benevolent severity, even a war of mercy."

"It is that small, still voice inside us all that says love is the way things are meant to be," the thoughtful pontiff said. "Did you know that the same letters in the word *earth* also spell *heart*? The important thing is to find some smiles along the way, especially in today's world with all its burdens."

"I couldn't agree more. We certainly don't want to keep these performers from the bacchanal," affirmed Cardinal Baltazar, who oddly enough was standing like a *ballerino* in fourth position, albeit in Roman sandals, his left foot in front, poised and pointing outward . . .

. . . as the pope next deigned to grant us a disquisition on the moral value of his favorite Buckaroo Banzai adventure stories, until the impatient cardinal again barked the time of day and nudged us toward the exit. Nor did we exactly protest.

"Yes, we need to mosey along as well, as I have a lecture to deliver at the Italian Astronomical Society and a concert sound check," Buckaroo said with typical mastery of the situation, embellishing our goodbyes with the fond expectation that we would see His Holiness that evening at the concert, to be followed by the unveiling of the fourth secret. Hopes for a lengthier conversation with the Holy Father, or a private one, were dashed, however, by Cardinal Baltazar's refusal to leave the pope's side even for an instant.

"Nice meeting you, Cardinal," Buckaroo said, heading out. "Thanks for your valuable time."

"Let not your heart be troubled. I am sure we'll meet again, Mr. Banzai . . . on the plain of Armageddon."

"Stay grounded, Padre."

"What an adorable guy," groused Pecos, whom we presently rejoined. "Mother Nature ruined a perfect asshole by giving him teeth."

AN AFFRAY THAT AFTERNOON

Because of Buckaroo's lecture and lengthy meet-and-greet session at the Enrico Fermi Astrophysical Society (with a queue around the block), we were unavoidably running behind schedule as we settled into the airy glass space at Palazzo. There were more than two dozen of us who had come directly from the Coliseum sound check: five of us touring Cavaliers (our lineup: Buckaroo, Pecos, Perfect Tommy, Hoppalong on bass, and me), our road crew (Webmaster Jhonny, Li'l Daughter, and Red Jordan, plus a small army of Italian sound and light technicians). To these must be added another dozen or so local Blue Blazes, including the *sindaco di Roma*, Mayor Agostinelli, and the odd traveling partners Jack Tarantulus and Mona Peeptoe, who by coincidence had shared a flight and would not have been themselves had they not arrived with complaints aplenty about airline schedules, subpar service, random searches, and an overall lack of respect.

"I don't care if the verdict is one penny in damages, I'm suing. And I happen to know the president of the American Bar Association," Jack was threatening, while Mona railed against everyone who had ever rejected her, including this author and high Vatican officials.

"Speaking of which," she ranted, "how flaky the people around Pope Innocent have become! I have it on good authority there's a lot of papal pill popping going on. What ever happened to sobriety? Personal integrity?"

Of course we hung breathlessly on her every word but somehow managed to continue eating, despite her matchless use of all her means of expression—the entire repertoire of vocal intonation, pause, gesture, attitude, and indescribable play of countenance . . .

. . . as she continued, "Or is it just me? Am I the only one who misses the old days when there was a modicum of etiquette and people actually answered emails and returned phone calls?"

On this point her eloquence made some headway, evoking general agreement and head nodding; and I myself was about to let my feelings be known when Buckaroo's hot phone buzzed and I experienced an urgent call of nature.

"High Sierra back in World Watch . . . about the Lectroid man-o'-war," Buckaroo whispered to me and got up to take the call away from the table . . .

. . . as I scooted back in my own chair, announcing with forced jocularity, "Time to move this show down the road, folks. No dancing on tables while I'm gone . . . at least not with your spurs on."

But Mona had overheard enough to ask, "What did Buckaroo mean, Reno . . . about High Sierra and the Lectroid . . . ? What man of war? Who . . . ?"

"I have no idea. You mean our next movie?" I said and marched quickly out of earshot, prompting her to shift her interrogation to Pecos.

"What's up with Reno and Buckaroo, Pecos? So secretive," she probed. "Are Lectroids in your new picture?"

"Unfounded gossip," Pecos instantly replied.

"Is it still called *Project Doom*? My sources who have seen the script are telling me Buckaroo takes over the president's job and issues a top-level directive from NORAD, placing US forces on worldwide alert . . . true or false?"

"Unfounded gossip," Pecos instantly replied . . .

. . . as Tommy thoughtlessly gushed, "DEFCON 2 . . ."

"DEFCON 2?" Mona said, taking out her pen and scribbling notes in the glow of her glittery pink Buckaroo Banzai phone, repeating to herself, "DEFCON 2 . . . can I quote you on that, Tommy?"

"Off the record, sorry," returned Pecos. "We can't be your source."

"Then just tell me, what's the threat in this movie? Who's the bad guy giving Buckaroo the finger? Hanoi Xan, as usual?" Mona asked. "Can someone connect the dots for me?"

By now I was just turning the corner toward the water closet when the sound of screams and a violent scuffle near the kitchen entrance caused me to pivot and freeze in my tracks. Torn by a physical need to be on my way and yet an inability to avert my eyes from the dramatic scene in front of me, I watched wide eyed as a restaurant cook and a pair of managers struggled to subdue a slight-built man who lay wriggling on the floor, his face shielded from me by his attackers and his filthy, ragged tunic and cowl.

A monk, then! At least this much was clear: a monk clutching a cheese sandwich.

"Kitchen thief! Filthy priest!" shouted the cook, who continued to strike the cowering victim with a sizzling-hot basket of wet pasta . . .

. . . while the meek monk cringed and whimpered in a mixture of Latin and Italian, pleading for God's mercy on grounds that he was pregnant (at least as far as I was given to understand), along with sporadic references to Buckaroo Banzai.

Please understand, dear reader, that all of this occurred within the span of several seconds, before my natural instinct as peacemaker took over and I took a tentative step to calm matters. A single step was indeed as far as I got, however, as suddenly the monk leapt to his feet and, in a voice that was at once unearthly and terrifyingly familiar to me, foamed at the mouth. "Shitebug! You mustache mama face!"

Cook and managers were sent flying with a flick of the mad monk's wrist; and the creature—for that was what he now was—turned to face me, the alien's old, familiar reeking odor even more hideous than I recalled, his Lectroid eyes like red cigarette embers that spewed only hatred. On the face of it, his very existence in this poor monk was preposterous, and yet I found myself forced to resist his will with every fiber of my mental and physical being.

"Whorfin . . . ?"

"'Your Majesty' to you, shitebug slurp pile . . . Reno Kid! Prepare freak your mind, fart hump!"

"Yes, who would believe it?" I mumbled, hearing my own voice quiver.

"Few believin' it, Reno . . . eye for eye, some shite like that," he replied and appeared to inhale, as if picking up a scent. "Buckaroo Banzai . . . need see Buckaroo . . ."

"That's a good one, but an old one. Everyone needs see Buckaroo. If you mean to harm him, you'll get phawked up pretty quickly, because this behavior is not acceptable to the human race," I warned and braced myself to do battle, for in the narrow hallway there was no room for evasive action . . . except to retreat.

As my fingers edged toward my pocket revolver, I overheard myself making the feeblest of attempts at small talk: "Long time, no see . . . I see you've changed partners. Is there a problem?"

"No problems, twat mongrel. Why got problems?"

"Where are you living these days?"

"Here, there, at the Vatican, layin' me down in green pasture . . . just dancin' my mess around . . ."

"Congratulations. That is truly sad, Your Majesty."

And with that, he opened his mouth, revealing flowy cilia, venom sacs, and a barbed stinger set to launch, when suddenly his hands grasped his own throat and dropped himself, kicking and screaming, to the floor.

" 'Vengeance is mine, saith the Lord!' "

"Dick biscuit! Dickhole! Your neck will know my boot!" wailed Whorfin . . .

. . . as the mad dyad in a single body continued to kick and throttle one another, barely able to squeeze out any speech—which in any case came now from the Italian speaker with a handlebar mustache. "*Per Dio!* Reno! Hear my words of truth! For the sake of all, for the sake of the world, I give myself to die! *Porca Madonna*, kill the demon and his lineage! Please, I beg, put an end to my guilt! Clean me out!"

XXIV. OUR LAST SUPPER?

> A net is spread,
> Gripping the towers about.
> —Aeschylus

Naturally I could not fulfill the stranger's request to kill an innocent man, namely himself, and in any case Whorfin now slipped his own chokehold and bowled over a waiter on his way out the back door. Whether sluggish from food and drink or more urgent biological needs, I confess I failed to pursue in timely fashion—although who could have divined such an unlikely scenario right under our noses, entwined as it was with our purpose?

But here I will dispense with excuses, for you who know me as one not given to sugarcoat or romanticize our history, or indulge in cheap stage drama, deserve no less than the unvarnished truth. So I will make a full confession: at that fraught moment I failed to do more, not only because I felt like a crisis actor in a staged event, but because I had pissed myself.

But put yourself in my shoes, dear reader. Yes, I did manage to scamper to the exit and peer out at a dark alleyway in time to observe several police officers toss a net over the monk and attempt to load him into a waiting van . . . when suddenly their quarry flicked them aside like so many toothpicks and, casting an eerie light from within, yelled what sounded like "little bitches" and fled off into the night!

A true story, albeit one even I had difficulty believing, despite witnessing the fantastic scene with my own eyes. I hardly need mention with what renewed urgency I hurried to the bathroom, where I relieved my bowels and dabbed my wet crotch. Several more crucial minutes were lost when I took off my trousers and attempted to dry them in front of the hot-air hand dryer.

My nerves at last settled, I noted that Buckaroo was still absent when I returned to the table and the following conversation.

"John Whorfin?! For real? Out to kill you in your next movie . . . ?" said Mona, wide eyed.

"We don't know. Maybe the Lectroids'll set us on fire or maybe they're just pretending," blurted Red Jordan at the next table. "Buckaroo is also afraid of a worldwide viral outbreak. We're still tinkering with the story."

"My God, no wonder you're all in Hulk mode," said Mona. "I see it in your faces. You're all in character."

"Yesiree, Mona," Tommy declared with steely, bloodshot eyes, alternating between sips of prosecco, beer, and Coca-Cola. "The shiteball's been rolling toward the fan for some time, but nobody at this table's throwing in the towel. We've got our britches pulled up, our hats turned the right way. I do not hate on my fellows or any other species, but I'll fight any attacks on our mother world to the last freckle on my ass. God bless America and semper paratus, meaning 'always horny.'"

"Yes, bubbly-wubbly . . . shoot fire and holy smoke, God bless us every one," Mona grumbled and tried to sneak out her phone, only to be quickly found out.

"This is off the record, Mona. You promised," Pecos reminded her in no uncertain terms . . .

. . . as Mona reluctantly put the phone away, grousing, "Well, that's damn inconvenient. Insane. Wake up, people. The world can't wait to hear about your next film or musical project."

"Relax, Mona, you'll still get your scoop," I assured her, perhaps lying and wondering myself why it mattered . . . indeed why anything mattered anymore.

"Yeah, let's just have dessert," Tommy said.

During my five-minute trip to the loo, in other words, everything and nothing had changed, as dear friends strung together another meaningless conversation, and Tommy, taking another gulp, said,

"Tyranny goes down smooth, that's the trouble. Paraphrasing the philosopher, I prefer liberty with danger to peace with slavery."

"Just paraphrasing? Do you honestly expect me to believe that, with Perfect Tommy's famous photographic memory?" Mona remarked, peering over her drink at Tommy and giving me an undeniable surge of jealousy.

"Thanks for believing in me, Mona," Tommy said coolly. "In the event of my death on the field of battle, I'd like to have my personal effects forwarded to you . . . if you don't mind."

"But that would mean giving you my location," she replied without blinking.

Webmaster Jhonny laughed at her retort and, itching for another go at Tommy, launched his fiercest attack yet: "You are on fire, Mona! Ha, ha! Tommy is rankled and fulminating some awful, so bitter like he is drinking vinegar! He can't handle it, because, Tommy, your mouth sprays only halitosis . . . ha, ha! What rolls downhill, poopy smelling like rotten fish and vinegar!"

"Humorous take, rookie, but try to hang with the subject matter," Tommy replied. "The rest of us have work to do, like eating these noodles."

"What do you want, a gold medal for spaghetti sucking?" Jhonny said. "That is your skill set? Please obtain a life, Tommy, as you are walking evidence of knuckle dragging . . . ha, ha, knuckle dragger who wears a dunce's hat, proving my point Tommy has trouble talking to girls who are not Neanderthals."

"Get straight in your penny loafers, kid. You'll have to get up at the butt crack of dawn to know more about women than I do," said Tommy through several strands of dangling spaghetti. "Mona's already mentioned relationship rule number one."

"And what is that, O Great Tommy?" Mona wanted to know. "What's your 'relationship rule number one'?"

"There's all manner of shite in my foolproof system, but I'll tell you," he said. "Rule number one: never tell her where you live."

"But you live in the freaking bunkhouse!" Mona howled loudly. "Ohmyfreakin'god, everybody knows that!"

"Ha, ha, Tommy is under attack and consternated [sic]," cackled Jhonny.

Hoping to head off trouble, Pecos now changed the subject, putting it to the webmaster: "So, tell us, Jhonny, apart from peeping on ladies when they sleep, and possibly in the shower, what do you know about women? Then we'll talk from there."

Jhonny, wearing a colorful roll-neck sweater inscribed with the motivational quote ALL I DO IS WIN, readily replied, "First of all, Pecos, as we discussed, I am unworthy of your opinion. I admit it was not mean [sic] to be. Among the vast of men [sic], I am maybe not the most handsomely, but I bring to the table class and gentleman manners and try to emulate Buckaroo with a love for everyone."

"You said a mouthful right there, Jhonny," she said . . .

. . . as the webmaster continued to expound in his unassuming way, "I am not over six feet or a former marine or horseback rider, but neither a horndoggy leg hound like Tommy without couth or moral . . ."

"Needless to say," said Tommy.

". . . whose animalistic erection makes for oxygenated blood deficit in his tiny brain," Jhonny went on. "Because, unlike Tommy, I bring honest emotions of love and do not go with hookerized ladies."

"Ha, ha, true comedic gold . . . like I give a twenty-dollar phawk," Tommy said halfheartedly between slurping noodles and barely listening. "Keep barking at the moon, kiddo, while I tell you how the story ends."

Jhonny flexed a fist and returned fire: "Ha, Tommy is mistaking intelligence for weakness! Wait until I chase you down and pugilize you in the fight of the century and beat you purple with my freight train! Ha, ha, Tommy is a train wreck! And a dumbbell!"

"Somebody hold me back," said Tommy. "I'm right here, pencil arms. Just gimme a minute to piss down my leg before I grab you by the oysters."

"Like you took a pee in my cat box one time?" Jhonny cackled exuberantly. "Tommy is a dumb-dumb with Dumbo ears! Enough is enough, dumbo loser with no life who did not get through grammar school! I will swat you and your banjo! Consider yourself warned and your attitude adjusted."

"My goodness," said Mona. "Jhonny does not mince words and is quite the expert in the art of humiliation, though I suspect both of you are in reality two cheeks of the same ass."

"Har," laughed Tommy. "Maybe Jhonny doesn't realize when people are just having a little fun at his expense."

Somehow encouraged, Jhonny continued: "Unlike Tommy the Perfect, however, I do not like flabby-gut grannies, bowlegged gold diggers, and pompous, agitating wildebeests with other womans' [*sic*] hair or hungry elephants with five o'clock shadows—in short, nickels masquerading as dimes . . ."

"In other words, women who are faker than you with your Chiclet denture," interjected Mona, whom he failed to hear or at least pretended not to hear.

". . . or ladies who wear pointed shoes or white hats in winter also," Jhonny ranted on. "When I am in a hardship and horned up and looking to spend some good time with ladies, I go for a shave and splurge for a clean-cut, manly look—handcrafted Mexican boots, a cowboy shirt and hard-starched blue dungarees or khaki pants, and a neat quilted vest. I do not go to a cheaters' bar like Tommy and parade around with a fat roll of twenties, making care to overtip so everyone notices me."

"For crying out loud," said Pecos. "Is that true, Tommy?"

"Of all the shady, low-down douchebaggery," Tommy replied, arching his eyebrows menacingly at Jhonny. "I smell a hidden traitor to the buddy code. An implacable madman."

"A madman who will stop at nothing," Jhonny confirmed in the same roguish vein. "Of course because Tommy is my tablemate and Welcome Ambassador to the Institute, I have accompanied him on what he calls possum hunting . . ."

"Feeling it my duty to teach young minds, perhaps I went beyond reasonable," Tommy said.

"Who, in consideration of this, sometimes asks my opinion, because I know his tricks of the trade. He bellies up to the bar with the look of a gentleman of ease, relative to a man who never looks is getting desperate [*sic*]. When he sees the right class single woman of good quality and congenial demeanor—the number-ten or trophy type—he sends her a tutti-frutti root beer float with two spoons and then makes his approach: 'Hey, you are cute. Do you like to share the float with Perfect Tommy, then maybe to retire to my rooms for a drink of Hong Kong Baijiu, official drink of the Hong Kong Cavaliers? Would you happen to have a light for my unfiltered Camel?'"

"I roll my own, Jhonny boy."

"Move over, Mr. Romance Novel, both of you," bleated Mona. "What a charmer you are, Tommy, and I bet you get plenty of play with the ladies yourself, Jhonny."

"Plenty of party play, Mona, I assure you," Jhonny said. "I am what I am. They do not call me Casanova for no reason."

"For no reason but none," Tommy interjected. "Simple pimple Jhonny . . . horny as a two-dick billy goat."

"Ha, ha . . . K-I-S-S . . . keep it simple, stupid Tommy! I deem you stupid because I bring more to the party than meets the eye," parried Jhonny.

"I've noticed," Mona said. "You're plenty fun, Jhonny, quite full of gas. What else do you do in the way of a-wad behavior?"

"Thank you, Miss Mona, for the honest comment. Being super knowledgeable, I am crime and disease free and do not pick up trash from the bottom of the barrel. That means I do not stoop so low for the drecks [sic] of society, low-hanging fruits or womans [sic] who some problem prevents them to be happy. Neither am I so much attracted to timeless hotties of high caliber and high cheekbones, especially beauty queens and volleyball blonds, but only if her hair matches her downtown or she benefits from smoothness. Neither do I care for womans [sic] who do not want to be productive in life or who talk long drivels. Or toothpick-thins, mad cow disease, big rumbling meatballs with two hundred pounds in her rears who will crush me, or tattooed like a scratch pad, but I do not mind a little text on a pretty foot."

"Ha, ha, Jhonny's snobby," Tommy said, trying to keep his eyes open. "Excuse while I snooze."

"So weird," opined Pecos. "Thanks for opening my eyes, Jhonny. I thought I was the only girl you spoiled rotten."

"What a full load of you-know-what," expressed Mona in response to Jhonny's newfound cockiness. "Seems the real Jhonny has woken up. Good luck finding someone to babysit your giant man-baby egos, both of you."

"Yes," agreed Jhonny, gulping another shot of *baijiu*. "We are polar opposite. Having forsaken all others, I have eyes only for one, i.e., Pecos."

"I.e., ayeeee," replied Pecos.

The webmaster drooled a little more and, lowering his straw fedora over his face, literally talked through his hat: "But making love or doing naughty with a sexy-sexy, I don't follow the rules—I rewrite them and take requests. My ear is glued to her body because she is running things, unless she is vegetative."

"Amen, brother. My hat is off to you, Jhonny," Mona said approvingly.

"Going to pains to flourish her and drive her crazy, I do not ignore your needs, taking proper care of my queen with butterfly kisses, super oral like a cat licks its rear parts, with good rhythmic movements, and the act of love with good rhythmic movements, boom-boom with my Cyclops." He continued, now in a high-pitched falsetto, " 'Oh no, Jhonny, your one-eyed Cyclops is too big for my belly button!' In short, do not let the book cover fool you. I am not so roided up like Tommy, but I am clean jacked like a horse nonetheless . . ."

"Jacked like a seahorse." Tommy snickered and reopened his eyes. "Or my name isn't Scrotum McTang-Tang."

"Straight up, I bring the beef to the burrito," Jhonny continued, unfazed and raising his voice. "I will say it out loud: I like it stank nasty and stupid, hot action of an adult nature, preferably on the flooring or eating table—all freak, all animal-style, delivered room service by my manly hood [sic]."

"Egad, ugh, you're freaking me out, Jhonny," grunted Mona, more or less gagging. "I want to like you. I just don't want to end up in your refrigerator."

"Good one, Mona . . . the perfect touch. Gets better by the minute," Tommy grumbled.

"My refrigerator of stainless steel," Jhonny continued. "My refrigerator which will be of stainless steel and one of the super big ones with a television set."

"Highly inappropriate," Tommy said.

"And then some," echoed Mona. "Gross and disturbing, worse than gross. I'm starting to doubt your sincerity, Jhonny."

Jhonny seemed flummoxed but bragged, "Just call me a no-count son of a B with nothing left to lose, only good at being no good."

"I call poser," Tommy said. "Show your face like a man."

"By all means, we want to see your pretty hazel eyes, Jhonny," Mona cajoled. "No need to be shy. We're a fun group."

"I am hiding from s-s-tupidity," Jhonny slurred.

"So sad," opined Pecos. "Painful to watch."

We all traded looks and Tommy, biting his tongue, interjected, "Painful is an understatement. Can we, please . . . ? Why are we letting this standard of indecency and dumbassness continue? I think it's all so ignorant. Let us take the high ground, brothers and sisters . . . especially you, Jhonny. Please respect yourself enough to change and cease being an object of ridicule."

"Appalled and disgusted, beyond disgraceful. I feel like throwing up," Jumbo Jack Tarantulus likewise weighed in with a patronizing tone of moral superiority. "You kiss your mother with that mouth, young man? Is it 'Johnny'? Is that your name, young fella? You're in desperate need of help. You need to spit that gum out and rinse your mouth out with soap, then apologize to the entire community for sprinkling all this sexual innuendo."

" 'Sprinkling' . . . ha, ha! Piss and moan," squealed Jhonny.

"I, too, am sad and ashamed, Jack," Tommy replied, obviously having his fun, "because Jhonny has failed the Institute, perhaps even flushed his future down the toilet to the extent a malodorous fetor hangs over this table . . . a new phawked-up. I believe childish is the word."

As if in response, Jhonny now downed another shot and tipped over his glass like a fallen chess piece, declaring, "Having drunk seven shots of Hong Kong Baijiu, two Jägermeister bombs, in addition two Honey Jack mind probes and two tall cool ones, my feelings are in shambles and I am one-half tilt [sic]. Ha, ha, I am hammered as phawk, so to speak!"

"I'm just in a state of stundation [sic]," Tommy said, although both he and Jhonny appeared to be growing weary of their juvenile badinage and had begun dueling with bread sticks. "Phawk you, Jhonny, in the fullest measure of 'phawk you,' for slandering my good name. You're cringey as phawk, dude."

"And guilty also stealing a pair of my workout socks from the laundry," claimed Jhonny, who now lowered his hat and closed one eye in order to see straight.

With reluctance I now fessed up: "Sorry, Jhonny, that was me. I used your socks for my malodorous plasma experiments. Case closed."

"See, another damnable lie!" said Tommy adamantly. "Lucky for Jhonny I'm a class act and in a good mood. That increases his odds of survival a thousand percent."

A LAST ROUND OF DRINKS

Tommy's boast drew a look of stern disapproval from Mona, who advised, "Don't interrupt the adults, Tommy—that's so remedial. And don't let Perfect Tommy dull your sparkle, Jhonny. His time is coming."

"Yeah, don't sell your sparkle short, Jhonny boy," Tommy sarcastically chimed in. "Sorry if I'm rough on you, especially now that the world's coming to an end."

It was an offhand remark, but it nonetheless prompted Pecos to direct a weighty glance my way, as Mona ordered more drinks and meanwhile had her fun with Jhonny, teasing, "Anyway, to a woman it's the little things that tickle her sweet spot, like a man's voice, good manners, and personal hygiene. And your dimpled chin with that hipster bristle . . . you can sweat out my hairstyle any day."

"I am Sagittarius, and my interests are anime, travel and food, movies, music, and computer languages," said Jhonny. "Who, valuing your age and wisdom, likes to suckle ladies' hind teat . . ."

"My age and wisdom . . . ?" Mona fired back. "What did you say? My hind tit?"

"Yeah, suckle what, fella?" asked Jack.

"Suckle my throbbing machete," Jhonny replied.

"Whoa, that's a dark twist. You're a bad apple, kid," said Jack.

"My hind tit, Jhonny?" Mona persisted. "What did you mean? You think I have extra ones? A surplus of tits?"

For once Jhonny lacked a reply, other than to say, "I will make you come and squirt honey."

"Make what squirt honey, Jhonny?" she demanded. "How many girlish parts do you think a woman has? Do you even know where a lady keeps her sugar?"

"Behind her badge of honor? I don't think I am far off," poor Jhonny theorized, tilting in his chair and in imminent danger of toppling over.

"An inch is as good as a mile, kid," Tommy laughed again. "Put on your big sister's pants and remind Uncle Tommy to tell you the story of the birds and the bees and the tortoise in the hair."

"You don't have to be a pig, Tommy," Mona griped and suddenly turned to me. "Reno, are you going to let Jhonny and Tommy assault ladies' sensibilities like that? Both are obviously insensitive clods."

Focused on my own recent disappointments for reasons already mentioned, I merely stared vacantly into space and gestured for their inane conversation to pass me by. But my neutrality only earned Mona's mockery: "What's the matter? Can't even squeak up a reply, Reno? How special, yet how typical. No comment? No dirty laundry to air?"

"You're messing with the wrong hombre, Mona," insisted Tommy, leaping to my defense. "Reno's as fine a straight-razor-shavin' fella as I've ever had the privilege to know—and I've known him since back when a buck was still silver. He's what you'd call righteous, comfortable in his boots, same as me, with a heart as big as the moon and tender as a woman, yet hard as a preacher's dick and ornery enough to sandpaper a bobcat's ass. You'll damn sure not find a better person or fishing buddy than the Reno Kid, and I'll fight any man or woman that says different! Right, Reno?"

"Tell me about it," replied Mona, smiling wickedly at me. "Kitty got your tongue, Reno?"

When I still did not reply, Tommy turned on me and unleashed, "Screw you, Reno. God bless your ignorance," then lifted a glass of *baijiu* in a toast. "Here's to Rome! The Eternal City of Love, so let bygones be bygones. To everybody in the trenches, citizens at the helm, to the True Blue everywhere . . . everybody who carries a Blue Blaze badge on their Blue Blaze sash and fights shady business! I drink to Dante's health . . ."

He did not mention—nor did he need to—that half the Blue Blazes in Rome, volunteers of all ages and from all walks of life, were busy looking for the enigmatic Abbot Costello, whom I had just encountered not ten minutes earlier. It ought to come as no surprise, however, that I said nothing about the incident, at least not at the crowded table.

At this point Mona turned her dark cat eyes back to me and, in her best throaty purr, said, "How about it, Reno? I bet you wouldn't lie to a girl. Tell me, what keeps you up at night?"

"Me? What keeps me up . . . ?" I said, bewitched by her sparkly eye shadow and finding myself weakening despite my best efforts. Did our eyes lock? It seems likely, as I was swimming in them; and that was before she crossed her legs and casually dangled one of her open-toed stiletto pumps, revealing tackets on its sole and the top of her foot

stamped with the tattoo of a red-assed monkey she once said was me
. . . her little toe meats and their cleavage visible enough through her
pantyhose stockings to produce an out-of-body experience that both
energized my powers and left me sad to be human. Phobia and
queasiness mixed with desire for this beautiful dom woman—these
and other rare feelings for her that I thought I had boxed up and packed
away now came roaring back to me.

"What are you thinking, Reno?" she cooed knowingly and with a
wink. "My binky all buttery? Baby needs milk? What say, Reno?"

Struggling to bear up under her stare, I was suddenly distracted by a
heated discussion, money related, between Jack and our head waiter, the
dashing Giuseppe.

It appeared that when Jack attempted to pay our enormous dinner
bill, things had not worked out with his credit card, through no fault
of his own.

"Very sorry but there is a bug in our system," Giuseppe was saying.

"A bug in your system? More like a rat," Jack said deliberately and
slowly, as if trying to communicate in a foreign language. "I'm starting
to question if you're even in your right mind. No credit cards, no biggie,
huh? That's a huge red flag. I'm promoting the biggest concert the
Roman Empire has ever seen, and you won't take my credit card? Where
the hell's the accountability? You think I carry this kind of wad? Maybe
we should've ordered off the dollar menu."

I could see his temperature rising and warned, "Take it easy, Jack—do
you really want to go back to jail? Remember that fado bar in Lisbon,
that whole fiasco when you lost control."

"Or the Pub in Valletta," Pecos recalled. "Reno's right, Jack. No sense
chewing the poor man out for something that's not his fault."

"I'll have a grape Fanta and a bag of Fritos for the road," Tommy
interrupted, further flustering Giuseppe. "Just put it on the consigliere's tab."

"I'm not sure he can handle that," ventured Jack. "This is Rome, a
cultural vacuum. What's wrong with simple potato crisps and a Coke?"

"Again, I apologize, signore. Our system is the problem," reiterated
Giuseppe, as we began digging deep in our pockets. "No Fritos, but we
do accept Mexican pesos and every major currency, except rubles."

"For crying out loud, Giuseppe, all I've got is a load of Russian
G-notes. All right, everybody, ante up," Jack said.

As the rest of us dug deep in our pockets, just at that moment Buckaroo returned with some melancholy news concerning the survival of the human race.

"Looks like they're here," he whispered to me matter-of-factly, pointing at the ceiling. "Huge, rapid-moving high-pressure system across the Northern Hemisphere. Before communications went dark, NORAD called it 'a queried unverified event under evaluation,' but confirmed it's not our secret bird or anyone else's . . ."

His portentous remarks and my indignant reaction were met by a general show of ignorance, hence Mona's question: "Who's here, Buckaroo? What do you mean? Are we under attack by little green men or something?"

As if in answer to her facetious question, the overhead lights abruptly flickered three times, and Jack glanced around the room.

"Somebody playing with us?" said Jack, jumping up. "Good grief, this place is a dump. Let's vamoose this clip joint. I'll fetch our limos."

Believe me, gentle reader, when I say Tommy, Pecos, and I were not far behind, hurrying to catch up to Buckaroo and Tommy—no easy task, as we found ourselves obliged to pause at nearly every table to satisfy fans clamoring for our attention. Out of the corner of my eye, it also happened that I glimpsed highly disturbing images on a television set behind the bar: live combat footage from Gaza, followed by a close-up of the leering, insolent face of Archangel Brother Deacon Jarvis. What he was saying, I could not quite make out; but the odds were good that every word came straight from the motherboard of whatever alien vessel was now on our horizon.

"So they're here?" I whispered to Buckaroo as we paused just long enough to have our picture taken with friends of Mayor Agostinelli. "It's confirmed? It's real?"

Buckaroo nodded gravely. "They apparently dropped some piece of hardware over Manitoba, which pinged on radar in World Watch One, and Strategic Air Command's not denying something big has uncloaked itself in the upper stratosphere."

"They actually answered the phone?" Pecos said.

"No. Basically all branches of the military are down. I talked to the president," Buckaroo explained. "He's working the phones trying to organize a unified global response, for all the good that's likely to do."

"But at least no one's shooting yet," I said, in search of a silver lining.

"No thanks to Baltazar," Buckaroo replied gravely while scrawling his name across a fan's napkin. "Mrs. Johnson and High Sierra, working with several of our ace Blue Blaze hackers and codebreakers, have discovered that Baltazar's been using encrypted messages over Vatican Radio to communicate with the alien ship, claiming to speak on behalf of the pope and everyone on the planet . . ."

"My God . . . that sonofabitch, negotiating on behalf of the pope," I said, barely able to contain my disgust, as the lights continued to flicker. "What's that demented headcase got to offer? Has he got Whorfin?"

"I mean to find out," Buckaroo vowed. "Possibly the only person who knows, besides Baltazar and possibly Pope Innocent, is Abbot Costello, the joker in the pack . . . if he ever turns up."

I cleared my throat. Here was my opening, and I informed Buckaroo of my surreal encounter with John Whorfin and his human host, the monk, and their spectacular escape from potential captors unknown. Whereas I had been prepared for a certain amount of mental anguish, remarkably there was no rift between us. Buckaroo simply listened in his wise way and summed things up by saying, "What else could you do? Shoot the poor monk? Brawl with Whorfin, who perhaps could have killed you with one poison dart? Relax, you did all you could do, Reno. Thanks to you, at least now it's obvious what kind of devilish deception we're dealing with," he said, "although a photograph would have been nice. Perhaps a camera in the alley captured the van's license number."

I made a note to follow up, saying, "It was a Vatican plate, yellow and white. I'm sure of that."

"Then let's assume Baltazar is behind his capture," said Buckaroo. "We also know that the cardinal is in daily communication with a secret group of certified underwriters . . ."

"Underwriters . . . ?"

I wasn't understanding all of this, but Buckaroo was walking fast and talking faster on his way out of the restaurant. "Our own Rainbow Trout, Postmaster General Mantooth, has intercepted certain documents in the mail revealing the existence of something called the Quisling Society and Project CURE—Certified Underwriters Research Engine—basically a data bank for our entire species, nine hundred million pages of files, full of intimate details and risk factors on every man, woman, and child in most of the developed world . . . as well as an estimated value for everything on our planet, which he's trying to sell to our visitors . . . his price being an unholy alliance with them . . ."

"Whoa . . . you mean a price tag for Mother Earth?" said Tommy. "I always wondered what insurance companies did, besides just grab your money."

"But Baltazar doesn't have Whorfin, at least not yet," I pointed out.

"A major bone of contention, no doubt putting him in a bind," Buckaroo replied, "and perhaps calling for a clever bit of bait and switch. If he can't give them Whorfin, he can offer them Earth, a society of worker ants, with himself the queen . . ."

"That sad bucket of piss," said Tommy scornfully.

"True," agreed Buckaroo, "but if you were offering a planet for sale, wouldn't you like to get your hands on that bank of metadata from the insurance industry and its private reporting bureaus? What could be more deadly efficient than a planet run by insurance underwriters . . . a.k.a. the Quisling Society?"

By now we had reached the street, where car alarms were blaring and awestruck pedestrians had begun to stare at the sky—or at least that portion which was visible through the city's smog blanket—for reasons yet unknown.

"See that?" said Buckaroo, pointing.

"That's an early moon," I replied, unsure what I was supposed to say . . . but reminded I had gazed up at the heavens from Apache land only a few nights earlier.

"Take a better look, Reno," Buckaroo urged. "Look closer."

This I did and at once caught myself gasping, "Insane . . . holy beans, mother of Jesus! The Big Dipper, the polar star moving . . . !"

"You can say that again," Tommy said, whistling through his teeth. "What the phawk, phawkin' A . . . ! Are you phawkin' me?!"

XXV. THE GREAT UNVEILING

> A frog in a well does not know the great ocean.
> —Japanese proverb

"The whole sky is in motion!" Tommy, Pecos, and I gasped in unison.

Or at least what appeared to be the sky at first glance was turning slowly like an old-fashioned phenakistoscope. In fact, it was the undercarriage of a gigantic spaceship projecting a planetarium-like artificial sky, complete with a waxing gibbous moon, star constellations, even wispy clouds; and now the giant visage of Brother Deacon Jarvis, in a Quaker hat, appeared alongside a running chyron in various languages:

IL TUO VERO PADRE

VOTRE VRAI PÈRE

YOUR REAL DADDY

"From the fruited plains to the corners of the woods, welcome to the Love Channel, and greetings to the misguided blind Earth moles, bodies of flesh and creatures of darkness!" the pixelated face also thundered in multiple tongues. "Do not be frightened, *Pithecanthropus erectus*. The Most Beautiful Flower of Heaven and Shining Star of Hope is coming! She is Your Real Daddy and Mother of Wonder, the sun upon your Earth! To all the phony preachers calling me a liar, that's a damn crock, for it's the liar who is telling you the truth and the one telling you the truth who is a liar! The dark lord, the false prophets, will be purged when your axial tilt hits the fan and Judgment Day arrives. Verily I say unto you, clean up your house, or your planet will be incinerated and its ashes shot from a cannon into deep space . . ."

He paused now, modulating his voice to a more relaxed and folksy tone, an almost jocular mood at odds with everyone around us, terrified witnesses gazing up in shock and tears, blocking traffic, clogging the street . . .

. . . as cars slammed on brakes, or into one another, and drivers flung insults and threats.

"Just stay cool," Jarvis purred perversely, plainly toying with us. "Take a breath, folks . . . breathe in the fresh taste of Salem menthol-filtered cigarettes, with the taste of springtime, soft and menthol fresh! See the USA in your Chevrolet, and remember, you won't get a lemon from Toyota of Orange! Can I get a hallelujah? Tell 'em the old traveling preacher Archangel Brother Deacon Jarvis sent you! Church ladies to the front! Can I get an amen, brother?"

"Lord redeemer, phawk me in the bosom of Abraham. That's some kind of whirligig," I heard Tommy murmur before he whistled in wide-eyed amazement of the same kind I was feeling.

"The angel of death with a word from our sponsor . . . ?" Buckaroo murmured softly . . .

. . . as the image of Jarvis abruptly zapped off, to be replaced by a pulsing flash brighter than the sun, so that we had to avert our eyes but could not resist glancing back.

"Hello, neighbor," I muttered, dumbfounded by the incomprehensible size of the thing. "Look, the fake Milky Way . . . there's the North Star. I'm getting dizzy."

"Yeah, can't say I'm enjoying the view," Buckaroo said. "But take it all in. Our whole lives have been preparing us for this moment."

"How big, Buckaroo . . . ?" Tommy asked.

"A big moment, Tom. Maybe the biggest in the history of the world."

"No, I mean the ghost ship. How big in terms of size?"

"Hard to say . . . just guessing . . . maybe a whole time zone, maybe the size of western Europe . . ." replied Buckaroo . . .

. . . as Tommy coughed and wheezed repeatedly, managing to squeeze out, "Sweet honey nuts, talk about a big circle jerk . . . the mother of 'em all, bigger'n damn Europe. You could park Texas and a double-wide in that thing and still have room to get out and slam the door. Some real bragging rights right there . . . I wonder who or what's driving that jalopy . . ."

"And who or what's got its finger on the trigger," I heard my own voice utter with tremolo effect. "I bet that thing can put some cold steel downrange, if it had to. Of course I could be guessing and guessing wrong . . ."

"Your guess is as good as mine, Reno," said Buckaroo. "The stage is set, I'd say. Now we're on the clock."

"Clock, hell," Tommy said. "Tell 'em to go kick rocks. If the sky is fake, maybe their ship is fake, too . . . a whadda you call it . . . Potemkin . . . made of nothing but ones and zeros."

"Wanna bet the planet on it, Tom?" replied Buckaroo. "Could backfire."

"At least with their shield down, they won't be sneaking up on us," Pecos pointed out.

"That's about the size of it," agreed Buckaroo. "But I wonder if their shield is truly down. How are we with the portable quark-gluon Jelly Beam, Reno?"

"It's in the equipment truck, along with the rest of the gear," I replied. "I serviced all the fluids, but I wouldn't say it's ready. Fact of the matter, it's still a big question mark . . . only worked a single time in the lab . . ."

"That's a relief—like hell!" Tommy retorted sarcastically. "Brute beasts just knocking on our damn door! What're we supposed to do, then? Invite 'em to tea and beg for mercy? Put a smile on their faces and reward their monkey business? Maybe hit 'em over the head with a pool cue?"

"If it comes to that, or even offer myself as a hostage," Buckaroo said shockingly.

"What the hell, no!" Tommy replied. "We need you here, Buck! I'm just hoping we have coffins in their size after we give them a little street justice they won't see coming if push comes to shove."

"If push comes to shove, I'll offer myself as a hostage, too," said Pecos.

"Me, too," I replied.

"Sterling suggestions, all, but they might give us a run for our money," said Buckaroo, as he peered through the artificial sky with his Go-Phone's infrared telescope and full-spectrum interferometer/dosimeter/spectrometer, measuring the alien ship's chemical traces, airflow rates, albedo, elevation, speed, and bearing, as well as any transmission frequencies.

"Just as we suspected: an array of supersnoop listening devices . . . radar-absorbing hull with hundreds of two-megawatt generators . . . literally one giant pixel projector screen . . . and lots of aftermarket hardware on that buggy," he proceeded, examining his Go-Phone and talking to himself. "Clogged drainage ducts and air portals . . . and someone forgot the fuel door . . . is that an open fuel nozzle or an exhaust bypass valve? And traces of barium and aluminum oxide . . . ?"

"Aluminum oxide . . . ?" I muttered in surprise. "As in chemtrails?"

He gave half a laugh and continued to scan the fake sky. "At this point I'm ruling nothing out . . . subgrade engineering, retrofitting, sloppy maintenance, or all three. She's been around the block a few times. Radiometric age dating suggests the barnacles on her hull may be two million years old . . . plus radioactivity readings off the charts, traces of tantalum 181 . . . and brimming with methane . . . ?"

Here he stared at the information stream on his device with evident surprise, which he did nothing to dissemble. "Methane? Possible game changer, suggesting low motility . . . but hard to judge what we don't know. It might be possible to do business with them, so let's not draw red lines or give in to the weirdness quite yet. No need to light a fire under them or invent unnecessary drama . . ."

THE FIRST LEVITATION

"Unnecessary drama? Damn, Buckaroo, that's some steaming shite!" Tommy uttered in disbelief, ranting angrily. "You really think they want to do business with us? Only if their business is to burn down our breadbaskets, our corn and wheat centers, and mutilate our cattle!"

"Thanks for the insight, Tom," replied Buckaroo, who continued to scan the sky with both the naked eye and one of his Go-Phones while pressing the other to his ear and conversing animatedly with someone I assumed to be President Monroe.

"If you can't trust a Lectroid, who can you trust?" I commented.

"Unnecessary drama?" Tommy repeated. "So when do they cross the line, Buck, and what do we do? Where's the damn red line when we use real steel?"

"Real steel?" said Buckaroo. "Like what?"

Tommy repeated, "I'm just saying, where do you draw the line?"

"Where's the damn limo?" I wondered.

"Good luck with that," said Tommy. "Everybody's gone nuts."

"Let's walk," Buckaroo replied, his next words lost in the blaring of a hundred car horns. "This isn't a video game where we can lose and play again. Any action we take now limits our future options. Shoot our wad now and we won't be around to help remedy things on the back end. Sometimes, like any doctor knows, all you can do is alleviate the severity of the condition. But even buying into your argument, it's true we could always launch some kind of kinetic military action just to make a point, but unless we have a magic bullet, an equalizer—if we shoot from the hip and misfire or blow up a city, and the planetoid strikes back with nukes or something worse, there's no sense even ringing the fire bell, because no one's going to be coming to our rescue. So happy hunting."

Tommy nevertheless remained defiant, insisting, "This ain't rocket surgery, Buckaroo. All this politeness—writing Xan a strongly worded letter or maybe playing kissy face and hoping for the best—makes me wonder if you haven't lost the hair off your nuts and turned into a bend-over Buckaroo! Sorry, but there's no other way to dice it—wake up and smell the truth, Buck! If human civilization falls, we're all screwed!"

Beyond angry, I gave Tommy a push and came to our chief's defense. "And he's supposed to take advice from you? Buckaroo's got more hair on his nuts than both of us combined."

"I'm not saying he's pubeless—"

"Are you saying I've fallen off, Tom?" said Buckaroo. "Do you know that in your heart, Tom? Am I going downhill so fast? In your professional opinion, do you see my illness progressing?"

Taken aback by Buckaroo's earnestness, Tommy could only stare ashamedly at his own cherry-red boots for a minute, groping for words.

"Hell, Buck, I'm talking the amazing that once was you. Truth of the situation, I admit it makes for a quandary, and I'm kind of a rambling mess right now myself. Don't know jack about jack. All I'm saying is it's time, damn time, to buck the phawk up. After what happened to Penny and with everything going on with you in the Godforsaken Eighth Dimension, maybe you've even checked out of reality. Hell, it wouldn't halfway surprise me if Lectroids took control of you . . ."

Directly he uttered these words, Buckaroo started to shine and fade slightly from view before rising off the sidewalk a full six inches. Also, strange to say, no passersby saw fit to comment on the phenomenon. Other than this I have nothing to say.

"Wait a minute," said Pecos.

"Good grief," was all Tommy could muster. "The future is now."

"For all practical purposes, Tom," Buckaroo calmly admitted. "My last trip into other dimensions came close to blowing the doors off my brain, not to mention the Jet Car, so maybe I'm not as quick on the draw as I used to be."

"But you can fly?" Tommy said.

"An odd side effect when I turn a certain way into a lightning storm or other powerful electron field and—" Buckaroo tried to explain before changing the subject. "All I'm saying is let's not labor under any preconceptions . . . such as crafting an enemy in our own likeness or selling ourselves a fake bill of goods. For all we know, that thing could be a gigantic seed bomb, carrying myriad life forms and viruses, never mind awash in radioactivity and Jupiter methane."

"Jupiter methane . . . ?" Tommy said.

"According to its spectrographic signature, unless this gadget's on the blink," Buckaroo replied, again studying his portable instrument and backing me up. "Even assuming you could pierce the ship's defenses with the Jelly Beam . . . and depending on which radionuclide we're talking about and who knows what other toxins and unknown bioagents . . . that thing looks like a giant gas bomb that could kill two-thirds of Europe."

"Like a thermonuke bug bomb, then?" Tommy interjected. "Burning down our own house in order to save it . . ."

"Good point, P. T. Like a giant *Hindenburg*, but incalculably more explosive, with resultant astronomical disease rates that could kill millions," Buckaroo affirmed. "And what is it I always say? Don't pick up something . . ."

Pecos completed the thought: "Don't pick up something you can't put back down."

Buckaroo nodded. "Exactly. So in the meantime, we need to warn all the world governments not to attack the planetoid. I'll call President Monroe, the Russians, and the Chinese myself. That's job one. Job two is find John Whorfin . . . our best hope."

"Maybe our only hope," said Pecos. "The show must go on."

"All roads lead to Rome . . . the Coliseum, to be precise," Buckaroo agreed and returned both feet to the ground.

"I'll liaise with Mrs. Johnson and home base," I said, already dialing the Institute.

ON MY LOVE FOR MOTHER EARTH

All of it true . . . not a drill, but true, I kept telling myself, as I got off the phone with Mrs. Johnson and peered out the limousine window at city life and peaceful genre scenes: people going about their daily chores, pushing the apple carts of their hopes and dreams, oblivious to any imminent threat or at least averting their eyes from it and pretending all was well.

"Icarus has fallen! The sky is falling!" I wanted to scream out the car window.

How could I not be reminded of *Landscape with the Fall of Icarus* by Brueghel—or perhaps a worthy imitator—wherein a humble plowman tills his field, his head lowered and utterly unaware of the tragedy that has occurred, while Icarus tumbles into the sea near a ship sailing uninterrupted on its way! Contemplating the same painting, Auden had written something about the dogs going on "with their doggy life" and the torturer's horse scratching its butt on a tree. Yes, exactly! But in a way I was also thankful that the same world for which we were preparing to fight to the death continued on in blissful ignorance, as on any other random day. After all, what was the real value of our superior knowledge? Even we Cavaliers—made steel by having been through the furnace on other occasions—could be accused of fiddling while Rome burned. What were we to do, aware of the near-impossible odds we were up against? Laugh or cry? Puff out our chests like Perfect Tommy and flail our fists?

Get carried away with our own comic book personas and put ourselves to some foolish test just to prove our bravery? Did we really think ourselves cockamamie superheroes, empowered to fight an alien man-o'-war with a buzzsaw?

You, dear reader, know better. Would that I possessed such sovereign powers to change the dreary facts—the arbitrariness of a writer of fiction—to say we stumbled upon a magic bullet to vanquish all adversaries and dictate a happy outcome, to worry only about plotting problems for our little adventure story! To be free of the truth and put forward my vision of Buckaroo Banzai as a composite of virtues in yet another festschrift, relating in addition his ability to float off the ground?! To promise, alas, to fling no more depressing news out into the universe?!

In other words, would that this were just another story in one more juvenile adventure book, for at that moment I was equal parts humbled and awed by the evening's events, but also equally overwhelmed by the sight of my fellow human beings going about their ordinary activities that we call life. Yes, all around us life appeared to be going on as normal; yet the nagging feeling in my gut said things were about to become worse in very short order.

XXVI. THE BIG SHOW

> Nothing great was ever achieved without enthusiasm.
> —Ralph Waldo Emerson

As I write these words now, images of our historic Coliseum performance in front of the pope and a crowd of thousands of Catholic youths come flying at me in a swirling light show of lasers, smoke machines and fireworks, deafening amplifiers, rhythmic dancers, television lights, and gyrocameras . . . but most of all, happy faces of all ages and colors, their exuberant screams soon to be followed by a shocking orgy of violence and death, all within a span of a couple of hours.

With reason, I was overexcited by the long-awaited arrival of the alien ship, as well as my customary bout of stage fright before a concert. Doubtless that was why I made a point of taking several long walks, expeditions really, all the way down to the labyrinthine tunnels beneath the ancient Roman structure. But my true purpose was more prosaic: to escape the infernal noise of our opening act, a super-loud quintet called Rooster and the Sidesaddle Boys, another of Jack's discoveries he touted as the next platinum-selling "big thing."

In that maze of dark tunnels, it was impossible not to think of the Ludus Magnus nearby and those poor souls who waited here before ascending to the arena . . . both professional gladiators and ordinary men and women who spent their last moments contemplating their fate before being ripped to shreds or burnt to death, all in plain view of the cynical Roman public. What terrible sights and sounds this place once held—groaning bodies and clanking chains—and seemed to hold them still.

GUITAR HEROES

While I shined my light on ages-old graffiti and Buckaroo greeted dignitaries backstage—and we all wrestled with the astonishing revelation that extraterrestrial aliens were somewhere above our heads—Tommy watched from the wings and quietly seethed, his blood boiling with professional jealousy at the sight of the Sidesaddle Boys' frontman, a beady-eyed guitarist who excited the crowd with his banshee-like vocal wailing, rapid finger work, and predictable stage attire of dangling spiked paddles and chains and a "Property of Satan" T-shirt.

"Awright, Rome! Thank you, Rome! Keep spreading the love! You're awesome!" the cocky Rooster shouted over a sea of applause. "Y'all ready to rock?! Knock these old walls down?! How about you, my holy man?! Pope Innocent, everybody!"

Here he pointed at an enthusiastic Pope Innocent in his bulletproof box seat between Baltazar and the Pomeranian Sokol, while sword-wielding bodyguards in the black tunics of the Hospitallers of Saint John prowled nearby. Along with the rest of the audience, the Holy Father appeared duly impressed by the band's half-shaved frontman who—working the fretboard of his vintage Les Paul with one hand while chugging a bottle of Tennessee whiskey with the other—suddenly launched himself into the air with the help of hidden wires and exhorted the crowd, "Let's get loud! Let's get rowdy!"

In the face of such pyrotechnics, the oohs and aahs of the crowd had the effect of making Tommy feel the sting of rejection; such is his insecurity.

"What the hell are we doing here?" he mumbled over and over. "Are we crazy? Fiddling while Rome burns . . ."

"Not just Rome. Maybe the whole world," echoed Pecos, who was practicing a drum roll on his taut shoulders. "But is that really what's bothering you?"

"Who is this lizard?" Tommy resumed, watching the skinny guitarist prance and gyrate.

"Pulling out all the stops, isn't he?" she said. "The chief wants to see you."

"This guy's the ultimate loser, packing nothing but shite," muttered Tommy, still obsessed with the guitar virtuoso. "Me and my Schecter Hellraiser could burn him and that toy axe he's playing to the ground."

"Of course you would—he's all window dressing. Just a pretty boy," Pecos reassured him.

"You really think he's good looking?" Tommy said, genuinely wanting to know.

"In a certain neutered, epicene kind of way . . ."

"Yeah, he looks like a horse all right," he agreed. "I'm the real rooster around here."

Was there ever a rogue so cheeky, or a mule so stubborn, as our own d'Artagnan, Perfect Tommy, whose rare medical condition permits him only to think when he is talking? Like a magnificent male baboon made jealous by a rival, Tommy now stripped to his skintight mariachi pants and puffed out his sculpted chest.

Recognizing these telltale signs of trouble, Pecos urgently asked, "Any advice for him, Tommy?"

"Advice?"

"Obviously, he's strutting his stuff because he knows the almighty Tommy's watching him . . . not only a force of nature, but the very example of music-business success," Pecos explained. "Meanwhile, he's just another decent player with a great look and a couple of tunes climbing the charts."

"You think he has a great look?" Tommy pressed her again, snorting with glee when Rooster accidentally became entangled in his puppet wires and very visibly pissed his codpiece—although he continued to play. "I'd say, 'Rooster, you'd better look over your shoulder, because I'm taking names and putting you on my list. In this business, one minute you're a butterfly and the next minute you're a hefty, bloated slug with a spare tire and a pork chop habit . . . and now your bubble has reached the bursting stage' . . . ha, ha! What'd I tell you? He doesn't even know his world's about to end. He's stuck!

"Stand tall, Rooster!" he yelled out and smugly snapped a photo of the ashen-faced fellow dangling upside down and beginning to flail helplessly . . .

. . . as Li'l Daughter arrived with an important invitation, announcing, "Hey, guys, Buckaroo has somebody who wants to see you. Come say hello to her, Tommy."

"One of my old flames?" Tommy asked.

"I wouldn't be surprised," Daughter said coyly. "How's that for a tease?"

RETURN OF A PRODIGAL SISTER

Sufficiently intrigued, we stepped into Buckaroo's dressing room and at once erupted into both howls of agonized laughter and yowls of delight, for there, in her skater shoes and moth-eaten Andean poncho, was our perky former bandmate and electric lutist Muscatine "Magnum" Wu, the prodigal player who had left our humble band to follow her personal white rabbit—this after repeatedly being called on the carpet by Buckaroo for her odd fetishes, repeated rules violations, and mood swings that would culminate typically in one of her suicidal spirals or fits of fury. These issues were now seen to be bygones, however, or at least set aside for the moment, to judge by the convivial faces crammed into the tiny dressing room: a slew of international celebrities I won't name, along with Jack Tarantulus, Hoppalong, Buckaroo, and a middle-aged couple who would identify themselves as the Italian prime minister and his wife, and the veritable elephant in the room: a seven-foot-tall, slick-skin robot with a swivel head and fake plastic hair gelled back and what appeared, disconcertingly, to be a corkscrew pig's tail for a nose.

"Well, I'll be got-damn. Looks like Muscatine Wu found a feller," Tommy quipped, indicating the big automaton. "Who's the good-looking wise guy, Muscatine?"

"Abysmo, meet Tommy. Tommy, meet Abysmo," she replied. "The first of eight hundred on order by the Pentagon. Don't worry, Tommy, I also make gorgeous humanoid gods and goddesses for the socially inept."

She laughed, but need I mention a telescoping hand that suddenly grabbed me with a grip of steel when I attempted to give her a hug and a squeeze?

"Me Abysmo, you wanker," the male-sounding machine threatened me, while its other hand hovered near my jugular with a razor-sharp blade attachment.

"Wanker . . . ?" I responded with more fear than indignation.

"Abysmo, enough argy-bargy!" Muscatine Wu commanded. "Put Reno down before he draws his sidearm."

With these words, however, a mischievous gleam came into her eyes; and in another instant, before any of us could react, Abysmo appeared to hum with a strange energy, and Tommy flew straight into the robot's arms, headfirst, exclaiming in pain, "For the love of God! The steel plate in my head!"

While my own encounter was less violent, my college class ring, light-carry revolver, and boot derringer likewise flew straight into the robot's steel paw, much to Muscatine's amusement.

"Miniature cyclotron electromagnets," she informed us. "Another of his self-defense applications, along with a Browning .30 caliber machine gun in his left arm."

"Yeah, and great interpersonal skills," I said, smoothing my mussed apparel . . .

. . . as Tommy struggled in vain to free his skull from Abysmo's powerful magnetic skin, despite repeating solicitously, "Mutual respect, you dip wad . . . !"

"He's just very protective—doesn't quite get the intangible, although he's getting better at banter," Muscatine said. "He also cuts my hair, paints my nails, and carried me up Mont Blanc on his big, strong shoulders. Plus, he flies . . . a little. Abysmo, bring us a dozen margherita pizzas from the best pizza maker in Rome. Oh, and include a love sonnet in iambic pentameter of your own composition."

"Yes, my darling," said the mechanical beast, who at once deactivated his magnetic force and fired up several directional-thrust jet nozzles that lifted him off the floor and nearly undressed us!

"Heads up!" Muscatine alerted us . . . a needless warning . . .

. . . as we ducked instinctively and her invention, despite a certain ungainliness, swooped in a low circle, inches above our heads, before flying through the low doorway and out of the room.

"See?" she said, as the rest of us traded incredulous expressions. "The only problem is his sex drive is too high. God knows I need the attention and crave a little corporal punishment, but his navigational skills are a little rough—"

"Perhaps a faulty rectifier," Buckaroo suggested. "I have always respected your personal road, Muscatine. It was your CIA funding that violated our rules."

She nodded and resumed, "I can easily see why, Buckaroo. My selfishness was extremely ignorant. But after leaving the Institute, I continued work on the problem, manipulating it every which way and always failing, until a few months ago, when Professor Hikita appeared to me in a dream and said, 'This is a nutty problem worthy of King Solomon. Here is King Solomon's nut.' And he held out to me this large coconut, which he opened to reveal the Big Bang, which produced a holy flame in which I saw all the laws of physics go up in smoke . . . and then I woke up with a sudden start and an amazing original thought."

"'Water in a sleeping ear'—old Japanese saying," noted Buckaroo. "So dear Hikita helped you overcome the unipolar paradox and the minor obstacle of Newton's second law!"

"Yes, exactly!" she said quite cheerfully.

"We saw the Professor, too, just the other day, but without the comedic value," I said, allowing her to put her arm around me and draw me close.

"Tommy and Reno . . . good ol' Reno!" she sighed. "And Tommy, you beast, still breaking all the girls' hearts?"

"More like the opposite, I'd say," Tommy wisecracked, with both fake humility and a grain of truth.

"A natural progression, then. Poetic justice," she declared, giving us all a hearty laugh.

"Where have you been keeping yourself?" Tommy asked her.

With a toss of her ponytail, she replied, "Launching a company, piling on debt, going to the poorhouse . . ."

"A startup robotics outfit she just sold for three billion dollars to a major multinational," Buckaroo cut in to inform us with obvious pride, "of which she's giving the Institute thirty million."

"Cool sense of humor, Buckaroo," Tommy said.

"Damn, woman, that's a pretty penny," whistled Pecos in disbelief . . .

. . . as Muscatine expressed her own appreciation instead. "It's the least I can do, Buckaroo, in return for the seed money, the use of the Institute's workshop, and Dr. Doe's professional help encouraging me to cast aside my fears and wake up my sleeping dragon . . . to satisfy my curiosity, in more ways than one. And to you—Reno, Tommy, Pecos, and Jack, the hardest-working agent in show business—for your friendship and collaboration and for reawakening the musical passion within me. I still feel our souls are connected. By your examples, I learned to stop just going through the motions, to face my demons in the mirror and unravel the real me . . . to dare to be different. After leaving the band, I hooked up for a while with Yngwie Malmsteen, then went to work on myself in Africa, where I realized I didn't need all the shiny stuff. For three years I lived in a hut made of elephant dung, though I spent most of the time inside my head restoring my soul and working out new ideas."

Caught up in the convivial spirit, I could only nod in agreement until Buckaroo added, "Muscatine wants to rejoin the band."

"Not to take food out of anyone's mouth," the great lutist hastened to add. "I won't need a full share. I just miss making beautiful music with you guys . . . oh, and possibly righting some wrongs, realizing I am ridiculously overpaid and I miss Mrs. Johnson's cheeseburgers. But it's up to you."

"Hell, yeah," said Pecos, applauding.

"No sweat off my behind," Tommy agreed. "Just don't mess with my stuff. You owe me a dozen guitar picks and a K-ration of potted meat for that time in the Kalahari, but if you want to choose us over the three billion . . ."

"Um, I'm keeping the money, Tommy," Muscatine explained. "It's not an either-or . . ."

"Tommy, you stereotypical retrograde dumbass," Pecos said.

"How about you, Reno?" Muscatine asked. "Let's just lay the shite bare. I know we've had our creative differences in the past when I was musical director."

"Differences out the wazoo, but not unacceptable ones. You brought something new and did funktify [sic] our sound," I freely admitted and looked to Buckaroo for guidance.

"You're musical director now, Reno. It's up to you," he said simply and glanced at his watch to let me know time was one variable.

"This is just like your dream, Buckaroo!" Pecos said, reminding us of that evening around the campfire I have described, which now seemed like eons ago. "Muscatine onstage with us at the Roman Coliseum . . ."

"If it was a dream," he joked, "I'm having it again."

Muscatine now spoke again on her own behalf, saying to me, "Let me simplify it for you, Reno. I'll compete to win a spot, but I won't plead or egg you on to accept me. I know I was a sour-on-life bullshitter who sponged off people in the past and left the Institute under less than auspicious circumstances. I struggled with addiction and attempted suicide. I was usually paired up with Jack Daniels and even drank hair tonic . . . a sorry excuse for a human being, something of a slave to my vices and a dominant mistress to my personal slaves, strong players I turned into little bitches . . ."

She mentioned no names but glanced at Tommy and continued, "Funny thing, Buckaroo always warned me to pace myself, but I was young and wild and didn't want to listen. And I remember you telling me that maybe the best life for a person isn't the life we're looking for but the life that's looking for us."

"I remember, too," said Buckaroo with fondness. "Water in a sleeping ear."

"Of course I didn't listen, then," she went on. "I kept wondering how far I could push, so I squandered human relationships because they took me away from my computations. To save time and energy, I immersed myself in hentai and realized that all I really wanted was a companion machine with a stick to grind, which I've now invented. You see, Abysmo isn't just my bodyguard, nutritionist, confidant, lover, and personal assistant—I myself am in transformer mode, on my way to becoming a cyborg and a better person."

She moved aside her hair to show us surgical scars; but if she was expecting us to be shocked by this confession, she was in for a letdown, for only Tommy pronounced a judgment. "Then congratulations, Muscatine. I hope he knows he's one lucky mechanical doofus. Speaking for myself, I've missed the crud outta you."

SHOWTIME

In the end, I had the final word. "It takes two to tango but only an individual to chart her own true path. As Fellows of the Banzai Institute, we are all in need of recovery and set forward certain things like shared respect and solidarity. We have rules but don't want for a heart. It's always been that way and always will. If you're willing to put in the work to pick yourself up, dust yourself off, and get back on the daily grind, then maybe it's time you came home. Welcome home . . . our beloved Muscatine. There's just one problem . . ."

I now looked from Muscatine to Buckaroo, who confirmed, "I've brought her up to speed on what's happening. She knows we may all get smoked at any minute."

"I'm down for the whole nine yards," she declared. "One for all and all for one . . ."

"Well, no worries, then," I said to nervous titters that served as a timely tension buster—for just at that moment Webmaster Jhonny appeared in the doorway, holding up five fingers.

"Live in five," he announced. "Five minutes."

There was just time for us to come together in our preconcert ritual of clasping hands and repeating together, *"Kaizen! Banzai! Fight the good fight!"*

"Lace up our boots! Kick ass!" yelled Muscatine.

"Hell, yeah—they can run but they can't hide!" echoed Tommy.

From our makeshift dressing room, we could hear the crowd, causing our nerves to tighten. Some of us, like Buckaroo, drank an extra portion of fizzy water mixed with something stronger and raised a mock toast to the thunderous shouts of "Buckaroo! Buckaroo! Buckaroo!" rocking the Coliseum . . .

. . . as Rooster What's-His-Name performed his final backflip and his Sidesaddle mates finished their last encore and brushed past us on their way offstage.

"We'll take it from here, boys. Nice set," Pecos informed the band's swaggering drummer in passing—a comment I did not hear myself, but which evidently irritated the scrawny fellow.

"Afraid you can't compete?" he reportedly said, to which Pecos responded with something that sounded like "I'll fix you, cupcake," setting off a brief flurry of fisticuffs and drumstick jabs before everything dissolved into chaos.

"Oww! Hairy-legged witch!"

"All that and more, big boy!" growled Pecos.

By the time I turned around, the drummer had fainted (courtesy of Pecos), and she and Jack were pulling Tommy away from Rooster, who made the near-fatal mistake of trying to truss Tommy up with an amplifier cord—something Tommy did not take well. Consequently, seeing his sick gambit fail, Rooster began to squeak in terrified anticipation of Tommy's revenge.

But Tommy merely told him, "Nice falsetto. Best note you've hit all day," and swung his leg over a police Moto Guzzi, which he and Buckaroo rode onstage to a deluge of wild excitement.

"*Signore e signori, Buckaroo Banzai!*" shouted an excitable local radio personality into the microphone. "Buckaroo Banzai and his all-star orchestra, the Hong Kong Cavaliers . . . !"

Thousands more yelled themselves hoarse and pelted us with bouquets of flowers and more personal items . . . as Buckaroo stepped to the mike and announced, "Fellow Romans! *Ave, Roma, amici! Pubblico romano!* For those about to rock, *saluti*! Any Blue Blazes out there?"

Another roar erupted from a sizable number of fans in Blue Blaze paraphernalia and our new Digitizer-Transcender earpieces, and we were off and running, as Hoppalong's rock-steady bass backed up the syncopated rhythm laid down by Pecos, and Muscatine's electric lute erupted in spurts like a fit of temper. Taking my cues from her, I leaned in, first on the harmonica and then on the moonshine jug, fluidly extemporizing as though we had been playing together all our lives.

Buckaroo likewise appeared to forget all our troubles and continued his sunny remarks to the crowd. "Tonight's a special night, but music is just one way we communicate our love for one another! Right now the whole planet's in serious trouble and needing every little bit of kindness and good vibes you can send its way, so raise your flowers and glow sticks and your positive energy to be absorbed into the ether! One people and one Earth with the universe!"

Pecos meanwhile banged away on her Ludwig skins as a wise guy shouted from the crowd, "But you say there's more than one universe!"

FORCE MAJEURE

Buckaroo has been accused not infrequently by his critics of spouting empty platitudes (cynically interpreted as self-righteousness) and a heavy dose of mumbo jumbo. But jibes aside—and I have heard too many—I will never accept that our syncopated music and psychic experiment had no effect on the Lectroid ship; at a very minimum I believe it bought us time. For that we have the word of John Singsong, whose odd scrawlings communicate the following:

. . . this rock bubbling with water and its bipedal perambulators who seem
to beguile us with no evil intention . . . not the abominable burning world
of monsters we were told, hence the unreasonable need to destroy them.
But who will take pity on us, and the dying world of discord and brother
against brother we inhabit? No, it is we who dance like grinning toads
even while questioning the basis of things . . .

Not for nothing, then, were our roles as intermediaries; and, despite
the great distraction literally looming over us, I doubt we ever played better
than during that historic performance shortened by events beyond our
control. Nor do I appear to be alone in this opinion, to judge by our fan
mail and sales of our *Alive in the Roman Coliseum* video. As many of you
have aptly noted, we were indeed "playing for our lives" with a certain
manic energy.

Let me put it another way. Only someone who has played in a musical
ensemble can know the joy and sense of inner peace—a place of sanctuary,
no matter what the world might throw at us—that comes from making
music in close concert with others. To say we were "in the pocket" or "in
the zone," musically speaking, that particular evening would be putting
it mildly, and it is my belief that such a syncopated rhythm has a magical
effect on the listener.

With our every atom of existence caught up in a swirling coalescence
of external stimuli and intense concentration, however, we were suddenly
jarred out of our reverie by a fresh series of electromagnetic pulses that
had the effect of intermittently plunging the Coliseum into darkness.
Although our stage equipment was backed up by mechanical generators,
the repeated blackouts were disconcerting, as despite our best efforts, the
audience's mood seemed to tip from merriment to a general anxiety . . .
a sense of foreboding in the air, a suffocating foreign consciousness that
weighed heavily over all.

With our emotions thus running unrestrained, I shivered from what
felt like a blast of refrigerated air and stepped to the microphone to
announce our next song, when the weather and wind direction abruptly
changed. A hot, miserable wind suddenly gusted out of the south and
began to blow sideways what the locals call "blood rain": desert sand
and pink slime from the Sahara that resembled great strands of linguini,
spattering over our stage equipment.

"*Dal diavolo*, something is wrong!" someone shouted. "Something is messed up!"

But Buckaroo continued to plead for calm: "*Pazienza, amici . . . con calma, con calma . . . !* Just someone upstairs trying to communicate with us! And that's okay, because we're strong enough to hear that voice and hear it correctly. Let's trust ourselves to feel that power and reflect it back with better thoughts! Right, Your Holiness?"

A glance at the pope in his plexiglass fish tank, however, revealed that His Holiness was as agitated as everyone else, albeit in the ecstatic way of a child with a sugar buzz. After first pumping his fist, he appeared to be collecting the blood-rain linguini but was ready to bolt when the simulated panorama overhead briefly projected the most ghastly image—the flaming gates of hell and a straightaway roller coaster drop into a lake of fire—which sowed no small amount of terror among us all! Yet through it all, we Cavaliers never broke stride, continuing to play in top form and lifting the spirits of all present; and as the mood reverted to celebration, Pope Innocent himself appeared to signal the heavens with his BB flashlight ring.

Next to His Holiness, Cardinal Baltazar was no less moved by these events, while remaining hypervigilant and alert to any signs of the pope's boyish excitability lest it get out of hand; indeed, at one point Baltazar appeared to restrain the pontiff from attempting to climb his way out of their plexiglass box. While concert security officials looked on with placid indifference, Baltazar and his black-clad Hospitallers grabbed Innocent and trundled him out of the papal box toward a side exit—leading Buckaroo to signal Red Jordan with urgency. At this juncture, however, the impetuous Tommy short-circuited matters by tossing his guitar to Muscatine and hurrying offstage.

What happened next can best be related by Tommy himself, who later would author the following for the venerable *New Yorker* magazine:

> *So I reach the loading zone in time to see Sir Ivanhoe and his knights of the Round Table [Hospitallers and Templars—Reno] hustling the pope into the popemobile. I yell, "Hey, Pope!" He looks worried, and then this little overcompensating Cardinal Baltazar and his musclebound knights get in my face.*

"Hey, how's the pope doin'? He okay?" I ask them.

"Who asked you?" this Black Knight Sir Pussy Cat [probably Sokol the Pomeranian—Reno] wants to know and moves to put his hands on me.

I go, "I asked you, Deputy Dawg. You're not shite without that costume. I'll drop you like a cheap transmission."

So then Peewee Napoleon Baltazar pipes up. "Said the man in the cowboy outfit! You're a dead yob, Tommy, because you're not authorized. I knew it was only a matter of time until we'd meet again. You're a long-ass way from home now, Tommy. Rome is my town."

"Oh yeah, Baltazar? Ten thousand fans in this joint say different," I say.

He goes, "Talk balls to me, I'll feed 'em to the band saw!"

I say, "Yeah, bullfrog?"

Then, out of nowhere, Baltazar goes ballistic and coldcocks me right in the kisser, thrusting his fingers up my nose and his thumb into my mouth, where it gets caught on my diamond grill. You should have heard him squeal as I started slapping him around.

"Save that scream—you might need it!" I grit out through clenched teeth. "I'll hit you faster than you can blink!"

"My thumb!" he shrieks. "You've cut the main artery!"

"That's a lie," I say. "I wonder what else you're lying about."

I'm surrounded, so I press my Blue Blaze alert bracelet and reach for my snub .357, when all the jolly knights body slam me and grab my snubby, and somehow in the melee I plain bite off the motherphawker, just plain bite it off, right through the bone.

Naturally he's screaming, and I'm laughing at him. I'm chewing his thumb, and I say, "How'd you like that for a manicure, lady?"

"Give me back my thumb!" he's screaming, holding his bloody hand, so I head-butt him and pop him a bloody harelip to go with it.

Meanwhile, two of them pin me while another one puts a sword to my Adam's apple and goes after my jaws, just about gives me a root canal, which is when I decide to educate them by swallowing the little phawker, just gulp it right down.

Maybe it's stupid, maybe it isn't, but I'm tired of the bulldog's bullhonkey.

"A cold day in hell, signore," I say. "You, sir, are a loser."

So they hit me good for that and throw me into the cardinal's processional tumbrel—this stagecoach horse-drawn wagon—where they work me over some more.

"Slug him in the stomach. Make him regurgitate my thumb," Baltazar orders his bullies, one of whom is wearing a gauntlet with a studded steel fist that hurts like hell and hurts worse the more the guy practices on me. Obviously he is looking to learn, and what he lacks in experience, he more than makes up for with fun and games. Just then I see Mona Peeptoe come running between two television trucks, and, before anyone can stop her, she jumps into the popemobile.

I can't say, but I must have passed out, though I continued to talk shite and at some point could hear the wagon wheels clattering over the cobblestones.

The last thing I remember saying was "I might as well warn you— I've got numerous well-balanced throwing blades hidden on my person."

I remember they laughed, and I laughed, too, at their arrogant stupidity.

DISQUIETUDE BACK HOME

Although Tommy makes no mention of it, he also managed to send an SOS over his wristband beacon, an emergency signal instantly received back at the ranch by Mrs. Johnson, who, with a Thought Digitizer-Transcender in her ear, was simultaneously sending friendly vibes into space and counting the evening's proceeds from her tips jar, all while fielding panicked phone calls from world leaders, virtually all of whom were in seclusion, if not outright hiding.

Licking her fingers and counting dollar bills, she said to the president of France, "*C'est la vie, m'sieur président.* I'll give Buckaroo the message."

To the Guatemalan head of state, and his Nicaraguan counterpart, she announced, "*Gracias, Dios, gracias*, yes, I am well, thank you. I'll pass the message on."

To President James Monroe—in the basement of US Postal Service headquarters watching our concert telecast—she put the question, "Have you tried all his private numbers, Mr. President? Do you need more B_{12} serum?"

Since she was watching the concert in addition to her other responsibilities, she naturally had not failed to notice that Tommy was no longer onstage with the band, but the possibility that he might be in some kind of real jeopardy had not occurred to her. Even now, making phone calls to world dignitaries and fielding their callbacks, she was suspicious of his alert on her phone, thinking it might be a false alarm, perhaps a malfunction of the emergency beacon or a side effect of her intense telepathic session with the alien ship somewhere up there.

"A dark place," she declared to the Marchioness and Jill of All Trades, two of our most powerful telepathic thinkers, who sat hunched over on the floor nearby, rocking back and forth as if either going into withdrawal or sending mental signals into space.

"Very dark," said the Marchioness. "I'm hearing these voices, but they're blathering crypto, except now . . . I'm getting some kind of programming code . . . squiggly numbers . . . but now into direct thought link . . ."

"From the ship?" asked Mrs. Johnson.

The Marchioness nodded, replying, "I think so . . . John . . . talk to me, John . . ."

"They're all named John, for whatever reason," noted Mrs. Johnson, sticking her spent chewing gum under a coffee table and fielding yet another call. "Hello, this is Mrs. Johnson . . . Who? . . . King of Norway? . . . I'm sorry, let me put you in a conference call with the king of Thailand and the king of the Zulu Nation. Buckaroo isn't available at the moment, but I'm sure he'll want to speak with you . . ."

The voice of the Marchioness meanwhile was growing more distant. "John Singsong-of-the-Narrows-of-No-Return . . . Not-Him-But-the-Other-One . . . yes, I feel you . . . I feel a chill . . ."

She puckered and made a noise, as if sucking in more deeply the troubling mental energy that caused her to rock to and fro in pain.

"I understand, John Singsong . . . I feel your digestive health problems and this tremendous loss of life and tears, the overwhelming sensation of death and despair you are feeling," she was saying.

"What does it want?" wondered Mrs. Johnson.

"He doesn't want to 'burn our house' . . . not the message I'm getting," the Marchioness said, furiously massaging her temples. "What I'm getting . . . they have a bird's-eye view of us, but they just want to go home. Sounds like they're living in some kind of hellish misery. Wow, I just need to decompress. What should I tell him?"

Mrs. Johnson gave no answer . . . as she was far more interested in our live show, where we Cavaliers were full throating a raucous version of "Hang On, Sloopy."

"Hang on, Sloopy, Sloopy, hang on! Hang on, Sloopy, Sloopy, hang on!" she sang along, getting an increasingly uneasy feeling in the absence of Tommy's vocal harmonies.

"Where is he?" she remarked to the Marchioness. "Something is wrong. I don't like this."

Hesitant to act on her own, she arose and strode the roughly fifty paces to World Watch One, where High Sierra and three others already were pursuing the mystery of Tommy's whereabouts, attempting to track him via the World Watch big board and its bank of monitors. At that moment, according to Tommy's satellite tracking chip, he in fact appeared to be in an automobile moving from the Coliseum toward Vatican City. Following the most basic dictum of the Institute—"ask questions"—High Sierra sent Tommy's alert on to Buckaroo, who also had received Tommy's signal but was presently constrained by circumstances beyond his control, which is to say singing "Hang On, Sloopy" to a live audience of billions around the world.

XXVII. A CALL TO ARMS

> Today I shod my death horse. Tonight I shall ride it.
> —traditional Hong Kong Cavaliers song

But let us momentarily leave Buckaroo and the Hong Kong Cavaliers and turn now to the redoubtable Mona Peeptoe, whose dramatic impromptu ride in the popemobile with the goodhearted Pope Innocent was to become the stuff of popular legend, seen and heard by millions, despite the shaky camera work and spotty audio clarity of her worldwide scoop. But these were the shoes Mona was born to fill . . . interviewing the most celebrated people on the planet and fighting to get the story, no matter what.

For our purposes, I will begin from the point on the video (5:47) where, amid cheers from spectators in the background—"*Viva il papa! Viva Innocente! Bravissimo!* Hey, Mona! It's Mona Peeptoe! Mona, we're from the USA! Marry me, Mona! *Vostro autografo! Per favore!*"—she surreptitiously films the pope with both the hidden camera in one of her Louboutin high heels and her camera phone held in the crook of her elbow, and a lighthearted misunderstanding ensues.

"Amazing . . . I can't believe I'm alone with the great Pope Innocent," she says.

"And I with the great Mona Peeptoe," the pope replies. "Can I offer you a libation for the weary feet? My tongue is hot and swollen."

"A libation?" she asks. "You mean now? With your tongue?"

"And lips," he says. "A little lubrication to wet your throat . . ."

"You want to get me wet?" she asks, sniffing a journalistic coup.

"Any way you enjoy it. It is free, just like the cup of kindness," the pope says.

"Wow. Too bad I'm wearing pantyhose," she utters cryptically from her bench seat, gazing up at him in his high chair and focusing her camera for several seconds on his smallish footwear.

"Tell me who you're wearing," she says. "I like your little boots."

"They're Justin Ropers, a gift from Buckaroo Banzai," Innocent replies. "Brand new and super comfortable. I enjoy putting on cowboy clothes and dressing up special."

"Very nice. I think Buckaroo endorses them," she points out, as he meanwhile extracts a colorful can of energy drink from the hollow armrest of his white leather chair.

"I enjoy the sizzle and effervescence of Go Fast," he says, pulling the tab on the canned drink in what is obviously a well-rehearsed gesture. "The most bubbles and pop in any leading energy drink. Then it's off to bed for an early morning of day drinking . . ."

Thinking better of the remark, he points to the can and explains, "Sure you won't share my favorite libation?"

She blushes, realizing she has misunderstood. "That's right, I've seen your commercial! I forgot Go Fast is one of your endorsements. This is so crazy, Your Holiness! Here I was thinking you wanted to wash my feet with your tongue . . ."

"Yes. If it would help you smile," he replies. "It seems your face has forgotten how to smile."

"Do I seem like an angry woman, Holy Father?"

He answers simply, "It would be a better world if everyone smiled in appreciation of God's grace. The best thing is that it's absolutely free, but so many of us carry only anger, dysfunction, and scars . . ."

Now it's her turn to speak; but because of her professional ground rule to refrain from making the story about herself, what follows is an awkward, thumb-twiddling silence. Then the "blood rain" I have mentioned begins to spatter on the plexiglass roof, obliging her to remark, "This weather is a mess. Those clouds are not even shaped like rain clouds. It's weird."

"Good point. It seems to have popped up out of nowhere," he agrees, "but the world does not spin according to its impact on our lives; nor is it easily traceable back to God, who has other responsibilities."

Something—his gentle voice or the way he now touches her hand— suddenly causes her to let go of her professional protocol and unleash a torrent of personal feelings, surprising even herself with her frankness.

"And whom we're supposed to follow blindly like sheep even when he plays us for a fool? Isn't it time we started acting like grownups?" she says, almost instantly regretting her aggressive tone. "I'm sorry, Father. I don't mean to be nasty. I guess you'd say I have daddy issues. I'm just so used to male filthbags going gaga over my toes and vulgar bits. They're like dogs on my leg—not that you're a man—I mean, sometimes I think it's the only part of me they care about . . . because so many have stomped my heart, not counting all the filthy hoops I've had to jump through to get where I am today. I'm a strong woman, Father, but I'm also broken. Does that make sense?"

"I'm also strong and also broken," he replies. "I hear Zion's trumpet and also see our Lord's tears in your eyes, for God loves all of you, every inch of your pretty toes and very much else. God is everywhere, my child. Just remember this is not our true home. We are here only temporarily while Jesus arranges our accommodations in a far better place."

"Believe whatever you want. Wishes are fishes," she replies with a shrug, "but thank you for taking the time to teach us these things, this advice on life. Something I've always wondered about, though: if God is everywhere, where does he go when he wants to be alone?"

"Simple answers are not always simple," the pope says with a hint of displeasure. "He loves us. Why would God want to be alone when we are the apple of his eye and the cherry topping of all creation?"

"Maybe because of stress, working, dealing with our relationships and trashy people . . . or just for fun. I just wondered if he had a place to go to be alone . . ."

A better answer now occurs to the pope, and he says, "He goes to church. That's where he goes when he wants to be alone."

"And heaven?" she queries. "What's heaven like? Are we all children again, like in a fairy tale?"

On more familiar ground, the holy man easily fields the question.

"Like children, except in heaven everyone is a thirty-third-degree

Mason and thirty-three years old—like Jesus. All the streets of gold are one way, and bears and lions are our pets and also thirty-third-degree Masons."

"In the big circle in the sky . . . ?" she asks. "Everyone is thirty-three in the big circle, with a big pet?"

"Not only that," he informs her. "A right-handed person always stands next to a left-handed person so they can hold hands."

"So left-handed people don't stand next to each other?"

"Not in heaven."

"But aren't there many more right-handed people than left-handed . . . ?"

Here again the pope flashes impatience and takes a gulp of Go Fast.

"That is some crazy flavor," he declares, but more urgent matters now intrude, as the peg-legged Pomeranian suddenly bounds alongside them, making threatening faces at Mona.

SOKOL THE JOYKILLER

"What's his problem?" she asks. "He looks like a one-legged elephant seal, like something tripped his wire and he's about to blow a blood vessel."

"Sokol the Joykiller and Protomartyr, a disciple of Cardinal Baltazar," the pope replies. "Grand marshal of the palace guard and first lord of the admiralty."

"The admiralty? A bit of a sham, that?" she questions.

"And first officer of my bedchamber, responsible for my safety," he adds, hastily drawing the curtains.

"It looks like he scares you, too. Why don't you tell him to hit the road?"

The pope recounts a brief history, explaining, "Because his brain is the size of a mustard seed. Called the Joykiller for his undying faith, in Pomerania he was caught in his own bear trap and sawed off his own leg, making it impossible for him to continue his job as a sheepherder . . . so he came to us, a flagellant submitting to pain to symbolize submission to God. He is a virgin with women and whips himself into a frenzy. His heart is pure, but he can be a bit fanatical, sometimes overprotective of me."

"I'll say. He's drunk the Kool-Aid the deepest, in other words . . . an ice-cold sociopath stirring up crap and throwing his weight around," she observes. "Does he always wear that Nazi boot on his wooden leg?"

"Perhaps he is misunderstood. He has a speech impediment . . . a stutter," Innocent replies, as if offering an explanation.

"If you watch my show, you know my motto: 'That chaps my nipples.' I call 'em like I see 'em because we live in an age of unaccountability . . . people who take advantage."

"Yes, you take the world on your shoulders, much as I, Miss Peeptoe."

"Then your people need to set a better standard. A man like that belongs in prison," she says.

Under his breath, barely audible on the grainy tape, the pope is heard to mutter, "I'm the one in prison, I'm afraid."

Here he is interrupted suddenly by the dim bulb at the door, by whom I mean the crazed Sokol! Desperate to break in, the wolfman curses and tugs at the door held shut by His Holiness, who tells Mona urgently, "Do you have your phone? Do you know Buckaroo Banzai's number?"

"Someone very close to him," she replies, jerking out her pink electric stun gun and gripping the pope's leg in an attempt to help. "How about the Reno Kid?"

"Yes, of course," he says breathlessly. "Tell Buckaroo and my true friends, the Cavaliers, that I have been cut off from all communications. Perhaps I have been too gullible, but I need their help in these perilous times. I have reason to fear a palace coup . . ."

"Seriously, Your Eminence? I find that hilarious, but not really," she says. "From whom? This man Sokol . . . ?"

Suddenly, the popemobile door flies open and Sokol bursts in, lunging for Mona, who kicks savagely while unleashing three million electric-pink volts . . . but wide of the target and instead zapping Innocent, who falls back in his chair with a howl.

"Jesus, the power! Come and get me . . . !"

Between syllables he accidentally spills Go Fast on Sokol, who jerks back in apparent agony, as if scalded, and continues to manhandle Mona, violently dragging her out of the popemobile, exclaiming, "F-f-fool w-w-woman! Snake creature!"

Spilling painfully into the street, she scrambles to avoid a speeding horse-drawn carriage that swerves in an attempt to run her down; and she considers that in her whole life she has never been dumped from a moving vehicle with such force. As she would tell me later, "All I remember thinking was, this is exactly how a bitch gets killed. Then the sky lit up, bright as day, and I assumed I was dead."

ON DEATH

What goes through one's mind when confronted by the specter of imminent death, the certain knowledge that one's time in the sun is at an end? I am reminded of a question that Buckaroo Banzai once put to me: "Reno, at the end of your life, face to face with your last memory of this world, will you wish you had done more, or done less?"

With typical drollery I said something like, "I suppose it would depend how old I was."

But age has little to do with it; he was asking something more profound, and I am still not sure how to answer him. Perhaps the best response is less and more at the same time, meaning we ought to do more with less . . . less for ourselves and more for others.

Given its universal application—we are all doomed to die—it is perhaps nevertheless a mistake to think in universal terms when subsets of humanity differ radically in their view of death. Certain religionists doubtless welcome it, or so they say, while I suspect the vast majority of us regard it with some degree of terror: the great unknown that may be eternal. I will go further: anyone who is not frightened by the thought of death is not quite sane. Who would not be frightened by such a prospect? What might be your last thoughts, young reader, with cold gun steel pressed to your head?

When I once put this same question to Buckaroo, he said, "I would hope my last thought would be the same as my tombstone: 'He did more good than harm.'"

My point here is that you almost surely cannot know until it happens, and with luck death will take you unawares, in your sleep. As a Hong Kong Cavalier and someone therefore used to being in the line of fire, I have communed with death, inhaled her bittersweet fragrance and felt the rustle of her dreaded skirts, yet resisted her cold kiss more times than I can count. Thankfully, our relationship has remained in the flirtatious stage, though on one occasion I deactivated the wrong wire on an explosive device and lay on an autopsy table for two hours while experiencing a flood of random memories, good and bad, over which I seemed to have no control—along with a feminine voice, presumably a woman but not specifically anyone from my past (at least no one I recognized), whispering sweetly, "I love you, baby, from the rock bottom of my heart."

Who might this mystery voice have been, who claimed to love me? The old death hag herself? A former companion or lover, hidden to my memory? The voice of God? A siren sent to guide me into the next life? I also had a dream once in which I communed with our Rawhide, famously killed by a Lectroid stinger. Asking him how things were in the afterlife, I heard him say, "Not bad, just boring. I'm here but I'm not here, you know what I mean? 'No matter where you go, there you are'? Not really."

So I have no answers; and even if I did, my experience might have nothing in common with yours. If there is one thing certain in the world, it is that each of us must die alone, a stranger to everyone in the end, even to ourselves. I have already recounted how Xan cut the beating heart out of the sacrificial Paraguayan, whom I will not identify out of respect to his family; but in his last breath, he appeared to have a religious experience—a not uncommon phenomenon among the dying, who with their last, gasping breath often have a conversation with mysterious figures standing in light.

TOMMY AND THE HAPPY HEADSMAN

As against that, when I asked Perfect Tommy what went through his mind when Cardinal Baltazar pressed a Beretta to his forehead in the cardinal's carriage, his reply was "I wished for a bottle of hooch."

"I want my thumb," demanded the cardinal.

"You can have your thumb, I'll keep my dignity," Tommy replied.

"You'll catch hell. Thanks for the laughs, Tommy, but I think we can do better than that," replied Baltazar, cocking the 9 mm and dry squeezing the trigger. "Git along, move along, little doggie . . ."

"It's *dogie*, pronounced *do-gie*," insisted Tommy through a bloody lip. "Is nothing sacred?"

"Is that right, Mr. Tommy? How do you pronounce *send your ass to Armageddon* . . . ?" the cardinal muttered and slapped Tommy with the pistol.

But it was not yet time for him to leave this earth. Moments later, the carriage clattered to a stop in the underground Vatican garage, and men in medieval knight regalia pummeled him and pulled him out, carrying him down an innocuous tunnel to a hidden door that opened with an ancient passkey . . . from there via rough-hewn steps that wound, for what seemed at least an eternity, to a narrow footpath carved out of solid rock peppered with two thousand years' worth of graffiti and handprints. Indeed do not think I am exaggerating by far when I say that as much of Rome lies below the surface as above it. They do not call it the Eternal City for nothing, when archaeologists are always making new discoveries of layer built upon layer, epoch upon epoch, so that much of what is hidden from view is found to be more magnificent than anything seen on picture postcards.

I am not speaking here of the maze of glorious catacombs and underground mausoleums for which Rome is justly famous, but of something even more fantastical and central to our chronicle: the secret cathedral just below Saint Peter's Basilica. Discovered only recently in the time of the great digger Pius XII and still in the process of being restored, it had been given the unpleasant sobriquet "the Dwarf Church" even before the ungodly events I am about to recount.

It is, as I have said, and properly speaking, a scale-model cathedral— whose provenance is said to date back to Constantine himself, the great friend of Christians and constructor of the original Saint Peter's. As the legend goes, the emperor ordered two basilicas built, one aboveground and one below, in keeping with the Hermetic scripture that says, "as above, so below." The problem with such a scenario, however, is that the underground cathedral is of Gothic design, meaning a style of architecture that did not appear until roughly eight hundred years after Constantine.

Who, then, built the magnificent, albeit miniature, structure which a bloodied and browbeaten Tommy now beheld by the glow of gas lighting as his captors dragged him through the low church entryway carved with impressive jamb figures of the twelve disciples and a sculpted tympanum depicting Christ as judge on the last day?

"Sweet Jesus retail, I'll be dang . . . damned awesome," he muttered in amazement, crawling on all fours and admiring the majestic nave's ribbed vaulting barely a few feet above his head and several tiny chapels radiating out from its cruciform floor plan.

"Indeed, it is a miracle, in the language of speaking," said Baltazar, "built over hundreds of years by little people of the catacombs, lepers and cripples, outcasts of society, nameless martyrs for the faith. Look, you can see their pitiful names scratched in the basalt."

"Then their treasure is in heaven," Tommy replied, in awe of the soaring ceiling and faded frescoes of biblical scenes . . . one of which depicted crusader knights battling turbaned Saracens at the foot of the cross.

"Ironic, isn't it?" said Baltazar. "These small crusaders for forces of light living down here in darkness. This was their entertainment. It is said there is a secret tunnel proceeding directly to the earth's core, perhaps even to hell."

"I thought it smelled like butt funkness," noted Tommy.

"It is called the Cloaca Maxima, where your remains will disappear for spewing your shite on me, you worthless rocket scientist," the cardinal angrily informed him, then performed a surprisingly agile jump kick to the back of Tommy's skull, propelling him forward and causing him to smack his head on a decorative crenelated battlement above the choir . . . merely the latest low blow to our dear Tommy.

"That one's on the house!" snickered Baltazar . . .

Wary of saying the wrong thing, Tommy wisely said nothing and allowed himself to be frogmarched through an adjoining chapel lined with reliquaries full of chicken and rodent bones and mummified flesh . . . then through another low door and another set of steps, down to a deeper catacomb, half-flooded, where humming generators, creaking metal doors, and groaning voices (Lectroid and human) became impossible to ignore.

"Down here is where we keep the demons . . . and my headsman." Baltazar kept on with his inane antics. "Ha, ha . . . there goes the neighborhood!"

Was that the sound of military boots, marching with parade-ground precision? Or simply Tommy's own pulse throbbing in his ears?

Through a jumble of smells—diesel, seeping sewage, cooking odors— the strangers dressed as medieval knights dragged him through a hole in a wall into a cavernous room housing assorted implements of torture, candy and soft drink vending machines, a wicker basket overflowing with human heads, and dimly lit cages packed with filthy, ragged prisoners who unanimously reacted with excitement to the sight of the new arrival.

"Perfect Tommy!" came their refrain, weak but insistent enough to interrupt the plain cause of their abject misery: a pear-shaped Vulcan in his forge, more flabby than muscular and with a Cro-Magnon head so large as to appear cartoonish. Naked except for a shiny gold jacket, bloody butcher's apron, and shoes with high, stacked soles, he stiffened at the sight of the cardinal.

"Yes, Your Eminence . . . ?" he said in a husky Scandinavian accent, raising a salute with a blowtorch and a pair of wire cutters. "Shave and a cut . . . ?"

Baltazar pointed at Tommy and replied, "I need my thumb that he ate. Slice him open, so I can have it reattached."

"Could get messy if it has gone into the intestines," demurred the man in the apron. "Let me work my methods, bringing him to a highly adrenalized state of catharsis. I mean to say he will expel the thing in harmony with nature. Then I will snip his wires."

"Bury him in the earth's core or sell him into slavery, as you wish . . . but keep things moving, now that Banzai has butted in," warned the cardinal, who lingered, examining the various implements of torture with a keen eye for detail.

The hooded man smiled knowingly and indicated a rotating sarcophagus, a homemade, barrel-like device lined with piston-firing wooden knobs, saying, "Don't worry, it will all come out in the wash. I'll give him a good cleansing in my electrified pounding machine and have him singing like a songbird."

"What a shocker . . . quite the handyman, aren't you?" remarked Tommy, nervously eyeing a Craftsman toolbox next to a macabre rotating contraption hooked up to a car battery.

"Thanks. I make all my own equipment," the headsman said with a laugh, pointing to the torture machine. "Lined with electrified three-inch drywall screws, it does a fair enough job of making chicken salad out of chickenshits . . . although I do get my fair share of complaints. Or maybe you'd prefer the smother box . . ."

Tommy felt his legs about to buckle but somehow found the wherewithal for a defiant rejoinder, saying, "No complaints outta me. I've been tortured by the best and pooped blood, but I didn't sing."

"Ha, ha, you'll sing and hit the high notes," the man parried. "Don't let this pretty face fool you: I'll have your cods in your mouth—stitched shut— by the time I'm done. I'm the buster! You haven't been tortured until you've been tortured by Pay Piggie. Pay Piggie now or pay Piggie later."

"So you're a special breed of knucklehead," Tommy joked and grimaced. "I see you wear high heels so your knuckles don't drag . . ."

"Indeed, my wires are crossed," laughed Pay Piggie, showing his yellow-butter teeth and practically shooting sparks through his eyeholes. "I like you, Tommy. If you're nice to me, I'll give you a choice: hammer or wire snips."

"Ha, ha . . . first I'll kick your carcass and make your girlfriend hold my coat," Tommy boasted unconvincingly, glancing with defiance at Cardinal Baltazar. "Just don't give me whole milk. My stomach can't handle it."

"The great Perfect Tommy . . . lactose intolerant, eh?" snickered Baltazar. "Your act's wearing thin, Mr. Perfect, so let's wind this charade on down. Wave goodbye: you have an appointment with the fun machine and I have a vendetta [sic] with destiny. Get well soon."

Turning, he instructed one of his knights to go in search of a gallon of milk and then was gone, leaving Tommy alone to confront the specter of torture and his own demise—and therein lies an unhappy dilemma. Although I would like to represent with some exactness Tommy's courage in the face of different torture techniques, it would not endear me to the Institute's censors or to the parents of my readers. Hopefully, it is enough to tell you that the pain he endured left him sorely tempted to accept, on the Piggie's return, the gift of a leather strap bearing the deep bite marks of previous victims.

"Here's a little something to chew on," said the leering sadist, "whilst I cut your ass from the bone."

"I smell your fear," spat Tommy, refusing the leather belt. "Just know this: your days as a free man are numbered."

"You crack me up," said Pay Piggie. "But now it's my turn."

No one is immune to pain or the weeping and wailing it can bring to even the bravest among us; and I have no intention of recounting such horrors to young readers—not even my own such dire experiences in other circumstances—so allow me now to leave poor Tommy to his torture session (at least temporarily) and turn our attention back to the Coliseum, where we, too, were bathed in light: the biggest and brightest full moon our planet has yet seen, made the more remarkable when the "moon" suddenly split in two for a twin effect. As bright as the sun, the enormous silver globes brought an artificial daylight so intense that some in the crowd began to faint, while others alternately cheered nervously or cried aloud, *"Impossibile! Figlio di merda! What is happening?!"*

BUCKAROO GOES SOLO

Doubtless our television viewers around the world were wondering the same; we continued to play, not taking a break even though we were smoldering in the festering artificial heat. In the midst of the surreal spectacle, Li'l Daughter answered my Go-Phone and, pretending to change the reed on my alto sax, brought me the news onstage. In such a roundabout way, I learned of Tommy's SOS call to Mrs. Johnson and the pope's troubling cry for help to Mona Peeptoe. In turn I conveyed both into the ear of Buckaroo Banzai, who almost immediately signaled Pecos to take an extended drum solo and thereupon departed the stage.

Since he offered no explanation, the motive for his exit in the middle of "Prettiest Eyes This Side of Heaven"—our best-selling record and a tribute to Penny—was unknown to the others. What was clear, however, was that we were now down to four musicians: Pecos on drums, Muscatine on guitar and electric lute, Hoppalong on bass, and yours truly on saxophone and keyboards. Just how long we were expected to hold down the musical fort was anyone's guess, but one other thing was certain: we would never quit without giving our fans their full allotted money's worth. Still, as Pecos sweated buckets and pounded her drum kit with zest—hitting her cymbals and rimshots with a power I have seldom seen before or since—my gut told me I was listening to war drums that had never been louder. It was rage I was hearing, and like Pecos, I was getting worked up.

But I risk getting off topic, since at that very moment Buckaroo Banzai was speeding across Saint Peter's Square on our borrowed police Moto

Guzzi. To say that he turned heads, riding hell bent for leather in full stage regalia, including a pair of six-guns, would be putting it mildly; but neither did he exactly sow panic. Recognizing him and thinking it all somehow connected to the astounding "special lighting effects" and the small army of television satellite trucks parked around the square, most visitors simply reacted with delight, raising their cameras to record the encounter. Among these was Mona Peeptoe, disoriented by the blazing double moons overhead and still nursing scrapes and bruises after her tumble from the popemobile. Like others, she squinted in stunned disbelief as Buckaroo, champion of the average man and the dispossessed, aimed the powerful motorcycle straight at the Apostolic Palace. Too late did it occur to her that she might be on the threshold of the greatest news story of her celebrated career . . . meaning she did not raise her camera in time to get the shot. On the other hand, what a night it had been already . . . with perhaps even more in store?

Nor did the quartet of ceremonial Swiss Guards on duty at the great bronze doors, the majestic entryway into the palace, regard Buckaroo with particular concern until he was almost upon them. Then, momentarily frozen by the sight of the lone cowboy bearing down fast, they quickly succumbed to panic, yet were able to cross their halberds in an attempt to deny Buckaroo entry.

"Alt! Alt!"

"Fat chance!" muttered Buckaroo, who merely took the crossed halberds as a challenge, trick-riding the Moto Guzzi by dropping the bike nearly on its side and racing toward the gleaming halberd blades that could easily decapitate any fool so reckless.

As I have hinted, after his last trip through solid matter and alternate dimensions, Buckaroo's neurologist had warned him against operating a motor vehicle, much less a high-performance motorcycle; and although the rare disorder (what other human being could share it?) lacked a name, Buckaroo has indicated that it was characterized by mini blackouts and swarms of eye floaters, as well as occasional hiccups in recognizing social and situational cues.

Whether his condition itself played a role in the following sequence of events is anyone's guess. I can only relate what Buckaroo has told me: how he felt a sudden fading effect and a kind of dead zone, his consciousness out of phase with his surroundings, almost as if he had entered another dimension. Perhaps the "midnight moons effect"—the glare from the artificial orbs overhead—also played a role . . .

. . . as he shot just beneath the gleaming halberds, through the doorway, and into the foyer of the palace . . . skidding across marble floors and past another security checkpoint before scattering a small conclave of visiting nuns . . . and a gaggle of guards who now came on the run, pistols drawn, yelling, "Get him! *Attenti . . . suoi rivoltelle!* Get his six-guns!"

"Ripe for the taking—all you gotta do is come get 'em!" Buckaroo chided, gunning the motorcycle once more and heading for the famous royal staircase.

"*Alt!* Closed! You can't . . . !"

"Can't . . . ?! You know that word's not in my dictionary, boys!"

What sounded like a backfire was actually a gunshot that zipped past Buckaroo's head and ricocheted off Bernini's colossal equestrian statue of Constantine the Great, miraculously causing both the Roman emperor and Buckaroo Banzai to drop lower in their saddles as Buckaroo accelerated jarringly up the steps of the colonnaded Scala Regia.

"Bernini, you sonofa . . . !" Buckaroo groaned through clenched teeth, cursing the great baroque master and architect of the staircase . . .

. . . before he at last mercifully bounded over the last steps and turned into the magnificent Sala Regia, where he paused to get his bearings on his Go-Phone, momentarily distracted by the floor-to-ceiling art treasures, but only for a moment . . . hearing a small army of clanking Swiss Guards headed his way.

Oh, for the opportunity to play such a game, he thought, rather enjoying it and giving thanks in this house of holies before suddenly reversing his course, speeding back down the stairs and out of the palace, leaving the guards to gloat giddily, "Buckaroo Banzai is frightened of our sharp halberds! *Buckaroo Banzai è un pollo . . . !*"

Again, the truth lay elsewhere. Behind our chief's change in plans lay an urgent alert received over his headset from the worldwide Banzai Institute network of concerned citizens. Local Blue Blazes were reporting, via World Watch One, that someone in a cheap lodging house, some twenty minutes away from Vatican City, was in urgent need of a doctor. The caller said his name was Costello, an abbot in the Franciscan order who wished to make full confession . . . to Buckaroo Banzai. As a physician—yes, first and foremost—but also as an extremely interested party, Buckaroo made his decision without hesitation.

XXVIII. AN UNNATURAL BIRTH

> Caligula is in each one of you.
> —Albert Camus

Not so many years ago, the Banzai Institute of Applied Sociology published a study on urban living patterns in the United States which delved heavily into the statistics of homelessness and the development of communal squatting into a new social order. While this is not the place to go into detail, the point I wish to make is that the phenomenon is already well entrenched in Rome and other Italian cities, and it was to such a squatter settlement that Buckaroo directed himself.

Overwhelmingly young and often from an immigrant background, urban settlers (to use a term they prefer) may posture as anarchists, but in reality they only desire to live in peace and with modest luxuries, like the rest of us. A consistent finding of the paper's authors (*Networking the Land: Conflicting Imperatives of the New Urban Settler Movement*, Berlin and Offenbach) was that in every settlement studied there was, for lack of a better word, a shot caller . . . a key man (usually) who calls the shots, deciding who may stay and who must go and in general what rules are to be enforced in the communal living space.

At the lodging house under discussion, an ancient, derelict five-story *questura* closed for renovations, this key individual happened through a lucky coincidence to be a Blue Blaze irregular, and it was he and two other settlers who averted their gaze from the ever-changing sky long enough to greet Buckaroo the instant he jumped off the Moto Guzzi.

"Buckaroo!" exclaimed the key man, a genial immigrant in an official Blue Blaze sash who clapped both hands gleefully before extending one in greeting. "Welcome to our digs! You bring honor upon us."

"Hopefully you bring honor upon yourselves," Buckaroo said. "Where's the monk?"

"I will show you," said the greeter and indicated his two associates, who continued gazing at the sky. "I am Blue Blaze Able Omar the Berber, an experienced mediator . . ."

"'Able Omar' . . . ?" queried Buckaroo.

"Short for Able Moammar. It was I who called you. My *ragazzi* will keep your Moto from harm and stand watch. But what is up? Is the end of the world, no?"

"I wish I knew what's up, Omar," Buckaroo replied.

Through the graffiti-covered entrance and up a dingy staircase, he then followed his guide, who was busy explaining, "I saw the official Blue Blaze worldwide alert, so of course I recognized the mad monk at once, because I am also an artist. I draw comic books and also do watercolors."

"Good luck," Buckaroo said. "Have you called anyone else? How many others know?"

"Only my *ragazzi*," the Blue Blaze replied, "and of course Sister Mary."

"Sister Mary . . . ?"

The name meant nothing to Buckaroo, but by the time they reached the fourth floor he had heard a short account of Omar's journey from the Levant and his efforts to get an internship in the beauty industry despite his main career as a freelance commercial artist.

"But now I get another letter which seems I must pay for beauty consultant certification, although I clearly stated I have ten years' experience, even executive experience. It is a lot of bullshit!"

"Yes, it is," Buckaroo agreed, though barely listening.

"Maybe if you wrote to them a letter on official Banzai Institute stationery, else no one would believe it. Meanwhile I am powerless," the young man complained as they turned from the stairs past more graffiti, holes in walls, and the smells of old urine, baked bread, and fried fish behind heavily locked doors.

"Send the details to Mrs. Johnson. I'll do my best to get to the bottom of it," replied Buckaroo, when a door opened at the end of the hallway and, as in a dream, a sweet oval face appeared to him, squinting meekly from beneath a nun's headdress.

"I told you I would bring him, Sister Mary," said Omar.

"Buckaroo Banzai! *Che sogno! Vergine santa!*" Sister Mary uttered with surprise. "*Dio* . . . the answer to my prayers! Like a dream, or an angel out of the blue . . ."

"I'm no angel, Sister, but you could be," he said and moved quickly toward her, taking in at a glance her auburn widow's peak, rosebud mouth, and inquiring eyes like blue crystal pools of pure benevolence and celestial light. No dead religion here, it occurred to Buckaroo, but a living faith. Yet far from beatific, her gentle expression was troubled, a flower in extremis . . . reflecting the agony of her savior and perhaps the messy job at hand that required her to wear glycerin gloves. In both hands she gripped household cleansers, yet her gentle mien seemed to transcend any such earthly concern. If ever a human's gaze was on heaven . . .

"Come in, Buckaroo Banzai," she said, opening the door wider and drawing her shawl more tightly around her, intently searching his face. "Have you a remedy for devilry?"

"You mean beyond the norm? I try to assemble the facts and go from there, Sister," he volunteered. "That's all any of us can do—and your accent . . . American?"

"I was raised in an American convent. Call me Mary, Mary Comfort. Somehow I knew you would come," she replied and admitted him to her chamber, her holy shrine . . . for her room gave every appearance of being a shrine, albeit to temporal love and Broadway musicals. There were show memorabilia and pictures of her Prince Charming, Abbot Costello, along with withered bouquets of flowers, stuffed animals, rag dolls, and packages of candy. Who could blame Buckaroo for scarcely believing his eyes and turning toward the closed bathroom, where the air seemed suffocatingly thick with a fetid smell he could not identify and the low-throated groans of someone in distress?

"Here, God bless," she said and at once began rubbing her slippery hands over his head. "It is oil from the Mount of Olives."

"Thanks for the thought, Sister," he replied.

"I have another Pampers bag, and I called an ambulance but they don't always show up," she informed him, as he pressed open the bathroom door and almost immediately flinched from the sight. The abbot lay in a bathtub breathing heavily, his face contorted, but the very human nature of the grimace told Buckaroo he was looking into the white eyes and drooping mustache of a man near death, a human at war with a deadly parasite. Perhaps thirty, he easily looked fifty.

"Buckaroo Banzai . . . *per favore*," the pale monk managed weakly, pointing at his crotch. "*Orribile* . . . horrible . . . little fireman hurt . . ."

"In *pericolo*, are you? In trouble? Going through some tough stuff, for sure . . . pain you don't deserve," Buckaroo said, gently hitching up the monk's garment and examining the private parts the monk seemed so intent on protecting fervently. "May I see your little fireman? You didn't try to hurt yourself, did you?"

"Hurts to pee," the monk groaned in agony. "Owchies! When I pee-pee, is burns. Aaaaaaayy, I ain't know what happen . . . my fire-rod baby man . . ."

Now Sister Mary Comfort spoke from the doorway, saying, "Part of God's plan we have to accept, like the demon of lust. Though I can never forgive myself, I ask God's forgiveness and pray for him to find peace from the demon who has taken possession of him and yet to whom I also surrendered."

"He needs a hospital. How long has he been like this?" Buckaroo asked.

"For an hour . . . but really since returning from America some weeks ago and announcing he was carrying a devil, a sack of . . . the word he used was *merda*," she said.

"A sack of . . . I understand," Buckaroo said out of respect for the nun's sensibilities, squeezing the monk's penis and abdomen to the point that the tortured wretch squirmed uncontrollably and cursed the Deity.

"I'm just of the thought that you reap what you sow," she said. "My father once told me that babies come from fruit juice when you're having too much fun."

"A wise man. Did you see any physical changes in him, such as—" Buckaroo began before he was interrupted by the monk's wild-eyed scream.

"May the heavens crumble to the earth! Bloated corpse of Jesus . . . stolen my dignity!"

Now the monk's increasingly obscene blasphemies, and total lack of respect for everything in the world, so affected her that she put her fingers in her ears and spoke louder than normal.

"Yes, he had an emergence of belly gas, little windstorms that used to chase me from the room. And he would become silent and very angry . . . behaving oddly and experiencing pain in his . . . I am embarrassed to say . . . his mouse . . . his carrot . . . his thingbob."

"His thingbob," repeated Buckaroo, "and small wonder, depending on the size of the stone. You say 'behaving oddly' . . . like a man possessed . . . ?"

"Yes," she agreed at once, "by a terrible guilt for which I blamed myself. This room was our little secret Garden of Eden, where Lucifer opened our eyes to love without measure, where I told him, 'Our souls have sought each other out. I want to love you all the ways there are.' So we tapped our toes to the music of you and the Hong Kong Cavaliers and threw ourselves into the flame of passion, playing pony ride or tickling one another in our self-induced hell on earth. Then one day we took a picnic to Villa d'Este . . . such fools but happy as children in the gardens of Tivoli . . . drinking cocoa . . . there, in the grotto and overcome with lust, I leaned to whisper something to him, and my tongue must have entered his ear, or perhaps I sneezed, because he made the cream cheese and became expectant."

"That would be a problem, if true," Buckaroo said, barely concealing his exasperation.

"Yes," she continued. "Then later, when he returned from America, he announced he was infected with a demon child . . . the devil's revenge, he said, for my dirty hands."

"That's a nice concept, but it's not your fault," Buckaroo told her. "Dirty hands and sneezing in his ear had zero to do with it."

"Even if I was menstruating? I did blame myself. Love blossomed and love is pain . . . as you know," she said, giving him a long look. "I'm so sorry about Penny."

"Thank you, Sister."

She brushed her hand against Buckaroo's cheek in sympathy and said, "When I confessed my shame to dear Innocent, it was the psychopath Cardinal Baltazar who, eavesdropping, learned of our relationship and threatened to expose us and my father as well."

"Your father . . . ?"

"Pope Innocent is my father. I am his illegitimate issue . . . but that isn't important."

Buckaroo scarcely had time to react to this extraordinary revelation before she revealed a further surprise. "Cardinal Baltazar is raising an army of demons. I've seen them down in the tunnels."

"Tunnels . . . ?"

"The catacombs . . . an army of monsters, evil Goliaths he makes from . . ." she said, momentarily too disgusted to continue. "He is playing God. He raises his hands and brings them into existence . . . sets of twins, triplets, like zombies. I once sent you a letter because our computers are monitored by the cardinal's men . . ."

Buckaroo snapped his fingers, instantly recalling, "Of course. It was you who sent that anonymous letter to us at the Institute."

"I do not claim vast knowledge," she said, "but I know trouble when I see it. They are like pack animals he keeps behind grates, not trusting them . . . not to mention yellow mustard gas."

"Mustard gas . . . ?"

"So I've heard, and smelled it. But what is his purpose?"

"That's what I'd like to know," Buckaroo replied. "It's about time I had a little talk with the cardinal. Can you take me down to the catacombs?"

With a nod she said, "I know them all like the back of my hand . . ."

"A valuable tip, Sister. It appears our time is running out," Buckaroo said. "I need to get to work."

The monk now began to grimace and thrash, spewing small words and sobbing loudly enough to be overheard outside the bathroom, as Buckaroo produced his Go-Phone with its Doc-in-a-Box application and retractable surgical blades.

"I know your nerves are scrambled right now," he told the desperate monk, "but this kidney stone in your ureter carries a dangerous risk. I need you to open your eyes and tell me you trust me to perform a ureteroscopy . . ."

"*Si, mi fido di te . . . ! Per favore . . . ayy, il dolore . . . !* My baby coming!"

"Not unless everything I learned during my OB clinicals was wrong," replied Buckaroo.

The monk did open his eyes, but their natural beauty was in the process of being eclipsed by an evil beyond imagination, as his white irises and white pupils turned reptilian and then rolled up, leaving only membrane. Hostage to a repulsive being within, he snarled in a deep, scratchy voice: "Ha, ha . . . see you in hell, Banzai . . . Banzai, the brainiac!"

For an instant Buckaroo froze and seemed not even to breathe, as if fearful of inhaling the same air in which resonated the voice of the degenerate Whorfin. But gathering himself, he said calmly, "Hell bound, are we? Glad to see you're still stuck in your ways, Whorfin, you freak . . . enjoying your old hobby as a leech."

"Whadda you want, a sorry?"

"Just take your medicine," Buckaroo declared, as he simultaneously emptied his Pez dispenser of Alka-Seltzer tablets down the poor abbot's throat, despite his feeble protests and an ominous hiss from deep in his bowels, like the muffled rage of a wild boar stuffed in a poke.

"Time to move on, clean house, and purge the parasitic element inside you," Buckaroo informed the monk. "Nod your head if you understand me. I'm giving you an alkalinizing agent. Hopefully, you're not on any amphetamine medication . . ."

"No more . . . no more," begged the monk, who was already changing colors, glowing red and hot from within. "Thank you, Buckaroo, for deliver me from evil! Anus of Satan, I have suffer so much, only can cry . . . !"

"I am sorry this happened to you. You're a good and decent man of the cloth who doesn't deserve this," said Buckaroo.

"What is happening?!" Sister Mary Comfort demanded to know, seeing her monk turn red as a radish. "*Per l'amor di Dio* . . . his soul is burning!"

"Mother Nature taking her own sweet time. He's having cramps and spasms," Buckaroo said, turning on the tub's cold-water spout. "I'm worried for his heart . . ."

"His heart is pure," the sister declared.

"It will be purer after this," Buckaroo said.

In this way he dismissed a more immediate danger to himself—a radiating rottenness inside the monk, something he had seen only once in his career—but in any case he was in no position to act upon it, since it was not his own well-being that now loomed paramount in his thoughts. The accursed monk, possessed by the demon John Whorfin and presenting classic signs of attempting to pass a kidney stone, plainly carried the heavier burden, and the Hippocratic Oath obliged Buckaroo, above all, to do no harm . . .

. . . when at that very instant Whorfin—the beast within—attacked with full fury and the speed of a viper, finding the strength to kick Buckaroo in the testes and seize his throat in a vise grip, pulling him on top of him and trying to grab his six-shooter.

"Choking you out, Banzai!" Whorfin screamed. "Those were fun times!"

The two of them (three of them? four of them?) thrashed and splashed in the tub in a slap fight, although primarily it was Buckaroo absorbing Whorfin's piston-like blows while refraining from counterpunching the hapless monk, whose latest misfortune was to ooze antacid fizz from his nose and mouth like a mad dog at the same time that he felt a painful rush in his urethra.

"Ayyy, ayyy! Is coming! *Nome di Gesù* . . . baby coming!"

It is safe to say that Buckaroo had a hunch already that he was dealing with something beyond a kidney stone, yet what else could he have done with such a radical suspicion? This is the question I put to you, reader. Who could guess that a man could give birth to an alien being through his urinary tract? Of prime concern to Buckaroo was simply the monk's pain, since passing a kidney stone is among the most excruciating of agonies a human being can endure, even without taking into account the monk's intense gastric upheaval and fissuring at the cellular level— analogous to being ball-gagged and anally fisted (although Costello had no knowledge of such things).

"Ha, ha, who put the blasting charge? What I'm drinking, moonshine? Delicious!" slurped Whorfin, drooling frothily, his stinger launcher protruding serpent-like from Costello's mouth when he guffawed. "Laugh while you can, monkey boy!"

"Back at you, Whorfin," came Buckaroo's indignant reply. "Because . . . cry, and you cry alone. Laugh and . . . time to go back to the pit hole of the Eighth Dimension . . ."

"Come and get me, monkey boy! Cob hole ass munch . . . snot-bubble slobber!"

"*Zitto! Santa Madonna!* Filthy!" Mary Comfort exclaimed and grabbed the nearest weapon handy—a toilet plunger—with which she smacked the monk's ear severely, upbraiding the evil one. "You want to play dirty?! *Porco cane* . . . ! He has the devil all over him!"

To this accusation Whorfin replied with a wink, saying, "Plastic whore doll! Ha, ha! Devil's daughter! I am Whorfin . . . emperor of Lectroids, master of the game!"

"Master of the scam, you mean . . . but starting to show your age," retorted Buckaroo, who now took a head butt to the nose and angrily retaliated with a mild slap to the monk's double chin, merely causing Whorfin to cackle.

"Donkey punch only makin' me stronger, Banzai! A fat one, slurp slurp!"

Of course it was the monk who absorbed the blow; Whorfin himself felt nothing. My point is that whatever spare capacity for tolerating pain that poor Costello once enjoyed was now exhausted. Miracle of miracles, his heart was still beating, albeit racing to an irregular rhythm. He alternately shivered and sweated, wept openly, talked to himself and to mankind, but mostly juggled thoughts of piety with pleas to God to lighten his load, though it would be foolish of me to try to simulate all his screams, juvenile curses, and drowning noises, both vocal and otherwise, on this page. It is enough simply to say that in the end he prayed for a final nail in his coffin, since death would be a mercy.

"Satan, come out of me!" he cried, struggling for one good breath. "By the Lord God of Hosts, I beckon you!"

"Beckon me, I beckonin' you!" Whorfin growled and landed another blow to Buckaroo, who shrank less from the punch than from the gentle monk's desperate prayer.

"Help me in my present urgent petition," the monk pleaded. "In return I promise to make your name known and cause you to be invoked. This novena has never been known to fail. This novena must be said for nine consecutive days . . ."

Abruptly realizing the hopelessness of his predicament, the abbot now accepted the inevitable . . . gurgling through a foaming mouthful of crackling and popping phlegm, "My life . . . no smoking, good nature, healing strangers . . . why you have left me hanging, Father . . . ? My hair is wet . . ."

"Help him, Buckaroo!" pleaded Sister Mary Comfort. "He's losing faith, perhaps even salvation . . . !"

"Push, Brother . . . it's trying to come through! Don't give up, push! Try!" Buckaroo urged.

"Some drug, please! Make feel better!" cried the monk.

"All I have is a cyanide capsule."

"Give to me! God will make a way! My soul, my soul . . . like a river to the sea," gasped Brother Costello, who now felt his loins move and a quickening in his member, as something passed—no, forced—its way through his urethra, causing him to empty his bladder and stiffen, contorting in pain and sexual ecstasy before exhaling an agonal last breath. "*Laus Deo!* Praise to the king . . . *il potere e la gloria* . . . fading fast . . . from my labor to my reward! Oh, crab of lust! Octopus of weak flesh! Beautiful Virgin . . . grant me a holy death! I wish to God! *Basta, cazzo!*"

With that, he began to sing Handel's "Hallelujah" and pissed out a bloody glob at the same moment his heart ceased to beat.

THE ASTONISHING AFTERBIRTH

"Damn you, brother!" Buckaroo exclaimed in the face of the abbot's cardiac arrest and a sickening, noxious odor (described to me as a gut-wrenching combination of sulphur, burnt plastic, and canine anal gland scent, all poured over a boatload of rotted carp) . . .

. . . as he flew into action at once, by turns performing manual cardiopulmonary resuscitation and pressing his Go-Phone in defibrillator mode against the abbot's chest.

"C'mon!" he exhorted, seeing the monk fade to blue. "This is your chance—empower yourself, Whorfin! You have to work, too! Get off your phawking ass! Rage, Whorfin! Where's your fighting spirit?!"

This scolding came to nothing. But as he repeatedly failed to shock the monk's heart back to life, the drowning, distant voice of Whorfin, by now more plaintive than belligerent, also sensed the end. "Gettin' sticky in here! Feelin' walled in! Gettin' squeezed! Pick it up, Banzai! Pick it up!"

"Aww, listen to the bawl baby. No use . . . pulseless . . . and no epinephrine," a disheartened Buckaroo muttered to himself, left once again to cradle his blade and contemplate more invasive measures . . .

although the thought almost certainly crossed his mind that such heroic measures were inappropriate in such a case. If the monk's death meant the end of Whorfin, then perhaps it was for the best . . . goodbye and good riddance, after all. And doubtless Abbot Costello would wear the crown of martyrdom gladly, for the sake of humanity.

But, moved by love, Sister Mary Comfort refused to let the monk leave this earth.

"Let me try!" she at once insisted and attacked the monk's bare chest with her toilet plunger, push-pulling in rapid strokes, frantically trying to gain suction.

"One for every minute we had together! You want to pierce my heart? Put a knife through my heart? Breathe, my sweetness!" she cried. "Always my sugar!"

Of course her actions were also a kind of madness; and as if in response, the murky water in the tub appeared to churn and now parted like the Red Sea to reveal the alien thing itself . . . the stone or bezoar or whatever word one might choose, for it was something else altogether that had passed out of the monk . . . something pulsing so supernaturally bright as to be beyond my present vocabulary, approximately the size and shape of a small garbanzo but like a bean only in the manner of the Mexican jumping variety . . . a tiny house for a living occupant such as a faerie or perhaps a darker entity.

And from that disquieting thought naturally sprouted another: could the thing be an egg?

A calcified microfetus?

"Hold on, little slugger," said Buckaroo, urgently defibrillating with one hand and with the other reaching for the tiny alien object . . . which on closer inspection seemed to be spinning simultaneously on both a vertical and a horizontal axis . . . that is, comprising a pair of perpendicular energy fields that teetered on the edge of weirdness yet somehow commingled in perfect equilibrium, ebbing and flowing with a reddish glow while smelling something awful.

"Little stinker, then," he called it, only to come close to retching, instantly finding himself under intense psychic attack from a power beyond the pale of all that was human . . . . as if the thing, this stinker, was skimming his brain until something captured its fancy. And then it bored in with bursts of blazing aqua-blue luminescence and countervailing dark energy on a scale Buckaroo had never experienced and a feeling of suffocation—as if the candle of his soul were burning out and sucking the life out of him to feed its dying flame. He felt abandoned by the world and yet free, empty, unladen of cares and without regrets.

A death wish, he supposed. Thanatos was its name.

Another curious finding: when the mystery object's brightness and rotation ebbed, its natural shape seemed to be a disk; only its rapid spinning gave it the appearance of a sphere. Was it his imagination or did time also seem to lag at such moments . . . a disjuncture of sequence and causation . . . in tandem with the overhead lights that flickered and dimmed?

"Amazing," thought Buckaroo. "So it absorbs light like any other energy . . . perhaps even time! Is there anything it can't do . . . ?"

By now mentally armed against the little bugger, he nonetheless found it useless to resist as he was transported deeper into his heart . . . "to a wild weird clime that lieth sublime" . . . lifted up above the earth to a place beyond time and space and all cares, all notions of past and future, to her rotting fragrance! Of course, who else but Penny! Her sigh, her dead lips on his, and the joy of complete submission to a feeling of pair bonding with destiny . . .

. . . as tears filled his eyes, and here he felt a shadow pass and at the same moment returned to himself. What staggering force lay behind this neural net and mystery energy field? An electromagnetic storm? Gravitational distortion? Or a universal field, under quantum rules, that unified binary bits across the whole spectrum? More than that, it seemed to be not only a force field but a field of value, a manifestation of the *cogito*, leading to the obvious questions. Was the little god seed conscious? Was it alive? Or . . . perhaps alive and also not alive? But what was life anyway but the oddest and most glorious of things? A preflexive consciousness, electrical impulses in response to stimuli—within a wider circuit perhaps, even a cosmic circuit—but what else? We do not understand fully the prebiotic chemistry of life on this planet, much less on other worlds.

All of this, and more, he considered in a matter of seconds.

In probing his vulnerabilities, had the little sponge—this nameless button—detected his inner turmoil concerning Penny's loss? That he had lost his path and in some sense was looking to chew himself to death?

Did that explain why his hand was on fire, as it seemed to be, from the thermal energy or other type of radiation generated by the mystery object, and why he did not have the strength to let it go?

These were questions for another day, however, as it was by now clear that Brother Costello would not be returning from the land of the dead. In another setting—a hospital operating room—the patient would already be on the table, hooked to an IV with his chest cavity stretched open, allowing Dr. Banzai to perform open-chest cardiac massage or direct defibrillation to the heart muscle. In real life, however, Buckaroo was holding only his multifunction Go-Phone with its retractable surgical blades and the little nugget that now spun faster and hotter, emitting a brighter red glow and causing his hand to tingle and become as transparent as glass . . . eerily revealing every bone, sinew, and blood vessel within.

Even rattled, the scientist in him could not help experiencing a certain thrill, for here was some new truth wrapped in fallacy, at least according to the old scientific paradigm that appeared all of a sudden full of holes and in need of reprogramming. What kind of alien essence was he holding? What of its structure and molecular composition? Was it made of ordinary atomic nuclei or something strange, like quark matter? He could not begin to understand any of this but sensed at once the thing's spectacular power, for better or worse, and realized there was nothing to lose by experimenting . . .

. . . as he now passed the tiny glowing orb over the monk's chest, illuminating his skeleton and everything within like a life-size anatomical model. There he saw plainly the toad-shaped lost soul of John Whorfin; and, to his astonishment (too trite a word), he found a bloodless portal through the monk's rib cage into the thoracic cavity . . . and to the heart itself.

A MIRACLE

Quite often I am asked if Buckaroo is religious. Other than being known as the eponym of Banzai-ism—a unique mix of Buddhist stoicism and the American can-do spirit—he is not what I would call a follower of any organized religion . . . although this page is not the place to answer such a complex question. Some readers will recall his cryptic words from another episode, which I will paraphrase: "I believe only God can save the world, but I am not a believer." I will say also that the only prayer I have heard him utter is the same one he intoned at the moment his hand entered the monk's chest without breaking the skin.

"By the universal law of Myoho, I now put my intention in motion," he murmured and began to massage the monk's heart with his bare hands.

But massaging the muscle and even seeing it twitch, he could not help wondering if his hands were in the monk's actual bio-body or in another dimension, courtesy of the little orb, which he now imagined to be a kind of miniature OSCILLATION OVERTHRUSTER. Or was he simply hallucinating . . . the result of whatever mental impairment he had contracted in his interdimensional travels? And yet there was ample evidence that he was exactly where he thought he was, right here in Sister Mary Comfort's bathtub, pounding the monk's true heart and feeling a faint pulsation.

"Yes, Brother Monk . . . !" he exclaimed. "Wake up!"

Was it his healing hands, the pocket defibrillator, or the mini orb—or all three—that kick-started the monk's heart? Factually speaking, there was no way to know, and yet another jolt to the muscle had the twofold effect of returning it to a regular rhythm and causing a great smoke bomb of foaming spume to billow forth from the monk's nose and mouth and float toward the ceiling . . . where the frothy substance began to coalesce into what appeared to be John Whorfin's corporeal form!

"Free, brothers! Gone the cement shoes!" rejoiced Whorfin, who clearly felt refreshed, reveling in his new freedom—but was he so twisted in the head that he did not understand that without a physical body he was helpless . . . a pathetic, free-floating malevolence with only the ability to rant and snivel? Even his present condition could only be temporary, as gobs of Alka-Seltzer bubbles were dropping away from him already.

AN EPIC BATTLE OF WILLS

There the matter stood while Sister Mary—rendered as numb and mute at the incredible sight as Buckaroo himself—swung her plunger heroically at the fizzing monstrosity that now appeared to her in the terrifying guise of a giant, hovering cockroach . . . the whole improbable sequence interspliced with Whorfin's snickering laughter and bombast from the lather.

"Fellow Lectroid soldiers! The future now! Power no longer our dreams but in our hands! All or none! Now work faster to finish the Great Vehicle so can enter the Eighth Dimension and free our trapped comrades! So return to our homestead and seize what is ours! Roll over the dying to degrade the dead! Build fortress walls with their useless carcasses! Mass death! Back to the Heroic Age!"

(If he was not merely delirious, however, exactly whom was he addressing? This was unclear, unless by some telepathic means he was able to communicate with the captive Lectroids in the Vatican tunnels and of course his army of followers not in our dimension—a possibility I do not discard.)

"Feeling your oats, eh, Whorfin? But maybe not for long," answered Buckaroo, who now withdrew his hands from Costello's cavity and passed the magical, gleaming pellet over the unbroken skin . . . marveling at how his stilled heart was now pumping strong, how the monk himself seemed disoriented but otherwise alert, suffering only from a running nose and a bad-tasting, hacking cough.

"Buckaroo . . . ? Why is fallen your countenance? What happen the demon?" he muttered with a sense of wonder. "So much pain . . . more sicker . . . my mouth is stink. Gargle *merda*?"

"That's actually good news," Buckaroo informed him. "It means the bad spirit's gone . . . in the twinkling of an eye . . ."

Feeling slightly reassured, the monk squinted to behold the great Whorfin floating overhead and dripping like creamy Bisquick, liberated from physical bonds and speaking with authority, calling to the magic kernel, "Speck! Shiny power child! Come back to me! You are lost!"

"Holy Father . . . ?" said the vexed monk, unsure of what was floating above his head. "This is heaven? *Santa Madonna . . . andiamo!* It's be liars!"

Buckaroo shook his head, saying, "Not liars—just good news. You're alive, and there's no higher being here, no greater power . . . just a bunch of fizz."

"Purgatory, then? For mercy sake . . ."

"Yes . . . a kind of limbo state, perhaps. You seem to be fine, but I can't guarantee I've fixed all the damage. You might need to visit a urologist to have some work done, not to mention counseling," Buckaroo said, and in the same breath found himself struggling to control the little dynamo in his hand that seemed to have become agitated and overheated . . . hot as a sizzling coal, in fact. Even so, Buckaroo tightened his grip, either oblivious to the pain or oddly craving it, but determined to protect the strange newborn that now passed through his flesh as easily as it had penetrated the monk only moments before . . . bloodlessly exiting through Buckaroo's closed fist and twirling in midair like a spritely bee or a firefly, apparently in response to Whorfin's booming voice.

"Tidbit, my nymph child of blood and most powerful, whose mighty will a blessing straight out of heaven . . . chosen seed of prophecy and I, John Whorfin, Trumpet of Heaven and All in All, your lord and master having borne you thirty thousand years! Come now to me, youngster, back into my habitation . . . by order your father, your king!"

"King of fools," muttered Buckaroo, and at that very instant he and the nun were joined by Blue Blaze Able Omar, who, drawn by Whorfin's voice, stepped in . . . only to hold his nose and stumble backward from the floating alabaster blob on the ceiling.

"Gross! What the hell? Is a fat djinni . . . ?" he said, shaken by the impossible sight.

"Something worse—get out of here . . . fast. And take him," Buckaroo said, indicating the monk.

"The ambulance is here, but I don't trust it," Omar blurted out. "Under escort by Cardinal Baltazar and his secret police . . . ! I heard them speak of a holy sword."

"The sword . . . ?" asked Buckaroo. "Of San Galgano . . . ?"

"The same. I have cleaned it with vinegar and mineral oil," Sister Mary announced.

"That gives me hope," he told her. "You have it here?"

She hesitated to say more, giving Omar a sidewise look and telling Buckaroo in a whisper, "I don't trust the Moor."

"He wears the badge of a Blue Blaze—that's good enough for me," Buckaroo retorted, telling Omar, "Go, hurry . . . take the abbot to the ambulance, stay with him. Sister, pray the beads."

"For you?" she queried.

"For the whole world," he replied, "that it doesn't end tonight. And try to find me an industrial-strength vacuum cleaner."

"My vacuum cleaner was stolen," she revealed sadly and made the sign of the cross, while Buckaroo lent a hand helping Abbot Costello only as far as the door. In this manner he stayed behind to face an uncertain fate that he preferred not to contemplate.

"Rise with me, junior! Little grub, cuddle buddy, shitebug gold mine! Let cover you . . . my embrace!" Whorfin cajoled. "Together we murder!"

By now all too familiar with the little nugget's unfathomable power, Buckaroo quickly made his own urgent plea via brain waves.

"Little firefly, whatever your name—" he began. "Whatever you are— baby lectroid, little deva, or author of the universe—I can't grasp what you are or everything going on with you but sense you are special and recognize your power. I sense goodness within you."

Or did he? Feeling at that moment a roaring gale of utter desolation blow through his soul, he had to brace himself and try to catch his breath . . .

. . . as Whorfin's *Geist* blew bubbles: "Imp! Squirt . . . buckle up and fly with me, our electrons spliced together forever! Together we are all-powerful, above, beneath, and throughout a thousand star pools!"

"No!" countered Buckaroo, likewise addressing the mystery speck. "Resist him, little friend! It's only a money game with him! Read my intentions and know that I am a man of goodwill who wishes you no harm, who only wishes you happiness . . ."

"Balls, Banzai! Shut you worm mouth! Anal sore! Bean fart!" screeched Whorfin, whose foaming paws now reached for the dancing particle, prompting Buckaroo to launch himself and slash at the white cloud of Alka-Seltzer bubbles with his surgical blades.

"Off to meet the wizard, Whorfin! Off you go!" he vowed, popping bubbles left and right. "Pretty soon there won't be anything left of you!"

"Banzai stink wipe! Filth dog spunk! Choke you grub hole, grub nuts! Piss crusty grub nuts! Bleed, you bastard!"

Now Buckaroo tasted his own blood despite the tape over his orifices; and his mental powers spun out of control, thrown haywire by a powerful force . . . but from what quarter? Whorfin? Or perhaps the mystery speck, which for a moment seemed to be gravitating toward Whorfin but now retreated to the tub, which it began orbiting at high velocity, seemingly

ready to drown its sorrows in the bloody water. Suffering, terror, grief—
all of these Buckaroo was experiencing through the particle of light; and
up above the thundering gale, Whorfin's incandescent bubble cloud
likewise could be seen dwindling, strewing its tendrils like snowflakes.

"Banzai cock knocker, let my spunk in!" Whorfin threatened . . .

. . . as Buckaroo wrapped himself tighter, against a howling wind that
came out of nowhere to rattle the room, bringing with it a shadow that
came over him and entered him like a dark reckoning: a vision of Penny
in a field of bluebonnets with a donkey-baying lover he recognized at
once as the jackass burro in Baltazar's ridiculous painting of Napoleon.

Speaking of the cardinal, now a fresh danger arose in the form of Sister
Mary's urgent voice on the other side of the door: "Buckaroo, Cardinal
Baltazar is coming with his forces! Oh, Jesus, be my refuge!"

He scrambled at once, keeping a careful eye on what remained of
Whorfin's ceiling perch. And the tiny entity? The little powerhouse?
Based upon the available evidence and nary a ripple in the bloody water,
it was nowhere to be found. Gone down the bathtub drain, then? Back
to Whorfin? Homeward bound to wherever home was? Or something
equally absurd? It was all too much to digest, and he already felt slightly
sickened, poking absently at what he believed to be a scratch on his arm
from the tussle with Whorfin. But the odd mark was more like an entry
wound . . . or a bite . . . from an insect? A spider? *Of all the things to worry
about*, he chided himself . . . and rushed out to do his duty.

XXIX. DR. BANZAI DRAWS BLOOD

> Beware the fury of a patient man.
> —John Dryden

Reader, if I have failed to serve your purpose or you are under the impression that I have teased or led you astray in any way with authorial ruses, please accept my sincere regrets and merely afford me your further indulgence for a few pages more. Ordinarily, at this key juncture I might extol Buckaroo Banzai as the moral center of gravity in our tale—his accustomed role—and a man who decries violent methods despite the hazards of living in the modern world among the criminal kind. Yet when a dangerous threat materializes on one's doorstep, sanctimony up to the eyeballs is of no use; it is a fearsome weapon one wants.

Already I can hear the ethical outcries concerning guns and gun-toting cowboys—indeed I have heard them all and have raised a few myself—yet despite our modern pretensions and thin veneer of civilized society, there exists a sacred bond dating back to the dawn of history between a man and his tool of self-defense. To my mind it is a phenomenon rooted in human nature and hence probably beyond the point of repair. Whether against a charging sabertooth or a band of rampaging marauders, it is force, not reason, that protects a man and his clan. Would that it were otherwise, but until that day when humanity undergoes a complete personality change . . .

Although Buckaroo Banzai is proficient in virtually all types of combat and is known to administer vigilante justice in extreme cases, he is seldom accused (except by his adversaries) of having an itchy trigger finger. The mainstay of his shooting repertoire is the classic Colt six-shooter, of which he owns perhaps a dozen, his favorite among them being a pair of Colt model 1873 single-action revolvers—hardly the weapon of choice for the modern-day merc, albeit one Buckaroo is famous for employing with lethal effect—along with the three-barreled derringer he wears in his boot.

But his twin ivory-handled Colts remained holstered as he emerged from the monk's bathroom to find the diminutive Sister Mary crouching inside her armoire, signaling with urgency and clutching what appeared to be an ancient battle sword.

"This way . . . the tunnel!" she cried out, gesturing for him to follow . . . but too late . . .

. . . as she quickly shuttered herself inside at the same instant Cardinal Baltazar kicked open the apartment door and barged in with his bodyguard Sokol the Joykiller and a dozen blade-wielding crusaders roughly divided between Templars in their white tunics with red crosses and black-garbed Hospitallers emblazoned with the white Maltese.

In the face of this almost incomprehensible flying squad straight out of the Middle Ages, Buckaroo was armed with only his multipurpose Go-Phone and its retractable tools and a four-inch Sebenza switchblade scalpel in his boot. ("Leery of drawing a firearm inside an inhabited building," he would later laugh: a quaint concern indeed, in light of all the mayhem that was to come!)

One against the many, then, and directly in his path stood a sneering Baltazar, who announced, "I have in my hand a *lettre de cachet* for the arrest of Buckaroo Banzai."

This statement was somewhat puzzling inasmuch as his hand held nothing but a bloody bandage.

"Nasty hand," observed Buckaroo. "I'd see a doctor if I were you."

"I am seeing one," replied Baltazar snidely.

"Careful, don't do anything drastic, Baltazar," Buckaroo mentioned matter-of-factly. "I have sovereign rights, diplomatic immunity from the Italian government."

"This is the Vatican, Banzai. My house, my rules."

"How grandiose of you. Says who?"

"Says me. Signed by me."

"And the pope?"

"The pretend pope? Sweet Pickles? Satan's boy?" scoffed the cardinal, whose faithful Pomeranian now leveled his machine pistol at Buckaroo and cautiously edged forward.

"Leash your animal before I neuter him, Cardinal. Tell the drooling ignoramus to keep his distance," Buckaroo warned.

"Or else what?" said the cardinal, stepping close enough to flick a glove under Buckaroo's chin. "The truth is, you'll do nothing, John Wayne proud guy with your cowboy hat and pointy boots, and good American shite talk! Ha, ha, last of the cowboys, defender of sodbusters and señoritas, you're a fossil in the modern world. What does *BB* stand for? Bitch boy? Can't even protect your girl . . ."

When Buckaroo instinctively curled his hands into fists, the overeager Pomeranian squeezed his weapon ever more tightly, saying in a fit of stuttering, "I-I-I c-c-could shoot him in the f-f-face . . . or turn him into a p-p-p-pincushion!"

"No, Admiral Sokol," said the cardinal, fixing his icy gaze on Buckaroo. "I need his surgical know-how to reattach my thumb. And besides putting his nose in my business, he interests me. Don't worry, he won't do anything. I've seen his movies—he never kills anyone until he puts on his killing clothes, his splash suit. These are his stage duds. I doubt his shootin' irons are even real six-guns."

"You don't want to find out," Buckaroo warned but offered no resistance when another of the cardinal's men crept up behind him and took both pistols from his holsters.

"Ha, ha, fill your hand, podner!" the cardinal taunted. "Without his merry band of borderline psychotics, the Hong Kong Cavaliers, he is gentle as a lamb . . . a drugstore cowboy, ha, ha! Nothing but a greenhorn! And a sissy! Buckaroo Banzai is a sissy! Isn't that right, Smartest Man in the World?"

"Go on, Baltazar, enjoy yourself," said Buckaroo calmly, with the slightest hint of bemusement. "I'll correct things in a minute."

"Well, we all need correction," replied Baltazar. "I pray for correction every day, so perhaps we can help one another. We are both servants of our fellow men and both do God's work in so many areas . . . weeding the garden by judging the living, condemning worthless nothings to the trash heap of society. Together, amid magnitudes of bloodshed and with the combined foot soldiers at our disposal—my golden knights of faith and your Cavaliers and Blue Blazes—we, the magnificent twain, could achieve an empire together!"

"Anything different would hardly be fair," Buckaroo said archly.

"Everybody loves a winner, Banzai."

"Then maybe you should go sit down somewhere, Baltazar. Satan the Lutheran is laughing at you and your medieval reenactors because you have eaten the apple full of bullshit to feed your own ego. Don't forget there's one big difference between us: one of us is a sociopath and an embarrassment to Bosnia . . . lacking in every decent attribute, a clown-ass little man hell bent on selling out the whole human race."

"Napoleon was also on the short side. Deal with it, Banzai, and say hello to a real hero," the cardinal retorted, assuming the fourth ballet position and spitting in contempt. "See, I know your tricks. You're confusing humor with sarcasm, so you may as well know I'm suing you for theft of intellectual property and deformation [sic] of character. I'll take your belt buckle and secret derringer, too."

"In your fairy tale. You and whose army?" Buckaroo replied, but still offered no resistance as the cardinal's men pinned his arms and unfastened his shiny belt buckle and the double-barreled derringer pistol behind it.

Far from troubled by the question, the cardinal smiled and proclaimed rhapsodically without taking a breath, "*My* army, the most powerful army the world has ever seen, *pro Deo* and the Holy Roman Empire, the prophesied one hundred forty-four thousand elect who will defeat Gog and Magog on the Plain of Megiddo. 'He will take your sons and make them serve with his chariots and horses, and they will run in front of his chariots. Some he will assign to be commanders of thousands and commanders of fifties': my Templars and Knights of Saint John, supported by the Germanic tribes and a secret uprising of the Salvation Army, who at this very moment are raiding the cache of biological weapons stored at Fort Detrick, Maryland—enough to kill the world several times over and bring sores upon the crotches of sodomites and women on birth control, who prowl the night in shorts, inflamed with carnal lust . . . all of them to be made into footstools for their shameless acts in a fallen world which I have been anointed to shepherd through seven years of terrible tribulation and throw into the fire all who are not well fortified in the faith, all who do not say grace and amen, all who do not have at least three months of freeze-dried food and fifty gallons of unfluoridated, alkaline water."

"Congratulations, quite a feather in your cap," retorted Buckaroo. "Just goes to show, nothing is impossible, even if the voices in your head have led you to the gates of fiery hell."

"The concentrated fire of my genius, limited only by my demented mind," the cardinal returned.

"Who loves to sing of it," parried Buckaroo. "'And they glory in their shame, with minds set on earthly things.' Or stop me if you've heard this one: 'As a dog returneth to its vomit, a fool returneth to his folly.'"

"So you know scripture . . ."

"I don't know all the trick lingo, Baltazar, but sounds like you've got it all figured out. Must be nice when your evil-genius plan comes together on the big chessboard."

"You are bang on the money, Banzai. Man's ceiling is God's floor, which is a chessboard, and he has given me seven gold ornaments with the power to send a great flood, to smite the sea into seven streams . . . seven rivers of fire upon the heads of the wicked," Baltazar continued with glazed eyes, "to give the planet a good pressure wash until the filth is gone—while we in the bosom of the faithful, blessed sevenfold, will be safe in treehouses on the isle of Pátmos and soon cozy as kittens in the space ark with the angels."

"The space ark? You mean Jarvis?"

"I mean the archangel Raphael, one of the seven archangels. Both his name and his pseudonym Jarvis are ruled by the number seven. You can—"

"Right, I can do the numerological calculation in my head," Buckaroo interrupted, glancing at Sokol the Joykiller, who was creeping around behind him. "If I were in your sandal boots, maybe I'd check into flotation devices, because this is too big for you, Baltazar. I can tell you're on the verge of a breakdown, most likely from handling Lectroid medical waste."

"Shut up, Banzai," Baltazar said sharply and whistle farted. "Just a bad case of gas."

"And about to get a lot worse. Tell me, does your angel Jarvis up in the mother ship know about your Red alien friends down in the catacombs?"

"You mean my pieces of meat? Those shallow assholes? I ran up a pretty tab trying to mold them into fighters, but they're children. All they want is candy . . ."

"And all you want is to rule the world. You're a nasty piece yourself," said Buckaroo.

"I can't help the way I am, no matter how hard I try," said Baltazar airily, twirling his tongue, as he was wont to do when thinking hard upon a matter; and before he could amuse himself further, the bathroom door rattled spookily as if someone were trying to open it from the other side, and what appeared to be soap bubbles began to ooze through the crack of daylight at the bottom.

"Someone is taking a bath? Who's in there?" the cardinal demanded. "The fool abbot, by any chance?"

"Not the fool abbot. But I wouldn't go in there," replied Buckaroo.

"Why?" the cardinal said, sniffing. "Because it stinks in here, you pig?"

"You could say that. It's full of psych energy . . . a demonic possession. I got a little on my boot, as a matter of fact," Buckaroo told him.

"Strip him," said the cardinal to Sokol. "See what else he's hiding."

Buckaroo was now grabbed from behind by Sokol, whose hands went to Buckaroo's fancy cowboy shirt and began unsnapping his mother-of-pearl buttons. At the same time Cardinal Baltazar took tentative steps toward the bathroom door that by now was seen straining against its hinges, emitting dazzling light and an ethereal high-pitched drone that sounded for all the world like a choir of prepubescent angels . . . punctuated by a ghostly, pompous voice speaking with an unidentifiable accent.

"Let me out, for it is I, the divine instrument! Open the door!"

This was immediately followed by, "Have heard of Moses, no? For it is I!"

"He's here! Moses, holy Moses . . . ?" muttered the cardinal excitedly, reaching to open the bulging door, behind which he no doubt expected to find the great patriarch and a face-to-face meeting he had anticipated since boyhood. But this was not to be, as events now spun out of control quickly and with tragic, bloody results in the tight quarters of the tiny apartment. As Sokol finished unbuttoning Buckaroo's shirt and tried to tear it away from his body, he experienced wild terror.

"He's wearing his splash suit!" he exclaimed in a panic, pointing to a rubberized blood-spattered bib now visible beneath Buckaroo's shirt.

"Just like in my dream," Buckaroo marveled to himself.

"Grab him, centurions! Bring it!" ordered Baltazar, judiciously disappearing into the bathroom before the door slammed shut behind him with thunderous force, followed almost immediately by tormented animal noises and the cardinal's own bloodcurdling screams . . .

. : . as Sokol and the knife-wielding Templars made their move against Buckaroo, setting in motion a chain of events I will attempt to lay out clearly and without injecting any artificial suspense.

THE SECOND LEVITATION

Like an out-of-body experience, accompanied by what Buckaroo interpreted as an odd vibration in the pineal gland, his sixth chakra, he once more felt himself floating off the floor and empowered to educate his unfortunate attackers. After demonstrating a savage midair spin kick against the first charging Templar, he cried out, "Shattered pelvis!"

Next, he paralyzed another knight with a strike to the throat, spinning him around and following with a jab of two spirit fingers to the spine, yelling out, "Busted clavicle, cracked vertebrae!"

Then hastily extracting the Sebenza surgical switchblade from his boot, he inflicted a well-aimed incision upon the abdomen of a third assailant, who in vain attempted to clutch his wriggling intestines like so many holiday sausages before they came slithering out.

"You're not well, friend. A chink in your armor," Buckaroo told him and dodged the dagger of another . . . slashing the knifeman across the forehead with the same razor-sharp scalpel, causing the man's face to fall away and dangle limply from the effect of gravity.

"I'm messed up! What's wrong?" the faceless fellow wailed in desperation, blinded by his own blood.

"Hang in there. I let this go out into the universe—so be it," Buckaroo asserted and ducked a roundhouse kick from another attacker, whom he handily dispatched by delivering a spinning back fist and a hard right cross, then letting the Templar's momentum do the rest . . .

. . . as a single upward thrust of the surgeon's bloody switchblade sliced chain mail and traveled beneath the third rib and hard sternum directly into his heart. At once the knight gasped, gurgled spasmodically, and collapsed into Buckaroo's arms, gushing blood onto his splash suit.

"Gurney to eternity, my friend. Good luck in sleepyland," Buckaroo dutifully informed him, simultaneously regretting the necessary taking of life and the hot mess of the knight's arterial spray . . . all of the above taking place at the same time Sister Mary Comfort threw open the doors of the armoire and Baltazar's helpless cries filtered out of the bathroom.

"Feed me grapes, priest! Man-dance, humphead! Shake that booty home!"

"Yes, John Whorfin!" ejaculated the cardinal, who now threw open the bathroom door and emerged with the look of a third-degree madman, spewing foam from every orifice and walking blindly into a wall, which he proceeded to punch and pound with his head. On his face was etched the aspect of a man who, having ventured into a bear's cave or an oracle's den, came back so enlightened as to be incomprehensible.

For brief seconds both Buckaroo and Sokol looked on in amazement, as Buckaroo reclaimed his pistols and it became apparent that something uncanny had occurred. Indeed it is unlikely we will ever understand by what mysterious process the *Geist* of Whorfin came to sit on the bully-boy cardinal's shoulder. Yet it was self-evident in the cardinal's bumbling motions that he was no longer alone in the driver's seat; instead he appeared dazed, spittle flecked, and constantly looking over his shoulder, while a voice inside his head rang like a fire alarm: "And there went out another horse that was red. What red horse? Phawk all that introspection! And power was given to him that sat thereon. John Whorfin will ride the red horse! John Whorfin will keep the red horse! Keep me happy, priest! There is Banzai, the serpent!"

It was Baltazar's tongue wagging, and yet it seemed to be joined to an entire race of Red Lectroids, an ancient hive mind that continued to speak despite his wishes . . .

. . . as Buckaroo dove into Sister Mary's armoire, thereby throwing Baltazar and Whorfin into a collective purple rage to match the color of the midnight suns slowly fading outside.

"Blazes! Stop him! Shoot!"

Taking his master at his word, Sokol fired a short and hurried burst of 7.62 x 51 mm NATO rounds at the armoire. It is Buckaroo's belief that there were six shots altogether . . . two triple taps . . . and I have no reason to doubt his word. He heard the sharp reports and also the unmistakable *crack* of the bullets ripping through the ornate wooden armoire. But this was not all he would claim, feeling Old Hag Mother Death wrapping her cold arms around him, poking and probing him here and there, talking seductively in his ear. Any last wishes? Of course the thought occurred to him . . . so many thoughts during this interstice, as if he had hit an air pocket and suddenly dropped into another dimension, soft as a cotton cloud. Was this the way his world would end? Had he already stepped into his coffin? Was he dead already without knowing it?

Perhaps not. Seeing was believing, and Sister Mary Comfort was waving him on, into the crawl space, then into the tunnel, where cool, musty air braced him like a tonic . . . where, still unbound by time, he gripped the cold steel of San Galgano barely ahead of the bullets that now whizzed past, missing them by inches.

"Calling Dr. Pariah," he joked to himself incautiously—recalling his dream—still feeling the effects of having left multiple victims squealing on the floor without medical attention . . . all in a matter of seconds. A senseless situation, but what was the point of having second thoughts after bloody deeds, except to call an ambulance? How many second thoughts could he afford in any case? This was him searching his conscience, his soft side—a man sworn to value and protect life—because his hard side terrified him and was nothing he cared to ponder or know intimately.

"Hurry!" Sister Mary whispered over her shoulder. "They're bound to follow!"

Heedful of the voices behind him, Buckaroo did not need the reminder. But what to do? The clock was ticking, and more of Cardinal Baltazar's so-called army was waiting in the wings to raise ten kinds of hell—not to mention there was the giant alien ship and the end of the world to consider.

BRAVE TOMMY IN THE HELLISH HOLE

Or consider poor Tommy, who already had spent nearly half an hour in Pay Piggie's electrified pounding machine and now was undergoing a double ordeal too terrible to relate. I refer of course to the twin effects of whole milk forced down his throat and whole patches of his skin stripped away by the torturer's homemade sandblaster. Yet all the while Tommy refused to regurgitate or loosen his sphincter. Instead, even with a plastic funnel in his mouth, he warbled, "Yippie yi ooh, yippie yi yay, ghost riders in the sky," before mangling one of our rockabilly originals: "Forgive me, cowgirls, if I'd rather come and go, free as the wind, a wild buck among does . . ."

"Ha, ha, your pain is music to my ears, and vice versa," Pay Piggie taunted him, as he blasted Tommy's back and buttocks with a high-pressurized abrasive that shredded his flesh. "Croon while you can, Perfect Tommy. Everyone has a breaking point. I'll make your shite flow like the Rio Bravo, cowboy!"

"Bury my heart in old El Paso, where I first learned to throw a lasso," Tommy continued to warble, singing for his life like a bluesy Scheherazade, one tune after another, but to what end? Buying time? But how much longer could he continue serenading his tormentor?

"The gloves are off! Gonna give me that thumb?" demanded Pay Piggie.

"I'm leaning into a yes," replied Tommy; but still stalling and still determined to live, he kept on singing. "Trouble ahead, lady in red, take my advice, you'd be better off dead."

"So you're a Dead fan. I'm a Deadhead, too. Hardcore," said his torturer, singing along. "Trouble ahead, trouble behind, you know that notion just crossed my mind . . . Sing me another, Perfect Tommy. Ha, ha, try 'Death by a Thousand Cuts'! Know that one?"

"What a comedy show of failures. I had really hoped this would turn into something good," Tommy whimpered amid repeated waves of nausea.

"How about 'Shoveling Shit's Hard on My Back' . . . ? Sing it! Or I'll break my leg in your ass!" the sadist threatened, landing another high-pressure blast that momentarily took Tommy's breath away. "Maybe I'll have to chop your ears to teach you some respect or neuter you like a cur . . ."

"You think I give two rat turds?" Tommy gasped in agony. "Try switching hands, you sorry sonofabitch . . . looks like you'll get tired before I will!"

"Maybe you prefer the electric boogaloo from Pay Piggie!"

Saying that, he flipped a switch and sent a powerful electric current coursing through Tommy . . . causing him to break into a series of involuntary facial tics and gesticulations.

"Dance, Perfect Tommy!"

"Phawk you, you phawkin' phawk-faced phawk!"

No natural lyricist, Tommy struggled to rhyme lines but nonetheless managed to wail a verse about a man in a halfway house of love who cut himself on divorce papers and bled to death. It was more a rambling vent than a song, but in fact his blood already flowed freely into the filthy gutter, mixing with that of others whose wild cacophony of suffering voices he could hear but not see in the shadowy corners of the underground torture chamber. "Please! . . . Water! . . . In the name of God! . . . Allah the merciful! . . . I confess I am a Jew! . . . A drop of water! . . . *Zitto*, let Tommy sing!"

And despite the heart-rending racket, Tommy continued to give his all with vocals of remarkable power and control, especially considering the circumstances, even when his torturer next slipped Tommy's feet into a pair of black compression stockings.

"What the hell kind of thing," muttered Tommy, who did not have long to wonder before he began to scream and flop like a fish, vainly attempting to extract his feet at all costs.

"Having fun yet, Tommy?" asked Piggie.

"You egg-sucking dog!"

"Brazilian bullet ants, the most painful bite on earth," chortled the torturer. "Hurts bad, does it not? I will make you mine, Tommy. Feel free to crap yourself when the urge strikes."

But Tommy, despite the terrible agony, still resisted succumbing to the Pig's will. Instead, against all odds, he took the following corrective measure: by imagining it was his body double being tortured rather than himself, he found a measure of peace in meditation and in the song "Bridge over Troubled Water," which he now sang repeatedly . . . attempting to ignore the great whooshing noise of the sandblaster that Pay Piggie once again started up.

FIREWORKS

As for the rest of us, our adventures paled in comparison with those of Buckaroo and Tommy; yet we, too, were swept along by the tsunami of history. The unexplained absence of Buckaroo and Tommy from the stage naturally provoked a general disquiet among our audience, an almost palpable sense of impending peril; and this seemed to be confirmed—as we held our breath—by the sudden destruction overhead of a jet fighter, seemingly evaporated by a bolt of lightning.

Against a backdrop of the same wild electrical disturbance, a wanted poster of John Whorfin appeared on the underside of the giant ship, and a now-familiar voice boomed down in a tone more ominous than anything heretofore.

"It's me, the old country boy Archangel Brother Deacon Jarvis, special emissary of Your Real Daddy, the Virgin Empress John Emdall, whose power is great and yet in no ways bloody minded. Whereupon let it be known by all present and by the instrument of her royal staff of authority, and in the name of all her noble earls and ministers, that Her Majesty claims this new world as her own and awaits in good earnest the king of the faith, the Innocent One, and the official handover of the monster John Whorfin!"

Following several minutes of silence, Jarvis continued with growing irritation: "Further, Her Majesty's patience is sorely tried by the gall of men and continued presence of the demon seed John Whorfin. Stop the stonewalling! Unless men pay what they owe, Her Majesty's engine of destruction will fling its thunderbolts and destroy your castle and all your impoverished lands, with your mighty, proud legions stopped in their smoking tracks!"

The great digital head of Jarvis repeated this warning via echo chamber numerous times; and as if this explicit threat were not enough, the voice of Johnny Cash now boomed down from the sky:

And it burns, burns, burns
That ring of fire, that ring of fire . . .

On cue, too, the sky suddenly came alive, lit by exploding orange blossoms that threw sparkling petals high and wide—mirages, I thought, but who could be sure?—while Jarvis, his face clouding, now announced in annoyance, "Get the picture now? They won't be flowers next time! Folks, we're looking for a high-value target with all the bells and whistles. We smell him, but until we find him, you're gonna all be pulled through the needle eye . . . culled by a generational curse, even an extinction event if need be. And so the heathens turn their eyes toward the firmament, asking, where is deliverance? Not in the church house, brothers and sisters, but smack dab in the high honcho, Your Real Daddy and Mother of all Fathers, John Emdall, who ordained the galaxies, named the stars, and placed each planet in its trajectory, who brings the nourishing rains and life-giving sunshine! Can't beat that anywhere! See the others first but see us last and tell 'em the old country preacher sent you! This is Paul Harvey! Good day!"

He then disappeared and the real fireworks began: a lightning storm, followed by a swirling display of dazzling northern lights and star fields, behind which could be seen the radiant outline of a figure in dream form, a shimmering spirit in the sky with arms outstretched and a face hidden behind a supernova. In the midst of this celestial display, a huge digital timer now appeared in the sky, its minutes and seconds counting down toward zero.

And yet toward what end? The end of the world, perhaps, and yet the timing of these things was not yet known.

"No pity! Won't be pretty!" Jarvis announced ominously, suddenly resurfacing. "Watch and learn, kiddos, you simple of Earth! Watch and learn and smell the coffee! Bad credit, no credit, no problem! You won't get a lemon from Toyota of Orange!"

By now, long, ungainly mechanical arms, resembling ghostly insect feelers or octopus tentacles, could be seen protruding from the planetoid: some kind of air sniffers, presumably looking for John Whorfin, although this was only a guess. At least the clown Jarvis had not made it sound as though the alien intruders were threatening to destroy the entire world in a single strike, as we had feared, but where were Buckaroo and Tommy? Minutes earlier, Pecos had received an alert from Mona Peeptoe, who claimed to have seen Buckaroo speeding across Saint Peter's Square on a police motorcycle—troubling news that made no sense, but we felt compelled to credit the report from one of the best newshounds in the business.

With our emotions thus running unrestrained, I nonetheless shivered from what felt like a blast of superheated air and stepped to the microphone to announce our last song of the evening.

"*Viva Roma! Viva romani! Viva la dolce vita!*" I began, attempting to speak over the dull roar of explosions that increasingly sounded like thundering hoofbeats, followed by the unthinkable . . .

. . . as in the next instant every face in the Coliseum looked skyward and to the east, to behold a giant nuclear mushroom cloud (its distance from us impossible to say) from which now erupted the Four Horsemen of the Apocalypse riding the nuclear wind across the sky! At least this was my first impression, for astride a flickering white stallion a holographic Buckaroo bore straight down upon us, flanked by Tommy on a big galloping black, Pecos on a bright-red chestnut, and your present narrator on the pale horse of Death!

"Get kaput, you *bandido*!" Tommy shouted and fired his trademark big-bore Henry rifle at an unseen outlaw.

Small comfort that I quickly recognized the images as a film loop from one of our TV westerns—whose psychological effect upon less discerning viewers cannot be overstated. Even to those in our audience who believed, or wished to believe, that the optical phenomena were part of the concert light show, the specter of the atomic blast that still billowed in the air like a gigantic fleur-de-lis could not be dismissed so lightly.

Nevertheless I did my utmost, announcing, "Don't panic—it isn't real! This isn't really happening! It's some kind of slick effect . . . !"

A bolt of lightning from the blue and a deafening crack of thunder cut me short, further spooking the crowd, but I continued, "This'll be our last tune of the night, folks! Please remain calm and join us in the Italian national anthem! Let them hear the roar of mighty Rome, whoever they are!"

While my attempt to maintain a stiff upper lip—amid similar assurances from Pecos and Muscatine Wu—had a certain calming effect on our audience, what were words against the staggering specter of the hallucinatory mushroom cloud and the devil wind that threatened to sweep all before it, carrying away hats and umbrellas and seeming to suck the life out of one and all? Yet I cannot help second-guessing myself, wondering what more I might have done to prevent the crowded stampede for the exits that cost more than a few lives. This feeling of guilt is something I must live with; but the truth is that I myself was filled with fear—not of death or of the "sky daddy" exactly, but of events beyond my ability to reconcile and even comprehend, resulting in a loss of critical coping mechanisms.

Mind control?

Almost certainly there was an element of it that paralyzed all my better instincts. Looking back, I do not doubt that I was telepathically manipulated—in some way joined to the hive mind of the alien visitors— to the point that it required every ounce of my strength even to grip the microphone.

But what drama! Like a volcanic eruption of emotions, tears streaming down our faces, thousands of us shared a single heartbeat, lifting the Italian anthem to the behemoth alien eye in the sky:

Siam pronti alla morte, l'Italia chiamò!

"Ready for death, Italy has called!" Even now, to recall how we strained our throats to drown our own sobs of grief transports me . . . still sends a chill of raw emotion up my spine. Among those sights never to be forgotten was Muscatine's robot, Abysmo, standing in the wings and singing in perfect Italian—a moment frozen in time for me . . .

. . . until we were unable to hear ourselves, drowned out by the moaning wind and the rising din of emergency sirens and car alarms across the city . . .

EVENTS ELSEWHERE . . . TOMMY'S RESCUE

Only a few kilometers distant, a self-propelled antiaircraft platform of Russian manufacture—a surplus Bulgarian Zenitnaya Samokhodnaya Ustanovka 23-4, to be exact, but better known as a "Shilka" system— rolled out of a nondescript warehouse on Via Gregorio VII and, disguised as a taco truck with billboards of rolled homogenous armor, lumbered toward Vatican City. Besides its normal complement of 23 mm autocannons and a triad of Buk antiaircraft missiles, it carried two Japanese Type 11 Nambu machine guns and a 29 mm spigot mortar, all of World War II vintage, and an improvised Roman-style trebuchet for extra firepower. Along for the ride were an uncertain number of Knights Templar fusiliers sporting camouflage tunics and the jaunty confidence of soldiers everywhere on the eve of war; and while the weapons and the carriage itself may have been military surplus—the Shilka's interior was practically held together with silicone gunk, electrical friction tape, Velcro, and bungee cords—its armaments and moving parts were entirely functional. Certainly its autocannons worked well enough to blast holes in a pair of police cars and various practice targets along the way.

But the story for our purposes remains with Tommy, still singing, however incoherently, his mind now a sad shambles: "Oh, Susanna . . . I come from Alabama with a banjo on my knee . . . from sea to shining sea . . ."

In response to these pathetic efforts, his torturer poured more milk down Tommy's gullet and sang his answer. "Never gonna let you go . . . gonna hold you in my arms forever . . . !"

And despite unwavering pain and stomach cramping, Tommy squeezed out his own lyrics: "Jimmy crack corn but I ain't bent . . ."

At last out of hope and out of prospects, out of the corner of his rheumy eyes he now glimpsed Pay Piggie preparing an "advanced pharmaceutical" in a medical syringe.

"Now the Kool-Aid," he pronounced almost gleefully. "All this goodness in a hot needle."

"You stinking bastard," growled Tommy through tears of hate.

"Red Devil lye, mate . . . worse than milk, tends to burn a bit. Cheers," replied the Pig, preparing to stick Tommy with the needle when a sudden disturbance in the darkness near the portal—a violent clash of steel, grunts and curses, screams, and bodies falling—caused him to drop the syringe and grab his blowtorch . . . a scenario in which poor Tommy, bound and naked to the world (save the compression socks), was unable to do more than clench his jawline and recite Rimbaud to Jesus and the bare light bulb overhead.

A LAST-MINUTE RESCUE

"*Tu viendras, tu viendras, je t'aime!*" he beseeched, even as Piggie fired up his torch flame and dashed out of view before quickly returning in the macabre form of his decapitated head that rolled across the floor with a final unspoken curse still on his lips . . . to be followed instantly by the appearance of Buckaroo Banzai clutching the bloody sword of San Galgano!

"If he hadn't lost his head, he'd still be alive," Buckaroo said tersely, as he sliced Tommy's bonds with the keen blade amid exuberant shouts of joy from the dank cages.

"*Impossibile . . . per i santi, è lui! Buckaroo Banzai!*" they called out. "*Canzone . . . a song!*"

"Maybe next time, fellas," announced Buckaroo, who for the moment had more urgent matters to attend to, informing Tommy, "Just because you're butt naked, don't think you're going to weasel out of your responsibilities, despite the fact the world would probably be a lot safer if you stayed home."

"Like hell. I owe you one," said Tommy, eyeing the legendary sword. "The saint's sword . . . ? No wonder I heard you wreaking havoc."

"Here, pagan," Buckaroo affirmed, handing the weapon to Tommy. "No need to thank me, except take off those silly black stockings. Honestly . . ."

Unashamed of his nakedness or his knee-high socks, Tommy said, "Nope, I'm keeping 'em on . . . as a little reminder. Yow! Sonofabitch! They've awakened a sleeping Rottweiler!"

Then, accepting the bloody sword with all due solemnity, he limped over to the vending machines and began whacking them with the hallowed relic.

"Who wants some? Who wants some peanut M&M's? Who wants a Payday bar? How about a soda?" he yelled to the caged wretches, until he had sliced the automated dispensers open and sent candy bars and Coke cans flying in all directions . . . whereupon, to the throaty cheers of the captives, he kicked the hated Piggie's large melon head like a soccer ball and turned his wrath to the cages themselves, attacking steel mesh with such fury that he failed to hear a female voice calling anxiously from the passageway.

"Someone's coming, Buckaroo . . . !"

"On our way, Sister!" Buckaroo answered, pausing for a moment to pocket a pair of Coca-Cola cans and signaling Tommy to pull himself together and follow . . .

. . . as Sister Mary Comfort simultaneously stepped into the dim light and shrank back in dismay on seeing the instruments of torture and scene

of mayhem. Yet she did not quickly take her eyes off Tommy, who looked
surprisingly well despite his harrowing ordeal. (And here a small caveat:
I have never known Tommy to read Rimbaud or poetry of any kind,
and his account of the torture session with Piggie is my only source.)

"Perfect Tommy . . . ! How you used to turn my knees to jelly on the
Grand Ole Opry!" she said in a soothing whisper, before her tone quickly
turned stern and combative. "But now we must resist and fight . . . defend
the castle!"

"That's what I've been saying. Defend our domicile, before somebody
brings the house down," Tommy replied with a reproachful look at
Buckaroo, who retrieved Pay Piggie's blowtorch from the floor and
handed it to the nun.

"Know how to use one of those?" Buckaroo asked her.

"If I need to. God will show me the way," she said demurely, studying
the wicked-looking tool with a sense of wonder. "And I in turn will
share it with others."

"Mighty Christian of you. A pleasure to watch you do the Lord's
work," Buckaroo told her, as he led our little trio out to fight the forces
of darkness.

"And my Blue Blaze name shall be Twisted Sister," she announced,
eyes blazing beneath her snow-white wimple.

XXX. THE END OF DAYS

> The Lord is a man of war: the Lord is his name.
> —Exodus 15:3

Let us then set the scene in as few words as possible: the sinking canopy of the metallic sky, a hot, swirling sandstorm that choked the lungs and burned the throat, and a kind of collective madness in the air which even now I am at a loss to describe in a coherent way. While I do not quarrel with those who frame the event as unique in our planet's history—an extraterrestrial enemy at our gates has never happened before—it does not follow that human behavior that evening in Rome and elsewhere was extraordinary. To the contrary, moments of duress have long been known for bringing out both the best and worst of human qualities. Most people behave well in a crisis; some even act nobly—may blessings alight upon them—and a few, with all fear of detection removed, take advantage of the situation to chase the fatted calf and serve themselves only. Thus it ever was, from the shadows of prehistory until the present.

Unlike some authors, I will not linger over lurid details of Romans and others feeling emboldened to pursue their crudest instincts—from pickpocketing and looting to copulating in public, running over one another with their cars and supermarket trolleys laden with everything under the sun. It was an orgy of lawlessness all of us would prefer to forget; and given the fact that the entire fabric of life had been rent

suddenly by raw fear, perhaps individuals even of good upbringing
need not be blamed for their behavior . . . which I mention only to
illustrate the thin veneer of civilization in general and provide the
reader an idea of what we were up against in our efforts. Suffice it to
say signs of the collective breakdown were everywhere, with armed
police pretending to enforce an illusion of order against the human
tide that rolled toward the gates of the ancient palatial city, slowed only
by traffic-clogged streets. To make matters worse, at odd intervals the
opaque ceiling rained down snakes and balls of naphtha as in city sieges
of old. Granted, these were amazing illusions only, but the panic was
real. Who knew if these little stunts might not be followed by a hundred
atomic missiles raining down across the globe? "It's just like the last
days of Pompeii and Herculaneum!" I heard people say more than once
while gazing upward . . . perhaps just long enough to smoke a cigarette
or guzzle whiskey, desperate to understand what was happening or to
ask questions in vain. Where was the Star of Hope? The guiding light?
Where had the twin moons gone? There was talk of a "space ark" from
the emissary Jarvis, but how many humans would gain admittance?
And why had the entire sky disappeared? All brightness had been stolen,
along with the fondest hopes, belief in a stable world and afterlife, and
any thought that things could go back to the status quo after that
evening. In other words it was not merely social continuity and civil
norms—such things as exchanging money for goods and obeying traffic
signals—that had been lost in the last hour, but also profound religious
notions like belief in God.

If there existed a silver lining, it lay in the fact that we Cavaliers
ourselves lifted many spirits—or at least we tried, by passing out coins
and little souvenirs to the children, while in general letting it be known
that we cared about their plight. Further, I believe the sight of us with
our weapons had its own salubrious effect and was doubtless of some
comfort to the man in the street, certainly more so than the various
emergency announcements from the civil authorities that included a plea
for calm from the prime minister: "God bless you" and so on. But the
material reality around us was starkly chaotic, with people of both high
and low station occupying the same space not altogether happily, milling
around and bumping into one another with nowhere to go—the rich
with their jewelry and art pieces, the bourgeoisie with their mattresses

and baby strollers, the poor with their ragged belongings, but all wearing the same uncomprehending, blank expressions, their voices hoarse and strangely muted.

The reader can imagine that amid the carnival-like atmosphere, street debaucheries abounded and need not be described here in explicit detail, other than to say it was a dark time in more ways than one. I personally saw a policeman simultaneously masturbate and beat himself with his own cudgel, while nearby a motorcycle ran over a bundle of clothes that had once been a man. Meanwhile, a pair of rivals stood glaring at one another and making threats over a woman, while a flamboyant streetwalker carried two cats and dragged a birdcage without so much as spilling the ash from her cigarette.

What I am getting at is that human nature remained unchanged even as ordinary life came to a stop. People continued to quarrel but also gave tokens of their feelings for one another: in some cases more than they wished to show because of the fear the world might end at any moment.

Doubtless many others refused to cross their thresholds, simply preferring to retire to their beds and pull the covers over themselves in an effort to forget or be forgotten; and I confess to wanting the same: to crawl into bed with someone, to inhale her sweet fragrance and feel a body next to me one last time, to lose all contact with the world outside.

Yes, absolutely, it was all like a dream . . . a mad party of a farce . . . as slowly, or suddenly, it began to dawn on even the slowest of wits that the whole idea of following the blazing star might be nothing but a cruel cosmic joke—either a form of extortion or a baseless provocation designed simply to amuse a higher power at our expense. Only one thing was clear: someone like a god had come calling, but who and from where? And why?

Yet another reaction—and I confess it was one with which I also wrestled—was one of docility and mute acceptance of a life without purpose from this day forward. And it was through this dispirited, jostling mob that our little band now pushed, having taken a few crucial minutes to retrieve the experimental Bubble Gun and the shoulder-carried Jelly Beam apparatus from the capable hands of our equipment managers, Li'l Daughter and Red Jordan, both of whom were fit to be tied at being left behind under such fraught circumstances.

"Guard the Bubble Gun and Jelly Beam with your life, Reno! Don't do anything I wouldn't do!" Red called.

"I'm sure Buckaroo's got things under control by now. We'll just handle the light work," I said, as our little expeditionary force followed Buckaroo's last-minute instructions and slathered on liberal doses of topical antifungal clotrimazole to our exposed skin, giving us a whitened, ghostly appearance.

Of course none in the crowd could have guessed that what I carried on my back—the Jelly Beam and Bubble Gun—likely had the power to wipe out the entire city . . . although certainly the thought crossed my mind and commingled with fears of the unknown.

Among our party, Muscatine and Jack Tarantulus (who had come at his own insistence) rode upon the back of the mechanical beast Abysmo, while Pecos, Jhonny, Hoppalong, and I brought up the rear, moving toward Vatican City at a snail's pace amid persistent rumors that the whole affair was somehow connected to the fourth secret of Fátima, which the pope had promised to reveal at midnight . . . odd timing said to be proof that the arrival of the spaceship could not be mere coincidence.

"All we can do is hope there is hope," I overheard someone say.

Perhaps there was a glimmer of hope if there existed some biblical text, viz., some helpful prophecy that the world would end not by random chance but by almighty design. Since God's divine wrath had been in the offing for millennia—and whose dread prospect was therefore well known to all—there seemed to be less justification for complaints . . . particularly in view of a promised paradise for the righteous. Or, and I come back to the dreaded dichotomy, was it the opposite case, that the alien ship signaled that there was no Supreme Being at all? In which case it was like watching a heroic figure die . . . the death of a living legend.

"They're laughing, watching us like rats," summarized this attitude; and given the immense size of the thing above us, it was indeed doubtful there could be either refuge or immunity from it. Put more perversely, immunity might be on offer, but no one would qualify. Nor, if all the old dogmas were suddenly only fossilized curiosities, was there salvation in connectedness to a favored group. No, the human herd would be thinned according to a new set of rules or perhaps even no criteria at all. Also heard, among other blasphemies: "Liar! Cheater Jesus! You have some nerve! Now the truth has come out!"

But my immediate concern at this point was not for the future of the planet, but that something might happen to the revolutionary directed-energy weapon in the unfolding chaos. Although I had programmed the Jelly Beam's biometric safeguards to allow only myself to operate it, I felt an undeniable paranoia as I absurdly pushed the multimillion-dollar weapon along in a wobbly shopping trolley behind Abysmo, who attempted to clear us a path through a combination of brusqueness and politeness.

"Keep moving! You, size of Tyrrhenian Ocean, looking for Sea of Troubles? Do you not see what I am? Oh, you are blind. I am automaton Abysmo. So sorry, my bad."

In sum, who knew anything? What single belief, what maxim, what "scientific fact" could be relied upon? To say the least, it was a fluid situation, and yet . . . in light of this singularity when all was open to doubt, including religious faith, there was also a renewed interest in old-time prayer, meaning the Latin. Particularly among those of us headed for *campo santo*, I heard some kind of Latin, educated or vulgate, on nearly every tongue.

LIVE FROM SAINT PETER'S SQUARE

Mona Peeptoe was already in situ at the Vatican, broadcasting live via her Go-Phone and a satellite link to a terrified audience in the United Kingdom, a country where the lights still shone through the darkness.

"I'm informed that Rome has gone dark—so lots of accidents, drive carefully—but the lights still burn late in the Apostolic Palace behind me. Make of that what you will. The question is whether anyone is home. Never have I seen such a cockamamie sight! This is crazy! A Mexican-food catering truck armed with machine guns and rockets and a crazy slingshot has just pulled into the square! Must have taken a wrong turn from Tijuana! Oh my, this is bigtime . . . either the greatest scam I have ever seen or the biggest event in human history. To give you some idea, there are actually two anomalies—the fake sky, which, we are told, extends over much of Europe and perhaps all the way to Russia, and the situation here in Saint Peter's Square, which is beginning to fill up with spectators, many with candles and flowers, despite efforts to keep them out by the Swiss Guards and so-called Knights of Malta, marginal losers in black-and-white tunics, who I am told are Cardinal in Chief Baltazar's private militia . . ."

As she slowly panned the spacious square with her Go-Phone, the Bulgarian light tank / food truck known in *Jane's Defence Review* as a Shilka pulled into the plaza, trailed by several cars full of Christian warriors in chain mail and crusader tunics of different designs and hues. These newcomers at once assembled in a makeshift marching formation and passed in review beneath the pope's traditional balcony, where a shirtless Sokol now appeared and raised a cigarette to salute their commanding officer and torchbearers.

"Archers! My English la-la-lads, sons of the w-w-war bow! R-r-raise high your arrows of ash and the sacred flame!" he exhorted them. "Let the w-w-weak know we are strong!"

"We march on, until victory is won!" the torchbearers shouted back.

With a fresh memory of her earlier violent run-in with Sokol, Mona momentarily took cover behind a television satellite truck, continuing the eyewitness reporting that later would win her a prestigious Peabody Award.

"I recognize this man. His name is Sokol . . . the Joykiller, they call him, and you can see why. He is a tweaked-out pile of you-know-what who ought to be strung up and shot. Good gravy, I don't know whether to laugh or cry . . ."

Here she seemed to laugh and cry equally, falling into a coughing fit but pressing on: ". . . but I will try to do it dispassionately, since my voice is a little shaky from too much wine at dinner and antibiotics . . ."

As she correctly assumed, not only was it the greatest story she had ever covered; it was quite likely the greatest story in the history of broadcast journalism. And she was the one telling it to millions, even billions, including a highly agitated North American audience whose regular programming of game shows and professional sports had now been interrupted to feature her report.

"The mood here, among those few tourists camped out, is one of running scared, just trying to get the lay of the land and waiting for the other shoe to drop. That goes for the clergy as well . . . one of whom, a visiting diocesan priest from New Jersey, just said to me that he believes the fourth secret of Fátima is that everyone who is not 'rhapsodied'—his word—will have to receive demonic DNA in the form of a microchip, signaling the Mark of the Beast and the beginning of the Great Tribulation. Of course the trick in this scenario is to be one of the rhapsodied ones [sic], to be uplifted to the mystery ship . . . which, according to my priest friend, could start happening at any moment. 'Pray for the Rhapsody. Repent! Pray Saint Jude's novena before it's too late—but it's already too late! Oh, sing with me!' he kept reiterating. Meanwhile I'm seeing the arrival of a number of red-robed cardinals, who appear to be finding themselves locked out of Saint Peter's and the Apostolic Palace and have begun milling about the plaza, looking as confused and frightened as the rest of us, as the questions keep coming and we wait and understand how rats in a laboratory maze must feel. Except for the hum of generators from television trucks and the intimidating army vehicle that has positioned itself strategically in front of the basilica, the place is unnaturally quiet and in lockdown mode, under extraordinary security from these lowlife paramilitaries whom I've been describing, who I hear have been cracking the heads of tourists trying to enter the square.

"In the meantime, it's been fifteen minutes since our taskmaster, the so-called country boy, Archangel Brother Deacon Jarvis, has taken our emotions on another goofy roller coaster ride with his scare tactics . . . alternately reviving our hope of salvation with talk of the True Light and putting his thumb in our eye by threatening to destroy the world if we don't turn over their favorite alien, the one called Red John Whorfin.

"But how will we even do that? Assuming Buckaroo Banzai or someone else has caught the so-called Red Whorfin and offers to give him up, without due process or human rights, will the space visitors drop down a little arm with a claw to fetch him? Will that make them happy? Will they then be appeased, or will they land and make a smorgasbord of further demands, like material goods for themselves, or command us to become their slaves? And will we obey like dancing puppets and crack addicts, or resist with every fiber of our being, even if it means blood in the streets? But surely that all depends on what they are—murdering maniacs, psychotic parasites, monstrous leeches, or angels with wings— and it probably depends on what we are as well, whether we are part of their preferred population or among the doomed.

"This is not some lying media hook, folks. Have they come to fix us or phawk us? Pardon my French to any young ones watching, but the decision seems to be out of our hands . . . in any case, a show not to be missed. I would like to put these transcendent questions to Dr. Buckaroo Banzai . . . as it occurs to me he is somewhere nearby, perhaps in that very building with the pope, who has yet to appear on that balcony illuminated by television lights powered by thirty-thousand-watt diesel generators. I think Buckaroo would say something to the effect that nothing is beyond the power of a proactive citizenry; but for now we're alone, so utterly alone . . . oh, ohhh . . . there goes another helicopter, down in flames! What a waste! Or is it simply a trick to distract us from a more elaborate hoax? What a terrible dichotomy . . . a massive power play in either case.

"An Associated Press reporter just asked me how to spell *apocalypse*. Things do seem to be spinning out of control . . . but spinning toward what? A dog toilet of radioactive ash? I've never sensed such evil in my lifetime, so if I start to cry or have a temper tantrum, forgive me, but I have no intention of shutting this down. I'm pretty sure this is my last gig, folks, but nothing will stop me from keeping you updated on this turn of events that is literally beyond all comparison . . . beyond all comprehension . . . and whoa! What was that? It sounded like the last trumpet!"

Automatically, she lifted her eyes, thinking the majestic trumpet had sounded from the big shrine in the sky . . . so loud and glorious was its sonic blast; but no sooner had the sparrows and pigeons around her taken flight than she realized the true source of the musical salvo: a trio of trumpeters in medieval garb, standing near the Shilka and heralding the improbable arrival of what was in fact a pizza delivery.

"Wow, give this guy a prize. Pizza driver of the year," she joked on air, albeit with a portentous edge in her voice, now observing a small cadre of foot soldiers and various swordsmen on horseback—resplendent in Templar tunics and shining armor with crepe paper streamers— surround the delivery van, forcing it to a stop in the center of the square.

"Not sure the meaning of this and not sure I like it. Maybe the taco dudes don't appreciate Pizza Guy horning in on their territory. They seem loaded for bear," she told her viewers, feeling tempted to look away; but it was her job, after all . . . so she watched as the knights jerked the driver from behind the wheel and plundered his cargo, sticking their swords through his dozen or so pizza boxes and carrying them away like so much booty.

"Dance, *carogna!*" they warned him.

"Gee, thanks for the pizza and peace be with you! We are all earthlings! Get over it! Of all the perverse things," she lamented between gasps of disbelief, watching as the swordsmen stuffed themselves and commanded the pizza driver to dance. "That poor, frightened man only trying to go about his business to earn his daily bread, attacked by street thugs out to undermine the public trust . . . with the world meanwhile on the threshold of . . . unless I'm mistaken . . . and we're starting to see it now . . . not to sugarcoat this: the implementation of fascism."

Her stark warning to the world was in large part due to Sokol the Joykiller's continued presence on the pope's balcony, beneath which several of the same pizza robbers now rode their mounts or goose-marched in review, executing a smart little hop every fifth step while chanting, "Sevastopol! Constantinople! Schleswig-Holstein! Our faith is our shield! On to Jerusalem!"

"*Deus vult!*" Sokol called back, returning their salute in his best Il Duce imitation and stuttering his way through some tangled Latin and Italian without a microphone, so that his meaning was entirely mystical. A moment later, one of the horsemen tossed him a pizza like a Frisbee, and Sokol ducked back inside, setting the stage for the real drama to come.

"At least speak intelligible Italian or English," Mona groused, sensing the presence of other things in the dark, not merely armed men but beasts, even demons, lurking in the shadows, as the thought now occurred to her that all of this was like a Passion play, and the pizza man was Jesus awaiting his fate. Above her, the great digital clock had ticked down to zero, and now the unthinkable occurred: a fiery stela resembling an Egyptian obelisk fell from the colossal artificial world above and crushed the pizza van on impact, causing Mona to jump nearly out of her skin and pinch her cheek in disbelief!

"My God!" she said, her voice quaking. "What just happened? What is that thing that fell out of the sky? It looks like a flaming sword, or an angry candlestick! What is happening?!"

"Welcome to *The Dating Game*! Love that crunchy goodness!" came the only response, however cryptic, from Archangel Brother Deacon Jarvis, who proceeded, "I hate to smear folks, even a race of pig monkey sinners, but when Your Real Daddy says move, you gotta move! We will now accept the captive John Whorfin and the notarized deed to Planet Earth from your surrender emissary and king of the past, the trollish lackey pope. On behalf of your new empress John Emdall Thunderpump, I accept total victory."

But no such emissary, indeed no one at all, appeared anywhere in sight.

An awkward silence and utter stillness followed, as spectators—mostly tourists, beggars, and prostitutes—alternated their gazes between the sky and the mysterious stela . . . until someone, most likely the priest from New Jersey, proclaimed, "Don't be fooled—he's no messenger from God! He stinks to high heaven! We are all emissaries, representing future generations, and we will be held accountable by history! Jarvis is a con artist, a mouthpiece for the antihumans, alien mutants seeking total privatization of our natural resources and public infrastructure! First Vatican City, and then the whole world! Pray for our laws and human decency, but on our feet! Better to live on our feet than—"

Just at that instant, however, a lightning bolt flashed from the glowing stela and obliterated the speaker and several others, of whom nothing remained except an inky stain . . . in response to which the only sign of protest was our open mouths.

"Wake up, be warned!" proclaimed Jarvis. "If you don't like it, tell the pope! Ha, ha!! The mighty Roman Empire cannot stand against the Star of Hope, Your Real Daddy and Mother of Wonder! For true humanity and a better tomorrow, things gonna get hot by divine direction . . . I'll pop your brains like popcorn! There ain't a chap as can outfight me! You hear me, Crown Prince Baltazar?"

But there was no sign of Baltazar or Pope Innocent or Buckaroo Banzai; and the fake evangelist was losing patience at being unable to find any human beings in high positions.

"*Roma delenda est*, bitches!" he warned, for starters. "Who's running the show? Where is Buckaroo Banzai? What is President Lincoln's location? Think I'm pranking? It's goodbye time."

THE BURNING SOFA

The night before departing with his armada for Rome, Hanoi Xan slept next to Penny, something he had never done in the past. Rather, I should say he tried to sleep but found it almost impossible since he was wrapped in plastic. Around three in the morning, Penny—who had fought sleep because she did not trust him—had fallen to dozing and dreaming of an unknown figure on horseback, a rider whose face lay hidden in shadow, whereupon the big horse rose on its hind legs and neighed at the same instant she sniffed the pungent combination of Moroccan hashish and burning animal hide and observed what appeared to be Xan's free-floating face on the horsehair sofa, now obscured by smoke.

"Help me, Mama! I can't breathe!" he managed to wheeze in a panic . . . bringing a pair of bodyguards, along with Satrap, who fetched a pry bar and at once began trying to rescue his master.

Despite the flurry of activity before her very eyes, because Xan's head seemed to be unattached to a body, she still believed herself to be dreaming; and in this we are reminded of Procopius's famous account of the emperor Justinian (identified by Carlyle as the dark lord Xan, though A. H. M. Jones disputes this), who "suddenly rose from his throne and walked about, and indeed he was never wont to remain sitting for long, and immediately Justinian's head vanished, while the rest of his body seemed to ebb and flow; whereat the beholder stood aghast and fearful, wondering if his eyes were deceiving him."

This was in fact something like the present case, as Penny scrambled out of bed and approached Xan's talking head—a lumpy and lopsided affair with festering polyps and various tics and twitches doubtless caused by the small army of bedbugs running roughshod over it—only slowly realizing that his head was still attached to the rest of him, which appeared to be woven somehow into the sofa; and she could swear the color of his eyes had lately changed to a darker, fathomless black. Even more disconcerting, his ever-present toupee had slipped, revealing sections of exposed brain through three syphilitic holes in his skull.

"Yes, yes, the pest. It was almost my exit. He fumbled me and I was smart enough to get away, to hide here in the cushions," he kept repeating to Satrap, who sprayed his master's face sparingly with a can of something that smelled like insecticide and at last prized him free by ripping the upholstery with the chisel bar.

"The Admin grabbed you?" Penny was curious to know. "Or the Selector?"

"Yes, the Mongol worm in the weeds," he explained, still catching his breath. "I had sat down to smoke and watch the football results on the telly. Right away I noticed that something was just a little off. My *Malleus Maleficarum* was there on the table when a beam of light shot from it and fell on me . . . a light, or a haze, something that made me drowsy and seemed to wrap me in plastic, rendering me immobile. Then I proceeded to have the strangest dream."

Xan licked insecticide off his lips, coughed, and continued: "I was watching a picture I produced with my old compatriot Léonide Moguy and Ava Gardner, and must have fallen asleep, so that in my second dream, within the first, the screen came closer and closer until I disappeared through it into darkness, like a dissolve, and found myself in an unexplored cave, going forward like a spelunker and wondering where the hell I was. Along one wall I saw a hideous red blob, like a tumor, and realized at once that I was inside my own rectum."

"At least you were safe there," remarked Satrap.

"Hardly," replied Xan. "The tumor turned into the Death Wyrm and I nearly fell into its clutches. Instead I ran and ran and soon emerged into a beautiful field of bluebonnets bathed in lovely light, and I experienced a sudden, childlike joy. I even turned a somersault. What do you think it means?"

Satrap demurred, and Xan looked at Penny, who said, "Whackadoodle . . . you should ask Hippolyte."

Xan nodded, saying thoughtfully, "I must ask Hippolyte. When I awoke, my buttocks were still wrapped in plastic and stuck to the settee, so that I was unable to get up. The horsehide would not release me, and then the cushions began to fold in on me and weigh me down under their heavy load. Sinking and sinking, my arms became pinned and my legs useless. Then the horsehide began to melt and biting crawlies practically covered my face. Only centimeters from the edge of the void, and I was groping."

"You fell asleep smoking and had a dream, that is all," she told him and could not hold back a certain look of satisfaction.

"And the horsehair sectional set?" he asked.

"Ruined, all ruined, by smoke and bedbugs," Satrap informed him.

"I've had it for a hundred years. The Kaiser himself gave it to me," he said ruefully—an absurd statement; and yet it was strange he had no injuries, no burns to speak of.

Only minutes later Satrap found his pipe in the still-smoldering sofa and picked it up by his fingertips without wanting to look at it, as if it were something loathsome, and not without reason . . .

. . . as an eddy of hashish smoke now emerged from the pipe's briarwood bowl and, attaining the shape of a worm in the Ba Gua mirror on the wall, darted out the window above the saltwater fish tank, leaving the curtains aflutter in its wake.

"That shit-burrowing Wyrm, he's just up from his hellhole on business," Xan muttered to himself. "But that is his technique to catch me napping, and I nearly swallowed him . . ."

So it was the worm, she decided—and the weight of her tormentor's guilt—that had pressed him so deeply into the cushions; but this was to assume, perhaps wrongly, that he had a conscience, something he had never demonstrated around her.

"I have to leave on business," he said, understandably irritable and seeming to be in the throes of depression as Satrap gently washed his face. "But I've left word for you to be taken care of, in the event of my . . . absence."

"You're not coming back . . . ?"

"Don't appear so disappointed, Princess," he said through a tight smile that showed his animal false teeth. "I know you wish me dead, although we are not so worthless to one another as you may think. I am a man in my dotage and have mentally deteriorated to the point that things may be winding down for me. Even I cannot skirt the law forever . . . not that I am frightened of death, but of the ninety-five percent of the universe that is unknown and open ended. My only hope is to be enclosed in a circle of love when I fall in the ring and the mules drag me away."

No, it was the opposite, she said, telling him how she often worried what would happen to her on that inevitable day when she failed to suit his fancy, and again he promised that she would be taken care of . . . whatever that meant.

"It's been a dangerous year," he added. "People have tried to walk over me, and it is not in my nature to turn the other cheek."

She shook her head but was not really arguing, saying, "I wish I could go away forever . . . nothing else. That's all I ask."

"That would be your loss, but someday, perhaps even soon, you'll have your wish. You can be happy as you please with Old Larry, who will put a fire under your ass," he replied, though it was not at all clear what he meant by this statement.

"O'Leary?" she asked. "Who is this person?"

"A once-good, good-looking shade," he told her. "He'll take you to live in his spiderweb until we meet again."

"What is the rush?" she said, beginning to feel nervous.

"Always best to be prepared when you're my age," he replied. "You've seen what happens when you're not looking. One never knows when the Selector may send his Wyrm."

Considering the supernatural spectacle she had just witnessed—the burning sofa—she didn't like the way he sounded. While it was her fervent fantasy to strike back at him when the moment came and thereby strip away the power he held over her, she worried that if he suddenly disappeared, she might be given or sold to some random goon of the less educated and cruder sorts who worked for him. In other words, despite her terrible abuse at his hands, it occurred to her that if he were blown off the face of the earth, perhaps she would do well to throw herself onto his flaming pyre, like he said his wives in India had done.

"You should put on something. Aren't you cold?" she told him with some genuine feeling and attempted to drape a shawl over his nightdress . . . an act of concern he angrily flicked away.

"You should ask yourself that question," he replied indignantly. "Do not think I am fooled by your seasonal cycles or pleased by your dead-fish imitation and our recent lack of fizz together. I hope this trend will not continue?"

A moment later Satrap went out and reappeared with his master's dark suit and bulletproof Chesterfield and announced that the car was ready, while Xan put his soft, liver-spotted hands on the folds of her belly. In fact he had the softest hands she had ever known, almost like a baby's. But how many men had touched her? She had no more idea about that than anything else.

"Your breasts droop like sad flowers, your rear is a shambles, and you're getting a potbelly. Too much cheese and butter sauce," he said, either trying to be humorous or simply being unkind, moving now to pinch her hip in a way that caused her pain. "Perhaps you're snacking and reading too much. I'm taking away your refrigerator. You need to be careful because your breasts, along with your dimples, are special points of interest, and you're not the prettiest girl . . . but also not the ugliest. Good looks will fade, and you're lucky I look beyond such things. You should exercise in the gym. Or is it your aim to curl up with a good book instead of a lover, and end up fat and bitter? Or perhaps eat yourself to death?"

She said nothing. What could she say to such silly questions?

He continued, "I've seen you browsing in the library . . . some of the ancient books. Be careful handling them, as they carry negative energy and can be toxic, even to the touch. Did you know they are all that remain from the House of Wisdom in ancient Baghdad . . . ? I paid a pretty penny, I assure you."

She shook her head, having no idea what he meant, but asked, "The rolled ones with the funny writing that smell funny? What are they about?"

"They can be difficult even for me. That is why I give you others, some of Henty's tales. *Under Drake's Flag* . . . ? *With Kitchener in the Soudan* . . . ? How about Og Mandino, whose positive energy might help your self-esteem and teach you how to better sell your ideas? Did you read his books I gave you, seeking nothing in return?"

"Og Mandino," she repeated under her breath, chewing the name like a magic herb. There was a power in those syllables and she felt inexplicably enriched.

"*The Greatest Secret in the World*," he reminded her.

"Og Mandino is the greatest secret in the world?" she said, trying to recall the name from another place and time . . . another library in her old life? So strange . . .

"As convenient an excuse as any . . . a funny name, so you throw a kink into everything?" Xan complained. "The man is in first place with Jesus Christ. Why do you want no part of anything I hand you with every decent intention? A hundred culinary delicacies, even a cookie, even a little trinket? Would it cost you so much to bolster your self-confidence? I don't believe you would quarrel with the results."

"The least movement of my eyes to read and I fall asleep, and you know it's true," she replied.

"Then perhaps circle back to one of your own books . . . *Atlas Shrugged* . . . *The Fountainhead* . . . do you remember writing those?"

She confessed to being in the dark about these as well, when something occurred to her and she pointed to his private bookcase behind locked glass.

"I'd rather read your books," she told him.

"My books?"

"By the one you hate, the Reno Kid."

Taken aback, Xan feigned amusement. "Reno, eh . . . the tingling excitement of his poor simple yarns . . . and not a chance in hell you would like them. I keep them under lock and key for a reason."

Just seeing his face, his head shaking, she knew something had changed inalterably.

"What is the reason?"

"I'm not going to pound the point," he said, reaching into his pocket but failing to withdraw his hand. "I don't think Reno is appropriate for you. He's profane and I doubt he's even a Christian. However, if you would prefer his stupid little stories aimed at youngsters . . ."

Here he took his hand from his pocket, holding something which he now revealed and lay on the night table. "As I'm going away and I see your nervous disorder returning . . . you can have my books, but only if I fall in battle."

"You can trust me," she told him as if swearing a vow, nonetheless eyeing the key to his bookshelves like a morsel to eat.

Perhaps reading her mind, he said, "Now I'm famished and must have a little something before I hit the road with my bravos."

Upon his signal, a pair of shield maidens next entered to wash and dress him, but Xan had first to bid her goodbye and shore her up. This he achieved with a rare bit of honesty and fingers that moved with fairy-like lightness across her face . . . however much his sulphurous exhalations made her wish to turn away.

"I am your jailer and have done you much harm, but remember I did not take your life," he emphasized. "Do you like the taste of me? No, but then you never did, and that is nothing new under the sun. We came from the same soul egg, the same slurry of spit and shite, and just as I pulled you out of your pestilent hole, you did the same, giving back exactly as you received. In other words, all has happened before. What has been will be, even if in a world of another sort. All is repetition. We are damned, Alisa . . . but damned to be together."

Inasmuch as she had heard the message many times, she nodded as expected and replied, "I should say so."

"And if it is happening again, it is only because in the scintillating vibrations of the universe we give tacit consent?"

"Truly this is one of nature's truths."

It was a morbid thing to say, but she had said it; and he looked relieved . . . satisfied. "Together we are shite in bloom. When I return, by God, we should marry . . . once you ditch your cowboy old man."

"My cowboy?"

"Your husband . . . Frank."

Without knowing why, she felt her pulse quicken and heard the words "Og Mandino, Og Mandino" pass her lips.

"Chant it with hope," he said, pinched her cheek, and jumped like a jackrabbit into the arms of the maidens, who carried him away to the wars.

"I'll miss you, Mama," was the last thing she heard until she was back in her room, where the only noises were the clatter of equipment and vehicles down in the yard and the fitful snoring of her new monitor and cleaning lady Sonya, an older shield maiden who sometimes fell asleep in a chair after a prior evening's bacchanal.

PENNY'S EMPTY MEMORY BOOK

Trying to clear her head about her situation never failed to leave her teetering on the brink of a meltdown . . . hanging by a thread to an identity she could remember only slightly. As best she could figure, having lost track of the exact number of days, she had spent seven months in this house and remembered practically nothing of what had come before. Who had she been before she began living this life? She had a feeling she had not had a strong home life, but sadly she had no information to confirm this. Had she lived in comfortable circumstances or been a pauper, living ten girls to a floor, as she did now? When he spoke of having "rebirthed" her through dark magic—sand drawings, precious stones, and crystals—what did he mean? That he had created her from dust? From vapor? But did that mean that she had been vaporized from something solid that had existed before? Did he think she was a child or a moron to believe such stupid things? Although she thought of herself as a spiritual person and seemed to possess fuzzy recollections and odd trivia gleaned from another existence, the notion of their crazy love affairs or entanglements, as he called them, across past lives defied common sense . . . and yet it was a knife twisting in her side all the same.

Sonya, or Caesonia, was a fiftyish Corsican, who, arriving in Paris as a footloose young woman decades earlier, had found work as an au pair for a sex- and organ-trafficking subboss of the World Crime League, a certain "Mr. Noone." Through him she had found employment with the military wing and moved eventually into the private security force of Sir Henry Shannon, the well-known business titan and aristocrat popularized in the British press as the "Coal King of Cornwall."

A frequent visitor to Satrap's vast bin of pharmaceuticals, she spoke freely of her life as a shield maiden, and Penny, starved for human company, welcomed her stories.

"You know, I was once Sir Henry's favorite," the older woman never tired of saying. "I was like you once, before I spiraled into a dark place with my Ho Hos and Ding Dongs."

"You could do worse, I guess," Penny would say. "Maybe it was even for the best . . ."

"I was working in the mailroom then, and as a street scout, but was also called upon for . . . special duties . . . because I was attractive. I got to know several of the big shareholders."

"You're still very pretty."

"Sir Henry would often parade me in front of them, naked, and say, 'Have you ever seen such a body?' That's when they began to call me Sonya."

"Oh . . . ?"

"After Caesonia, beautiful bride of Caligula. I had the goods, all right, and the best smile. I came to Paris to dance in a music hall revue. Did I ever tell you that, Alisa?"

On this particular occasion, the day of Xan's departure for the front, she propped open one eye and stared intently at Penny for what seemed an eternity.

"What is it, Sonya?" Penny finally asked, looking up from her needlecraft.

"You look a lot like her."

"Like Alisa . . . ?"

Sonya shook her head. "Like Penny Priddy . . ."

"Who?"

"Why, Penny Priddy . . . Buckaroo Banzai's girlfriend, except she was a blondie."

"Buckaroo Banzai . . . ?"

"The one and only, whose young wife was killed on their honeymoon to Bhutan. The Jet Car crashed into a mountain—it was only all over the news! How long have you been locked away in here . . . ?"

Word of this tragedy naturally startled Penny, at least what little was left of her that wasn't completely numb and incapable of feeling emotion, though she wondered why it seemed to strike so close to home . . . why it awoke echoes in the back of her brain and caused her to put her guard up. It was as if she were isolated in a specimen jar—the term *bell jar* came to mind, perhaps from something she had read—yet she had no difficulty picturing herself unconscious on a fog-shrouded mountain, its massive silhouette looming above her. But her tormentor Sir Henry, the man of riches, had told her she was married to "Frank," a cowboy.

At the same time the news of Penny's death struck her as something dangerous, even a danger to herself, although why this should be so remained maddeningly dim and just beyond the horizon of her brain power to comprehend.

"Please, for the love of all things, make yourselves known!" she wanted to scream at her rambling memories that remained always behind a gauze veil. At her best moments, they were like bees buzzing in her head around a hive of fuzzy reality . . . while at her worst, excruciating flare-ups of the worst pain ever. When would they all come together on her screen as some sort of life journey instead of a pounding migraine?

How could she remember such things, if they were in fact memories? From school? Books? Had she traveled? Been brought back to life, as he said? Despite intense soul searching—which amounted to little in the enormous and useless region of her traumatized psyche—she could not unlock these secrets. But now Sonya was saying that Buckaroo Banzai was dead, and she was feeling an incalculable sadness, to the point of biting her lip until it bled.

"What? No, you misunderstood. Buckaroo's still okay, Alisa," Sonya clarified. "Penny is the one who died in the crash. At least that's what they say—they never found her body."

Now she was spooked. Later, in the middle of the night, she was standing in front of the bathroom mirror examining her scarred-over wounds when her knees began to buckle. Shuffling back to bed, she tried to feel comfortable in her skin, but felt she had been duped by a man she had never trusted in the first place. Was it possible she was the famous Penny Priddy, Buckaroo Banzai's deceased sweetheart and wife? Was that even an allowable thought? No, that had to be a mistake—her heart was beating, pounding so hard in fact that it seemed about to jump out of her chest when she closed her eyes and watched herself die in a violent, flaming crash. What could be more nonsensical than wondering if she had died already?

And yet she could not deny that on occasion there were gauzy glimpses of something, like scattered pages of an epic tale coming into focus . . . passages of happiness, of holding someone in her sleep, of the coolness of fresh sheets and the smell of a man, of the sun shining on their shoulders and birds somewhere singing, followed by pain and loss; and, in fact, only the other evening she had glimpsed someone in the corner of her eye: a handsome cowboy standing at dusk under a cottonwood tree and gesturing for her to join him in a romp, a kind of lucid hallucination between sleep and wakefulness, bathed in strange light like the glow of a heat lamp that ultimately washed him away. But before he vanished, she felt a gruesome end: screams, her body torn apart, hot blood and a warm embrace pulling her toward a pool of iridescent light deep and wide, a disconsolate man asking her questions and holding her desperately in his arms, his voice suddenly fragmented and warbling: "Penny, don't die on me! Penny! Can you hear me?"

Then, as now, she remembered attempting to wake up, telling herself, "It must be a joke. There's no such place, no such place . . . no such beautiful man!"

"Buckarooooooo . . . be strong, be happy . . . for me," she whispered . . .

. . . as his face now faded, replaced by a stranger's snarling voice. "Buckaroo can't hear you. It's me, O'Leary . . . Louie, Louie . . ."

Now it was singing, or growling, words she couldn't understand, and off she went, feeling herself swept into darkness. Or was she imagining it all? Then the pills and laudanum kicked in and she drifted, trying to think with her head and not her heart; yet the only thought that came to her was a desire that it could all be over, that she could grab the broom she kept in the corner and sweep her life into the dustpan and then fly away through the clouds.

And in the same dream, or perhaps in a different dream but during the same sequence, there appeared to her another vision in which the cowboy kissed her good night at one door, and she gave him a welcome-home kiss at another. And there was more: by carefully shifting two letters in the name *Alisa*, she formed the word *alias*. She could not say why, but in her dream this little revelation gave her cause for hope . . . a reason at least to watch and wait and go on, with the understanding that a monster had put her in this spot, this staged situation in which she found herself governed by him as his property. The only thing he ever told her that she found believable was that her story was a long one. She would have to work to put the pieces together, but she knew her present condition was not her natural one, not who she was. Her story was much more than this and too long to state here.

XXXI. THE DIE IS CAST

> Sweet is war to him who knows it not.
> —Pindar

There is a quotation attributed to Buckaroo Banzai that has become the stuff of lore among his admirers—as I say, attributed and perhaps apocryphal, because I have been unable to find the exact source of the remark, and the modest Buckaroo himself has been of little help. I have the following testimony from Tommy, however, concerning the specific event:

"It was in a country I can't name for diplomatic reasons, because officially we were never even there—so officially what happened in Borneo never happened. We had just had a shootout with some of Xan's boys, several of whom we sent to meet their maker, when a local reporter walked up and asked Buckaroo, in broken English, how he was feeling. I was standing right next to him, wrapping a tourniquet around my flesh wound, when I heard him say, 'I'm fine. I feel bad people had to die.' That's all there was to it, initially."

So there you have it, not exactly from the horse's mouth, but close enough; and what at first glance seems like a simple-enough statement has turned into something of a parlor game with many academics, particularly among practitioners of literary criticism. What did Buckaroo mean by the remark "I feel bad people had to die"? Was he saying he felt bad that lives had been lost? Or did he mean to say that certain "bad people" deserved to die? Since I am unable to come down authoritatively on either side of the question, I leave it to my readers' interpretation; but let us proceed with the present chronicle, especially inasmuch as events were by now coming to a rapid boil.

Guided by Buckaroo's Go-Phone interferometer and EMF detector, our trio of tunnel fighters had detected traces of mustard gas, radioactivity, and signs of unusual electromagnetic contamination—not to mention idiot babbling in the dark—and more than once had reversed course to avoid encounters with unknown bands of armed men and distinctive Lectroid energy fields. Forced to take one too many turns, however, even Sister Mary Comfort had become disoriented, and Tommy meanwhile was growing impatient in his shivering nakedness.

"Maybe we're getting too picky," he kept saying. "Anyone can play hide-and-seek . . . no real challenge in that."

"If it's action you want, Tommy, then we can split up," Buckaroo told him.

"Hell, I don't wanna die alone," Tommy replied with a whimper.

In rapid succession they had sought refuge in a hastily abandoned mess hall and a munitions storage room; and just now, hearing voices approaching, they ducked into a makeshift ossuary featuring a lime pit filled with half-dissolved, half-burnt human and Lectroid remains. I feel no need to describe further the rot of the place or its odor of sulphur and swamp gas, except to recount that they had little choice in the matter (or else would have fled in disgust), and poor Sister Mary Comfort meanwhile drew her habit around her face and intoned scripture . . . doubtless so as not to witness the most disgraceful spectacle that presently unfolded, when a pair of rudimentary, half-formed Lectroids crawled from the foul pit and made clumsy movements toward them.

Virtually faceless but fairly sizzling with electricity, their body language exhibited signs of aggression and blind rage, though there was not really time to take careful stock of their mood or capabilities. Their powers of camouflage were still plainly in evidence, however, as Buckaroo adjudged one of the beasts to be a sprightly elf and the other a rough version of Lady Liberty herself, complete with smeared lipstick and an obscene, leering expression.

What the others saw in their own reality-distortion fields is unknown, but Tommy blurted out, "Nasty stuff! I can't wait to put these guys on the extinct list!" and raised the fabled sword to smite the advancing creatures in their reality-distortion field. Buckaroo at once signaled him otherwise, however, and instead produced a small spray canister, which he shook vigorously and spurted its overflow at the oncoming beasts. In this manner events ran their course: the miserable creatures recoiled in agony from contact with the aerosol discharge and fell at once into a kind of seizure . . . dancing spasmodically and prompting Tommy to educate the unhappy creatures. "No good, my friends—you can't undo the damage. Imagine what the stuff does to a car engine."

He said this as he put one writhing Lectroid out of its misery with a powerful swing of the saint's blade and Sister Mary torched the other with her lethal holy blowtorch and watched the writhing beast slowly melt away.

"Smoke your socks off!" she murmured, averting her eyes from her gruesome handiwork and crossing herself.

"Let's go find your old man," Buckaroo reminded her with a nudge, as the voices from the passageway now dissipated and the trio resumed their journey to the surface.

DISARRAY IN THE PAPAL APARTMENT

But the quest would not be easy, for at that moment no one knew where Innocent was. Even in his private apartments—in fact, there most of all—a certain state of confusion verging on full-blown panic was beginning to take hold. While Sokol the Joykiller stuffed himself with ill-gotten pizza, a crack of thunder exploded seemingly just outside the windows, violently rattling the glass and illuminating the night, while a recon patrol of Templars returned at roughly the same time with the bad news they had failed to locate the head man.

Several of these Sokol punched in the gut and sent on their way once again, as Cardinal Baltazar and half a dozen of the world's foremost insurance executives meanwhile emerged through a pair of gilded double doors. These were not men with a utopian vision but corporate bosses intent on closing a business deal and signing a contract . . . a project at some risk, they must have believed, to judge by their tense and frankly dyspeptic facial expressions. This was above all the case with the cardinal, who carried a golden Styrofoam fasces—a gift from the insurance magnates—in his thumbless hand and a Gucci briefcase in the other. While the firm set of his jaw projected fearlessness and a readiness for any eventuality, on closer inspection he exhibited bulging, hyperthyroidal eyes, inexplicable nervous tics in a face that now assumed puffy proportions, and a swollen tongue withal, to judge by his semigarbled words.

"Any word from the East? Metropolitan Spiro and his hieromonks?"

"Nothing."

"Archimandrite Zalman's auxiliaries?"

"The reinforcements have yet to leave his skete at Pskov," Sokol replied. "The French appear to have put the knee down, as always, and similarly the Macedonian schismatics . . ."

"Bastards. And the Germanic tribes . . . welfare sissies . . . refusing to cross the Alps," he uttered with disgust, although it was not clear whom he was addressing. In fact, he seemed to be engaging in debate with himself, twitching his nose and flicking his tongue from side to side in a kind of smell test . . . simultaneously talking out of both sides of his mouth in a troubling display of psychic turmoil.

Now a gleam—the smile of a mad cat toying with a mouse—came over him, and he shouted in an alien voice that even Sokol failed to recognize at first. "Moving forward! Busting my ass! I sense General Warts!"

As startled as anyone by the bombastic, theatrical persona that had suddenly erupted into the room, the cardinal quickly demanded of the nearest insurance tycoon, "Did you say something?"

"Did you say *genital warts* . . . ?" the executive replied. "Are you unwell, Cardinal?"

When the other executives averted their eyes somewhat uncomfortably, the cardinal began to strangle the upstart fellow before appearing to apply concentrated effort to keep himself under control. Using his natural slurred voice, he demanded, "Any news on Sweet Pickles . . . ?"

The question was put sharply to Sokol, who was busy retrieving a dropped piece of Canadian bacon, and now rose to salute—much to the disgust of the cardinal, who gave him a backhand across the kisser along with a scolding. "You only salute with your hat on!"

This warning was followed by another, delivered in a guttural and bizarre tone of voice. "On our way to genocide! It will not be done for us but by our hand alone! God bless us!"

"We are looking high and low, Your Excellency. We found his hat," replied Sokol, pointing to the pope's white fishtailed miter on a nearby divan.

"Look under the Chair of Peter! He's a mental midget—he could be anywhere, sneaking around in the shadows," the cardinal snapped in a breaking voice. "Do your job and find the traitorest pope! And where is my donkey? Walk military!"

Sokol at once grabbed his machine pistol and a golden knight's casque, complete with plume and visor, and "walked military," albeit with a limp, out of the room, but this hardly improved Baltazar's disposition. I will not get into high-flown matters of his deep unconscious—the tangled, deep-seated schism between his two halves—for I do not feel equipped to address such a complex subject as dissociative identity disorder; and more powerful minds than my own have failed to account for it. More importantly, the cardinal himself could have had no understanding of what was happening to him, but what a show it must have been to watch him pacing under ungodly pressure and seeming about to burst into tears at any moment . . . all of this as the spectacle down in Saint Peter's Square continued to unfold.

"Where is my ride? And why has there been no cybersignal or direct message in the sky?" he fretted, shakily pouring a glass of the pope's Hennessey and beginning to worry that perhaps he had gotten crossed signals on the dating website from the heavenly host; but how could he have gotten things wrong if he lacked clear instructions from Archangel Brother Deacon Jarvis—the pixelated prophet Elijah, as Baltazar still judged him to be—and the Merkabah mother ship?

He lamented that his negotiations with the visitors had not progressed as he would have liked, having heard nothing from the heavenly beings for the past twenty-four hours. Had they sold him empty promises, just as he had sold them a bill of goods? Indeed, he was one to complain, having lied to the angels through his teeth when he promised them John Whorfin, who now turned out to be himself . . . or at least partially himself . . .

. . . so that now, in a situation worthy of the Mad Hatter's tea party, he was not only unable to hold up his end of the deal, but through no fault of his own had given refuge unwittingly to the most wanted fugitive in many a star system. What a tangled web it all was! He now faced the dilemma of whether to attempt to reconnect with Jarvis—Elijah, Michael, or Gabriel, whichever was his true identity—or slink away with his tail between his legs, thereby giving up God's work, even to the point of sabotaging his plan. But that would amount to selling his soul to the forces of darkness, an indignation against almighty God, and he almost could hear the narrow gate of heaven closing against him; and in any case, where could he hide from the Lord? He thought of Adam in the garden, poor Job, the sons of Ornan, and all the tormented others, hiding their faces.

Even in the deepest cave, even wearing the best disguise, he knew there was no escaping from the Lord at the end of the day, or the end of days. Yet at his most lucid, he imagined that the entire affair might be merely a means of testing him, as Jehovah toyed with Abraham and Satan tempted Jesus; and in the case that Whorfin was not Satan or a demon at all, a verse from the Book of Hebrews came to mind: "Do not neglect to show hospitality to strangers, for thereby some have entertained angels unawares."

Or was all of this so much dancing upon the head of a pin, when one considered that the whole chain of events had to be overseen by an omniscient Almighty who got up every morning, already knowing the day's events and so on into eternity? In other words, the Lord had to have known that he would be attacked by the thing called Whorfin (however one defined his black energy); and yet, of all the candidates in the College of Cardinals, the same God had appointed him, Baltazar of Bosnia, to enforce his will on earth due to the cardinal's unbesmirched righteous character.

Armed with this somewhat reassuring thought, he believed he had enough clues to take it on faith that he was still the Anointed One; and he still felt the chemical spark that passed from him to the Lord and vice versa. At the same time he realized that being called as God's good servant meant that he would be attacked by Satan the Lutheran in all his dark forms and forced to mingle with the flesh, including something along the lines of alien experimentation. On a tactical level, this struggle presented him with two conflicting choices: either suppress the evil inside himself or make a clean breast of it and confess his condition to the angelic newcomers. This dilemma only became more difficult, and by a power of ten, when the chemical spark in his head somehow short-circuited and came under the control of the tyrant Whorfin—akin to dialing a wrong number or having a call intercepted by a third party—something that was occurring now, as he directed himself toward the double doors leading out of the apartment and toward the basilica.

With every step, the demon and its horrid out-of-this-world stink in his nostrils filled him with the panic of a cornered animal: a false hope that this couldn't be happening and yet a feeling of physical and mental instability manifested in nausea and wavy vision, a kind of stupor and difficulty in walking . . . his head jerking spasmodically, bobbing like a cork on waves of free-ranging consciousness. From this dream cycle or ecstatic state, there arose nightmarish thoughts and the snake's lies: invitations to Dionysian debauchery, demonic images of irregular sexual congress, public restrooms, and rocket explosions that threatened to override his holy armor and spiritual immune system. Battleground zero was now between his ears, a maelstrom of desire and shame that he desperately prayed would pass.

Still, fortune favored the bold; and even in those dire moments of moral upheaval when he battled the foreign infiltrator and Satan the Lutheran for control of his mind, the faith of a martyr—*mit dem Mut der Verzweiflung*—impelled him forward to his assigned task and even bore him aloft, above the howling wind and storm waves of temptation, enabling him to understand that this onslaught of infernal desires arose not from his own uniquely sinful character but from universal mankind's fallen nature, in which light all his failings were only human and forgiven in advance by the gift of salvation, the miracle of the blood, and therefore cause to give thanks . . . which he gave with his hands clasped, for this day was given unto him.

Rejoicing, then, he directed his mind to cling to the rock of faith against all comers, particularly the panicked executive vice president from Lloyd's of London who seemed to be running amok and addressed him with an air of agitation, bordering on contempt.

"Do you hear the music? Do you know what that is?! Archangel Jarvis is playing 'The Final Countdown' . . . !"

"'The Final Countdown' . . . by Europe?" the cardinal replied with pleasure, hearing now the music filtering down from the rafters. It was perhaps his favorite song by the band known as Europe, and for a shining moment he was one with it and in awe of himself.

"My God, all this terribleness, and for what? Does this mean . . . ?" the insurance executive stammered breathlessly, blinking back tears. "Does this mean that when the song ends, it is the end . . . ?"

"I am blotted to the whole question," replied the cardinal, who felt now the sudden imposition of John Whorfin. "But we must not give in to terror, which only begets more terror. We will fight them from holes, we will fight them in the ditches . . . we will never surrender."

"Are you phawking crazy?" exclaimed the executive. "It means they're tired of waiting for the notarized deed from us, signed in blood by the pope . . . tired of waiting for the pope's special worldwide address you promised us! Your plan! You said—"

"Forget that simpleton. I'll hand over the articles of surrender myself with a special dispensation," Cardinal Baltazar vowed . . .

. . . as Sokol now returned, leading a nervous donkey, and announced, "Here is your ride, master."

On his third awkward attempt, and with two hands from Sokol, the cardinal now climbed atop the gentle ass. Then picking up the pope's pointy hat and placing it upon his own cuspidate head, he exited the apartment with a small entourage, including the man from Lloyd's.

Along his short journey through the palace's corridors, however, the tide of events presently overtook the cardinal and moved toward a certain logical conclusion; and for a moment his brain seemed to experience an out-of-body misfire or ceased to function at all, when a bold voice, hinting at demonic possession, rode a tide of bile from his lower gut, swept upward, and belched, "Lord Whorfin crap on a donkey! Slop donkey spatter shite! Hell gonna pay!"

Yet when Whorfin-in-Baltazar tried to dismount, Sokol simply righted the cardinal on the animal's back, and the procession continued on down the hallway.

THE DJINN OF BATTLE

Cardinal Baltazar had no idea why such words, encapsulated in a large, filmy bubble, had escaped his lips; all he knew was that he had not spoken them. Or if they had come from his lips, he was not the one doing the speaking, just as he was not the one whose left hand now moved involuntarily to prevent his right hand from opening the doors leading out to the famous balcony, the Loggia of Blessings, from which the pope customarily addressed his world audience.

"Emdall hag queen lookin' for Big John Whorfin!" his growling belly cursed subvocally between sharp pangs, as he sniffed the air and peeked through the curtains at the lightning-generating obelisk down in the plaza. "Ha, ha . . . torch for Big John . . . nobody give her florescence what Big John give her . . ."

"Big John . . . Whorfin," repeated the bifurcated Baltazar with a certain familiarity, as if speaking of a special friend, while continuing to sneer at the spewing pillar, reveling in the thought that John Emdall still longed for his charismatic electric field—insofar as Lectroids were capable of such sentiments—but that did not mean he could be certain of her affection, for he no longer had a powerful physique, or even existed in physical form apart from this fester of a cardinal. Yet despite his outward cockiness, he quavered from both fear and excitement to think of confronting once again the dark beauty who had led her mottled race against him, captured him with uncanny treachery (as he viewed the matter), and shot him into the formless hell of the Eighth Dimension.

"Holy mother Devil Bug! Payback laughing slick whore bitch!" announced Whorfin weakly, sounding like a faint speaker rattle.

"Don't blaspheme the Holy Mother," warned his host.

"Hindquarters!"

"What?"

"Hindquarters! Hindquarters soldier love!"

What followed, however, was an interiorized *cri de coeur* with the emotional edge of nails on a chalkboard; and it was perhaps only at that moment, when Baltazar tried to block the demon's thought waves and take back possession of his own brain—his hands still pitted against one another—that he realized the psychic attack in his head was probably not going away and, without divine intervention, he might never be the same.

If all of this is a long-winded way of saying that the two halves were of two minds whether to proceed out to the balcony, I ask the reader to indulge my rambling prose. I simply wish to emphasize the magnitude of the moment and the cardinal's own crisis of doubt, since his original plan had called for Innocent to reveal, *ex cathedra*, the fourth secret and in the process to confer his holy authority upon his handpicked successor, who would hand Whorfin to his enemies as expiation for the sins of the Earth. If for obvious reasons, this ideal scenario now had been thrown into disarray, a terrible judgment upon the wicked was sadly a real likelihood, and untold suffering awaited billions of souls living in darkness, and doubtless even a few innocents.

Do not think he took lightly the assignment and its daunting responsibility, however.

"I can't do this," he thought for an instant, heeding the little buzzing conscience that he kept submerged and hardly ever allowed to speak. "The crushing weight . . . the bloodshed . . . is more than I can handle. On the other hand, self-doubt will not buy even a submarine sandwich."

With this argument he overcame his indecision; and given the present state of emergency with all hell about to break loose, he reckoned that the college of cardinals would have no feasible choice but to march in lockstep and confirm him as *pontifex inquisitor maximus*, or even the first Pope Baltazar. Indeed this line of fanciful thinking gained even greater traction, as the heady confidence of John Whorfin fed his own. In a telling moment he was suddenly the Lectroid lord studying the Catholic cardinal observing the Lectroid hive mind in a never-ending series of reflections, images in a mad carnival funhouse chasing their single tail round and round.

It is frankly no use attempting to describe his state of mind adequately. I have never experienced such an indwelling, viz., a foreign agent passing into my consciousness; but the physical sensation, as recounted by Abbot Costello, is one of crossed neural circuits combined with a kind of feverish euphoria and a leakage into thought bubbles of Lectroid lingo and wild Lectroid ways . . . an alien experience spinning in Baltazar's head and causing a certain shifting in his skull, like a rolling marble or oblong egg with the ability to pass through the brain-body membrane and control the motor system. As if this tortured interior dilemma were not enough, awaiting him outside lay the great unknown, a convoluted existential mess that needed to be cleaned up; but here also was his opportunity to strut upon the international stage, to bestride a world in extremis.

Above all, what was lacking at this tipping point was a leap of faith. "What is happening?" the cardinal asked himself, but who was "himself"? And who was asking the question?

Indeed, it was safe to say he no longer knew himself; and he now began to pray, seeking divine understanding, remediation, and above all, a gatekeeper to filter his thoughts and help him regain his self-control and sense of identity.

But these feelings were as nothing compared to the sounds of gunfire and the cries of men that now reached his ears from the corridor he had traversed only moments earlier. "My poor little ass," was his first thought, but "Banzai!" was his automatic utterance; and suddenly he felt hot and agitated, feeling something like a fiery embrace from his new partner that interrupted his moment of indecision.

"Yes, Banzai!" cried Whorfin in a rare show of unity. "Spineless dog bitch weasel Banzai!"

With a quick gesture to the panicked man from Lloyd's of London, Baltazar shouted, "Don't just stand there! Help me move my hand!"

"Your hand . . . ? What's happening, Cardinal?" said the underwriter.

More gunshots! And louder, meaning closer . . .

"Take my left hand from my right, now!" Baltazar yelled with urgency and in the same breath commanded Whorfin, "Let go of my hand!"

"What?!" said Lloyd's of London, more confused by the second.

"Take my hand and bring my donkey!" Baltazar repeated, having two conversations at once. "Let go, you demon! I'll press charges!"

"Whorfin not your puppet!" shot back his indwelling.

"No, you're a coward!"

"Coward? Take it outside, fart box! Say it my face, butt crack belcher!" said Whorfin.

"What face, lizard?"

"Whippin' you one hand behind my back, fry fart! Cluck, cluck, chicken poop cutter! You'll sing a different tune when—"

"Mumbo jumbo, sew your lips, moron!" answered Baltazar, painfully striking himself in the testicles with his left hand, while his right hand gripped the door handle. But who controlled the left and who controlled the right? Where did one end and the other begin?

"So sassy! Pop you head like egg!" Whorfin fired back from within.

There was much more to their exchange of epithets; but it is important to capture its spirit only, while redacting the more offensive sequences. No one had ever spoken to the cardinal in such a manner—certainly not the pope or even Hanoi Xan. As a result of the tirade, he now realized that he was not talking to a rational being; and against this threatening alien invader, he now summoned reinforcements, invoking the "blessed Virgin Queen"—which was a mistake.

"The whore, you mean?" protested Whorfin . . .

. . . as with a mighty heave-ho from the helpful man from Lloyd's, the cardinal was at last able to wrench free his right hand and use every muscle to push open the double doors and take a step outside, whereupon one side of his body immediately went limp. If it was not a heart attack or a stroke, it was at the very least a violent psychotic episode, complete with dyspepsia and a fragrant stench in his nose that emanated from only God knew where. Searching for relief as he had done for decades, he sought refuge in scripture, reciting, "Blow a horn in Zion! Let all the inhabitants of the land tremble!"

In this effort at least, his fighting morale was bolstered both by God's hortatory message—"Go, Baltazar!"—and a pugnacious Whorfin.

"No dogma me! Hurt feelings? Enough womankind, dipwit—I don't give damned! Fight like a Lectroid, be worthy to die! Today we march to bloody victory or the gated entrance of hell . . . !"

"I'll help you pack," muttered Baltazar.

"We'll go together, Zoran Caiaphas Baltazar, as we mental graft one piece at a time. What's happening? Feelin' you clutching . . ."

"I'm having a heart attack, you fat phawk!" the other returned. "You infected sore in the devil's grip, big zero before the one revealed God."

"No flatter you self! Stop overtalking me!" hissed Whorfin. "Disrespect! I'll deal with you when I get home to Number 10!"

The cardinal's reply was weak . . . so weak it probably would not have registered on a Breathalyzer. And so they emerged onto the balcony as one, two strangers avoiding one another like the plague, straining under their mutual bipolarity.

THE BATTLE OF THE PAPAL APARTMENT

Meanwhile, the violent fracas out in the hallway now spilled into the pope's apartment, with Sokol the Joykiller and several of the bloodied palace guard reeling backward, under savage attack from Buckaroo, Tommy, and Sister Mary Comfort. At the same time, the insurance underwriters fled the chaos en masse, many on all fours, in order to duck Tommy's sword and Buckaroo's deadly six-guns that now traded fire with a pair of Templars, disarming them both and sending them and their comrades scurrying to safety in other rooms . . .

. . . in the process abandoning Sokol, who now whirled to meet his fate, lowering his steel face mask against what might come next: a bullet, a blade, or the blowtorch that Sister Mary Comfort now fired up.

"What do you say now, hard body? You and your big weights?" she asked him provocatively.

"I am cooked," he bleated, creeping one hand to his flank, "but will wear the martyr's crown."

"What do you want, a medal?! Let's tangle ass!" Tommy yelled and at once hastened to make the fight more equal by handing the sword of San Galgano to Sister Mary Comfort.

"I'll play," declared Sokol, who in one motion drew a dagger from beneath his loincloth and adopted a combat stance.

"Your last mistake, karate man! Do your parents have any other children?" Tommy inquired.

"I have an older brother in Pomerania who is a truck driver," the knight replied inside his helmet.

"Pomeranian?" questioned Tommy. "I thought you were Dalmatian."

"No. I am a Pomeranian."

"Good . . . that makes it easier to knock your top off. I didn't start this bull, but let's go until one of us stops kickin'!" said Tommy, who suddenly launched himself across a refectory table and tackled the Pomeranian, tumbling with him over upholstered chairs and priceless objets d'art.

"Need help, pard?" Buckaroo now called from a doorway.

"He tore a hole in my lip and smells like day-old beans, but I'm still whippin' the dog piss outta him!" Tommy shouted back.

"Is that a yes or a no?!" yelled Buckaroo, who by now was already past Tommy and moving into the interior rooms of the apartment . . . whence moments later came sounds of fresh gunfire—Kalashnikovs, answered by thunderous six-guns—and panicked voices:

"Don't shoot, Buckaroo Banzai! We are private contractors! No shoot!"

Sister Mary Comfort meanwhile felt stuck, as if her feet were glued to the floor, watching two practically naked men bear hug one another and roll across the floor, first one on top and then the other, biting and brawling and bellyaching like a pair of truant schoolboys. How playful their grappling seemed, with nothing to indicate that each intended to destroy the life of the other! Seen in slow motion, they might be roughhousing on the playground, tussling and throttling one another over the merest of gripes, but that was before the Pomeranian managed to land a solid kick with his peg leg and thrust with his sharp weapon.

"Tommy! Look out!" she cried in alarm.

"Balls out!" he shouted back, heeding her warning but momentarily losing control of Sokol's knife hand that appeared first as a shadow on the wall and in another instant as glinting steel looking for work, a purpose to fulfill . . . its sharp point directed now toward Tommy's throat . . . when Sister Mary Comfort's acetylene torch suddenly spat fire, evoking screams of agony from both men.

"Sonofabitch!"

"Enough is enough!"

"Damn, learn how to shoot that thing, Mama!"

"Goes double for me!"

Besides scorching Tommy's facial hair and Sokol's knife hand, her action had another unforeseen effect, which was to set ablaze the gilded curtains behind the two men. Other than a momentary panic attack, however, she paid scant attention to the rising flames, which she attacked only with kicks from her sturdy brogans. In inadequate proportions, then, she worried about Tommy and too late looked for something with which to douse the fire.

Tommy also made a lunge for the flaming curtains but found himself otherwise detained by his own vise grip on Sokol's wrist, which forced the Pomeranian to drop the blade and leave himself open to body blows, including Tommy's signature two-handed hammer strike to the solar plexus—something that had never before failed to stop a beating human heart.

"End of lesson. No charge for the schooling," an exhausted Tommy told his conquered foe, whose trembling fingers surreptitiously found his second, secret dagger; and as Tommy tried to scramble to his feet, Sokol jerked him back down hard and simultaneously head-butted him with his iron visor and jabbed him in the gut.

"No charge for the extra hole!" heckled Sokol, who now purposed to plunge the blade again into Tommy's gullet, when Sister Mary—whirling with religious rage—hefted San Galgano's unwieldy sword overhead with all her might and let it drop.

"Here you go, meathammer!" she cried out. "Have a great weekend."

In this manner she did nothing more than was necessary, as the legendary sword did the rest, falling point first and of its own weight, passing directly through the right eyehole of Sokol's visor and impaling his brain. Although her own effort had been minimal—her fingers had merely let go—the fact that it had happened within her line of sight caused her acute anxiety. Worse, Sokol's open left eye could still be seen blinking through the other slit, and his expression appeared less dead than embarrassed . . . altogether awakening in her an uncontrollable flood of tears.

"It's okay—I'll be okay—it's only a bruise, only a concussion," said Tommy woozily, tasting a sudden saltiness but nonetheless struggling to his feet despite the blood pouring out of his mouth and from the fresh orifice in his stomach.

THE POPE, WHO WAS LOST, NOW IS FOUND

And what is to be said of the combat in the other rooms of the apartment? I refer of course to what befell the other Templars whom Buckaroo relentlessly pursued, shooting and reloading as he went. I will not hazard a guess as to intervening events, but ten minutes later much blubbering and wailing streams of consciousness could still be heard, with rivers of bodily fluids distributed over several hundred feet of Persian rugs.

As for the effect of these events on our hero, this was a more difficult question. Indeed, how can anyone answer such a question except the protagonist himself? Had he committed crimes or acted in self-defense?

In the larger picture, was it a confrontation that could have been avoided or a dirty job that had to be done? From the peanut gallery the perspective may be one thing, while those of us actually working through events on the ground may see matters in quite another way; and the physician among us is required to have an even different point of view. Must he forgive and succor all, even victims of his own hand who were still alive and now cried out in pain? One now had a face full of blood freckles and the other, a big man, had been made considerably shorter, practically sliced in half by friendly fire. Should the doctor now go to them, even though he had more urgent work to do and was pressed for time?

No, it was too late in more ways than one. Buckaroo's own head was pounding, not merely from the aftermath of gunplay, but inflamed from the killing. He had often heard the term *blood drunk* but had not experienced such a seasick feeling until now . . . muddle headed with elevated blood pressure and temperature, a racing heart, and above all, a thirst for more of the same. Had his feet really left the floor as he spun around the rooms like a whirling dervish, managing to shoot with deadly accuracy between his own heartbeats? But otherwise how was it possible, except for a trifling flesh wound on his arm—actually the same insect bite or oozing eschar he had noticed in the monk's bathroom—that he had not been hit by any of the dozen shooters arrayed against him?

He could not explain the strange phenomenon any more than he could account for the rising tide of nausea he was now feeling, a heaviness and sickness of the soul akin to the stupefaction of the holiday reveler who cannot pull away from the feast even when he has stuffed himself to the point of gagging. That is to say, his blood lust had not yet been sated. He was left still thirsting for more; and catching an unwanted glimpse of himself in a gilded mirror, he saw a cockeyed smile that held the warrior's reproach to the civilized man . . . the contemptuous leer of one who has glimpsed the unspeakable and perhaps even committed the crime. Blood engorged and yet oxygen deprived, he momentarily gasped achingly for air, reloaded his pistols, and looked about for fresh prey. And it was just at this moment that a desperate Sister Mary appeared in the doorway to announce: "Tommy's hurt, Buckaroo! And there's a fire!"

"On my way," Buckaroo said, already sniffing the smoke and a hint of something sweeter . . . no, not perfume exactly, but the refreshing scent of vintage after-shave lotion.

"Pope Innocent?!" he called out and followed the faint fragrance of Heaven Scent by Aqua Velva mixed with Camel Blacks to a grandfather clock, stepping over bodies as he went.

"Your Eminence . . . ?" he said softly, knocking on the clock's wooden panel.

"Papa . . . ? Are you in your cubbyhole?" the nun called out, quickly answered by a wary voice from inside the compartment.

"Sister . . . my child . . . ?"

"Your Eminence . . . are you all right?" Buckaroo demanded impatiently; but the pope refused to come out.

"I'm completely all right," he said sheepishly and with a thick tongue. "I often come in here to find release when I am too uptight to carry out my mission."

"Oh, Father, carry us thither!" Sister Mary pleaded. "We all need you . . . !"

"There is no sublimer work, but I am unfit at present. My most productive time is after everyone goes to bed. Call me when it's over," the voice came back, asking only to be allowed to pray for the broken world in solitude . . .

. . . prompting his disappointed daughter to whisper to Buckaroo, "Sometimes when he's stressed, he drinks Heaven Scent."

"Blessed is the drunkard," spoke the clock, "for they shall see God twice."

XXXII. THE MOTHER OF ALL BATTLES

> I want no prisoners. I wish you to kill and burn;
> the more you kill and burn the better you will please me.
> —General Jacob Smith

It is a point not to be argued that events were now accelerating toward a climax, as all now know. Barely an instant before Cardinal Baltazar stepped into view on the Loggia of Blessings, the sky roiled, and atop the mysterious stela there now appeared, behind a salad of cloud shapes and rainbow colors, the ethereal, luminous head of John Emdall. Her countenance, still hidden, was ringed by a bluish halo and Medusa-like tendrils of flowing water . . . a dazzling visage, to be sure, and a welcome one in the unstinting heat, but nonetheless terrifying.

"I am the well, the wishing well," she announced, giving the world a shy peek-a-boo glimpse of her face, which was that of a medieval Madonna forged from gold leaf. "Come drink yourselves full and make a wish, my precious shaved monkeys, my starving little people, and it shall be granted. I have seen your world of tears and heard your cries for true peace and love, freedom from greed and lies, an end to poverty and nagging arguments. This, along with Lectroid management according to the intelligence and goodness of our nature, I, John Emdall Thunderpump—Virgin Queen of Heaven and Empress of India, Mother of All Fathers—promise you in exchange for the rascal John Whorfin. Let us proceed with the burnt offering."

Here, then, was a pagan heresy on bold display, but where was the true God? Turning their eyes to the basilica's famous balcony, the spectators naturally wondered: Where was Innocent? Where was the man from Galilee? But for now there was only John Emdall Thunderpump in the sky with her court of angels and her surrogate Jarvis, who persisted with his corny witticisms: "People of Earth, nice planet you got here . . . it'd be a shame if anything happened to it! Ha, ha! 'And what was left of them, the beast trampled underfoot! It was different from all the other beasts, and it had ten horns!' Here's the kicker: no big loss, folks! The old world passeth away, the next world cometh! Who's Your Real Daddy now? Only Empress John Emdall Thunderpump, the King and the Queen and Mother of All Fathers, is willing to take a paternity test!"

Emdall smiled, then, at a multicolored flame that appeared in the palm of her hand, and the entire artificial sky was at once filled with clock faces—each star became a little clock with fast-moving hands—along with smiling cherubs and harp-strumming angels: a breathtaking panorama Emdall punctuated by bizarre jerky dance movements, as awestruck spectators lit candles and craned their necks to behold the dancing deity and mysterious spinning clocks.

Inasmuch as your narrator was still some blocks away, we are fortunate to have on record Mona Peeptoe's own words, spoken in wonderstruck tones, to describe the scene: "What's been happening in the last few minutes? As we record these incredible events for posterity, I look around and see people running about, but also a growing contingent of people on their knees, some mothers hiding their children and others holding them up to be washed in the cool, refreshing waters gushing from the glowing pillar. Do I fully get this . . . this signal day in the history of the world? Harbinger of a new age? Or the end of ages? No, but I feel something in my bones, some bad business down the road . . . just putting the entire world on notice. Of exactly what, something tells me we'll know soon enough. I hope so. If you see me squirming, it may or may not be because I need to use the restroom, but not to worry: I'm here for the duration, even to the end of the world and the last torch light of life on this planet or the last tweet on my Twitter feed . . . only barefoot now in case I have to wet myself, so I won't flood my Louboutins . . ."

This was not the normal hyperbole of the television reporter seeking to stir up controversy or gloating over the misfortune of others; her lament was genuine. But just then she interrupted her train of thought to announce, "Wait, he's walking out now, possibly something to do with his revelation of the fourth secret of Fátima . . . let's listen."

CARDINAL BALTAZAR'S MOMENT

It was not the pope, however, who stepped out onto the balcony and into the glare of television lights, but Cardinal Baltazar . . . or at least a poor likeness of him . . . on a recalcitrant donkey. Televised footage of the cardinal's bizarre demeanor, seen these days on the Travel Channel and elsewhere, requires no commentary from me. No doubt in response to his own tumult of emotions—having finally arrived at his lifelong destination but at such great personal cost—he appears discolored, either drugged or deranged; and for a moment it is only his index finger that appears to work, as it moves in the air to form odd signs and the shape of the cross, before he at last takes a deep breath and abruptly shakes himself in an attempt to cast off the unknown agent of his misery.

To those in the square, and billions more tuning in around the world watching the events live, it was apparent that his brain was trying to work out certain things, its squeaking wheels turning dangerously fast. While it was impossible to understand by what biological processes the adjoining halves of his gray matter were descending into chaos, its physical effects were plain—profuse sweating, labored breathing, and all the symptoms of a stroke—causing his left eye to darken, while the right retained its cerulean color and lunatic glow . . . not to mention his mouth that appeared to be twisting into a blasphemous articulation that demanded to be spoken.

"I took an antihistamine and have chronic sinusitis" was his offhand excuse, uttered as an aside to no one but picked up by parabolic microphones and even Mona Peeptoe's standard Go-Phone . . .

. . . as she continued in her increasingly hazardous location despite a slip of the tongue that transported her back to one of her earliest jobs in television:

"Mona Peeptoe reporting, live for *9 on Your Side*: the only thing that keeps me going is that maybe all this is so absurd that it must be staged, as in fake—someone's idea of a joke, just having fun with us—but even if it's not, then maybe it's supposed to happen as part of the big plan, like an informative update to the written scriptures. I mean the Big Day! Oh my, oh my goodness, it looks like things are about to get down and dirty! Dear God, thank God, it's the Hong Kong Cavaliers! Will they be able to get us all out of hot water yet again . . . ?"

To be sure, our little band had entered the great square only moments earlier and now strode with a sense of urgency toward the balcony of the basilica. While we had not planned it quite this way and doubtless appeared to many as something out of a dream, who could guess that the firing tube and bulky power supply I pushed in the wobbly shopping cart was a directed-energy weapon, the much-vaunted Jelly Beam prototype? Indeed, who had even heard of it? On the other hand, I do not mean to make it sound as though we were relishing a bloodbath or even spoiling for a fight. Our purpose, as always, was to find truth and produce results . . . and leave none of our own fighters behind.

Even at this watershed moment in world history, our priority was the fate of our friends, particularly Buckaroo and Tommy, not to mention a world seemingly gone out of control. Yet even as the bigger picture caused our heads to spin, our legions of fans brought sweet relief—for, as we rolled forward, we encountered milling crowds who had been waiting for us and in their excitement frequently even blocked our progress.

"Look, it's Muscatine Wu and the Reno Kid! With Pecos! And a freak of a robot!" they cheered boisterously and quickly besieged us, slowing us unnecessarily while tittering like birds in a kind of daze; at least that is how I remember it.

"And look! New Jersey!" a voice exclaimed.

I jerked round in disbelief, yet the living truth could not be denied, for over my shoulder I glimpsed our old bandmate New Jersey, waving and running our way. Unbelievably, he was trailed by dozens of ruby-cheeked choirboys in sailor suits who seemed nothing short of delighted by our show of weapons.

"Reno, what happened to your mustache?" he spouted good-naturedly, awkwardly embracing me and trying to shake my gun hand. "Speaking of close shaves, our plane was forced down at the airport and I heard there was trouble!"

"Trouble?" I said incredulously. "And plenty more where that came from! Are you crazy, Sidney? Get those kids outta here! Can't you see we're at war?"

As if for the first time, he looked left and right at the overwhelming forces arrayed against us and seemed to sense the gravity of the situation . . . and the danger to his young singers.

"Ah, the mess of it all," he sighed, while adding a warning: "If we have to cancel our tour, I'm suing for double damages. I'll be right back—I shall return!"

Knowing better, I said, "Don't worry about us. Those kids are counting on you."

"Stand tall, comrades!" he called back.

Although the encounter lasted perhaps less than a minute, I believe his effect on our cohort was real. We all echoed his warm sentiments, and I believed I detected a trace of nostalgia in his gaze before he gathered his flock and departed as quickly as he had arrived—a brief appearance that might be called a cameo in motion-picture jargon.

"See you back at the clubhouse," Pecos called after him rather too cheerfully; and I suspect we were a little jealous of him as well, knowing we were pushing our luck in the face of severe odds. Other than the weapons of mass destruction strapped to my back, we were armed relatively lightly. Muscatine, as far as I could see, packed a pair of Glock 10s, one of which she unselfishly passed to Jack. As for myself, my 1911 Colt .45 continued to ride my hip, while I carried my Vepr 12 scattergun with a drum magazine in one hand and the Jelly Beam nozzle, calibrated to plasma cutter mode, in the other. Off to my right marched Pecos, freely swinging the pink-and-yellow plastic hydrocannon full of our new toxic concoction along with a custom diamond-studded pistol-grip Moss 8, loaded with 00 buck pellets and white phosphorous for night fighting. On the immediate left came Jhonny, brandishing his Institute-issued H&K special operations .45 and his personal Pistola con Caricato—a triple-barreled eighteen-shot revolver—snapping his fingers in a mood that was almost manic and jocular, while a few steps away Hoppalong protected our left flank, draped in multiple bandoleers and gripping the barrel of our M60 machine gun with an oven mitt.

Just what our fans saw in us, what hopes we embodied for them and the entire world—other than as cultural icons—I cannot say. All the same, they could not hide their relief on seeing us, much as we could not disguise our fatigue and sickness of heart that we were perhaps taking our last steps on this earth.

Yet if we hurt a little, it would be as nothing compared to the pain we would feel if we failed and the aliens came barging into our world, so we prepared to fight tooth and nail. But fight whom? The impregnable ship and its artificial sky? Or the buffoonish Cardinal Baltazar, who one moment seemed full of swagger, only to appear visibly agitated a few seconds later by the magnitude of the storm gathering on all sides. Making a clumsy show of unfurling his cape and waving his fake fasces at the television lights, he first paused to wipe the sweat from his face, mumbling, "Warm night . . . hot as a pot roast."

Now he began in earnest, his voice by turns ominous and giddy: "College of cardinals, insurance underwriters, Holy Office of the Directorium, Orthodox primates, friends and neighbors in the faith, condottieri, *episkopos* and the worldwide apostolic family and peoples beyond the Po, elements of the armed forces of God . . . the Equestrian Order of the Holy Sepulchre of Jerusalem, Knights Templar, Knights of Columbus, Grenadieri of the Holy Basilica, pure as impeccable Mary . . . and special visitors from heaven . . . I am pope pro tempore . . . uh . . . Cardinal Shine Shine of Bosnia and the Sovereign Order of Malta . . . *Vicarius Filii Dei* . . . ! Me against the world, all eyes on me . . . !"

Once more he sopped up perspiration and gazed heavenward, crossing himself and waiting for what light applause did come, as well as a thrown tomato and a tin of cannellini beans that struck his backside and caused him to become sullen, albeit not for long . . .

. . . as the mounted knights and a short column of jackbooted footmen now began to march vigorously in place, or as energetically as could be expected, given their bulky suits of homemade armor. Indeed, several swooned from the heat while making esoteric hand signs and singing boisterously, "And as I go, I love to sing, my nutsack [*sic*] on my back . . . valdaree, valdaraa, valdaree, valdaraa ha ha ha ha ha! Valdareeee . . . it's a long way to Tipperary . . . my nutsack on my back!"

The impromptu performance continued until Templar snipers on the rooftops spotted smoke coming from the papal apartments and the cameras shifted momentarily in that direction, eliciting cries of "Fire! Fire!"

Fire or no, hotter than ever, Baltazar resumed his statement for the cameras. "At this hour of flagrant conflict, in the decisive moment in our long and winding human destiny of never-ending wars, I reach out to inform you that our beloved Pope Innocent the Incorruptible is inside the palace in a deep gloom, wrestling the devil of melancholia who has emerged from hell's portal, and he has asked me to reveal the secret fourth secret of Our Lady of Fátima . ... given to the young and free children but never revealed until now. Let us learn together just what is the story, ha, ha . . . ! Three guesses, and the first two don't count . . ."

He now made a show of waving the sacred envelope, which he had difficulty opening and which he now began to pummel with his thumbless fist in exasperation, meanwhile dropping the fasces and proclaiming theatrically, "No sense waiting. I will now open the seal!"

With this pronouncement, he at last ripped the envelope open, along with its contents, clumsily ripping the paper in two and feeding half to the donkey. Nevertheless, he began to read from one half of the torn page, intoning each word like a scratchy phonograph disk and always with an awareness of the cameras.

"My dearest children, who have forgotten where your heart belongs, yet whose knock on my door I have never failed to answer even from far away, I did not come to bring peace but the sword! Come hither and commend yourselves to Cardinal Baltazar, my Shine Shine and the last great knight and my champion, commander of armies and succulent fruit of righteousness, the right hand of God, the hope and resurrection of the Holy Roman Empire who brings joy to the faithful and terror to the infidel, to whom I give authority over all the earth's kingdoms and principalities—with the battle cry 'Santiago! For God and for Spain! For the empire!"

Somewhere below, a pair of trumpeters blew; but here the cardinal's façade cracked again and he paused to light a cigarette, which only served to provoke a coughing spasm and no little anxiety. Consequently his brain grew further clouded and his tongue flicked, drooling a literal pool of an oleaginous substance that resembled bacon grease or maple syrup, while his bifurcated gaze once more darted about like unaligned headlights, crazed eyes lolling in their sockets . . . the left rotating toward the right so that their gazes seemed to meet in a cross-eyed look of . . . what? Mutual understanding? Recognition of the fragility of life? Gastric issues? But what was the focal point? Had he seen our advance across the square and felt the noose tightening? Or perhaps John Whorfin—now put on notice by Emdall—had panicked and was either trying to jump ship or seize total control of Baltazar's human form.

"Hurry up, tart! Errand boy! I bash you brains!" came Whorfin's gruff voice that only the cardinal could hear.

Whatever the source of Baltazar's despondency and tortured existence, the trouble was sufficient to cause the cardinal to burrow down into his innermost self . . . and as a siren's oscillating crescendo could be heard approaching, he now read from the other half of the torn page. "Here is my secret and the whole of the holy mystery: all the popes and saints are hilarious devils, and the church is a dwelling of harlots and losers. But rejoice and hail my sweet Cardinal Shine Shine, bringer of the sword and vicar of Satan, God's true prodigal son and bride of Christ! *Sanctus Satanas Diabolus, domine noster, quam admirabile est nomen tuum in universa terra . . . exurgat . . . !* Arise, all-powerful Dark One! Hail Wotan! Hail Odin! Almighty Satan, Prince of the Power of the Air, I invoke thee in the flesh! *Ein Volk, ein Reich! Heil Hitler! Heil great Luther! O Lucifer!*"

A small number of doubters and conscientious objectors—and even among his followers there were a few—echoed feebly, "Vicar of Satan . . . ?"

As I say, these voices were a minority; yet to note that these words, along with his demonic facial aspect, set off a furor among most of the few remaining faithful would be putting it mildly. Many hurled their shoes and screamed invective such as "It's not real! He's a hologram!" Or "A bloody crock! Perversion of the magisterium! He's in bed with the devil and he's not even the pope!"

In the face of such outrage, the agonized cardinal appeared to choke. Bubbles of foaming saliva dangled from the corners of his mouth, and he seemed to be struggling even more desperately with himself. Clearly, he was in the fight of his life and able to continue for only a few seconds more.

"*Ave Satanas* . . . breath of the serpent and of life, by whom all things are set free, I cast myself utterly into thine open arms and place myself unreservedly under thine all-powerful protection!"

"Pompous jerk!" came back his own fragmented rejoinder. "Treasonous whore! Shame!"

Having committed his soul to hell so publicly, Baltazar now appeared momentarily nonplussed by his own words . . . if in fact he had been the one speaking them. Or had he merely gotten carried away with excitement? Tears filled his eyes and seemed to speak of regrets and second thoughts, the feel and taste of the body of Christ, and even a glimmer of humanity; yet a cynic might say he had cast his lot much earlier, so that the outcome was only a formality, a fulfillment of a contract between his own ego and the Deceitful One. As a result, he had the contentious aspect of someone who, while wishing to seem light and breezy, laughed obnoxiously and stomped his feet like a man who had lost his mind.

"Hail his lordship John Whorfin!" he announced, with one hand signing the cross and the other forming the sign of the horns. "Together, we have crossed the Rubicon and are en route to Olympus!"

Events now interceded in quick succession, too rapidly and too many to be detailed in this brief space, much less to my satisfaction and with sufficient conviction that they are true. As I present a laundry list of items which I will call facts—whether or not I can explain or debunk them or whether I was even in a position to see them clearly—I extend an apology in the hope that the reader nevertheless will not be unappreciative of my best efforts. Did I see what I thought I saw? This is a key question but far from the only one. Of equal importance, did I see what I saw but lacked the conceptual awareness to process it? In other words, were we simply dealing with forces we could not understand? If so, I remain in the same boat as television viewers who shared the same hair-curling feeling of unease as those of us present: a disconcerting sense of peeking, indeed of being sucked, through an interdimensional gateway into an alternative history. Therefore putting aside all grand notions of "truth," let us agree to believe in the simple power of photographic evidence and eyewitness testimony, even if it is only the smallest bit, glimpsed through a raging sandstorm and the fog of war.

HELL BREAKS LOOSE

As if on devilish cue, swirling wind gusts now blew garbage and stray rats across the plaza. These were joined by vultures that settled upon the fountains and the colonnade, while Baltazar created a further sensation by seeming to enter a trance-like state and hissing a spate of jibber-jabber, possibly glossolalia, that had the immediate effect of agitating the mysterious stela whose tendrils of life-giving water were transformed now into crackling lightning bolts forming the head of John Emdall juxtaposed over a mélange of aliens of diverse species.

"Welcome to the Planet 10 family of planets," Emdall's voice spoke soothingly over images of happy aliens of various worlds, at work and at leisure, projected onto a sky that began to roll up and dissolve into a blinding fireball, bright as the sun, with Brother Jarvis at its white-hot center.

"Better listen up, kiddos!" interjected Jarvis. "I would if I were you. Submit to your mama or she'll phawk you like nobody else! John Whorfin, tyrant and traitor, come out with your hands up!"

This ultimatum—indeed the mere mention of Whorfin's name—was answered by more foaming glossolalia from Baltazar, followed by a muffled primal scream from deep within his entrails. The high-pitched caterwaul, like the screech of a band saw, seemed to harmonize with the oncoming siren noise and was promptly emulated by an overstimulated Red Lectroid foot soldier below who now revealed his true appearance—one-eyed and with an egg-shaped, tumorous head— eliciting screams of grief from the public as he pranced buck naked through a war dance, unabashedly exhibiting his rosy backside and pantomiming something like the following: "Bring it hard, Lord Whorfin! Give us the smallest opening and we shall squeeze an army through! Your serf, sweet-hearted General Warts, kisses your big black boot!"

"Wear it with pride! We, swindled by fate, you are my frontline!" returned Baltazar with equal swagger, albeit involuntarily and vexed that the Lectroid apparently had mistaken him for someone else.

"In black boots we sweep all before us, to build greatness through steel! None can list the sorrows!" continued the Lectroid Warts.

"Santiago, son of Zebedee!" a plainly addled Baltazar responded, watching Warts perform his little jig that was both an exhibition of physical prowess and a motivational message that none but his own species could understand in its fullest measure. While the power of his dance to influence his fellows cannot be known, directly had he finished his war dance, a motley column of Lectroids in surplus forage caps and puttees (albeit barefoot) quick marched forth from a darkened portico. Most lacked fully formed faces and one or more appendages, yet all did their best to hobble in loose formation, brandishing an unwieldy assortment of potato-masher stick bombs, pineapple grenades, and Kalashnikovs and swearing personal oaths to the commanding figure on the balcony.

"Lord Whorfin, I am drunk with your strong hand!" shrieked various Lectroids seemingly in unison. "Neither am I a newcomer but one of the magnificent few, it will please you to know, being present at the battle of—"

Next arose a collective litany commemorating various campaigns and battles; and in reply Lord Whorfin—through the intermediary of Baltazar—remained quiet, giving no signal to his Lectroid loyalists other than his eye pupils, which were glowing excitedly now, blazing white in pools of black.

But let us now turn to the blistering response that was not long in coming. Other accounts have alluded to the burst of white noise from the mother ship, followed by the blinding flash of a nuclear blast that momentarily disoriented us and sent all but a handful of spectators fleeing in panic. Of course such terror was the general idea, and the rude and abusive Brother Deacon Jarvis was its face.

"What's the matter? Sun in your eyes? Ha, ha, no one lives forever!" he boomed down through a motionless mouth . . . accompanied by a special lighting effect of a blazing half sphere that now descended slowly toward Earth like a guillotine blade.

"I smell you, Whorfin the Worthless! Fungus breath!" he jeered . . .

. . . as Baltazar pressed his mouth closed so that no foreign breath or words might escape, yet managed a tightlipped reply. "No, it's me, Brother Jarvis: Cardinal Baltazar from the Holy Office! From the chatroom! The dating verification website! I do not know this thief Whorfin! Do not know him! I do not know the man!"

Almost instantly his brain experienced a sharp whiplash effect not unlike an aneurysm, and Jarvis, in any case, gave no sign of recognizing him and continued to bellow, "There's no turning around! No exit door! What's your choice? A fire that burns everlasting? Hell's coming! Ten minutes! Gonna be a bumpy ride! Gonna shove it right at you!"

Because he had been taught respect for authority at an early age, however, General Warts the Sweet-Hearted continued his slow dance in honor of Lord John Whorfin, until the stela's tendrils of life-giving water suddenly crackled and shot forth as lightning bolts, instantly incinerating the loyal officer and several of his motley adjutants at the same time a psychic attack caused the very earth to appear to fall away beneath our feet, revealing a churning sea of red-hot lava where paving stones presumably still supported us.

"It's only a show! Phawk that noise and phawk these Christmas lights!" I heard Pecos yell somewhere off to my right.

Through it all, however, Mona continued to broadcast: "Folks, bear with me. My priest friend keeps shouting at me . . . what? . . . Something about the goat Baphomet . . . the black goat . . . the Greatest of All Time? Oh, my God, that poor thing! There it is!"

Viewers at home next got a blurry view of a half-crazed black-and-white goat with its fur ablaze that had wandered into the plaza and apparently lost all sense of direction. Despite being on fire, it displayed a certain bravado that was in some way supernatural and frightening, before someone with good intentions and a bottle of water ran after it. Without further ado, the poor beast fled into the night, its hooves throwing off sparks, chased by both the Good Samaritan and a stray dog.

"So sad, the sick minds!" Mona resumed. "On my knees now, keeping my head down. The real shit's about to hit, people. Maybe I'm losing it—in case you couldn't guess—but this is hell in my heart, people, that hurts even to breathe! I want to vomit . . . trying to push the feelings down, but I'm crying . . . sick and worn out, waiting for the end of the world and just feeling so useless. I've also just been informed that there's some kind of battle going on with terrorists trying to steal our biological-weapons surplus at Fort Detrick, Maryland, within a stone's throw of our nation's capital. Our planet is under attack, people. The only question is whether it is a wound that will heal or will slowly bleed the life out of us.

"Thank you—someone just handed me a chocolate bar, and several good folks have offered me stuffed animals and candles, even balloons—but phawk balloons! Pardon my French, but what good are balloons or teddy bears or standing around and waving candles at a time like this? Anyway, I'm not going anywhere. Work has always been my way of dealing with barbarism and the extra-bad people. I realize how many times I've used the same words that utterly fail to describe the insanity, the abomination of the desolation unfolding before my eyes, but I'm out of adjectives, superlatives, out of metaphors and metonymies or nouns in apposition . . . standing here trembling like a leaf and not just because the very ground is shaking. No, it's because I'm angry at those who would use violence or the threat of violence to violate our inalienable rights as human beings. These people deserve nothing but our contempt.

"I use the word *people* loosely. In my career I've seen my fair share of things I never would have believed before . . . but what are these deformed monstrosities I'm looking at? Hybrid human mongrels? Zombie soldiers? Men wearing animalistic masks, or . . . I no longer trust my eyes, much less have faith in people, but we'll get through this together."

(Sometime later in a candid interview, Mona would reveal that the Lectroids were something of a turn-on for her, confessing, "They looked like the biggest imbeciles on Earth, literally, but also kind of heroic and intimidating . . . the way they moved, powerful and unclothed. In the event, I seemed to have feelings that I had trouble admitting to myself. There was a level of darkness in me that frankly took me by surprise.")

"Fry and die, sour tripe! Where are you, John dog?" Jarvis continued in a blind rage, prompting another inchoate, misshapen Red Lectroid to step into the open, on hearing his name called.

"I am called John Dogg! Leftenant Major John Dogg, Seventy-Second Imperial Hoplites," he announced and was instantly incinerated . . . literally left sizzling in his own juices by a bolt from the blue by way of the stela.

"Surprise! All there is to it, assbag!" Jarvis hooted.

"Virgin whore! Plague on your meat!" Dogg's Lectroid comrades erupted in anger and fired wildly at John Emdall's ethereal head and the artificial sky, some of their venomous darts and electrical charges ricocheting off the stela and striking down numerous Templars, including a cuirassier in gleaming armor unceremoniously zapped out of his saddle. Witnessing this, the English bowmen loosed a volley of their yard-long arrows at their erstwhile alien allies and reaped the whirlwind.

WAR!

In just this manner, hell on earth erupted all around us, as the skittish Templars and Lectroids traded gunfire and electrical voltage, and we fired in the direction of both. Exactly who was our enemy I cannot say with any degree of certainty, but what difference does it make? Given the existing fraught state of affairs, the plaza was a tinderbox; and if one thing had not sparked the explosion, some other catalyst would have served. Certainly there was no shortage of martyrs-in-waiting eager to bring heaven to earth or transport themselves to heaven—whichever came first. But, as I say, all of this mattered very little, as in an instant the plaza was convulsed by warfare, screams, and chaos, in addition to a number of events which cannot be explained to anyone's satisfaction.

Over the first volley between the Templars and the Lectroids and the close-quarter fighting that ensued, our band ducked behind Abysmo and continued to advance . . . turning over in our minds a range of emotions and possible outcomes limited only by our own creativity. Certainly it did seem as though we were pitted against a whole family of devils: John Whorfin, Cardinal Baltazar, and even the enigmatic John Emdall, whose intentions were as unknown to us as the machinations of a bumblebee or a butterfly. And I have not mentioned lately the boundless villain Hanoi Xan, who would soon make his presence known to all. What I mean to say is that in an ideal world, we would have bided our time and assayed the disposition of the battlefield—but as matters stood, it was too late; we were already in the thick of it, caught in the crosshairs of a crossfire.

"Stand ye steady! If any man defile the temple of God, him shall God destroy; for the temple of God is holy!" seemed to be the ironic *cri de guerre* of the Christian knights, who uttered the sentiment repeatedly . . . even as they toppled off their horses in battle.

And emotions ran high among us as well, as off to my immediate left I heard Jhonny yell out, "Time to bang heads, sling snot against this pathetic lot! Cavaliers, what are we waiting for?"

"Legal reasons, kiddo!" announced Jack Tarantulus. "You want to get your ass sued? Land in court?"

"Gotta love a plainspoken man. Keep all options open," Pecos yelled back over the resounding crack of gunshots from a rooftop.

"Sniper at two o'clock!" Muscatine shouted. "Another one at ten! Heads down, tails tucked!"

"Circle wagons, huh . . . we just gonna watch show unfold?" complained Hoppalong, impatiently squeezing the M60. "Enlighten me. What in hell are our ROE?"

"Hold fast but hold your fire. Anyway, good luck finding a target," I informed him, referring to the curious tactic of the Lectroids, who by now had encircled the crusaders in an ever-tightening, ever-faster movement, such that they became a blur to our eyes.

"Yes, look!" exclaimed Hoppalong. "They are running around like bunch of wild animals, like cyclone. I have seen this in Siberia, among deer and antelope. It is herd mentality."

"Just be ready. My squirt gun's ready," I said, stroking the Jelly Beam nozzle and now ducking as stray bullets ripped above our heads and caused the big robot to lurch and begin to limp, wounded.

"Abysmo is hit!" exclaimed Jhonny, audibly growing more desperate. "I am losing it! Does no one give a flip? Are we going to join the fracas or not?!"

"Hold your fire, kid! Leave it to the morons!" Muscatine urged, and for good reason . . .

. . . as Whorfin's Lectroids unleashed a barrage of electric-shock throat darts, quickly imposing their will on Cardinal Baltazar's weighted-down troops in their clanking metal armor and seizing control of the taco truck / transporter / erector / launcher. The result indeed was so swift and one sided that Baltazar appeared to have trouble digesting it. Or did he have mixed feelings, fighting a duel within his schizoid self?

"Abandon the field to prepare the counterattack!" he shouted, although it is questionable whether he was heard, much less heeded . . . particularly the words he uttered under his breath. "I will say this sucks. Father, why hast thou forsaken me to mine enemies, the demons?"

From the same mouth, Whorfin called out grandiloquently, "My shock troops! Gone electric! Fulfill your cosmic destiny!"

As I say, the swaggering Lectroids strangely served to boost Baltazar's flagging spirits even after he had watched his prized knights drop like flies in the internecine bloodbath. He was by now little more than John Whorfin's wingman and, as such, could not conceal a certain pride in the Lectroids' momentary victory. As for the "demons," he was not the only one who saw something of the kind. I myself observed ethereal beings of the most freakish sort slithering and flitting about in the superheated air. Perhaps they were delusions cast by the Lectroids' electronic camouflage, perhaps not; to this day I remain uncertain. If they were delusions, then others had to share my fantasy or the same personality disorder, because they saw them similarly.

At all events, the Lectroids chirped and ululated in celebration; and now they were in business, mounting the Shilka in an effort to familiarize themselves with the vehicle's controls, promptly causing its gun carriage and missile pod to rotate and sway erratically from side to side.

"Wuzzah, O Whorfin! We will storm the heavens!" the creatures boasted and puffed their throats, enraging the sun god Jarvis.

"Think you're tough? Toilet paper's tougher! I wipe my ass with John Whorfin and Planet Earth!" Jarvis ranted through the hellish haze. "You see where I'm going with this, losers?! Got a light?! Ha, ha, lemme reach back and hand out a blessing!! You listening, suck monkeys?!"

Brother Jarvis was a hothead and running his mouth; but there was more than bluster in his threat against our world, as his colossal fiery guillotine blade now belched forth a solar flare that rolled across the plaza, incinerating a cluster of outdoor toilets and a portable generator.

"Just for that, I'm tacking on a restocking fee! I break it, you bought it! At double retail!" the preacher's snarling image threatened, as a Templar fireball emerged from one of the toilets and jumped in the Bernini fountain in a vain attempt to save himself; and now Whorfin's Red fighters replied with the Shilka's quadruple 23 mm guns . . . firing a wild cannonade at John Emdall's floating image, which the stela avoided by bending from side to side, while neutralizing other shells harmlessly with its mysterious spin energy and some kind of reactive armor.

All the same, the red-hot shrapnel rained over us; and while I have no intention of embarking on a morbid roundabout describing every horror of combat, I ask you in the same breath to imagine the effect of such alien phenomena—appearing to our human eyes almost as sorcery—on our own kill-or-die mentality. None of us had ever seen anything like these hellish marvels, which were followed almost immediately by the *whoompf* of a spigot mortar and a moment later a faint whistling noise somewhere high above us and in free fall . . . reminding me of the old dictum that being shot at significantly improves one's powers of concentration.

"Mortar! Heads up!" I cried at the top of my lungs, sending us diving for the nearest cover—with the exception of Jhonny, now upright and marching stiffly behind a rudderless Abysmo, whose powerful magnetic arms had begun to suck away weapons and anything metallic, including pieces of its own hardware blown apart by bullets.

"Abysmo! Halt!" shouted Muscatine, since her remote control of the robot had ceased to function.

"Jhonny! You crazy ass . . . !" I screamed equally to no avail, finding myself curled up next to our peerless showbiz agent, who would not, or could not, cease his infantile babbling.

"Stupid idea. What a total disaster," Jack kept whimpering. "Mother of God, just give me rat poison. What is that intoxicating smell? Come a crapper, I'm about to lay a gold nugget . . . !"

"Try to hold it!" I warned, holding him down by the scruff of his neck and reminding him that he had forced himself upon our party.

"That's not very brotherly love," he prattled. "Attack after attack after attack . . . smells like Mrs. Johnson's burnt eggs . . . !"

"It's called gunpowder and high explosives," I said.

"Whiskey sours, out the butt . . . ! Or is it Guinness lager? I need to make a dump run! Gotta make it to the can, maybe the fountain . . ."

"There's snipers! Try to hold it!"

"Hold it? I'm about to give birth here!" he exclaimed.

"Damn right," I scolded him. "What's a bullet compared to a lump in your shorts?"

We had, in fact, a short discussion concerning the small cluster of burnt-out porta-potties I have mentioned; but do not think, dear reader, that the absurdity of our conversation and situation—splayed prostrate and hugging some of the holiest ground in Christendom (although this still appeared to us as hellish red-hot lava)—was lost on me. Perhaps the reader is tempted to ridicule; and it is all too easy, from our present vantage point, to make a joke of it all. Yet at the time we could afford to be under no such delusions, even if it were possible; and to say that we overall goodhearted people saw our afterlives flash before our eyes at that moment would be risible understatement. Above us, the burning guillotine was still descending; and the great stela seemed to fume and fulminate and vibrate anew, shooting forth a flurry of terrifying lightning bolts. Without shame or apology, I confess I called upon the Great Spirit and all the saints for protection, focusing on my pranayama breathing technique until the mortar shell landed on an unfortunate fire truck just entering the square . . . exploding it into bright pieces like a jumbo bag of Skittles.

No sooner had the concussion sucked the air out of our lungs than the din of battle was joined by the chirping alarms from the air packs of the luckless Roman firemen who were no longer moving. Nor was there time to mourn them, for in another instant more shots ripped through the satellite truck like hot knives through butter, forcing us to keep our heads down.

And yet there was Jhonny still on spindly legs, a one-man frontal assault firing hot sparks from his H&K Mark 23 and Pistola revolver at Templar stragglers, Lectroids, Swiss Guards, the armored Shilka, insurance executives, red-coated cardinals, rooftop snipers, fleeing rats, and the odd bewildered tourist . . . but particularly the stone sentinels atop the colonnade. More than a few of these holy saints and martyrs he shot down from their lofty nests, while demonstrating no emotion other than strange sobs of laughter and robotic utterances as he blasted away.

"Bugger off, you cockups . . . nincompoops . . . last chance, scumbags . . . !"

But our relief at seeing Jhonny still on his feet, however emotionally disconnected he appeared, was moderated by our certitude of what was to come and therefore a sense of disbelief that he had not lit up like a firework already—a fact doubtless due to an assist from our barrage of covering fire and the timely emergence of our own Buckaroo and his blazing six-guns spewing lead from the papal balcony.

"Here's my message from heaven!" some heard him shout.

"It's Chief!" shouted Hoppalong gleefully. "And he's not pussyfooting around!"

This was something Baltazar and Whorfin in their mutual predicament well understood, as both dropped to their belly in mortal terror of a man known for backing up his talk.

XXXIII. ON THE KNIFE'S EDGE

> The war has not necessarily proceeded to our advantage.
> —Emperor Hirohito

Would that this were masterful storytelling, dear friends, but if I am entitled to any credit, it is for simply allowing the truth to be told without flattery or undue embellishment. Indeed, as I have mentioned, in many ways what happened in the next minutes is beyond my scope as a fictionist.

Let us just say Buckaroo was intensely engaged, penetrating psychological camouflage to shoot Lectroids but watching in frustration as these only tended to fall and rise again, even when hit; moreover, his bullets had no chance against the armored Shilka. Nevertheless, as the Lectroids shifted their firepower toward the balcony, Jack Tarantulus made a desperate beeline for the Bernini fountain, nearly tripping over his unbuckled pants, and Pecos and Muscatine likewise jumped to their feet, availing themselves of Jack's diversionary feint and Buckaroo's introduction of a second front in the great battle. In this way both Jack's bowel issues and Buckaroo's rear-guard attack were shown to be advantageous to our team.

"Cover us!" Pecos and Muscatine yelled, running after Jhonny and the damaged robot Abysmo, which zigzagged even more erratically before finally tottering over with a deafening racket and an almost human-like groan . . .

. . . while Jhonny, out of ammo and with the smug look of a man who may not have done things in quite the correct fashion but had avoided a waste of time, tried to reload his break-action Pistola in plain sight. As I fight back tears, I ask myself now as I asked myself then: did he wish to commit suicide, or did he fancy himself immortal? I confess that even today I am vexed by this question. All I know is that having fed the beast inside him and boiled over, Jhonny now was cooling off, causing his still-smoking empty gun to feel heavy indeed.

In retrospect, perhaps, one sees it was his fate that Pecos should take the weapon from him only seconds later, but a second too late, at the very instant a 23 mm shell busted Jhonny's gut, blowing him back several feet and dropping him near Abysmo, which lay on its side, almost in a fetal position . . . its arms and legs continuing to move like a giant battery-operated plaything. Jhonny, too, quivered for a moment, staring into the face of his beloved Pecos, who dragged him to cover but scarcely knew how to hold him, given his delicate condition.

THE DEATH OF WEBMASTER JHONNY

"Pecos, precious pearl, Pecos," he wheezed through blood. "Afraid I have gone south to rot in hell. Luck is not my gift . . ."

"You took one for the team, Jhonny . . ."

"I took a cannonball . . ."

"Because you're a force to reckon with. You took a stand, for us all," she told him over the noise of the battlefield. "To make a commitment in blood and sacrifice yourself for others, the most noble thing a man can do . . . a standup man, Jhonny."

"Team building, to belong in the palm of my friends"—he coughed with strenuous effort—"to sit at the table of Buckaroo Banzai instead of to sit home in my country and watch life pass me by, wishing I had not given up on my dreams. I take pride . . ."

"That's right—don't give up, Jhonny. We'll follow our dream together . . ."

"Because I am the webmaster. I can do a reboot and live happily ever after," he joked and winced in pain.

"Not too much to ask," she said with the same tight smile.

He shook his head, knowing better.

"If wishes were fishes and pigs had dreams . . . that's false. I am grave, I think, my innards blown the phawk out, but perhaps my debt is paid to the Institute. I gave all I had. I always wanted to be first at something. Now I am first to die . . ."

She begged him to save his strength, but he continued, "It burns but I can't get warm, so shivering . . ." His teeth were chattering now, like clicking castanets, but his wetness was hot to her touch, oozing through his combat vest and the blood-soaked red-and-green sweater beneath.

"Oh, Jhonny . . . my Christmas sweater . . . ?" she said.

"I never take it off," he affirmed, his voice alternately husky and pubescent falsetto. "Thank you for it. But why are you spinning, Pecos? You are spinning round and round. I am already in the red zone, bound for the pillars of fire . . . with a yappy black dog, the hound of hell . . . I see Lonesome Town . . . is this all there is? All there is . . ."

He had begun to jabber to himself, settling in for the short time remaining. Maybe Lonesome Town was his destination, because now he tried to raise both middle fingers at the heavens. Or was the gesture directed at this world instead?

"Like my dream!" he suddenly erupted, his eyes bulging in their sockets. "Riding in a casket, but I see the mules pulling me, sinking into quicksand, going down to Lonesome Town! To Tommy, whom I do not hold a grudge, I will my Dingo boots, Beatle boots, and carton of nonfilter Camels . . . to Reno, my tennis racket, my Pistola, my Stevens .22 and Mauser 98 . . . and my onesie, all my Magic cards, my kitty cat Libby, and my lucky rubber bands . . ."

He looked at her through a glaze of tears, continuing, ". . . to you, my precious Pecos, I am sorry . . . all my sweaters and kisses. I wish you all the best in life. All I ever dreamed was to die in your arms . . ."

"And now your dream is true," she sobbed gently, realizing that at this stage of the tragedy all she could do was grant his wish . . .

. . . as he squeezed out his final words. "Game over. Now I go to the great whore, to wage spiritual warfare in the eternal pit . . . my God, the stench! The waiting room is full, a sold-out house. Is there a place for the hopeless sinner when they call the roll up yonder? No, no, it is rhetorical bullshit . . . chimes and circus music, but there is no show, and I can't leave except through admission of my own death . . . the price of admission! Seriously I am scared now, but tell my mother and father my underwear is clean and I did not cry like a baby . . ."

"I'll tell your loved ones, Jhonny. I promise . . . and Buckaroo."

"Don't let them throw dirt . . ."

"I'll remember."

Now, with one final effort, he gripped her tightly and tried to drag her along with him into the hereafter, exclaiming with a mad burst, "They're calling the roll! I bid you adieu . . . *ave atque vale* . . . Webmaster Jhonny has left the building! Fire up the music!"

"Jhonny, yes, I'm listening! Still here . . ."

"Thanks for listening, thank you very much," he whispered and shrank back, staring at her with the eyes of old age.

It is a commonplace that a dying man tells the truth. But if Jhonny wished to be cremated, it would have been included in his personnel file, where his instruction called for an Apache-style burial in a hollow log. It may be that he said something more in his own native tongue, though Pecos failed to hear it over the rising theme music . . . which we may call a source of wonder because the actual origin of the music—our platinum-selling single, "Blue Bottle Fly"—was not clear. Some remember it as having a local source, such as a radio in a window or even the Vatican public address system, while others argued that it was connected to, and perhaps dependent upon, alien energy.

As if in reverence, Pecos lifted her eyes but spied only the play-dough face of Archangel Brother Deacon Jarvis glaring through the hellish haze and still prattling on: "Tits up and gettin' cold! Can't say I didn't warn you, so suck your snot up! Food for thought, folks . . ."

What else to say about Jhonny? As the one who personally selected him for the tour, I will feel guilt always, remembering our final meal together and imagining him smiling and still safe at his computer keyboard . . . his lucky rubber bands and prized Pistola now a keepsake paperweight on my desk as I write these words:

In pace requiescat.

BUOYED BY BUCKAROO

Through it all Jarvis thundered on, evidently alluding to the Shilka's SAM pod that had now begun to spin and agitate up and down like a washing machine. "I'm warning you—now I'm mad something fierce! I'll put it on you strong, like the fires of Nineveh! Don't make me do it! Don't pull that trigger! Stir the shit, you gonna get hit! Can I get an amen?"

Lightning bolts now flashed from the stela, carbonizing more Lectroids, whose gaseous products yielded a hallucinatory cloud in which I saw John Whorfin with white hair and fiery eyes and wearing a golden girdle, and now a great sword came out of his mouth. And from her hiding place nearby, I heard Mona's broken voice sobbing, ". . . I have lived a loose life, a low life . . . a hypocrite who caused more pain and suffering than I exposed in others . . . who, in order to advance my career, changed my name from Desdemona Pepitone and became the whore of Lucifer. I faked interest, faked passion, faked sources, faked ego stroking . . . cheated on my lovers, cheated on my taxes, scalped my complimentary Super Bowl tickets . . . ! Before God Almighty I have faked it all except my love for Jesus . . ."

Hearing the pain in her labored breathing, I called out, "Need a crying towel, Mona? Let us all cry together!"

With a full-throated laugh, she returned, "Good old Reno! I love you, Reno!"

"I love you, too, Mona!"

Perhaps it was only common decency—high sentiments in a dire moment—but I believe we both meant what we said. Perhaps we did not even need to say it: I loved her. Certain people come back into our lives repeatedly for a reason, which is often to grow old together and effect a future that is somehow supposed to be. I could see myself getting rid of a lot of things, people in my life, but never Mona. We have soul ties.

I have mentioned Buckaroo's statement that the purpose of time is to keep everything from happening all at once. If that statement is accurate—and what fair-minded person would dispute it?—we now had arrived at a moment when time ceased to exist . . . because everything was happening simultaneously. As Buckaroo would say later, this was the ball game for the survival of our planet with multiple balls in play; yet as we did our best juggling routine, it is incumbent upon the historian not only to chronicle the parts with care but to make some sense of the whole.

For that reason, I have given myself the task of presenting Buckaroo Banzai the man, and not a mere persona: the man of the hour but a man all the same . . . who now unleashed a barrage of hot lead at the Red Lectroids, along with several spewing cans of carbonated beverage that he hurled like grenades. By means of these, he dropped various of the craggy beasts before trick shooting the release button of the Shilka's trebuchet and thereby launching several Lectroids across the plaza like crash-test dolls.

"Buckaroo Banzai . . . you pick up my spirits! I believe in you!" sputtered the heartless cardinal, who, crouching at Buckaroo's feet safely out of the line of fire, both moaned in agony and applauded with one hand while reaching into his cassock with the other. "You don't trust me, but I'm telling you the truth! I'll be the bigger man and martyr myself!"

"Great idea, Baltazar. Why don't you take a baby step and a flying leap? I hope it was all worth it," retorted Buckaroo.

"Yes, it's killing me inside," the simpering cardinal continued. "I just want to go home to Sarajevo . . ."

No, his actual objective was a secreted German Luger in a hidden pocket, but amid this bit of misdirection he was caught by Buckaroo's left cowboy boot, which kicked him squarely across the balcony in the direction of a seminude figure who had just stepped into view carrying a bloody sword and earning a heartfelt hurrah from the smattering of spectators still in the great plaza.

"It's Special Tommy!" voices shouted.

"Damn it, Tommy," Buckaroo upbraided him, less than pleased to see his sidekick clad only in makeshift bandages . . . mostly swatches of velvet curtain. "I thought I told you to stay put! You're in no condition—"

"You know me, Buck—I can't stay outta the spotlight for long, much less the grand finale," Tommy retorted, deftly aiming the tip of his sword at Cardinal Baltazar's Adam's apple while lifting the German Luger from his secret pocket.

"I'll take this, turkey buzzard . . . er, I mean red bird . . . Cardinal . . ."

"Perfect Tommy!" reacted Baltazar groggily, rubbing an apparently broken jaw and frozen facial expression, as a result of which he could barely say a word, other than to throw his voice like a ventriloquist . . . but it was not his own voice that was thrown. It was that of John Whorfin.

"Judgment Day is upon us and Jesus in his mercy will put me back together," Whorfin's disembodied voice said with a throaty cackle, at once causing Buckaroo to turn his head at the telltale sound; but it was not at all clear where it was coming from.

"Whorfin?"

"Ha, ha, Banzai . . . suck a fat one. My blade is rusty but thirsty, to drink your blood . . . oh, dear, I have let in the devil and left the good and narrow path, knowing I am guilty of something but don't know what. How could my shame be any greater?"

At the first sound of his voice, however, a number of winged Lectroids—perhaps all who were able—flew up to the balcony and fluttered like hungry pigeons or a flock of seagulls drawn to their master's voice.

"The hell . . . ? Damn it!" Tommy exclaimed and shot at several with Baltazar's Luger, while Buckaroo tried to fight off the winged creatures with kicks and punches, between quick looks at Baltazar.

"Of course," Buckaroo muttered, putting one and one together. "The two of them . . . together for the first time!"

"Who . . . ?" said Tommy.

"Baltazar and Whorfin . . . in the monk's bathroom. They copulated . . ."

"Though I did not know it," Baltazar tried to squeeze out through his broken jaw. "As God is my witness . . ."

"Toilet slave! Took my odor rocket and liked it! What'd you expect, Balty? A peppermint stick?"

A gigantic audible fart now issued from the cardinal's buttocks, further sending the winged Lectroids into an ecstatic warbling frenzy.

"Chili cook-off! Tonight we rise steely eyed! Back to 10! Home!"

"Home!"

"On that ship!" the ex-emperor-god proclaimed, pointing at the sky . . .

. . . as Jarvis continued with the threats. "What're you looking at me for, monkey boys? What are you waiting for? Some music video with good vibes of peace and love? You know what I want. Give me Whorfin or I'll shoot the screws to you and this mud ball you call a world!"

Tommy waved at the sky, but was Jarvis actually looking at us? Was he even conscious of anything happening down here below? Who could say? But his threat had its intended effect on Tommy, who tried to pick up Baltazar but quickly found himself outnumbered two to one.

"Baltazar, you subpar sack of stink . . . !" Tommy grunted, finding himself unexpectedly caught in a leg-scissors hold.

"Don't forget I was a professional wrestler," the cardinal managed to whisper.

"And I am Lord John Whorfin!" said the voice of the air, using Baltazar's fists, albeit with Lectroid strength, to punish Tommy.

"The last straw," groused Tommy when one of Whorfin's hammer blows to his gut, added to the power of Baltazar's leg vise, caused him to spit up a small mangled bone.

"Mine!" squealed Baltazar, who relaxed his leg hold to scoop up his thumb, and, no doubt animated by Whorfin, now took a well-nigh-impossible leap for a man of his age and outward condition, launching himself from the balcony into the welcoming arms of the Lectroid fighters massed on and around the Shilka below.

Watching this whole sequence of events I have just described, I could not shake the feeling that our old world was passing from us self-important humans into the clutches of its new masters, one group of Lectroids or the other, while all we humans could do was observe.

I have noted our own helplessness. What a worthless group we were so far, pinned down by a handful of Templar snipers firing at anything that moved. Unable to do more than watch, we could only shout encouragement at Buckaroo, who was fighting against impossible odds, battling Lectroids from the four corners of creation; and there was our stalwart Tommy on his knees, still folded over, his strength dissipated by the day's prior combats and now this latest indignity . . . having been bested in a scrap with a middle-aged cardinal. On the other hand, we were still alive, and it was with growing pride I watched Tommy raise himself and go to Buckaroo's aid against the airborne Lectroids, many of whom fortunately elected to follow their leader to the missile platform.

"Huzzah! Huzzah!" the beasts and even the remnants of beasts celebrated on the Shilka, crowding so close together around their exalted leader they became as a single body.

"Sorry, Buck, I couldn't hold him," I heard Tommy say over my earpiece.

"And I couldn't help you," Buckaroo replied, after which neither could bring himself to say another word for several seconds.

"You gave it your best. It's okay, guys," Pecos weighed in.

"It won't be okay if those fools figure out how to work those missiles," Muscatine Wu said.

"Is no light thing," added Hoppalong. "Is no light thing what is happening."

"True enough . . ."

"Poor Jhonny . . ."

"Given a bad hand . . ."

"What a great guy . . . I really valued his friendship."

"You okay, Pecos?"

"Anybody seen Jack?"

"He was washing his pants in the fountain, the last I saw him . . ."

"Probably having a cappuccino somewhere . . ."

We may have laughed at the thought, I'm not sure. Then, as if on cue, we heard signals from the Shilka's cab, where a trio of Lectroids, bathed in eerie green LED light, were playing with the controls.

"I feel ill," Pecos said. "Somehow we've gotta take that truck."

"I've still got the Jelly Beam and Bubble Gun, if worse comes to worst," I said.

"How could it get worse?" noted Pecos.

"In the wrong hands either one could destroy half of Rome," said Muscatine.

"In the right hands either one could destroy half of Rome," remarked Buckaroo.

"What's the answer then?" I posed.

"The answer . . . ? If only this were an equation," pondered Buckaroo, his voice sounding suddenly far away as if thinking now on other matters about to intrude into the calculus . . . for, as we now know, his superkeen, catlike senses—that evolutionary mix of human and animal faculties dating back to our origins in the mud—detected at that instant a scent on the breeze, a sweet-smelling smoke masking an odor of waste, like old fish grease or feces bleaching in the sun.

Whorfin? No, this was not the stench of rotting Lectroid, but a roughly equivalent human smell and one he recognized as a physician. Almost certainly a festering canker or a cancer . . .

"Then let this be the hill we die on," I said before raising a bone-chilling war cry in response to the others.

"All the beans and bullets you can eat! Banzai!"
"Banzaaaaaaaai! Let's go!"

XAN'S ARRIVAL ON THE FIELD

Directly had our fierce cries arisen, however, I heard the tinkle of a livestock bell heralding the arrival of an extraordinary procession whose centerpiece—a wizened, pipe-puffing dandy draped in silk, peacock feathers, and a faded tartan carpet—rode a solid gold, diamond-encrusted mobility scooter beneath a Mongol warlord's *tug*, consisting of horse tails dangling from a high pole. More remarkable still, the entire machine was borne aloft like a litter by a dozen robotic commandos goose-stepping in perfect lockstep in their identical glow belts and black armor, the frontmost of whom—appearing to be of a lower caste of robot—swept the path clean with whisk brooms for the advancing litter and the motorized toilet and artillery piece that brought up the rear of the column.

Such was my initial impression, at least. In fact they were fleshy humans—at least for the most part—because they bled; indeed their blood was to flow in streams over the Vatican paving stones. But they might as well have been automata. Either they could not comprehend the extent of the disaster that awaited them or they did not care. But do not simply take my word for it. No doubt owing to a case of taut nerves and the fact that we had been out in the blazing artificial sun for too long, others saw things differently, leading to a hodgepodge of opinions about the color of the scooter and the *tug*, the size and demeanor of the hunchbacked smoker and the nature of his or her bodyguards; and for the same reason video images have failed to settle the issue. Let us merely consider the facts that are not in dispute, however.

In a matter of seconds—everything happened so quickly, before they even knew what hit them—the warlord's little parade was ripped to pieces by the battle truck's autocannons and aftermarket flamethrower that the Lectroids had wasted little time in mastering and were now firing indiscriminately. Yet as soon as one goose-stepping bravo dropped and departed for the rewards of martyrdom, another moved up to occupy the space of the former; and in this way the sacred *tug* and mobility scooter were held aloft and never allowed to touch the ground.

"It's a damn turkey shoot!" marveled Pecos, nonetheless disgusted by the scene of such wanton carnage. "Morons! Lunatics! Welcome to the hornets' nest . . . the World Crime League pennant?! No . . ."

"My God! Is it him?" Muscatine Wu screamed. "Think about it."

"I thought I smelled a rat!" said Pecos.

The air immediately surrounding the mysterious marching column was indeed putrid, but markedly different from the plaza's overall stench of death, Lectroid musk, and acrid cordite. Was the rider with a bell around his neck in fact the mysterious and notorious man of shadows, Hanoi Xan? In retrospect, the answer is yes; but at that dire moment when the world was a ticking bomb, who could bear faithful witness? Again, in this regard I speak for myself alone when I say that even though I would not be able to pick the "stranger" out of a police lineup, I experienced a wave of revulsion and intense negative energy at the mere sight of him . . . above all, his sickly, cloying scent; and it was mainly this that gave him away—a blend of treacle and iodoform with traces of skunk oil, ambergris, and rotting meat—for his face itself was but scantly visible, obscured by the tartan rug around his head and shoulders that had the effect of a cowl.

"Where is old fart going on his merry way?" remarked Hoppalong incredulously.

Almost numb and at a loss for words myself, I could say only, "Lower your voice. That old fart just happens to be human quicksilver—"

When I faltered at saying the name, he read my thoughts in an almost reverent whisper: "Hanoi Xan? That little guy . . . no hooves, no horns, or a tail . . . the All-Destroyer? That's crazy . . ."

If I still failed to make reply, it was because at that instant Xan's *tug* and the last of his bodyguards crashed to earth and the golden mobility scooter suddenly rose into the air without any visible means of support, floating overhead like some kind of balloon animal, unbound by gravity and seemingly impervious to all manner of gunfire.

While it is likely that the four-wheeled single-seater possessed variable jet thrusters, such armchair ratiocination did little to allay the extent to which his flight played with our minds at that moment, and I found myself watching the airborne scooter in eye-popping bewilderment.

There had to be some natural explanation, we told ourselves . . . some ingenious antigravity innovation afoot that we did not yet understand but would surely learn in due time.

On the other hand, were we witnessing reality? A master magician's trick? An illusionist's sleight of hand, suggesting hidden wires? Perhaps a cloud of camouflage similar to the ruse employed by the Lectroids? Or a level of the preternatural beyond our comprehension, as I have hinted already?

The old man himself appeared to show no emotion other than tiny pinpricks of light in his peculiar goat eyes, which Mona was to liken to those of a cunning lynx. He seemed to be babbling to himself in a tongue I couldn't make out and fading in and out, as if from one energy level to another, radiating a color as well as an odor . . . silver from my point of view, to match his seamless garment of argent silk and recalling Forbes's description of him as "a silver blaze . . . an ominous glitter"; but the video footage is inconclusive on this. In his right hand he carried his gnarled walking stick, a holy relic from the true cross, as I have related, with added wires and a stingray tail, extended forward like a rudder or a crude guidance system—reminiscent of Michelangelo's outstretched Creator God inside this very palace—and pointing directly at the Loggia of the Blessings, where you may imagine Xan's arrival, even without a supporting cast, was already having its due effect.

"Hanoi Xan . . . ?" Tommy urgently asked Buckaroo, whose normal fixed expression had hairline cracks.

"Him? Here? Am I really watching this?" Buckaroo almost certainly said to himself and instinctively hefted his pistol at the sight of his ancient rival, whom he knew by blood. Then a second voice—not the impulsive voice of vengeance but of reason—uttered, "The *kenka* can wait. Anyway, you forgot your silver bullets!"

The *kenka*—understatement of understatements!—their age-old feud that predated Edo and even the Mongol khanate, harking back to the dawn of time . . . and all over a mathematical formula and a spilled cup of tea at a banquet no one could remember!

In the disorder of his mind, how he had dreamt lately of Xan and inclined all his energies toward revenge! And how often across the span of history had he inhaled the fiend's trace on his travels, just as he breathed it now: the dirt particle of human erosion that floated—yes, deigned to hover like the insect he was—before his very eyes, causing his heart to race and skip a beat! And yet what did any of it matter now, even sweet retribution, at the end of the world?

This was all fine wisdom, but in actual practice his free and natural thoughts were overtaken by a more pressing matter, as it could not have escaped his attention that Templar bullets and Lectroid mouth darts spewed at Xan seemingly all sailed wide or passed through the man-rascal without effect. For this claim I can likewise offer no proof; but to all members of our team, it appeared that Xan was immune to physical harm and isolated from the rest of us, as if occupying his own special spacetime frame between two dimensions and with nothing better to do than mock our helplessness. For this reason and others mentioned, I remind the reader that the anomaly we know as Hanoi Xan—his very quiddity—belongs to the realm of shadows and the undefined.

But what to do with the information that an enemy walks and talks but both is and is not a living being like others? As a problem solver and the chief hope of humanity, Buckaroo Banzai was scarcely the type to make alibis; nor was he out to prove a point, simply preferring to compose himself and resolve to fit together all pieces of a given puzzle. Only those of us who were his intimates could sense the volcanic upheaval within his soul, made worse on this night by an agonizing headache, burning eye sockets, and the feeling that something unintelligible—even a whole bloodthirsty other—was roaming free inside him, inciting him to hatred.

Despite his doubts and afflictions, however, he remained the outward picture of self-control, raising his own left hand—inscribed with our Coliseum song list in smeared ballpoint ink—as an antidote against Xan's mystical force field. In an instant it was as though a thousand years had come and gone and they were back in old Mongolia swimming in the same gene pool and asserting their iron wills through games, combat, and throat singing. Just as the enchanter Xan raised his holy stick, Buckaroo spring-cocked his powerful spirit fingers, throwing sovereign Pythagorean signs very like the Masonic square and compass, bringing his ancient rival's blood to a slow boil.

(The reader may recall Buckaroo's statement "things we don't understand we call woo or pseudoscience." All the same, I do not mean to ascribe to their mental tug of war anything beyond the power of suggestion. Their respective energy fields obviously relied upon one another's belief for some of their efficacy, but that is not to say that this belief was mere superstition and not the product of a thick stack of empirical evidence gathered over many centuries.)

"I feel thy warm feelings for an uncle! Has something happened?" Xan returned with false jocularity, although he did not take his teeth from his pipe, and these were not the exact words that reverberated around the plaza's semicircular walls without an identifiable origin. By that I mean that his language was Old Enochian, as I was to discover: the tongue of angels and the learned ones, the Nephilim of olden times.

At the same time, Buckaroo felt Xan's power and pushed back against it in a simple game of dominance and submission, the oldest sport on earth. For Xan, this was a reclamation project—to exert control over his righteous younger nemesis—whereas Buckaroo's every fiber screamed questions about Penny; but Xan's voice on the wind answered only, "A long time since Edo when last we spoke face to face. Thou hast shaved thy goat tuft, nephew, but this is no time for making fun. Such wonders in the heavens . . ."

"And on the earth," Buckaroo concurred. "A shakedown from the horror story above . . ."

"There's always that one neighbor," Xan said half in jest, but guessing at once the situation. "An encore of Lectroid simpletons, by thine hand? When all the world was ordered so, in perfect spheres, thou hast broken the rhyme by thy foolishness."

"Then the world is not so stable and wonderfully made as thou makest it, if by my own hand I could uncobble its spheres," Buckaroo replied. "But I agree it is no time to be sitting in judgment of one another for aberrations from the old cults and sacred books. That way lies madness. Let us extend the hand of peace, rather than vendettas and threats of comeuppance!"

"If thou seekest me from the bottom of thine heart, of course the answer will be yes, nephew . . . a business-type arrangement, then? A new chapter?" said Xan.

"For a limited time."

"A limited offer!" Xan roared with laughter and began singing his own joke lyric, "Homunculus, why so blue," to the tune of our hit recording "Blue Bottle Fly" before firing off a plume of smoke from his pipe that seemed to carry his words away like dust on the wind. In any case, reader, have no doubt that in those precious seconds more was said between them, involving stories of true life that would hold no meaning for the reader, rooted as they were in centuries-old events. This increasingly heated dialogue, in their esoteric language and now lost to posterity, I will not pretend to convey . . .

. . . as Tommy interrupted, shouting, "You've got this, Buckaroo!"

"I would need a better answer, a good-faith gesture," Buckaroo calmly informed Xan.

"A limited time only . . . whatever maketh thee happy," replied Xan, dripping sarcasm. "I want what maketh thee happy, nephew."

"I think you have what makes me happy," Buckaroo snapped, unable to conceal his emotion even at this historic moment. "You know her name."

"Yes, thou hast lost all and are in danger of falling apart . . ."

"Keep her from harm or I'll—"

"How high thy wall, cowboy? Not high enough!" uttered Xan, as an exhalation from his pipe now became a swirling penumbra, a smoke ring sent on its way by an acoustic blast from his cane, packing such a punch that it struck Buckaroo and Tommy with the force of a bullwhip and even smoked their hair and eyebrows . . .

. . . infuriating Tommy, who now made a threatening gesture with the sword of San Galgano before Buckaroo rebuked him, saying, "Give him the sword, Tommy."

"I've a mind to give it to him real good," swore Tommy ill-temperedly. "Him and his black rites . . ."

"No. Give it to him as a gift."

Tommy's singed eyebrows shot sky high. "You mean Xan? Give Hanoi Xan the sword of San Galgano?"

"Give it to him before he takes it. This is the foundation of the old teaching," Buckaroo told him. "Just do it, Tom."

"Great. Under protest and against my better judgment," Tommy whined, tossing the sword toward Xan, who by some unknown means accelerated the weapon's flight so that it flew directly into his hands. There it remained for only seconds, however, before he hurled it across the square.

"Fake!" he pronounced. "And to someone who has stood by you through a thousand dangers!"

"And I," returned Buckaroo, "nettled by thy rudeness!"

Visibly shaken—as were we all by this display of Xan's dark arts and the overall spine-tingling bad energy in the air—Tommy may have eyed the door with thoughts of retreating, but said only, "Now what? So much for our good-faith offering. Now we're ripe for the pluckin'."

Xan's demonstration also had its due effect aboard the Shilka, where the phantom Whorfin felt this new dark force and murmured, "Holy shit a brick. Who that good-looking dog rides such a bicycle?"

"Hanoi Xan," Baltazar answered and could not have been more terrified if Jesus himself had suddenly shown up. "Oh, Father, I seek thy rapture and righteous protection. I feel my welcome here has worn out."

For my part, with Xan in my sights, I could have easily blown him out of the sky, but equivocated by double-checking the Jelly Beam's settings, making sure I had switched it from continuous fire to single-shot mode and in my nervousness trying to remember the appropriate power-augmentation tables. In the end I selected a half-charge bolt setting; or at least so I believed, taking into account my white knuckles and trembling hands.

"Ripe for the pluckin'" . . . weren't we all? Seeing Buckaroo's woeful appearance, I heard the phrase like an echo of the age-old feud between the two rivals and from my front-row seat witnessed Xan hurl a psychic blow to Buckaroo's solar plexus and show his teeth to say, "Thy mother! How I love her sticky spot and intimate things!"

"She remained faithful to the end," Buckaroo returned, endeavoring to summon his better angels. "Yet it is true we must all suffer the errors of our mothers who bring us into this world. And Penny . . . ?"

"I am teaching her the Kama Sutra, having sucked her soul into hell! God, she is a little phawk engine . . . fifteen hours a day!"

Reader, bear in mind this is illustration dialogue only. I am only guessing what was said—and much more was exchanged between them—yet this grotesquerie at Penny's expense incited Buckaroo to deliver a sharp counterattack that spiked Xan's blood pressure and nearly stopped his pickled heart . . . to which Xan retaliated by sucking the wind from our chief's lungs, leaving Buckaroo staggering on his feet and the rest of us in serious fear for his life.

Meanwhile, once more I had Xan dead to rights and shouldered the Jelly Beam; but beset by doubts and considering the possibility of collateral damage to the Vatican's priceless art treasures, again I failed to pull the trigger despite my own bitter imprecations.

"Kill him, damn it, while you have the chance! Get rid of Xan once and for all!" I cursed myself for doing nothing and yet for a second time did nothing, feeling the monster's light-absorbent gaze fall upon me with all the atavistic nightmares of our race, taking me to a place beyond my understanding where it was all I could do to breathe between his soul-piercing mental attacks. Or perhaps it was the smokescreen he unleashed, simultaneously jerking his scooter wildly from side to side, either by design or malfunction, and leading me to question why he failed to kill me when he had the chance. Hadn't he recognized me?

Still riding his scooter like a bucking horse, Xan then returned to his truculent negotiations with Buckaroo Banzai. What agreement they may have reached, what rules bound them, I'll likely never know; and I confess my thoughts at that moment were traveling elsewhere. From somewhere above I heard Jarvis: "Big sound for the big town! Annihilation, baby!"

And phantom Whorfin, too, speaking to his eager sad sacks on the Shilka battle truck. "Total war!" he howled. "Look sharp, you sniveling rejects! Together we storm the heavens, ya? To regain what we have lost, take back what was stolen! Back to our home where we were happy and worth a shite!"

"Wuzzah! Wuzzah, Whorfin!" the Lectroid chorus sang back.

"Think with your blood, comrades! Let us do the dirty work, kill wholesale and consummate the genocide! You believin' . . . ?"

"We believin' . . . !" echoed the Lectroid chorus, freeing themselves of their sorrows and despair; and while we are inclined to ridicule their expectations, the fact is that they were sick of their lodgings on Earth and he was their knight, their messiah, whose happy proverbs and language of the clergy, handed down through collective memory, had kept them going through many a difficult year.

Sometimes I am asked, "Are Lectroids seriously that stupid? Was John Whorfin seriously that stupid?" My reply is usually something on the order of "Is an ice-pick killer seriously that stupid?" Perhaps a better description than "stupid" in this instance would be "goal oriented," and in this light Whorfin's ravings may be seen as not entirely so much hot air. While it is true he lacked a physical Lectroid body and certain other ingredients of his former existence, he at least had at his disposal a missile launcher and a loyal cadre who may have revered him all the more, now that he had apparently passed over into the spirit realm of everlasting life, home of the immortals.

In a sober moment may we not even admire their bravery in a bad cause? Indeed, how could Whorfin not take heart from the raucous cry that now went up from his ragtag army—some of them little more than pieces of appendages—the voice of the powerless who have been wronged?

"As for me, my money is on John Whorfin!" they roared back.

HAND-TO-HAND COMBAT

Imagine now, reader, billions of eyes on Buckaroo Banzai and Perfect Tommy, the two weary men on the pope's balcony to whom the world now turned. It is a famous image but I prefer the impression in my memory—and it is a strong one. Between the two men, they have a pair of six-guns, an empty Luger, assorted knives, and a spray can of special anti-Lectroid repellent. They have endured more physical depredations in a day than many men in a lifetime; they are hurting mightily but speak stoically; not given to pessimism, through it all their eyes still shine. On another occasion they might be heading off into the sunset, and perhaps they will do that today . . . if the sun returns and there is another sunset.

Below them in the great plaza, dozens of Lectroids swarm atop the Shilka, crowding so close together as to appear a single writhing organism. Several more sit in the vehicle cab, eerily illuminated by LED lights, playing with the foreign controls.

Nor can our two heroes expect any help from a magical man in the sky, unless you count a suspicious, vibrating Jarvis looking down from on high, and, just above their heads, circling the plaza like a vulture in search of carrion—of which there is no shortage this night—a certain Hanoi Xan lingering for no apparent reason other than to dive down at a given moment.

In my earpiece I hear them even now.

"How're you feeling, old man?" says Buckaroo.

"A little sluggish," Tommy replies.

"Changes can come over a man when he gets older . . ."

Tommy laughs and winces. "I'll come back and tell you when I get there."

"Don't worry. I'll keep you in sight," Buckaroo says, now indicating the Shilka. "Best not to linger. If they figure out how to work that launcher, we're cooked."

"The whole world's cooked."

"Midnight in the world," Buckaroo remarks, glancing at his Go-Phone, and pointing its laser aiming beam at Xan, who signals back by flashing his headlights. "Just watch the road. Ready?"

"You talking to me?" Tommy asks.

"I don't see anybody else up here. Wanna go together?"

"I don't see why not."

Buckaroo now inserts two fingers in the corners of his mouth to produce a loud foghorn of a whistle—signaling a suicide charge—and holds out his other hand to Tommy. With an offensive holler the two then take a flying leap, hand in hand, over the balustrade and into the middle of the churning Lectroid scrum below.

Into the eyes of the savages, then! Shooting, stabbing, spraying, and kicking!

"Dread Lord Whorfin . . . !" the stricken beasts cry.

"This is what troubles you? Seize them! Do something!" the phantom Whorfin demands, yet nervously retreats.

"Whoop! Whoop!" Tommy yells, spinning and slashing with Buckaroo's switchblade scalpel and firing a six-gun. "Tarnation, there's too dang many of 'em!"

Tommy once remarked to me that he thought he would die in an insane asylum. At the time I believed he was not serious. Now I know he was being the optimist, as mind searches memory and I see him there on the Shilka with the simple choice to fight or be dead. Even now I pay them tribute.

"Looks like we're done, old pard! Hanging out with some bad company!" Buckaroo declared with typical aplomb under pressure and over the snarling, teeming mob.

"Great work if you can get it! Boot Hill, here we come!" Tommy growled maniacally.

"Any day's a good day to die for one's world!" Buckaroo answered.

"Always knew we'd have a special kind of ending . . . side by side! Nothing lives forever!" echoed Tommy.

"Not even this spinning globe, unless by some miracle . . . !" lamented Buckaroo, attempting to shrug off the nick of a poison dart that in an instant reduced him to a one-armed fighter . . . even as he picked up a heavy chain which he wielded like a bludgeon against all comers.

"Out of ammo!"

"Me, too!"

Such was the gist of it. Meanwhile the rest of us were not idle . . . advancing in three relief columns, as I shall describe; but more immediate help came now from an unexpected source . . .

. . . as Buckaroo, his back against the radar dish and out of time and space in which to maneuver, took another poison dart and dropped to one knee. Watching the conquering horde close in, he called out, "Looks like my destiny's writ!"

In no less of a tight spot, Tommy nonetheless clawed his way toward his friend. "I'm coming! If I'm not there by Saturday—"

"Ha, ha! Good one!" Buckaroo forced a laugh and prepared to go down swinging. The problem, as always, was that a Lectroid could be beaten to pieces but every piece would do its utmost to continue the fight. One detached arm would be picked up by another and swung like a weapon, a decapitated head hurled like a slingshot; in this way every available piece was consigned back to the fight.

Innumerable stories have been written about the strange flickering light that was next reflected on Buckaroo's face—not a halo but from a shadowy fire wheel that swept overhead, startling his attackers and causing them to fall back in confusion.

"Xan!" he exclaimed.

"Thy will be done!" came the voice of Xan, his scooter surrounded by a swirling ring of black fire which, joined by powerful sonic pulses from his ancient walking stick, now threw the Lectroids into further disarray.

"By the power of the cross . . . ! So that everything we do shall prosper . . ."

"Rather later than expected, but . . ."

"Ah, the martyr's agony. Art thou angry? In thy place I would feel the same."

"Hanoi Xan? My friggin' nerves," said Tommy, who took advantage of the respite to go on the attack; but the battle was far from over . . .

. . . as the gun pods and radar dish suddenly began to rotate and an electronic voice speaking Bulgarian could be heard from the cab in what sounded like a countdown. But for how long?

"Two minutes!" Buckaroo translated, simultaneously spotting Cardinal Baltazar climbing a missile tube against his better judgment, appearing in fact to be pushed by an unseen force—which of course we know was John Whorfin; and from this higher vantage point the Lectroid warlord sought to rally his troops.

"Lectroids of Planet 10! Blood and iron! Greed and power! Long live war!" he thundered in one of his finest speeches. "Where are my old boys who split hell open?"

"We are here, Lord Whorfin, greatest of warmongers, we are here and have not lost that loving feeling! Long live war! Long live Planet 10!" came the mob's feverish response.

"Planet 10, the place to be!" Whorfin's voice shrieked. "The place called home, the place of our downfall and stories of our race! Cry havoc, you sugar-fed lames in the ranks, and drive the monkey boys back with our boots! Yoke them to the whipping post!"

"We are Lectroids! Cry, cry! Back to home, where we were happy and worth a shite! The good old days once again! Listen! The trumpet is blowing, 'Hail! Hail Victory!'"

Here, Whorfin's voice made noises that imitated a crude trumpet and apparently constituted their tribal anthem. While I do not brush aside the tune's psychological effect or anything else that fell from his lips, I think it questionable whether any such nostalgia for home even existed in the collective memory of his fighters, or whether their enthusiasm derived simply from a fascination with other places, not unlike the longing common to many of our own religions: to leave this world in favor of a happier one.

"Where are we going?" he cried out and prodded Baltazar to keep climbing toward the top of the launch tube that by now had assumed a near-perpendicular position.

"The reason for this?" Baltazar had the temerity to ask.

"Going home, honey tongue, through a cheese hole. Where are we going, boys?"

"Home!" the Lectroid chorus screeched back.

"When are we going?"

"Soon!"

"Sooner than soon!" Whorfin replied. "When?!"

"Sooner than soon! Real soon! Right now!"

"Why? I live here. Rome is my home. I've acquired social position," the cardinal tried to explain, yet feeling at sea himself. An earthling at heart, he was nevertheless terrified of Hanoi Xan's retribution, all the more so since the wheel of fire still encircled his mobility scooter.

Meanwhile, what was Whorfin thinking? To students of the great battle, this question remains a source of bafflement. Doubtless his goal was to save his own "skin"—all jokes aside—and pick up where he left off as divine absolute ruler of Planet 10; but a goal is not the same as a strategy, and to the extent he was any longer a coherent entity capable of ratiocination, how did he expect to achieve any such result? Alas, like you, I would like to know the answer myself. What follows, then, is the best I can offer, because I am not convinced I know.

We may stipulate at the outset that his ambition far exceeded his grasp. Painted as he was into a corner, even the madman had to realize that his fearsome reputation and the luster of his legend were no substitute for a capable fighting force, that under these conditions his few woefully mismatched fighters were useless to his plans, which likely anticipated a journey back through the Eighth Dimension in order to be reunited with his biomass and material form. But for this purpose he would require something like an OSCILLATION OVERTHRUSTER, and unfortunately for him only two vehicles were within the range of possibilities: Buckaroo Banzai's Jet Car, securely hidden in the Apache silver mine, and Emdall's siege vessel overhead. Had Whorfin, then, at long last and like so many other criminals before him, become tired of being a fugitive and consequently wished to surrender himself? In some sense to become whole again in the Eighth Dimension? Or was he mad enough to think he could somehow, by sheer force of will, defeat the massive ship and all its firepower? Or, finally, did he simply wish to go down fighting, to "go out with a big bang" in a final operatic climax worthy of Wagner?

And while I am no exopsychologist and any analysis of Whorfin's mental state (by human standards) is doubtless a complete waste of time, I might speculate that he likely relished the idea of causing the Earth and its population to be destroyed in the bargain . . . thereby cementing his legend as the bloodiest Lectroid of all time. No mean feat, I might add.

Was this the paramount thought going through his mind, then? The thought of smashing Earth with the hammer of the mother ship—of going out in a blaze of glory and taking billions of earthlings with him—the thrilling feeling of power in one last exhilarating moment. If our death warrant had been issued by John Emdall's alien expedition, John Whorfin was ready to sign it of his own volition, feeling no compunction about destroying our world.

Suicide, then, destroying himself and our world as if it were his own, a grandiose go-out-with-a-bang ending, in other words . . . even as master of nothing, not even his own demented consciousness: was that his twisted thinking?

I will leave that for the reader to decide, with the proviso that one might liken our own behavior to a death wish, as Buckaroo's suicide whistle crackled over our earpieces and we charged into the valley of death.

INTO THE CAULDRON

I have stated already that the rest of us had not exactly been waiting in reserve, and it is only the barest truth to say we had been advancing under fire, steadily clearing pockets of resistance from one Lectroid redoubt to the next; and now, upon hearing Buckaroo's suicide whistle and his explanation of what was at stake—the countdown to Armageddon, now with approximately one minute left—we threw caution to the wind.

Carrying out an enveloping action on the left flank, Hoppalong and I formed a single fire team, while the other half of the pincer movement, Muscatine and Pecos, assembled behind Abysmo, who—apparently resuscitated by Buckaroo's two-finger whistle or some quick troubleshooting by Muscatine Wu—now rolled over onto all fours and loped forward like man's best friend or a fearless Arabian, charging into the terrible thick of it, over the strewn bodies of men and their animals and shrieking mounds of degraded Lectroid biomass.

My own role thus far has been relatively minor, owing to the constraints imposed upon my maneuverability by the bulky weight of the Bubble Gun and the Jelly Beam, which, due to their immense theoretical destructive capacity and ability to unpack superstring, Buckaroo still judged too risky to employ, especially in a highly populated zone. Were they therefore useless? I feared so, until the voice of Buckaroo crackled in my ear.

"Reno, is the Bubble Gun good to go?" he yelled hoarsely; and I spotted him now through the smoke, at the base of the missile launch tube and beginning his ascent in pursuit of Baltazar and the phantom Whorfin.

So why did he want the Bubble Gun? He has said that in view of the short time window and his own predicament, he adjudged it impossible to stop the launch by gaining access to the Shilka's controls. Rather, his plan was twofold: to capture Whorfin-in-Baltazar and shoot the missile out of the sky in the event the worst happened. As a third option, and without putting myself in the great man's boots, my hunch is that he might also have been considering blowing the Shilka—and himself, along with Tommy—to smithereens. No matter his plan, the fact was that he required the experimental Bubble Gun and at this desperate hour there was no room for argument.

"Yes, no—not a hundred percent!" I shouted back. "More yes than the other, but suboptimal . . . !"

"Then I'll fix it! Heave it, won't you, Reno!"

To make himself clear, he repeated his demand . . . although, as I say, the sight of him and Tommy still in the throes of hand-to-hand combat made me leery of hurling the bulky weapon prototype onto the Shilka from any distance. But damn the torpedoes and my own vertigo (I had been grazed by a Lectroid dart); now it was my duty to do as told or die trying.

I gave the order: "Time to jump! I don't think these clowns can shoot."

"Sure, forward march. I feel like stretching my legs," joked Pecos.

"Oh, joy, I love freelancing!" Muscatine shouted back . . .

. . . as she and Pecos moved forward in a center thrust behind Abysmo and Hoppalong and I skirted their flanks, running in opposite directions.

"Just keep breathing," I reminded the others. "Don't forget to breathe."

"*Da*, always good idea," agreed Hoppalong, who dodged a sniper and a stream of napalm at the same moment I saw an unfinished Lectroid straggler blow his bellows and throw a pair of darts my way. The insolent fellow was foaming and I could have ventilated him with my Vepr scattergun, but I was in a mad rush, breathing the spirit of Rawhide and Geronimo . . . while breaking into a dead run toward the Shilka . . .

. . . as the air crackled with more gunfire from Lectroid and Templar shooters that threw up sparks from paving stones but failed to slow our offensive . . . a subject to which I might someday devote an entire history as some "military experts" have already done. But, for now, suffice it to say our sole focus was the Shilka and its imbecilic Lectroid pirates who stupidly flattered themselves by thinking they had cornered Buckaroo and Tommy by "chasing" them up the missile tube, thus trapping our heroes between the shrieking horde below and the phantom Whorfin, who, as one with Baltazar, presently sat astride the rocket warhead at the very summit of the ascent!

One does not need an exceedingly clever mind to recognize that this was Buckaroo's destination all along; but we are talking now about Lectroids, who naturally boasted of their "victory" by puffing and beating their chests in view of the phantom Whorfin, who was not pleased.

"Fools! You hillbilly idiots with no scrap of brains!" he berated them, simultaneously using Baltazar's foot to kick at Buckaroo on his way up—a freak show with its comic elements.

Yet are we humans not equally tempted to show off? Certainly we Hong Kong Cavaliers, in the best show business tradition, were playing to an audience of our own, by which I mean the television cameras and odd cameramen lurking about.

"*Banditi!* That way, Reno!" one of these helpfully pointed for my benefit shortly before I was knocked off my feet by the same grenade blast that put Abysmo down for the final count and sent a searing shard of him through Muscatine's arm. Seeing the robot burnt black and hearing my old pal's pain, I felt her love for the big guy; but for the moment these were lost thoughts, as we both picked ourselves up and continued to tread our way forward.

"Those savages . . . I'll peel their phawking skulls!" she vowed. "Stay safe, guys!"

"You, too!" echoed Pecos. "Going in with my hydrocannon . . ."

"*Da! Da! Ya tozhe!* Engaging vermin now," hollered Hoppalong, barely audible over his clattering M60.

At the same time Buckaroo came through loud and clear. "Reno!"

"Present!"

"Now, damn it! I need that Bubble Gun! Trust me, I'll catch it!" he yelled in my ear; and without another moment's hesitation, I did as commanded and hurled the Bubble Gun backpack with all my strength, momentarily exposing myself in the process, before diving for cover behind a pile of wriggling "dead" Lectroids gnawing on Templar flesh. Yet it was not this horrid scenario that nearly gave me a heart attack and drove my scream of fury in the next moment—no, it was the sight of Hanoi Xan on his scooter, swooping in out of nowhere to snag the Bubble Gun out of midair with his ancient walking stick!

"Cockroach! Snake! You Godforsaken man-rascal! Burn in hell, you shite for a soul!"

All that and then some I howled, as did the others—every epithet you would expect on the last day, at the last hour—and yet directly did Xan grab the backpack, he flew straight at Buckaroo.

"What?! What the . . . are you kidding me? Bull caca?!" Our voices merged and our minds raced, and who could blame us? Had Xan come to the rescue once again? Performing his second good deed in under a minute? It did appear, on this day at least, that he had left his black intentions behind.

Let us now revisit the next minute—arguably the most momentous in world history—looking at it in light of what we now know, at least to the best of my memory, ordinarily like an elephant's, which may differ from the official account, however.

Odds and ends: my grimy hands, the smell and taste of cordite in my mouth and nostrils, my eyes scanning slug-faced Lectroids falling on top of each other, the face of Jarvis—"Every damn time I turn around! Open your eyes, people, before I crank it up!"—a hawk leisurely gliding across the square, beer cans, blood and waste, a pair of dead vacationers with their accumulation of personal belongings . . . why, oh why? Out of the corner of my eye, I catch sight of Mona on all fours, carrying her stiletto heels and still filming with her Go-Phone . . . making her way toward Jack Tarantulus, who is crouching behind the Bernini fountain in his boxer shorts.

Under any other circumstances, such a ridiculous sight would send me into paroxysms of laughter—and I may have laughed on this occasion anyway—but my thoughts are of her, amazing Mona.

"Brave Mona," I say to myself, picturing her red-rimmed blues staring up at me during our last breakup . . . this time in Nairobi . . . when tears overflowed and all that came out of my mouth was baby noise.

"What the hell are we saving ourselves for? How do I light a fire under you, Reno?" she had said and reached for me . . . but I pulled back.

"Maybe I don't have the heart. Don't pin all your hopes on me, Mona."

The story of my life, the postponement of adult commitments . . . there's always tomorrow, until there isn't. Now it occurs to me that with a little effort and a little fruit of the vine, a man could damn near manage to be happy with a woman like Mona. I'm breathing her, inhaling her scent, and then . . .

"Xan, thou daemon! Thou viper!" Buckaroo is hollering in a rage, and in the same instant I hear Baltazar's mutant scream . . .

. . . as Buckaroo, Tommy, and Xan grab hold of Cardinal Baltazar atop the missile cone, but not exactly in concert . . . Buckaroo and Tommy with their bare hands and Xan in his hovering scooter by some invisible force, tugging the cardinal from both directions. So our bitter enemy is back, and in a way it is even strangely comforting that things are back to normal, back to what they have always been. Not only has Xan pilfered the experimental Bubble Gun, it seems he also has his eye on Baltazar!

Does Xan already know Baltazar is inhabited by Whorfin? If not, he will learn momentarily, as Whorfin's voice comes alive and screams for help from his "old guard," his "old boys," and Buckaroo hollers at me with equally wild alarm, pointing to a patch of sky above the missile.

"There, Reno! The Jelly Beam! Get ready!"

"What?"

"Jarvis's nose! Aim and shoot on launch!"

"Shoot Jarvis?"

He doesn't answer back, continuing the tug-of-war with Xan, as the missile countdown continues and Jarvis is moaning and groaning upstairs, practically crying, "No, no, nooo! Nothing left to be said, fools . . . lemme just reach back . . ."

Meanwhile Hoppalong is spraying the Shilka cab with the machine gun and Pecos and Muscatine Wu have brought Lectroid poison and a storm of lead to bear, but none of that stops the digital clock; and suddenly Xan skewers Baltazar with his ancient splinter of the true cross at the same instant the ground beneath us trembles! Baltazar screams like a stuck pig and I see fire erupt from the missile!

"Reno! Shoot!" Buckaroo commands and, still not letting go of Baltazar, points his Go-Phone mini oscillating laser at the nose of Jarvis, just as I aim the Jelly Beam and curl my finger around its firing lever.

"Five seconds!" I hear Hoppalong, who knows enough Bulgarian to hit the deck, but a lot can happen in five seconds. A man can get religion, a man can get a conscience or recall the one he used to have, a man can get cold feet and a case of the nerves . . . something about myself I've been unable to admit, indeed have chosen not to talk about until now. This, then, is the gut-wrenching confession I'm giving for the first time to you, dear reader—you to whom I do not know how to lie—that my mind was perhaps not in sync with my destiny. Or, as the saying goes, was the moment simply too big for me?

Is it my imagination, or is the Jelly Beam quivering? No doubt it's Hoppalong at my side, turning knobs on the power pack. "Buckaroo says max power. I'll feed you!"

"Jump, Buckaroo!" Muscatine Wu yells. "Jump, Tommy!"

In the same instant Xan plucks the roly-poly cardinal off the rocket warhead as effortlessly as a cheese ball on a toothpick and the missile streaks upward still carrrying Buckaroo and Tommy. Somebody's crying, wailing over the din, and I squeeze the trigger, sending a superexcited stream of plasma the color of the rainbow straight at Jarvis's ugly mug! Oh, Xan, wretch of a devil, is there another word for you I haven't used? My thoughts race like mad to match the headlong pace of events . . . all of this in the same instant the pulsing Jelly Beam overtakes the missile, converging with Buckaroo's oscillating aiming dot and the missile warhead at a single point in spacetime.

"What is happening?" Pecos screams.

"See you on the eleven o'clock news!" yells Muscatine.

Then the air above us superheats and explodes, but in the strangest way, like a flash of ball of lightning that spreads from east to west. There is no fire. The missile has disappeared and the deafening thunder hits, the shock wave throwing me through the air like a rag doll, headlong over paving stones and into a dreamlike state . . . on the great utopian plain where I blow my saxophone a hundred times better than I've ever played in my life, soaring and honking like Coltrane, all of it cut and mixed into the master track of my life . . . then losing my human form but with an understanding of my own insignificance and constant in my thankfulness to the universe, while in my last thought I wonder what photograph of me the media will use to announce my death, quickly followed by a second last thought—what media? What world?

Then the steady blue screen and the lights go out.

LIVE FROM THE END OF THE WORLD

Lying there in my reduced state of consciousness, I could be forgiven for thinking the centrifugal force of chronological time was already spinning faster and out of control, for at virtually the same moment Xan's light-absorbent eyes fell upon me with all the atavistic nightmares of our race—taking me to a place beyond my understanding where it was all I could do to breathe and convince myself I was still alive. I heard two voices in my ear, only one of which came through my headset.

"Reno! You got this! Open your eyes!"

But whence the command? Who uttered it? None of our remaining team—of that I'm certain. My hunch is that the voice belonged to my old bunkmate Rawhide calling long distance through what sounded like a tin can on the moon; but of course I can offer no proof of this, other than the fact I answered him.

"Rawhide?" I blurted out and opened my eyes to see Xan's scooter looming dimly above me.

"Is it fire? Where's the fire?"

The second voice was Pecos, speaking for us all, repeating the question as another way of asking what had just happened . . . of expressing our despair that Buckaroo and Tommy were gone.

In that sense our world had ended. Granted, the rest of us were still alive—as was our bitter enemy Hanoi Xan, who strangely enough was once again hovering above me in his scooter—but without the unique talents of Buckaroo, what were our chances against the World Crime League, much less an organization that now possessed the Bubble Gun and John Whorfin? Although Buckaroo has often stated that the cemeteries of the world are full of irreplaceable people, in this war there was no one to take his place, no one else to take the measure of Hanoi Xan.

Yet it occurred to me that if the long game—what I may generally call the "future"—was over and we were withal powerless to prevent its loss, the least I could do was this close work, this proper act of ridding the world of this execrable gargoyle and his black malevolence that fate had placed once again directly in my line of sight. Though I normally placed little faith in the lofty sphere of the preordained, my actions already loomed as inevitable; and in my fresh rage I could taste the blood lust in my mouth.

My disgust was further intensified by the pathetic sight of Cardinal Baltazar, crouching before Xan in the scooter like a cowed penitent, fanning himself with one hand and licking his thumbless other like a miserable cur, all while smacking his lips . . . thus fulfilling Xan's prophecy that he would "horse-phawk him until he squats to pee and quacks like a duck."

My finger was again on the Jelly Beam trigger, for how long I cannot say. What was the key to replenish my confidence, to repair the world in some way, if not my finger? But time, in my bubble of solitude, had ceased to flow, and apart from sweating and swearing, for a third time I failed to lay the demon to rest for no reason other than a weakness of the spirit, a dissipation of the will, compounded by the sheer difficulty of absorbing this reality. But reader—having come this far with me—do you think you would not have had the same crisis of doubt? The same comedy of indecision? Call it a cosmic joke if, like me, you take into account all the frivolous killings you have committed in your life, every fly you have swatted, roaches and ants you have sprayed, mosquitoes you have smushed without a second thought, even human beings you may have eliminated, only to hesitate at ridding the earth of its ultimate pest Hanoi Xan, and likely Cardinal Baltazar in the bargain, though his quick death could be considered merciful euthanasia under the circumstances.

As I cursed my fate and Xan's scooter passed within earshot overhead, I overheard the following conversation:

"You are funny . . . such a disappointment to me. Did you think I would dismiss such impertinent behavior?"

"I went in search of trouble, and trouble I have found," the cardinal moaned. "*Ego sum vermis non homo . . . !* A worm, lower than a worm . . . a snake *in herba*, a lost cause whose only hope is forgiveness from the merciful Xan! O Xan, *miserere mei et salva me* . . . ! I am not worth the bullet I deserve, but I am open to your mercy. Perhaps just send me away supperless . . . ?"

Then the voice of Whorfin, rising with great effort and grave misgivings: "Great Xan, belle of Babylon, I know you comin' back for John! Small world, sincerest pleasure! Careful on your bicycle, Hanoi, no speedin', ha, ha! We still got mathematical chance . . ."

"Shut the phawk up. You work for me now," Xan said and slapped both of them across the mouth.

"*Consummatum est,*" whimpered the cardinal and burst into tears; and in another second, still defying all laws of physics, Xan flew low and attempted to take possession of Pecos.

"Ride with me, Pecos!" he offered, probing her mind and affecting to befriend her; but she sprayed him with the hydrocannon and he flew away.

I, Reno of Memphis, being present in the great piazza of Saint Peter, witnessed this with my own eyes.

XXXIV. IN NO MAN'S LAND

> Why is there woe in thy heart?
> And why is thy face like one who has made a far journey?
> —Epic of Gilgamesh

The last thing Buckaroo remembered, prior to riding the missile through a pinhole in time crystals, was aiming his Go-Phone mini oscillating beam with its advanced SQUID at a convergence of violent shock waves that suddenly grew from a swirling counterclockwise ink spot into a dreamlike horizon, a spacetime ripple capable of swallowing the entire Vatican—perhaps the entire Earth—when a synapse buzzed in: "You are a tachyon in a roundabout. Nothing can hurt you. Due to a one-in-a-gazillion shot, your account is still open."

And the deluge of colors! The swirling wonders . . . wheels within wheels of light . . . a spiral galaxy moving like a Ferris wheel of stars, like a million shiny fairies, washing over him unrestricted by causation, gravity, or time and space, but, no, that was wrong; there was no "washing over," no up or down, no inside or out, no *noesis*, no *noema*, no *am I*, just all as one and the wholeness of primordial being! No limits, no borders, no body, no *sensum*, only the collapse of time and a fading away of his ego and his faith in reason—his very identity—into oblivion. Terror! *Jouissance!* Transcendence! But here was the fussy little aporia: *"Everything is a lie," says the liar.* To whom was this great illumination, the presence of his absence, appearing?

Then a violent lurch back to the time horizon, the phenomenal world, culminating in a flight through gales of wind and crashing waves, past the Pillars of Hercules and up to heaven through a series of celestial spheres . . . each a more sublime and fragrant nut garden than the last, and along whose paths of precious stones he encountered many of history's greatest figures.

"Welcome to the company of heaven, where zephyrs of delight blow," said a swarthy, unshaven Jew who identified himself as "Yeshua Ha-Nozri. Also known as Jesus, from Nazara, Judea, by way of Bethlehem. Son of . . . it's a little complicated . . ."

Then there were the three white-robed old-timers—two of whom looked up from a golden table of dainty meats and other culinary delights to greet him, and the third who held only a rice bowl and a seaweed stick.

"A pleasure, Buckaroo. Come, let us argue logic. I am called Socrates of Athens, son of Sophroniscus and Phaenarete, though some disavow my existence also . . ."

"My name is Master Kong, known to billions as Confucius. Allow me to introduce you to Prince Siddhartha. We have been expecting you for lunch . . ."

In another sphere Einstein arrived with those he called "some of the old hands"—Galileo, Leibniz, and Newton—and in all these encounters Buckaroo had many questions; but the bearded worthies spoke only in riddles or verse, with the exception of Sun Tzu, who told him bluntly, "Enough of this rambling bullshit. Just handle this business."

Buckaroo nonetheless felt greatly animated in their company and, after brief conversations, resumed his flight toward the highest sphere—a palace of immeasurable brightness in infinite space—and it was this blinding purple light that bore down on him when he opened his eyes to discover his form once again had assumed a steady state, albeit suspended on a huge rotating spinner rack and surrounded by the contours of a magnificent chamber in which unseen witnesses buzzed in the shadows. Along the way he had lost his colorful stage outfit and wore only tattered boxer shorts and one cowboy boot; yet he rejoiced to be alive in spite of feeling like he weighed a ton and was submerged in a big glob of pudding, having survived an undeniable trauma to the brain despite a self-scan that revealed only a mild concussion. It made no sense, but this obviously meant nothing.

"Ooh, someone turned the lights back on," he said, blinking and gasping for breath (low-oxygenated air and heavy gravity?), trying to pinch himself, desperate for a heartbeat; but there was no need, because he was roused by the pungent scent of something like formaldehyde and a crush of Lectroids who were already probing him with cone-shaped trocars and glass magnifying eyes, squeezing and tugging at fasteners that seemed to hold him together, twisting his skin; but, strangely, the process was not painful. So not heaven, but a physical exam by aliens . . . meaning he was alive . . . but in what universe?

By what route, by what dimension, by what timeline had he traveled to this place? He vaguely remembered the blast and the flow upward through the heavenly spheres full of tranquility and forgiveness, for how long he didn't know. Meeting Jesus and the Buddha . . . both with aristocratic British accents . . . and then a muddled feeling of switching between life and death and back again, before being pulled finally into terrible cold darkness and demoralization, with pieces of himself floundering, rudderless, amid attacks from his own conscience—all his doubts and shame, the wreckage from all the wrongs he had committed— that crawled over him like soul-sucking leeches; and from somewhere the blues of Robert Johnson nearly lost in a howling wind and the thudding pulse of heavy metal Megadeth over a Mexican radio station: "You take a mortal man and put him in control, watch him become a god, watch people's heads a-roll . . ."

But in what sense were these qualia real? And what was reality anyway, but a transactional state agreed upon by a network of nodes? How long, and in what uncharted regions, had he been adrift? How much time had passed back on Earth? Had he even gone forward or perhaps back to an age long ago? The thought caused his mind to spiral, to take apart and put together a thousand possibilities. Could he be there and here at the same time? Was he, in effect, still back on Earth? In the Eighth Dimension? Was he, in effect, even alive in the understood sense of the word?

There was worse to come, all too terrible to replay, until he managed to close the spigot of onrushing horrors and squint into the otherworldly light above, hearing Jimi Hendrix now—"Purple haze, all in my brain. Lately things they don't seem the same . . . don't know if I'm coming up or down"—and heaving a sigh of relief to be back in cyclic time. Or was he?

"I'm not dead yet, fellas, so hold off the postmortem!" he managed to complain, despite his psychic discomfort at being so probed by the repugnant examiners. "And what else have you touched with those scaly appendages? Where's Perfect Tommy? Where's my telephone?"

His examiners offered no reply, other than to spray him again with the same odorant which was likely not a preserving liquid but an antidote or a sanitizer for a particular stench (possibly thermite or rocket propellant?) arising from himself; and it occurred to him that perhaps he was embalmed already.

Through the purple fog, he could see a number of "ordinary" Lectroids in ice cream suits who appeared to have just gotten off work—although he didn't know why he thought this, other than the fact that they carried what could have been lunch pails and seemed to share a certain easy camaraderie—and white-veiled medical students on their way to class. Or perhaps this was the class and he was the model patient or curiosity piece they were meant to observe.

Somewhere a door now opened to admit other Lectroids in elaborate purple gowns and tall hats of the same color—high priests he would learn—and up above, in a high alcove, still other Lectroids played a game like dice . . . or were they tossing and reading auguries? Deciding his future on a coin toss? Or . . . who could say? And these were only the known unknowns.

Where to begin to describe the present strangeness? He tried to guess the age of the Lectroids and his surroundings but found it impossible. From what he could see, the great room abounded in symmetries: double stairways that each led to double balconies which were themselves divided into four mirrored segments, each containing eight statues of what he judged to be eminent Lectroids (medical professors, perhaps?), angled in such a way that the multiplier effect continued indefinitely in the imagination.

Then there was the odd light emanating from a huge skylight that appeared artificial—fake sunshine—and beyond these features I have mentioned stretched a vast darkness from which he heard much wing flapping, leading him to wonder how many more Lectroids were present. Dozens? Hundreds? Since there was no basis on which to venture even an estimate of their number, he stayed with his senses, studying and smelling only the handful of Lectroid figures I have described, until a radiant "Penny Priddy" came into view.

"Penny!" he thought, thrilled beyond belief; and it was only a thought and nothing more, for his joy was beyond words and no sound escaped his lips. His flight—above all his journey through multiple mesovortices and a final sloughing off into whatever dimension he now occupied—had taken too much out of him, leaving him with the aforementioned injuries in addition to aching muscles and blurred vision from the concussion of either the explosive takeoff or the rocky landing.

"Buckaroo, my darling. You can't say I haven't been patient, waiting to rekindle our tender affections," his Penny told him in that gentle voice he knew so well. "Welcome to Cloud Nine . . ."

"Cloud Nine . . . ? A ninth dimension?"

"Nine and a half of your minute units," she replied. "Nine and a half minutes of putting your life in a dangerous situation in order to meet your lovesick lady. But what a stunt . . ."

"A stunt, as I live and breathe," he coughed between huffing and puffing for oxygen. "Of all the speakeasies in the universe, you had to walk into this one. You must be—"

"I am Penny from Planet 10. Would you like to step in for a dip?" she said with a smile that for all its seeming glory left him only suspicious. "Am I not good to see, a sight for your sore eyes?"

"Oh, you're good . . . very good. When is your birthday, Penny?" he asked her. "Come to think of it, what was your mother's maiden name?"

Getting only garbled responses to either security query, he was no longer able to delude himself, with the result that he made an outcry—"Damn you!"—and her visage metamorphosed into her true form, a Lectroid who viewed him with something like a pitiful expression.

"Just trying to help," the beast seemed to say.

"A little too busty, but thanks," he replied. "Not sure my legs work— am I okay? Gonna need a wheelchair?"

Receiving no answer, he watched with concern and fascination as the parabolic disk shone its eerily beautiful violet light on his every blemish—a few prematurely gray hairs and facial wrinkles, tooth fillings, moles, and patches of cellulite—before appearing to extract his entire spine and bloated stomach to examine both from various perspectives inside the disk itself . . . all by virtue of a power he did not understand and could do nothing to stop.

"Seriously humiliating, friends, thanks—peace and harmony—but it's mostly my head that hurts. Careful that thing doesn't run out of batteries," he complained, squinting his eyes to perceive a shaft of light and a flowery scent and a royal procession of dark Lectroid lords and courtiers wafting down one of the stairways on pillows of pure light; and in their midst floated an immense, shrouded figure he could only assume was the empress John Emdall Thunderpump—flying literally by the seat of her pants in a spectacular padded costume of the purest white girded with a belt of iridescent crystal and topped by a halo-like tiara that resembled Yogo sapphires and diamond tassels like twinkling stars. She was more roundish than the virtual figure he had glimpsed in their holographic encounters years earlier—indeed she appeared to be the largest Lectroid he had ever seen, having the inflated aspect of a blowfish—but perhaps it was this quality which provided her sufficient buoyancy to carry her bejeweled staff, a large glowing cudgel fashioned after the greater obelisk hurled from the sky into Saint Peter's Square; and her face appeared to emit a similar glow beneath her dark veil and crown of life, as if she and the symbol of her power were naturally of one and the same immutable substance.

At once his Lectroid examiners bowed down reverently to her, although rather pointedly the priests did not follow suit and continued to gab among themselves. But as for the rank and file, even their shadows showed obeisance, according to the old saying; and while it is tempting to ask with what state of mind he witnessed her dramatic entrance, realistically how could he view her with anything other than awe and trepidation? As he later said to me, the sight of her was like gazing at shiny pixels that disguised her true appearance. Even closing his eyes, he continued to see her brilliant raiments but almost nothing of her face.

Her reaction to the sight of him was less transparent and may never be understood completely, except to say that she appeared to puff herself up even further and "spoke" to him telepathically through body movements, much as one communicates with exaggerated excitement to a dog or small child.

"Buckaroo Banzai . . . how was your ride?"

"A little bumpy," he expressed as a thought.

"This is Buckaroo Banzai," she communicated to her underlings. "He is something special, a monkey boy who rises to the level of our science, a semi-immortal doubtless needing elbow room away from his dysfunctional planet."

"Semi-immortal . . . ?" our disoriented hero managed to question, getting her attention.

"After all this passage of time, hello and good evening, Buckaroo Banzai! Cheers to you, for making it through the Eighth Dimension, because you are beautifully intact, all things considered," she made him understand.

"John Emdall? Or her close relative . . . I must be dreaming," he murmured.

"A dream come true, for us both," she replied, if not audibly. "You have channeled your energy well, as usual, Buckaroo Banzai."

"I try not to waste it, but to give it my all every time," he said.

"Because you are a passionate being . . . a passionate, good-looking class of monkey boy, the dearest I have found, who lives life to the fullest and cares deeply about other beings. But what were you trying to prove?"

Trying to prove? For a moment he drew a blank and could come up with nothing, unable to recall his last moments on Earth and very little of anything afterward.

"How could I ever forget? I came on a mission for peace, in search of Your Excellency's patience and understanding," he said nevertheless and struggled to formulate his own questions. "How long—? How did I—?"

"How did you get here? That is still pending investigation by our engineers and line of command. You were a long time in oblivion, nearly nine and a half minutes according to our estimations, without protection from gamma radiation—and you fell a long distance. I know many who have never returned . . ."

"If it was easy, anyone could do it," he commented, performing a deep breathing exercise and still trying to shake the cobwebs out of his head. "My OVERTHRUSTER phone app could never quite lock in. Getting a vector was the best I could do . . . and it feels like it got pretty ugly. Looks like I'm hooked up to the works."

"Sorry we could not offer you a softer landing, Buckaroo Banzai, but you were lucky, for it is our solstice day and a holiday from killing. For that reason our vessel *Imperatrix* did not destroy you but corrected your course toward us, where we caught you on the spinner, covered in quantum foam and fuzziness, smelling of urine and mumbling about 'the giants' . . ."

"Tokyo Giants?" he said, searching his foggy memory of the trip.

"You would know better than I," she replied. "A matter of the heart, perhaps."

"Yes, a matter of the heart, my life flashing before my eyes," he reflected, still struggling to recall. "And Tommy?"

She made a noise that sounded like an exhalation, a whoosh of air that conveyed a certain depth of emotion: "Tommy has never awakened in the regeneration capsule. It is too bad—he was a very special human but also suffering extensive injuries . . ."

"He fought like the dickens, with all he had," Buckaroo replied, pained beyond words; and directly he heard this devastating news, she gave him worse:

"We thought we could do business with you and for that reason looked kindly upon your planet, but now you're here and John Whorfin still wanders Earth. Therefore without further ceremony I had to give the order . . ."

". . . To destroy the whole world?" Buckaroo gasped, his chest growing even tighter at the enormity of what he was hearing, while simultaneously detecting a foreign presence—alien to his body and yet seeming to emanate from his fourth chakra—caused by what? A heart blockage? The rotating mirror disk? A chemical injection? John Emdall herself? Or the same foreign agent he had sensed earlier in his pineal gland?

"It is not the whole world, it is only *your* world, a baby world out of billions," she made clear without any great concern, yet seeking to tranquilize him. "Strong planets do what they wish, and weak planets accept what they must. But let us not be doomsayers. Even galaxies have collided, but who mourns their loss? What is important is that once again our paths have crossed, meaning our souls have connected . . . brought together like the first time . . . meaning it is no accident that we find ourselves at this crossroads."

"You perverse royal butcher! Slaughtering billions, when all we asked was to survive—my God!" he erupted in disgust at her icy lack of concern for his world, straining against his invisible restraints.

"No need for words, no need for drama," she hushed him.

"No, no need for anything now, not if it's all over," he muttered morosely but caught himself before surrendering altogether to defeatism. "But even if I'm the last earthling, the human spirit will survive in me."

"Yes, unfortunate . . . the loss of life. So sad to give up on humanity," she informed him.

An interval of indefinite duration passed in which he heard his own voice still screaming, reminding him that time in this place seemed to drag and even loop back on itself. Since Emdall did not "speak" but communicated instantaneously, she seemed unbothered by the awkward lag effect; yet the phenomenon raised a question that long had fascinated him: did a sense of time, even time itself, depend upon inherited physiology?

"You failed yet again but did your best, so give your wings a little shake and go on . . . since there's no going back. Order had to be restored," she pointed out, while inquiring of the Lectroids around the floating exam table, "His functions?"

Buckaroo already had self-diagnosed the symptoms of a serious concussion, a separated shoulder, a broken large toe, and a collapsed lung; and now in a painful intake of breath, he watched the parabolic disk mark up his neck with bursts of radiant energy that caused a taste of alien swill to rise in his throat, along with an intense burning sensation on his tonsils and a sudden hacking cough and hiccups, as if he had ingested something spicy that threatened to culminate in what? Heartburn? A cry in vain that was to be a requiem? His *finalis*?

"Some monkey vomit and a degree of mutation on a cellular level from photon exposure," his examiners reported.

"Mutation? You mean my DNA? What are you hitting me with now?" Buckaroo anxiously inquired, eyeing the disk as a further radiation source.

"But his functions are excellent . . . a high traffic of thoughts and good meat on the bone," his examiners continued, squeezing his muscles. "A complex but serviceable structure, courtesy of the Great Architect. Much like the brain of a Voltymion ooze slug . . . and here, see the shiny pump, it takes the blood . . . the bloodsucker. Let us pull the parts."

"Have a heart," Buckaroo managed to jest. "Let's not get carried away, boys . . . as if I cared anymore . . ."

"Yes, I believe it is called a heart," explained John Emdall. "Buckaroo Banzai, the golden man, is known to have a heart of gold."

"Not gold, but fire!" a Lectroid examiner claimed with animated movements.

Translation: "Because, look—a luminous kernel! He has a supernal soul? . . . On my oath!"

Either as cause or consequence, it seemed that the overhead disk was turned suddenly to a higher setting and sharper focus, causing it to spin incomprehensibly fast and glow more brightly. Without going into graphic detail, I further will report that the Lectroids present began to chatter animatedly among themselves, goosing and prodding every part of him with sudden enthusiasm and anticipation . . . particularly his head and chest; and John Emdall herself hovered closer to see a tiny orb—a minuscule stone or a seed—embedded in his heart muscle, revealing with every throbbing pulse a tiny flame, blindingly bright, within the particle's protective coating . . . a phenomenon that caused the Lectroids to vibrate in a state of supreme agitation.

"A holy seed! Do you see the numen? The colors! A flare off the sacred rainbow flame!" they exclaimed. "From Planet 1, garden of the primordial gods!"

"A little hazy on the worship picture, but feel free," Buckaroo gamely murmured to himself. "I've got all the time in the world . . ."

Of course he spoke in jest, but his examiners were apparently in deadly earnest, arguing so vehemently over what Buckaroo interpreted as differences of opinion over divine signs, colors, and gemstones—it was all so confusing—that John Emdall at last demanded, "The priests must decide! What say the priests?"

In fact she doubtless spoke because the high priests were already involved, having flitted down from their perches to inspect this rare human specimen . . . even as she regarded their every move with what Buckaroo judged to be antipathy and intense excitement.

"It is written," expressed one who appeared to be the head priest. "Six colors and six steps to the throne, seven rays of light behind a veil of stone. And within the flame, the Bloody One alone, smaller than small yet greater than all that is known."

"Reborn as the divine child and Superpartner who will lead us to a new land of plenty, according to the ancient sources!" rejoiced a lesser holy man.

"Or tall tale! There are many stories."

"But also correct doctrine and true teachings that he could not have known . . . yet arriving on the solstice in accord with the old pattern."

"But the kernel of the Bloody One in a homeless outsider?"

"How better to test our faith? Where better to hide the secret?"

"But a hairy monkey boy? Yes, perhaps a transman or demigod offering another way, but this is a naive belief!"

"Remember the parable of the monkey paw that fell from the sky! And the black beast who walks at midnight . . ."

"As do daemons and spies!"

The priests continued to argue vehemently among themselves—their verbal fencing escalating at times to physical blows—only to declare at last, "We cannot judge. He must be put to the question! A report must be made!"

None of this made much sense to Buckaroo, but he had a feeling it did not bode well. Something about the mood in the room had shifted, and something extremely irregular, with a high asking price, was about to happen. He naturally would not whimper to his captors or beg for his life—not after these murderous creatures had terminated his world, lopped it off as casually as an arm or a leg—but he could be forgiven for cursing them, and himself. If only he had never gone into the Eighth Dimension the first time, John Whorfin would have remained locked inside the lunatic inmate Emilio Lizardo, who would have died and been buried on the grounds of the asylum. No, the blame for all of this . . . the resurrection of Whorfin, Emdall's intervention, the end of the world . . . lay squarely at the feet of Buckaroo Banzai and the Pandora's box he had opened.

"Look, the little jewel is moving again . . . !" one of the priests exclaimed through squeaking noises . . .

. . . as Buckaroo experienced the sensation for himself, feeling now an unmistakable ripple of energy moving from the sixth chakra down to the third, into the area of his solar plexus. So the little intruder seemed to be traveling, but why . . . ? And why at that precise moment, seeing his distorted reflection and the entry wound on his neck in the whirling disk, did he think of the missing particle, the little "firefly" . . . last seen where? Creeping into—no, breaking into—his flesh and down the memory hole?

"The monkey seems sexually flustered!" the one I have identified as the head priest gesticulated. "His seeding rod is growing, standing! And strongly so!"

"Let us ease up! Enough with your probe, which may jeopardize the safety of the little godling!" the empress now commanded, ordering the priests to refrain from striking his manhood like a punching bag, or worse, as they were intent on doing.

A FLIGHT TO THE CASTLE

Aroused or not—an involuntary reaction, after all, that need not be sexual—Buckaroo felt himself levitating, rising from the spinning table and alighting on something so wonderfully soft it might have been a cloud. As to the duration of this small journey, indeed how to measure time in this world, he had no idea; but he found himself sitting in the sumptuous lap of John Emdall's royal padded garment that enveloped him like a fluffy clamshell; and in the next instant they flew together out of the dank chamber through the upper hatch into what felt like another atmosphere, indeed an altered state of being: a palatial room of thin black marble as clear as the dark sea, lit by pale gaslights in geometric designs and murmuring fountains of incandescent liquid, like something out of old Araby. Despite its immense size, the entire structure—a magnificent purple pyramid atop four golden plinths—seemed to float miles above the surface, giving a panoramic view of a dim dwarf star and twin reddish sun dogs that formed something like a triangle—and below these, a smoke-shrouded baby "moon" that emanated a mournful tone, audible even here below.

"It's called the Moon of the Misbegotten," she purred in her gravelly voice, interrupting his reverie.

"And that droning noise ⸱ . . ?" he queried. "It sounds like a tidal wave."

"The collective soul of prisoners locked in the azure vault," she replied with no trace of emotion. "Since it is the occasion of our principal solstice and crescent moons, they cry out for my grace."

"That rock is a prison?"

"It is not a rock but a piece of blue ice," she informed him.

"No shouts of joy, then . . ."

"But who does not love a good prayer uttered in earnest? All of Planet 10 resounds with their groans, their sobs. It is something I have to do, like an acting . . ."

"An acting gig?" he said.

"'An acting gig,'" she repeated. "It sounds hollow, doesn't it? Monotonous."

When he said nothing, she made a sweeping gesture. "Above and below, to the farthest points and farther than the eye can see . . . I am the monarch of heaven."

He returned his gaze to the planet's surface, where—seen through drifting gas and particulate matter—great dust storms swept over an arid landscape of orange regolith and robotic diggers at work in ponds of boiling water and swarming mounds of overabundant giant "insects" . . . while, beyond, a vast lava lakebed stretched toward a vanishing point of jagged massifs, fiery volcanoes, and an electric-blue-edged horizon.

"Not too hot and not too cold," she continued.

"Maybe a mite drafty . . ." he noted, feeling a chill from perhaps a number of factors.

"You are cold? I'll get you a suit. And of course we have the volcanoes to heat our hives."

"And the combustible air which can be fatal if swallowed," he joked.

"How you tickle me with your mind and clever wit, Buckaroo Banzai. But how does a monkey boy preach to a Lectroid with forty thousand years of life experience? That is most humorous."

He conceded her point and said nothing, as she continued to extol the glories of her world: "From here you cannot see the great orchards on Mount Wah-Wah or the spectacle of our brick and ironwork bunkers below the surface, our mammoth electricity generators, famous libraries and centers of learning, or even the great orbiting stations by which we coax water from the clouds into the largest system of modern aqueducts and irrigation canals in the known universe and many other big pieces of work—all of which I have engineered, including many inventions, and made my mission in life despite all odds."

"A legacy they will put on your statues, no doubt," he said. "One for the history books."

"Yes, I expect the good to be returned to me," she conveyed to him, going on to boast of the planet's other attractions: the oracle of Mount Wah-Wah, recreational activities such as spelunking and hunting giant shaggy grasshoppers—and their eggs that "are good and affordable"—as well as the low crime rate and moneymaking opportunities in a modernizing economy that she had managed to wean off several hundred thousand years of tenant farming and the barter system.

"I have broken up the landlord class and the power of the crooked priests," she added. "In the process I have incurred many enemies and seriously so. I will even tell you a secret because my heart is open to you: sometimes I do not hold my own race blameless."

"Modernization can be difficult," he said, "yet an easy trick played on ourselves."

"Yes, in some ways we are still backward, preferring to be lazy and eat our newborns and younglings . . ."

There was a smell in the air of something cooking; but he felt it unwise to ask questions, saying instead, "I guess there are no free lunches."

"Oh, it is free to eat one's own," she explained. "How is it not free if it is one's own?"

"A concept in natural law, then," he said.

"Yes, natural law of the Lectroid," she communicated. "A Lectroid can do anything it wants as long as it is not disadvantageous to the colony as a whole, in which case they must be held accountable."

"A convivial prospect," he said. "Perhaps some even attain enlightenment."

"I do," she allowed. "To be all-knowing. I am already a god who can do anything I want."

"Who has no equal . . ."

She stared at him but said blithely, "I do not share my perch. For that reason I am sometimes lonely, to say the truth."

"Do you eat your younglings?"

"I am a virgin."

"Of course you are," he said, and she again looked at him askance.

"You have the spark of danger, Buckaroo Banzai, and none too subtle," she communicated before turning her attention to blue lightning in the distance. "We have six moons. How many does Earth have? Beware, I know the answer."

"Only one. But we have trees."

Fearing an ungovernable rage, he caught himself. He was ranting, talking as if he still had a world to go back to . . .

. . . as she continued on about the moons, "Of course they are little ones, but there are those who love each of them and even send them love messages. One is a war god, another a large toad, and so on. As the chief deity, I am like their mother and they are like my children . . ."

"Family," he said.

"Yes, we Lectroids are a big family, a proud and handsome race. I think you would grow to love us in the end."

"The future is now . . . ?" he speculated.

"Yes, isn't it beautiful?" she assented, adding, "Of course I want to conquer new worlds and have done so, from one end of the galaxy to the other. I want to do it all . . . to learn new information, to experience all that can be experienced . . . to pursue excellence in all things."

Communicating these thoughts, she projected a feeling that felt like an embrace, which he felt wise to turn away. All the same, he complimented her: "You are Faustian Lectroid."

"I do not know what that means but feel we are in many ways alike," she expressed. "Perhaps that is your purpose, to teach me new things. Something even tells me you will grow to love Planet 10 and accept our ways."

"Absolutely," he insisted. "I shall give the place a five-star review upon my return home."

A home he no longer had? A planet that no longer existed? Now another of her psychic embraces washed over him so intensely that he sensed he was nearing a breaking point, prompting him to change the subject.

"It's never enough, though, is it?" he queried her. "That's why you send ships across the galaxy in search of a new home . . . because your collapsing sun is dying and, with it, your world. The Ice Age cometh."

She evaded the matter of climate change, instead boasting, "Indeed our war fleets fly all the skies like watchful dogs. No one has the strength to challenge our race, or we will engineer disasters against them, and it will go badly for their home."

"And for you," he suggested, "when your puny star burns away to nothing and turns the lights out."

But how long would that take? Thousands of Earth years? What was ordinary time in this place anyway? *Ordinary time . . .* he had a glimpse of his mother in a small New Mexico church, the sun illumining her face through stained glass windows in adobe walls; but he said nothing else in order to save his breath; and this she provided suddenly—or was it slowly?—by pressing her oral groove against his lips and filling his lungs with her exhalation, which gave off a whiff of methane and sensuality. But it was not his mother whose icy fuzz nuzzled his ear.

"That is another topic," Emdall purred. "Perhaps you know of a more beautiful world we would like better . . . ? In that case we shall happily take it . . ."

"Or destroy it? And all that world had to offer?" he lamented.

"It wouldn't be the first time."

"And for what? Bragging rights?"

It was unclear if she understood he was talking about Earth. She projected merely, "So witty. Since we first looked down on this wonderful, clever monkey man with amazing qualities of strength and wisdom, a multidimensional man who admits no limitations, a man beloved by the gods—"

He interrupted to say, "Thank you, but why do I feel my bubble is about to burst?"

She ignored the remark and merely continued, "Beloved by the gods and perhaps a god himself . . ."

"I am no god, only a human being with all my imperfections," he declared.

"Yet carry the seed of a god . . . back to its mother."

He failed to detect her drift and replied, "I believe all humans carry such a seed. It is a human seed, which is why I believe in people."

"I believe in Lectroids, and it is a Lectroid seed. And I am most appreciative," she expressed, as in dramatic fashion she now lifted her veil to reveal half a dozen polychrome eyes clouded by something like cataracts and set in a chiseled, scarred face with a hanging jaw and slathered in what looked like war paint but stank of tallow . . . or, as he would later describe her to me, "the face of a gargoyle on a battlement." But scarred from what? Fire? Acid? A possible medical condition? Or was it simply her natural appearance? That he reacted to her unveiling as calmly as he did can be credited to the fact that in his life as a physician he had seen much worse.

"Our royal imperfections do not bother you, Buckaroo Banzai?"

"Is the scarring only local or . . . ?" he asked, unable to resist touching her scarred and pitted surface—something she took as an intimate gesture.

"Do you wish to see our nakedness . . . ?" she lowed seductively.

"Maybe in the big picture. Right now, I would rather . . . not . . ." he stammered, trembling from the cold, as she moved closer to him and he felt a further mood disorder, a sinking feeling of losing his mental alertness and ability to resist her powers of concentration. At the same time he recognized this diagnosis as merely a failure to understand the bigger issue of her mysterious influence over him.

"We have thought of you often," she informed him, "and wished you only the best since our first encounter so long ago, even though we never got to feel your touch."

"Long-distance relationships are difficult," he conceded. "I have thought of you, too, in my sleep."

She seemed to understand, letting him know, "We have searched for company many places in creation only to get hurt or second-guess ourselves, and the tension builds for both. So we have felt your pain. We, too, know what it is to be plagued by a fruitless search, to lose someone, to open one's heart only to sink into black despair and find yourself alone in the dark next to no one except pieces of yourself lying broken on the ground, bleeding and crying for love and yet wallowing in loneliness until not even the usual distractions can afford pleasure . . . as if the world has stopped and one's hopes are dead, even to feel that you deserve to be alone. Of course you, too, understand how life can be cruel."

"My background speaks for itself," he said. "I have failed my world and everyone I ever loved."

"We all have to pick up after ourselves," she informed him. "But let us drop formalities, allowing us a certain intimacy so that I sense I need hold back nothing from you . . ."

"Your darkest secrets are safe with me."

"So I will let you in on the darkest secret," she told him softly, not in words but in a single outpouring of information. "In my tender years, I was what you call a high-price pleasure slave. It was a job—I won't go into details. You see, I grew up in the refuse pits, eating scraps. It is also the custom among us to have coital relations with family members, which, despite my misspent youth, I did not wish. I was desperate to escape my daddy, so I preferred to sell myself. One night a wealthy Red bought me off the floor of a nightclub . . . an important Red who sent me to finishing school to prepare me for concubinage."

"Like an *oiran*," he guessed.

"A pleasure toy, yes."

"And this Red was Whorfin? He was your lover who inflicted the scars on you?"

"Some are battle scars I wear proudly. As for others, I give the credit where credit is due," she related before revealing more: "With great uneasiness I came to know him quite well, and my proximity to his affairs afforded me information which allowed me to rise in rank among the vigilantes who were to become our revolutionary cadre. Then came the great struggle, and I was to lead our race to victory in the decisive battle on the Plain of Odors, where I activated the stones and rained them down upon the Red Army. It is said I even caused the mountains to sway and tremble."

"That can be risky," he said.

"We were in a hurry to win," she answered.

"No doubt. And I have no problem believing there was a revolution led by yourself," he said. "A struggle of epic scale that closed the door on Whorfin . . ."

"The Red scum had killed us Darklings by the millions and beat us down into bondage for a long time, so our revenge was terrible but not surprising, and the fighters naturally wanted to capture John and stretch him apart. But we shared a secret, a larva between us, so I hid him from the mob in potting soil and arranged instead to have him and his top officers decerebrated and teledeported into another dimension with the new technology. Unfortunately, what a bad idea it was to send him to hell along with his plots! I let my feelings interfere, and then your Dr. Lizardo allowed him to escape from his exile and you shot him down in the sky over New Jersey . . . and at last I thought our dear John was finished, though I mourned my larva, if true . . ."

Overhead, the shadow of something—a bird?—passed and cawed something like a song. With a little premeditation our hero might have pursued this business of the larva or the god seed, but until he was able to collect his strength, it all seemed too much to grapple with . . . marred and defective as his brain was at present.

So he said merely, "I'm afraid I don't yet understand the scheme of things with you Lectroids. I can only try to be a good student who wishes to learn and teach my fellow earthlings something of your genius."

"As you may teach me something of rock 'n' roll since I do not have a taste for it. I am afraid it passes me by."

"You must come to Earth to visit. I'll offer you a full tour . . ."

Another fairy tale . . . his world, all that he ever accomplished or loved, his friends, Penny, gone in a whiff of smoke? It was too much to conceive of, much less bear; and she was going on now about rock 'n' roll?

"Your honest enthusiasm for it puzzles me," she continued, her every word sending him into a deeper tailspin. "It seems to awaken the lowly life in humans, yet you love to sing it."

"I like serene music as well," he said, "and look forward to taking some of your Lectroid tunes back with me."

"We have only one song," she revealed, "but with as many variations as there are stars in the sky. I am well known for my own version and have absolute pitch."

"Then I hope to hear it before I die."

"You shall."

"Thank you."

"It is nothing."

He felt her probing his mind and suspected she could see his true motives and all else . . . his boiling anger at the fate of his world, his terror and sense of helplessness at being utterly dependent on her goodwill.

"Trying to read your thoughts . . . you are worried you will perish in this wilderness?"

"Not exactly—"

"Then perhaps you've caught a fever."

"Perhaps it is only homesickness."

Her eyes flashed with amusement. "You have ridden to heaven and are here as my guest. Nothing can hurt you."

"That is joy to my ears, Your Majesty."

"Call me John. What are you frightened of? Rocks?"

"Lots of rocks . . . and the future."

"To us, rocks betoken cheeriness and the constant renewal of hope. If you are homesick, there is also a nitrate sea full of blossoms, a valley full of snow. We can ride the high country on a prodigious toadster. In my perfect dream, one day you will look around and your Earth will be only a dim memory."

"I am incapable of imagining such happiness," he said with more than a little sarcasm.

"We will have a rich reproductive life," she continued, as his heart sank further.

"Even a modest output would be wonderful, now that you have wiped out my entire species," he replied. "Any chance there are any of my kind left?"

"We will have to take stock after the dust settles. I have just given the order," she informed him.

At that instant everything was suddenly jumbled and hope returned for him . . . or at least appeared on the surreal horizon.

"Just given the order . . . ?" he gasped. "Then—"

Then there was still a chance; and with thoughts of home and loved ones and renewed hopes of life on Earth, he resolved to fight until the very last by any means possible. Of a sudden the milk-white desert of Planet 10 and the belching Vesuvius of Mount Wah-Wah were still bleak but also vaguely beautiful; there was grandeur in its rocky desert and its dazzling firmament of unknown star constellations.

"Yes, isn't it strange how fate contrives a solution?" she was musing. "Two grown individuals catching one another on the rebound and against all the intelligence of nature. But I am ancient now and don't care. I am wanting a soulmate, a twin flame to experience together the miracle of life all around us . . ."

"The miracle of life . . . ? If only . . ."

Perhaps reading his feelings, she explained, "Do not assume it is false hyperbole, Buckaroo Banzai. There has not been a day when my heart has not thought of you; furthermore, the roots of our passion lie in prophecy and the Akashic compendium."

"I never thought of it that way," he said, feeling more and more uncomfortable under her unrelenting gaze.

"You are a tall drink, Buckaroo Banzai, and I mean to have you," she told him bluntly. "I want your holy spark as the prophecy requires."

"You want to fool around."

"In the worst way," she expressed. "You are cold and shivering. Let me put you in my warm pocket."

Beware, he warned himself in vain, as she now enveloped him within her wingspan, pulling something like wool over his eyes—preparatory to force-feeding him her frigid teat, or whatever it was!

How cold to his lips, her noxious taste!

"Maybe I could give you a foot massage instead. Maybe I could just adore your feet, wherever they are," he attempted to say, but his words were virtually smothered by her copious excretion and his own gritted teeth.

"I have enough worshipers," she purred. "Maybe I could give you a woman show."

"A woman show?"

"And you could teach me lady tricks. Teach me, Buckaroo Banzai. My frustration is beyond belief and my hind gut is clean. You have what I want."

"I will do my duty. Is that your clitellum I feel?" he inquired gravely.

"Oh yes! How you delight me! A feather is heavier than my heart!"

THE UNSPEAKABLE ACT

Before proceeding, the more youthful reader may deem it prudent to turn the page, because she next explored him with her spidery feelers and wrapped her moist, mushy region around his proud, erect humanity. May we say therefore he was sexually attracted to a Lectroid? Certainly many have wondered and consulted my opinion on the question; and, insofar as Buckaroo Banzai has made his feelings known to me, I would answer in the following manner. While coital coupling occurred and a degree of tactile pleasure on his part cannot be gainsaid, the word *attraction* may be misapplied under the circumstances. He indulged Emdall in order to survive—requiring her constant kisses in order to fill his lungs—and subsequently likened the experience to hypoxic euphoria and the feeling of being a helpless marionette dancing to an alien tune.

Along with the lack of oxygen flowing to his brain, he was deluged with guilt over thoughts of Penny and the unnatural act he was committing with this alien species and without protection; and this feeling of self-loathing arose from the darkest corner of himself—the self-doubter and luckless impostor who would get the punishment he deserved, the same voice that in a moment of deepest alienation could mourn his own birth and indeed despise the creation of the whole universe, happily telling himself that it was all drawing to a close . . .

. . . as he and Emdall moved in unison, rolling and rising together, exploring the topography of the palace and one another.

Let us just say that he had crossed borders not meant to be crossed, leaving it to this writer of juvenilia to describe the horrid incident that defies description.

"How you electrify me! Spooning with Buckaroo Banzai! The smell of love fills me!" she murmured.

"My intentions are pure, I promise you," he gasped like a drowning man.

"Drive slow, you fool! I am a slave to your rhythm," she cooed, showing the wiggly, ululating stinger in her mouth. "You sexual athlete, you chiseled piece, oh my dumpling, give me your man musket, your hard dawber! How long have I waited for this . . . !"

"Yes, I've heard you're a virgin," he blurted sarcastically and immediately feared for his life, but nothing came of the remark.

"Get back to work, Buckaroo Banzai," she simply ordered; and he himself was building toward a climax against his will and therefore doing his best to concentrate on the little hissing noise inside himself:

"I won't go. I'd rather stay here, sheltered within you, where I have no obligations. I'm merely a diminutive individual, a little squirt, a flare off the big eruption. I didn't ask for this job. Why must I be dragged into the drama and asked to sacrifice myself for this dung heap of a planet? And for what, exactly? More wars and conquests? More killing and cruelty? And after this long? And now it's all on my shoulders? What am I, God?"

Unsure about the source of the small voice but sensing its awful agony, our hero felt like a spectator watching the distressing scene like some dramatic reenactment, as he went zombie-like through the motions of lovemaking . . . if that was what anyone could call it. The empress was blowing like an elephant and seemed to be hemorrhaging something—was she a virgin? Absurd . . . she had been John Whorfin's consort, and what was a virgin Lectroid anyway amid her mounds and tangled hedges he could not even identify? Maybe he was thinking of Penny and even hearing Penny murmuring in his head, all of it so strange as to be almost unbelievable . . .

. . . as he struggled to hold back the discharge she seemed intent on snatching from him . . . this Circe who had claimed him as her own and now brought him to the threshold of death, the "little death" of his life force, his seed, and after all the other injuries life had lately wreaked on him! Did he not have every right to complain if she took his ill-fated soul as well?

On the other hand, was it not an experiment in natural selection? What made Earth so special . . . the human race, including himself? Matter was matter, which begat the amoeba, which begat the worm, which begat the fish . . . which begat the . . . how did the process go? . . . The amphibian, the lemur, which begat the monkey, which begat the man, which begat God and the devil, which, playing outside the rules, begat the Lectroid! My God, he trembled . . . talk about being in the wrong place at the wrong time! He tried to blot her out, but if it was the way of the universe, maybe he had to be okay with it . . . so be it.

It was the little voice that made things worse and brought a lump to his throat.

Believing the voice to emanate from his own innermost confessional, Buckaroo answered, "Right on all points. There's no shame in having doubts and second thoughts—it is said the ancient gods required three tries to make a human being and still didn't get it right—but you can't let the perfect be the enemy of the good. Otherwise you'll always make excuses for putting forth no effort. Not to preach, but—"

"But maybe I would rather fly to the stars and explore all of Mother Nature, even if it means exile from the irresistible force . . ."

"Meaning your destiny?" replied Buckaroo. "Conscientious objector . . . I get it. It's rough out there dealing with the hurts in life. I often have the same urge to pack my bags and hit the highway, but as a physician, I have a duty to help those in need to the best of my ability, especially when I'm their only hope . . . the end of the tunnel."

"I can see the end of the tunnel, but it is still dark."

"I hope you would never harm yourself," Buckaroo thought, disturbed by the voice's cynicism.

"Don't worry," the little voice said. "I would never take my life by my own hand. If I really wanted to escape my lot, I would have done it already. I know that in the end I must do my duty."

"And teach others. You won't fight single-handed," came Buckaroo's promise.

But was he reading the situation properly? Addressing his own insecurities with psychobabble and trite advice? He had doubts; but directly did a few more words pass between them, Emdall dug her claws deeply into his back and cried out, "That's it—come, precious one! Come unto me! Out you come! Happy ending!"

"What's next? Loneliness! I go to die!" exclaimed the little voice, and in a show of unity Buckaroo Banzai likewise cried out a monster scream of ecstasy and pain! An eruption followed, along with the explosive release of energy many magnitudes more intense than anything he had ever experienced, like a heart attack, sending him into spasm after rising spasm of *jouissance*! But, good God, how it hurt! Or was there even a difference? Pain, pleasure . . . was either ever singular and alone?

During the contractions and tremors that followed, Emdall collapsed atop him and gave a fearful shudder, imploring him, "You have melted me, yet given me chills and stolen my heart . . . perhaps even blinded me to the truth. Hold me, Buckaroo Banzai."

"Do I have a choice? I am beneath you in so many ways," he noted, still delirious with the feelings I have described, yet also beginning to itch from some sort of crawling crotch infestation.

"Something I have not felt in my forty thousand years . . . a queer fluttering inside me," she let him know. "Some powerful force came into my brood chamber, almost with contempt, and yet knowing I am its mother."

"Spooky," he said. "Like the prophecy . . ."

"Do you think I believe such mumbo-jumbo? That is for the priests and my masses to entertain themselves. Why do you think I did not destroy your Earth long before, Buckaroo Banzai?"

Utterly depleted, his brain spun aimlessly. "You mean—"

"I thought there was a chance my larva still existed. Even though you swore Whorfin was dead, something told me otherwise. Call it a mother's intuition from halfway across the galaxy."

He shook his head and made an empty joke, saying, "I suppose a paternity test is out of the question."

"You are a sporty monkey man," she expressed, nestling him amid snorts of what sounded like confessionary tears, "but you have a Lectroid level of wisdom. You are the only sweetheart I have had since John Whorfin. Other pretenders I have shaken off like sand fleas and kept by the wayside. And yet I fear our union has created a spark which may burn and consume us."

"How comforting. Be careful what you wish for," he said with fresh urgency. "And now that you have your little precious one, there's nothing to prevent you from destroying Earth."

"I would not be empress of the Lectroids if I did not understand your reservations," she commiserated.

"Reservations . . . ?!"

"A son of Earth who has disappointed everyone after much luck in life had come your way."

"You understand me well, Your Grace."

"John."

"I could kick myself for not obliterating Whorfin and yet perhaps it was not fated to be. I am thinking now of your precious embryo."

"And now you seek happiness in vain, seeing me perhaps as forbidden fruit, the sweetest apple on the highest branch, untouchable by mortals . . . but you have touched me, Buckaroo, and found me juicy, I trust."

In fear of my life, Buckaroo nearly let slip, but assented with a nod. "I only wish we could be on Earth together so you could understand the workings of my human mind."

She appeared not to reject his reasoning and gently pressed his nose like a button. "I have watched many of your concerts and TV shows that tell the story of your life."

"Not exactly . . ."

"Hanoi Xan is a rat."

"That much is true."

"Hanoi Xan stole Penny Priddy."

"It seems so."

"Hanoi Xan is a polecat and a mangy coyote."

"I think he might even have John Whorfin," he said, having learned that the glint in her eyes, along with a slight buzzing noise, meant she was thinking; and she seemed now to be deep in thought.

"I should have tasked Hanoi Xan with the job," she eventually revealed. "But he is a hard man to lasso. No one can lasso him, much less John Whorfin."

"I can lasso him," he said. "I can lasso both of them in three days. If I fail, you can always destroy Earth later."

"Destroy it later . . . ?"

"That's the plan," he said, bringing all his mental powers into play, setting her mind to buzzing for another good minute or so.

"It is too bad you ran out of ammo for your carbine that time," she recalled. "You had the varmint dead to rights in that box canyon—no, it was the Valley of Mystery—out on the big federal range."

"You know all the finer points," he said. "But I'm sure I could find Xan again. And after I do, I'll buy you a margarita at Ramon's."

"Ramon's . . . ! Where you and Tommy eat nachos, drink margaritas, and leave a sawbuck for a tip. No, I am wrong . . . Tommy only drinks Nehi grape soda. What is a Nehi? Nehi to a grasshopper?"

At the mention of Tommy, his expression soured and her thoughts returned to the moment at hand.

"Yes, I know you love me, but perhaps you are not *in* love with me. You love me as an empress but perhaps not as a lover. I am an empress and a goddess but that's not all I am. I dabble in poetry and design stone carving and tattoo art; and although I rule over many worlds, I am still the same coppery Lectroid of humble origin who remembers well her early misfortunes to the point of melancholy and even despising my present responsibilities. In spite of this, I try to live by the rules of life and shall be the kind of spouse to render you good service and loyally love you, never to disappoint you, a partner not lacking in intelligence and warm caring in her heart . . . a caregiver to give a damn about you, to sit by the fire and enjoy its popping sound when we are old, to be terminally happy in other words, occupying one another's genitals."

"Everything but the white picket fence," he commented.

"Yes, we have no wood. But you are getting up in years, Buckaroo Banzai. Look to me for all your longings in one package, and you will never have to knock on the doors of brothels. You will want nothing."

"I want nothing now," he said, "except to go home . . . to show you my moon through the branches."

"Until the cows come home? To live miles from the nearest settlement . . . ?"

"That would be great."

"Why? Because I am not pretty enough?" she suggested and in the next instant appeared to him as the floating head of Penny Priddy . . . causing him to become notably agitated, even unhinged.

"Damnable, you Lectroid scarecrow!" he muttered, only to feel her iron grip at once around his throat.

"Your words cut us deeply and the empress cannot be responsible if . . ." she hissed before hesitating and softening, ". . . if I give you the peace you have been looking for. We shall be together always, even if I have to put you in my pocket."

She gave him a kiss of oxygen and he said with a grimace of gratitude, "I do not find you unattractive. What I have found on this lonely world is the love of my life."

Not another word was spoken then, but his eyes said enough.

THE TEMPTATION OF BUCKAROO BANZAI

Sometime later (as I say, he had lost all sense of time), her royal virgins and privy council arrived. Among the latter, Buckaroo recognized an old friend: John Emdall's former envoy to Earth, first introduced in the adventure *Buckaroo Banzai Across the Eighth Dimension.*

"John Parker? Is it John Parker? I can't tell—seems my head is full of bats!"

Unlike the others, Parker vocalized in English: "Vice Commander John Parker, Buckaroo Banzai. I apologize for the shortage of oxygen, but we didn't know you were coming! Always a pleasure, regardless! The universe is truly a small town!"

"Truly so, Vice Commander John Parker!" agreed Buckaroo. "Yet I am sorry you disappeared from my world without notice."

"He was highly decorated for his dangerous hard work," the empress noted.

"Yes, he made quite an impact on all of us," said Buckaroo, noting that Parker, too, had earned many gruesome battle scars since the last time he had seen him.

"Like you, Buckaroo Banzai, I believed our work was done," replied Parker, who gave him a balloon-like oxygen concentrator and dressed him in antigravity boots and a sparkly padded garment of an unknown material. Trailed now by two attendants who carried his royal train, he followed Empress Emdall out onto the balcony, there to be greeted by military horn blowers down below and an immense horde of her subjects, whose numbers could no more be estimated than the infinitude of stars overhead. Some threw little crackling bombs in celebration, while others carried offerings of delicacies such as fruitcakes and flower blossoms and dispatched these sweet scents upward, flapping their wings at the first sight of their queen—at whose insistence Buckaroo Banzai rested his weary soul in the hollow of a large, decorative stone that served as her royal divan or perhaps even her throne. Nor, given his evident depleted condition and overall muscle laxity, did he object to her hospitality, but watched with rapt fascination as Emdall adjusted her crown before taking wing from the balcony, swooping above her subjects to the accompaniment of martial music and spectacular fireworks issuing from her imperial staff.

"How my love soars!" her dancing and pantomimed message began. "Cheers and long life to my Lectroids of strength and wisdom! Your Virgin Empress and living god speaks to you of interests in her heart so that together we may drink spice syrup and eat candy-flowery bits in honor of our newest colony, the planet called Earth, in whose honor special privileges will also be given!"

Such big news naturally excited the huge crowd while having quite a different effect on Buckaroo Banzai. Still, he designed to hide his alarm, as she gave a brief history of the winged Lectroid race, tracing its survival through a prophetic trek across ten planets.

"Eternal thanks and glory to the miraculous Bloody One," she proclaimed, pointing to the dying red dwarf in the sky and its shimmering sun dogs, "our Superpartner who brought us this far, with the promise to return and carry all true Lectroids to a better world beyond!"

How familiar it all sounded on the one hand; and at the mention of the Bloody One, Buckaroo pricked his ears and had to marvel at the spectacle, the intricacy of nature's plan . . . how the tiny seed had found its way from the dying Lizardo cocoon to himself by way of the monk Costello . . . and how he himself, no doubt doomed, in turn passed the god particle to John Emdall, who at this moment was delivering a lengthy homily of self-adulation to her vast audience, touting her accomplishments as revolutionary leader and mother of the nation, the essence of which may be paraphrased as "Lectroids, whose greatest joy is to suffer and die for your empress, we salute you. Yet under our guidance, you never had it so good. You have lived better than the hypertrophic Red hyenas, whose bonds we threw off . . . better than the kings of many a planet we have conquered in our name. All of this has been our true vision, to which we have dedicated our life and talents, protecting you while you slumbered, leading you in front of enemy forces and against all cases of shady underhanded dealings . . ."

What was certain was that John Emdall looked particularly grand and glowing on this ceremonial occasion, gliding on the shifting breezes and frequently waxing a fluorescent turquoise during sections of her lengthy address to the nation . . . speaking almost entirely with her movements and amazing eyes.

Then, rising to a crescendo, she appeared to look toward the priests before concluding, "And yet we have walked among you as your mother, living simply in the public service with few goods to sustain us and never taking a lover . . ."

Her adoring masses quickened at this last remark—indeed it seemed to arouse a titter for an instant—before they settled back into the kind of reverence and acquiescence reserved for a divine figure, in keeping with her next revelation: "Then one night the Bloody One appeared and a holy wind came upon me in my sleep, causing my opening to vibrate with air noise and filling me with his buzz, saying, 'This is not flatus but a telling sign to the emperor of Planet 10. Where the devil John Whorfin fell, I will give you a new home. This marks the promise to the Lectroids of my own rebirth as crown prince to my carnal mother John Emdall and the chosen guardian of my holy seed, the angel Buckaroo of that far planet."

To say this news set off an uproar of wild shrieks and delirium among the amassed throng below would be to put it mildly, but the excitement was decidedly not shared by the high priests floating off to his right in their purple and Christmas-style spangles. One of these—taken by Buckaroo as the foremost among them—now even made a point of turning his back on the emperor's speech, simultaneously causing a shower of stones to fall from the sky and provoking a general clamor. All of this Buckaroo watched in stunned silence, theorizing only that a volcanic eruption somewhere beyond the horizon might offer a scientific explanation for the deluge of stones that gave no hint of abating.

"The gods are displeased!" the priests protested in a highly agitated song and dance.

"Maybe he means the volcano god," Buckaroo said to himself.

Yet even more frightful portents were in store. Directly the stones struck the surface, they shot back skyward; and the vast array of statuary within the palace and upon its grounds began to quake and pour out something like blood. Among these works was a great stone monument to war martyrs, capped by an image of John Emdall; and this, too, now fell, crushing a number of Lectroids and inciting the general masses to stampede and trample one another.

"It is her! And him! The monkey boy! Mount Wah-Wah is speaking!" clicked the high priest amid the widespread panic that seemed to have unnerved even John Emdall, whose controlled demeanor appeared to slip, however slightly, upon hearing the odd exhortation from the crowd in support of the "baby eater" known as John Red and Raw.

"Seems things are coming a little uncorked, Your Majesty," Buckaroo said, trying simultaneously to remain calm, draw oxygen, and disguise his own motives in the matter. "An awkward position . . . I would hate to think I am a liability to you."

When she failed to answer or crack her frozen demeanor, he followed by saying, "Perhaps I should go silently into the night. I mean leave the planet altogether . . . although that would be the spineless way out and I would of course prefer to leave with you."

To any of this, she did not reply directly, but communicated, "Thank you, Buckaroo Banzai, but I am afraid we are standing on the precipice."

"Indeed the shocks are getting stronger. I trust your world is not in danger?" he replied, leaning on her substantial mass for physical support.

"I mean we are on the precipice of civil war and the end of the peace I have built with nothing but my force of will," she explained.

"It does seem the masks have fallen. The priests look hopped up on something, almost rabid," he noted.

"Doubtless from eating bug nuts," she informed him in a cold fury; and indeed the head priest did appear to be chewing a charcoal-like substance, drooling its black juice over his vestment and multiple amulets.

"Or high on themselves," he speculated.

"Indeed, Buckaroo Banzai, they have long been skimming off the gross in a large way and flying in tight circles with General Red and Raw and delusions of power."

(It is worth noting that this was the first time Buckaroo had heard the name of General John Red and Raw, who would figure so prominently in the next volume of this series.)

"'Red and Raw,' huh? And the horse he rode in on," he mused, observing that only a handful of her equerries on their giant toads stood between the royal throne and the hostile priests who by now were circling overhead in tight formation.

"Self-promoters" was how she described them. "They mean to do me in. I know their agenda but not their plan, and I do not wish to be blamed for delivering the first blow. Do something, Buckaroo Banzai, before I give them mob justice and there is no going back."

"Out to stuff their own pockets?" he said. "We call them confidence men where I come from . . ."

It is well known that Buckaroo Banzai has faced many a daunting challenge in his varied careers as scientist, adventurer, and musical entertainer, but nothing in this life had prepared him for this moment. Having traveled through another dimension and experienced a rough go of it already—something of an understatement—he now stood shivering and oxygen depleted beneath a hailstorm of stones, facing a sea of hostile Lectroids (at least he imagined them to be hostile behind their cold, flinty exteriors) in a foreign world and possible war zone whose ground rules he had no way of knowing. How else could they view him but with condescension, as another conquered species, a prisoner of war, a barbarian freak, a trophy, a crazy monkey man?

And, to be honest, who could blame them? A tale this lurid and fantastical could only be told by an idiot, giving him the idea that his trip through the Eighth Dimension might have gone awry and landed him in the Seventh, territory of dreams and the make-believe. In other words, was it possible he was only putting in a performance on a page of fiction, or as a character in a role-playing video game of his own making, in which case the dangers facing him might be only allegorical and having to do with personal growth? Or was he simply hallucinating, suffering from the effects of oxygen depletion?

Maybe, maybe not . . . there was no way of knowing, short of actually losing his life, whether he was in physical danger: a fatal paradox. He had, then, to assume the worst, make peace with the prospect, and yet fight to the end. But how and with what? His natural first instinct as a scientist was to search his mind and its vast store of knowledge for answers. Under the circumstances, this was a time-consuming fool's errand, however; and at all events his superior powers of ratiocination only fostered in him a sense of his own futility, a defeatism he tried to suppress, but in vain . . . so that in this unprecedented crisis, and perhaps the final minutes of his life, he had but two terrible options: to feel sorry for himself or begin to clap his hands in an attempt to feel better. After all, he was not a rock but a living, feeling being, just as Lectroids, too, were sentient and self-aware creatures, not punch-pressed robots. This much he knew from his interaction with John Emdall and John Parker, both of whom seemed to reflect certain basic human emotions. In addition, although he had a troubling tendency to attribute to strangers his own patterns of thinking—a trait he called narcissistic—he believed that Lectroids, like human children and animals on Earth, paid particular attention to noise and moving objects. But let us be frank; it was also likely the case that he may have had little choice but to believe this, for the situation exhibited every sign of deteriorating into mass hysteria among her minions . . .

. . . as more Lectroids, including some in military regalia, now flocked to join the priests in a formation of concentric circles revolving around Emdall's imperial palace. Yet the question is a nagging one and has been asked of me countless times: what gave Buckaroo, despite his injuries, the courage to get up and dance at that moment in an alien world? Perhaps it is as simple as his answer to me: "Haven't I told you, Reno, that I was tired of living? But I thought I might still be able to do something for Earth. I danced for our planet . . . to save our home."

So it happened that Buckaroo Banzai, the natural-born entertainer, began to whirl and high step, not in the jagged Lectroid style, but with fluid human motion—or as smoothly as one can move when hampered by hypoxia, a fractured large toe, a dislocated shoulder, and a bulky royal cape with a long train—accompanying his dance with a rousing, soulful American anthem that came to him unbidden.

"War!" he shouted with all the depth of feeling he could muster. "Huh! Yeah! What is it good for? Absolutely nothin', uh-huh, uh-huh . . . !"

Although the elaborate outfit he was wearing granted him surprising buoyancy under the heavy gravity, it did little for his spasms of pain and shortness of breath, such that he paid scant attention to John Emdall's booming order: "Quiet, so that all should hear him!"

Was it to the heavens or her millions of followers she spoke? At all events he spent his remaining energies performing for an audience that was next to impossible to read, other than the fact that the massed Lectroids grew quiet and seemingly attentive the moment he opened his mouth and began to gyrate in the style of Elvis Presley or James Brown. Beyond that, who could guess? Were they sullen? Fascinated? Absorbed in what must have been for them his odd and exotic antics? It was his intuition only but he felt from multiple corners of the crowd a psychic wave of peace and agreement—"with you one hundred percent" seemed to be the message—and with even greater satisfaction he noticed that the underground quakes, too, had ceased, and the mysterious stones now paused in midair! This extraordinary phenomenon alone may have accounted for the sense of awe that came over the crowd; and in this he felt the hand of another, most likely John Emdall, not to say the little egg inside her. Not for a moment did he believe such extraordinary power came from within himself, unless he was the avatar of a foreign operator . . . again leading him to theorize he was actually back at the Institute watching and enjoying all this on his computer monitor, though plainly not in his right mind.

"You and I have this understanding," he thought, "and now the proof. I still feel your distress, but you have the power—no sense hoarding it—to repair everything that has been damaged and to see to my safety, or at least give me what I deserve. C'mon, Buckaroo!"

As an afterthought, he added, "Amen."

If he received a timely answer, he failed to hear it. But he could not fail to notice when, upon Emdall's signal, an attendant unwound the empress's shining girdle and wrapped it several times around his waist— such was the length of it—doubtless as a symbol of their union. In this way, he and the empress began to move as one, as partners.

"Are you sure this is a good idea? Should we snuggle so in public?" he wondered; and indeed a wave of childlike surprise now spread through the audience, who saw their divine ruler moving sensuously in concert with the earthling interloper. To add to the spectacle, military drummers now began to pound their skins and Emdall herself began to chirp and squeal—perhaps translating song lyrics, perhaps not—while her royal attendants began to sway and make odd background noises that sounded like crystal singing bowls or an old-fashioned four-chime doorbell.

(Again, for the record, I remind the reader that Buckaroo did not "speak" the Lectroid idiom. His understanding of their communications came only through his extraordinary ability to read thought transmissions.)

"As you can see, music is my passion. I am known as something of a crooner myself," she revealed.

"Or better known as the only game in town," he commented, continuing to mesmerize a crowd he estimated in the millions with his full-throated soul shouting. "Say it again, y'all! War! Huh! Good God! . . . What is it good for? Absolutely nothing!"

"You are giving me everything I want, Buckaroo Banzai, and everything I need!" she gushed. "A good hot breeze is blowing, if you believe in superstitions! As a duet, we have placed the heavenly stones in abeyance and pacified the gods!"

"Perhaps the gods but not your priests," he told her, pausing only to inhale deeply from his oxygen balloon. "And I am tiring, Your Grace, dying a slow death on this platform. I'm only human and can't keep this up. Do you have any water?"

"I will order it," she promised, but with a warning. "I don't like things to end, Buckaroo Banzai. I even start my song over before it ends. Let us continue while I think of what to do with the traitors."

"Yes, let us think things through. The reality is that your subjects will stop paying attention when this song and dance ceases to be new. We would do well to take this show on the road."

"On the road?"

"My work is on Earth, Your Grace."

"Good Buckaroo Banzai, speaking in the air of one so loyal and upright, but I see deceit in your human eyes. Do you expect me to abdicate? That is nonsense," she expressed, her tone turning indignant. "We both know better. And I have already given the command to put an end to Earth and John Whorfin. Order must be restored."

"Order. Of course . . . order. Who would not be in favor . . . ? It's just this unreal moment, things happening so quickly . . . I need time to catch my breath."

"Doubtless your pallor is human emotion. You are anticipating our vows."

"Vows? Yes," he managed. "I vow my loyalty and friendship . . . so much so that you have made me the happiest man on Planet 10."

"Then why do I fear you are formulating a scheme?"

"Scheme? Maybe I just need to sort things out. It's not every day a man falls for an empress, much less an empress of another planet, another culture, and a whole other species. It could be an uplifting story, but also a tragic one. What if we fight like cats and dogs . . . ?"

"Then you will be fed to the toadsters of my royal stable. Who are you calling a dog?"

"No, no, no. We are destined to be bound forever—as you say, it cannot be mere coincidence—but the situation has sadly arisen where I need to return my comrade Tommy, a young man who stood in a class by himself, to Earth for a proper burial. I'll probably be expected to give his eulogy and his final paycheck to his family . . ."

"I said he has not awakened," she explained. "Perhaps he never will, but he may be nonetheless alive and should remain in the regeneration chamber."

His spirits soaring with this bit of news, Buckaroo recalibrated his appeal: "Then he may need urgent care in a human hospital with competent medical staff. If I had my OSCILLATION OVERTHRUSTER, I could go and be back before—"

Such talk again only seemed to annoy her. "I fear your health does not permit that, and you are trying to dictate my course, Buckaroo Banzai . . . to persuade me of something you do not believe. I offer you irrevocable love and a pact between us, and you would depart from me? Spurn me in front of my own subjects?"

Now he was the one who pretended not to hear, but continued to press his argument in his own way, saying, "As you know, I also have a happy musical band, the Hong Kong Cavaliers, with concert dates. Thousands of people have already paid for tickets, and it would be wrong to keep them in the dark. Where I come from, a man's word is his bond."

"A frontier trait, I reckon," she expressed with no trace of mockery. "Just the way your mama and daddy . . ."

". . . Just the way my mama and daddy raised me," he said, finishing the well-known line from our weekly television series. "I wish you could have met them before we tied the knot. I guess that makes me old fashioned."

"I am old fashioned, also," she declared. "Perhaps I can meet them in the Eighth Dimension, along with Rawhide and Professor Hikita . . . and Penny . . ."

"Ah," he said as if punched in the gut.

"Do you think she would like me?"

Still speechless, he scrambled to say, "That would be wonderful. In the meantime I could plan a big wedding on Earth and straighten out my affairs. There are contracts, radio and television shows, a lot of money involved, and I could get in a lot of trouble. In addition, there is my research and various properties I own, employees who must be paid. If you would give me a little time to appoint an administrator in my absence and seek instructions from my government . . ."

"Instructions? If you suspect someone represents a danger, simply put them on the conveyor belt and tear their skins off with a grater to make them reveal other traitors," she instructed.

"Hmm, I see what you mean," he pretended to ponder.

"You must be proactive and not reactive to learn their number exactly. And don't forget the hoodlum Hanoi Xan, who is behind so much of your trouble . . ."

"Exactly. That's the plan, to put Xan on the grater until he gives up John Whorfin," he replied.

"And then grate him further, because he is a no-account sidewinder."

"Yes. It is important to exercise my authority to the fullest."

"Yes, for a ruler it is important that there is moral ground that the ruler is free to manipulate," she informed him authoritatively. "Also give traitors blows without shirking so that fear is always at hand. At the end of the day, your integrity is all you've got left."

"Agreed," he hastened to add. "I need to go at once and handle such sensitive matters, so that my world understands the new rules."

"And leave me lonely? That would not be healthy for either of us."

"I could commute. I'm used to living out of a suitcase and need to ready everything for your triumphal entrance. There's a lot to be done. I don't think you would find the bunkhouse adequate, especially for a growing family."

"Most naturally," she seemed to agree. "Once order has been restored, and without human beings, Earth could be a pretty place. I would give it to you as my gift. We could live in the big canyon, the grand one."

"Indeed, Arizona is nice this time of year, and next to it is New Mexico . . ."

"Mexico . . . ?"

"New Mexico. Like Mexico, but newer . . . the Land of Enchantment," he said eagerly.

"The Land of Enchantment," she repeated as if savoring each syllable.

"Because the people are enchanting. We could take a long honeymoon and just see where the trail takes us . . . no schedule, no destination, no worries . . ."

"On a horse? I do love to ride and am praised highly."

"Of course . . . on a horse . . . horses," he said, considering her size. "As many as we need."

"In the Land of Enchantment," she fantasized. "I would like to go there to obtain a Mexican sombrero . . . but also atomic bombs, no? Your parents and Professor Hikita worked on the reservation . . ."

"In secret and in isolation, because of false accusations that they would spill the beans," he confirmed. "They lived among the Apache tribe during their work on the Manhattan Project."

"Those bombs and all the parts and laboratories used to make them must be turned over to our forces before incineration. I desire a clean planet without atomic radiation."

"That will be my job," he said eagerly. "Certain governments might object but—"

She cut him off, slapping his head. "Then thwack them thus! They have no right to speak to you. Dead, gone, done."

"Loud and clear," he said.

She heaved a sigh. "Oh, Buckaroo, you cannot know how tempting it all sounds, to free my soul from all my heavy memories and responsibilities and traitorous religionists, if only for a little while. To write the greatest song, to paint the greatest picture, to climb the highest mountain! You and me and Mrs. Johnson, Buckaroo Banzai!"

"Don't forget Tommy," he said.

"You and me and frozen Tommy and Mrs. Johnson!" she went on, happily entertaining herself. "Then there is nothing more to talk. Just the four of us in the new Lectroid Earth. I give it my noblest blessings."

"Then you may wish to change your order for its destruction," he urged . . .

. . . as she raised an appendage, but only to make the momentous announcement: "At this time the Most High Priest, Sacred John Tail Crab, will deliver the 'push-pull' oath to your faithful empress and her prince-consort-to-be Buckaroo Banzai . . ."

These words, needless to say, set off an uproar of excitement among the ordinary Lectroids (Buckaroo could not honestly judge if their outward display was feigned or genuine or indeed whether it sprang from happiness or another emotion) that only seemed to further enrage the priests. Among these, their leader, Sacred John Tail Crab, appeared to consider Buckaroo an easy target and a useful means by which to destroy the true object of his hate, the empress John Emdall; and Buckaroo returned Tail Crab's hostility with his own death stare.

BLOOD WEDDING

"I know you are a man who questions, Buckaroo Banzai," she expressed with renewed urgency, "especially if you are a god in whom divinity has only now awakened. You may be like the beast who does not recognize its own odor."

"I have had this very conversation with myself," he said to her.

"Then I may get under your skin," she conveyed. "But one thing you are not is a backstabber playing a double game. You must see it is in your own interests to do as I say, inasmuch as I am your sole protector."

Sensing the imminent threat represented by the priests, he readily understood, saying, "I will stand with you, Your Grace, shoulder to shoulder."

"Of course you will die for me, Buckaroo Banzai. I have no doubt. We will sign in blood after the tossing of my staff," she expressed, indicating the great carved club she bore. "Symbolizing my supposed defloration to come."

"Right . . ."

"Which you will then hurl straight up into the air. If the club returns to you, it means our marriage is blessed."

"That's easy enough," he said.

"Then you will execute the traditional flying leap with the symbolic matrimonial stone," she conveyed.

"What?"

Here she motioned toward John Parker, who reappeared with what appeared to be a heavy round stone whose girth easily exceeded that of a man, prompting Buckaroo to peer down at the swelling crowd far below with natural anxiety.

"Jump? From here?" he questioned.

"Don't worry, Buckaroo Banzai," said John Parker. "Your special royal garments will give you buoyancy, and Her Majesty's subjects who love her will rise up to catch you."

"But let us not tarry, lest the oracle again shall change its mind," she expressed and gestured to the priests, whose sullen anger by now had only intensified. Yet they dared not defy her openly and approached as beckoned, presenting a small dish of delicacies and a united front of enshrouded belligerence.

Presenting himself with an extravagant salute, the head priest Tail Crab held up something like caramelized blood grapes and small white wafers and intoned a series of bass notes signifying, "With notice to the gods and ample respect due Her Imperial Highness John Emdall Thunderpump, we proceed to a matter of state, the union of our beloved empress and this . . ."

With a haughty turn, the priest fixed his gaze upon our hero and appeared to struggle in search of a proper means of introduction, before bellowing loudly to the assembly, "This . . . the monkey in question . . ."

"Proceed, Priest," ordered John Emdall sharply.

Unswayed, Tail Crab resumed, "The Earth monkey and galactic tripper named Buckaroo Banzai, of whom an official security assessment has not been made, yet who, I am informed, has a long list of works and whose travels have been rewarded by our empress's friendship . . ."

There now was felt a sharp tremor, to which John Tail Crab reacted predictably by pausing and asking the sky theatrically, "Has something happened? Does the oracle of Mount Wah-Wah wish to speak?"

"I will interpret the oracle," Emdall interrupted at once. "The oracle has no objections. Get on with it . . ."

The priest now turned to address Buckaroo Banzai, offering him the bitter "grapes" symbolizing "all curses and false promises," asking, "Do you eat the sour grapes and swear by the fortune of the empress John Emdall Thunderpump to fulfill your purpose and bring honor to her crown?"

"A whole lot of nothing, but yes, I do so eat and swear," replied Buckaroo, who nonetheless struggled to ingest the highly unappetizing fare. The fruit was indeed rotten and sour and the accompanying "sweet" wafer was even worse—likely the worst thing he had tasted in his life—mostly gypsum with a yeasty bacterial smell, topped with a sticky, syrupy icing. He was still chewing when he noticed that John Parker had taken Emdall's portion of both and, doubtless as a matter of caution, ingested it all himself.

The high priest glared at Buckaroo once more and continued, "Do you wish to say something, monkey?"

"Happily, no. Keep doing the Lord's work," Buckaroo conveyed to him. "Or is the honeymoon over?"

With the same dour look, the priest expressed, "Do you reproach all other gods, save one: the empress John Emdall?"

"Save one, I reproach them all," Buckaroo swore, looking at Emdall, the alien creature he was about to marry—no, *he* was the alien in her world, the circus freak, the barbarian monkey man—and waging a war in his head that found expression in another fresh rumble underfoot. Yet, strange to say, he did not feel unwelcome among them, for at each sound from his mouth, he had noted how the Lectroid audience slapped their wings as one and made clicking noises he translated as approval, even applause. This was particularly the case when Buckaroo accepted Emdall's imperial staff from John Parker and tossed it above his head, drawing a roar from the mob; but it was at this juncture that the priests made their fateful move and fired a flurry of poison darts, felling two of Emdall's retainers who had loyally interposed their bodies between the empress and the traitors and taken the barbs themselves.

At the same instant, Tail Crab rose in the air and grabbed the staff himself, wielding it as a war club against John Parker, who received the full impact of the priest's first strike but nonetheless fought back with a vengeance. In this he was joined by our hero, who, enraged by the brazen attack upon his allies, came to Parker's aid by delivering a head butt, a throat punch, and a knee thrust that sent another of the clerics tumbling out of control over the parapet—where the unhappy creature met a violent end, to be intercepted and torn apart in the air by Emdall's loyalists . . . much to the apparent delight of a majority of the mob.

The other three priests took due notice of events and cowardly flitted away, leaving only Tail Crab to absorb the ultimate punishment from John Parker and the empress's virgins, who began to rain down hammer blows upon her would-be assassin.

"No end in sight to your lack of respect, fool? I will hold your brains!" Emdall raged and picked up her imperial staff with every intention of using it to bash the priest; yet something prevented her from doing this.

"The fight has gone out of the fool," Buckaroo weighed in. "Perhaps he could be of more use to you alive. Remember your advice . . . the cheese grater . . ."

"Mind your business, Buckaroo Banzai," she commanded sharply.

"I couldn't agree more," he said, but not before the priest fired a wild last-gasp volley of darts, one of which Buckaroo caught in his hand before it could strike the empress.

"You are hurt, Buckaroo Banzai!" she reacted with alarm.

"It is nothing or it is everything," he said, at once removing the barb and sucking out the poison. "I won't live long if the poison went deep enough . . . only a few minutes . . . and I am already feeling a little faint . . ."

"This is not a safe location," she informed him. "You must hurry below and get treatment from my medical staff while I quench the embers of this mutiny."

These were in fact more than embers; and as she appeared preoccupied with skirmishes among rival swarms of Lectroids, he took the opportunity to retreat inside . . . but not before John Parker delivered Tail Crab's coup de grâce by dropping the heavy matrimonial stone upon the squawking cleric's brain. At once, Emdall reacted by defiantly waving her staff and signaling her drummers and horn blowers to calm the surly crowd by blowing the lugubrious national anthem.

"We are well! Your empress has survived!" she announced, impressing upon them their responsibility to notify the security police of any seditious talk or suspicious behavior.

"They infest us! Kill all with the stink upon them!" returned the mob. "Silence is betrayal!"

Amid their loud cheers, she went on to announce an impromptu military parade and a strict new curfew, yet threatened no new purges or decimations and surprised many by neither throwing Tail Crab's brains to the mob nor eating them herself, instead tossing them into a nearby brazier, where they produced a supernatural display of ungodly noises and grotesque shadows. As against this, she called for reconciliation, saying, "Now is not the time to gyrate or challenge or eat brains or react to misinformation pointed against us and our overall betterment. The hate is theirs! Let our enemies keep it and not get under our skins! We are all Lectroids, who once walked Planet 1 together in peace and mutual trust! Only our markings and odors are different!"

These sentiments, anodyne as they were, gave rise to much unfavorable speculation among her audience, who were accustomed to hearing her describe the Reds in the most scurrilous of terms, and her next remarks confounded them even further.

"Two wrongs don't make a right! Love will conquer but expects no returns!" she expressed, causing the airborne stones to fly back to heaven and leading many to wonder where she had gotten such dangerous ideas.

TILL DEATH DO US PART

Back inside the palace, Buckaroo heard the commotion of the parade and felt an electric chill, whether from the dart's venom or his own heightened sense of danger, when John Parker touched him on the shoulder and directed him toward a contraption like an old-fashioned pneumatic tube.

"This way, Buckaroo. You must seek treatment," he warned.

Behind Parker followed two additional Lectroids who attempted to carry Buckaroo's lengthy train, but these arrived a fraction of a moment too late, as Buckaroo and Parker hastened into the tube and the portal closed behind them.

By quick turns during the rapid descent and their arrival in a cavernous underground city of mud hives and hibernation chambers, Buckaroo could not help but notice Parker's worried countenance and the furtive, envious glances his royal garment and crystal girdle aroused in ordinary Lectroids. He had to remember, he told himself, that they likely harbored a strong dose of fear based on the extraordinary fact that their maximum leader had chosen him, of all beings, as her mate. In a real sense he was higher than they, and on this account he wore a scowl and made grim faces in order to give them an idea of his ferocity.

"You look pained, John Parker. Do I look mad at the world? That doesn't mean I am mad at you," he said by way of reassuring his Lectroid companion.

"It is the empress," Parker replied with notable anxiety. "There is considerable trouble afoot . . ."

"Many warning signs and a lot of bad players, as we have seen," said Buckaroo. "If you feel you must go to your empress, John Parker . . ."

"I am to stay with you, Buckaroo Banzai. You are hurt and it is necessary to seek treatment."

"You are appreciated, John Parker . . ."

But his grimace also reflected a spreading numbness in his body. No matter how hard he sucked on his oxygen concentrator, he felt his strength deserting him, leaving him no choice but to reach out and lean on John Parker, saying, "Before I receive treatment, I need to visit my friend Tommy and gather our effects. Do you have my Go-Phone?"

When John Parker only appeared to mull over the request, Buckaroo reminded him, "You will take me to my friend and fetch my Go-Phone because I am the emperor's favorite and of a higher echelon than you. I count you a friend, but you must follow my orders. Otherwise, you deserve to die . . ."

Such a threat was of course not in his nature but it seemed to have its due effect, as Parker now guided him into another speedy capsule that carried them through an immense underground complex of factories and living blocks on multiple decks. Counted among these was a cathedral-ceilinged landing dock of enormous proportions housing a dozen or more flying ships in uneven states of repair; and it was to this multitiered hangar that Buckaroo was directed: a cavern lit by trellises of iridescent crystal so high and bright that his eyes shrank from their brilliance and focused instead on the horrors of the place, the brutal gears of the planet's system of control laid bare.

If their arrival in any way drew attention or interrupted the room's macabre assembly-line teamwork, there was no evidence of it. Perhaps this was because the air in the place already seemed charged with electric tension, accompanied by dizzying fluctuations in air pressure and heavy doses of what Buckaroo believed to be tranquilizer mist from spray dispensers. Whether these conditions were designed to bring the occupants' stress level up or down was an open question—as was the possible motive. Like the priests on the surface, however, dozens of nervous Lectroids appeared to have "bugged out," wagging their wings and rising above the masses of their fellow technicians who went about their businesslike routine of tending their enterprises or amusements in what was a combination workshop, torture chamber, and design studio— while above it all arose the pitiful whines and cries of their prisoners: various Lectroid types and alien creatures on conveyor belts, to be experimented upon before being sent elsewhere. Resounding above it all were the howls of shackled captives fed into the hall's centerpiece, a doughnut-shaped particle accelerator atop its fuel source and in-ground cooling pool that was itself teeming with odd life forms.

"Talk about a graveyard shift," Buckaroo muttered.

"We do not play games, Buckaroo Banzai," Parker replied. "A Lectroid's goal is always to dominate rather than be dominated. There is no middle ground. It has been this way since time out of mind and is something we are proud of."

"That is behavior that is familiar to me," noted Buckaroo; but even as he said this, several howling prisoners disappeared into the tubular structure, where with a great whirring and whooshing noise, they disappeared as if flushed down a drain.

"Where are they going, John Parker? The Eighth Dimension?"

"Another dimension," Parker said noncommittally, "or perhaps the Moon of the Misbegotten. There are many such prison planets and destinations."

The two of them continued across a broad gutter full of running ooze and ground flesh, then through an archway and down a corridor of closed hatches and bags of plunder guarded by more security officers and the boxy security droids that reminded him of kitchen appliances. Despite their implacable demeanor, however, he showed himself to be unafraid and even snapped at them.

"I've come for the monkey boy," he barked, adding his voice to John Parker's orders to various of the guards; and after another moment a hatch opened, through which he was permitted to pass alone into a fresh scene from hell: a low-ceilinged cage where a bruised and battered Tommy lay unconscious amid filth and sundry alien beings of diverse origins.

Several of these were making unintelligible noises, perhaps even singing their own dirges, as Buckaroo sharply gestured them aside and knelt beside Tommy, feeling his pulse.

"Tommy, old man . . ."

Silence. But the epithet was an apt one. Tommy was long bearded and nearly bald, as if thirty years had fallen on him overnight.

"Tommy, old man, talk to me," Buckaroo urged with emotion. "I'll do my best to patch you up, but you gotta get up. I'm here, Tom—get up and seize the day!"

"Just playin' possum, bud," groaned Tommy, opening his eyes in response to Buckaroo's nudging.

"Can't say I blame you, considering. Welcome to Planet 10. How're you doing?" Buckaroo replied, eyeing Tommy's eclectic band of roommates: a Mr. Peanut with one bird leg; a floating, regurgitating loaf of meat that seemed to be nothing but a locomotive alimentary canal; an invisible something or other inside a spacesuit; and a coiled thing in a corner, resembling a cross between a toothbrush and one of the giant shaggy grasshoppers Emdall had mentioned.

"Pretty crummy. Feels like I partied a little too much with these swamp zombies that eat their own shite," Tommy said gamely, but feebly. "This whole place has an undercurrent of weird."

"You can say that again, but nothing that getting outta here can't fix," Buckaroo told him. "Wanna have some fun? Think you can get up, maybe do a little fighting?"

"Until they rip my heart out, and that's the proven truth. You know me, Buck . . . I'm no crybaby," Tommy said and promptly began to sob. "Come hell or high water . . ."

"You'll have to get under my skirt and hug my hairy leg," Buckaroo informed him without fair warning.

"Beg your pardon . . . ?" Tommy said before comprehending quickly. "Hell, bring it on—beats dying in here, laughing my ass off. Why are you wearing this crazy getup anyhow?"

"This old quilty, fluffy thing? Just a little something I threw together," Buckaroo said before chiding him. "Why, do I look bloated??"

"Maybe a little. But it's a great outfit to go out on. I mean, if you never wear another outfit," Tommy replied. "Truth is, next to you, I always feel like used goods anyway . . . especially now. I feel worn to the bone."

"Then save your breath," Buckaroo said. "Gravity is approximately three and a half times that of Earth. Just hang on to me—we'll get through this together."

"Think we burnt all our bridges?"

"I'll let you know when I get my Go-Phone. Be quiet now," Buckaroo replied, throwing his long train over his garrulous comrade.

"Annoying as shit," Tommy complained in a muffled voice. "I think I got salt water in my eyes and ears. Did we go through salt water?"

"Could be your tears, Tommy. But I thought the Sea of Tears in the Land of the Giants was only in my Seventh Dimension, not yours . . ."

"The Seventh . . . ?"

"We went through the Seventh on our way to the Eighth . . ."

"Right, stands to reason," Tommy said. "Buck—"

"Yeah, Tom?"

"You could've left me for dead, dude. Thanks."

With a tender pat, Buckaroo gave no reply other than "Let's go home."

Moments later, they emerged into the hallway, where John Parker was waiting with his Go-Phone, a mangled, misshapen mess which he handed over with a certain note of sadness, saying, "I can tell this instrument has powerful meaning for you, Buckaroo Banzai."

"Yes, it is . . . or was . . . unique," Buckaroo said, stroking the melted plastic and feeling his hopes sink anew. Here was his phone and lifeline—cold and dead or at least in critical condition—which he only pretended to examine, as John Parker watched carefully to see if there was a way to unlock the instrument.

Could he trust John Parker? Did he have a better option?

"You want me to crack it open? I share your view, John Parker. Looks like it got a blistering," Buckaroo said, crestfallen but reminding himself this was no time for self-pity with Tommy rustling beneath his royal skirt.

It was a simple matter now, albeit in the face of long odds. Without another word, he began retracing his steps back toward the spaceship repair dock, a relatively short walk he recently described to me as the most nerve-racking of his life, with his fate, and Tommy's, depending upon a number of variables out of his control. What if his Go-Phone was truly dead? What then? Or, conversely, what if he unlocked it and the Lectroids took it from him? How much time did he have before some cocky Lectroid called his bluff? Or before John Parker, or even John Emdall herself, objected?

Now he stumbled, prompting Parker to say, "You are weak, Buckaroo. Allow me to carry your royal cloak."

"Nonsense, John Parker," he replied. "I am the royal-consort-to-be . . . in other words, a royal pain in the ass. Do not touch me."

"But you are making a wrong turn. I was trying to back you up. The hospital is not this way."

"Do not speak, John Parker. I know where I'm going, on secret orders from the empress."

"That does not match with the truth, Buckaroo Banzai," Parker reproached him.

"Let us not jump to conclusions, John Parker. Perhaps you were not listening when the empress spoke to me personally and intimately," Buckaroo said, wincing to himself.

Even the mere mention of her caused a gob of bile to rise in his throat. What a nightmare, the prospect of living on Planet 10 as John Emdall's royal consort! What a travesty and a disgusting feeling to be controlled by another, not to mention having been taken by her and violated—by a life-sucking creature with lobster claws and a tail!—after which more of the same was bound to follow from a thief who could never give back what she had taken from him, so how could there be room for compromise? But without his OVERTHRUSTER, what choice would he have? In more ways than one, then, he had traveled to a dark place from which he was not sure he could come back, even if he managed to survive the rising poison in his system. If he failed to escape, in other words, he would die willingly . . . somehow wander off and die rather quickly from exposure. In this he was certain he spoke also for Tommy, whose labored breathing and heartbeat he believed he could hear through the garment.

And yet . . . a contrary view might have it that he was not doing the daring thing by trying to escape but the detrimental thing, the selfish thing, the cowardly thing. Of course, assuming his world still existed, he would fight for it, but would not Earth be better served if he remained on Planet 10 and exercised his influence on John Emdall, here in the seat of Lectroid power? It bothered him that he could not refute this argument to his satisfaction—primarily because of his degraded physical condition, he figured—but he also knew that too much thinking under the circumstances could be fatal. Only later would there be time to substantiate his decision or second-guess how history would judge him.

Or would there even be a historical account? If so, who would write it? The Reno Kid? Did Reno even still exist, or had his noble pen been quieted forever?

By now they had crossed the floor of the industrial slaughterhouse and were approaching the spaceship hangar, where drones and Lectroid workers appeared to watch enthralled as Buckaroo approached the smallest of the docked ships, a two-seater no larger than a school bus.

When a trollish Lectroid officer moved into their path on the narrow rampway, yammering a series of clicks and holding a weapon that resembled a yo-yo, Buckaroo said arrogantly to John Parker, "To this I say bullshit, Parker. Tell this good fellow who I am and that I need this ship for an important mission."

"But this ship cannot carry you, Buckaroo Banzai," Parker warned.

"I'm not going far, only through that solid wall and into the Eighth Dimension," Buckaroo replied.

Parker strenuously denied this, saying, "Not the case, Buckaroo Banzai. Indeed you will not take that ship anywhere!"

No longer inexperienced in their ways, Buckaroo understood that a direct command to a Lectroid, backed by a threat of force, was the only thing they respected. Hence he bore down and demanded, "John Parker, if you need to be taught a lesson, I'll provide the education. Tell me only the truth."

"Now you wish me to speak?" said John Parker. "The truth is, I thought you were smarter than to try to make your getaway in a flight simulator."

"Simulator??"

What terrible indecision Buckaroo experienced at that instant, not knowing whether John Parker was telling the truth, which is to say whether Parker supported him! On the other hand, why should Parker assist him? Parker was a Lectroid, presumably loyal to Empress Emdall and with her best interests at heart. What reason did he have to be grateful to Buckaroo Banzai? Indeed Buckaroo could see no reason at all and regretted that such a dilemma now fell on his old friend, whose very life he likely was putting in jeopardy . . . not to mention Tommy's and his own.

To make matters worse, a group of Lectroids and security drones had begun to take notice of the alien stranger in their midst and came trotting over, at which point everything might have been lost if Tommy had not unexpectedly chosen this moment to peek out from beneath Buckaroo's garment—the sight of which, a second human head, so astonished the Lectroids that they momentarily shrank back in terror!

"Perfect Tommy?" expressed John Parker in surprise, recognizing the famous human whom he had met during his brief sojourn on Earth.

"John Parker! Where are we? What's going on?" Tommy asked anxiously, no less frightened than the fascinated Lectroid spectators surrounding them.

"Keep looking at them, without sticking your tongue out," Buckaroo told him cautiously, at once marking his decision to change plans by informing John Parker, "We will go as we please, but in a different ship. Can you point us in the right direction?"

As Parker appeared dazed by these sudden developments, Buckaroo read his thoughts: "I have done my job at work and built a career . . . shown up on time all my life, but now if I lose Buckaroo Banzai or any harm comes to him or Perfect Tommy, I will be accused and lose everything: all this that is mine, my rank, even my retirement bonus, even my life . . . perhaps to be injected or even boiled alive. I fear the wrath of John Emdall, lest she see me as worthless or disloyal."

Buckaroo then continued, "I understand your position, John Parker, but I must get to where I am going, to see what must be done if the existence of my world is in doubt. Earth may be a small imperfect planet, but we will also not be anyone's doormat. If attacked, we will fight; and Perfect Tommy and I must be at the forefront."

"We all have our pride, Buckaroo Banzai. You are much beloved, but I cannot contribute to this," Parker declared.

"You have been a brave and helpful friend, John Parker, inviting many dangers," continued Buckaroo, who momentarily wobbled on his feet, doubtless still feeling the effects of Tail Crab's poison dart.

"Buckaroo, you are all right?" a concerned John Parker inquired and embraced our hero, helping to steady him.

"Good John Parker," said Buckaroo, who now easily overpowered the Lectroid and grabbed his furry nape, for in truth Parker resisted but little. "And in return for your labors, I pay you thus."

"Thank you, Buckaroo Banzai," whispered Parker.

Without another word Buckaroo hurled Parker at the Lectroid officer and the curious onlookers I have described, all of whom were knocked back and sent sprawling like so many dominoes.

The pace of events now accelerated, as Tommy emerged from Buckaroo's skirt and the two men together scrambled to the next bay, where crews had been busy readying a sleek ship the length of a football pitch.

"Looks badass. This baby looks like it can haul," Tommy said, receiving an assist from Buckaroo into the cockpit, where Buckaroo wasted precious time laboring to close the hatch before settling in at the ship's controls and attempting to activate his Go-Phone . . . with the result that in the span of seconds their narrow view from the flight deck was obscured by a swarm of Lectroids bent on retribution.

"Cockroaches!" Tommy ejaculated nervously. "At least move away from the window, assholes. Where's my Raid?"

Buckaroo said nothing, but his furrowed brow and growing frustration spoke volumes . . . a brutal reality that naturally failed to reassure Tommy, who anxiously searched the ship's strange control board for anything familiar.

"Kudos to you, Buckaroo, as long as you understand the locomotion of this buggy," he said, "because I'm clueless."

"It's not exactly the locomotion I'm worried about," Buckaroo replied. "It's that solid rock wall in front of us and no book of spells."

"You mean no OVERTHRUSTER?"

"That's the idea," said Buckaroo, still repeatedly tapping in the Go-Phone's activation code to no avail, while a barrage of Lectroids continued to throw themselves violently against the cabin porthole, in some cases leaving chemical stains.

"Two more blobs and one slop. Here comes the heavy equipment," noted Tommy with remarkable equanimity, hearing the whine of cutting instruments. "Well, we gave it a good try. Buckaroo, do you ever look in the mirror and think you weren't always crazy?"

Buckaroo, too, replied calmly, "Starting to feel sorry for yourself, Tom? You need to stop taking things so seriously."

Tommy laughed and mused grimly, "Yeah, maybe we'll win the Planet 10 lottery."

"We're not goners yet," Buckaroo replied and now once more attempted the critical activation of his Go-Phone, noticing that one of the crucial buttons in the sequence seemed to be inoperative. Borrowing Tommy's knife, he ran the tip of the blade carefully around the edges of the recalcitrant plastic button, cleaning its contact point and punching the entry code in again . . . an operation followed eerily by strains of a symphony orchestra he could not reconcile with pounding Lectroids and power tools.

"Funeral dirge?" Tommy wisecracked, not immediately recognizing the charred and battered Go-Phone as the music's source.

"Just hope it's not ours," replied Buckaroo. "Beethoven's *Eroica* . . . what a gift. How excruciatingly beautiful . . ."

"Hallelujah," was all Tommy could say, staring at Buckaroo's glowing Go-Phone with misty eyes and a sense of reverence . . . both men thinking of home but knowing full well that in another moment, barring a last-second miracle, they would either be recaptured or explode on impact with the solid wall ahead of them.

"Okay, let's fire it up," Buckaroo announced, rotating several balls on the master console and bringing the musical prelude to an end . . . before an image of an animated John Emdall suddenly appeared on an overhead screen, her wild, clownish movements incomprehensible until he realized she was trying to mimic his face.

"So this is how you repay my favors, Buckaroo Banzai?! Leaving me is my reward?" she demanded, pounding the screen with her staff. "I have been wronged! Wronged by your disgusting nature! You have neither soul nor integrity, Buckaroo Banzai! I am meaningless to you!"

"Your Grace . . . I was just expecting your call. Face time is good," he said, at once scrambling to coordinate his Go-Phone with the ship's instruments.

"You do not deserve my time, Buckaroo Banzai! Keep your trash in your mouth! You will get the bad end of this! I will pull your teeth and destroy your world!"

"Then you will destroy one who is faithful to you, Your Majesty. Of course you are disappointed, as am I, having to leave our little love nest, but I told you Tommy needed treatment and that I'm always here for you in time of need. Earth is practically your backyard . . ."

"Animal beast! You need correction!"

"Please, no name-calling. I see the light in your eyes and can't imagine life without you, but we both need to move on . . ."

"Move on?!" reacted Emdall with predictable rage. "We will settle this debt!"

"Speaking of moving on," Tommy muttered to Buckaroo, peeking out as the craft lurched without warning. "I think we're getting towed, Buck. Damn, they're towing us . . . !"

"That bird will be your cage, Perfect Tommy! You will be shredded, you and your doomed comrade!" expressed Emdall, whom Tommy had difficulty comprehending.

"Relax," Buckaroo told him. "All I need is a little polarity guidance to get our angle . . ."

"You mean a compass?" asked Tommy.

"Close enough," Buckaroo replied, clicking more keys.

"We're on?" said Tommy excitedly.

"We're on."

"You are delusional!" warned the empress. "Utter lunacy! You've been warned!"

"I didn't say there wasn't work to be done. Anything else you want to share before I go?" Buckaroo asked.

A second later, as they felt another jolt and the cockpit began to crack under heavy assault, Buckaroo revved the craft to maximum throttle and pointed his quivering Go-Phone forward.

"How you like our odds . . . ?" Tommy muttered.

"Odds of surviving? Not insignificant if we stick to the one true path and avoid glitches. All we can do is give it a whirl," Buckaroo answered tersely, his expression bearing every sign of the strain and physical duress he was under. "We've got a shot, depending on whether this phone's been cooked, how fast this buggy can do zero to six hundred, and provided we find an exit portal and I can master the fly-by-wire to bend the universe to our will."

"Sounds good," Tommy said, still seeking reassurance. "But will it work? Just the synopsis . . ."

"Just the synopsis? If you know the right people," Buckaroo replied, forcing a last smile and blowing a kiss at the cursing John Emdall. "I think somebody up there likes me."

Now, as he performed a last-second fix to the SQUID and oscillation overthruster applications that suddenly produced a singular note on his device, he remarked with obvious relief to Tommy, "Hear that? That's a handshake dial tone, the frequency of our world . . ."

"The Pythagorean monochord . . . ?" queried Tommy incredulously.

"At a higher pitch than ever, like a cry for help. Let's hope something is still the way we left it."

"And not a big glob of crap. Need my help?"

"Only if we swerve and get lost or I pass out," Buckaroo said and now manipulated the controls, removing all restraint, whereupon the sleek ship levitated.

"You can run, but . . . I'll follow you to hell, Buckaroo Banzai!" snarled John Emdall, whose other choice words may be imagined.

"Do, please come visit," he replied . . .

. . . as the ship shot forward and disappeared with a roar through solid terrylium rock, engulfed in flames.

"I'm out! No offense," he informed her . . . and the universe.

XXXV. DEUS EX MACHINA

> Another world is not only possible, She is on her way.
> —Arundhati Roy

They traveled—according to both men—via the Fifth Dimension, that realm of perfect memories and recorded experience. Without getting into the unsettled scientific business of whether they chose the route or the route chose them, I will note only that Tommy returned to his days of high-school gridiron glory, while Buckaroo relived a wondrous summer afternoon with Penny, despite an unwelcome interruption to their picnic from obnoxious honeybees. But these memories, as I say, may have been affective, arising from feelings of nostalgia. What conclusively identified this zone as Fifth Dimensional was a visit by Buckaroo to his boyhood summer home in Hiroshima.

In Buckaroo's own words, "I couldn't have been much more than a toddler and had totally forgotten about the incident until our journey through the Fifth Dimension, when I wandered into our kitchen. I remember now my favorite team, the Hiroshima Carp, was playing the Giants on the radio, and standing around were my parents and a special family friend, the great actor Nakajima Haruo, who played the role of Godzilla in my favorite movies. As soon as I saw him, my eyes lit up and I pointed. '*Gojira! Gojira!*' I shouted, making everyone laugh!"

In fact, Buckaroo has said he was enjoying a moment of neutral observation within the boyhood incident when, like a hammer blow, their ship slammed down upon a viscous surface thick as molasses, and powerful g-forces pressed them back in their seats until the ship at last came to a soft stop in the black mire and began to settle.

"Holy hell, I thought we were cruising! What we get for taking the laws of nature into our own hands . . . collapsing everything into infinity!" Tommy ejaculated. "Maybe if you were a better driver . . . hell, you know I'm the better driver! I'm king of the road!"

"I could say I'm sorry, Tom, but save the smart stuff. You might need it," Buckaroo warned, intently checking his Go-Phone.

"Where are we?" Tommy asked anxiously.

"The real address? Good question," Buckaroo replied, adding, "Sorry to put it to you like this, Tommy, but looks like we're back in Planet 10 atmosphere and gravity."

"Jesus crap, you mean we're right back . . . ?" Tommy erupted in disbelief. "Damn, I thought we sealed the deal . . . caught the bypass all right. It felt like first we hauled ass, had a free lane, and swerved and hit a pothole, then got our ass stomped. Nothing like kicking a fella while he's down. Good thing I didn't get too wrapped up into coming home."

"Wise words, Tommy, but maybe we dodged a bullet in any case," said Buckaroo. "Let's be proactive and not blame ourselves for trying . . ."

"Hell, I'm ready for anything. What's out there?"

"Another experience, looks like," replied Buckaroo. "We can't just turtle up here. The lake means to keep this buggy. Plus, I'm hungry and tired and at the end of my rope, too."

"What a day," remarked Tommy with a fatalistic air, although the aging effects of their previous voyage had been noticeably reversed and both appeared as they had on Earth.

A moment later, the two of them climbed out onto the ship's sinking hull and surveyed the desolate scene around them: a sulphurous black lake stretching endlessly in every direction and littered with unidentifiable creature carcasses and other floating detritus.

"Smells like a low-end dive I remember, or an outhouse," Tommy commented with a grimace, trying to catch a breath despite the stench of the place.

Without another word Buckaroo extended a hand to his junior partner, who at first rejected the offer, until one look at the jiggling sludge below changed his mind. Then, arm in arm, they jumped, sinking for a terrifying instant before bobbing atop the surface.

"Over there," Buckaroo said and pointed toward a wall of flames in the far distance, the only source of light in the featureless landscape.

"No sky—where in hell's the horizon? Some kind of underground ocean," Tommy complained. "Sure to shit, this place is literally a shit hole."

In that same frame of mind they set out across the unknown sea—or rather Buckaroo bore Tommy's weight in addition to his own, breathing mightily despite the stifling stench of the place.

"That's some low-quality air. You okay, Buck? Hell, I'm watching you do all the work," Tommy wheezed.

"Just . . . tired . . . hurts like hell . . . gonna have to . . ." Buckaroo said, attempting in a moment of frustration to remove his crystal girdle and bulky royal garment that had grown wet and doubly heavy. But this proved too exhausting even for Buckaroo Banzai, who until now had surpassed all records of human endurance but at last faltered and knelt on the gelatinous surface, seemingly speaking gibberish to himself.

"What're we looking for?" Tommy asked with an air of helplessness, unable to do more. "Maybe I can . . ."

"Besides a shoulder to cry on? There's nothing, old man," replied Buckaroo, his gaze forlornly searching for any sort of identifying landmark.

"Reckon we're at that point," said Tommy. "Fit to be stuffed. This is the hill of shit we die on!"

"If it happens, it happens," countered Buckaroo. "Let's not be champing at the bit."

"Hey! Hey!" Tommy shouted at the top of his lungs and heard back a weak echo . . .

. . . when, without warning, a shaft of light from above momentarily blinded the two earthlings and a flying pod's antigravity beam lifted them up and sped them toward a shoreline where a herd of dark black figures awaited. As the pod illumined the two famous faces, the mood of their greeters appeared to change dramatically. Of a sudden the Darkling Lectroids seemed to awaken and twist themselves into new,

conjoined shapes, swinging together and raising muffled, fluttery noises
before appearing to be in the process of bowing down.

"What's all this?" Tommy wondered aloud.

"Enjoy it while you can," cautioned Buckaroo, who hovered next
to him.

Now the air was saturated with buzzing Lectroid voices: "Emperor
Consort Buckaroo Banzai! And Tommy!"

Our companions floated to rest near a covered causeway, through
which the waiting party carried them like returning heroes. Just why
this was happening—that is, the Lectroids' motives—could only be
guessed at by Buckaroo and Tommy, who, having been storm tossed
long enough by the Fates, longed only for the pleasures of home or,
failing that, an expeditious resolution of their case; and perhaps it is the
same with you, dear reader. Having come a long way together, you and
I may wish for the same, to move events along with dispatch.

From the causeway, then, to a vacuum capsule that carried them
directly to an observation deck with a spectacular nighttime view of
Europe . . . the boot of Italy dimly but clearly visible.

"The world! Is that reality?" Tommy murmured with astonishment . . .

. . . as Buckaroo's lips seemed to formulate a similar half question
before mustering a reply. "Yes. I believe we're expected."

Here the Lectroid welcoming party was more corpulent—heavy-
bodied officers in wilted plumage and tarnished gold buttons and an even
fatter, purple-wrapped priest of the kind seen on Planet 10—and they
received the two men with a formal courtesy that bordered on servility.
Yet, to use Tommy's phrase, there was an "undercurrent of weird" as
well . . . as if at any moment the Lectroids' true intentions might become
distressingly clear.

"Do come in, come in. Welcome aboard the interstellar *Imperatrix*,"
the ship's tumor-ridden commander—whose biological sex was
impossible to identify—welcomed them robustly and genuflected toward
Buckaroo's crystal girdle. "We were about to sanitize Earth when at the
last moment the empress rescinded the order and we received news of
your impending arrival. Please make yourselves at home."

"What fortunate timing. We are anxious to get home, unsanitized as
it may be," remarked Buckaroo acerbically, peering out at the magnificent
full moon and blue globe that apparently still continued to spin in space,

undamaged. So it seemed his decision to flee had been the correct one; it was even possible he had saved the world, at least for the time being. If nothing else—assuming their effusive welcome was genuine—he and Tommy had survived to fight another day.

In the words of the ship's commander, "There are few things better in life than to share conversation over a pleasant meal."

"I agree completely, Commandant," returned Buckaroo with practiced haughtiness. "What is your name, sailor?"

"Fleet Marshal John Double Bottom, Baron of Orange, at your pleasure, my lord."

"Baron of Orange . . . ? You won't get a lemon!" said Tommy.

". . . From Toyota of Orange!" enthused John Double Bottom.

Buckaroo's head suddenly hurt. He needed to go and repair himself; hence he replied simply, "I'm good with that. Fleet Marshal Double Bottom, is it?"

"You may call me John," expressed the fleet marshal.

"How'd I know that?" quipped Buckaroo.

"What's cooking?" Tommy said, introducing himself to Lectroids who of course already had recognized him.

Platters of strange food, carried by stick-figure waiters resembling walking tapeworms, now arrived in waves, and Buckaroo and Tommy ate hungrily in the Lectroid style, upright and without utensils. Tommy believed he was eating "good breakfast chow" from a country buffet back home and licked clean his fingers, while Buckaroo sampled each dish only sparingly . . . correctly guessing its true source.

And what do you suppose they were eating in fact, dear reader? Shall we agree to leave the meat a mystery?

Throughout the meal, the ship's commander chain-smoked cigarettes (obtained how?) and carried the conversation by reciting an encyclopedic litany of facts about his ship and Earth's ant and termite species, delivered in the condescending tone of a lecture to the newcomers. Such hubris, along with an unawareness of irony, was common to Lectroids, Buckaroo had learned; yet he did not raise a peep in protest, as his intention at this point was to hold his tongue and not put Tommy and himself in additional jeopardy.

"True, Earth is not pristine," Buckaroo commented in a firm, professorial manner. "Uncontrolled population growth of my own species unquestionably contributes to methane production, but your comparison of people to unneeded life, and Earth to a toxic dumpster fire, is off the mark. I admit there is a problem, but we don't want to throw the baby out with the bath water . . ."

Just as the Lectroids appeared collectively puzzled by the phrase "throw the baby out," a small glass eye on the commander's grease-laden uniform lit up red. Glancing at it, the Lectroid officer signaled Buckaroo with the message, "Your bride . . . for you, my lord."

Was there an undertone of sarcasm in his words? Envy perhaps—but, as I have said, irony is not a concept known to Lectroids, whose chief shared quality may be described as a kind of delusional confidence, not to say racial arrogance. Thus, the creature simply passed the magic ball to Buckaroo, whose heart had faltered nearly at once, thinking of his bride, Penny Priddy. But, alas, no . . . for materializing within the cloudy ball was an image of the empress John Emdall alongside John Parker.

"Excuse me," he said to the others and made his way over to the enormous arched windows that looked out upon our planet, steeling himself for a moment before gazing intently at the smaller ball in his hands and the powerful being who held sway over his fate.

"Good John Parker and Your Grace, how appropriate! You are the breath of fresh air we are missing!" he greeted them exuberantly. "I was just talking to Fleet Marshal Double Bottom about the importance of preparing the way for you. You must know I am working in our mutual best interests and desire nothing more than to take a walk with you on my planet."

There was a slight delay as Emdall clicked and gestured angrily and Parker translated: "Enough foolery, Buckaroo Banzai—almost all of you is a liar. I gave in to your desires, and you used me . . . stole my royal caravel in further insult, along with personal belongings, which have now sunk in deep shite. You do not deserve to live."

"Yes," Buckaroo agreed, thankful that her demeanor was less angry than he had expected. "I behaved like a monkey swine toward you and deserve to be buried, but wished only to be interred on my natural planet, which by your mercy happily still exists. Long live our empress John Emdall, for whom my love is unconditional."

In response a smoky haze presently filled the scrying ball; and a pair of ideograms—clapping hands and a pile of crap—swirled into view, causing Buckaroo to smile at John Parker despite the latter's harsh words on Emdall's behalf: "The empress wants you to know she would rather throw you into the lake of offal, but for the fact she is with larva and dealing with urgent matters of statecraft and may require your hospitality in the future."

"My door is always open," said Buckaroo. "How bad are things?"

John Parker continued: "And she has told you she is not a one-night stand and does not like endings . . ."

"How well I recall, and I don't like endpoints, either. I would prefer to go on forever myself . . ."

"Tell her again of your love, for she is feeling rather painted blue."

Without a second thought, Buckaroo said, "You have entered my heart, John," and extemporized a haiku:

Entering my heart
Your memory takes refuge
My sentries stand guard . . .

After a silence, Emdall appeared to rise and fall in ecstasy, and Parker said, "I will love you a thousand years, Buckaroo Banzai. I carry your issue and will see you shortly, my husband."

"Yes, please don't work too hard in your delicate condition, John. Don't let the bastards wear you down."

"I give you the same advice, Buckaroo Banzai: show leadership from the top down and with a hard hand. Call me soonest, before I come and take you! Now comes tomorrow!"

Her image at last dissolved, and Buckaroo turned to see Double Bottom, the planetoid commander, staring down at the Earth intently. With no preamble, the Lectroid said flatly, "I am charged to assist you with security and your projects but also to inform you that we are only half strength as a result of disease, violent outbursts, and much bitching on my ship . . ."

"They appear to have shat on you, as well. You need to clean up that uniform," Buckaroo noted.

The Lectroid genuflected and confessed with frustration, "That is true, due to circumstances beyond my control."

"Beyond your control? Meaning?"

"Sickness, hunger, insomnia, allergies, the humdrum life far from home, Buckaroo Banzai; we are the dead generation."

"As are we all," Buckaroo replied. "But no need to hasten things along . . ."

The officer appeared not to hear these remarks and continued, "My troops need much food and supplies: baby pablum, boxes of confectionery, and many tons of your minnows and worms, even a little of your famous earthly sunshine and blue skies, such as the Italian Riviera or a reservoir where we might bathe and make repairs . . ."

Utterly drained and half-convinced he was hallucinating, Buckaroo had no intention of making any decisions after only a first meeting— hence he merely said, "A little rest and relaxation? I sympathize, but isn't there a saying on Planet 10 that a faultfinder will find fault even in paradise?"

"I am not one to ask. I have been busy repelling hordes and swatting beasts and have not set foot on Planet 10 in three hundred years. In addition, my digestion is upset," the Darkling Lectroid communicated, quickly adding, "Of course you are free to beat me for whatever reason."

With a shake of his head, Buckaroo said, "Let me work on it. All I demand from you is honesty, even if it is a difference of opinion. Do not blow hot air."

"Hot air? I find the climate on your world quite vital and ideal."

"One further question," said Buckaroo. "What do you know about General John Red and Raw?"

Double Bottom's demeanor seemed to harden as he revealed, "He was once the boy wonder groomed for big things before the revolution, to which he lent his support. It is said he is handsome and glows in the dark, but I do not trust his hue; nor does the empress, who has banished him to a distant system. He has no powers here."

"I hope not," said Buckaroo. "But we must trust one another, John Double Bottom. Make me a full list of what you need. In the meantime . . ." Buckaroo glanced around, adding, "I would like to meet Jarvis."

Double Bottom signaled and in short order a smallish Lectroid appeared through a doorway, advancing tentatively, his head encased in a boxy monstrosity of a helmet.

"This is Jarvis," announced Double Bottom . . .

. . . as the helmet lit up and came alive with the pixelated toothy face of Archangel Brother Deacon Jarvis and his big-ass drawl: "Awright, awright, right on, right on! How about a big standing O for Buckaroo Banzai . . . ?! Can I get an amen, brother? Let's nut it up . . . !"

"Amen, brother!" Buckaroo and Tommy both howled with knee-slapping laughter and Buckaroo said, "Well done, fellow! Fleet Marshal Double Bottom, get me that list of requirements and take your ship behind the moon until you hear from me. I'll plan my official visit and a full inspection tour of the vessel soon."

The Lectroid officer bowed once more, and when Buckaroo offered to return the glass eye, the creature demurred, saying, "Our empress wishes you to have it. I have another of my own."

"I'm not surprised," replied Buckaroo. "Very well, who will drive me home? I must announce my return and get to work."

"I will activate the rainbow," said John Double Bottom.

THE THIRD LEVITATION

In what Mona Peeptoe described as "a biblical moment," there were in fact three rainbows that crisscrossed the night sky to the blaring accompaniment of Beethoven's *Emperor* Concerto. Otherwise, dear reader, how do I describe the very instant in which the blinding light and shock wave of the terrible explosion disappeared from memory? How our empty-handed defeat turned to delirious victory? How our mopping-up operations were interrupted the instant we were blown through space, only to resume and sputter seconds later with the unannounced arrival of a pod in the sky! As we looked on, firing wildly, screaming hoarsely with excitement and scarcely believing our eyes, the pod paused in midflight and out stepped Buckaroo in his voluminous padded garment, crystal girdle, and antigravity boots, moving through the air with no visible means of assistance, casually waving at everyone below in the cavernous plaza, very much like a man taking a Sunday stroll.

But what fanfare from our end! And with what utter bafflement all eyes in the square turned upward to gape at the brilliant colors and the incomprehensible spectacle of Buckaroo and Tommy appearing to slide down a rainbow!

So high were our feelings, so deep our relief, the newly appointed "Emperor of Earth" had no choice but to roll with the punches as we playfully boxed and hugged him while dancing and jumping about, happy as fleas on a dog. Even if the world was still in danger and the alien planetoid had not officially called it quits, at least we were not yet in servitude, but still living freely and capable of fighting another day.

Who will forget that night? Certainly not the two time-traveling protagonists, Buckaroo and Tommy, or any of the others present: this author, Pecos, Muscatine, Hoppalong, Jumbo Jack Tarantulus, the award-winning Mona Peeptoe, along with the late-arriving Li'l Daughter and Red Jordan, various bedraggled spectators, insurance executives, and a handful of Knights Templar and Hospitallers who initially had fled the battle and now limped back to pose for tourist photographs. Moments later, Sister Mary Comfort and her father Pope Innocent also appeared in a public embrace on the Loggia of the Blessings, serenaded by the cherubic Viennese boy singers under the baton of New Jersey.

Nearby, a despondent Lectroid moaned and cried out in vain to his lord John Whorfin, who was of course nowhere to be seen, while, of our group, only Jhonny lay still on the cold, gray stones, having both covered himself in glory and died of hotheadedness, but none of that mattered now; and as Buckaroo made his way among the casualties, tending the wounded who might be saved, we could only guess his thoughts as he knelt beside our still companion. Imagine having just returned from the harrowing odyssey I have related—now perhaps in possession of the power of life or death over the entire world—and yet lacking any remedy for poor Jhonny, who was already walking in glorious sunshine to the bunkhouse in the sky . . . to be greeted there by Rawhide, Professor Hikita, and our other martyrs.

Meanwhile, Mona wasted no time taking Tommy aside for an exclusive live interview. Panting with excitement, she hugged him and shouted, "Tommy, you look terrible! Like you've been through a war! Ha, ha! Do you love life, Tommy?! Oh, do you love life?! Are we back to good?"

"Back to good?" he repeated, still somewhat disoriented.

"Let freedom ring!" she rejoiced, throwing her fist in the air; and almost at once a divine wind arose, causing chimes and church bells to begin to peal, first in the basilica and then citywide . . . an ecstatic, riotous clash of frequencies stretching as far as the sea and the lands beyond . . .

. . . as she bubbled over, unable to be heard above the tumult in the plaza but interfacing with her audience of millions: "No, not back to good! Not 'good enough,' but better than ever! Why do I feel this is only the beginning, the beginning of a second chance to get our business in order and our priorities straight? To know the truth and leave our lies and hypocrisy behind! Like newborns! In a golden age! No more preaching love while living with hate! No more war! Was there ever a better time to be alive? To remodel the world? With so much more to say, so much more to learn . . ."

Here she gave a whoop of hurt and confusion and shook her head, trying to convince herself of her own words: "Looking around, I'm alive! Oh my goodness, smiling but I'm weeping . . . I love life, although for a minute there, I wasn't sure! When I saw you and Buckaroo ride the rocket, I thought I would never see you again! Then the strange purple explosion! I saw stars, cried tears, and was blinded and actually felt myself burning, and yet here I am and with a heightened sense of gratitude, understanding how flimsy life is, and how I almost lost it! There, but for the grace of God, go I—look at me now, just a celebration of life and the hero who won our cause! O lucky day, and heartfelt thanks . . . and to you, too, Tommy . . ."

Her voice trailed off and Tommy nodded, fatigued beyond human endurance but mostly distracted by a small boxy object he was holding, opening it and closing it, before saying softly, "I don't know anything about all that, but I have love, too. It's been a real learning experience—humbling, I guess you could say—leading me to kind of examine my life. A Lectroid named John Singsong-of-the-Narrows just gave me this little box before I came down here from the mother ship. Inside is a little scroll with his writing on it, and when you open the cube, with all the flaps, it forms the shape of a cross, see . . ."

"I'll be darned, look at that. Will every cube do that?" Mona asked, pointing her Go-Phone at the box, whose sides indeed did unfold to reveal the shape of a cross.

"Every one," he said. "Every cube in the universe since the beginning of time . . . but their time's different."

"And you say one of the aliens in the ship gave it to you? And he wrote a little something. Or is it a she . . . ?"

"John Singsong's his name . . . he had a special vibe about him, next to no English but a kind of laughing-Buddha thing. Then I look around," he said in a daze, still trying to digest everything, "and I see all these dead knights who gave their lives—not to take anything away from them—I don't mean to vent, but it just seems kind of depressing . . ."

"No, no, you have a right to express your feelings, Tommy, after all you've been through . . ."

But Tommy's words did not come easily or even sound particularly coherent.

"I mean, up to now we've failed this world miserably . . . then tried to sweep everything under the carpet. It just seems so inconceivably stupid. How ignorant . . . we keep being beasts in this, our little comfort zone: our tribe against their tribe, this one against that one. Even on this big stage, where we pulled Earth's chestnuts out of the fire by the skin of our teeth . . . but then I think one day everyone in the audience will be dead, and all that will remain to remember us by will be John Emdall's stela, if even that. God help us . . ."

Like a prayer raised up, his words moved the pope himself to fling open his arms and announce to the worldwide flock, "Cometh the hour, cometh the man! The light from heaven named Buckaroo Banzai . . . !"

"Buckaroo Banzai! Buckaroo Banzai!"

The chant spread like wildfire among the witnesses, and all eyes turned to the great man walking and kneeling among the afflicted, offering help and comfort, while the rest of us continued to spin and whirl, one and all now, joyously dizzying ourselves like Sufi dervishes in a dance of dispossession, attempting to rid our minds of the recent traumatic events . . .

. . . as Tommy gazed up in wonder at the great stela; and it must be said that time has proved him correct, dear reader, for if you visit Saint Peter's Square, the only evidence to be seen of the epic battle I have just described is John Emdall's towering obelisk, her staff of authority that still dominates that famous plaza today.

True story.

TO BE CONTINUED IN

BUCKAROO BANZAI, EMPEROR OF EARTH

NEXT VOLUME IN THE THRILLING SERIES